P9-DYE-751

"[A] PHANTASMAGORIC MASTERPIECE . . . THE BOOK LEFT ME BREATHLESS WITH ADMIRATION."
—BRIAN STABLEFORD

"New Crobuzon combines equal parts Dickens and Kafka, Dick and Cronenberg to generate 700-odd pages of moving freak show, united into a single urban organism through the matter-of-fact deadpan of Miéville's assured narration. *Perdido Street Station* combines audacious invention with surprising detail and grace, and gives a complex amalgam of grotesque and mundane without flinching or smirking."
—*City Paper* (Philadelphia)

"[This] darkly imaginative and complex story whirls along to its final resolution with the reader's own imagination locked in tow."
—*The Anniston Star*

"An astonishing fantasy tale that is a must reading . . . Creative, satirical, and witty . . . Fans of epic fantasy will reread this classy tale many times over."
—Booksnbytes.com

Please turn the page for more reviews . . .

"AUDACIOUSLY IMAGINED . . . AN IMPRESSIVE AND ULTIMATELY PLEASING EPIC."
—*Publishers Weekly*

"Wiggy, weird, and way cool . . . *Perdido Street Station* is set in a world that is a cross between *Blade Runner* and the London of Charles Dickens. And it's populated with characters borrowed from mythologies from all over the world that are given China's own unique twist. . . . Considering that *Perdido Street Station* is only his second book, he's a writer to keep our eyes on."
—WARREN JAMES
Hour 25

"The most exciting, enthralling novel I have read in a long time. It is about everything important—love, work, hope, worlds we knew were out there but needed a writer like Miéville to show them to us. His imagination is vast, his talent volcanic. Read this book. It just might be a masterpiece."
—JONATHON CARROLL

"China Miéville's cool style has conjured up a triumphantly macabre technoslip metropolis with a unique atmosphere of horror and fascination."
—PETER F. HAMILTON

Perdido Street Station

Also by China Miéville

KING RAT
THE SCAR

Books published by The Random House Publishing Group
are available at quantity discounts on bulk purchases for
premium, educational, fund-raising, and special sales use.
For details, please call 1-800-733-3000.

Perdido Street Station

China Miéville

DEL
REY

BALLANTINE BOOKS • NEW YORK

Sale of this book without a front cover may be unauthorized. If this book is coverless, it may have been reported to the publisher as "unsold or destroyed" and neither the author nor the publisher may have received payment for it.

A Del Rey® Book
Published by The Random House Publishing Group

Copyright © 2000 by China Miéville

All rights reserved under International and Pan-American Copyright Conventions. Published in the United States by The Random House Publishing Group, a division of Random House, Inc., New York, and simultaneously in Canada by Random House of Canada Limited, Toronto. Originally published in Great Britain by Macmillan Publishers Ltd., London, in 2000.

Perdido Street Station is a work of fiction. Names, places, and incidents either are a product of the author's imagination or are used fictitiously.

Del Rey is a registered trademark and the Del Rey colophon is a trademark of Random House, Inc.

www.delreydigital.com

ISBN 0-345-45940-7

Manufactured in the United States of America

First American Edition: March 2001
First Mass Market Edition: August 2003

OPM   10 9 8 7 6 5 4 3 2 1

to Emma

ACKNOWLEDGEMENTS

With love and thanks to my mother, Claudia, and my sister, Jemima, for their help and support. Huge thanks to everyone who gave me feedback and advice, especially Scott Bicheno, Max Schaefer, Simon Kavanagh and Oliver Cheetham.

Deep love and gratitude to Emma Bircham, again and always.

Thanks to all at Macmillan, most especially to my editor Peter Lavery for his incredible support. And infinite gratitude to Mic Cheetham, who has helped me more than I can say.

I don't have space to thank all the writers who've influenced me, but I want to mention two whose work is a constant source of inspiration and astonishment. Therefore to M. John Harrison, and to the memory of Mervyn Peake, my humble and heartfelt gratitude. I could never have written this book without them.

"I even gave up, for a while, stopping by the window of the room to look out at the lights and deep, illuminated streets. That's a form of dying, that losing contact with the city like that."

Philip K. Dick, *We Can Build You*

Veldt to scrub to fields to farms to these first tumbling houses that rise from the earth. It has been night for a long time. The hovels that encrust the river's edge have grown like mushrooms around me in the dark.

We rock. We pitch in a deep current.

Behind me the man tugs uneasily at his rudder and the barge corrects. Light lurches as the lantern swings. The man is afraid of me. I lean out from the prow of the small vessel across the darkly moving water.

Over the engine's oily rumble and the caresses of the river small sounds, house sounds, are building. Timbers whisper and the wind strokes thatch, walls settle and floors shift to fill space; the tens of houses have become hundreds, thousands; they spread backwards from the banks and shed light from all across the plain.

They surround me. They are growing. They are taller and fatter and noisier, their roofs are slate, their walls are strong brick.

The river twists and turns to face the city. It looms suddenly, massive, stamped on the landscape. Its light wells up around the surrounds, the rock hills, like bruise-blood. Its dirty towers glow. I am debased. I am compelled to worship this extraordinary presence that has silted into existence at the conjunction of two rivers. It is a vast pollutant, a stench, a klaxon sounding. Fat chimneys retch dirt into the sky even now in the deep night. It is not the current which pulls us but the city itself, its weight sucks us in. Faint shouts, here and there the calls of beasts, the obscene clash and pounding from the factories as huge machines rut. Railways trace urban anatomy like protruding veins. Red brick and dark walls, squat churches like troglodytic things, ragged awnings flickering, cobbled mazes in the old town, culs-de-sac, sewers riddling the earth like secular sepulchres, a new

*landscape of wasteground, crushed stone, libraries fat with for-
gotten volumes, old hospitals, towerblocks, ships and metal
claws that lift cargoes from the water.*

*How could we not see this approaching? What trick of topog-
raphy is this, that lets the sprawling monster hide behind corners to leap out at the traveller?*

It is too late to flee.

*The man murmurs to me, tells me where we are. I do not turn to
him.*

*This is Raven's Gate, this brutalized warren around us. The
rotting buildings lean against each other, exhausted. The river
smears slime on its brick banks, city walls risen from the depths
to hold the water at bay. There is a vile stink here.*

*(I wonder how this looks from above, no chance for the city to
hide then, if you came at it on the wind you would see it from
miles and miles away like a dirty smear, like a slab of carrion
thronging with maggots, I should not think like this but I cannot
stop now, I could ride the updrafts that the chimneys vent, sail
high over the proud towers and shit on the earthbound, ride the
chaos, alight where I choose, I must not think like this, I must not
do this now, I must stop, not now, not this, not yet.)*

*Here there are houses which dribble pale mucus, an organic
daubing that smears base façades and oozes from top windows.
Extra storeys are rendered in the cold white muck which fills
gaps between houses and dead-end alleys. The landscape is defaced with ripples as if wax has melted and set suddenly across
the rooftops. Some other intelligence has made these human
streets their own.*

*Wires are stretched tight across the river and the eaves, held
fast by milky aggregates of phlegm. They hum like bass strings.
Something scuttles overhead. The bargeman hawks foully into
the water.*

*His gob dissipates. The mass of spittle-mortar above us ebbs.
Narrow streets emerge.*

*A train whistles as it crosses the river before us on raised
tracks. I look to it, to the south and the east, seeing the line of little lights rush away and be swallowed by this nightland, this be-
hemoth that eats its citizens. We will pass the factories soon.
Cranes rear from the gloom like spindly birds; here and there
they move to keep the skeleton crews, the midnight crews, in*

their work. Chains swing deadweight like useless limbs, snapping into zombie motion where cogs engage and flywheels turn.

Fat predatory shadows prowl the sky.

There is a boom, a reverberation, as if the city has a hollow core. The black barge putters through a mass of its fellows weighed down with coke and wood and iron and steel and glass. The water here reflects the stars through a stinking rainbow of impurities, effluents and chymical slop, making it sluggish and unsettling.

(Oh, to rise above this to not smell this filth this dirt this dung to not enter the city through this latrine but I must stop, I must, I cannot go on, I must.)

The engine slows. I turn and watch the man behind me, who averts his eyes and steers, affecting to look through me. He is taking us in to dock, there behind the warehouse so engorged its contents spill out beyond the buttresses in a labyrinth of huge boxes. He picks his way between other craft. There are roofs emerging from the river. A line of sunken houses, built on the wrong side of the wall, pressed up against the bank in the water, their bituminous black bricks dripping. Disturbances beneath us. The river boils with eddies from below. Dead fish and frogs that have given up the fight to breathe in this rotting stew of detritus swirl frantic between the flat side of the barge and the concrete shore, trapped in choppy turmoil. The gap is closed. My captain leaps ashore and ties up. His relief is draining to see. He is wittering gruffly in triumph and ushering me quickly ashore and away and I alight, as slowly as if onto coals, picking my way through the rubbish and the broken glass.

He is happy with the stones I have given him. I am in Smog Bend, he tells me, and I make myself look away as he points my direction so he will not know I am lost, that I am new in the city, that I am afraid of these dark and threatening edifices of which I cannot kick free, that I am nauseous with claustrophobia and foreboding.

A little to the south two great pillars rise from the river. The gates to the Old City, once grandiose, now psoriatic and ruined. The carved histories that wound about those obelisks have been effaced by time and acid, and only roughcast spiral threads like those of old screws remain. Behind them, a low bridge (Drud Crossing, he says). I ignore the man's eager explanations and walk away through this lime-bleached zone, past yawning doors that promise the comfort of true dark and an escape from the river stench. The bargeman is just a tiny voice now and it is a small pleasure to know I will never see him again.

It is not cold. A city light is promising itself in the east.

I will follow the trainlines. I will stalk in their shadow as they pass by over the houses and towers and barracks and offices and prisons of the city, I will track them from the arches that anchor them to the earth. I must find my way in.

My cloak (heavy cloth unfamiliar and painful on my skin) tugs at me and I can feel the weight of my purse. That is what protects me here; that and the illusion I have fostered, the source of my sorrow and my shame, the anguish that has brought me to this great wen, this dusty city dreamed up in bone and brick, a conspiracy of industry and violence, steeped in history and battened-down power, this badland beyond my ken.

New Crobuzon.

PART ONE

Commissions

CHAPTER ONE

A window burst open high above the market. A basket flew from it and arced towards the oblivious crowd. It spasmed in mid-air, then spun and continued earthwards at a slower, uneven pace. Dancing precariously as it descended, its wire-mesh caught and skittered on the building's rough hide. It scrabbled at the wall, sending paint and concrete dust plummeting before it.

The sun shone through uneven cloud-cover with a bright grey light. Below the basket the stalls and barrows lay like untidy spillage. The city reeked. But today was market day down in Aspic Hole, and the pungent slick of dung-smell and rot that rolled over New Crobuzon was, in these streets, for these hours, improved with paprika and fresh tomato, hot oil and fish and cinnamon, cured meat, banana and onion.

The food stalls stretched the noisy length of Shadrach Street. Books and manuscripts and pictures filled up Selchit Pass, an avenue of desultory banyans and crumbling concrete a little way to the east. There were earthenware products spilling down the road to Barrackham in the south; engine parts to the west; toys down one side street; clothes between two more; and countless other goods filling all the alleys. The rows of merchandise converged crookedly on Aspic Hole like spokes on a broken wheel.

In the Hole itself all distinctions broke down. In the shadow of old walls and unsafe towers were a pile of gears, a ramshackle table of broken crockery and crude clay ornaments, a case of mouldering textbooks. Antiques, sex, flea-powder. Between the stalls stomped hissing constructs. Beggars argued in the bowels of deserted buildings. Members of strange races bought peculiar things. Aspic Bazaar, a blaring mess of goods, grease and tallymen. Mercantile law ruled: *let the buyer beware.*

The costermonger below the descending basket looked up into flat sunlight and a shower of brick particles. He wiped his eye. He plucked the frayed thing from the air above his head, pulling at the cord which bore it until it went slack in his hand. Inside the basket was a brass shekel and a note in careful, ornamented italics. The food-vendor scratched his nose as he scanned the paper. He rummaged in the piles of produce before him, placed eggs and fruit and root vegetables into the container, checking against the list. He stopped and read one item again, then smiled lasciviously and cut a slice of pork. When he was done he put the shekel in his pocket and felt for change, hesitating as he calculated his delivery cost, eventually depositing four stivers in with the food.

He wiped his hands against his trousers and thought for a minute, then scribbled something on the list with a stub of charcoal and tossed it after the coins.

He tugged three times at the rope and the basket began a bobbing journey into the air. It rose above the lower roofs of surrounding buildings, buoyed upwards by noise. It startled the roosting jackdaws in the deserted storey and inscribed the wall with another scrawled trail among many, before it disappeared again into the window from which it had emerged.

Isaac Dan der Grimnebulin had just realized that he was dreaming. He had been aghast to find himself employed once again at the university, parading in front of a huge blackboard covered in vague representations of levers and forces and stress. Introductory Material Science. Isaac had been staring anxiously at the class when that unctuous bastard Vermishank had looked in.

"I can't teach this class," whispered Isaac loudly. "The market's too loud." He gestured at the window.

"It's all right." Vermishank was soothing and loathsome. "It's time for breakfast," he said. "That'll take your mind off the noise." And hearing that absurdity Isaac shed sleep with immense relief. The raucous profanity of the bazaar and the smell of cooking came with him into the day.

He lay hugely in the bed without opening his eyes. He heard Lin walk across the room and felt the slight listing of the floorboards. The garret was filled with pungent smoke. Isaac salivated.

Lin clapped twice. She knew when Isaac woke. Probably because he closed his mouth, he thought, and sniggered without opening his eyes.

"Still sleeping, shush, poor little Isaac ever so tired," he whimpered, and snuggled down like a child. Lin clapped again, once, derisory, and walked away.

He groaned and rolled over.

"Termagant!" he moaned after her. "Shrew! Harridan! All right, all right, you win, you, you . . . uh . . . virago, you spitfire . . ." He rubbed his head and sat up, grinned sheepishly. Lin made an obscene gesture at him without turning around.

She stood with her back to him, nude at the stove, dancing back as hot drops of oil leapt from the pan. The covers slipped from the slope of Isaac's belly. He was a dirigible, huge and taut and strong. Grey hair burst from him abundantly.

Lin was hairless. Her muscles were tight under her red skin, each distinct. She was like an anatomical atlas. Isaac studied her in cheerful lust.

His arse itched. He scratched under the blanket, rooting as shameless as a dog. Something burst under his nail, and he withdrew his hand to examine it. A tiny half-crushed grub waved helplessly on the end of his finger. It was a refflick, a harmless little khepri parasite. *The thing must have been rather bewildered by my juices*, Isaac thought, and flicked his finger clean.

"Refflick, Lin," he said. "Bath time."

Lin stamped in irritation.

New Crobuzon was a huge plague pit, a morbific city. Parasites, infection and rumour were uncontainable. A monthly chymical dip was a necessary prophylactic for the khepri, if they wanted to avoid itches and sores.

Lin slid the contents of the pan onto a plate and set it down, across from her own breakfast. She sat and gestured for Isaac to join her. He rose from the bed and stumbled across the room. He eased himself onto the small chair, wary of splinters.

Isaac and Lin sat naked on either side of the bare wooden table. Isaac was conscious of their pose, seeing them as a third person might. It would make a beautiful, strange print, he thought. An attic room, dust-motes in the light from the small window, books and paper and paints neatly stacked by cheap wooden furniture. A dark-skinned man, big and nude and detumescing, gripping a knife and fork, unnaturally still, sitting opposite a khepri, her slight woman's body in shadow, her chitinous head in silhouette.

They ignored their food and stared at each other for a moment. Lin signed at him: *Good morning, lover.* Then she began to eat, still looking at him.

It was when she ate that Lin was most alien, and their shared meals were a challenge and an affirmation. As he watched her, Isaac felt the familiar trill of emotion: disgust immediately stamped out, pride at the stamping out, guilty desire.

Light glinted in Lin's compound eyes. Her headlegs quivered. She picked up half a tomato and gripped it with her mandibles. She lowered her hands while her inner mouthparts picked at the food her outer jaw held steady.

Isaac watched the huge iridescent scarab that was his lover's head devour her breakfast.

He watched her swallow, saw her throat bob where the pale insectile underbelly segued smoothly into her human neck . . . not that she would have accepted that description. *Humans have khepri bodies, legs, hands; and the heads of shaved gibbons,* she had once told him.

He smiled and dangled his fried pork in front of him, curled his tongue around it, wiped his greasy fingers on the table. He smiled at her. She undulated her headlegs at him and signed, *My monster.*

I am a pervert, thought Isaac, *and so is she.*

Breakfast conversation was generally one-sided: Lin could sign with her hands while she ate, but Isaac's attempts to talk and eat simultaneously made for incomprehensible noises and food debris on the table. Instead they read; Lin an artists' newsletter, Isaac whatever came to hand. He reached out between mouthfuls and grabbed books and papers, and found himself reading Lin's shopping list. The item *a handful of pork slices* was ringed and underneath her exquisite calligraphy was a scrawled question in much cruder script: *Got company??? Nice bit of pork goes down a treat!!!*

Isaac waved the paper at Lin. "What's this filthy arse on about?" he yelled, spraying food. His outrage was amused but genuine.

Lin read it and shrugged.

Knows I don't eat meat. Knows I've got a guest for breakfast. Wordplay on "pork."

"Yes, thanks, lover, I got that bit. How does he know you're a vegetarian? Do you two often engage in this witty banter?"

Lin stared at him for a moment without responding.

Knows because I don't buy meat. She shook her head at the stupid question. *Don't worry: only ever* banter *on paper. Doesn't know I'm bug.*

Her deliberate use of the slur annoyed Isaac.

"Dammit, I wasn't insinuating anything . . ." Lin's hand waggled, the equivalent of a raised eyebrow. Isaac howled in irritation. "Godshit, Lin! Not everything I say is about fear of discovery!"

Isaac and Lin had been lovers nearly two years. They had always tried not to think too hard about the rules of their relationship, but the longer they were together the more this strategy of avoidance became impossible. Questions as yet unasked demanded attention. Innocent remarks and askance looks from others, a moment of contact too long in public—a note from a grocer—everything was a reminder that they were, in some contexts, living a secret. Everything was made fraught.

They had never said, *We are lovers,* so they had never had to say, *We will not disclose our relationship to all, we will hide from some.* But it had been clear for months and months that this was the case.

Lin had begun to hint, with snide and acid remarks, that Isaac's refusal to declare himself her lover was at best cowardly, at worst bigoted. This insensitivity annoyed him. He had, after all, made the nature of his relationship clear with his close friends, as Lin had with hers. And it was all far, far easier for her.

She was an artist. Her circle were the libertines, the patrons and the hangers-on, bohemians and parasites, poets and pamphleteers and fashionable junkies. They delighted in the scandalous and the outré. In the tea-houses and bars of Salacus Fields, Lin's escapades—broadly hinted at, never denied, never made explicit—would be the subject of louche discussion and innuendo. Her love-life was an avant-garde transgression, an art-happening, like Concrete Music had been last season, or 'Snot Art! the year before that.

And yes, Isaac could play that game. He was known in that world, from long before his days with Lin. He was, after all, the scientist-outcast, the disreputable thinker who walked out of a lucrative teaching post to engage in experiments too outrageous and brilliant for the tiny minds who ran the university. What did he care for convention? He would sleep with whomever and whatever he liked, surely!

That was his persona in Salacus Fields, where his relationship with Lin was an open secret, where he enjoyed being more or less open, where he would put his arm around her in the bars and whisper to her as she sucked sugar-coffee from a sponge. That was his story, and it was at least half true.

He had walked out of the university ten years ago. But only because he realized to his misery that he was a terrible teacher.

He had looked out at the quizzical faces, listened to the frantic scrawling of the panicking students, and realized that with a mind that ran and tripped and hurled itself down the corridors of theory in anarchic fashion, he could learn himself, in haphazard lurches, but he could not impart the understanding he so loved. He had hung his head in shame and fled.

In another twist to the myth, his Head of Department, the ageless and loathsome Vermishank, was not a plodding epigone but an exceptional bio-thaumaturge, who had nixed Isaac's research less because it was unorthodox than because it was going nowhere. Isaac could be brilliant, but he was undisciplined. Vermishank had played him like a fish, making him beg for work as a freelance researcher on terrible pay, but with limited access to the university laboratories.

And it was this, his work, which kept Isaac circumspect about his lover.

These days, his relationship with the university was tenuous. Ten years of pilfering had equipped him with a fine laboratory of his own; his income was largely made up of dubious contracts with New Crobuzon's less wholesome citizens, whose needs for sophisticated science constantly astounded him.

But Isaac's research—unchanged in its aims over all those years—could not proceed in a vacuum. He had to publish. He had to debate. He had to argue, to attend conferences—as the rogue, the rebellious son. There were great advantages to renegacy.

But the academy did not just play at being old-fashioned. Xenian students had only been admitted as degree candidates in New Crobuzon for twenty years. To cross-love openly would be a quick route to pariah status, rather than the bad-boy chic he had assiduously courted. What scared him was not that the editors of the journals and the chairs of the conferences and the publishers would find out about Lin and him. What scared him was that he be seen not trying to hide it. If he went through the motions of a cover-up, they could not denounce him as beyond the pale.

All of which Lin took badly.

You hide us so you can publish articles for people you despise, she had signed at him once after they had made love.

Isaac, in sour moments, wondered how she would react if the art-world threatened to ostracize her.

That morning the lovers managed to kill the nascent argument with jokes and apologies and compliments and lust. Isaac smiled at Lin as he struggled into his shirt, and her headlegs rippled sensuously.

"What are you up to today?" he asked.

Going to Kinken. Need some colourberries. Going to exhibition in Howl Barrow. Working tonight, she added mockominously.

"I suppose I won't be seeing you for a while, then?" Isaac grinned. Lin shook her head. Isaac counted off days on his fingers. "Well . . . can we have dinner at The Clock and Cockerel on, uh . . . Shunday? Eight o'clock?"

Lin pondered. She held his hands while she thought.

Gorgeous, she signed coyly. She left it ambiguous as to whether she meant dinner or Isaac.

They piled the pots and plates into the bucket of cold water in the corner and left them. As Lin gathered her notes and sketches to go, Isaac tugged her gently onto him, on the bed. He kissed her warm red skin. She turned in his arms. She angled up on one elbow and, as he watched, the dark ruby of her carapace opened slowly while her headlegs splayed. The two halves of her headshell quivered slightly, held as wide as they would go. From beneath their shade she spread her beautiful, useless little beetle wings.

She pulled his hand towards them gently, invited him to stroke the fragile things, totally vulnerable, an expression of trust and love unparalleled for the khepri.

The air between them charged. Isaac's cock stiffened.

He traced the branching veins in her gently vibrating wings with his fingers, watched the light that passed through them refract into mother-of-pearl shadows.

He rucked up her skirt with his other hand, slid his fingers up her thigh. Her legs opened around his hand and closed, trapped it. He whispered at her, filthy and loving invitations.

The sun shifted above them, sending shadows of the windowpane and clouds moving uneasily through the room. The lovers did not notice the day move.

CHAPTER TWO

It was 11 o'clock before they disentangled. Isaac glanced at his pocket-watch and stumbled around gathering his clothes, his mind wandering to his work. Lin spared them the awkward negotiations that would surround leaving the house together. She bent and caressed the back of Isaac's neck with her antennae, raising goosebumps, and then she left while he still fumbled with his boots.

Her rooms were nine floors up. She descended the tower; past the unsafe eighth floor; the seventh with its birdlime carpet and soft jackdaw susurrus; the old lady who never emerged on the sixth; and on down past petty thieves and steel workers and errand-girls and knife-grinders.

The door was on the other side of the tower from Aspic Hole itself. Lin emerged into a quiet street, a mere passageway to and from the stalls of the bazaar.

She walked away from the noisy arguments and the profiteering towards the gardens of Sobek Croix. Ranks of cabs were always waiting at their entrance. She knew that some of the drivers (usually the Remade) were liberal or desperate enough to take khepri custom.

As she passed through Aspic the blocks and houses grew less salubrious. The ground undulated and rose slowly to the southwest, where she was heading. The treetops of Sobek Croix rose like thick smoke above the slates of the dilapidated housing around her; beyond their leaves poked the stubby high-rise skyline of Ketch Heath.

Lin's bulging mirrored eyes saw the city in a compound visual cacophony. A million tiny sections of the whole, each minuscule hexagon segment ablaze with sharp colour and even sharper lines, super-sensitive to differentials of light, weak on details unless she focused hard enough to hurt slightly. Within each segment, the dead scales of decaying walls were invisible to her, architecture reduced to elemental slabs of colour. But a precise story was told. Each visual fragment, each part, each shape, each shade of colour, differed from its surroundings in infinitesimal ways that told her about the state of the whole structure. And she could taste chymicals in the air, could tell how many of which race lived in which building: she could feel vibrations of air and sound with precision enough to converse in a crowded room or feel a train pass overhead.

Lin had tried to describe how she saw the city to Isaac.

I see clearly as you, clearer. For you it is undifferentiated. In one corner a slum collapsing, in another a new train with pistons shining, in another a gaudy painted lady below a drab and ancient airship . . . You must process as one picture. What chaos! Tells you nothing, contradicts itself, changes its story. For me each tiny part has integrity, each fractionally different from the next, until all variation is accounted for, incrementally, rationally.

Isaac had been fascinated for a week and a half. He had, typically, taken pages of notes and sought books on insectile vision, subjected Lin to tedious experiments in depth-perception and distance-vision; and reading, which impressed him most, knowing as he did that it did not come naturally to her, that she had to concentrate like someone half-blind.

His interest had quickly waned. The human mind was incapable of processing what the khepri saw.

All around Lin the duckers and divers of Aspic filled the streets on their way to scrape for money, stealing or begging or selling or sifting through the piles of rubbish which punctuated the street. Children scampered by carrying engine parts cobbled together into obscure shapes. Occasionally gentlemen and ladies strode by with an air of disapproval on their way Somewhere Else.

Lin's clogs were wet with organic muck from the street, rich pickings for the furtive creatures peering from drains. The houses around her were flat-roofed and looming, with plank walkways slung across gaps between houses. Getaway routes, alternative passageways, the streets of the roofworld above New Crobuzon.

Only a very few children called names at her. This was a community used to xenians. She could taste the cosmopolitan nature of this neighbourhood, the minute secretions of a variety of races, only some of which she recognized. There was the musk

of more khepri, the dank odour of vodyanoi, even, from somewhere, the delicious taste of cactacae.

Lin turned the corner onto the cobbled road around Sobek
Croix. Cabs waited all along the iron fence. A massive variety.
Two-wheelers, four-wheelers, pulled by horses, by sneering ptera-
birds, by steam-wheezing constructs on caterpillar treads . . .
here and there by Remade, miserable men and women both cabdriver and cab.

Lin stood before the ranks and waved her hand. Mercifully,
the first driver in line geed his ornery-looking bird forward at her
signal.

"Where to?" The man leaned down to read the careful instructions she scrawled on her notepad. "Righto," he said, and jerked
his head, motioning her in.

The cab was an open-fronted two-seater, giving Lin a view of
her passage through the south side of the city. The great flightless bird moved with a bobbing, rolling run that translated
smoothly through the wheels. She sat back and read over her instructions to the driver.

Isaac would not approve. At all.

Lin *did* need colourberries, and she was going to Kinken for
them. That was true. And one of her friends, Cornfed Daihat,
was having an exhibition in Howl Barrow.

But she would not see it.

She had already spoken to Cornfed, asking him to vouch that
she had been there, should Isaac ask (she could not foresee that
he would, but she might as well be safe). Cornfed had been delighted, flicking his white hair out of his face and flamboyantly
begging eternal damnation for himself should he breathe a word.
He clearly thought she was two-timing Isaac, and considered it a
privilege to be part of this new twist to her already scandalous
sex life.

Lin could not make it to his show. She had business elsewhere.

The cab was progressing towards the river. She swayed as the
wooden wheels hit more cobblestones. They had turned onto
Shadrach Street. The market was to their south now: they were
above the point where the vegetables and shellfish and overripe
fruit petered out.

Swelling fatly above the low houses before her was the Flyside militia tower. A vast, filthy, pudgy pillar, squat and mean,
somehow, for all its thirty-five storeys. Thin windows like arrow-

slits peppered its sides, their dark glass matt, immune to reflection. The tower's concrete skin was mottled and flaking. Three miles to the north Lin caught a glimpse of an even taller structure: the militia's hub, the Spike, that punctured the earth like a concrete thorn in the heart of the city.

Lin craned her neck. Oozing obscenely over the top of the Flyside tower was a half-inflated dirigible. It flapped and lolled and swelled like a dying fish. She could feel its engine humming, even through the layers of air, as it strained to disappear into the gun-grey clouds.

There was another murmur, a buzzing dissonant with the airship's drone. Somewhere nearby a support strut vibrated, and a militia-pod streaked northwards towards the tower at breakneck speed.

It careered along way, way above, suspended from the skyrail that stretched out on either side of the tower, threaded through its summit like wire through some colossal needle, disappearing to the north and the south. The pod slammed to a sudden stop against the buffers. Figures emerged, but the cab passed on before Lin could see any more.

For the second time that day Lin luxuriated in the taste of cactus-people sap, as the pterabird loped towards the Greenhouse in Riverskin. Shut out of that monastic sanctuary (the twisting, intricate panes of its steep glass dome looming to the east, in the heart of the quarter), despised by their elders, small gangs of cactus youth leaned against shuttered buildings and cheap posters. They played with knives. Their spines were cropped in violent patterns, their spring-green skin savaged with bizarre scarification.

They eyed the cab without interest.

Shadrach Street dipped suddenly. The cab was poised on a high point, where the streets curved sharply down away from it. Lin and her driver had a clear view of the grey, snow-specked jags of mountains rising splendidly to the west of the city.

Before the cab trickled the River Tar.

Faint cries and industrial drones sounded from dark windows set into its brick banks, some of them below the high-water mark. Prisons and torture-chambers and workshops, and their bastard hybrids, the punishment factories, where the condemned were Remade. Boats coughed and retched their way along the black water.

The spires of Nabob Bridge appeared. And beyond them, slate

roofs hunching like shoulders in the cold, rotten walls held at the point of collapse by buttresses and organic cement, stinking a unique stink, was the shambles of Kinken.

Over the river, in the Old City, the streets were narrower and darker. The pterabird paced uneasily past buildings slick with the hardened gel of the home-beetle. Khepri climbed from windows and doors of the refashioned houses. They were the majority here, this was their place. The streets were full of their women's bodies, their insectile heads. They congregated in cavernous doorways, eating fruit.

Even the cabdriver could taste their conversations: the air was acrid with chymical communication.

An organic thing split and burst under the wheels. *A male, probably,* thought Lin with a shudder, imagining one of the countless mindless scuttlers that swarmed from holes and cracks all around Kinken. *Good riddance.*

The shying pterabird balked at passing under a low arch of brick that dripped stalactites of beetle mucus. Lin tapped the driver as he wrestled with the reins. She scrawled quickly and held up her pad.

Bird not too happy. Wait here, I'll be back five minutes.

He nodded gratefully and extended a hand to help her down. Lin left him trying to calm the irritable mount. She turned a corner into Kinken's central square. The pale exudations that drooled from rooftops left street-signs visible at the edges of the square, but the name they declared—Aldelion Place—was not one that any of Kinken's inhabitants would use. Even the few humans and other non-khepri who lived there used the newer khepri name, translating it from the hiss and chlorine burp of the original tongue: the Plaza of Statues.

It was large and open, ringed by ramshackle buildings hundreds of years old. The tumbledown architecture contrasted violently with the great grey mass of another militia tower looming to the north. Roofs sloped incredibly steep and low. Windows were dirty and streaked with obscure patterns. She could feel the faint therapeutic humming of nurse-khepri in their surgeries. Sweet smoke wafted over the crowd: khepri, mostly, but here and there other races, investigating the statues. They filled the square: fifteen-foot figures of animals and plants and monstrous creatures, some real and some that had never lived, fashioned in brightly coloured khepri-spit.

They represented hours and hours of communal labour. Groups of khepri women had stood for days, back-to-back, chewing paste and colourberries, metabolizing it, opening the gland at the hindpart of their beetle-heads and pushing out thick (and misnamed) khepri-spit, that hardened in the air in an hour to a smooth, brittle, pearly brilliance.

To Lin the statues represented dedication and community, and bankrupt imaginations falling back on cod-heroic grandiosity. This was why she lived and ate and spat her art alone.

Lin walked past the fruit and vegetable shops, the handwritten signs promising home-grubs for hire in large uneven capitals, the art-exchange centres with all the accoutrements for the khepri gland artist.

Other khepri glanced at Lin. Her skirt was long and bright in the fashion of Salacus Fields: human fashion, not the traditional ballooning pantaloons of these ghetto-dwellers. Lin was marked. She was an outsider. Had left her sisters. Forgotten hive and moiety.

Damn right I have, thought Lin, defiantly swishing her long green skirt.

The spittle-store owner knew her, and they politely, perfunctorily, brushed antennae.

Lin looked up at the shelves. The inside of the store was coated in home-grub cement, rippling across walls and blunting corners with more care than was traditional. The spittle goods perched on shelves that jutted like bones from the organic sludge were illuminated by gaslight. The window was artistically smeared with juice from various colourberries, and the day was kept out.

Lin spoke, clicking and waving her headlegs, secreting tiny mists of scent. She communicated her desire for scarletberries, cyanberries, blackberries, opalberries and purpleberries. She included a spray of admiration for the high quality of the storekeeper's goods.

Lin took her wares and left quickly.

The atmosphere of pious community in Kinken nauseated her.

The cabdriver was waiting, and she leapt up behind him, pointed north-east, bade him take them away.

Redwing Hive, Catskull Moiety, she thought giddily. *You sanctimonious bitches, I remember it all! On and on about community and the great khepri hive while the "sisters" over in*

Creekside scrabble about for potatoes. You have nothing, sur-rounded by people that mock you as bugs, buy your art cheap and sell you food dear, but because there are others with even less you style yourselves the protectors of the khepri way. I'm out. I dress how I like. My art is mine.

She breathed easier when the streets around her were clean of beetle cement, and the only khepri in the crowds were, like her, outcasts.

She sent the cab under the brick arches of Spit Bazaar Station, just as a train roared overhead like a great petulant steam-powered child. It set off towards the heart of the Old Town. Su-perstitiously, Lin directed the cab up towards Barguest Bridge. It was not the nearest place to cross the Canker, the Tar's sister; but that would be in Brock Marsh, the triangular slice of the Old City wedged between the two rivers as they met and became Gross Tar, and where Isaac, like many others, had his laboratory.

There was no chance at all he would see her, in that labyrinth of dubious experiments, where the nature of the research made even the architecture untrustworthy. But so that she need not even think of it for a moment, she sent the cab to Gidd Station, where the Dexter Line stretched out to the east on raised tracks that stretched higher and higher above the city as they moved further from the centre.

Follow the trains! she wrote, and the cabdriver did, through the wide streets of West Gidd, over the ancient and grand Bar-guest Bridge, across the Canker; the cleaner, colder river that flowed down from the Bezhek Peaks. She stopped him and paid, with a generous tip, wanting to walk the last mile herself, not wanting to be traceable.

She hurried to make her appointment in the shadow of the Ribs, the Bonetown Claws, in the Thieves' Quarter. Behind her, for a moment, the sky was very full: an aerostat droned in the distance; tiny specks lurched erratically around it, winged fig-ures playing in its wake like dolphins round a whale; and in front of them all another train, heading into the city this time, heading for the centre of New Crobuzon, the knot of architectural tissue where the fibres of the city congealed, where the skyrails of the militia radiated out from the Spike like a web and the five great trainlines of the city met, converging on the great variegated fortress of dark brick and scrubbed concrete and wood and steel and stone, the edifice that yawned hugely at the city's vulgar heart, Perdido Street Station.

CHAPTER THREE

Opposite Isaac on the train sat a small child and her father, a shabby gent in a bowler hat and second-hand jacket. Isaac made a monster face at her whenever she caught his eye.

Her father was whispering to her, entertaining her with prestidigitation. He gave her a pebble to hold, then spat on it quickly. It became a frog. The girl squealed with delight at the slimy thing and glanced shyly up at Isaac. He opened his eyes and mouth wide, mumming astonishment as he left his seat. She was still watching him as he opened the door of the train and stepped out onto Sly Station. He made his way down and onto the streets, wound through the traffic for Brock Marsh.

There were few cabs or animals in the narrow twisting streets of the Scientific Quarter, the oldest part of the ancient city. There were pedestrians of all races, as well as bakeries and laundries and guildhalls, all the sundry services any community needed. There were pubs and shops and even a militia tower; a small, stubby one at the apex of Brock Marsh where the Canker and the Tar converged. The posters plastered on the crumbling walls advertised the same dancehalls, warned of the same coming doom, demanded allegiance to the same political parties as elsewhere in the city. But for all that apparent normality, there was a tension to the area, a fraught expectancy.

Badgers—familiars by tradition, believed to have a certain immunity to the more dangerous harmonics of hidden sciences—scampered past with lists in their teeth, their pear-shaped bodies disappearing into special flaps in shop doorways. Above the thick glass storefronts were attic rooms. Old warehouses on the waterfront had been converted. Forgotten cellars lurked in temples to minor deities. In these and all the other architectural crevices, the Brock Marsh dwellers pursued their trades: physicists; chimerists; biophilosophers and teratologists; chymists;

necrochymists; mathematicians; karcists and metallurgists and
vodyanoi shaman; and those, like Isaac, whose research did not
fit neatly into any of the innumerable categories of theory.

Strange vapours wafted over the roofs. The converging rivers
on either side ran sluggishly, and the water steamed here and
there as its currents mixed nameless chymicals into potent compounds. The slop from failed experiments, from factories and
laboratories and alchymists' dens, mixed randomly into bastard
elixirs. In Brock Marsh, the water had unpredictable qualities.
Young mudlarks searching the river quag for scrap had been
known to step into some discoloured patch of mud and start
speaking long-dead languages, or find locusts in their hair, or
fade slowly to translucency and disappear.

Isaac turned down a quiet stretch of the river's edge onto the
decaying flagstones and tenacious weeds of Umber Promenade.
Across the Canker, the Ribs jutted over the roofs of Bonetown
like a clutch of vast tusks curling hundreds of feet into the air.
The river sped up a little as it bore south. Half a mile away he
could see Strack Island breaking its flow where it met the Tar and
curled away grandly to the east. The ancient stones and towers of
Parliament rose hugely from the very edges of Strack Island.
There was no gradual incline or urban scrub before the blunt layers of obsidian shot out of the water like a frozen fountain.

The clouds were dissipating, leaving behind a washed-out
sky. Isaac could see the red roof of his workshop rising above the
surrounding houses; and before it, the weed-choked forecourt of
his local, The Dying Child. The ancient tables in the outside yard
were colourful with fungus. No one, in Isaac's memory, had ever
sat at one of them.

He entered. Light seemed to give up the struggle halfway
through the thick, soiled windows, leaving the interior in shadows. The walls were unadorned except by dirt. The pub was
empty of all but the most dedicated drinkers, shambolic figures
huddled over bottles. Several were junkies, several were Remade. Some were both: The Dying Child turned no one away. A
group of emaciated young men lay draped across a table twitching in perfect time, strung out on shazbah or dreamshit or very-
tea. One woman held her glass in a metal claw that spat steam
and dripped oil onto the floorboards. A man in the corner lapped
quietly from a bowl of beer, licking the fox's muzzle that had
been grafted to his face.

Isaac quietly greeted the old man by the door, Joshua, whose Remaking had been very small and very cruel. A failed burglar, he had refused to testify against his gang, and the magister had ordered his silence made permanent: he had had his mouth taken away, sealed with a seamless stretch of flesh. Rather than live on tubes of soup pushed through his nose, Joshua had sliced himself a new mouth, but the pain had made him tremble, and it was a ragged, torn, unfinished-looking thing, a flaccid wound.

Joshua nodded at Isaac and, with his fingers, carefully held his mouth closed over a straw, sucked greedily at his cider.

Isaac headed for the back of the room. The bar, in one corner, was very low, about three feet from the ground. Behind it, in a trough of dirty water, wallowed Silchristchek the landlord.

Sil lived and worked and slept in the tub, hauling himself from one end to the other with his huge, webbed hands and frog's legs, his body wobbling like a bloated testicle, seemingly boneless. He was ancient and fat and grumpy, even for a vodyanoi. He was a bag of old blood with limbs, without a separate head, his big curmudgeonly face poking out from the fat at the front of his body.

Twice a month he scooped the water out from around him and had his regulars pour fresh buckets over him, farting and sighing with pleasure. The vodyanoi could spend at least a day in the dry without ill-effects, but Sil could not be bothered. He oozed surly indolence, and chose to do so in his filthy water. Isaac could not help feeling that Sil debased himself as a kind of aggressive show. He seemed to relish being more-disgusting-than-thou.

In the early days, Isaac had drunk here out of a youthful delight in plumbing the depths of squalor. Mature now, he frequented more salubrious inns for pleasure, returning to Sil's hovel only because it was so close to his work, and, increasingly, unexpectedly, for research purposes. Sil had taken to providing him with experimental samples he needed.

Stinking piss-coloured water slopped over the edges of the tub as Sil wriggled his way towards Isaac.

"What you having, 'Zaac?" he barked.

"Kingpin."

Isaac flipped a deuce into Sil's hand. Sil brought down a bottle from one of the shelves behind him. Isaac sipped the cheap beer and slid onto a stool, grimacing as he sat in some dubious liquid.

Sil sat back in his tub. Without looking at Isaac, he began a monosyllabic, idiot conversation about the weather, about the beer. He went through the motions. Isaac said just enough to keep the discourse alive.

On the counter were several crude figures, rendered in water that seeped into the grain of the old wood before his eyes. Two were rapidly dissolving, losing their integrity and becoming puddles as Isaac watched. Sil idly scooped up another handful from his tub and kneaded it. The water responded like clay, holding the shape Sil gave it. Scraps of the dirt and discoloration of the tub eddied inside it. Sil pinched the figure's face and made a nose, squeezed the legs to the size of small sausages. He perched the little homunculus in front of Isaac.

"That what you're after?" he asked.

Isaac swallowed the rest of his beer.

"Cheers, Sil. Appreciate it."

Very carefully, he blew on the little figure until it fell backwards into his cupped hands. It splashed a little, but he could feel its surface tension hold. Sil watched with a cynical smile as Isaac scurried to get the figurine out of the pub and to his laboratory.

Outside the wind had picked up a little. Isaac sheltered his prize and walked quickly up the little alley that adjoined The Dying Child with Paddler Way and his workshop-home. He pushed open the green doors with his bum and backed into the building. Isaac's laboratory had been a factory and a warehouse years ago, and its huge, dusty floorspace swamped the little benches and retorts and blackboards that perched in its corners.

From the two corners of the floor came yelled greetings. David Serachin and Lublamai Dadscatt—rogue-scientists like Isaac, with whom he shared the rent and the space. David and Lublamai used the ground floor, each filling a corner with their tools, separated by forty feet of empty wooden boards. A refitted waterpump jutted from the floor between their ends of the room. The construct they shared was rolling across the floor, loudly and inefficiently sweeping up dust. *They keep the useless thing out of sentimentality,* thought Isaac.

Isaac's workshop, his kitchen and his bed, were on the huge walkway that jutted out from the walls halfway up the old factory. It was about twenty feet wide, circumnavigating the hall, with a ramshackle wooden railing miraculously still holding from when Lublamai had first hammered it in.

The door slammed heavily shut behind Isaac, and the long mirror that hung beside it shuddered. *I can't believe that thing doesn't break,* thought Isaac. *We must move it.* As always, the thought was gone as soon as it had come.

As Isaac took the stairs three at a time, David saw how he held his hands and laughed.

"More of Silchristchek's high art, Isaac?" he yelled.

Isaac grinned back.

"Never let it be said I don't collect the best!"

Isaac, who had found the warehouse all those years ago, had had first pick of the working space, and it showed. His bed and stove and chamberpot were in one corner of the raised platform, and at the other end of the same side were the bulky protuberances of his lab. Glass and clay containers full of weird compounds and dangerous chymicals filled the shelves. Heliotypes of Isaac with his friends in various poses around the city and in Rudewood dotted the walls. The warehouse backed onto the Umber Promenade: his windows looked out over the Canker and the Bonetown shore, gave him a splendid view of the Ribs and the Kelltree train.

Isaac ran past those huge arched windows to an esoteric machine of burnished brass. It was a dense knot of pipes and lenses, with dials and gauges shoved roughly wherever they would fit. Ostentatiously stamped on every component of the whole was a sign: PROPERTY OF NC UNIVERSITY PHYSICS DEPT. DO NOT REMOVE.

Isaac checked and was relieved to see that the little boiler at the machine's heart had not gone out. He shoved in a handful of coal and bolted the boiler closed. He placed Sil's little statue on a viewing platform under a glass bell, and heaved at some bellows just beneath it, siphoning out the air and replacing it with gas from a slender leather tube.

He relaxed. The integrity of the vodyanoi waterpiece would hold a little longer, now. Outside vodyanoi hands, untouched, such works would last perhaps an hour before slowly collapsing back into their elemental form. Interfered with, they dissolved much more quickly: in a noble gas more slowly. He had perhaps two hours to investigate.

Isaac had become interested in vodyanoi watercræft in a roundabout way, as a result of his research in unified energy theory. He had wondered whether what allowed vodyanoi to mould water was a force related to the binding force that he sought, that held matter together in certain circumstances, dispersed it violently in others. What had happened was a common pattern of Isaac's research: a byway of his work had taken on a momentum of its own, and had become a deep, almost certainly short-lived, obsession.

Isaac bent some lens-tubes into position and lit a gasjet to illuminate the waterpiece. Isaac was still piqued by the ignorance surrounding watercræft. It brought home to him, again, how much mainstream science was bunk, how much "analysis" was just description—often bad description—hiding behind obfuscatory rubbish. His favourite example of the genre came from Benchamburg's *Hydrophysiconometricia*, a hugely respected textbook. He had howled when he read it, copied it out carefully and pinned it to his wall.

The vodyanoi, by means of what is called their *watercræft*, are able to manipulate the plasticity and sustain the surface tension of water such that a quantity will hold any shape the manipulator might give it for a short time. This is achieved by the vodyanois' application of an *hydrocohesive/aquamorphic energy field of minor diachronic extension*.

In other words, Benchamburg had no more idea how the vodyanoi shaped water than did Isaac, or a street urchin, or old Silchristchek himself.

Isaac pulled a set of levers, shifting a series of glass slides and sending different coloured lights through the statuette, which he could already see beginning to sag at the edges. Peering through a high-magnification eyepiece, he could see tiny animalculae squirm mindlessly. Internally the water's structure changed not at all: it merely wanted to occupy a different space from its usual.

He collected it as it seeped through a crack in the stand. He would examine it later, though he knew from past experience he would find nothing of any interest in it.

Isaac scribbled notes on a pad beside him. He subjected the waterpiece to various experiments as the minutes went by, piercing it with a syringe and sucking some of its substance away, taking heliotypic prints of it from various angles, blowing tiny air-bubbles into it, which rose and burst out of its top. Eventually he boiled it and let it dissipate in steam.

At one point Sincerity, David's badger, ambled up the stairs and sniffed at his dangling fingers. He stroked her absently and when she licked his hand, he yelled to David that she was hungry. He was surprised by the silence. David and Lublamai had left, presumably for a late lunch: several hours had passed since he had arrived.

He stretched and paced over to his pantry, throwing Sincerity a twist of dried meat, which she began to gnaw happily. Isaac was growing conscious of the world again, hearing boats through the walls behind him.

The door swung open and shut again below.

He trotted to the top of the stairs, expecting to see his colleagues returning.

Instead, a stranger stood in the centre of the great empty space. Air currents adjusted to his presence, investigated him like tentacles, sending a whirligig of dust spinning around him. Spots of light littered the floor from open windows and broken bricks, but none fell directly on him. The wooden walkway creaked as Isaac rocked, very slightly. The figure below jerked its head back and threw off a hood, hands clasped to its chest, very still, staring up.

Isaac gazed in astonishment.

It was a garuda.

He nearly stumbled down the stairs, fumbling with the rail, loath to take his eyes off the extraordinary visitor waiting for him. He touched earth.

The garuda stared down at him. Isaac's fascination defeated his manners, and he stared frankly back.

The great creature stood more than six feet tall, on cruel clawed feet that poked out from under a dirty cloak. The ragged cloth dangled down almost to the ground, draped loosely over every inch of flesh, obscuring the details of physiognomy and musculature, all but the garuda's head. And that great inscrutable bird face gazed down at Isaac with what looked like imperiosity. Its sharply curved beak was something between a kestrel's and an owl's. Sleek feathers faded subtly from ochre to dun to dappled brown. Deep black eyes stared at his own, the iris only a fine mottling at the very edge of the dark. Those eyes were set in orbits which gave the garuda face a permanent sneer, a proud furrow.

And looming over the garuda's head, covered in the rough sackcloth it clasped about itself, projected the unmistakable shapes of its huge furled wings, promontories of feather and skin and bone that extended two feet or more from its shoulders and curved elegantly towards each other. Isaac had never seen a garuda spread its wings at close quarters, but he had read descriptions of the dust-cloud they could raise, and the vast shadows they threw across the garuda's prey below.

What are you doing here, so far from home? thought Isaac with wonder. *Look at the colour of you: you're from the desert! You must have come miles and miles and miles, from the Cymek. What the spit are you doing here, you impressive fucker?*

He almost shook his head with awe at the great predator before he cleared his throat and spoke.

"Can I help you?"

CHAPTER FOUR

Lin, to her mortal horror, was running late.

It did not help that she was not an aficionado of Bonetown. The cross-bred architecture of that outlandish quarter confused her: a syncresis of industrialism and the gaudy domestic ostentation of the slightly rich, the peeling concrete of forgotten docklands and the stretched skins of shantytown tents. The different forms segued into each other seemingly at random in this low, flat zone, full of urban scrubland and wasteground where wild flowers and thick-stemmed plants pushed through plains of concrete and tar.

Lin had been given a street name, but the signs around her crumbled on their perches and drooped to point in impossible directions, or were obscured with rust, or contradicted each other. She concentrated to read them, looked instead at her scribbled map.

She could orient herself by the Ribs. She looked up and found them above her, shoving vastly into the sky. Only one side of the cage was visible, the bleached and blistered curves poised like a bone wave about to break over the buildings to the east. Lin made her way for them.

The streets opened out around her and she found herself before another abandoned-looking lot, but larger than the others by a huge factor. It did not look like a square but a massive unfinished hole in the city. The buildings at its edge did not show their

faces but their backs and their sides, as if they had been promised neighbours with elegant façades that had never arrived. The
streets of Bonetown edged nervously into the scrubland with ex-
ploratory little fringes of brick that petered quickly out.

The dirty grass was dotted here and there with makeshift
stalls, foldaway tables put down at random places and spread
with cheap cakes or old prints or the rubbish from someone's attic. Street-jugglers chucked things around in lacklustre displays.
There were a few half-hearted shoppers, and people of all races
sitting on scattered boulders, reading, eating, scratching at the
dry dirt, and contemplating the bones above them.

The Ribs rose from the earth at the edges of the empty
ground.

Leviathan shards of yellowing ivory thicker than the oldest
trees exploded out of the ground, bursting away from each other,
sweeping up in a curved ascent until, more than a hundred feet
above the earth, looming now over the roofs of the surrounding
houses, they curled sharply back towards each other. They
climbed as high again till their points nearly touched, vast
crooked fingers, a god-sized ivory mantrap.

There had been plans to fill the square, to build offices and
houses in the ancient chest cavity, but they had come to nothing.

Tools used on the site broke easily and went missing. Cement
would not set. Something baleful in the half-exhumed bones
kept the gravesite free of permanent disturbance.

Fifty feet below Lin's feet, archaeologists had found vertebrae
the size of houses; a backbone which had been quietly reburied
after one too many accidents on-site. No limbs, no hips, no gargantuan skull had surfaced. No one could say what manner of
creature had fallen here and died millennia ago. The grubby
print-vendors who worked the Ribs specialized in various lurid
depictions of *Gigantes Crobuzon*, four-footed or bipedal, humanoid, toothed, tusked, winged, pugnacious or pornographic.

Lin's map directed her to a nameless alley on the south side of
the Ribs. She wound her way to a quiet street where she found
the black-painted buildings she had been told to seek, a row of
dark, deserted houses, all but one with bricked-up doorways and
windows sealed and painted with tar.

There were no passers-by in this street, no cabs, no traffic. Lin
was quite alone.

Above the one remaining door in the row was chalked what
looked like a gameboard, a square divided into nine smaller

squares. There were no noughts or crosses, however, no other mark at all.

Lin hovered in the vicinity of the houses. She fidgeted with her skirt and blouse until, exasperated with herself, she walked up to the door and knocked quickly.

Bad enough that I'm late, she thought, *without pissing him off even more.*

She heard hinges and levers slide somewhere above her, and detected a tiny glint of reflected light over her head: some system of lenses and mirrors was being deployed so those within could judge whether those without were worthy of attention.

The door opened.

Standing before Lin was a vast Remade. Her face was still the same mournful, pretty human woman's it had always been, with dark skin and long plaited hair, but it supplanted a seven-foot skeleton of black iron and pewter. She stood on a tripod of stiff telescoping metal. Her body had been altered for heavy labour, with pistons and pulleys giving her what looked like ineluctable strength. Her right arm was levelled at Lin's head, and from the centre of the brass hand extended a vicious harpoon.

Lin recoiled in astonished terror.

A large voice sounded from behind the sad-faced woman.

"Ms. Lin? The artist? You're late. Mr. Motley is expecting you. Please follow me."

The Remade stepped backwards, balancing on her central leg and swinging the others behind it, giving Lin room to step around her. The harpoon did not waver.

How far can you go? thought Lin to herself, and stepped into the dark.

At the far end of an entirely black corridor was a cactacae man. Lin could taste his sap in the air, but very faintly. He stood seven feet tall, thick-limbed and heavy. His head broke the curve of his shoulders like a crag, his silhouette uneven with nodules of hardy growth. His green skin was a mass of scars, three-inch spines and tiny red spring flowers.

He beckoned to her with gnarled fingertips.

"Mr. Motley can afford to be patient," he said as he turned and climbed the stairs behind him, "but I've never known him relish waiting." He looked back clumsily and raised an eyebrow at Lin pointedly.

Fuck off, lackey, she thought impatiently. *Take me to the big man.*

He stomped off on shapeless feet like small tree-stumps.

Behind her, Lin could hear the explosive bursts of steam and thumps as the Remade took the stairs. Lin followed the cactus through a twisting, windowless tunnel.

This place is huge, Lin thought, as they moved on and on. She realized that it must be the whole row of houses, dividing walls destroyed and rebuilt, custom-made, renovated into one vast convoluted space. They passed doors from which suddenly emerged an unnerving sound, like the muffled anguish of machines. Lin's antennae bristled. As they left it behind, a volley of thuds sounded, like a score of crossbow bolts fired into soft wood.

Oh Broodma, thought Lin querulously. *Gazid, what the fuck have I let you talk me into?*

It was Lucky Gazid, the failed impresario, who had started the process leading Lin to this terrifying place.

He had run off a set of heliotypes of her most recent batch of work, hawked them around the city. It was a regular process, as he attempted to establish a reputation among the artists and patrons of New Crobuzon. Gazid was a pathetic figure forever reminding anyone who would listen of the one successful show he had arranged for a now-dead æther sculptress thirteen years previously. Lin and most of her friends viewed him with pity and contempt. Everyone she knew let him take his heliotypes and slipped him a few shekels or a noble, "an advance on his agent's fee." Then he would disappear for a few weeks, to emerge again with puke on his trousers and blood on his shoes, buzzing on some new drug, and the process would begin again.

Only not this time.

Gazid had found Lin a buyer.

When he had sidled up to her in The Clock and Cockerel she had protested. It was someone else's turn, she had scribbled on her pad, she had "advanced" him a whole guinea only a week or so ago; but Gazid had interrupted her and insisted she retreat from the table with him. And as her friends, the artistic elite of Salacus Fields, laughed and cheered them on, Gazid had handed her a stiff white card stamped with a simple crest of a three-by-three chessboard. On it was a short printed note.

Ms. Lin, it said. *My employer was most impressed with the examples of your work your agent showed him. He wonders whether you might be interested in meeting him to discuss a possible commission. We look forward to hearing from you.* The signature was illegible.

Gazid was a wreck and an addict of most things going, who could not help going to any lengths to secure money for drugs; but this was not like any scam that Lin could imagine. There was no angle for him, unless there was indeed someone wealthy in New Crobuzon prepared to pay for her work, giving him a cut.

She had dragged him out of the bar, to catcalls and whoops and consternation, and had demanded to know what was going on. Gazid was circumspect at first, and seemed to rack his brains to think of what lies to spout. He realized quite quickly that he needed to tell her the truth.

"There's a guy I buy some stuff from occasionally . . ." he started shiftily. "Anyway, I had the prints of your statues lying around . . . uh . . . on the shelf when he came round, and he loved them and wanted to take a couple away, and . . . uh . . . I said 'yeah.' And then a while later he told me that he showed them to the guy who supplies *him* with the stuff I sometimes buy, and *that* guy liked them, and took them away, and showed them to *his* boss, and then they got to the kind of top man, who's huge into art—bought some of Alexandrine's stuff last year—and he liked them and wants you to do a piece for him."

Lin translated the evasive language.

Your drug dealer's boss wants me to work for him??? she scrawled.

"Oh shit, Lin, it's not like that . . . I mean, yeah, but . . ." Gazid paused. "Well, yeah," he finished lamely. There was a pause. "Only . . . only . . . he wants to meet you. If you're interested he has to actually meet you."

Lin pondered.

It was certainly an exciting prospect. Judging by the card, this was not some minor hustler: this was a big player. Lin was not stupid. She knew that this would be dangerous. She was excited, she could not help it. It would be such an event in her art-life. She could drop hints about it. She could have a criminal patron. She was intelligent enough to realize that her excitement was childish, but not mature enough to care.

And while she was deciding that she didn't care, Gazid named the kinds of sums the mysterious buyer was quoting. Lin's headlegs flexed in astonishment.

I have to talk to Alexandrine, she wrote, and went back inside.

Alex knew nothing. She milked the kudos of having sold canvases to a crime boss for what she could, but she had only ever met an at-best middle-ranking messenger, who had offered her enormous sums for two paintings that she had just finished. She had accepted, handed them over, and never heard anything again.

That was it. She had never even known the name of her buyer.

Lin decided that she could do better than that.

She had sent a message through Gazid, down the illicit conduit of communication that led fuck-knew-where, saying that yes, she was interested, and would be prepared to meet, but she really must have a name to write in her diary.

The New Crobuzon underworld digested her message, and made her wait a week, and then spat back an answer in the shape of another printed note, pushed under her door while she slept, giving her an address in Bonetown, a date, and a one-word name: *Motley.*

A frenetic snapping and clatter sifted into the corridor. Lin's cactacae escort pushed open one dark door among the many, and stood aside.

Lin's eyes adjusted to the light. She was looking into a typing pool. It was a large room with a high ceiling, painted black like everything in this troglodytic place, well-lit with gaslamps, and filled with perhaps forty desks; on each was a bulky typewriter, at each a secretary copying from reams of notes by their sides. Mostly human and mostly women, Lin also caught smell and sight of men and cactacae, even a pair of khepri, and a vodyanoi working at a typewriter with keys adapted for her huge hands.

Around the room Remade were stationed, mostly human, again, but of other races too, rare as xenian Remade were. Some were organically Remade, with claws and antlers and slabs of grafted muscle, but most were mech, and the heat from their boilers made the room close.

At the end of the room was a closed office.

"Ms. Lin, finally," boomed a speaking-trumpet above its door as soon as she entered. None of the secretaries looked up. "Please make your way across the room to my office."

Lin picked her way between the desks. She looked closely at

what was being typed, hard though it was, and harder in the odd light of the black-walled room. The secretaries all typed expertly, reading the scribbled notes and transferring them without looking at their keyboards or their work.

Further to our conversation of the thirteenth of this month, read one, *please consider your franchise operation under our jurisdiction, terms to be arranged.* Lin moved on.

You die tomorrow, you fuck, you wormshit. You're going to envy the Remade, you cowardly cunt, you're going to scream till your mouth bleeds, said the next.

Oh . . . thought Lin. *Oh . . . help.*

The door to the office opened.

"Come in, Ms. Lin, come in!" The voice boomed from the trumpet.

Lin did not hesitate. She entered.

Filing cabinets and bookshelves filled most of the small room. There was a small, traditional oil painting of Iron Bay on one wall. Behind a large darkwood desk was a folding screen illustrated with silhouettes of fish, a large version of the screens behind which artists' models changed. In the centre of the screen, one fish was rendered in mirrored glass, giving Lin a view of herself.

Lin hovered uncertainly in front of the screen.

"Sit, sit," said a quiet voice from behind it. Lin pulled up the chair in front of the desk.

"I can see you, Ms. Lin. The mirrored carp is a window on my side. I think it's polite to let people know that."

The speaker seemed to expect a response, so Lin nodded.

"You're late, you know, Ms. Lin."

Devil's Tail! Of all the appointments to be late to! Lin thought frantically. She began to scribble an apology on her pad when the voice interrupted her.

"I can sign, Ms. Lin."

Lin put down her pad and apologized profusely with her hands.

"Don't worry," said her host disingenuously. "It happens. The Bonetown is unforgiving to visitors. Next time you'll know to leave earlier, won't you?"

Lin agreed that she would, that that was exactly what she would know to do.

"I like your work a great deal, Ms. Lin. I have all the heliotypes that made their way from Lucky Gazid. He is a sad, pathetic, broken cretin, that man—addiction is very sad in most of its forms—but he does, strangely enough, have something of a nose for art. That woman Alexandrine Nevgets was one of his, wasn't she? Pedestrian, unlike your own work, but pleasant. I'm always prepared to indulge Lucky Gazid. It will be a shame when he dies. It'll doubtless be a sordid affair, some dirty stubby knife gutting him slowly for the sake of small change; or a venereal disease involving vile emissions and sweat caught from an underage whore; or perhaps his bones will be broken for snitching—the militia, after all, do pay well, and junkies can't be choosers when it comes to income."

The voice that floated over the screen was melodious, and what the speaker said scanned hypnotically: he spoke everything into a poem. His sentences lilted on gently. His words were brutal. Lin was very afraid. She could not think of anything to say. Her hands were still.

"So having decided that I like your art I want to talk to you to discover whether you would be right for a commission. Your work is unusual for a khepri. Would you agree?"

Yes.

"Talk to me about your statues, Ms. Lin, and don't worry, were you about to, that you might sound precious. I have no prejudices against taking art seriously, and don't forget that I started this conversation. The key words to bear in mind when thinking how to answer my question are 'themes,' 'technique' and 'aesthetics.' "

Lin hesitated, but her fear drove her on. She wanted to keep this man happy, and if that meant talking about her work, then that was what she would do.

I work alone, she signed, *which is part of my . . . rebellion. I left Creekside and then Kinken, left my moiety and my hive. People were miserable, so communal art got stupidly heroic. Like Plaza of Statues. I wanted to spit out something . . . nasty. Tried to make some of the grand figures we all made together a little less perfect . . . Pissed off my sisters. So turned to my own work. Nasty work. Creekside nasty.*

"That is exactly as I had expected. It is even—forgive me—somewhat hackneyed. However, that doesn't detract from the power of the work itself. Khepri spit is a wonderful substance. Its lustre is quite unique, and its strength and lightness make it convenient, which I know is not the sort of word one is supposed to think of in connection with art, but I am pragmatic. Anyhow, to have such a lovely substance used for the drab wish-fulfilment of depressed khepri is a terrible waste. I was so very relieved to see someone using the substance for interesting, unsettling ends. The angularity you achieve is extraordinary, by the way."

Thank you. I have powerful gland technique. Lin was enjoying the licence to boast. *Originally I was a member of the Outnow school which forbids working on a piece after spat out. Gives you excellent control. Even though I have . . . reneged. I now go back while the spit is soft, work it more. More freedom, can do overhangs and the like.*

"Do you use a great deal of colour variation?" Lin nodded. "I saw only the sepia of the heliotypes. That is good to know. That is technique and aesthetics. I'm very interested to hear your thoughts on themes, Ms. Lin."

Lin was taken aback. Suddenly she could not think what her themes were.

"Let me put you in an easier position. I'd like to tell you what themes I am interested in. And then we can see if you'd be right for the commission I have in mind."

The voice waited until Lin nodded assent.

"Please tilt your head up, Ms. Lin." Startled, she did so. The motion made her nervous, exposing as it did the soft underbelly of her beetle head, inviting harm. She held her head still as eyes behind the mirror-fish watched her.

"You have the same cords in your neck as a human woman. You share the hollow at the base of your throat beloved by poets. Your skin is a shade of red that would mark you out as unusual, that's true, but it could still pass as human. I follow that beautiful human neck up—I have no doubt you won't accept the description 'human,' but indulge me a minute—and then there is . . . there is a moment . . . there is a thin zone where that soft human skin merges with the pale segmented cream underneath your head."

For the first time since Lin had entered the room, the speaker seemed to be searching for words.

"Have you ever created a statue of a cactus?" Lin shook her head. "Nonetheless you have seen them up close? My associate who led you here, for example. Did you happen to notice his feet, or his fingers, or his neck? There is a moment when the skin, the skin of the sentient creature, becomes mindless plant. Cut the fat round base of a cactus's foot, he can't feel a thing.

Poke him in the thigh where he's a bit softer, he'll squeal. But there in that zone . . . it's an altogether different thing . . . the nerves are intertwining, learning to be succulent plant, and pain is distant, blunt, diffuse, worrying rather than agonizing.

"You can think of others. The torso of the Cray or the Inchmen, the sudden transition of a Remade limb, many other races and species in this city, and countless more in the world, who live with a mongrel physiognomy. You will perhaps say that you do not recognize any transition, that the khepri are complete and whole in themselves, that to see 'human' features is anthropocentric of me. But leaving aside the irony of that accusation—an irony you can't yet appreciate—you would surely recognize the transition in other races from your own. And perhaps in the human.

"And what of the city itself? Perched where two rivers strive to become the sea, where mountains become a plateau, where the clumps of trees coagulate to the south and—quantity becomes quality—are suddenly a forest. New Crobuzon's architecture moves from the industrial to the residential to the opulent to the slum to the underground to the airborne to the modern to the ancient to the colourful to the drab to the fecund to the barren . . . You take my point. I won't go on.

"This is what makes the world, Ms. Lin. I believe this to be the fundamental dynamic. Transition. The point where one thing becomes another. It is what makes you, the city, the world, what they are. And that is the theme I'm interested in. The zone where the disparate become part of the whole. The hybrid zone.

"Could this theme interest you, d'you think? And if the answer is yes . . . then I am going to ask you to work for me. Before you answer, please understand what this will mean.

"I will ask you to work from life, to produce a model—life-size, I fancy—of me.

"Very few people see my face, Ms. Lin. A man in my position has to be careful. I'm sure you can understand. If you take this commission I will make you rich, but I will also own a part of your mind. The part that pertains to me. That is mine. I do not give you permission to share it with any. If you do, you will suffer greatly before you die.

"So . . ." Something creaked. Lin realized that he had sat back in his chair. "So, Ms. Lin. Are you interested in the hybrid zone? Are you interested in this job?"

I cannot . . . cannot turn this down, thought Lin helplessly. *I cannot. For money, for art . . . Gods help me. I cannot turn this down. Oh . . . please, please let me not regret this.*

She paused, and signed her acceptance of his terms.

"Oh, I am so glad," he breathed. Lin's heart raced. "I really am glad. Well . . ."

There was a shuffling sound behind the screen. Lin sat very still. Her antennae moved tremulously.

"The blinds are down in the office, aren't they?" said Mr. Motley. "Because I think you should see what you will be working with. Your mind is mine, Lin. You work for me now."

Mr. Motley stood and pushed the screen to the floor.

Lin got half to her feet, her headlegs bristling with astonishment and terror. She gazed at him.

Scraps of skin and fur and feathers swung as he moved; tiny limbs clutched; eyes rolled from obscure niches; antlers and protrusions of bone jutted precariously; feelers twitched and mouths glistened. Many-coloured skeins of skin collided. A cloven hoof thumped gently against the wood floor. Tides of flesh washed against each other in violent currents. Muscles tethered by alien tendons to alien bones worked together in uneasy truce, in slow, tense motion. Scales gleamed. Fins quivered. Wings fluttered brokenly. Insect claws folded and unfolded.

Lin backed away, stumbling, feeling her terrified way away from his slow advance. Her chitinous headbody was twitching neurotically. She shook.

Mr. Motley paced towards her like a hunter.

"So," he said, from one of the grinning human mouths. "Which do you think is my best side?"

CHAPTER FIVE

Isaac waited, facing his guest. The garuda stood silent. Isaac could see it was concentrating. It was preparing to speak.

The garuda's voice, when it came, was harsh and monotone.

"You are the scientist. You are . . . Grimnebulin."

It had difficulty with his name. Like a parrot trained to speak, the shaping of consonants and vowels came from within the throat, without the aid of versatile lips. Isaac had only ever conversed with two garuda in his life. One was a traveller who had long-practised the formation of human sounds; the other was a student, one of the tiny garuda community born and raised in New Crobuzon, which grew up shouting the city slang. Neither had sounded human, but neither had sounded half so animal as this great birdman struggling with an alien tongue. It took Isaac a moment to understand what had been said.

"I am." He held out his hand, spoke slowly. "What is your name?"

The garuda looked imperiously at his hand, then shook it with a strangely fragile grip.

"Yagharek . . ." There was a shrieking stress on the first syllable. The great creature paused, and shifted uncomfortably, before continuing. It repeated its name, but this time added an intricate suffix.

Isaac shook his head.

"Is that all your name?"

"Name . . . and title."

Isaac raised an eyebrow.

"Am I, then, in the presence of nobility?"

The garuda stared at him blankly. Eventually it spoke slowly without breaking his gaze.

"I am Too Too Abstract Individual Yagharek Not To Be Respected."

Isaac blinked. He rubbed his face.

"Um . . . right. You have to forgive me, Yagharek, I'm not familiar with . . . uh . . . garuda honorifics."

Yagharek shook his great head slowly.

"You will understand."

Isaac asked Yagharek to come upstairs, which he did, slowly and carefully, leaving gouges in the wooden stairs where he gripped with his great claws. But Isaac could not persuade him to sit down, or to eat, or to drink.

The garuda stood by Isaac's desk, while his host sat and stared up at him.

"So," said Isaac, "why are you here?"

Again, Yagharek gathered himself for a moment before he spoke.

"I came to New Crobuzon days ago. Because this is where the scientists are."

"Where are you from?"

"Cymek."

Isaac whistled quietly. He had been right. That was a huge journey. At least a thousand miles, through that hard, burning land, through dry veldt, across sea, swamp, steppe. Yagharek must have been driven by some strong, strong passion.

"What do you know about New Crobuzon's scientists?" asked Isaac.

"We have read of the university. Of the science and industry that moves and moves here like nowhere else. Of Brock Marsh."

"But where do you hear all this stuff?"

"From our library."

Isaac was astonished. He gaped, then recovered.

"Forgive me," he said. "I thought you were nomads."

"Yes. Our library travels."

And Yagharek told Isaac, to Isaac's growing amazement, of the Cymek library. The great librarian clan who strapped the thousands of volumes into their trunks and carried them between them as they flew, following the food and the water in the perpetual, punishing Cymek summer. The enormous tent village that sprung up where they landed, and the garuda bands that congregated on the vast, sprawling centre of learning whenever it was in their reach.

The library was hundreds of years old, with manuscripts in uncountable languages, dead and alive: Ragamoll, of which the language of New Crobuzon was a dialect; hotchi; Fellid vodyanoi and Southern vodyanoi; high khepri; and a host of others. It even contained a codex, Yagharek claimed with discernible pride, written in the secret dialect of the handlingers.

Isaac said nothing. He was ashamed at his ignorance. His view of the garuda was being torn up. This was more than a dignified savage. *Time to get me down* my *library and learn about the garuda. Pig ignorant bastard,* he reproached himself.

"Our language has no written form, but we learn to write and read in several others as we grow," said Yagharek. "We trade for more books from travellers and merchants, of whom many have passed through New Crobuzon. Some are native to this city. It is a place we know well. I have read the histories, the stories."

"Then you win, mate, because I know shit about your place," said Isaac despondently. There was a silence. Isaac looked back up at Yagharek.

"You still haven't told me why you're here."

Yagharek turned away and looked out of the window. Barges floated aimlessly below.

It was difficult to discern emotion in Yagharek's scraping voice, but Isaac thought he could hear disgust.

"I have crawled like vermin from hole to hole for a fortnight. I have sought journals and gossip and information, and it led me to Brock Marsh. And in Brock Marsh it led me to you. The question that led me has been: 'Who can change the powers of material?' 'Grimnebulin, Grimnebulin,' everyone says. 'If you have gold,' they say, 'he is yours, or if you have no gold but you interest him, or if you bore him but he pities you, or if a whim takes him.' They say you are a man who knows the secrets of matter, Grimnebulin."

Yagharek looked directly at him.

"I have some gold. I will interest you. Pity me. I beg you to help me."

"Tell me what you need," said Isaac.

Yagharek looked away from him again.

"Perhaps you have flown in a balloon, Grimnebulin. Looked down at roofs, at the earth. I grew up hunting from the skies. Garuda are a hunting people. We take our bows and spears and long whips and we scour the air of birds, the ground of prey. It is what makes us garuda. My feet are not built to walk your floors, but to close around small bodies and tear them apart. To grip dry trees and rock pillars between the earth and the sun."

Yagharek spoke like a poet. His speech was halting, but his language was that of the epics and histories he had read, the curious stilted oration of someone who has learnt a language from old books.

"Flight is not a luxury. It is what makes me garuda. My skin crawls when I look up at roofs that trap me. I want to look down at this city before I leave it, Grimnebulin. I want to fly, not once, but whenever I will.

"I want you to give me back flight."

Yagharek unclipped his cloak and threw it away across the floor. He stared at Isaac with shame and defiance. Isaac gasped.

Yagharek had no wings.

Strapped across his back was an intricate frame of wooden struts and leather straps that bobbed idiotically behind him as he turned. Two great carved planks sprouted from a kind of leather jerkin below his shoulders, jutting way above his head, where they hinged and dangled down to his knees. They mimicked wingbones. There was no skin or feathers or cloth or leather stretched between them, they were no kind of gliding apparatus. They were only a disguise, a trick, a prop on which to drape Yagharek's incongruous cloak, to make it seem as if he had wings.

Isaac reached out for them. Yagharek stiffened, then steeled himself and let Isaac touch them.

Isaac shook his head in astonishment. He caught a glimpse of ragged scar tissue on Yagharek's back, until the garuda turned abruptly to face him.

"Why?" breathed Isaac.

Yagharek's face creased slowly as he screwed up his eyes. A thin, utterly human moan started from him, and it grew and grew until it became a bird of prey's melancholy war-cry, loud and monotonous and miserable and lonely. Isaac gazed on in alarm as the cry became a barely comprehensible shout.

"Because this is my *shame*!" screamed Yagharek. He was silent for a moment, then he spoke quietly again.

"This is my shame."

He unclipped the uncomfortable-looking bulk of wood from behind him, and it fell with a flat clatter to the floor.

He was nude to the waist. His body was thin and fine and tight, with a healthy emaciation. Without the looming bulk of his fake wings behind him, he looked small and vulnerable.

He turned slowly, and Isaac caught his breath as the scars he had glimpsed were brought into view.

Two long trenches of flesh on Yagharek's shoulderblades were twisted and red with tissue that looked as if it were boiling. Slice marks spread like small veins from the main eructations of ugly healing. The strips of ruined flesh on either side of his back were a foot and a half long, and perhaps four inches at their widest point. Isaac's face wrinkled in empathy: the torn holes were criss-crossed with rough, curving slice marks, and Isaac realized that the wings had been *sawed* from Yagharek's back. No single, sudden cut but a long, drawn-out torturous disfigurement. Isaac winced.

Thinly hidden knobs of bone shifted and flexed; muscles stretched, grotesquely visible.

"Who did this?" breathed Isaac. *The stories were right,* he thought. *The Cymek is a savage, savage land.*

There was a long silence before Yagharek responded.

"I . . . I did this."

At first Isaac thought he had misunderstood.

"What do you mean? How the fuck could you . . . ?"

"I brought this onto me." Yagharek was shouting. "This is justice. It is I who did this."

"This is a fucking punishment? Godshit, fuck, what could . . . what did you do?"

"Do you judge garuda justice, Grimnebulin? I cannot hear that without thinking of the Remade . . ."

"Don't try to turn it round! You're absolutely right, I've no stomach for the law in this city . . . I'm just trying to understand what happened to you . . ."

Yagharek sighed, with a shockingly human slump of the shoulders. When he spoke, it was quiet and pained, a duty that he resented.

"I was too abstract. I was not worthy of respect. There . . . was a madness . . . I was mad. I committed a heinous act, a heinous act . . ." His words broke down into avian moans.

"What did you do?" Isaac steeled himself to hear of some atrocity.

"This language cannot express my crime. In my tongue . . ." Yagharek stopped for a moment. "I will try to translate. In my tongue they said . . . they were right . . . I was guilty of choice-theft . . . choice-theft in the second degree . . . with utter disrespect."

Yagharek was gazing back at the window. He held his head high, but he would not meet Isaac's eyes.

"That is why they deemed me Too Too Abstract. That is why I am not worthy of respect. That is who I am now. I am no longer Concrete Individual and Respected Yagharek. He is gone. I told you my name, and my name-title. I am Too Too Abstract Yagharek Not To Be Respected. That is who I will always be, and I will be true enough to tell you."

Isaac shook his head as Yagharek sat slowly on the edge of Isaac's bed. He cut a forlorn figure. Isaac stared at him for a long time before speaking.

"I have to tell you . . ." said Isaac. "I don't really . . . uh . . . Plenty of my clients are . . . not entirely on the right side of the law, shall we say? Now, I'm not going to pretend that I even slightly understand what you did, but as far as I'm concerned it's not my business. Like you said, there's no words for your crime in this city: I don't think I could ever understand what it was you'd done wrong." Isaac spoke slowly and seriously, but his mind was already racing away. He began to speak with more animation.

"And your problem . . . is interesting." Representations of forces and lines of power, of femtomorphic resonances and energy fields were beginning to leap into his consciousness. "It's easy enough to get you *into* the air. Balloons, force manipulation and whatnot. Even easy to get you up there more than once. But to get you up there *whenever you want it*, under your *own steam* . . . which is what you're after, yes?" Yagharek nodded. Isaac stroked his chin.

"Godspit . . . ! Yes . . . now that is a much more . . . interesting conundrum."

Isaac was beginning to retreat into his computations. One prosaic part of his mind recalled that he had no appointments for some time, and that meant he could immerse himself in research for a little while. Another pragmatic level did its job, evaluating the importance and urgency of his outstanding work. A couple of piss-easy analyses of compounds that he could put off more or less indefinitely; a half-promise to synthesize an elixir or two—easy to get out of . . . apart from that, it was only his own research into vodyanoi watercræft. Which he could put to one side.

No, no, no! he contradicted himself suddenly. *Don't have to put watercræft aside . . . I can integrate it! It's all about elements arsing about, misbehaving . . . liquid that stands free, heavy matter that invades the air . . . there's got to be something there . . . some common denominator . . .*

With an effort he brought himself back to his laboratory, realized that Yagharek was staring at him impassively.

"I'm interested in your problem," he said simply. Immediately Yagharek reached into a pouch. He held out a huge handful of twisted, dirty gold nuggets. Isaac opened his eyes wide.

"Well . . . uh, thank you. I'll certainly accept some expenses, hourly rates, etc . . ." Yagharek handed Isaac the pouch.

Isaac managed not to whistle as he weighed it in his hand. He peered into it. Layer on heavy layer of sifting gold. It was undignified, but Isaac felt almost spellbound. This represented more money than he had ever seen in one place, enough to cover a lot of research costs and still live well for months.

Yagharek was no businessman, that was certain. He could have offered a third, a quarter of this and still had almost anyone in Brock Marsh panting. He should have kept most of it back, dangled it if interest waned.

Maybe he has *kept most of it back*, thought Isaac, and his eyes widened even further.

"How do I reach you?" said Isaac, still gazing at his gold. "Where are you living?"

Yagharek shook his head and was silent.

"Well, I have to be able to reach you . . ."

"I will come to you," said the garuda. "Every day, every two days, every week . . . I will make sure you do not forget my case."

"No danger of that, I assure you. Are you really saying I can't get messages to you?"

"I do not know where I will be, Grimnebulin. I shun this city. It hunts me. I must keep moving."

Isaac shrugged helplessly. Yagharek stood to leave.

"You understand what I want, Grimnebulin? I do not want to have to take a potion. I do not want to have to wear a harness. I do not want to climb into a contraption. I do not want one glorious journey into the clouds, and an earthbound eternity. I want you to let me leap from the earth as easily as you walk from room to room. Can you do that, Grimnebulin?"

"I don't know." Isaac spoke slowly. "But I think so. I'm your best bet, I reckon. I'm not a chymist, or a biologist, or a thaumaturge . . . I'm a dilettante, Yagharek, a dabbler. I think of myself . . ." Isaac paused and laughed briefly. He spoke with heavy gusto. "I think of myself as the main station for all the schools of thought. Like Perdido Street Station. You know it?" Yagharek nodded. "Unavoidable, ain't it? Fucking massive great thing." Isaac patted his belly, maintaining the analogy. "All the train-lines meet there—Sud Line, Dexter, Verso, Head and Sink Lines; everything has to pass through it. That's like me. That's my job. That's the kind of scientist I am. I'm being frank with you. Thing is, you see, I think that's what you need."

Yagharek nodded. His predatory face was so sharp, so hard. Emotion was invisible. His words had to be decoded. It was not his face, nor his eyes, nor his bearing (once again proud and imperious), nor his voice that let Isaac see his despair. It was his words.

"Be a dilettante, a sciolist, a swindler . . . So long as you return me to the sky, Grimnebulin."

Yagharek stooped and picked up his ugly wooden disguise.

He strapped it to himself without obvious shame, despite the indignity of the act. Isaac watched as Yagharek draped the huge cloak over himself and stepped quietly down the stairs.

Isaac leant thoughtfully on the railing and looked down into the dusty space. Yagharek paced past the immobile construct, past haphazard piles of papers and chairs and blackboards. The light beams that had burst through walls pierced by age were gone. The sun was low, now, behind the buildings across from Isaac's warehouse, blocked by massed ranks of bricks, sliding sideways across the ancient city, lighting the hidden sides of the Dancing Shoe Mountains, Spine Peak and the crags of Penitent's Pass, throwing the jagged skyline of the earth into silhouettes that loomed up miles to the west of New Crobuzon.

When Yagharek opened the door, it was onto a street in shadow.

Isaac worked into the night.

As soon as Yagharek left Isaac opened his window and dangled a large red piece of cord from nails in the brick. He moved his heavy calculation engine from the centre of its desk to the floor beside it. Sheafs of programme cards spilt from its storage shelf to the floor. Isaac swore. He patted them together and replaced them. Then he carried his typewriter to his desk and began to make a list. Occasionally he would leap upright and pace over to his makeshift bookshelves, or rummage through a pile of books on the floor, till he found the volume he was looking for. He would take it to the desk and flick through from the back, searching for the bibliography. He laboriously copied details, stabbing with two fingers at the typewriter keys.

As he wrote, the parameters of his plan began to expand. He sought more and more books, his eyes widening as he realized the potentiality of this research.

Eventually he stopped and sat back in his chair, pondering. He grabbed some loose paper and scrawled diagrams on it: mental maps, plans of how to proceed.

Again and again he returned to the same model. A triangle, with a cross firmly planted in the middle. He could not stop himself grinning.

"I like it . . ." he murmured.

There was a knock at the window. He rose and paced over to it.

A small scarlet idiot face grinned at Isaac from outside. Two stubby horns jutted from its prominent chin, ridges and knobs of bone unconvincingly imitated a hairline. Watery eyes gazed above an ugly, cheerful grin.

Isaac opened the window onto the rapidly dwindling light. There was an argument between klaxons as industrial boats fought to crawl past each other in the waters of the Canker. The creature perched on Isaac's window-ledge hopped up into the open window-frame, grasping the edges with gnarled hands.

"Wotcher, captain!" it gabbled. Its accent was thick and bizarre. "Saw the red wossname, scarf thing . . . Says to meself, 'Time for da bossman!' " It winked and barked stupid laughter. "Wossyer pleasure, captain? Atcher service."

"Evening, Teafortwo. You got my message." The creature flapped its red batwings.

Teafortwo was a wyrman. Barrel-chested creatures like squat birds, with thick arms like a human dwarf's below those ugly, functional wings, the wyrmen ploughed the skies of New Crobuzon. Their hands were their feet, those arms jutting from the bottom of their squat bodies like crows' legs. They could pace a few clumsy steps here and there balancing on their palms, if they were indoors, but they preferred to career over the city, yelling and swooping and screaming abuse at passers-by.

The wyrmen were more intelligent than dogs or apes, but decidedly less than humans. They thrived on an intellectual diet of scatology and slapstick and mimicry, picking names for each other gleaned without understanding from popular songs and furniture catalogues and discarded textbooks they could just about read. Teafortwo's sister, Isaac knew, was called Bottletop; one of his sons Scabies.

The wyrmen lived in hundreds and thousands of nooks, in attics and annexes and behind hoardings. Most picked a living from the margins of the city. The huge dumps and rubbish-heaps at the outskirts of Stoneshell and Abrogate Green, the wastescape by the river in Griss Twist, all swarmed with wyrmen, squabbling and laughing, drinking from stagnant canals, fucking in the sky and on the earth. Some, like Teafortwo, supplemented this with informal employment. When scarfs flapped on roofs, or chalk marks defaced walls near attic windows, the odds were that someone was calling some wyrman or other for a task.

Isaac foraged in his pocket and held up a shekel.

"Fancy earning this, Teafortwo?"

"Betcha, captain!" shouted Teafortwo. "Look out below!" he added and shat loudly. The stool spattered on the street. Teafortwo guffawed.

Isaac handed him the list he had made, rolled into a scroll.

"Take that to the university library. You know it? Over the river? Good. It's open late, you should catch 'em open. Give that to the librarian. I've signed it, so they shouldn't give you any trouble. They'll load you up with some books. Think you can bring them back to me? They'll be pretty heavy."

"No problem, captain!" Teafortwo swelled his chest like a bantam. "Big strong lad!"

"Fine. Manage it in one go and I'll slip you a bit more moolah."

Teafortwo clutched the list and turned to go with some rude childish yell, when Isaac grabbed the edge of his wing. The wyrman turned, surprised.

"Problem, boss?"

"No, no . . ." Isaac was staring at the base of his wing, thoughtfully. He gently opened and closed Teafortwo's massive wing with his hands. Under that vivid red skin, horny and pockmarked and stiff like leather, Isaac could feel the specialized muscles of flight winding through the flesh to the wings. They moved with a magnificent economy. He bent the wing through a full circle, feeling the muscles tug it into a paddling, scooping motion that would shovel air out and under the wyrman. Teafortwo giggled.

"Captain tickle me! Saucy devil!" he screamed.

Isaac reached for some paper, having to stop himself from dragging Teafortwo with him. He was visualizing the wyrman wing represented mathematically, as simple component planes.

"Teafortwo . . . tell you what. When you get back, I'll toss you another shekel if I can take a few heliotypes of you and do a couple of experiments. Only half an hour or so. What do you say?"

"Lovely-jubbly, captain!"

Teafortwo hopped onto the window-sill and lurched out into the gloaming. Isaac squinted, studying the rolling motion of the wings, watching those strong muscles unique to the airborne send eighty or more pounds of twisted flesh and bone powering through the sky.

When Teafortwo had disappeared from sight, Isaac sat and made another list, by hand this time, scribbling at speed.

Research, he wrote at the top of the page. Then below it:

physics; gravity; forces/planes/vectors; UNIFIED FIELD. And a little below that, he wrote: *Flight i) natural ii) thaumaturgical iii) chymico-physical iv) combined v) other.*

Finally, underlined and in capitals, he wrote PHYSIOGNOMIES OF FLIGHT.

He sat back, not relaxed but poised to leap. He was humming abstractedly. He was desperately excited.

He fumbled for one of the books he had fished from under his bed, an enormous old volume. He let it topple flat onto the desk, relishing the heavy sound. The cover was embossed in unrealistic fake gold.

A Bestiary Of The Potentially Wise: The Sentient Races Of Bas-Lag.

Isaac stroked the cover of Shacrestialchit's classic, translated from the Lubbock vodyanoi and updated a hundred years ago by Benkerby Carnadine, human merchant, traveller and scholar of New Crobuzon. Constantly reprinted and imitated, but still unsurpassed. Isaac put his finger on the G of the thumb-index and flipped the pages, until he found the exquisite watercolour sketch of the Cymek bird-people that introduced the essay on the garuda.

As the light ebbed from the room he turned on the gaslamp that sat on his desk. Out in the cool air, away to the east, Teafortwo beat his wings heavily and grasped the sack of books that dangled below him. He could see the bright glimmer of Isaac's gasjet, and just beyond it, outside the window, the sputtering ivory of the streetlamp. A constant stream of night-insects spiralled it like elyctrons, finding their occasional way through a crack in the glass and immolating themselves in its light with a little combustive burst. Their carbonized remains dusted the bottom of the glass.

The lamp was a beacon, a lighthouse in that forbidding city, steering the wyrman's way over the river and out of the predatory night.

In this city, those who look like me are not like me. I made the mistake once (tired and afraid and desperate for help) of doubting that.

Looking for a place to hide, looking for food and warmth at night and respite from the stares that greet me whenever I set foot on the streets. I saw a young fledgling, running easily along the narrow passageway between drab houses. My heart nearly burst. I cried out to him, this boy of my own kind, in the desert tongue . . . and he gazed back at me and spread his wings and opened his beak and broke into some cacophonous laughter.

He swore at me in a bestial croaking. His larynx fought to shape human sounds. I cried out to him but he would not understand. He yelled something behind him and a group of human street-children congregated from holes in the city, like spirits spiteful to the living. He gesticulated at me, that bright-eyed chick, and he screamed curses too fast for me to understand. And these, his comrades, these dirty-faced roughnecks, these dangerous brutalized amoral little creatures with pinched faces and ragged trousers, spattered with snot and rheum and urban dirt, girls in stained shifts and boys with jackets too big, grabbed cobblestones from the earth and pelted me where I lay in the darkness of a decaying threshold.

And the little boy whom I will not call garuda, who was nothing but human with freakish wings and feathers, my little lost non-brother threw the stones with his comrades and laughed and broke windows behind my head and called me names.

I realized then as the stones splintered my pillow of old paint that I was alone.

And so, and so, I know that I must live without respite from this isolation. That I will not speak to any other creature in my own tongue.

I have taken to foraging alone after nightfall when the city quiets and becomes introspective. I walk as an intruder on its solipsistic dream. I came by darkness, I live by darkness. The savage brightness of the desert is like some legend I heard a long time ago. My existence grows nocturnal. My beliefs change.

I emerge into streets that wind like dark rivers through cavernous brick rockfaces. The moon and her little shining daughters glimmer wanly. Cold winds ooze like molasses down from the foothills and the mountains and clog the night-city with drifting rubbish. I share the streets with aimlessly moving scraps of paper and little whirlwinds of dust, with motes that pass like erratic thieves under eaves and through doors.

I remember the desert winds: the Khamsin that scourges the land like smokeless fire; the Föhm that bursts from hot mountainsides as if in ambush; the sly Simoom that inveigles its way through leather sandscreens and library doors.

The winds of this city are a more melancholy breed. They explore like lost souls, looking in at dusty gaslit windows. We are brethren, the city-winds and I. We wander together.

We have found sleeping beggars that clutch each other and congeal for warmth like lower creatures, forced back down evolutionary strata by their poverty.

We have seen the city's night-porters fish the dead from the rivers. Dark-suited militia tugging with hooks and poles at bloated bodies with eyes ripped from their heads, the blood set and gelatinous in their sockets.

We have watched mutant creatures crawl from sewers into cold flat starlight and whisper shyly to each other, drawing maps and messages in the faecal mud.

I have sat with the wind at my side and seen cruel things, wicked things.

My scars and bonestubs itch. I am forgetting the weight, the sweep, the motion of wings. If I were not garuda I would pray. But I will not obeise myself before arrogant spirits.

Sometimes I make my way to the warehouse where Grimnebulin reads and writes and scrawls, and I climb silently to the roof, and I lie with my back to the slate. The thought of all that energy of his mind channelled towards flight, my flight, my deliverance, lessens the itching in my ruined back. The wind tugs me harder when I am here: it feels betrayed. It knows that if I am made whole it will lose its nighttime companion in the brick mire and midden of New Crobuzon. So it chastises me when I lie there, suddenly threatening to pull me from my perch into the wide stinking river, clutching my feathers, fat petulant air warning me not to leave it; but I grip the roof with my claws and let the heal-ing vibrations pass up from Grimnebulin's mind through the crumbling slate into my poor flesh.

I sleep in old arches under the thundering railtracks.

I eat whatever organic thing I find that will not kill me.

I hide like a parasite in the skin of this old city that snores and farts and rumbles and scratches and swells and grows warty and pugnacious with age.

Sometimes I clamber to the top of the huge, huge towers that teeter like porcupine spines from the city's hide. Up in the thin-ner air, the winds lose the melancholy curiosity they have at street level. They abandon their second-floor petulance. Stirred by towers that poke above the host of city light—intense white carbide lamps, smoke-burnished red of lit grease, tallow twin-kling, frenetic sputtering gas flare, all anarchic guards against the dark—the winds rejoice and play.

I can dig my claws into the rim of a building's crown and spread my arms and feel the buffets and gouts of boisterous air and I can close my eyes and remember, for a moment, what it is to fly.

PART TWO

Physiognomies of Flight

CHAPTER SIX

New Crobuzon was a city unconvinced by gravity.

Aerostats oozed from cloud to cloud above it like slugs on cabbages. Militia-pods streaked through the heart of the city to its outlands, the cables that held them twanging and vibrating like guitar strings hundreds of feet in the air. Wyrmen clawed their way above the city leaving trails of defecation and profanity. Pigeons shared the air with jackdaws and hawks and sparrows and escaped parakeets. Flying ants and wasps, bees and bluebottles, butterflies and mosquitoes fought airborne war against a thousand predators, aspises and dheri that snapped at them on the wing. Golems thrown together by drunken students beat mindlessly through the sky on clumsy wings made of leather or paper or fruit-rind, falling apart as they flew. Even the trains that moved innumerable women and men and commodities around New Crobuzon's great carcass fought to stay above the houses, as if they were afraid of the putrefaction of architecture.

The city thrust upwards massively, as if inspired by those vast mountains that rose to the west. Blistering square slabs of habitation ten, twenty, thirty storeys high punctuated the skyline. They burst into the air like fat fingers, like fists, like the stumps of limbs waving frantically above the swells of the lower houses. The tons of concrete and tar that constituted the city covered ancient geography, knolls and barrows and verges, undulations that were still visible. Slum houses spilt down the sides of Vaudois Hill, Flyside, Flag Hill, St. Jabber's Mound like scree.

The smoky black walls of Parliament jutted from Strack Island like a shark's tooth or a stingray's jag, some monstrous organic weapon rending the sky. The building was knotted with obscure tubes and vast rivets. It throbbed with the ancient boilers deep within. Rooms used for uncertain purposes poked out of the main body of the colossal edifice with scant regard for buttresses or braces. Somewhere inside, in the Chamber, out of reach of the sky, Rudgutter and countless droning bores strutted. The Parliament was like a mountain poised on the verge of architectural avalanche.

It was not a purer realm that loomed vastly over the city. Smokestacks punctured the membrane between the land and the air and disgorged tons of poisonous smog into that upper world as if out of spite. In a thicker, stinking haze just above the rooftops, the detritus from a million low chimneys eddied together. Crematoria vented into the airborne ashes of wills burnt by jealous executors, which mixed with coaldust burnt to keep dying lovers warm. Thousands of sordid smoke-ghosts wrapped New Crobuzon in a stench that suffocated like guilt.

The clouds swirled in the city's filthy microclimate. It seemed as if all of New Crobuzon's weather was formed by a massive, gradual crawling hurricane that centred around the city's heart, the enormous mongrel building that squatted at the core of the commercial zone known as The Crow, the coagulate of miles of railway line and years of architectural styles and violations: Perdido Street Station.

An industrial castle, bristling with random parapets. The westernmost tower of the station was the militia's Spike, that loomed over the other turrets, dwarfing them, tugged in seven directions by taut skyrails. But for all its height the Spike was only an annex of the enormous station.

The architect had been incarcerated, quite mad, seven years after Perdido Street Station was completed. He was a heretic, it was said, intent on building his own god.

Five enormous brick mouths gaped to swallow each of the city's trainlines. The tracks unrolled on the arches like huge tongues. Shops and torture chambers and workshops and offices and empty spaces all stuffed the fat belly of the building, which seemed, from a certain angle, in a certain light, to be bracing itself, taking its weight on the Spike, preparing to leap into the enormous sky it so casually invaded.

Isaac did not look with eyes clouded by romance. He saw flight wherever he looked in the city (his eyes were swollen: behind them buzzed a brain wired with new formulae and facts all furnished to slip gravity's clutches), and he saw that it was not an escape to a better place. Flight was a secular, profane thing: simply a passage from one part of New Crobuzon to another.

He was cheered by this. He was a scientist, not a mystic.

Isaac lay on his bed and gazed out of his window. He followed one flying speck after another with his eyes. Scattered around him on the bed, spilling onto the floor like a paper tide, were books and articles, typewritten notes and long sheaves of his excited scrawl. Classic monographs nestled under the musings of cranks. Biology and philosophy jostled for space on his desk.

He had sniffed his way along a contorted bibliographical trail like a bloodhound. Some titles could not be ignored: *On Gravity* or *The Theory Of Flight*. Some were more tangential, like *The Aerodynamics Of The Swarm*. And some were simply whims that his more respectable colleagues would surely frown at. He had yet, for example, to browse the pages of *The Dweomers That Live Above The Clouds And What They Can Tell Us*.

Isaac scratched his nose and sipped the beer balancing on his chest through a straw.

Only two days working on Yagharek's commission, and the city was completely changed for him. He wondered if it would ever change back.

He rolled onto his side, rummaged around underneath him to shift the papers that were making him uncomfortable. He tugged free a collection of obscure manuscripts and a sheaf of the heliotypes he had taken of Teafortwo. Isaac held those prints in front of him, examined the intricacies of the wyrmen musculature that he had made Teafortwo show off.

Hope it's not too long, Isaac thought.

He had spent the day reading and taking notes, grunting politely when David or Lublamai yelled greetings or questions or offers of lunch up to him. He had munched some bread and cheese and peppers which Lublamai had dumped on his desk in front of him. He had gradually shed layers of clothing as the day grew warmer and the little boilers on all the equipment heated the air. Shirts and kerchiefs littered the floor by his desk.

Isaac was waiting for delivery of supplies. He had realized early in his reading that for the purposes of this commission there was a massive hole in his scientific knowledge. Of all the arcana, biology was his weakest. He was quite at home reading about levitation and countergeotropic thaumaturgy and his beloved unified field theory, but the prints of Teafortwo had made him realize how little he understood the biomechanics of simple flight.

What I need's some dead wyrmen . . . no, some live one to do experiments on . . . Isaac had thought idly, staring at the heliotypes the previous night. *No . . . a dead one to dissect* and *a live one to watch flying . . .*

The flippant idea had suddenly taken a more serious shape. He had sat and pondered for a while at his desk, before taking off into the darkness of Brock Marsh.

The most notorious pub between the Tar and the Canker lurked in the shadow of a huge Palgolak church. It was a few dank streets back from Danechi's Bridge, which joined Brock Marsh to Bonetown.

Most of the denizens of Brock Marsh, of course, were bakers or street-sweepers or prostitutes, or any of a host of other professions unlikely ever to cast a hex or look into a test-tube in their lives. Similarly, the inhabitants of Bonetown were, for the most part, no more interested in grossly or systematically flouting the law than most of New Crobuzon. Nevertheless, Brock Marsh would always be the Science Quarter: Bonetown the Thieves' District. And there where those two influences met—esoteric, furtive, romanticized and sometimes dangerous—was The Moon's Daughters.

With a sign depicting the two small satellites that orbited the moon as pretty, rather tawdry-looking young women, and a façade painted in deep scarlet, The Moon's Daughters was shabby but attractive. Inside, its clientele consisted of the more adventurous of the city's bohemians: artists, thieves, rogue scientists, junkies and militia informants jostling under the eyes of the pub's proprietor, Red Kate.

Kate's nickname was a reference to her ginger hair, and, Isaac had always thought, a damning indictment of the creative bankruptcy of her patrons. She was physically powerful, with a sharp eye for who to bribe and who to ban, who to punch and who to ply with free beer. For these reasons (as well, Isaac suspected, as a small proficiency with a couple of subtle thaumaturgical glamours), The Moon's Daughters negotiated a successful, precarious trail evading any of the competing protection rackets in the area. The militia raided Kate's establishment only rarely and perfunctorily. Her beer was good. She did not ask what was being discussed in huddles and knots at corner tables.

That night, Kate had greeted Isaac with a brief wave, which he had returned. He had gazed around the smoky room, but the person he had been seeking was absent. He had made his way to the bar.

"Kate," he shouted over the din. "No sign of Lemuel?"

She shook her head and handed him, unbidden, a Kingpin ale. He paid and turned to face the room.

He was rather thrown. The Moon's Daughters was Lemuel Pigeon's office, as near as dammit. He could usually be relied on to be here every night, wheeling, dealing, taking a cut. Isaac guessed he was out on some dubious job or other. He paced through the tables aimlessly, looking for someone he knew.

Over in the corner, grinning beatifically at someone, wearing the yellow robes of his order, was Gedrecsechet, the librarian of the Palgolak church. Isaac brightened and headed towards him.

He was amused to see that the forearms of the scowling youth arguing with Ged were tattooed with the interlocking wheels that proclaimed her a Godmech Cog, doubtless attempting to convert the ungodly. As Isaac drew closer the argument became audible.

". . . if you approach the world and God with one iota of the *rigour* and the *analysis* you claim, you'd see that your pointless sentientomorphism would simply be untenable!"

Ged grinned at the spotty girl and opened his mouth to reply. Isaac interrupted.

"Pardon me, Ged, for butting in. Just wanted to say to you, young Flywheel, whatever you call yourself . . ."

The Cog tried to protest, but Isaac cut her off.

"No, shut up. I'll say this very clearly . . . *piss off*. And take your rigour with you. I want to talk to Ged."

Ged was giggling. His opponent was swallowing, trying to maintain her anger, but she was intimidated by Isaac's bulk and cheerful pugnacity. She gathered herself to go with a semblance of dignity.

As she stood, she opened her mouth with some parting shot she had clearly been preparing. Isaac pre-empted her.

"Speak and I'll break your teeth," he advised amiably.

The Cog closed her mouth and stalked off.

When she was gone from view both Isaac and Ged burst into laughter.

"Why do you put up with them, Ged?" howled Isaac.

Ged, crouched like a frog before the low table, rocked back

and forth on his legs and arms, his big tongue flapping in and out of his huge loose mouth.

"I just feel *sorry* for them," he tittered. "They're so . . . *intense*."

Ged was generally held to be the most anomalously good-humoured vodyanoi anyone had ever met. He had absolutely none of the glowering snappiness typical of that cantankerous race.

"Anyway," he continued, calming down a little, "I don't mind the Cogs nearly as much as some. They don't have half the rigour they think they do, of course, but at least they're taking things seriously. And at least they're not . . . I don't know . . . Compline or Godling Brood, or something."

Palgolak was a god of knowledge. He was depicted either as a fat, squat human reading in a bath, or a svelte vodyanoi doing the same, or, mystically, both at once. His congregation were human and vodyanoi in roughly equal proportions. He was an amiable, pleasant deity, a sage whose existence was entirely devoted to the collection, categorization, and dissemination of information.

Isaac worshipped no gods. He did not believe in the omniscience or omnipotence claimed for a few, or even the existence of many. Certainly there were creatures and essences that inhabited different aspects of existence, and certainly some of them were powerful, in human terms. But worshipping them seemed to him rather a craven activity. Even he, though, had a soft spot for Palgolak. He rather hoped the fat bastard *did* exist, in some form or other. Isaac liked the idea of an inter-aspectual entity so enamoured with knowledge that it just roamed from realm to realm in a bath, murmuring with interest at everything it came across.

Palgolak's library was at least the equal to that of the New Crobuzon University. It did not lend books, but it did allow readers in at any time of the day or the night, and there were very, very few books it did not allow access to. The Palgolaki were proselytizers, holding that everything known by a worshipper was immediately known by Palgolak, which was why they were religiously charged to read voraciously. But their mission was only secondarily for the glory of Palgolak, and primarily for the glory of knowledge, which was why they were sworn to admit all who wished to enter into their library.

Which was what Ged was gently complaining about. The

New Crobuzon Palgolak Library had the best collection of religious manuscripts known in the world of Bas-Lag, and it attracted pilgrims from a huge variety of religious traditions and factions. They thronged the northern ends of Brock Marsh and Spit Hearth, all the worshipping races of the world, in robes and masks, sporting whips, leashes, magnifying glasses, the whole gamut of religious paraphernalia.

Some of the pilgrims were less than pleasant. The viciously anti-xenian Godling Brood, for example, was growing in the city, and Ged saw it as his unfortunate sacred duty to assist these racists who spat and called him "toad" and "riverpig" in between tracing passages from their texts.

Compared to them, the egalitarian Godmech Cogs were a harmless sect, even if their belief in the mechanicity of One True God was aggressively asserted.

Isaac and Ged had had many long arguments over the years, mostly theological, but also over literature and art and politics. Isaac respected the friendly vodyanoi. He knew him to be fervent in his religious duty of reading and, accordingly, hugely knowledgeable about any subject Isaac could think of. He was always at first a little circumspect with *opinions* about the information he shared—"Only Palgolak has enough knowledge to offer *analysis*," Ged would proclaim piously at the start of an argument—until three or so drinks had obscured his religious non-dogmaticism and he would hold forth at the top of his voice.

"Ged," Isaac asked. "What can you tell me about the garuda?"

Ged shrugged, and he grinned with pleasure at imparting what he knew.

"Not very much. Bird-people. Live in the Cymek, and the north of Shotek, and the west of Mordiga, reputedly. Maybe also on some of the other continents. Hollow bones." Ged's eyes were fixed, focused on the remembered pages of whatever xenthropological work he was quoting. "Cymek garuda are egalitarian . . . *completely* egalitarian, and completely individualistic. Hunters and gatherers, no sexual division of labour. No money, no rank, although they do have sort of *uninstitutional* ranks. Just means you're worthy of more respect, that sort of thing. Don't worship any gods, although they do have a devil-figure, which may or may not be a real eidolon. Dahnesch, it's called. Hunt and fight with whips, bows, spears, light blades. Don't use shields: too heavy to fly with. So they sometimes use two weapons at once.

Have the occasional rumble with other bands or species, probably over resources. You know about their library?"

Isaac nodded. Ged's eyes glazed with an almost obscene look of hunger.

"Godspit, I'd love to get to that. It'll never happen." He looked glum. "Desert's not really vodyanoi territory. Bit dry . . ."

"Well, seeing as you know so arsing little about them, I might as well just stop talking to you," said Isaac.

To Isaac's astonishment, Ged's face fell.

"Joke, Ged! Irony! Sarcasm! You know fucking *loads* about them. At least compared to me. I've been browsing Shacrestial-chit, and you've just exceeded the sum of my knowledge. Do you know anything about . . . uh . . . their criminal code?"

Ged stared at him. His huge eyes narrowed.

"What you up to, Isaac? They're so egalitarian . . . well . . . Their society's all based on maximizing choice for the individual, which is why they're communistic. Grants the most uninhibited choice to everyone. And as far as I remember the *only* crime they have is depriving another garuda of choice. And then it's exacerbated or mollified depending on whether they do it with or without respect, which they absolutely *love* . . ."

"How do you steal someone's choice?"

"No idea. I suppose if you nick someone's spear, they don't have the choice of using it . . . What about if you lie about where some tasty lichen is, so you deprive others of the choice of going for it . . . ?"

"Maybe some choice-thefts are analogies of stuff we'd consider crimes and some have absolutely no equivalent," said Isaac.

"I'd imagine so."

"What's an abstract individual and a concrete individual?"

Ged was gazing at Isaac in wonder.

"My good arse, Isaac . . . you've made friends with some garuda, haven't you?"

Isaac raised one eyebrow, and nodded quickly.

"Damn!" Ged shouted. People at the surrounding tables turned to him with brief surprise. "And a Cymek garuda . . . ! Isaac, you *have* to make him—him? her?—come and talk to me about the Cymek!"

"I don't know, Ged. He's a bit . . . taciturn . . ."

"Oh please oh *please* . . ."

"All right, all right, I'll *ask* him. But don't get your hopes up.

Now tell me what the difference is between a fucking abstract and concrete individual."

"Oh, this is *fascinating*. I suppose you aren't allowed to tell me what the job is . . . ? No, didn't think so. Well, put simply, and as far as I understand it, they're egalitarian because they respect the individual so much, right? And you can't respect other people's individuality if you focus on your own individuality in a kind of abstract, isolated way. The point is that you *are* an individual inasmuch as you exist in a social matrix of others who respect your individuality and your right to make choices. That's concrete individuality: an individuality that recognizes that it owes its existence to a kind of communal respect on the part of all the other individualities, and that it had better therefore respect them similarly.

"So an abstract individual is a garuda who forgot, for some time, that he or she is part of a larger unit, and owes respect to all the other *choosing* individuals."

There was a long pause.

"Are you any wiser, Isaac?" asked Ged gently, and broke off into giggles.

Isaac wasn't sure if he was or not.

"So look, Ged, if I said to you 'second-degree choice-theft with disrespect,' would you know what a garuda had done?"

"No . . ." Ged looked thoughtful. "No, I wouldn't. Sounds bad . . . I think there are some books in the library that might explain, though . . ."

At that moment, Lemuel Pigeon strode into Isaac's view.

"Ged, look," Isaac interrupted hurriedly. "Beg pardon and all that, I really have to have a word with Lemuel. Can I talk to you later?"

Ged grinned without rancour and waved Isaac away.

"Lemuel . . . a word in your ear. Could be profitable."

"Isaac! Always a pleasure to deal with a man of science. How's the life of the mind?"

Lemuel leant back in his chair. He was dressed foppishly. His jacket was burgundy, his waistcoat yellow. He wore a small top hat. A mass of yellow curls burst out from under it in a ponytail they clearly resented.

"The life of the mind, Lemuel, has reached something of an impasse. And that, my friend, is where *you* come in."

"Me?" Lemuel Pigeon smiled lopsidedly.

"Yes, Lemuel," said Isaac portentously. "You too can forward the cause of science."

Isaac enjoyed bantering with Lemuel, although the younger man made him a little uneasy. Lemuel was a chancer, a snitch, a fence . . . the quintessential go-between. He had carved a profitable little niche for himself out of being a most efficient middleman. Packages, information, offers, messages, refugees, goods: anything that two people wanted to exchange without actually meeting, Lemuel would courier. He was invaluable to those like Isaac who wanted to dredge the New Crobuzon underworld without getting their feet wet or their hands dirty. Similarly, the denizens of that other city could use Lemuel to reach into the realm of the more-or-less legal without beaching, flopping helplessly at the militia's door. Not that all of Lemuel's work involved both worlds: some was entirely legal or entirely illegal. It was just that crossing the border was his speciality.

Lemuel's existence was precarious. He was unscrupulous and brutal—vicious when necessary. If the going ever got dangerous, he would leave anyone with him in a trail of his dust. Everyone knew that. Lemuel never hid it. There was a certain honesty about him. He never pretended that you could trust him.

"Lemuel, you young science fiend, you . . ." Isaac said. "I'm conducting a little research. Now, I need to get hold of some specimens. I'm talking anything that flies. And that is where you come in. See, a man in my position can't be trogging around New Crobuzon looking for fucking *wrens* . . . a man in my position should be able to put the word out and have winged things fall into his lap."

"Put an ad in the newspapers, Isaac old chum. Why're you talking to me?"

"Because I'm talking *plenty plenty*, and I don't want to know where it comes from. And I'm talking *variety*. I want to see as many different little flying things as I can, and some of them ain't easy to come by. Example . . . if I wanted to get hold of, say, an aspis . . . I could pay some buccaneer of a ship's captain top dollar for a mange-ridden half-dead specimen of same . . . *or* I can pay you to arrange for one of your honourable associates to liberate some poor stifled little aspis from some fucking gilded cage up in East Gidd or Rim. Capiche?"

"Isaac old son . . . I begin to understand you."

"Of course you do, Lemuel. You're a businessman. I'm looking for *rare* flying things. I want things I've never seen before. I want inventive flying things. I will not be paying top whack for a basket full of blackbirds—although please don't take that to mean that blackbirds aren't wanted. Blackbirds are welcome, along with thrushes, jackdaws and what have you. Pigeons, Lemuel, your very own namesake. But what's even *more* welcome are, say, dragonfly-snakes."

"Rare," said Lemuel, looking intently at his pint.

"Very rare," agreed Isaac. "Which is why serious amounts of dosh would change hands for a good specimen. You get the idea, Lemuel? I want birds, insects, bats . . . also eggs, also cocoons, also grubs, anything which is going to turn *into* a flying thing. That could be even more useful, actually. Anything which looks set to be up to dog-sized. Nothing too much bigger, and nothing dangerous. Impressive as it would be to catch a drud or a wind-rhino, I don't want it."

"Who would, Isaac?" agreed Lemuel.

Isaac stuffed a five-guinea note into Lemuel's top pocket. The two men raised their glasses and drank together.

That had been yesterday evening. Isaac sat back and imagined his request worming its way through New Crobuzon's criminal alleys.

Isaac had used Lemuel's services before, when he had needed a rare or forbidden compound, or a manuscript of which there were only a few copies in New Crobuzon, or information on the synthesis of illegal substances. It appealed to Isaac's sense of humour to think of the hardest elements of the city's underworld earnestly scrabbling for birds and butterflies in between their gangfights and drugs deals.

It was Shunday the next day, Isaac realized. It had been several days since he had seen Lin. She didn't even *know* about his commission. They had a date, he remembered. They were meeting for dinner. He could put his research aside for a little while and tell his lover everything that had happened. It was something he enjoyed, emptying his mind of all its accumulated odds and ends, and offering them to Lin.

Lublamai and David had gone, Isaac realized. He was alone.

He undulated like a walrus, scattering papers and prints all over the boards. He turned his gasjet off and peered up out of the dark warehouse. Through his dirty window he could see the great cold circle of the moon and the slow pirouettes of her two daughters, satellites of ancient, barren rock glowing like fat fireflies as they spun around their mother.

Isaac fell asleep watching the convoluted lunar clockwork. He basked in the moonlight and dreamt of Lin: a fraught, sexual, loving dream.

CHAPTER SEVEN

The Clock and Cockerel had spilt out of doors. Tables and coloured lanterns covered the forecourt by the canal that separated Salacus Fields from Sangwine. The smash of glasses and shrieks of amusement wafted over the dour bargemen working the locks, riding the sluicing water up to a higher level, taking off towards the river, leaving the boisterous inn behind.

Lin felt vertiginous.

She sat at the head of a large table under a violet lamp, surrounded by her friends. Next to her on one side was Derkhan Blueday, the art critic for the *Beacon*. On the other was Cornfed, screaming animatedly at Thighs Growing, the cactacae cellist. Alexandrine; Bellagin Sound; Tarrick Septimus; Importunate Spint: painters and poets, musicians, sculptors, and a host of hangers-on she half-recognized.

This was Lin's milieu. This was her world. And yet she had never felt so isolated from them as she did now.

The knowledge that she had landed *the* job, the huge request they all dreamed of, the one work that could see her happy for years, separated her from her fellows. And her terrifying employer very effectively sealed her isolation. Lin felt as if suddenly, without warning, she was in a very different world from the bitchy, game-playing, lively, precious, introspective Salacus Fields round.

She had seen no one since she had returned, shaken, from her extraordinary meeting in Bonetown. She had missed Isaac badly, but she knew that he would be taking the opportunity of her supposed work to be drowning himself in research, and she knew also that for her to venture to Brock Marsh would anger him greatly. In Salacus Fields, they were an open secret. Brock Marsh, though, was the belly of the beast.

So she had sat for a day, contemplating what she had agreed to do.

Slowly, tentatively, she had cast her mind back to the monstrous figure of Mr. Motley.

Godspit and shit! she had thought. *What* was *he?*

She had no clear picture of her boss, only a sense of the ragged discordance of his flesh. Snippets of visual memory teased her: one hand terminating in five equally spaced crabs' claws; a spiralling horn bursting from a nest of eyes; a reptilian ridge winding along goat's fur. It was impossible to tell what race Mr. Motley had started out as. She had never heard of Remaking so extensive, so monstrous and chaotic. Anyone as rich as he must be could surely afford the best Remakers to fashion him into something more human—or whatever. She could only think that he chose this form.

Either that, or he was a victim of Torque.

Lin wondered if his obsession with the transition zone reflected his form, or if his obsession came first.

Lin's cupboard was stuffed with her rough sketches of Mr. Motley's body—hastily hidden on the assumption that Isaac would stay with her tonight. She had made scrawled notes of what she remembered of the lunatic anatomy.

Her horror had ebbed, over the days, leaving her with crawling skin and a torrent of ideas.

This, she had decided, could be the work of her life.

Her first appointment with Mr. Motley was the next day, Dustday, in the afternoon. After that, it was twice a week for at least the next month: probably longer, depending on how the sculpture took shape.

Lin was eager to begin.

"Lin, you tedious bitch!" yelled Cornfed and threw a carrot at her. "Why are you so quiet tonight?"

Lin scrawled quickly on her pad.

Cornfed, sweetheart, you bore me.

Everyone burst into laughter. Cornfed returned to his flamboyant flirtation with Alexandrine. Derkhan bent her grey head towards Lin and spoke softly.

"Seriously, Lin . . . You're hardly speaking. Is something up?"

Lin, touched, shook her headbody gently.

Working on something big. Taking up a lot of my mind, she signed at her. It was a relief to be able to speak without writing every word: Derkhan read signing well.

I miss Isaac, Lin added mock-forlornly.

Derkhan creased her face sympathetically. *She is,* Lin thought, *a lovely woman.*

Derkhan was pale, tall and thin—though she had gained a small gut as she passed into her middle years. Though she loved the outrageous antics of the Salacus set, she was an intense, gentle woman who avoided being the centre of attention. Her published writing was spiky and merciless: if Derkhan had not liked her work, Lin did not think she could have been Derkhan's friend. Her judgements in the *Beacon* were harsh to the point of brutality.

Lin could tell Derkhan that she missed Isaac. Derkhan knew the true nature of their relationship. A little over a year ago, when Lin and Derkhan were strolling together in Salacus Fields, Derkhan had bought drinks. When she handed over her money to pay, she had dropped her purse. She had bent quickly to retrieve it, but Lin had beaten her to it, picking it up and pausing only very slightly when she saw the old, battered heliotype of the beautiful and fierce young woman in a man's suit that had fallen from it onto the street, the xxx written across the bottom, the lipstick-kiss. She had handed it back to Derkhan, who had replaced it in the purse without hurrying, and without looking Lin in the eyes.

"Long time ago," Derkhan had said enigmatically, and immersed herself in her beer.

Lin had felt she owed Derkhan a secret. She had almost been relieved a couple of months later when she found herself drinking with Derkhan, depressed after storming out of some stupid row with Isaac. It had given Lin the opportunity to tell Derkhan the truth that she must already have guessed. Derkhan had nodded with nothing but concern for Lin's misery.

They had been close since then.

Isaac liked Derkhan because she was a seditionist.

Just as Lin thought of Isaac, she heard his voice.

"Godshit, everyone, sorry I'm late . . ."

She turned and saw his bulk pushing through tables towards them. Her antennae flexed in what she was sure he would recognize as a smile.

A chorus of salutation greeted Isaac as he approached them. He looked straight at Lin and smiled at her privately. He caressed her back as he waved at everyone else, and Lin felt his hand through her shirt clumsily spell out *I love you.*

Isaac yanked a chair over and forced it between Lin's and Cornfed's.

"I've just been to my bank, depositing a few sparkly little nuggets. A lucrative contract," he shouted, "makes a happy scientist with very bad judgement. Drinks on me." There was a raucous and delighted crowing of surprise, followed by a group yell for the waiter.

"How's the show going, Cornfed?" said Isaac.

"Oh splendid, splendid!" shouted Cornfed, and then bizarrely added, very loud, "Lin came to see it on Fishday."

"Right," said Isaac, nonplussed. "Did you like it, Lin?"

She briefly signed that she had.

Cornfed was only interested in gazing at Alexandrine's cleavage through her unsubtle dress. Isaac switched his attention to Lin.

"You would not *believe* what's been happening . . ." Isaac began.

Lin gripped his knee under the table. He returned the gesture.

Under his breath, Isaac told Lin and Derkhan, in truncated form, the story of Yagharek's visit. He implored them to silence, and glanced around regularly to make sure that no one else was listening in. Halfway through, the chicken he had ordered arrived, and he ate noisily while he described his meeting in The Moon's Daughters, and the cages and cages of experimental animals he expected to arrive at his laboratory any day soon.

When he was finished, he sat back and grinned at them both, before a look of contrition washed over his face, and he sheepishly asked Lin: "How's your work been going?"

She waved her hand dismissively.

There's nothing, dear heart, she thought, *that I can tell you. Let's talk about your new project.*

Guilt passed visibly over his face at his one-sided conversation, but Isaac could not help himself. He was utterly in the throes of a new project. Lin felt a familiar melancholy affection for him. Melancholy at his self-sufficiency in these moments of fascination; affection for his fervour and passion.

"Look, look," Isaac gabbled suddenly, and tugged a piece of paper from his pocket. He unfolded it on the table before them.

It was an advertisement for a fair currently in Sobek Croix.
The back was crisp with dry glue: Isaac had torn it from a wall.

MR. BOMBADREZIL'S UNIQUE and WONDERFUL FAIR, guaranteed
to astound and enthral the most JADED PALATE. The PALACE OF
LOVE; The HALL OF TERRORS; The VORTEX; and many other attractions for reasonable prices. Also come to see the extraordinary freakshow, the CIRCUS OF WEIRD. MONSTERS and
MARVELS from every corner of Bas-Lag! SEERS from the FRAC-
TURED LAND; a genuine WEAVER'S CLAW; the LIVING SKULL; the
lascivious SNAKE-WOMAN; URSUS REX, the man-king of the
Bears; DWARF CACTUS-PEOPLE of tiny sizes; a GARUDA, bird-man
chief of the wild desert; the STONE MEN of Bezhek; caged DÆ-
MONS; DANCING FISH; treasures stolen from THE GENGRIS; and
innumerable other PRODIGIES and WONDERS. Some attractions
not suitable for the easily shocked or those of a NERVOUS DISPO-
SITION. Entrance 5 stivers. Sobek Croix gardens, 14th Chet to
14th Melluary, 6 to 11 o'clock every night.

"See that?" Isaac barked, and stabbed the poster with his
thumb. "They've got a garuda! I've been sending requests all
over the city for dubious bits and bobs, probably going to end up
with loads of horrible disease-riddled jackdaws, and there's a
fucking *garuda* on the doorstep!"

Are you going to go down? signed Lin.

"Damn right!" snorted Isaac. "Straight after this! I thought we
could all go. The others," he said, his voice dropping, "don't
have to know what it is I'm doing there. I mean, a fair's always
fun anyway. Right?"

Derkhan grinned and nodded.

"So are you going to spirit the garuda away, or what?" she
whispered.

"Well, presumably I could arrange to take heliotypes of it, or
even ask it to come for a couple of days to the lab . . . I don't
know. We'll organize something! What do you say? Fancy a
fair?"

Lin picked a cherry tomato from Isaac's garnish and wiped it
carefully clean of chicken stock. She gripped it in her mandibles
and began to chew.

Could be fun, she signed. *Your treat?*

"Absolutely my treat!" boomed Isaac, and gazed at her. He
stared at her very close for a minute. He glanced round to make

sure that no one was watching, and then, clumsily, he signed in front of her.

Missed you.

Derkhan looked away for a moment, tactfully.

Lin broke off the moment, to make sure that she did it before Isaac. She clapped loudly, until everyone at the table was staring at her. She began to sign, indicating Derkhan to translate.

"Uh . . . Isaac is keen to prove that the talk of scientists being all work and no play is false. Intellectuals as well as dissolute aesthetes like us know how to have a good time, and thus he offers us this . . ." Lin waved the sheet, and threw it into the centre of the table where it was visible to all. "Rides, spectacles, marvels and coconut shies, all for a mere five stivers, which Isaac has kindly offered to underwrite . . ."

"Not for *everyone*, you sow!" Isaac roared in mock-outrage, but he was drowned out by the drunken roar of gratitude.

". . . offered to underwrite," continued Derkhan doggedly. "Accordingly, I move that we drink up and eat up and hightail to Sobek Croix."

There was loud, chaotic agreement. Those who had finished their food and drink gathered their bags. Others tucked with renewed gusto into their oysters or salad or fried plantain. Trying to organize a group of any size to do anything in synchronicity was an epic struggle, Lin reflected wryly. It would be some time before they set off.

Isaac and Derkhan were hissing to each other across the table in front of her. Her antennae twitched. She could pick up some of their murmurs. Isaac excitedly talking politics. He channelled his diffuse, undirected, pointed social discontent into his discussions with Derkhan. He was posing, she thought with amused pique, out of his depth, trying to impress the laconic journalist.

She could see Isaac pass a coin carefully across the table, and receive a plain envelope in return. Undoubtedly the latest issue of *Runagate Rampant*, the illegal, radical news-sheet for which Derkhan wrote.

Beyond a nebulous dislike of the militia and the government, Lin was not a political being. She sat back and looked up at the stars through the violet haze of the suspended lantern. She thought about the last time she had been to a fair: she remembered the mad palimpsest of smell, the catcalls and screeches, the rigged competitions and cheap prizes, the exotic animals and bright costumes, all packed together in a seedy, vibrant, exciting whole.

The fair was where normal rules were briefly forgotten, where bankers and thieves mingled to *ooh*, scandalized and titillated. Even Lin's less outrageous sisters would come to the fair.

One of her early memories was of creeping past ranks of gaudy tents to stand next to some terrifying, dangerous, multi-coloured ride, some giant wheel at the Gallmarch Fair twenty years ago. Someone—she never knew who, some khepri passer-by, some indulgent stallholder—had handed her a toffee-apple, which she had eaten reverentially. One of her few pleasant memories of childhood, that sugared fruit.

Lin sat back and waited for her friends to finish their preparations. She sucked sweet tea from her sponge and thought of that candied apple. She waited patiently to go to the fair.

CHAPTER EIGHT

"Come try, come try, come try your luck!"

"Ladies, ladies, tell yer fellers to win you a bouquet!"

"Spin in the Whirligig! It'll spin your mind!"

"Your likeness affected in only four minutes! No faster por-traiture in the world!"

"Experience the hypnagogic mesmerism of Sillion the Extraordinary!"

"Three rounds, three guineas! Stand for three rounds against 'Iron Man' Magus and take home three Gs! No cactus-people."

The night air was thick with noise. The challenges, the shouts, the invitations and temptations and dares sounded around the laughing party like bursting balloons. Gasjets, mixed with select chymicals, burnt red, green, blue and canary yellow. The grass and paths of Sobek Croix were sticky with spilt sugar and sauce. Vermin scampered from the skirts of stalls into the dark bushes of the park clutching choice morsels. Gonophs and cutpurses slipped predatory through the crowds like fish through weeds. Indignant roars and violent cries sounded in their wake.

The crowd was a moving stew of human and vodyanoi, cactus, khepri, and other, rarer breeds: hotchi and strider and stilts-pear and races the names of which Isaac did not know.

A few yards out from the fair, the darkness of the grass and trees was absolute. The bushes and boughs were fringed with bunting of ragged paper, discarded and ensnared and slowly shredded by the wind. Paths criss-crossed the park, leading to lakes and flower beds and acres of untended growth, and the old monastic ruins at the centre of the huge common.

Lin and Cornfed, Isaac and Derkhan and all the others strolled past enormous contraptions of bolted steel, garishly painted iron and hissing lights. Delighted squeals sounded from little cars swinging on flimsy-looking chains above them. A hundred different manically cheerful tunes sounded from a hundred engines and organs, an unsettling cacophony that ebbed and flowed around them.

Alex munched honeyed nuts; Bellagin salted meat; Thighs Growing a watery mulch delicious to cactus-people. They threw food at each other, caught it in their mouths.

The park was thronging with punters, throwing hoops over poles, firing children's bows at targets, guessing under which cup the coin was hidden. Children screamed with pleasure and misery. Prostitutes of all races, sexes and descriptions sashayed exaggeratedly between the stalls or stood by the beerhalls, winking at passers-by.

The party disintegrated slowly as they passed into the heart of the fair. They hovered a minute while Cornfed showed off his archery. He ostentatiously offered his prizes, two dolls, to Alex and a young, beautiful whore who cheered his triumph. The three disappeared arm in arm through the crowd. Tarrick proved adept at a fishing game, pulling three live crabs from a big swirling tub. Bellagin and Spint had their futures read in the cards, squealing in terror when the bored witch turned over The Snake and The Old Crone in succession. They demanded a second opinion from a wide-eyed scarabomancer. She gazed theatrically at the images skittering across the carapaces of her pattern beetles as they bumbled through their sawdust.

Isaac and the others left Bellagin and Spint behind.

The remnants of the party turned a corner beside the Wheel of Destiny and a roughly fenced-off section of the park came into view. Inside a line of small tents curved away from view. Above the gateway was a crudely painted legend: *The Circus of Weird*.

"Now," said Isaac ponderously. "Reckon I might have a little look at this . . ."

"Plumbing the depths of human squalor, 'Zaac?" asked a young artist's model whose name Isaac could not remember. Besides Lin, Isaac and Derkhan, only a few others of the original group were left. They looked mildly surprised at Isaac's choice.

"Research," Isaac said grandly. "Research. Fancy joining me, Derkhan? Lin?"

The others took the hint with reactions ranging from careless waves to petulant flounces. Before they all disappeared, Lin signed rapidly to Isaac.

Not interested in this. Teratology more your thing. Meet you at the entrance in two hours?

Isaac nodded briefly and squeezed her hand. She signed good-bye to Derkhan and trotted off to catch up with a sound-artist whose name Isaac had never known.

Derkhan and Isaac stared at each other.

". . . and then there were two," sung Derkhan, a snatch of a children's counting song about a basket of kittens that died, one by one, grotesquely.

There was an additional charge to enter the Circus of Weird, which Isaac paid. Though hardly empty, the freakshow was less crowded than the main body of the fair. The more monied the punters inside looked, the more furtive their air.

The freakshow brought out the voyeur in the populace and the hypocrisy in the gentry.

There seemed to be some kind of tour starting, which promised to view each exhibit in the Circus in turn. The bawls of the showman bade the assembled stick close together and prepare themselves for sights such as mortal eyes were not meant to see.

Isaac and Derkhan hung back a little and followed the troupe. Isaac saw that Derkhan had a notebook out and a pen poised.

The bowler-hatted Master of Ceremonies approached the first tent.

"Ladies and gents," he whispered loudly and huskily, "in this tent lurks the most remarkable and terrifying creature ever seen by mortal man. Or vodyanoi, or cactus, or whatever," he added in a normal voice, nodding graciously to the few xenians in the crowd. He returned to his bombastic tones. "Originally described fifteen centuries ago in the travelogues of Libintos the Sage, of what was then just plain ol' Crobuzon. On his trips south to

the burning wastes, Libintos saw many marvellous and monstrous things. But none more terrifying than the awesome . . .
mafadet!"

Isaac had been sporting a sardonic smile. But even he joined
the mass gasp.

Have they really got a mafadet? he thought as the MC drew
back the curtain from the front of the little tent. He pushed forward to see.

There was another, louder gasp, and people at the front fought
to move back. Others shoved to take their place.

Behind thick black bars, tethered by heavy chains, was an extraordinary beast. It lay on the ground, its huge dun body like a
massive lion's. Between its shoulders was a fringe of denser fur
from which sprouted an enormous serpentine neck, thicker than
a man's thigh. Its scales glistened an oily, ruddy tan. An intricate pattern wound up the top of that curling neck, expanding to
a diamond shape where it curved and became an enormous
snake's head.

The mafadet's head lolled on the ground. Its huge forked tongue
flicked in and out. Its eyes glistened like jet.

Isaac grabbed Derkhan.

"It's a fucking *mafadet*," he hissed in amazement. Derkhan
nodded, wide-eyed.

The crowd had drawn back from the front of the cage. The
showman grabbed a barbed stick and poked it through the bars,
goading the enormous desert creature. It gave forth a deep, rumbling hiss and batted pathetically at its tormentor with a massive
forepaw. Its neck coiled and twisted in desultory misery.

There were small screams from the crowd. People surged at
the little barrier before the cage.

"Back, ladies and gents, back, I beg of you!" The showman's
voice was pompous and histrionic. "You are all in mortal danger! Don't anger the beast!"

The mafadet hissed again under his continued torments. It
wriggled backwards along the floor, crawling out of range of the
vicious spike.

Isaac's awe was waning fast.

The exhausted animal squirmed in undignified agony as it
sought the rear of the cage. Its threadbare tail lashed the stinking
goat carcass presumably provided for its nourishment. Dung and
dust stained the mafadet's pelt, along with blood that oozed thickly

from numerous sores and nicks. Its sprawled body twitched a little as that cold, blunt head rose on the powerful muscles of the snake-neck.

The mafadet hissed and, as the crowd hissed in turn, its wicked jaws unhinged. It tried to bare its teeth.

Isaac's face curled.

Broken stubs jutted from the creature's gums where cruel fangs a foot long should have glinted. They had been smashed out of its mouth, Isaac realized, for fear of its murderous, poisonous bite.

He gazed at the broken monster whipping the air with its black tongue. It laid its head back down.

"Jabber's arse," Isaac whispered to Derkhan with pity and disgust. "Never thought I'd feel sorry for something like that."

"Makes you wonder what state the garuda's going to be in," Derkhan replied.

The barker was hurriedly drawing the curtain on the miserable creature. As he did so he told the crowd the story of Libintos's trial by poison at the hands of the Mafadet King.

Nursery tales, cant, lies and showmanship, thought Isaac contemptuously. He realized that the crowd had only been given a snatch of a view, a minute or less. *Less chance anyone will notice how moribund the poor thing is,* he mused.

He could not help but imagine the mafadet in full health. The immense weight of that tawny body padding through the hot dry scrub, the lightning strike of the venomous bite.

Garuda circling above, blades flashing.

The crowd were being shepherded towards the next enclosure. Isaac was not listening to the roar of the guide. He was watching Derkhan jot quick notes.

"This for *RR*?" whispered Isaac.

Derkhan looked around them quickly.

"Maybe. Depends what else we see."

"What we'll *see*," hissed Isaac furiously, dragging Derkhan with him as he caught sight of the next exhibit, "is pure human viciousness! I fucking despair, Derkhan!"

He had stopped a little way behind a group of dawdlers who were gazing at a child born without eyes, a fragile, bony human girl who cried out wordlessly and waved her head at the sound of the crowd. *SHE SEES WITH INNER SIGHT!* proclaimed the sign over her head. Some before the cage were cackling and yelling at her.

"Godspit, Derkhan . . ." Isaac shook his head. "Look at them tormenting that poor creature . . ."

As he spoke, a couple turned from the exhibited child with disgust in their faces. They turned as they left and spat behind them at the woman who had laughed the loudest.

"It *turns*, Isaac," said Derkhan quietly. "It turns quickly."

The tour guide strode the path between the rows of little tents, stopping here and there at choice horrors. The crowd was breaking apart. Little clots of people milled away under their own volition. At some tents they were stopped by attendants, who waited until a sufficient number had congregated before unveiling their hidden pieces. At others the punters walked right in, and shouts of delight and shock and disgust would emanate from within the grubby canvas.

Derkhan and Isaac wandered into a long enclosure. Above the entrance was a sign rendered in ostentatious calligraphy. *A PANOPLY OF WONDERS! DO YOU DARE ENTER THE MUSEUM OF HIDDEN THINGS?*

"Do we dare, Derkhan?" muttered Isaac as they passed into the warm dusty darkness within.

The light ebbed slowly into their eyes from the corner of the makeshift room. The cotton chamber was full of cabinets in iron and glass, stretching out before them. Candles and gasjets burned in niches, filtered through lenses that concentrated them into dramatic spots, illuminating the bizarre displays. Punters meandered from one to another, murmuring, laughing nervously.

Isaac and Derkhan wandered slowly past jars of yellowing alcohol in which broken body parts floated. Two-headed foetuses and sections of a kraken's arm. A deep red shining jag that could have been a Weaver's claw, or could have been a burnished carving; eyes that spasmed and lived in jars of charged liquid; intricate, infinitesimal paintings on ladybirds' backs, visible only through magnifying lenses; a human skull scuttling in its cage on six insectile brass legs. A nest of rats with intertwined tails that took it in turns to scrawl obscenities on a little blackboard. A book made of pressed feathers. Druds' teeth and a narwhal's horn.

Derkhan scribbled notes. Isaac gazed avariciously about him at the charlatanism and cryptoscience.

They left the museum. To their right was Anglerina, Queen of the Deepest Sea; to their left Bas-Lag's Oldest Cactus-Man.

"I'm getting depressed," said Derkhan.

Isaac agreed.

"Let's find the Bird-Man Chief of the Wild Desert quickly, and fuck off. I'll buy you some candyfloss."

They wound through the ranks of the deformed and obese, the bizarrely hirsute and the small. Isaac suddenly pointed above them, at the sign that had come into view.

KING GARUDA! LORD OF THE AIR!

Derkhan tugged at the heavy curtain. She and Isaac exchanged glances, and entered.

"Ah! Visitors from this strange city! Come, sit, hear stories of the harsh desert! Stay a while with a traveller from far, far away!"

The querulous voice burst out of the shadows. Isaac squinted through the bars before them. A dark, shambolic figure stood painfully and lurched out of the darkness at the back of the tent.

"I am a chief of my people, come to see New Crobuzon of which we have heard."

The voice was pained and exhausted, high-pitched and raw, but it made nothing like the alien sounds that burst from Yagharek's throat. The speaker stepped out of obscurity. Isaac opened his eyes and mouth wide to bellow in triumph and wonder, but his shout mutated as it began and died in an aghast whisper.

The figure before Isaac and Derkhan shivered and scratched its stomach. Its flesh hung heavy off it like a pudgy schoolboy's. Its skin was pale and pockmarked with disease and cold. Isaac's eyes wove all over its body in dismay. Bizarre nodes of tissue burst from its bunched toes: claws drawn by children. Its head was swathed in feathers, but feathers of all sizes and shapes, jammed at random from its crown to its neck in a thick, uneven, insulating layer. The eyes that peered myopically at Isaac and Derkhan were human eyes, fighting to open lids encrusted in rheum and pus. The beak was large and stained, like old pewter.

Behind the wretched creature stretched a pair of dirty, foul-smelling wings. They were no more than six feet from tip to tip. As Isaac watched, they half-opened, jerked and twitched spastically. Tiny pieces of organic muck spilt from them as they shuddered.

The creature's beak opened and, underneath it, Isaac caught a glimpse of lips forming the words, nostrils above. The beak was nothing but a roughly made fixture shoved and sealed into place like a gas-mask over the nose and mouth, he realized.

"Let me tell you of the times I have soared into the air with my prey . . ." began the pathetic figure, but Isaac stepped forward and held up a hand to cut it off.

"Please gods, enough!" he shouted. "Spare us this . . . *embarrassment* . . ."

The false garuda staggered backwards, blinking in fear.

There was silence for a long time.

"What's the matter, guvnor?" whispered the thing behind bars eventually. "What'd I do wrong?"

"I came here to see a fucking garuda," rumbled Isaac. "What d'you take me for? You're Remade, mate . . . as any fool can see."

The big dead beak clicked together as the man licked his lips. His eyes darted left and right nervously.

"Jabber's sake, squire," he whispered pleadingly. "Don't go complaining. This is all I got. You're obviously a gentleman of education . . . I'm as close as most get to garuda . . . all they want's to hear a bit about hunting in the desert, see the bird-man, and that way I earn."

"Godspit, Isaac," whispered Derkhan. "Go easy."

Isaac was crushingly disappointed. He had been preparing a list of questions in his mind. He knew exactly how he had wanted to investigate the wings, which muscle-bone interaction currently intrigued him. He had been prepared to pay a good rate for the research, had prepared to get Ged to come down to ask questions about the Cymek Library. To be faced instead with a scared, sickly human reading from a script that would have disgraced the lowest playhouse depressed him.

His anger was tempered with pity as he stared at the miserable figure before him. The man behind the feathers nervously clutched and unclutched his left arm with his right. He had to open that preposterous beak to breath.

" 'Stail," Isaac swore softly.

Derkhan had walked up to the bars.

"What did you do?" she asked.

The man looked around again before answering.

"Did thieving," he said quickly. "Got caught trying to get an old painting of a garuda from some ancient cunt out in Chnum. Worth a fortune. Magister said since I was so impressed with garuda I could—" his breath caught for a moment "—I could be one."

Isaac could see how the feathers of the face were shoved ruthlessly into the skin, doubtless bonded subcutaneously to make removal too agonizing to consider. He imagined the process of insertion, one by torturing one. When the Remade turned slightly to Derkhan, Isaac could see the ugly knot of hardened flesh on his back where those wings, torn from some buzzard or vulture, had been sealed together with the human muscles.

Nerve endings bonded randomly and uselessly, and the wings moved only with the spasms of a long drawn-out death. Isaac's nose wrinkled at the stench. The wings were rotting slowly on the Remade's back.

"Does it hurt?" Derkhan was asking.

"Not so very much any more, miss," the Remade answered. "Anyway, I'm lucky to have this." He indicated the tent and the bars. "Keeps me eating. That's why I'd be obliged more'n I can say if you'd refrain from telling the boss that you clocked me."

Did most who came here really accept this disgusting charade? wondered Isaac. *Were people so gullible as to believe that something as grotesque as this could ever fly?*

"We'll say nothing," said Derkhan. Isaac nodded curtly in agreement. He was full of pity and anger and disgust. He wanted to leave.

Behind them, the curtain swished and a group of young women entered, laughing and whispering lewd jokes. The Remade looked over Derkhan's shoulder.

"Ah!" he said loudly. "Visitors from this strange city! Come, sit, hear stories of the harsh desert! Stay a while with a traveller from far, far away!"

He moved away from Derkhan and Isaac, gazing at them pleadingly as he did so. Delighted screams and astonishment burst from the new spectators.

"Fly for us!" yelled one.

"Alas," heard Isaac and Derkhan as they left the tent, "the weather in your city is too inclement for my kind. I have caught chill and temporarily cannot fly. But tarry and I will tell you of the views from the cloudless Cymek skies . . ."

The cloth closed behind them. The speech was obscured.

Isaac watched as Derkhan scribbled in her notepad.

"What are you going to turn in?" he asked.

" 'Remade Forced by Magister's Torture into Living as Zoo

Exhibit.' I won't say which one," she answered without looking up from her writing. Isaac nodded.

"Come on," he murmured. "I'll get that candyfloss."

"I'm fucking depressed now," said Isaac heavily. He bit at the sickly-sweet bundle he carried. Wisps of sugar fibres stuck to his stubble.

"Yes, but are you depressed because of what'd been done to that man, or because you didn't get to meet a garuda?" asked Derkhan.

They had left the freakshow. They munched earnestly as they walked past the garish body of the fair. Isaac pondered. He was a little taken aback.

"Well, I suppose . . . probably because I didn't meet a garuda . . . But," he added defensively, "I wouldn't be half so depressed if it'd just been a scam, someone in a costume, something like that. It's the . . . fucking *indignity* of it that really sticks in the craw . . ."

Derkhan nodded thoughtfully.

"We could look around, you know," she said. "There's bound to be a garuda or two here somewhere. Some of the city-bred must be here." She looked up, uselessly. With all the coloured lights, she could hardly even see the stars.

"Not now," said Isaac. "I'm not in the mood. I've lost my momentum." There was a long, companionable silence before he spoke again.

"Will you really write something about this place in *Runagate Rampant*?"

Derkhan shrugged, looked around briefly to make sure no one was listening.

"It's a difficult job, dealing with the Remade," she said. "There's so much contempt, prejudice against them. Divide, rule. Trying to link up, so people don't . . . judge them as monsters . . . it's really hard. And it's not like people don't know they've got fucking horrendous lives, for the most part . . . it's that there's a lot of people who kind of vaguely think they deserve it, even if they pity them, or think it's Gods-given, or rubbish like that. Oh, Godspit," she said suddenly, and shook her head.

"What?"

"I was in court the other day, saw a Magister sentence a woman to Remaking. Such a sordid, pathetic, miserable crime . . ." She winced in remembrance. "Some woman living at the top of one

of the Ketch Heath monoliths killed her baby . . . smothered it
or shook it or Jabber knows what . . . because it wouldn't stop
crying. She's sitting there in court, her eyes are just . . . damn
well *empty* . . . she can't believe what's happened, she keeps
moaning her baby's name, and the Magister sentences her.
Prison, of course, ten years I think, but it was the Remaking that
I remember.

"Her baby's arms are going to be grafted to her face. 'So she
doesn't forget what she did,' he says." Derkhan's voice curdled as
she mimicked the Magister.

They walked in silence for a while, dutifully munching
candyfloss.

"I'm an art critic, Isaac," Derkhan said eventually. "Remaking's art, you know. Sick art. The imagination it takes! I've seen
Remade crawling under the weight of huge spiral iron shells
they retreat into at night. Snail-women. I've seen them with big
squid tentacles where their arms were, standing in river mud,
plunging their suckers underwater to pull out fish. And as for the
ones made for the gladiatorial shows . . . ! Not that they admit
that's what they're for . . .

"Remaking's creativity gone bad. Gone rotten. Gone *rancid*. I
remember you once asked me if it was hard to balance writing
about art and writing for *RR*." She turned to look at him as they
paced through the fair. "It's the *same thing*, Isaac. Art's something you choose to make . . . it's a bringing together of . . . of
everything around you into something that makes you more human, more khepri, whatever. More of a person. Even with Remaking a germ of that survives. That's why the same people who
despise the Remade are in awe of Jack Half-a-Prayer, whether or
not he exists.

"I don't want to live in a city where Remaking is the highest
art."

Isaac felt in his pocket for *Runagate Rampant*. It was dangerous even to hold a copy. He patted it, mentally thumbing his nose
to the north-east, at Parliament, at Mayor Bentham Rudgutter
and the parties squabbling over how to slice up the cake amongst
themselves. The Fat Sun and Three Quills parties; Diverse Tendency, whom Lin called "comprador scum"; the liars and sed-
ucers of the Finally We Can See party; the whole pompous
bickering brood like all-powerful six-year-olds in a sandpit.

At the end of the path paved with bon-bon wrappers, posters,
tickets and crushed food, discarded dolls and burst balloons,

stood Lin, lounging by the entrance to the fair. Isaac smiled with unfeigned pleasure at seeing her. As they neared her she stood straighter and waved at them. She sauntered in their direction.

Isaac saw that she had a toffee-apple gripped in her mandibles. Her inner jaw chewed with gusto.

How was it, treasure? she signed.

"An unmitigated arsing disaster," Isaac huffed miserably. "I'll tell you all about it."

He even risked grasping her hand briefly as they turned their backs on the fair.

The three small figures disappeared into the dimly lit streets of Sobek Croix, where gaslight was brown and half-hearted where it existed at all. Behind them the enormous imbroglio of colour, metal, glass, sugar and sweat continued to pour its noise and light pollution into the sky.

CHAPTER NINE

Across the city, through the shady alleys of Echomire and the hovels of Badside, in the lattice of dust-clogged canals, in Smog Bend and the faded estates of Barrackham, in towers in Tar Wedge and the hostile concrete forest of Dog Fenn, came the whispered word. Someone's paying for winged things.

Like a god, Lemuel breathed life into the message and made it fly. Small-time hoods heard it from drug dealers; costermongers told it to decayed gentlemen; doctors with dubious records got it from part-time bouncers.

Isaac's request swept through the slums and rookeries. It travelled the alternative architecture thrown up in the human sumps.

Where putrefying houses loomed over courtyards, wooden walkways seemed to self-generate, linking them together, connecting them to the streets and mews where exhausted beasts of burden hauled third-rate goods up and down. Bridges jutted like splinted limbs across cess-trenches. Isaac's message was couriered across the chaotic skyline in the paths of the feral cats.

Little expeditions of urban adventurers took the Sink Line

train south to Fell Stop and ventured into Rudewood. They walked the deserted train tracks as long as they could, stepping from slat to wooden slat, passing the empty, nameless station in the outlands of the forest. The platforms had surrendered to green life. The tracks were thick with dandelions and foxgloves and wild roses that had shoved pugnacious through the railway gravel and, here and there, bent the tracks. Darkwood and banyan and evergreen crept up on the nervous invaders until they were surrounded, enclosed in a lush trap.

They went with sacks and catapults and big nets. They hauled their clumsy urban carcasses through the tangled roots and thick tree-shadows, yelling and tripping and breaking branches. They tried to pinpoint the birdsong that disoriented them, sounding on every side. They made faltering, useless analogies between the city and this alien realm: "If you can find your way through Dog Fenn," one might say fatuously and wrongly, "you can find your way anywhere." They would spin, look for and fail to find the militia tower of Vaudois Hill, out of sight behind the trees.

Some did not return.

Most came back scratching at burrs, stung and torn and angry, empty-handed. They might as well have hunted ghosts.

Occasionally they triumphed, and some frantic nightingale or Rudewood finch would be smothered with rough cloth to a chorus of ludicrously overblown cheers. Hornets buried their harpoons into their tormentors as they were swept into jars and pots. If they were lucky, their captors remembered to pierce airholes in the lids.

Many birds and more insects died. Some survived, to be taken into the dark city just beyond the trees.

In the city itself, children scaled walls to pull eggs from nests in decaying gutters. The caterpillars and maggots and cocoons they kept in matchboxes and bartered for string or chocolate were suddenly worth money.

There were accidents. A girl in pursuit of her neighbour's racing pigeon fell from a roof, breaking her skull. An old man scrabbling for grubs was stung by bees until his heart stopped.

Rare birds and flying creatures were stolen. Some escaped. New predators and prey briefly joined the ecosystem in New Crobuzon's skies.

Lemuel was good at his job. Some would only have plumbed the depths: not he. He made sure that Isaac's desires were communicated uptown: Gidd, Canker Wedge, Mafaton and Nigh Sump, Ludmead and The Crow.

Clerks and doctors, lawyers and councillors, landlords and men and women of leisure . . . even the militia: Lemuel had often dealt (usually indirectly) with New Crobuzon's respectable citizenry. The main differences between them and the more desperate of the city's inhabitants, in his experience, were the scale of money that interested them and the capacity they had not to get caught.

From the parlours and dining rooms there were cautious murmurings of interest.

In the heart of Parliament a debate was taking place about levels of business taxation. Mayor Rudgutter sat regally on his throne and nodded as his deputy, MontJohn Rescue, bellowed the Fat Sun party's line, poking his finger aggressively across the enormous vaulted chamber. Rescue paused periodically to rearrange the thick scarf he wore around his neck, despite the warmth.

Councillors dozed quietly in a haze of dust motes.

Elsewhere in the vast building, through intricate corridors and passages that seemed designed to confuse, suited secretaries and messengers brushed busily past each other. Little tunnels and stairs of polished marble bristled from main thoroughfares. Many were unlit and unfrequented. An old man pulled a decrepit trolley along one such passage.

With the bustling noise of Parliament's main entrance hall receding behind him, he dragged the trolley behind him up steep stairs. The corridor was barely wider than his trolley: it was a long, uncomfortable few minutes until he had reached the top. He stopped and wiped sweat from his forehead and around his mouth, then resumed his trudging plod along the ascending floor.

Ahead of him the air lightened, as sunlight tried to finger its way around a corner. He turned full into it, and his face was splashed with light and warmth. It gushed in from a skylight and, beyond that, from the windows of the doorless office at the corridor's end.

"Morning, sir," croaked the old man as he reached the entrance.

"Good morning to you," came the reply from the man behind the desk.

The office was small and square, with narrow windows of

smoked glass that looked out over Griss Fell and the arches of
the Sud Line railway. One wall was flush with the looming dark
bulk of Parliament's main edifice. Set into that wall was a small
sliding door. A pile of crates teetered in the corner.

The little room was one of the chambers that jutted from the
main building, high over the surrounding city. The waters of the
Gross Tar surged fifty feet below.

The delivery man unloaded his trolley of parcels and boxes in
front of the pale middle-aged gentleman sitting before him.

"Not too many today, sir," he murmured, rubbing his moaning
bones. He went slowly back the way he came, his trolley jouncing lightly behind him.

The clerk sifted through the bundles and rattled out brief
notes on his typewriter. He made entries in an enormous ledger
labelled "Acquisitions," skimming the pages between sections
and recording the date before each item. He opened up the packages and recorded the contents in a typewritten day-list and in
the big book.

*Militia reports: 17. Human knuckles: 3. Heliotypes (incrimi-
nating): 5.*

He checked for which department each collection of items
was bound, and he separated them into piles. When one pile had
grown big enough, he put it in a crate and carried it over to the
door in the wall. It was a four-by-four-foot square, which hissed
with a rush of siphoned air and opened at the behest of some hidden piston when he tugged a lever. At its side was a little slot for
a programme card.

Beyond it a wire cage dangled beneath Parliament's obsidian
skin, with one open side flush with the doorway. It was suspended above and on either side by chains that swung gently, rattled and disappeared into an eddying darkness that loomed off
without remission in all directions that the clerk could see. The
clerk lugged the crate up into the passageway and slid it along
into the cage, which pitched a little under the weight.

He released a hatch which closed sharply, enclosing the crate
and its contents with woven wire on all sides. Then he closed the
sliding door, reached into his pocket and pulled out the thick
programme cards he carried, each clearly marked: *Militia; Intelligence; Exchequer*; and so on. He slid the relevant card into the
slot beside the door.

There would be a whirr. Tiny, sensitive pistons reacted to the
pressure. Powered by steam driven up from the vast basement

boilers, gentle little cogs rotated the length of the card. Where their spring-loaded teeth found sections cut from the thick board, they slotted neatly inside for a moment, and a minuscule switch was thrown further along the mechanism. When the wheels had completed their brief passage, the combination of on-off switches translated into binary instructions that raced in flows of steam and current along tubes and cables to hidden analytical engines.

The cage jerked free of its moorings and began a swift, swinging passage beneath the skin of Parliament. It would travel the hidden tunnels up or down or sideways or diagonally, changing direction, transferring jerkily to new chains, for five seconds, thirty seconds, two minutes or more, until it arrived, slamming into a bell to announce itself. Another sliding door opened before it, and the crate was pulled out into its destination. Far away, a new cage swung into place outside the clerk's room.

The Acquisitions clerk worked quickly. He had logged and sent on almost all the assorted oddities before him within fifteen minutes. That was when he saw one of the few remaining parcels shaking oddly. He stopped scribbling and prodded it.

The stamps that adorned it declared it newly arrived from some merchant ship, the name obscured. Neatly printed across the front of the package was its destination: *Dr. M. Barbile, Research and Development.* The clerk heard a scraping. He hesitated a moment, then gingerly untied the string that bound it and peered inside.

Inside, in a nest of paper shavings that they nudged fitfully, were a mass of fat grubs bigger than his thumb.

The clerk recoiled and his eyes widened behind his glasses. The grubs were astonishingly coloured, beautiful dark reds and greens with the iridescence of peacock feathers. They floundered and wriggled to keep themselves on their stubby, sticky legs. Thick antennae poked from their heads, above a tiny mouthpiece. The hind part of their body was covered in multicoloured hairs that bristled and seemed coated in thin glue.

The fat little creatures undulated blindly.

The clerk saw, too late, a tattered invoice attached to the back of the box, half-destroyed in transit. Any invoiced package he was supposed to record as whatever was listed, and send on without opening.

Shit, he thought nervously. He unfolded the torn halves of the invoice. It was still quite legible.

SM caterpillars x 5. That was all.

The clerk sat back and pondered for a moment, watching the hairy little creatures crawl over each other and the paper they sat in.

Caterpillars? he thought, and grinned fleetingly, anxiously. He kept glancing at the corridor before him.

Rare caterpillars . . . Some foreign breed, he thought.

He remembered the whispers in the pub, the winks and nods. He'd heard a chap at his local offering money for such creatures . . . The rarer the better, he'd said . . .

The clerk's face wrinkled suddenly in avarice and fear. His hand hovered over the box, darting back and forth inconclusively. He got up and stalked over to his room's entrance. He listened. There was no sound from the burnished corridor.

The clerk returned to his desk, calculating risk and benefit frantically. He looked closely at the invoice. It was stamped with an illegible crest, but the actual information was handwritten. He fumbled in his desk drawer without giving himself time to think, his eyes darting constantly back to the deserted passage outside his doorway, and brought out a paper-knife and a quill. He scratched with the sharp knife at the straight line on the top and the end of the curl on the bottom of the 5 on the invoice, gently, gently, shaving them away. He blew away paper- and ink-dust, smoothed the roughened paper carefully with the feathered end of his quill. Then he turned it around and dipped the fine point in his inkwell. Meticulously, he straightened the curling base of the digit, converting it into crossing lines.

Eventually, it was done. He straightened up and squinted critically down at his handiwork. It looked like a 4.

That's the hard bit, he thought.

He felt about him for some container, turned his pockets inside out, scratched his head and thought. His face lit, and he pulled out his glasses case. He opened it and filled it with shredded paper. Then, his face wrinkling with anxious disgust, he pulled the edge of his sleeve down over his hand and reached into the box. He felt the soft edges of one of the big caterpillars between his fingers. As gently and quickly as he could, he plucked it squirming from its fellows and dropped it into his glasses case. Quickly, he closed the case around the frantically twitching little creature and fastened it.

He buried his glasses case at the bottom of his briefcase, behind mint-sweets and papers and pens and notebooks.

The clerk retied the string on the box, then sat back quickly and waited. His heart was very loud, he realized. He was sweating a little. He breathed deeply and squeezed his eyes closed.

Relax, now, he thought soothingly to himself. *That's your bit of excitement over.*

Two or three minutes passed, and no one came. The clerk was still alone. His bizarre embezzlement had gone unnoticed. He breathed easier.

Eventually he looked again at his forged invoice. It was, he realized, very good. He opened the ledger and entered, in the section marked *R&D*, the date and the information: *27th Chet, Anno Urbis 1779: From merchant ship X. SM caterpillars: 4.*

The last number seemed to glare at him as if it was written in red.

He typed the same information onto his day-sheet before picking up the resealed box and carrying it over to the wall. He opened the sliding doors and leaned into the little metal threshold, pushed the box of grubs into the waiting cage. Gusts of stale, dry air billowed onto his face from the dark cavity between the hide and guts of Parliament.

The clerk pulled the cage shut and closed the door before it. He fumbled for his programme cards, eventually pulling the one marked *R&D* from the little pack with fingers that still trembled, just a little. He slotted it into the information engine.

There was a juddering hiss and a ratcheting sound as the instructions fed along pistons and hammers and flywheels and the cage was pulled vertiginously up, away from the clerk's office, beyond Parliament's foothills, into the craggy peaks.

The box of caterpillars swung as it was tugged through the darkness. Oblivious to their journey, the grubs circumscribed their little prison with peristaltic motion.

Quiet engines transferred the cage from hook to hook, changing its direction and dropping it onto rusted conveyor-belts, retrieving it in another part of Parliament's bowels. The box spiralled invisibly around the building, rising gradually and inexorably towards the high-security East Wing, passing through mechanized veins to those organic turrets and protuberances.

Finally the wire cage dropped with a muted chime onto a bed of springs. The vibrations of the bell ebbed into the silence. After a minute the door to the shaft snapped open and the box of larvae was yanked brusquely into a harsh light.

There were no windows in the long white room, only incandescent gasjets. Every cranny of the room was visible in its sterility. No dust, no dirt invaded here. The cleanliness was hard and aggressive.

All around the perimeter of the room, white-coated figures were huddled in obscure tasks.

It was one of those bright, hidden figures who untied the box's string and read the invoice. She gently opened the box and peered inside.

She picked up the cardboard box and carried it at arms' length through the room. At the far end one of her colleagues, a thin cactacae with his spines carefully secured beneath thick white coveralls, had opened the large bolted door for which she was heading. She showed him her security clearance and he stood aside to let her precede him.

They walked carefully down a corridor as white and sparse as the room from which they had come, with a large iron grille at the far end. The cactus saw that his colleague was carrying something gingerly in both hands, and he reached past her and fed a programme card into an input slot in the wall. The slatted gate slid open.

They entered a vast dark chamber.

Its ceiling and its walls were far enough away to be invisible. Weird wails and lowing sounded distantly from all sides. As their eyes adjusted, cages walled with dark wood or iron or reinforced glass loomed at them irregularly in the enormous hall. Some were huge, the size of rooms: others were no larger than a book. All were raised like cabinets in a museum, with charts and books of information slotted before them. White-clad scientists moved through the maze between the blocks of glass like spirits in a ruin, taking notes, observing, pacifying and tormenting the cages' inhabitants.

Captive things sniffed and grunted and sang and shifted unreally in their dim prisons.

The cactus walked briskly off into the distance and disappeared. The woman carrying the grubs made her way carefully through the room.

Things lunged at her as she walked past and she shuddered with the glass. Something swirled oleaginously through a huge vat of liquid mud: she saw toothy tentacles slapping at her and scouring the tank. She was bathed in hypnotic organic lights.

She passed a small cage smothered in black cloth, with warning signs plastered ostentatiously on all sides and instructions on how to deal with the contents. Her colleagues drifted up to her and away again with clipboards and children's coloured bricks and slabs of putrefying meat.

Ahead, temporary black wooden walls twenty feet high had been thrown up, surrounding a floor-space forty feet square. Even a corrugated iron ceiling had been hammered over the top. At the padlocked entrance to the room-within-a-room stood a white-suited guard, his head braced to take the weight of a bizarre helmet. He carried a flintlock rifle and a back-slung scimitar. At his feet were several more helmets like his.

She nodded to the guard and indicated her desire to enter. He looked at the identification around her neck.

"You know what to do, then?" he asked quietly.

She nodded and put the box carefully on the floor for a moment, after testing that the string was still tight. Then she picked up one of the helmets by the guard's feet and slipped the unwieldy thing over her head.

It was a cage of brass pipes and screws that slotted around her skull, with one small mirror suspended a foot and a half in front of each of her eyes. She adjusted the chinstrap to keep the heavy contraption steady, then turned her back on the guard and fiddled with the mirrors. She angled them on their swivelling joints until she could see him clearly directly behind her. She switched focus from eye to eye, testing the visibility.

She nodded.

"All right, I'm ready," she said, and picked up the box, untying it as she did so. She stared intently into the mirrors while the guard unlocked the door behind her. When he opened it he averted his eyes from the interior.

The scientist used her mirrors to walk backwards quickly into the dark room.

She was sweating as she saw the door close in front of her face. She switched her attention again to the mirrors, moved her head slowly from side to side to take in what was behind her.

There was a huge cage of thick black bars filling almost the whole space. From the dark brown light of burning oil and candles she could make out the desultory, dying vegetation and small trees that filled the cage. The gently rotting growth and the darkness in the room were thick enough that she could not see the far side of the room.

She scanned quickly in the mirrors. Nothing was moving.

She backed quickly up to the cage, to where a small tray slotted back and forth through the bars. She reached behind her and tilted her head up such that the mirrors angled down and she could see her hand groping. It was a difficult, inelegant manoeuvre, but she managed to grip the handle and tug the tray out towards her.

She heard a heavy beating in the corner of the cage, like thick rugs being slammed quickly together. Her breath came faster and she fumbled to pour the grubs onto the tray. The four little undulating lozenges slipped in a shower of paper debris onto the metal.

Immediately, something changed in the quality of the air. The caterpillars could smell the inhabitant of the cage, and they were crying out to it for succour.

The thing in the cage was answering.

These cries were not audible. They vibrated in wavelengths other than sonar. The scientist felt the hair all over her body bristle as the ghosts of emotions fleeted through her skull like half-heard rumours. Snippets of alien joy and inhuman terror wafted in her nostrils and ears and behind her eyes, synaesthetically.

With trembling fingers she pushed the tray into the cage.

As she stepped away from the bars, something stroked her leg with a lascivious flourish. She gave a moaning grunt of fear and yanked her trouser out of reach, clamped down on her terror, resisted the instinct to look behind her.

In her head-mounted mirrors, she glimpsed dark brown limbs uncurling in the rough undergrowth, the yellowing bone of teeth, black ocular pits. The ferns and scrub rustled and the thing was gone.

The scientist knocked brusquely on the door as she swallowed, holding her breath until it was opened and she stumbled out nearly into the arms of the guard. She snatched at the clasps under her head, pulling herself free of the helmet. She stared intently away from the guard while she heard him closing and locking the door.

"Is it done?" she whispered eventually.

"Yes."

She turned back slowly. She could not look up, but kept her eyes firmly on the floor, checking that he told the truth by looking at the base of the door, then slowly and with a rush of relief raising her line of sight to eye-level.

She handed the helmet back to the guard.

"Thanks," she murmured.

"Was it all right?" he asked.

"Never," she snapped, and turned.

Behind her, she thought she heard a massive fluttering through the wooden walls.

She walked briskly back through the chamber of strange animals, realizing halfway through that she still clutched the now-empty box in which the grubs had come. She folded it and put it in her pocket.

She pulled the telescoping gate closed behind her on the massive chamber full of shadowy, violent shapes. She returned the length of the scrubbed white corridor and at last back into the Research & Development antechamber, through the first heavy door.

She pushed it closed and bolted it, before turning happily to join her white-suited fellows staring into femtoscopes or reading treatises or conferring quietly by the doors that led to other specialist departments. Each had a legend stencilled on it in red and black.

As Dr. Magesta Barbile walked back to her bench to make her report, she glanced briefly over her shoulder at the warnings printed on the door she had taken.

Biohazard. Danger. Extreme Caution Required.

Chapter Ten

"Are you a dabbler in drugs, Ms. Lin?"

Lin had told Mr. Motley many times that it was difficult for her to speak when she was working. He had affably informed her that he got bored when he was sitting for her, or for any portraits. She didn't have to answer him, he had said. If anything he said really interested her, she could save it up for afterwards and discuss it with him at the end of the session. She really mustn't mind him, he had said. He couldn't possibly stay still for two, three, four hours at a time and say nothing. It would drive him mad. So she listened to what he said and tried to remember one or two remarks to bring up later. She was still very careful to keep him happy with her.

"You should give them a try. I'm sure you have, actually. Artist like you. Plumbing the depths of the psyche. Such-like." She heard a smile in his voice.

Lin had persuaded Mr. Motley to let her work in the attic of his Bonetown base. It was the only place with natural light in the whole building, she had discovered. It was not only painters or heliotypists who needed light: the textures and tactility of surfaces that she evoked so assiduously in her gland-art was invisible by candlelight, and exaggerated in gasjets. So she had wrangled with him nervously until he had accepted her expertise. From then on, she was greeted at the door by the cactus valet and led to the top floor, where a wooden ladder dangled from a trapdoor in the ceiling.

She came and went into the attic alone. Whenever Lin arrived she would find Mr. Motley waiting. He would stand in the enormous space a few feet from where she pulled herself into his view. The triangular cavity seemed to stretch at least a third the length of the terrace, a study in perspective, with the chaotic agglutination of flesh that was Mr. Motley poised at its centre.

There were no furnishings. There was one door leading to some little corridor outside, but she never saw it open. The attic air was dry. Lin trod over loose boards, risking splinters with every step. But the dirt on the large dormer windows seemed translucent, admitting light and diffusing it. Lin would gently sign for Mr. Motley to position himself below the wash of sun, or cloudlight. Then she would pace around him, reorienting herself, before continuing with her sculpture.

Once she had asked him where he would put a life-size representation of himself.

"It's nothing for you to worry about," he had answered with a gentle smile.

She stood before him and watched the lukewarm grey light pick out his features. Every session before she started she would spend some minutes making herself familiar with him again.

The first couple of times she had come here, she had been sure that he changed overnight, that the shards of physiognomy that made up his whole reorganized when no one was looking. She became frightened of her commission. She wondered hysterically if it was like a task in a moral children's tale, if she was to be punished for some nebulous sin by striving to freeze in time a body in flux, forever too afraid to say anything, starting each day from the beginning all over again.

But it was not long before she learnt to impose order on his chaos. It felt absurdly prosaic to *count* the razor-sharp shards of chitin that jutted from a scrap of pachyderm skin, just to make sure she had not missed one in her sculpture. It felt almost vulgar, as if his anarchic form should defy accounting. And yet, as soon as she looked at him with such an eye, the work of sculpture took shape.

Lin would stand and stare at him, switching focus rapidly from visual cell to cell, her concentration fleeting across her eyes, gauging the aggregate that was Mr. Motley through the minutely changing parts. She carried dense white sticks of the organic paste she would metabolize to make her art. She had already eaten several before arriving, and as she took the visual measure of him, she would chew rapidly on another, stolidly ignoring the dull, unpleasant taste, and rapidly passing it through her headbody to the sac inside the hindpart of her headthorax. Her headbelly would swell visibly as she stored up her mulch.

She would turn and pick up the beginnings of the work, the three-toed reptile claw that was one of Mr. Motley's feet, and she would tie it into place on a low bracket. Then she would turn back and kneel, facing her subject, opening the little chitin case protecting her gland and fastening the nether lips at the rear of her headbody with a gentle *slup* onto the edge of the sculpture behind her.

First, Lin would gently spit a little of the enzyme that broke down the integrity of the already hardened khepri-spit, returning the edge of her work-in-progress to a thick sticky mucus. Then she would focus hard on the section of the leg she was working on, taking in what she could see and remembering the features out of her sight, the exoskeletal jags, the muscular cavities; she would begin gently to squeeze the thick paste from her gland, her sphincter-lips dilating and contracting and extending, rolling and smoothing the sludge into shape.

She used the opalescent nacre of the khepri-spit to good effect. At certain places, though, the hues of Mr. Motley's bizarre flesh were too spectacular, too arresting, not to be represented.

Lin would glance down and grab a handful of the colourberries arrayed on her pallet before her. She would take them in subtle combinations and quickly eat them, a careful cocktail of redberries and cyanberries, say, yellowberries and purpleberries and blackberries.

The vivid juice would be spat through her headguts, down peculiar intestinal byways and into an adjunct of her main thoracic sac, and within four or five minutes she could push the mixed colour into the diluted khepri-spit. She would smear the liquid froth into careful position, slopping astonishing tones in suggestive patches and scabs, where it coagulated quickly into shape.

It was only at the end of hours of work, bloated and exhausted, her mouth foul with berry acid and the musty chalk of the paste, that Lin could turn and see her creation. That was the skill of the gland-artist, who had to work blind.

The first of Mr. Motley's legs was coming along, she had decided, with some pride.

The clouds just visible through the skylight moiled vigorously, dissolving and recombining in scraps and shards in new parts of the sky. The air in the attic was very still, by comparison. Dust hung motionless. Mr. Motley stood poised against the light.

He was good at staying very still, as long as one of his mouths kept up a rambling monologue. Today he had decided to talk to Lin about drugs.

"What *is* your poison, Lin? Shazbah? Tusk has no effect on khepri, does it, so that's out . . ." He ruminated. "I think artists have an ambivalent relationship with drugs. I mean, the whole project's about unlocking the beast within, right? Or the angel. Whatever. Opening doors one thought were jammed closed. Now, if you do that with drugs, then doesn't that make the *art* rather a let-down? Art's got to be about communication, hasn't it? So if you rely on drugs, which are, I do not care what any proselytizing little ponce dropping a fizzbolt with chums at a dancehall tells me, which are an intrinsically *individualized* experience, then you've opened the doors, but can you communicate what you've found on the other side?

"Then on the other hand, if you remain stubbornly straightedged, keep sternly to the mind as she is more usually found, then you can communicate with others, because you're all speaking the same language, as it were . . . but have you opened the door? Maybe the best you can do is peer through the keyhole. Maybe that'll do . . ."

Lin glanced up to see which mouth he was speaking from. It was a large, feminine one near his shoulder. She wondered why it was that his voice remained unchanged. She wished she could reply, or that he would stop talking. She found it hard to concentrate, but she thought she had already extracted as good a compromise as she would get from him.

"Lots and lots of money in drugs . . . of course you know that. D'you know what your friend and *agent* Lucky Gazid is prepared to pay for his latest illicit tipple? Honestly, it would astonish you. Ask him, do. The market for these substances is extraordinary. There's room for a few purveyors to make quite tidy sums."

Lin felt that Mr. Motley was laughing at her. Every conversation he had with her wherein he disclosed some hidden details of New Crobuzon's underworld lore, she was embroiled in something she was eager to avoid. *I'm nothing but a visitor,* she wanted to sign frantically. *Don't give me a streetmap! The occasional shot of shazbah to come up, maybe a jolt of quinner to come down, that's all I ask . . . Don't know about the distribution and don't want to!*

"Ma Francine has something of a monopoly in Petty Coil. She's spreading her sales representatives further afield from Kinken. D'you know her? One of your kind. Impressive businesswoman. She and I are going to have to come to some arrangement. Otherwise it's all going to get messy." Several of Mr. Motley's mouths smiled. "But I'll tell you something," he added softly. "I'm taking a delivery very soon of something that should rather dramatically change my distribution. I may have something of a monopoly myself . . ."

I'm going to find Isaac tonight, decided Lin nervously. *I'm going to take him out to supper, somewhere in Salacus Fields where I can touch his toes with mine.*

The annual Shintacost Prize competition was coming up fast, at the end of Melluary, and she would have to think of something to tell him as to why she was not entering. She had never won— the judges, she thought haughtily, did not understand gland-art— but she, along with all her artist friends, had entered without fail for the last seven years. It had become a ritual. They would have a grand supper on the day of the announcement, and send someone to pick up an early copy of the *Salacus Gazetteer,* which sponsored the competition, to see who had won. Then they would drunkenly denounce the organizers for tasteless buffoons.

Isaac would be surprised that she was not taking part. She had decided to hint at some monumental work-in-progress, something to keep him from asking questions for some time.

Of course, she reflected, *if his garuda thing's still going on, he won't really notice if I enter or not.*

There was a sour note to her thoughts. She was not being fair, she realized. She was prone to the same kind of obsessing: she found it difficult, now, not to see the monstrous shape of Mr. Motley hovering at the corner of her vision at every hour. It was just bad timing that Isaac should be obsessed at the same time as her, she thought desultorily. This job was swallowing her up. She wanted to come home every night to freshly mixed fruit salad and theatre tickets and sex.

Instead, he scribbled avidly in his workshop, and she came home to an empty bed in Aspic Hole, night after night. They met once or twice a week, for a hurried supper and a deep, unromantic sleep.

Lin looked up and saw that the shadows had moved some way since she had come into the attic. Her mind felt foggy. Her delicate forelegs cleaned her mouth and eyes and antennae in quick passes. She chewed what she had decided would be the day's last clutch of colourberries. The tartness of the blueberries was tempered by the sweet pinkberries. She was mixing carefully, adding an unripe pearlberry or a nearly fermenting yellowberry. She knew exactly the taste she was striving for: the sickly, cloying bitterness of a colour like vivid, greying salmon, the colour of Mr. Motley's calf muscle.

She swallowed and squeezed juice through her headgullet. It squirted eventually onto the shimmering sides of the drying khepri-spit. It was a little too liquid: it spattered and dribbled as it emerged. Lin worked with it, rendering the muscle tone in abstract streaks and drips, a spur-of-the-moment rescue.

When the spit was dry she disengaged. She felt a sticky seal of mucus stretch and snap as she pulled her head away from the half-finished leg. She leaned to one side and tensed, pushing the remaining paste through her gland. The ribbed underbelly of her headbody squeezed itself out of its distended shape, into more usual dimensions. A fat white glop of khepri-spit dropped from her head and curled on the floor. Lin stretched her gland-tip forwards and cleaned it with her rear legs, then carefully closed the little protective case below her wingtips.

She stood and stretched. Mr. Motley's amiable, cold, dangerous little pronouncements broke off sharply. He had not realized she was finished.

"So soon, Ms. Lin?" he cried with theatrical disappointment.

Losing my edge if not careful, she signed slowly. *Takes a lot out of you. Got to stop.*

"Of course," said Mr. Motley. "And how is the meisterwork?"

They turned together.

Lin was pleased to see that her impromptu recovery from the watery colourberry juice had created a vivid, suggestive effect. It was not entirely naturalistic, but none of her work was: instead, Mr. Motley's muscle seemed to have been thrown violently onto the bones of his leg. An analogy perhaps close to the truth.

The translucent colours spilt in uneven grots down the white that glinted like the inside of a shell. The slabs of tissue and muscle crawled over each other. The intricacies of the many-textured flesh were vivid. Mr. Motley nodded approvingly.

"You know," he ventured quietly, "my sense of the grand moment makes me wish there was some way I could avoid seeing anything more of this until it's finished. I think it is very fine so far, you know. *Very* fine. But it's dangerous to offer praise too early. Can lead to complacency . . . or to the opposite. So please don't be downhearted, Ms. Lin, if that is the last word I say, positive or negative, on the matter, until the very end. Are we agreed?"

Lin nodded. She was unable to take her eyes from what she had created, and she rubbed her hand very gently over the smooth surface of the drying khepri-spit. Her fingers explored the transition from fur to scales to skin below Mr. Motley's knee. She looked down at the original. She looked up at his head. He returned her gaze with a pair of tiger's eyes.

What . . . what were *you?* she signed at him.

He sighed.

"I wondered when you'd ask that, Lin. I did hope that you wouldn't, but I knew it was unlikely. *It makes me wonder if we understand each other at all,*" he hissed, sounding suddenly vicious. Lin recoiled.

"It's so . . . predictable. You're still not looking the right way. At all. It's a wonder you can create such art. You still see *this*—" he gesticulated vaguely at his own body with a monkey's paw

"—as pathology. You're still interested in what *was* and how it went *wrong*. *This is not error or absence or mutancy: this is image and essence* . . ." His voice rang around the rafters.

He calmed a little and lowered his many arms.

"This is totality."

She nodded to show that she understood, too tired to be intimidated.

"Maybe I'm too hard on you," Mr. Motley said reflectively. "I mean . . . this piece before us makes it clear that you *have* a sense of the ruptured moment, even if your question suggests the opposite . . . So maybe," he continued slowly, "you yourself *contain* that moment. Part of you understands without recourse to words, even if your higher mind asks questions in a format which renders an answer impossible."

He looked at her triumphantly.

"You too are the bastard-zone, Ms. Lin! Your art takes place where your understanding and your ignorance blur."

Fine, she signed as she gathered her things. *Whatever. Sorry I asked.*

"So was I, but not any more, I think," he replied.

Lin folded her wooden case around her stained pallet, around the remaining colourberries (she needed more, she saw) and the blocks of paste. Mr. Motley continued with his philosophical ramblings, his ruminations on mongrel theory. Lin was not listening. She tuned her antennae away from him, felt the tiny ructions and rumblings of the house, the weight of the air on the window.

I want a sky above me, she thought, *not this ancient dusty brace of beams, this tarred, brittle roof. I'm walking home. Slowly. Through Brock Marsh.*

Her resolution increased as her thoughts progressed.

I'll stop at the lab and nonchalantly ask Isaac to come with me, and I'll steal him away for a night.

Mr. Motley continued sounding.

Shut up, shut up, you spoilt child, you damn megalomaniac with your crackpot theories, thought Lin.

When she turned to sign *goodbye*, it was with only the faintest semblance of politeness.

CHAPTER ELEVEN

A pigeon hung cruciform on an X of darkwood on Isaac's desk. Its head bobbed frantically from side to side, but despite its terror, it could only emit a bathetic cooing.

Its wings were pinned with thin nails driven through the tight spaces between splayed feathers and bent hard down to pinion the wingtip. The pigeon's legs were tied to the lower quarters of the little cross. The wood beneath it was spattered with the dirty white and grey of birdshit. It spasmed and tried to shake its wings, but it was held.

Isaac loomed over it brandishing a magnifying glass and a long pen.

"Stop fucking about, you vermin," he muttered, and prodded the bird's shoulder with the tip of the pen. He gazed through his lens at the infinitesimal shudders that passed through the tiny bones and muscles. He scribbled without looking at the paper beneath him.

"Oy!"

Isaac looked round at Lublamai's irritated call, and left his desk. He paced to the balcony's edge and peered over.

"What?"

Lublamai and David were standing shoulder to shoulder on the ground floor, their arms folded. They looked like a small chorus line about to burst into song. Their faces were furrowed. There was silence for some seconds.

"Look," began Lublamai, his voice suddenly placatory, "Isaac . . . We've always agreed that this is a place we can all do the research we want to do, no questions asked, back each other up, that sort of thing . . . right?"

Isaac sighed and rubbed his eyes with the thumb and forefinger of his left hand.

"For Jabber's sake, boys, let's not play old soldiers," he said with a groan. "You don't have to tell me we've been through thick and thin, or what have you, I know you're arsed off, and I don't blame you . . ."

"It smells, Isaac," said David bluntly. "And we're treated to the dawn chorus every minute of the day."

As Lublamai spoke, the old construct wheeled its way uncertainly behind him. It stopped and its head rotated, its lenses taking in the two poised men. It hesitated a moment, then folded its stubby metal arms in clumsy imitation of their poses.

Isaac gesticulated at it.

"Look, look, that stupid thing's losing it! It's got a virus! You'd better have it trashed or it'll self-organize; you'll be having existential arguments with your mechanical skivvy before the year's out!"

"Isaac, don't change the fucking subject," said David irritably, glancing round and shoving the construct, which fell over. "We all have a bit of leeway when it comes to inconveniences, but this is pushing it."

"All right!" Isaac threw up his hands. He looked slowly around. "I suppose I sort of underestimated Lemuel's abilities to get things done," he said ruefully.

Circumscribing the entire warehouse, the whole length of the raised platform was crammed with cages filled with flapping, crying, crawling things. The warehouse was loud with the sounds of displaced air, the sudden shifts and fluttering of beating wings, the spatter of droppings, and loudest of all, the constant screech of captive birds. Pigeons and sparrows and starlings registered their distress with their coos and calls: feeble on their own, but a sharp, grating chorus en masse. Parrots and canaries punctuated the avian wittering with squawked exclamation marks that made Isaac wince. Geese and chickens and ducks added a rustic air to the cacophony. Hard-faced aspises flung themselves through the air the short distance of their cages, their little lizard bodies banging against the chickenwire fronts. They licked their wounds with their tiny lions' faces and roared like aggressive mice. Huge glass tanks of flies and bees and wasps, mayflies and butterflies and flying beetles sounded a vivid aggressive drone. Bats hung upside down and regarded Isaac with fervent little eyes. Dragonfly-snakes rustled their long elegant wings and hissed loudly.

The floors of the cages had not been cleaned and the acrid smell of birdshit was very strong. Sincerity, Isaac saw, was wobbling up and down the room shaking her striped head. David saw where Isaac was looking.

"Yeah," he shouted. "See? The stink's making her miserable."

"Fellows," said Isaac, "I appreciate your forbearance, I really do. It's give and take, isn't it? Lub, remember when you were doing those experiments in sonar and you had that chap in banging that huge drum for two days?"

"Isaac, it's already been nearly a week! How long's it going to be? What's the schedule? At the very least clean their mess up!"

Isaac looked down at the irate faces below him. They were very pissed off, he realized. He thought quickly for a compromise.

"Fine, look," he eventually said, "I'll clean them out tonight— I promise. And I'll work flat fucking out . . . I know! I'll work hard on the *loud* ones first. I'll try and get rid of them within . . . two weeks?" he finished lamely. David and Lublamai expostulated, but he interrupted their jeers and catcalls. "I'll pay a little extra rent for the next month! How's that?"

The rude noises died down instantly. The two men stared at him calculatedly. They were scientific comrades, the Brock Marsh bad boys, friends; but their existence was precarious, and there was limited room for sentimentality where money was concerned. Knowing that, Isaac tried to forestall any temptation they might have to seek alternative space. He, after all, couldn't afford the rent here alone.

"What are we talking?" asked David.

Isaac pondered.

"Two extra guineas?"

David and Lublamai looked at each other. It was generous.

"And," said Isaac casually, "while we're on the subject, I'd appreciate a hand. I don't know how to manage some of these . . . uh . . . scientific subjects. Didn't you do some ornithological theory once, David?"

"No," said David tartly. "I was an assistant to someone who did. I was bored shitless. And stop being so transparent, 'Zaac. I'm not going to resent your pestilential pets any less if you *involve me in your projects* . . ." He laughed with a trace of genuine humour. "Have you been taking Introductory Empathic Theory, or something?"

But despite his scorn, David was ascending the stairs, with Lublamai behind him.

He paused at the top and took in all the jabbering captives.

"Devil's Tail, Isaac!" he whispered, grinning. "How much has this lot set you back?"

"Haven't entirely settled with Lemuel yet," said Isaac dryly. "But my new boss should see me all right."

Lublamai had joined David on the top step. He gesticulated at a collection of variegated cages in the far corner of the walkway.

"What's over there?"

"That's where I keep the exotica," said Isaac. "Aspises, lasifly . . ."

"You've got a lasifly?" exclaimed Lublamai. Isaac nodded and grinned.

"Don't have the heart to do any experiments with the beautiful thing," he said.

"Can I see it?"

" 'Course, Lub. It's over there behind the cage with the batkin in it."

As Lublamai trooped over between the tightly packed cases, David looked briskly about him.

"So where's your ornithological problem, then?" he asked and rubbed his hands.

"On the desk." Isaac indicated the miserable, trussed pigeon. "How do I make that thing stop wriggling. I wanted it to at first, to see the musculature, but now I want to move the wings myself."

David stared levelly at him as if at a halfwit.

"Kill it."

Isaac shrugged hugely.

"I tried. It wouldn't die."

"Oh for *fuck's* sake . . ." David laughed exasperatedly, and strode over to the desk. He wrung the pigeon's neck.

Isaac winced ostentatiously and held up his massive hands.

"They're just not subtle enough for that sort of work. My hands are too clumsy, my sensibilities too damned delicate," he declared airily.

"Right," agreed David sceptically. "What are you working on?"

Isaac was instantly enthusiastic.

"Well . . ." He strode over to the desk. "I've had fuck-all luck with the garuda in the city. I heard rumours about a couple living in St. Jabber's Mound and Syriac, and I sent word that I was willing to pay good moolah for a couple of hours' time and some heliotypes. I've had absolutely nil response. I've whacked a couple of posters up in the university as well, asking for any garuda student ready and willing to drop by here, but my *sources* tell me there's been no intake this year."

" 'Garuda aren't . . . *adept* at abstract thought.' " David imitated the sneering tone of the speaker from the sinister Three Quills party, which had held a disastrous rally in Brock Marsh the previous year. Isaac and David and Derkhan had gone along to disrupt proceedings, hurling abuse and rotten oranges at the man on stage to the delight of the xenian demonstration outside. Isaac barked in recollection.

"Absolutely. So anyway, short of going to Spatters, at the moment I can't work with actual garuda, so I'm looking at the various flight mechanisms you . . . uh . . . see around you. Amazing variation, actually."

Isaac sheafed through piles of notes, holding up diagrams of finches' and bluebottles' wings. He untied the dead pigeon and delicately traced the movement of its wings through a rolling arc. He pointed wordlessly at the wall around his desk. It was covered with carefully rendered diagrams of wings. Close-up sections of the rotating joint at the shoulder, pared-down representations of forces, beautifully shaded studies of feather patterns. Here too were heliotypes of dirigibles, with arrows and question marks scrawled on them in dark ink. There were suggestive sketches of the mindless men-o'-war, and hugely enlarged pictures of wasps' wings. Each was carefully labelled. David moved his eyes slowly over the hours and hours of work, the comparative studies of the engines of flight.

"I don't think my client's too fussy about what his wings—or whatever—look like, as long as he can get airbound as and when." David and Lublamai knew about Yagharek. Isaac had asked them for secrecy. He trusted them. He had told them in case Yagharek visited when they were in the warehouse, although so far the garuda had managed to avoid them on his fleeting visits.

"Have you thought about just, y'know, sticking some wings back on?" said David. "Remaking him?"

"Well, absolutely, that's my main line of enquiry, but there're two problems. One is what wings? I'll have to build them. Second is, do *you* know any Remakers prepared to do that on the quiet? The best bio-thaumaturge I know is the despised Vermishank. I'll go to him if I fucking *have* to, but I'll be sorely desperate before I do that . . . So at the moment I'm doing preliminary stuff, trying to work out the size and shape and power-source of something that would hold him up at all. If I go that way, eventually."

"What else have you got in mind? Physico-thaumaturgy?"

"Well, you know, UFT, my old favourite . . ." Isaac grinned and shrugged self-deprecatingly. "I have a feeling his back's too messed up for easy Remaking, even if I could get the wings sorted out. I'm wondering about combining two different energy fields . . . Shit, David, I don't know. I've got the beginnings of an idea . . ." He pointed vaguely at a roughly labelled drawing of a triangle.

"Isaac?" Lublamai's yell sailed over the relentless squawks and screeches. Isaac and David looked over at him. He had wandered on past the lasifly and the pair of gild-parakeets. He was pointing at a smaller set of boxes and cases and vats. "What's all this?"

"Oh, that's my nursery," shouted Isaac with a grin. He strode towards Lublamai, pulling David with him. "I thought it might be interesting to see how you progress from something that can't fly to something that can, so I managed to get hold of a bunch of neonates and unborns and baby things."

He stopped by the collection. Lublamai was peering into a small hutch at a clutch of vivid cobalt eggs.

"Don't know what they are," said Isaac. "Hope it's something pretty."

The hutch was on the top of a pile of similar open-fronted boxes, in each of which a clumsy little hand-made nest contained between one and four eggs. Some were astonishing colours, some a drab beige. A little pipe coiled away behind the hutches and disappeared over the railings into the boiler below. Isaac nudged it with his foot.

"I think they prefer it warm . . ." he muttered. "Don't really know . . ."

Lublamai was bending down to peer into a glass-fronted tank.

"Wow . . ." he breathed. "I feel like I'm ten again! Trade you these for six marbles."

The tank's floor writhed with little green caterpillars. They munched voraciously and systematically on the leaves stuffed rudely around them. The stems were crawling with little bodies.

"Yeah, that's quite interesting. Any day now they should go into their cocoons, and then I think I'm going to ruthlessly cut them open at various stages to see how they transmogrify themselves."

"Life as a lab assistant is cruel, isn't it?" murmured Lublamai into the tank. "What other disgusting grubs do you have?"

"Bunch of maggots. Easy to feed. That's probably the smell that's got Sincerity upset." Isaac laughed. "Some other grubs that promise to turn into butterflies and moths, horribly aggressive water-things that *I am told* turn into damask-flies and what have you . . ." Isaac pointed at a tank full of dirty water, behind the others.

"And," he said, swaggering over to a little mesh cage some feet away, "something *rather* special . . ." He jabbed his thumb at the container.

David and Lublamai crowded round. They gazed with open mouths.

"Oh, now that is *splendid* . . ." whispered David, after a while.

"What *is* it?" hissed Lublamai.

Isaac peered over their heads at his star caterpillar.

"Frankly, my friends, I have not an arsing clue. All I know is that it's huge, pretty, and not very happy."

The grub waved its thick head blindly. It shifted its massive body sluggishly around the wire prison. It was at least four inches long and one inch thick, with bright colours slapped randomly around its chubby cylindrical body. Spiky hairs sprouted from its rump. It shared its cage with browning lettuce leaves, little snips of meat, slices of fruit, paper strips.

"See," said Isaac, "I've tried to feed the thing everything. I've put in as many herbs and plants as exist, and it doesn't want any of them. So I tried it on fish and fruit and cake, bread, meat, paper, glue, cotton, silk . . . it just roots aimlessly around being hungry, staring at me accusingly."

Isaac leaned in, planting his face between David's and Lublamai's.

"It obviously wants to eat," he said. "Its colour's fading, which is worrying, both aesthetically and physiologically . . . I'm at a loss. I think the beautiful thing's going to sit there and die on me." Isaac sniffed matter-of-factly.

"Where did you get it from?" asked David.

"Oh, you know how this stuff works," said Isaac. "I got it from a cove who got it from a man who got it from a woman who got it . . . and so on. I've no idea where it came from."

"You're not going to cut this open, are you?"

" 'Stail, no. If it lives to build a cocoon, which I'm afraid I doubt, I'll be very interested to see what comes out. I might even donate it to the Science Museum. You know me. Public-spirited . . . So anyway, this thing's not really much use to me for research. Can't even make it eat, let alone metamorphose, let alone *fly*. So everything else you see around you—" he spread his arms wide, wriggled his wrists to take in the room "—is grist to my counter-gravitational mill. But this little geezer—" he pointed at the listless caterpillar "—this is social work." He grinned widely.

There was a creaking from below. The door was being pushed open. All three men lurched dangerously over the side of the walkway and peered down, expecting to see Yagharek the garuda, with his false wings under his cloak.

Lin peered up at them.

David and Lublamai started in confusion. They were embar-rassed at Isaac's sudden cry of irritated welcome. They found something else to look at.

Isaac was scurrying down the stairs.

"Lin," he bellowed. "Good to see you." When he reached her he spoke quietly.

"Sweetheart, what are you *doing* here? I thought I was going to see you later in the week."

As he spoke he saw her antennae quivering miserably, tried to temper his nervous irritation. It was clear that Lub and David understood what was going on—they'd known him a long time: he did not doubt that his evasion and hints about his love life had left them guessing reasonably close to the truth. But this was not Salacus Fields. This was too close to home. He might be seen.

But then, Lin was clearly miserable.

Look, she signed rapidly, *want you to come home with me, don't say no. Miss you. Tired. Difficult job. Sorry for coming here. Needed to see you.*

Isaac felt anger and affection jostle. *This is a dangerous precedent,* he thought. *Fuck!*

"Hang on," he whispered. "Give me a minute."

He raced up the stairs.

"Lub, David, I'd forgotten I'm supposed to be out with friends this evening, so someone's been sent to fetch me. I *promise* I'll muck out all my little charges tomorrow. On my honour. They're all fed, that's taken care of . . ." He was looking around him rapidly. He forced himself to meet their eyes.

"Right," said David. "Have a nice evening."

Lublamai waved him away.

"Right," said Isaac heavily, looking around him. "If Yagharek comes back . . . uh . . ." He realized he had nothing to say. He grabbed a notebook from the desk and bounced downstairs without looking behind him. Lublamai and David studiously did not watch him go.

He seemed to carry Lin with him as if he was a gale, billowing her helplessly with him through the door and into the darkening streets. It was only as they left the warehouse, when he looked at her clearly, that he felt his own irritation diminish to a low burn. He saw her in all her exhausted dejection.

Isaac hesitated a moment, then took her arm. He slipped his notebook into her bag, which he snapped closed.

"Let's have us a night," he whispered.

She nodded and leaned her headbody against him, briefly, held him tight.

They disengaged, then, for fear of being watched. They walked to Sly Station together slowly, at a lovers' pace, a few careful feet apart.

CHAPTER TWELVE

If a murderer stalked the mansions of Flag Hill or Canker Wedge, would the militia waste any time or spare resources? Why, no! The hunt for Jack Half-a-Prayer proves it! And yet, when the Eyespy Killer strikes in *Smog Bend*, nothing happens! Another eyeless victim was fished from the Tar last week—bringing the number killed to five—and not a word from the blue-clad bullies in the Spike. We say: *it's one law for the rich, another for the poor!*

Around New Crobuzon the posters are appearing demanding *your vote*—should you be lucky enough to have one! Rudgutter's Fat Sun huffs and puffs, Finally We Can See spout weasel-words, the Diverse Tendency lies to the oppressed xenians, and the human dust of the Three Quills spread their poison. With this sorry crew as the "choice," *Runagate Rampant* calls on all "winners" of the vote to spoil their ballots! Build a party from below and denounce the Suffrage Lottery as a cynical ploy. We say: *votes for all and vote for change!*

The vodyanoi stevedores of Kelltree are discussing strike action after vicious attacks on wages by the dock authorities. Disgracefully, the Guild of Human Dockers has denounced their actions. We say: *towards an all-race union against the bosses!*

Derkhan looked up from reading as a couple entered the carriage. Casually and surreptitiously, she folded her copy of *Runagate Rampant* and slipped it into her bag.

She sat at the very front end of the train, facing backwards, so she could see the few people in her carriage without appearing to spy on them. The two young people who had just entered swayed as the train left Sedim Junction and sat quickly. They were dressed simply but well, which marked them out from the majority of those travelling to Dog Fenn. Derkhan pegged them as Veruline missionaries, students from the university up the road in Ludmead, descending piously and sanctimoniously into the depths of Dog Fenn to improve the souls of the poor. She sneered at them mentally as she took out a little mirror.

Glancing up again to ensure she was not observed, Derkhan looked critically at her face. She adjusted her white wig minutely, and pressed at her rubber scar to make sure it was solid. She was dressed carefully. Dirty and torn clothes, no hint of money to attract unwanted attention in the Fenn, but not so fouled as to attract the opprobrious wrath of travellers in The Crow, where she had started her journey.

Her notebook was on her lap. She was taking some time during her journey to make preparatory notes on the Shintacost Prize. The first round was taking place sometime at the end of the month, and she had in mind a piece for the *Beacon* about what did and did not get through the early stages. She intended to make it funny, but with a serious point about the politics of the judging panel.

She stared at her lacklustre beginning and sighed. *Now,* she decided, *is not the time.*

Derkhan stared out of the window to her left, across the city. On this branch of the Dexter Line, between Ludmead and the industrial zone of New Crobuzon's south-east, the trains passed at about the midpoint of the city's tussle with the sky. The mass of roofs was pierced by militia towers in Brock Marsh and Strack Island, and far away in Flyside and Sheck. Sud Line trains passed south beyond the Gross Tar.

The bleached Ribs came and went beside the tracks, towering over the carriage. Smoke and grime built up in the air until the train seemed to ride on a smog tide. The sounds of industry increased. The train flew through clutches of vast, sparse chimneys like blasted trees as the train passed through Sunter. Echomire was a savage industrial zone a little way to the east. *Somewhere below and a little to the south,* realized Derkhan, *a vodyanoi picket is probably massing. Good luck, brothers.*

Gravity pulled her to the west as the train turned. It broke off from the Kelltree Line and veered away to the east, gearing up to leap the river.

The masts of tall ships in Kelltree swung into view as the train turned. They teetered and swayed gently in the water. Derkhan glimpsed the furled sails, the massive paddles and yawning smokestacks, the excited, tightly reined seawyrms of trading ships from Myrshock and Shankell and Gnurr Kett. The water boiled with submersibles carved from great nautili shells. Derkhan turned her head to stare as the train arced.

She could see the Gross Tar over the roofs to the south, wide and relentless and bristling with vessels. Antique ordinances stopped the large ships, the foreign ships, half a mile downriver of the confluence of Canker and Tar. They collected beyond Strack Island, in the docklands. For a mile and a half or more, the north bank of the Gross Tar thronged with cranes loading and unloading constantly, bobbing like massive feeding birds. Swarms of barges and tugs took the transferred cargos upriver to Smog Bend and Gross Coil and the mean slum-industries of Creekside; they hauled crates along New Crobuzon's canals, linking minor franchises and failing workshops, finding their way through the maze like laboratory rats.

The clay of Kelltree and Echomire was gouged by fat square docks and reservoirs, huge culs-de-sac of water that jutted into the city, linked by deep channels to the river, thronging with ships.

There had once been an attempt to replicate the Kelltree

docks in Badside. Derkhan had seen what remained. Three massive stinking troughs of malarial slime, their surfaces broken with half-sunk wrecks and twisted girders.

The rattle and boom of the tracks beneath the iron wheels changed suddenly as the steaming engine hauled its charges onto the great girders of Barley Bridge. It veered a little from side to side, slowing on the unkempt tracks as it rose as if with distaste over Dog Fenn.

A few grey blocks rose from the streets like weeds in a cesspool, their concrete seeping and rotten. Many were unfinished, with splayed iron supports fanning out from the ghosts of roofs, rusting, bleeding with the rain and the damp, staining the skin of the buildings. Wyrmen swirled like carrion crows over these monoliths, squatting on the upper floors and fouling their neighbours' roofs with dung. The outlines of Dog Fenn's slum landscape bloated and burst and changed every time Derkhan saw them. Tunnels were dug into the undercity that stretched in a network of ruins and sewers and catacombs below New Crobuzon. Ladders left against a wall one day were hammered into place the next, reinforced after that, and within a week had become the stairwells to a new storey, thrown precariously between two drooping roofs. Wherever she looked, Derkhan could see people lying or running or fighting on the roofscape.

She stood wearily as the smell of the Fenn seeped into the slowing carriage.

As usual, there was no one to take her ticket at the station exit. Had it not been for the profound consequences of discovery, however small the possibility, Derkhan would never have bothered buying one. She flung it down on the counter and descended.

The doors of Dog Fenn Station were always open. They had rusted into position, and ivy had anchored them against the walls. Derkhan stepped out into the squalls and stench of Silverback Street. Barrows were thrown against walls slick with fungus and rotting paste. All manner of wares—some of surprisingly high quality—were available here. Derkhan turned and walked deeper into the slum. She was surrounded with a constant hubbub of shouts, advertising that sounded more like riotous assembly. For the most part, it was food that was announced.

"*On*ions! Who'll buy my fine *on*ions?"

"Whelks! Stick to whelks!"

"Broth to warm yer!"

Other goods and services were plainly available on every streetcorner.

Whores congregated in wretched, raucous gangs. Filthy petticoats and tawdry flounces of stolen silk, faces smeared white and scarlet over bruises and broken veins. They laughed with mouths full of broken teeth and sniffed tiny stains of shazbah cut with soot and rat-poison. Some were children who played with little paper dolls and wooden quoits when no one watched them, pouted lasciviously and tongued the air whenever a man walked by.

The Dog Fenn streetwalkers were the lowest of a despised breed. For decadent, inventive, obsessive, fetishized corruption and perversion of the flesh, the connoisseur looked elsewhere, in the red-light zone between The Crow and Spit Hearth. In Dog Fenn, the quickest, simplest, cheapest relief was available. The clients here were as poor and dirty and diseased as the tarts.

At the entrances to clubs already ejecting comatose drunks, industrial Remade worked as bouncers. They teetered aggressively on hooves and treads and massive feet, flexing metal claws. Their faces were brutalized, defensive. Their eyes would lock at the taunts from a passer-by. They took gobs of spit in the face, unwilling to risk their jobs. Their fear was understandable: to Derkhan's left a cavernous space opened in an arch below the railway. From the darkness came the reek of shit and oil, the mechanical clank and human groans of Remade dying in a starving, drunken, stinking huddle.

A few ancient, tottering constructs staggered through the streets, clumsily ducking the rocks and mud thrown by ragged street-children. Graffiti covered every wall. Rude poems and obscene drawings jostled with slogans from *Runagate Rampant* and anxious prayers:

Half-a-Prayer's coming!
Against the Lottery!
Tar and Canker spread like legs / City wonders where her Lover went / Cos now she's being Ravished blind / by the Prick that is the Government!

The walls of churches were not spared. The Veruline monks stood in a nervous group and wiped at the scrawled pornography that had appeared on their chapel.

There were xenians in the crowds. Some were being harassed, notably the few khepri. Others laughed and joked and swore with their neighbours. On one corner a cactus was arguing fiercely with a vodyanoi, and the mainly human crowd was cat-calling equally for both sides.

Children hissed and called for stivers from Derkhan as she walked past. She ignored them, did not pull her bag closer to herself and identify herself as a victim. She stomped aggressively into the heart of Dog Fenn.

The walls around her suddenly sealed over her head as she passed under rickety bridges and ersatz rooms thrown up as if by aggregated filth. The air in their shadow dripped and creaked ominously. A whoop sounded from behind her, and Derkhan felt a rush of air on her neck as a wyrman dived aerobatically through the short tunnel and took off again into the sky, cackling madly. She stumbled as he passed and fell against a wall, adding her voice to the chorus of abuse that travelled in the wyrman's wake.

The architecture she passed seemed governed by rules quite distinct from those in the rest of the city. There was no functional sense here. Dog Fenn seemed born of struggles in which the inhabitants were unimportant. The nodes and cells of brick and wood and palsied concrete had gone rogue, spreading like malignant tumours.

Derkhan turned into a mildewed brick cul-de-sac and looked around her. A Remade horse stood by the far end, its hind legs enormous piston-driven hammers. Behind it, a covered cart was backed nearly to the wall. Any one of the dead-eyed figures loitering around could be militia informers. It was a risk she would have to take.

She walked around to the back of the cart. Six pigs had been loaded out of the cart into a makeshift pen open on the side nearest the wall. Two men were chasing the pigs comically around the little space. The pigs squealed and screeched like babies as they ran. The pen led onto a semicircular opening about four feet high set into the wall at ground level. Derkhan peered through this space into a foetid hole ten feet below, barely lit with gasjets that flickered unreliably. The burrow boomed and hissed and gleamed red in the gaslight. Figures came and went below her, bent double under dripping burdens like souls in some lurid hell.

A doorless opening to her left led Derkhan down steep stairs towards the sunken slaughterhouse.

      *   *   *

The spring warmth was magnified here as if by infernal energy. Derkhan sweated and picked her way through swinging carcasses and slicks of congealing blood. At the back of the room a raised belt dragged heavy meathooks along the ceiling in a remorseless circuit, disappearing into the darker bowels of the charnel-house.

Even the glints of light from knives seemed filtered through ruddy gloom. Derkhan held a posset to her nose and mouth and tried not to gag at the rancid, heavy stench of blood and warm meat.

At the far end of the room, she saw three men congregated below the open arc she had seen from the street. In this dark and stinking place, the Dog Fenn light and air that spilt through from above was like bleach.

At some unspoken signal, the three slaughtermen stood back. The pig-men in the alley above had got hold of one of the animals, and in the midst of a rising wave of curses and grunts and terrified sounds, they hurled her enormous weight through the opening. The pig screamed as she pitched into the darkness. She was rigid with terror as she hurtled towards the waiting knives.

There was a sick-making crack and snap as the sow's stiff little legs shattered on flagstones slimy with blood and shit. She collapsed on legs bleeding from bone-shards, thrashing and screeching, unable to run or fight. The three men moved forward with practised precision. One leaned on the pig's rump in case she jackknifed, another pulled back her head by those lolling ears. The third man split the skin of her throat with his knife.

Her cries ebbed quickly with the gouts and wash of blood. The men hauled her huge, twitching body onto a waiting table by which a rusted saw leaned. One man saw Derkhan. He nudged another.

"Ay ay, Ben, you dark horse, you rogue! It's your fancy tart!" he shouted good-naturedly, loud enough for Derkhan to hear. The man he spoke to turned and waved at her.

"Five minutes," he yelled. She nodded. Her posset was clamped to her mouth as she swallowed back bile and spew.

Again and again the massive, terrified pigs dropped from the alley in a flailing organic mess, legs folded in unnatural angles against their guts, again and again they were cut open and bled dry on ancient wooden stands. Tongues and flaps of ragged skin dangled, dripping. The channels cut in the abattoir floor burst their banks as a swamp of dirty blood lapped against buckets of giblets and bleached, boiled cows' heads.

Eventually, the last pig had fallen. The exhausted men swayed where they stood. They were awash with gore, and steaming. There was a brief conference and raucous laughter, and the one called Ben turned away from his fellows and approached Derkhan. Behind him, the two remaining men split the first carcass and swept innards into a huge trough.

"Dee," said Flex quietly, "I'll not kiss you hello." He gestured briefly at his saturated clothes, his bloody face.

"I'm obliged," she replied. "Can we get out of here?"

They ducked under the jerkily progressing meathooks and picked their way towards the dark exit. They took stairs up towards ground level. The light became less livid as the blue-grey tint of the sky filtered through dirty skylights in the narrow corridor's ceiling, a long way above.

Benjamin and Derkhan turned into a windowless room filled with a tub, a pump and several buckets. Some tough robes hung behind the door. Derkhan watched quietly as he stripped off his fouled clothes and threw them in a pail with water and powdered soap. He scratched himself and stretched luxuriously, then pumped water vigorously into the tub. His naked body was streaked with oily blood as if he was newborn. He shook some of the soap under the sputtering pump, swirled the cold water to make suds.

"Your mates are very understanding about you just up and taking a fuck-break, aren't they?" said Derkhan mildly. "What have you told them? Did I steal your heart, you mine, or are we in a purely business arrangement?"

Benjamin sniggered. He spoke with a strong Dog Fenn accent, in distinction to Derkhan's uptown tones.

"Well, I've been working an extra shift, ain't I? I'm already working over my time. I told them you'd be along. Far as they're concerned you're just a tart who's taken to me, and I to you. That wig, afore I forget, is a marvel." He grinned lopsidedly. "Suits you, Dee. You look a smasher."

He stood in the tub, slowly lowered himself into it, goose-bumps peppering him. He left a thick scum of blood on the surface of the water. Gore and grime lifted slowly from his skin and billowed lazily towards the surface. He closed his eyes a minute.

"I won't be long, Dee, I promise," he whispered.

"Take your time," she replied.

His head slid below the bubbles, leaving thin fronds of hair to coil on the surface and be sucked slowly under. He held his breath a moment, then began to scrub his submerged body vigorously, coming up and sucking air, then ducking below again.

Derkhan filled a bucket with water and stood behind the bath. As he broke the surface she poured it slowly over his head, rinsing him free of bloody soap stains.

"Oooh, lovely," he muttered. "More, I beg you."

She obliged him.

Eventually he stepped out of the bath, which looked like the site of violent murder. He tipped the slimy residue into a sluice hammered into the floor. They heard it slosh through the walls.

Benjamin stepped into a rough robe. He wagged his head at Derkhan.

"Shall we get down to business, love?" He winked at her.

"Just tell me what services you require, squire," she replied.

They left the room. At the end of the passage, picked out in the wash from the skylight, was the little room where Benjamin slept. He closed and locked the door behind them. The room was like a well, far taller than it was wide. Another grubby window was set into the square ceiling space. Derkhan and Benjamin stepped over the flimsy mattress to the ramshackle old wardrobe at its foot, a relic with a decaying grandeur at odds with the slum setting.

Benjamin reached inside and swept a few greasy shirts out of the way. He reached into the fingerholds drilled strategically in the wardrobe's wooden back, and with a little grunt, lifted it away. He turned it gently sideways and laid it on the cabinet's floor.

Derkhan looked into the small brick doorway Benjamin had uncovered while he reached onto a little shelf in the wardrobe and took down a matchbox and a candle. He lit the candle in a burst of sulphur, shielding it from the cool air that wafted from the hidden room. With Derkhan behind him, he stepped through the wardrobe and lit up the office of *Runagate Rampant*.

Derkhan and Benjamin lit the gaslamps. The room was large, dwarfing the adjoining bedroom. The air inside was heavy and sluggish. There was no natural light. High above, the frame of a skylight was visible, but the glass was painted over in black.

Around the room were dotted tumbledown chairs and a couple of desks, all covered in paper and scissors and typewriters. On one chair sat an inactive construct, its eyes dim. One of its legs was crushed and ruined, bleeding copper wire and splinters of glass. The wall was papered with posters. Stacks of mouldering *Runagate Rampant*s lined the room. Against one damp wall was the unwieldy-looking press, a huge iron thing coated in grease and ink.

Benjamin sat at the largest desk and tugged a chair over next to him. He lit a long, drooping cigarillo. It smoked profusely. Derkhan joined him. She jerked her thumb at the construct.

"How's that old thing?" she asked.

"Too bloody noisy to use during the day. I have to wait till the others have gone, but then the press is hardly silent itself, so that makes no difference. And it ain't half a relief not to have to spin that damn wheel over and over and over all fucking night, once a fortnight. I just chuck a bit of coal in his innards, point him at it, and have a snooze."

"How's the new issue?"

Benjamin nodded slowly and pointed at a bound pile beside his chair.

"Not too bad. Going to print off a few more. We're running a little thing about your Remade in the freakshow."

Derkhan waved her hand.

"It's not a big story."

"No, but it's . . . y'know . . . *toothy* . . . We're leading on the election. 'Fuck the Lottery,' in slightly less strident terms." He grinned. "I know it's pretty much the same as last issue, but that's the time of year."

"You weren't a lucky winner in the lotto this year, were you?" asked Derkhan. "Your number come up?"

"Nah. Only once in me life, years ago. Ran out to the ballot clasping me prize voucher proudly and voted Finally We Can See. Youthful enthusiasm." Ben sniggered. "You don't qualify automatically, do you?"

"Devil's Tail, Benjamin, I don't have that kind of money! I'd give a damn sight more to *RR* if I did. No, and I didn't win this year, either."

Benjamin split the string on the pile of papers. He shoved a handful at Derkhan. She picked up the top copy and glanced at the front. Each copy was a single large sheet of paper folded in half and half again. The font on the front page was about the same size as that used in the *Beacon* or the *Quarrel* or any other of New Crobuzon's legal press. However, inside the folds of

Runagate Rampant stories and slogans and exhortations jostled with each other in a thicket of tiny print. It was ugly but efficient.

Derkhan pulled out three shekels and pushed them across to Benjamin. He took them with a murmur of thanks and put them in a tin at the front of his desk.

"When are the others coming?" asked Derkhan.

"I'm meeting a couple in the pub in an hour or so, then the rest this evening and tomorrow." In the oscillating, violent, disingenuous and repressive political atmosphere of New Crobuzon, it was a necessary defence that except in a few cases, the writers for *Runagate Rampant* did not meet. That way the chance of infiltration by the militia was minimized. Benjamin was the editor, the only person on the constantly shifting staff whom everyone knew, and who knew everyone.

Derkhan noticed a pile of roughly printed sheets on the floor by her seat. *Runagate Rampant*'s fellow seditionist papers. Halfway between comrades and rivals.

"Anything good?" she asked, and indicated the stack. Benjamin shrugged.

"*The Shout*'s rubbish this week. Decent lead in *Forge* about Rudgutter's dealings with the shipping companies. I'll get someone to chase it, actually. Apart from that it's slim pickings."

"What do you want me to get onto?"

"Well . . ." Benjamin flicked through papers, consulted his notes. "If you can just keep your ear to the ground about the dock strike . . . Canvass opinion, try and get a few positive responses, a few quotes, you know. And how about five hundred words on the history of the Suffrage Lottery?"

Derkhan nodded.

"What else've we got coming up?" she asked.

Benjamin pursed his lips.

"There's some rumour about Rudgutter having some illness, dubious cures: that's something I'd like to chase, but you can tell it's been filtered by Jabber knows how many mouths. Still, keep an ear open. There's something else as well . . . very tentative at this stage, but interesting. I'm talking to someone who claims *they're* talking to someone who wants to blow the whistle on links between Parliament and mob crime."

Derkhan nodded slowly and appreciatively.

"Sounds *very* tasty. What are we talking? Drugs? Prostitutes?"

"Shit, sure as eggs Rudgutter's got fingers in every fucking pie you can think of. They all have. Churn out the commodity,

grab the profit, get the militia to tidy up your customers afterwards, get a new crop of Remade or slave-miners for the Arrowhead pits, keep the jails full . . . nice as you like. I don't know
what this grass has in mind particularly, and they're fucking nervous, apparently, ready to do a bunk. But you know me, Dee.
Softly softly." He winked at her. "I won't let this one get away."

"Keep me posted, won't you?" Derkhan said. Benjamin
nodded.

Derkhan bundled her collection of papers into a bag, hiding
them under assorted detritus. She stood.

"Right. I have my orders. That three shekels, by the way, includes fourteen copies of *Double-R* sold."

"Good stuff," said Benjamin, and found a particular notebook
among the many on his desk to record the fact. He stood and gestured Derkhan through the doorway and the wardrobe. She
waited in his tiny bedroom as he shut off the lights in the press.

"Is Grimwhatsisname still buying?" he asked through the
hole. "That scientist geezer?"

"Yes. He's quite good."

"I heard a funny rumour about him the other day," said Benjamin, emerging through the wardrobe, wiping his oily hands on
a rag. "Is he the same one who's after *birds*?"

"Oh, yes, he's doing some experiment or other. You been listening to *criminals*, Benjamin?" Derkhan grinned. "He's collecting wings. I think he makes it a point of principle never to
buy things officially when he can go through illicit channels."

Benjamin shook his head appreciatively.

"Well, the cove's good at it. He knows how to get word out."

As he spoke, he was leaning into the wardrobe and tugging
the wooden rear back into position. He fastened it and turned to
Derkhan.

"Righto," he said. "We'd best get into character."

Derkhan nodded curtly, and ruffled her white wig somewhat.
She undid her intricate shoelaces. Benjamin untucked his shirt.
He held his breath and swung his arms from side to side, until he
went deep red. He exhaled in a sudden burst, and breathed hard.
He squinted at Derkhan.

"Come on," he said imploringly. "Cut me some slack. What of
me reputation? You could at least look tired . . ."

She grinned at him and, sighing, rubbed her face and eyes.

"Oooh, Mr. B," she squeaked absurdly. "You're the best I ever
had!"

"More like it . . ." he muttered, and winked.

They unlocked the door and stepped out into the corridor. Their preparations had been unnecessary. They were alone.

Far below, the sound of meat-grinders could be heard.

CHAPTER THIRTEEN

When Lin woke with Isaac's head next to hers, she stared at it for a long time. She let her antennae flutter in the wind from his breath. It had, she thought, been much too long since she had enjoyed the sight of him like this.

She rolled slightly to her side and stroked him. He muttered and his mouth set. His lips pursed and popped open as he breathed. She ran her hands over his bulk.

She was pleased with herself, pleased and proud at what she had effected last night. She had been miserable and lonely, and she had taken a risk, angering Isaac by coming unbidden to his side of town. But she had managed to make the evening work.

Lin had not intended to play on Isaac's sympathy, but his anger had turned so quickly to concern at her demeanour. She had realized with a vague satisfaction that she was visibly exhausted and low, that she did not have to convince him of her need for mollycoddling. He was even recognizing emotions in the movement of her headbody.

There was one positive side to Isaac's attempts not to be seen as her lover. When they walked the streets together, without touching, at a gentle pace, it mimicked the shyness of young humans courting.

There was no equivalent for khepri. Headsex for procreation was an unpleasant chore carried out for demographic duty. Male khepris were mindless scarabs like the females' headbodies, and to feel them crawling and mounting and rutting one's head was something Lin was glad not to have experienced for years. Sex for fun, between females, was a boisterous, communal business, but rather ritualized. The signs of flirtation, rejection and acceptance between individuals or groups were as formal as dances.

There was nothing of the tongue-tied nervous eroticism of young humans.

Lin had steeped herself enough in human culture to recognize the tradition that Isaac was pulled back to when they walked together through the city. She had been enthusiastic about sex with her own kind before her illicit cross-affair, and intellectually she scorned the wasteful, pointless stammered conversations she heard from humans in snatches around New Crobuzon. But to her surprise, she felt that same coy and uncertain companionship from Isaac sometimes—and she rather liked it.

It had grown the previous night, as they walked cool streets towards the station, and rode across the top of the city towards Aspic Hole. One of the best effects, of course, was to make the sexual release, when it was finally possible, all the more charged.

Isaac had grabbed her as the door closed, and she had squeezed him back, wrapping her arms around him. Lust came quickly. She had held him back, opened her carapace and made him stroke her wings, which he did, with trembling fingers. She made him wait while she enjoyed his devotion, before pulling him to her bed. She rolled with him, till he lay on his back. She threw off her clothes and tugged his from him. She mounted him and he stroked her hard headbody, ran his hands down her body, over her breasts, clutching at her hips as they moved.

Afterwards he made her supper. They ate and talked. Lin told him nothing of Mr. Motley. She was uneasy when he asked her why she was so melancholy that night. She began to tell him a half-truth about a vast, difficult sculpture that she could show no one, that meant she would not compete in the Shintacost Prize, that was draining her away to nothing, in a space in the city she had found and could not tell him.

He was attentive. Perhaps it was studied. He knew Lin was sometimes offended by his absent-mindedness when he was on a project. He begged to know where she was working.

Of course, she would not tell him.

They went to bed wiping away crumbs and seeds. Isaac clutched her in his sleep.

When she woke, Lin spent long slow minutes enjoying Isaac's presence, before rising and frying bread for his breakfast. When he rose to the smell, he kissed her neck and headbelly playfully. She stroked his cheeks with her headlegs.

Do you have to work this morning? she signed at him from across the table, while her mandibles chewed grapefruit.

Isaac peered up from his bread a little uneasily.

"Uh . . . yeah. I really do, sweety." He munched at her.

What?

"Well . . . I've got all this stuff at home, all these birds and whatnot, but it's a bit ridiculous. See, I've studied pigeons, robins, merlins, Jabber knows what else, but I've not yet seen a fucking *garuda* up close. So I'm going to go hunting. I've put it off, but I think the time's come. I'm going to Spatters." Isaac grimaced and let that sink in. He took another big bite. When he had swallowed, he looked at her from under his brows. "I don't suppose . . . D'you want to come?"

Isaac, she signed immediately, *don't say that if you don't mean it because I* do *want to come and I'll say yes if you're not careful. Even to Spatters.*

"Look . . . I really . . . I *do* mean it. I'm serious. If you're not working on your magnum opus this morning, come and knock about." The conviction in his voice strengthened as he spoke. "Come on, you can be my mobile lab assistant. No, I know what you can do: you can be my heliotypist for the day. Bring your camera. You need a break."

Isaac was getting bolder. He and Lin left the house together, without him displaying any signs of unease. They wandered a little way north-west along Shadrach Street, towards the Salacus Fields Station, but Isaac became impatient and hailed a cab on the way. The hirsute driver raised his eyebrows at Lin, but he kept any objections quiet. He inclined his head while he murmured to his horse, indicating Isaac and Lin inside.

"Where to, guv?" he asked.

"Spatters, please." Isaac spoke rather grandly, as if making up in his tone of voice for his destination.

The driver turned to him incredulously. "You've got to be joking, squire. I ain't going into Spatters. I'll take you as far as Vaudois Hill, but that's your lot. Ain't worth my while. Down Spatters way, they'll have the wheels off me cab while I'm still driving."

"Fine, fine," said Isaac irritably. "Just get us as close as you *dare.*"

As the rickety hansom cab rolled across the cobbles through Salacus Fields, Lin caught Isaac's attention.

Is it really dangerous? she signed nervously.

Isaac glanced round, then answered her with signs himself.

He was much slower and less fluent than her, but using signing he could be ruder to the cabdriver.

Well . . . just fuck poor. They'll nick whatever's going, but not especially violent. Arsehole here's just cowardly. Reads too many . . . Isaac faltered and screwed up his face with concentration.

"Don't know the sign," he murmured. "*Sensational.* Reads too many sensational papers." He sat back and looked out of the window at the skyline of Howl Barrow that wobbled unsteadily to his left.

Lin had never been to Spatters. She knew it only by its notoriety. Forty years previously, the Sink Line had been extended south-west of Lichford, past Vaudois Hill and into the spur of Rudewood that abutted the southern reaches of the city. The planners and money-men had built the tall shells of residential blocks: not the monoliths of nearby Ketch Heath, but impressive nonetheless. They had opened the railway station, Fell Stop, and had started building another in Rudewood itself, before anything more than a narrow strip around the railway had been cleared. There had been plans for another station beyond that, and the tracks had extended into the forest accordingly. There had even been tentative, absurdly hubristic schemes to extend the rails hundreds of miles south or west, to link New Crobuzon to Myrshock or Cobsea.

Then the money had run out. There had been some financial crisis, some speculative bubble had burst, some trade network had collapsed under the weight of competition and a plethora of too-cheap products no one could buy, and the project had been killed in its infancy. The trains had still visited Fell Stop, pointlessly waiting a few minutes before returning to the city. Rudewood quickly reclaimed the land south of the empty architecture, assimilating the nameless empty station and the rusting tracks. For a couple of years, the trains at Fell Stop waited empty and silent. And then, a few passengers had started appearing.

The empty integuments of grand buildings began to fill. Rural poor from Grain Spiral and the Mendican Foothills began to creep into the deserted borough. The word spread that this was a ghost sector, beyond Parliament's ken, where taxes and laws were as rare as sewage systems. Rough frameworks of stolen wood filled the empty floors. In the outlines of stillborn streets shacks of concrete and corrugated iron blistered overnight. Inhabitation spread like mould. There were no gaslamps to take the edge off the night, no doctors, no jobs, yet within ten years the area was dense with ersatz housing. It had acquired a name, Spatters, that reflected the desultory randomness of its outlines: the whole stinking shantytown seemed to have dribbled like shit from the sky.

The suburb was beyond the reach of New Crobuzon's municipality. There was an unreliable alternative infrastructure: a self-appointed network of postal workers, sanitary engineers, even a kind of law. But these systems were inefficient and partial at best. For the most part, neither the militia nor anyone else went in to Spatters. The only visitors from outside were the regular trains appearing at the incongruously well-maintained Fell Stop Station, and the gangs of masked gunmen who appeared sometimes at night to terrorize and murder. The Spatters streetchildren were particularly vulnerable to the ferocious barbarism of the murder-squads.

The slum-dwellers of Dog Fenn and even Badside considered Spatters beneath their dignity. It was simply not part of the city, nothing but a strange little town that had grafted itself onto New Crobuzon without a by-your-leave. There was no money to entice industry, legal or illicit. The crimes in Spatters were nothing but small-scale acts of desperation and survival.

There was something else about Spatters, something that brought Isaac to visit its unwelcoming alleys. For the past thirty years, it had been New Crobuzon's garuda ghetto.

Lin watched the huge towerblocks of Ketch Heath. She could see tiny figures riding the updrafts that they created, swirling above them. Wyrmen, and maybe a couple of garuda. The cab was passing under the skyrail that dipped gracefully out of the militia tower that loomed near to the blocks.

The cab pulled to.

"All right, guv, this is where I stop," said the driver.

Isaac and Lin disembarked. On one side of the cab was a row of neat white houses. Each was fronted with a small garden, most of which were assiduously maintained. The street was lined with shaggy banyan trees. Opposite the houses, on the other side of the cab, was a long thin park, a strip of greenery three hundred or so yards wide that sloped steeply down and away from the street. This thin slip of grass acted as a no-man's-land between the polite houses of Vaudois Hill inhabited by clerks and doctors and lawyers, and the crumbling chaos beyond the trees, at the bottom of the hill: Spatters.

"It's no fucking wonder Spatters isn't the most popular place, is it?" breathed Isaac. "Look, it's ruined the view for all these nice people up here . . ." He gave an evil grin.

In the distance, Lin could see that the edge of the hill was split with the Sink Line. The trains passed through a chasm cut into the parkland of the hill's western flank. The red brick of Fell Stop Station loomed out over the quagmire of Spatters. In this corner of the city, the tracks were only fractionally above the level of the houses, but it did not take much architectural grandeur for the station to tower over the surrounding makeshift dwellings. Of all Spatters' buildings, only the refitted towerblock shells were taller.

Lin felt Isaac nudge her. He pointed at one clutch of blocks, close to the railway.

"See that?" She nodded. "Look up top."

Lin followed his fingers. The bottom half of the big buildings looked deserted. From the sixth or seventh floor up, however, wooden boughs poked at odd angles out of crevices. The windows were covered with brown paper, unlike the empty sockets. And way up on the flat roofs, at nearly the same level as Lin and Isaac, little figures were visible.

Lin followed Isaac's gesture up into the air. She felt a jolt of excitement. Winged creatures were visible sporting in the sky.

"Those are garuda," Isaac said.

Lin and Isaac walked down the hill towards the railway lines, bearing slightly to their right to arrive at the garudas' looming makeshift eyries.

"Almost all the garuda in the city live in those four buildings. There probably aren't two thousand in the whole of New Crobuzon. That makes them about . . . uh . . . nought point fucking nought three per cent of the population . . ." Isaac grinned. "I've been doing my research, see?"

But they don't all live here. What about Krakhleki?

"Oh sure, I mean, there *are* garuda that get out. I taught one once, nice geezer. There's probably a couple in Dog Fenn, three or four in Murkside, six in Gross Coil. Jabber's Mound and Syriac each have a handful, I've heard. And once or twice a generation, someone like Krakhleki makes it big. I've never read his stuff, by the way. Is he any good?" Lin nodded. "Right, so you've got people like him, and others . . . you know, what's the name of that fucker . . . the one in the Diverse Tendency . . . Shashjar, that's the one. They stick him in to prove the DTs are for *all* xenians." Isaac made a rude noise. " 'Specially the rich ones."

But most of them are here. And when you're here, it must be difficult to get out . . .

"I'd suppose so. Bit of an understatement, in fact . . ."

They crossed a brook and slowed as they approached the outlands of Spatters. Lin crossed her arms and shook her headbody.

What am I doing here? she signed sardonically.

"You're expanding your mind," said Isaac cheerfully. "Important to learn how other races live in our fair city."

He tugged at her arm until, mock-protesting, Lin allowed him to drag her out of the shade of the trees and into Spatters.

To get into Spatters, Isaac and Lin had to cross rickety bridges, planks thrown across the eight-foot ditch that separated the township from Vaudois Hill park. They walked in single file, their arms sometimes outstretched for balance.

Five feet below them, the trench was filled with a noisome gelatinous soup of shit and pollutants and acid rain. The surface was broken with bubbles of fell gas and bloated animal corpses. Here and there bobbed rusting tins and knots of fleshy tissue like tumours or aborted foetuses. The liquid undulated rather than rippled, contained by a thick surface tension so oily and strong that it would not break: the pebbles that fell from the bridge were swallowed without the slightest splash.

Even with one hand clapped over his mouth and nose against the stench, Isaac could not contain himself. Halfway across the plank he let out a bark of revulsion that turned into a retch. He controlled himself before he puked. To stagger on that bridge, to lose one's balance and fall, was too utterly vile a thought to consider.

The taste of the slurry in the air made Lin feel nearly as queasy as Isaac. By the time they stepped onto the other side of the wooden slats, both Lin's and Isaac's good humour had entirely worn off. They trudged in silence into the maze.

Lin found it easy to orient herself with such low buildings: the copse of blocks they sought was clearly visible just before the station. Sometimes she walked ahead of Isaac, sometimes he ahead of her. They picked their way over channels of sewage that ran between houses. They were unmoved. They were beyond disgust.

The inhabitants of Spatters came to stare.

Sour-faced men and women, and hundreds of children, all dressed in bizarre combinations of rescued clothes and sewn sackcloth. Little hands and fingers clutched at Lin as she passed. She slapped at them, walked in front of Isaac. Voices all around them started murmuring, and then a clamouring for money started up. No one made any attempt to stop them.

Isaac and Lin trudged stolidly through the twisted streets, keeping the towerblocks in their sights. They trailed a crowd. As they grew closer, the shapes of the garuda fleeting through the air above became clear.

A fat man nearly as large as Isaac stepped out in front of them.

"Squire, bugger," he shouted curtly, nodding at both of them. His eyes were quick. Isaac nudged Lin, indicated her to stop.

"What d'you want?" said Isaac impatiently.

The man spoke very quickly.

"Well, visitors being unco down the Spatters I was chewing on whether you'd fancy a little helpster, like."

"Don't be an arse, man," Isaac roared. "I'm not a *visitor*. Last time I was here I was the guest of Savage Peter," he continued ostentatiously. He paused for the whispers that the name invoked. "Now, at the present I'm after a little chinwag with them." He jerked his finger at the garuda. The fat man recoiled slightly.

"You're for conflabbing with the bird-boys? What's that about, squire?"

"None of your sodding business! Question is, do you want to take me to their mansion?"

The man held up his hands, conciliatory.

"Shouldn't have pried, squire, none of my concerns. Smiley to take you to the bird-boxes, for a measly little recompo."

"Oh, for Jabber's sake. Don't worry, you'll be taken care of. Just *don't*," yelled Isaac at everyone in the staring crowd, "be arsing around with ideas of muggery and thievery. I've just enough to pay a decent guide on me, not a stiver more, and I know that Savage will be *screaming fucking livid* if anything happened to an old mate on his turf."

"Please, guvvo, you're insultering the Spatterkin. Not another sound, just be tracing on me tail, how's that?"

"Lead on, man," said Isaac.

As they wound through the dripping concrete and rusted iron roofs, Lin turned to Isaac.

What in Jabber's name was all that? Who's Savage Peter?
Isaac signed as he walked.

Load of bollocks. Came here once with Lemuel on a . . . dubious errand, met Savage. Local big man. Didn't even know for sure he was still alive! Wouldn't remember me.

Lin was exasperated. She could not believe the Spatterkin were taken in by Isaac's preposterous routine. But they were definitely being led towards the garudas' tower. Maybe what she'd witnessed was more like a ritual than any real confrontation. Maybe, alternatively, Isaac had kidded and scared no one at all. Maybe they were helping him out of pity.

The makeshift hovels lapped up against the bases of the towerblocks like little waves. Lin's and Isaac's guide beckoned them enthusiastically and gesticulated at the four blocks positioned in a square. In the shadowy space between them a garden had been planted, with twisted trees desperately reaching for direct light. Succulents and hardy weeds burst from the scrubland. Garuda circled under the cloud-cover.

"There's your aim, squire!" said the man proudly.

Isaac hesitated.

"How do I . . . I don't want to just plough on up unannounced . . ." he faltered. "Uh . . . how can I attract their attention?"

The guide held out his hand. Isaac stared at him a minute, then fumbled for a shekel. The man beamed at it and put it in his pocket. Then he turned and stepped a little way back from the building's walls, put his fingers to his mouth and whistled.

"Oy!" he yelled. "Bird-bonce! Squire wants to parley!"

The crowd that still surrounded Isaac and Lin took up the yells enthusiastically. A raucous yelling announced to the garuda above that they had visitors. A contingent of the flying shapes congregated in the air above the Spatters crowd. Then with an invisible adjustment of the wings, three of them plummeted spectacularly towards the ground.

There was a gasp and appreciative whistling.

The three garuda dropped like the dead towards the waiting crowd. Twenty feet from the ground they twitched their outstretched wings and broke their precipitous falls. They beat the air heavily, sending massive gusts of wind and dust into the faces and eyes of the humans below them as they hovered up and down, sinking a little, then rising, just out of reach.

"What you all shouting for?" screeched the garuda on the left.

"It's fascinating," whispered Isaac to Lin. "His voice is avian, but nothing like as difficult to understand as Yagharek . . . Raga-moll must be his native language, he's probably never spoken anything else."

Lin and Isaac stared at the magnificent creatures. The garuda were nude to the waist, their legs covered in thin brown pan-taloons. One had black feathers and skin; the other two were dark tan. Lin gazed at those enormous wings. They stretched and beat with a massive span, at least twenty feet.

"This squire here . . ." began the guide, but Isaac inter-rupted him.

"Good to meet you," he yelled up. "I've got a proposal for you. Any chance we could have a chat?"

The three garuda looked at each other.

"What you *want?*" yelled the black-feathered one.

"Well, look—" Isaac gesticulated at the crowd "—this isn't really how I was envisaging this discussion. Is there anywhere private we could go?"

"You bet!" said the first one. "See you up there!"

The three pairs of wings boomed in concert and the garuda disappeared into the sky, leaving Isaac wailing behind them.

"Wait!" he shouted. It was too late. He looked around for the guide.

"I don't suppose," Isaac asked him, "the lift's working in there, is it?"

"Never got put in, squire." The guide grinned wickedly. "Best be getting started."

"Dear sweet Jabber's arse, Lin . . . go on without me. I'm dying. I'm just going to lie here and die."

Isaac lay on the mezzanine between the sixth and seventh floors. He hissed and wheezed and spat. Lin stood over him, her hands on her hips with exasperation.

Get up, you fat bastard, she signed. *Yes, exhausting. Me too. Think of the gold. Think of the science.*

Moaning as if he were being tortured, Isaac staggered to his feet. Lin chivvied him to the edge of the concrete stairs. He swal-lowed and braced himself, then staggered on up.

The stairwell was grey and unlit except by light filtering round corners and through cracks. Only now, as they emerged onto the seventh floor, did the stairs look as if they had ever been used. Rubbish began to build up around their feet. The stairs were grubby rather than thick in fine dust. At each floor were two doors, and the harsh sounds of garuda conversations were audible through the splintered wood.

Isaac settled into a slow, miserable pace. Lin followed him, ignoring his declarations of imminent heart attack. After several long, painful minutes, they had reached the top floor.

Above them was the door onto the roof. Isaac leaned against the wall and wiped his face. He was drenched in sweat.

"Just give me a minute, sweetheart," he murmured, and even managed to grin. "Oh gods! For the sake of science, right? Get your camera ready . . . All right. Here we go."

He stood and breathed slowly, then strode slowly up the last flight to the door, opened it and walked out into the flat light on the roof. Lin followed, her camera in her hands.

Khepri eyes needed no time to adjust from light to darkness and back again. Lin stepped out onto a rough concrete roof littered with rubbish and broken concrete and saw Isaac desperately shielding his eyes and squinting. She looked coolly around her.

A little way to the north-east rose Vaudois Hill, a sinuous wedge of high land which rose up as if trying to block the view to the centre of the city. The Spike, Perdido Street Station, Parliament, the Glasshouse dome: all were visible, butting their way over that raised horizon. Opposite the hill, Lin saw miles and miles of Rudewood disappear over uneven ground. Here and there little rock knolls broke free of the leaf-cover. Off to the north there was a long uninterrupted line of sight over to the middle-class suburbs of Serpolet and Gallmarch, the militia tower of St. Jabber's Mound, the raised tracks of the Verso Line cutting through Creekside and Chimer. Lin knew that just beyond those soot-stained arches two miles away was the twisting course of the Tar, bearing barges and their cargo into the city from the steppes of the south.

Isaac lowered his hands as his pupils tightened.

Whirling over their heads aerobatically were hundreds of garuda. They began to drop, to spiral neatly out of the sky and drop to their clawed feet in rows around Lin and Isaac. They fell thickly from the air like overripe apples.

There were two hundred at least, Lin estimated. She moved a little closer to Isaac nervously. The garuda averaged at least a couple of inches over six feet, not counting the magnificent peaks of their folded wings. There was no difference in height or musculature between men and women. The females wore thin shifts, the males wore loincloths or cut-off trousers. That was all.

Lin stood five feet tall. She could see no further than the first circle of garuda who surrounded her and Isaac at arms' length, but she could see more and more dropping from the sky; she had the sense of the numbers building up around her. Isaac patted her shoulder absently.

A few shapes still swept and hunted and played in the air around them. When the garuda had stopped landing on the roof, Isaac broke the silence.

"Righto," he yelled. "Thanks very much for inviting us up here. I want to make a proposition to you."

"To who?" came a voice from the crowd.

"Well, to all of you," he replied. "See, I'm doing some work on . . . well, on *flight*. And you are the only creatures in New Crobuzon who can fly *and* have brains in your bonces. Wyrmen aren't renowned for their conversational skills," he said jovially. There was no reaction to his joke. He cleared his throat and continued.

"So, anyway . . . uh . . . I'm wondering whether any of you would be willing to come and do a couple of days' work with me, show me some flight, let me take a few prints of your wings . . ." He took hold of Lin's hand that contained the camera and waved it around. "Obviously I'll pay for your time . . . I'd really appreciate some help . . ."

"What you doing?" The voice came from one of the garuda in the front row. The others looked to him when he spoke. *This,* thought Lin, *is the boss man.*

Isaac looked at him carefully.

"What am I doing? You mean . . ."

"I mean what for d'you need pics? What you up to?"

"It's . . . uh . . . research into the nature of flight. See, I'm a scientist and . . ."

"Horsecrap. How we know you don't kill us?"

Isaac started in surprise. The congregated garuda nodded and cawed in agreement.

"Why by *damn* would I want to kill you . . . ?"

"Just fuck off, mister. No one here wants to help you."

There were a few mutterings of unease. It was clear that a few of the assembled might, in fact, have been prepared to take part.

But none of them challenged the speaker, a tall garuda with a long scar linking his nipples.

Lin watched as Isaac opened his mouth slowly. He was trying to turn the situation round. She saw his hand go to his pocket and come away again. If he flashed money on the spot, he could seem like a spiv or a wide-boy.

"Listen . . ." he said hesitantly. "I really didn't realize there'd be a problem with this . . ."

"No, well, see, that may or may not be true, mister. Might be you're militia." Isaac snorted derisorily, but the big garuda continued in his sneering tone. "Might be that the murder squads've found a way to get to us bird-boys. 'Just come along to do research . . .' Well, none of us is interested, ta."

"You know," said Isaac, "I understand that you're concerned at my motives. I mean, you don't know me from Jabber and . . ."

"Ain't none of us going with you, mister. Simple."

"Look. I can pay well. I'm prepared to pay a shekel a day for anyone prepared to come to my lab."

The big garuda stepped forward and prodded Isaac aggressively in the chest.

"Want us to come to your *lab* to cut us open, see what makes us tick?" The other garuda stepped back as he circled Lin and Isaac. "You and your bugger friend want to cut me into pieces?"

Isaac was expostulating and trying to deny the charge. He turned slightly away and looked over at the surrounding crowd.

"So am I to understand that this *gent* speaks for all of you, or would someone here like to earn a shekel a day?"

There were a few mutterings. Garuda looked shiftily and uneasily at each other. The big garuda facing Isaac threw up his hands and shook them as he spoke. He was incensed.

"I speak for *all*!" He turned and stared slowly at his kin. "Any *dissenters*?"

There was a pause, and a young male stepped forward slightly.

"Charlie . . ." He spoke directly to the self-appointed leader. "Shekel's a lot of moolah . . . what say a bunch of us go down, make sure there's no monkey-business, keep it sweet . . ."

The garuda called Charlie strode over as the other male was speaking and punched him hard in the face.

There was a communal shriek from the congregation. With a tumult of wings and feathers, great numbers of the garuda burst up and out from the roof like an explosion. Some circled briefly and returned to watch warily, but many others disappeared into the upper floors of other blocks, or off into the cloudless sky.

Charlie stood over his stunned victim, who had fallen to one knee.

"Who's the big man?" shouted Charlie in a strident bird-call. "Who's the big man?"

Lin tugged at Isaac's shirt, began to pull him towards the stairwell door. Isaac resisted half-heartedly. He was visibly appalled at the turn his request had taken, but he was also fascinated to see the confrontation. She dragged him slowly away from the scene.

The fallen garuda looked up at Charlie.

"You the big man," he muttered.

"*I'm* the big man. I'm the big man 'cause I take care of you, right? I make sure you're all right, don't I? Don't I? And what'd I always tell you? Steer clear of groundcrawlers! And steer clearest of the anthros. They're the worst, they'll tear you up, take your wings away, kill you dead! *Don't trust any of 'em!* And that includes fatboy with the fat wallet over there." For the first time in his tirade he looked up at Isaac and Lin. "You!" he shouted, and pointed at Isaac. "Fuck off out of it 'fore I show you exactly what it's like to fly . . . straight fucking down!"

Lin saw Isaac open his mouth, attempt one last conciliatory explanation. She stamped in irritation and pulled him hard through the door.

Learn to read a damned situation, Isaac. Time to go, Lin signed furiously as they descended.

"All right Lin, Jabber's arse, I get the idea!" He was angry, stamping his great bulk down the stairs without any complaints this time. He was energized by his blistering irritation and bewilderment.

"I just don't see," he continued, "why they were *so fucking antagonistic . . .*"

Lin turned to him in exasperation. She made him stop, would not let him pass.

Because they're xenian and poor and scared, you cretin, she signed slowly. *Big fat bastard waving money comes to* Spatters, *for Jabber's sake, not much of a haven but all they've got, and starts trying to get them to leave it for reasons he won't explain. Seems to me that Charlie's bang-on right. Place like this needs someone to look after its own. If I was garuda, I'd listen to him, I tell you.*

Isaac was calming down, even looking a little shamed.

"Fair enough, Lin. I take your point. I should've scouted it out first, gone through someone who knows the area or whatever . . ."

Yes, and you've blown that now. You can't, it's too late . . .

"Yes, quite, thanks ever so for pointing that out . . ." He scowled. "Godspit fuck damn! I ballsed it up, didn't I?"

Lin said nothing.

They did not speak much as they returned through Spatters. They were watched from bottle-glass windows and open doors as they came back the way they'd come.

As they retraced their paths over the foul pit of nightsoil and rot, Lin glanced back at the tumbledown towers. She saw the flat roof where they had stood.

Isaac and she were being followed by a small swirling mass of garuda youth, sullenly trailing them in the sky. Isaac turned and his face lightened briefly, but the garuda did not come close enough to talk. They gesticulated rudely from on high.

Lin and Isaac walked back up Vaudois Hill towards the city.

"Lin," Isaac said after minutes of silence. His voice was melancholy. "Back there you said if you'd been garuda you'd have listened to him, right? Well, you're not garuda, but you *are* khepri . . . When you were ready to leave Kinken, there must've been plenty of people telling you to stick to your own, that humans couldn't be trusted, and whatnot . . . And the thing is, Lin, you *didn't* listen to them, did you?"

Lin thought quietly for a long time, but she did not answer.

CHAPTER FOURTEEN

"Come on old thing, old plum, old bugger. Eat something, for Jabber's sake . . ."

The caterpillar lay listlessly on its side. Its flaccid skin rippled occasionally, and it waved its head, looking for food. Isaac clucked over it, murmured at it, prodded it with a stick. It wiggled uncomfortably, then subsided.

Isaac straightened up and tossed the little stick to one side.

"I despair of you, then," he announced to the air. "You can't say I haven't tried."

He walked away from the little box with its mouldering piles of foodstuffs.

Cages were still piled high on the warehouse's raised walkway; the discordant symphony of squawks and hisses and avian screams still sounded; but the store of creatures was much depleted. Many of the pens and hutches lay open and empty. Less than half of the original store remained.

Isaac had lost some of his experimental subjects to disease; some to fights, both in- and inter-species; and some to his own research. A few stiff little bodies were nailed in various poses to boards around the walkway. A vast number of illustrations were plastered to his walls. His initial sketches of wings and flight had multiplied by a massive factor.

Isaac leaned against his desk. He ran his fingers over the diagrams that littered its surface. At the top was a scribbled triangle containing a cross. He closed his eyes against the continuing cacophony.

"Oh *shut up*, all of you," he yelled, but the animal chorus went on as before. Isaac held his head in his hands, his frown growing more and more piercing.

He was still stinging from his disastrous journey to Spatters the day before. He could not help running over the events again and again in his mind, thinking about what he could and should have done differently. He had been arrogant and stupid, wading in like an intrepid adventurer, flailing his money as if it were a thaumaturgic weapon. Lin was right. It was no wonder he had managed to alienate probably the city's entire garuda population. He had approached them as a gang of rogues to be wowed and bought off. He had treated them like cronies of Lemuel Pigeon. They were not. They were a poor, scared community scrabbling for survival and maybe a scrap of pride in a hostile city. They watched their neighbours picked off by vigilantes as if for sport. They inhabited an alternative economy of hunting and barter, foraging in Rudewood and petty pilfering.

Their politics were brutal, but totally understandable.

And now he had blown it with the city's.garuda. Isaac looked up at all the pictures and heliotypes and diagrams he had made. *Just like yesterday,* he thought. *The direct approach isn't working. I was on the right track at the very start. It's not about aerodynamics, that's not how to proceed* . . . The squalls of his captives intruded on his thoughts.

"Right!" he shouted suddenly. He stood up straight, and glared at the trapped animals, as if daring them to continue with their noise. Which, of course, they did.

"Right!" he shouted again, and strode over to the first cage. The brace of doves inside puffed and billowed explosively from one side to the other as he tugged them over to a large window. He left the box facing the glass and fetched another, within which a vivid dragonfly-snake undulated like a sidewinder. He placed that one on top of the first. He grabbed a gauze cage of mosquitoes, and another of bees, and dragged them over too. Isaac woke cantankerous bats and aspises basking in the sun, pulled them over to the window overlooking the Canker.

He cleared all his remaining menagerie over to that pile. The animals looked out at the Ribs, which curved cruelly over the eastern city. Isaac piled all the boxes containing living things into a pyramid in front of the glass. It looked like a sacrificial pyre.

Eventually the job was done. Predators and prey fluttered and screeched next to each other, separated only by wood or thin bars.

Isaac reached awkwardly into the thin space in front of the cages and swung the great window open. It hinged horizontally, opening at the top of its five-foot height. As it opened onto the warm air, a great rush of city sounds washed in with the evening heat.

"Now," yelled Isaac, beginning to enjoy himself. "I wash my hands of you!"

He looked around and strode back to the desk for a moment, returning with a long cane he had used many years before to point at blackboards. He poked it at the cages, knocking hooks out of eyes, fumbling till he undid latches, ripping holes in wire as thin as silk.

The fronts to the little prisons began to fall away. Isaac speeded up, opening all the doors, using his fingers where the cane was not delicate enough.

At first, the creatures within were bewildered. For many, it was weeks since they had flown. They had eaten badly. They were bored and frightened. They did not understand the sudden

vista of freedom, the twilight, the smell of the air before them.
But after those long moments, the first of the captives bolted for
freedom.

It was an owl.

It hurled itself through the open window and sailed off towards the east, where the sky was darkest, out towards the
wooded lands by Iron Bay. It glided between the Ribs on wings
that hardly moved.

The escape was a signal. There was a storm of wings.

Falcons, moths, batkin, aspises, horseflies, parakeets, beetles,
magpies, creatures of the upper air, little water-top skimmers,
creatures of the night, the day and the gloaming burst from
Isaac's window in a shimmering explosion of camouflage and
colour. The sun had sunk on the other side of the warehouse. The
only light that caught the clouds of feather, fur and chitin was
from streetlamps and shards of sunset reflected on the dirty river.

Isaac basked in the glory of the sight. He exhaled as if at a
work of art. For a moment he looked around for a box-camera,
but then he turned back and was contented just to stare.

A thousand silhouettes eddied in the air by his warehouse-
home. They swirled together, aimless for a moment, then felt the
currents of the air and were whisked away. Some went with
the wind. Some tacked and fought the gusts and wheeled over
the city. The peace of that first confused moment broke down.
Aspises flew through the shoals of disoriented insects, their tiny
leonine jaws closing on fat little bodies with a crunch. Hawks
skewered pigeons and jackdaws and canaries. Dragonfly-snakes
corkscrewed in thermals and bit at prey.

The flight-styles of the liberated animals were as distinct as
their silhouetted forms. One dark shape flitted chaotically
around the sky, sinking towards a streetlamp, unable to resist the
light: a fell-moth. Another rose with a majestic simplicity and
arced into the night: some bird of prey. This one opened momentarily like a flower then squeezed and jetted away with a squirt of
discoloured air: one of the small wind-polyps.

Bodies of the exhausted and the dying fell out of the air with a
little patter of flesh. The ground below would be discoloured
with blood and ichor, Isaac realized. There were gentle splashes
as the Canker claimed victims. But there was more life than
death. For a few days, a few weeks, Isaac mused, the sky over
New Crobuzon would be more colourful.

Isaac sighed beatifically. He looked around and ran over to the few boxes of cocoons and eggs and grubs. He shoved them over to the window, leaving only the big, dying, multicoloured caterpillar undisturbed.

Isaac grabbed handfuls of eggs and hurled them out of the window after the fleeing shapes. He followed them with caterpillars that twisted and jack-knifed as they fell towards the paved ground. He shook cages that rattled with delicate pupating shapes, and emptied them out of the window. He poured out a tank of waterborn larvae. For these young, it was a cruel liberation, a few seconds of freedom and rushing air.

Eventually, when the last tiny shape had disappeared below, Isaac closed the window. He turned back and surveyed the warehouse. He heard a faint drone of wings, and saw a few airborne shapes circulating the lamps. An aspis, a handful of moths or butterflies, and a couple of small birds. *Well,* he thought, *they'll find their own way out, or they won't last long and I can clear them out when they starve.*

Littering the floor in front of the window were some of the runts and the dying, the weaklings, that had fallen before they could fly. Some were dead. Most crawled feebly this way and that. Isaac set to cleaning them out.

"You have the advantage that you are *(a)* rather beautiful; and *(b)* rather interesting, old chum," he said to the huge, sickly grub as he worked. "No, no, don't thank me. Just consider me a *philanthrope.* And also, I don't understand why you don't eat. You're my project," he said, jettisoning a dustpan full of feebly crawling bodies into the night air. "I doubt you'll last the night, but fuck it, you've appealed to my pity and my curiosity and I'll have one last stab at rescuing you."

There was a shuddering bang. The door to the warehouse had been hurled open.

"Grimnebulin!"

It was Yagharek. The garuda stood in the dimly lit space, legs apart and arms clutching at his cloak. The jutting shape of his wooden wing disguise swayed unrealistically from side to side. It was not properly attached. Isaac leaned over the rail and frowned.

"Yagharek?"

"Have you forsaken me, Grimnebulin?"

Yagharek was shrieking like a tortured bird. His words were almost impossible to understand. Isaac gesticulated at him to calm down.

"Yagharek, what the fuck are you *talking* about . . . ?"

"The birds, Grimnebulin, I saw the birds! You told me, you showed me, they were for your research . . . what has happened, Grimnebulin? Are you giving up?"

"Hang on . . . how in the name of Jabber's arse did you see them fly away? Where've you been?"

"On your roof, Grimnebulin." Yagharek was quietening. He was calmer. He radiated a massive sadness. "On your roof, where I perch, night after night, waiting for you to help me. I saw you release all the little subjects. Why have you given up, Grimnebulin?"

Isaac beckoned him up the stairs.

"Yag, old son . . . Damn, I don't know where to start." Isaac stared up at the ceiling. "What the *arse* were you doing on my roof? How long have you hung about up there? 'Stail, you could've kipped down here, or something . . . that is *absurd*. Not to say a bit eerie, thinking of you up there while I work or eat or shit or whatnot. And—" he held up his hand to cut off Yagharek's response "—and I have *not* given up on your project."

He was silent for a while. He let the words sink in. He waited for Yagharek to calm, to return from the miserable little hollow he had carved for himself.

"I haven't given up," he repeated. "What's happened is quite *good*, actually . . . We've entered a new phase, I think. Out with the old. That line of research has been . . . ah . . . terminated."

Yagharek bowed his head. His shoulders shuddered slightly as he breathed out lengthily.

"I do not understand."

"Right, well, look, come over here. I'm going to show you something."

Isaac led Yagharek over to the desk. He paused momentarily to tut at the huge caterpillar that sagged on its side in the box. It stirred weakly.

Yagharek did not spare it a glance.

Isaac pointed to the various bundles of paper that propped up overdue library books and teetered on his desk. Drawings, equations, notes and treatises. Yagharek began to sift slowly through them. Isaac guided him.

"Look . . . See all the damn sketches everywhere. Wings, for the most part. Now, the starting point for the research was the wing. Seems sensible, don't it? So what I've been about is understanding that particular limb.

"The garuda who live in New Crobuzon are useless for us, by the way. I put up notices in the university, but apparently there're no garuda students this year. I even tried to argue for the sake of science with a garuda . . . uh . . . *community leader* . . . and it was a bit of a disaster. Let's put it that way." Isaac paused, remembering, then blinked himself back to the discussion. "So instead, let's look to the birds.

"Now, that leads us to a whole new problem. The *little* beggars, the humming birds and wrens and whatnot are all interesting and useful in terms of . . . y'know . . . broad background, the physics of flight and what have you, but basically we're looking at the big boys. Kestrels, hawks, eagles if I'd got hold of any. Because at this stage I'm still thinking *analogously*. But I don't want you to think I'm close-minded . . . I'm not studying the mayfly or whatever just out of *interest*, I'm trying to work out if I can apply it.

"I mean, I'm presuming you're not fussy, right, Yag? I'm presuming that if I graft onto your back a pair of bat or bluebottle wings, or even a wind-polyp's flightgland, you're not going to be fussy. Might not be pretty, but it's just about getting you into the air, right?"

Yagharek nodded. He was listening fiercely, sifting through the papers on the desk as he did so. He was intent on understanding.

"Right. So it seems reasonable, even given all that, that it's the big birds we should be looking at. But of course . . ." Isaac rummaged among the papers, grabbed some pictures from the wall, handed sheafs of the relevant diagrams to Yagharek. "Of course, that turns out not to be so. I mean, you can get so far on the aerodynamics of birds, all useful stuff, but it's actually *very misleading* to be looking at them. Because the aerodynamics of your body are so fucking different, basically. You *ain't* just an eagle with a scrawny human body attached. I'm sure you never thought you were . . . I don't know how your maths and physics are, but on this sheet *here*—" Isaac found it and passed it over "—are some diagrams and equations which show you why big birds' flight ain't the direction to be looking. Lines of force all wrong. Not strong enough. That sort of thing.

"So, I turn to the other wings in the collection. What if we tacked on dragonfly wings or what have you? Well, first of all there's the problem of getting hold of insect wings big enough. The only insects big enough already aren't going to just hand 'em over. And I don't know about you but I don't fancy fucking off into the mountains or wherever to ambush an assassin beetle. Get our arses kicked.

"What about building them to our specifications? Then we can get the size right *and* the shape. We can compensate for your . . . *awkward* form." Isaac grinned and continued. "Trouble is, material science being what it is, we *might* be able to make them exact enough, and light enough, and strong enough, but I honestly doubt it. I'm working on designs that *might* work, but might not. I don't think the odds are good enough.

"Also, you've got to remember that this whole project is dependent on you getting Remade by a virtuoso. I'm glad to say I don't know any Remakers, which is the first thing, and the second is they're usually more interested in humiliation, industrial power or aesthetics than in something as intricate as flight. There are shitloads of nerve endings, loads of muscles, ripped-up bones and the like floating around in your back, and they'd have to get *every one* exactly right if you were going to have the slightest chance of getting airborne."

Isaac had steered Yagharek into a chair. He pulled up a stool and sat opposite him. The garuda was completely silent. He gazed at Isaac with powerful concentration, then at the diagrams he held. This was how he read, Isaac realized, with this intensity and focus. He was not like a patient waiting for a doctor to get to the point: he was taking in every single word.

"I should say that I'm not totally finished with this. There's one person I know who's adept at the sort of bio-thaumaturgy you'd need to have working wings grafted to you. So I'm going to go round and pick his brains about the chances of success." Isaac grimaced and shook his head. "And let me tell you, Yag old son, that if you knew this geezer you'd know how damn noble that is. There's no sacrifice I won't make it for you . . ." He paused lengthily.

"So there's the chance this chap could say 'Yes, wings, no problem, bring him round and I'll do it on Dustday afternoon.' That *is* possible, but you employ me for my scientific nous, and I'm telling you that it's my professional opinion that that won't happen. I think we have to think laterally.

"My first forays down this route were to look at the various things that fly without wings. Now, I'll spare you the details of my schemes. Most of the plans are . . . *here,* if you're interested. A subcutaneous self-inflating mini-dirigible; a transplant of mutant wind-polyp glands; integrating you with a flying golem; even something as prosaic as teaching you basic physical thaumaturgy." Isaac indicated the notes on each of these plans as he mentioned them. "All unworkable. Thaumaturgy's unreliable and exhausting. Anyone can learn some basic hexes, given application, but constant countergeotropy *on demand* would take a damn sight more energy and skill than most people have got. Do you have powerful sortilege in the Cymek?"

Yagharek shook his head slowly. "Some whispers to call prey to our claws; some symbols and passes that encourage bones to knit and blood to clot: that is all."

"Yeah, that doesn't surprise me. So best not to rely on that. And trust me when I tell you that my other . . . er . . . *offbeat* plans were unworkable.

"So I've been spending all my time working on stuff like this, and getting nowhere, and I realized that whenever I stop for a minute or two and just have a think, the same thing comes into my head. Watercræft."

Yagharek frowned, drawing his already heavy brows into an overhanging crag of almost geological aspect. He shook his head to show his confusion.

"Watercræft," Isaac repeated. "You know what that is?"

"I have read something of it . . . The skill of the vodyanoi . . ."

"Bang on, old son. You'll see the dockers doing it sometimes, in Kelltree or Smog Bend. A whole gang of them can shape quite a bit of the river. They dig holes in the water down to where spilt cargoes lie on the bottom, so the cranes can hook them. Fucking amazing. In rural communities they use it to cut trenches of air through rivers, then drive fish into them. They just fly out of the flat side of the river and flop onto the ground. Brilliant." Isaac pursed his lips in appreciation. "Anyway, these days it's mostly just used to arse about, make little sculptures. They have little competitions and whatnot.

"The point *is,* Yag, that what you've got there is water behaving very much as it *shouldn't.* Right? And that's what you want. You want heavy stuff, this thing here, this body—" he poked Yagharek gently in the chest "—to fly. Are you with me? Let's turn our minds to the *ontological conundrum* of persuading matter to break habits of aeons. We want to make elements misbehave. This isn't a problem of advanced ornithology, it's *philosophy*.

" 'Stail, Yag, this is stuff I've been working on for years! It'd almost turned into a kind of *hobby*. But then this morning I looked again at some notes I'd made early on in your case, and I linked it up with all my old ideas, and I saw that this was the way to go. And I've been wrestling with it all day." Isaac shook a piece of paper at Yagharek, a piece of paper on which was a triangle containing a cross.

Isaac grabbed a pencil and wrote words at the three points of the triangle. He turned the diagram to face Yagharek. The top point was labelled *Occult/thaumaturgical*; the bottom left *Material*; the bottom right *Social/sapiential*.

"Righto, now, don't get too bogged down with this diagram, Yag old son, it's supposed to be an aid to thought, nothing more. What you've got here is a depiction of the three points within which all scholarship, all knowledge, is located.

"Down here, there's material. That's the actual physical stuff, atoms and the like. Everything from fundamental femtoscopic particles like elyctrons, up to big fuck-off volcanos. Rocks, elyctromagnetism, chymical reaction . . . All that sort of thing.

"Opposite, that's social. Sentient creatures, of which there's no shortage on Bas-Lag, can't just be studied like stones. By reflecting on the world and on their own reflections, humans and garuda and cactacae and whatnot create a different order of organization, right? So it's got to be studied in its own terms—but at the same time it's also obviously linked to the physical stuff that makes everything up. That's what this nice line is here, connecting the two.

"Up top is occult. Now we're cooking. Occult: 'hidden.' Takes in the various forces and dynamics and the like that aren't just to do with physical bits and bobs interacting, and aren't just the thoughts of thinkers. Spirits, dæmons, gods if you want to call them that, thaumaturgy . . . you get the idea. That's up at that end. But it's linked to the other two. First off, thaumaturgic techniques, invocation, shamanism and so on, they all affect—and are affected by—the social relations that surround them. And then the physical aspect: hexes and charms are mostly the manipulation of theoretical particles—the 'enchanted particles'—called *thaumaturgons*. Now, some scientists—" he thumped his chest "—think they're essentially the same sort of thing as protons and all the physical particles.

"This . . ." said Isaac slyly, his voice slowing right down, "is where stuff gets *really* interesting.

"If you think of any arena of study or knowledge, it lies somewhere in this triangle, but *not* squarely on one corner. Take sociology, or psychology, or xenthropology. Pretty simple, right? It's down here, in the 'Social' corner? Well, yes and no. That's definitely its closest *node*, but you can't study societies without thinking about the questions of physical resources. Right? So straight away, the physical aspect is kicking in. So we have to move sociology along the bottom axis a little bit." He slid his finger a fraction of an inch to the left. "But then, how can you understand, say, cactacae culture without understanding their solar-focus, or khepri culture without their deities, or vodyanoi culture without understanding shamanic channelling? You *can't*," he concluded triumphantly. "So we have to shift things up towards the occult." His finger moved a little, accordingly.

"So that's roughly where sociology and psychology and the like are. Bottom right-hand corner, little bit up, little bit along.

"Physics? Biology? Should be right over by material sciences, yeah? Only, if you say that biology has an effect on society, the reverse is also true, so biology's actually a tiny bit to the right of the 'Material' corner. And what about the flight of wind-polyps? The feeding of soul trees? That stuff's occult, so we've moved it again, up this time. Physics includes the efficacy of certain substances in thaumaturgic hexes. You take my point? Even the most 'pure' subject's actually somewhere between the three.

"Then there's a whole bunch of subjects that *define* themselves by their mongrel nature. Socio-biology? Halfway along the bottom and a little bit up. Hypnotology? Halfway up the right flank. Social/psychological and occult, but with a bit of brain chymistry thrown in, so that's over a bit . . ."

Isaac's diagram was now covered in little crosses where he located the various disciplines. He looked at Yagharek and drew a neat, final, careful x in the very centre of the triangle.

"Now what are we looking at *right here*? What's bang in the middle?

"Some people think that's mathematics there. Fine. But if maths is the study that best allows you to *think your way* to the centre, what're the forces you're investigating? Maths is totally abstract, at one level, square roots of minus one and the like; but the world is nothing if not rigorously mathematical. So this is a way of looking at the world which unifies all the forces: mental, social, physical.

"If the subjects are located in one triangle, with three nodes and one centre, then so are the forces and dynamics they study. In other words, if you think this way of looking at things is interesting or helpful, then there's basically *one* kind of field, one kind of force, being studied in its various aspects here. That's why this is called 'Unified Field Theory.' "

Isaac smiled, exhausted. *Godspit,* he realized suddenly, *I'm doing rather a good job of this . . . Ten years of research have improved my teaching . . .* Yagharek was watching him carefully.

"I . . . understand . . ." the garuda finally said.

"I'm glad to hear it. There's more, old son, so gird your loins. UFT's not very accepted as a theory, you know. It's probably about the status of the Fractured Land Hypothesis, if that means anything to you." Yagharek nodded. "Fine, you know what I mean, then. Just about respectable, but a bit crackpot. However, to shred the last vestiges of credibility I might have been able to muster, I subscribe to a minority view among UFT theorists. That's over the nature of the forces under investigation.

"I'll try and keep this simple." Isaac squeezed his eyes closed for a minute and gathered his thoughts. "Right. The question is whether it's *pathological* for a dropped egg to fall."

He paused and let the image hang for a minute.

"See, if you think that matter and therefore the unified force under investigation are essentially *static*, then falling, flying, rolling, changing your mind, casting a spell, growing older, moving, are basically *deviations* from an essential state. Otherwise, you think that motion is part of the fabric of ontology, and the question's how best to theorize that. You can tell where my sympathies lie. Staticists would say I'm misrepresenting them, but fuck it.

"So I'm a MUFTI, a Moving Unified Field Theorist. Not a SUFTI, a Static Unified . . . you get the idea. But then, being a MUFTI raises as many problems as it solves: if it *moves*, how does it move? Steady gait? Punctuated inversion?

"When you pick up a piece of wood and hold it ten feet above the ground, it has more energy than when it's on the ground. We call that potential energy, right? That's not controversial among *any* scientist. Potential energy's the energy that gives the wood the power to hurt you or mark the floor, a power it doesn't have when it's just resting on the ground. It has that energy when it's motionless, like it was before, but when it *could fall*. If it does, the potential energy turns into kinetic energy, and you break your toe or whatever.

"See, potential energy's all about placing something in a situation where it's teetering, where it's about to change its state. Just like when you put enough strain on a group of people, they'll suddenly explode. They'll go from grumpy and quiescent to violent and creative in one moment. The transition from one state to another's affected by taking something—a social group, a piece of wood, a hex—to a place where its interactions with other forces make its *own energy* pull against its current state.

"I'm talking about taking things to the point of *crisis*."

Isaac sat back for a minute. To his surprise, he was loving this. The process of explaining his theoretical approach was consolidating his ideas, making him formulate his approach with a tentative rigour.

Yagharek was a model pupil. His attention was totally unwavering, his eyes as sharp as stilettos.

Isaac took a long breath and continued.

"This is major shit we're dealing with here, Yag mate. I've been nibbling at crisis theory for arsing *years*. In a nutshell: I'm saying it's in the *nature of things* to enter crisis, as part of what they are. Things turn themselves inside out by virtue of being things, understand? The force that pushes the unified field on is *crisis energy*. Stuff like potential energy, that's one aspect of crisis energy, one tiny partial manifestation. Now, if you could tap the reserves of crisis energy in any given situation, you're talking about *enormous* power. Some situations are more crisis-ridden or -prone than others, yes, but the point of crisis theory is that things are in crisis just as part of *being*. There's *loads* of sodding crisis energy flowing around all the time, but we haven't yet learnt how to tap it efficiently. Instead it bursts over unreliably and uncontrollably every so often. Terrible waste."

Isaac shook his head at the thought.

"The vodyanoi can tap crisis energy, I think. In a tiny, tiny way. It's paradoxical. You tap the existing crisis energy in the water to hold it in a shape it fights against, so you put it in *more* crisis . . . but then there's nowhere for the energy to go, so the crisis resolves itself by breaking down into its original form. But what if the vodyanoi used water they'd already ... uh ... *water-cræfted,* and used it as a constituent for some experiment that drew on the increased crisis energy ... Sorry. I'm digressing. The point is, I'm trying to work out a way for you to tap into your crisis energy, and channel it to flight. See, if I'm right, it's the only force that's always going to be ... *suffusing* you. And the more you fly, the more you're in crisis, the more you should be able to fly ... That's the theory, anyway ...

"But to be honest, Yag, this is much bigger than that. If I can *really* unlock crisis energy for you, then your case becomes, frankly, a pretty paltry concern. We're talking about forces and energy that could *totally* change ... everything ..."

The incredible idea stilled the air. The dirty environs of the warehouse seemed too small and mean for this conversation. Isaac stared out of the window into the grubby New Crobuzon night. The moon and her daughters were dancing sedately above him. The daughters, smaller than their mother but bigger than stars, shone hard and cold above him. Isaac thought about crisis.

Eventually Yagharek spoke.

"And if you are right ... I will fly?"

Isaac burst into laughter at the bathetic demand.

"Yes, yes, Yag old son. If I'm right, you'll fly again."

CHAPTER FIFTEEN

Isaac could not persuade Yagharek to stay in the warehouse. The garuda would not explain his objections. He simply slipped away into the evening, a wretched outcast for all his pride, to sleep in some ditch or chimney or ruin. He would not even accept food. Isaac stood at the door to the warehouse and watched him go. Yagharek's dark blanket swung loosely from that wooden framework, those false wings.

Eventually, Isaac closed the door. He returned to his ledge and watched lights slide along the Canker. He rested his head on his fists and listened to the tick of his clock. The feral sounds of New Crobuzon at night inveigled their way through his walls. He heard the melancholy lowing of machines and ships and factories.

In the room below him, David and Lublamai's construct seemed to cluck gently in time to the clock.

Isaac collected his drawings from the walls. Some that he thought were good he stuffed into an obese portfolio. Many he squinted at critically and threw away. He got onto his big belly and rooted under the bed, bringing out a dusty abacus and a slide-rule.

What I need, he thought, *is to get to the university and liberate one of their difference engines.* It would not be easy. The security for such items was neurotic. Isaac realized suddenly that he would have the chance to scope out the guard systems for himself: he was going to the university the next day, to talk to his much-loathed employer, Vermishank.

Not that Vermishank employed him much these days. It had been months since he had received a letter in that tight little hand telling him his services were required to research some abstruse and perhaps pointless bywater of theory. Isaac could never refuse these "requests." To do so would have been to risk his access privileges to the university's resources, and hence to a rich vein of equipment he plundered more or less at his leisure. Vermishank did not make any move to restrict Isaac's privileges, despite their attenuating professional relationship, and despite probably noticing a correlation between disappearing resources and Isaac's research schedule. Isaac did not know why. *Probably to try to keep power over me,* he thought.

It would be the first time in his life he had sought out Vermishank, he realized, but Isaac had to go and see him. Even though he felt committed to his new approach, his crisis theory, he could not entirely turn his back on more mundane technologies such as Remaking without asking one of the city's foremost biothaumaturges' opinions on Yagharek's case. It would have been unprofessional.

Isaac made himself a ham roll and a cup of cold chocolate. He steeled himself at the thought of Vermishank. Isaac disliked him for a huge variety of reasons. One of them was political. Biothaumaturgy after all, was a polite way to describe an expertise one of whose uses was to tear at and recreate flesh, to bond it in unintended ways, to manipulate it within the limits dictated only by imagination. Of course, the techniques could heal and repair, but that was not their usual application. No one had any proof, of course, but Isaac would not be at all surprised if some of Vermishank's research had been carried out in the punishment factories. Vermishank had the skill to be an extraordinary sculptor in flesh.

There was a thump on his door. Isaac looked up in surprise. It was nearly eleven o'clock. He put down his supper and hurried down the stairs. He opened the door on a debauched-looking Lucky Gazid.

What the fuck is this? he thought.

" 'Zaac, my brother, my ... bumptious, bungling ... beloved ..." Gazid screamed as soon as he saw Isaac. He groped for more alliteration. Isaac pulled him into the warehouse as lights went on across the road.

"Lucky, you fucking *arse*, what do you *want?*"

Gazid was pacing from side to side much too quickly. His eyes were stretched wide open, and virtually spiralling in his head. He looked hurt by Isaac's tone.

"Steady on, guv, ease up, ease up, no need for *nastiness*, now is there? Eh? I'm looking for Lin. She here?" He giggled abruptly.

Ah, thought Isaac carefully. This was tricky. Lucky was a Salacus Fields man, he knew the unstated truth about Isaac and Lin. But this was not Salacus Fields.

"No, Lucky, she's not here. And if she were here, for some reason, you'd have absolutely no right to come crashing round here in the middle of the night. What do you want her for?"

"She's not at home." Gazid turned and walked up the ladder, speaking to Isaac without turning his head. "Just been round there, but I s'pose she's hard at *art*, eh? She owes me money, owes me *commission*, for getting her the *plumb job* and setting her up for life. Guess that's where she is now, eh? I want some *dosh* ..."

Isaac banged his head in exasperation and leapt up the stairs behind Gazid.

"What the fuck are you talking about? *What* job? She's doing her own stuff right now."

"Oh yes, course, righto, yup, that's the size of it," agreed Gazid with peculiar absent-minded fervour. "Owes me *money*, though. I'm fucking desperate, 'Zaac ... Stand me a noble ..."

Isaac was getting angry. He grabbed Gazid and held him still. Gazid had the junkie's scrawny arms. He could only struggle pathetically in Isaac's grip.

"Listen, Lucky, you little puke. How can you be *hurting*, you're so strung out now you can hardly stand. How dare you crash round my house, you fucking junkie . . ."

"Oy!" Gazid shouted suddenly. He sneered up at Isaac, breaking his flow. "Lin isn't here now, but I'm *hungry* for something, and I want you to *help me* or I don't know what I might end up saying, if Lin won't help me, *you* can, you're her knight in shining armour, her *love-bug*, she's your ladybird . . ."

Isaac drew back a fat meaty fist and smashed Lucky Gazid in the face, sending the little man yards through the air.

Gazid squealed in astonishment and terror. He scraped his heels on the bare wood and scrabbled towards the stairs. A star of blood radiated out from below his nose. Isaac shook blood from his knuckles and stalked towards Gazid. He was cold with rage.

Think I'm going to let you talk like that? Think you can blackmail me, you little shit? he thought.

"Lucky, you should leave right fucking now if you don't want me to take your head off."

Gazid crawled to his feet and burst out crying.

"You're fucking *crazy*, Isaac, I thought we were *friends* . . ."

Snot and tears and blood dripped onto Isaac's floor.

"Yeah, well, you thought wrong, didn't you, old son? You're nothing but a fucking dreg, and I . . ." Isaac broke off from his contumely and stared in astonishment.

Gazid was leaning against the empty cages on which the caterpillar's box lay. Isaac could see the fat grub wriggling, jack-knifing in excitement, twisting desperately against the wire front, squirming with sudden reserves of energy towards Lucky Gazid.

Lucky hovered, terrified, waiting for Isaac to finish.

"What?" he wailed. "What are you going to *do*?"

"Shut *up*," hissed Isaac.

The caterpillar was thinner than it had been on its arrival, and its extraordinary peacock-feather colours were dulled, but it was undoubtedly alive. It rippled its way around its little cage, feeling through the air like a blind person's finger, faltering towards Gazid.

"Don't move," hissed Isaac, and edged closer. The terrified Gazid obeyed. He followed Isaac's line of sight and his eyes

widened at the sight of the huge grub rooting its way around the
little cage, trying to find a way towards him. He snatched his
hand from the box with a little cry and started backwards. Instantly, the caterpillar changed direction, trying to follow him.

"This is *fascinating . . .*" said Isaac. As he watched, Gazid
reached up and clutched his head, shaking it suddenly and violently as if it was full of insects.

"Oh, what is happening in my *head*?" Gazid stuttered.

As he drew closer, Isaac could feel it too. Snatches of alien
sensation slithered like lightning-quick eels through his cerebellum. He blinked and coughed slightly, in thrall suddenly and
briefly to the sensation of emotions that were not his clogging up
his throat. Isaac shook his head and squeezed his eyes hard shut.

"Gazid," he snapped. "Walk slowly round it."

Lucky Gazid did as he was told. The caterpillar toppled over
in its eager attempts to right itself, to follow him, to track
him down.

"Why does the thing want *me*?" moaned Lucky Gazid.

"Well I don't *know*, Lucky," said Isaac tartly. "The poor
thing's *hurting*. Looks like it wants whatever you've got, Lucky
old son. Empty your pockets slowly. Don't worry, I'm not going
to nick anything."

Gazid began to pull strips of paper and handkerchiefs from
the folds of his soiled jacket and trousers. He hesitated, then
reached inside and pulled two fat packets from his inner pockets.

The grub went berserk. The disorienting shards of synaesthetic feeling whirled through Isaac's and Gazid's heads again.

"What the fuck've you got?" said Isaac through clenched
teeth.

"This one's shazbah," said Gazid hesitantly and waved the
first packet at the cage. The grub did not react. "This one's dreamshit." Gazid held the second envelope over the caterpillar's head,
and it all but balanced on its rear end to reach it. Its piteous wails
were not quite audible, but they were acutely sensible.

"There we go!" said Isaac. "That's it! The thing wants dreamshit!" Isaac held out his hand to Gazid and clicked his fingers.
"Give it to me."

Gazid hesitated, then handed over the packet.

"Lot of stuff there, man . . . that's a lot of moolah there,
man . . ." he whimpered. "You can't just *take* it, man . . ."

Isaac hefted the pouch. It weighed about two or three pounds, he estimated. He pulled it open. Again the emotional wails burst piercingly up from the caterpillar. Isaac winced at the poignant and inhuman begging.

The dreamshit was a mass of brown, sticky pellets that smelt like very burnt sugar.

"What is this stuff?" Isaac asked Gazid. "I've heard of it, but I know arse-all about it."

"New thing, 'Zaac. Expensive stuff. Been around a year or so. It's . . . heady stuff . . ."

"What does it do?"

"Couldn't describe it really. Want to buy some?"

"No!" said Isaac sharply, then hesitated. "Well . . . Not for me, anyway . . . How much would this packet cost, Lucky?"

Gazid hesitated, doubtless wondering how much he could exaggerate.

"Uh . . . about thirty guineas . . ."

"Oh fuck *off*, Lucky . . . You're such a piss-artist, old son . . . I'll buy this off you for . . ." Isaac hesitated. "For ten."

"Done," said Gazid instantly.

Shit, thought Isaac. *I've been stung.* He was about to quibble, when he suddenly thought better of it. He looked carefully at Gazid, who was beginning to swagger again, even with his face slick and ugly with gore and mucus.

"Righto, then. Deal. Listen, Lucky," said Isaac evenly, "I might want more of this stuff, you know what I mean? And if we stay on good terms, there's no reason not to keep you on as my . . . exclusive supplier. Know what I mean? But if anything came up to spread *discord* in our relationship, distrust and the like, I'd have to go elsewhere. Understand?"

" 'Zaac, my man, say no more . . . Partners, that's what we are . . ."

"Absolutely," said Isaac heavily. He was not so foolish as to think he could trust Lucky Gazid, but at least this way Isaac could keep him vaguely sweet. Gazid was unlikely to bite the hand that fed him, at least not for a while.

This can't last, thought Isaac, *but it'll do for now.*

Isaac plucked one of the moist, sticky lumps from the packet. It was the size of a large olive, coated in a thick and rapidly drying mucus. Isaac pulled back the lid of the caterpillar's box an inch or two and dropped the nugget of dreamshit inside. He squatted down to watch the larva through the wire front.

Isaac's eyelids flickered as if static coursed through him. For a moment, he could not focus his vision.

"Whoa . . ." moaned Lucky Gazid behind him. "Something's fucking with my head . . ."

Isaac felt briefly nauseous, then aflame with the most consuming and uncompromised ecstasy he had ever felt. After less than half a second the inhuman sensations spewed instantaneously out of him. He felt as if they left by his nose.

"Oh by Jabber . . ." Isaac yelped. His vision fluctuated, then sharpened and became unusually clear. "This little fucker's some sort of empath, ain't it?" he murmured.

He gazed at the caterpillar feeling like a voyeur. The creature was rolling around the drug pellet as if it were a snake crushing its prey. Its mouthpart was clamped hugely onto the top of the dreamshit, and it was chewing it with a hunger that seemed lascivious in its intensity. Its side-split jaws oozed with spit. It was devouring its food like a child eating toffee-pudding at Jabber's Feast. The dreamshit was rapidly disappearing.

"Hell's Ducks," said Isaac. "It's going to want a lot more than that." He dropped another five or six little lozenges into the cage. The grub rolled happily around in the sticky collection.

Isaac stood up. He regarded Lucky Gazid, who watched the caterpillar eating and smiled beatifically, swaying.

"Lucky, old son, seems like you might've saved my little experiment's bacon. Very much obliged."

"I'm a *lifesaver*, aren't I, 'Zaac?" Gazid spun slowly in an ugly pirouette. "Lifesaver! Lifesaver!"

"Yes, that'll do, that's what you are, old son, hush now." Isaac glanced at the clock. "I really have to get a bit more work done, so do the decent thing and push off, eh? No hard feelings, Lucky . . ." Isaac hesitated and thrust out his hand. "Sorry about your nose."

"Oh." Gazid looked surprised. He prodded his bloody face experimentally. "Well . . . whatever . . ."

Isaac strode away towards his desk.

"I'll get your moolah. Hang on." He rummaged in the drawers, eventually finding his wallet and drawing out a guinea. "Hold on, I've more somewhere. Bear with me . . ." Isaac knelt by the bed and began to throw piles of paper aside, collecting the stivers and shekels he unearthed.

Gazid reached into the packet of dreamshit which Isaac had left on the caterpillar's box. He looked thoughtfully at Isaac, who was scrabbling under the bed with his face on the floor. Gazid plucked two dreamshit pellets from the sticky morass and glanced over to Isaac, to see if he was watching. Isaac was saying something in a conversational tone, his words muffled by the bed above him.

Gazid sauntered slowly over towards the bed. He took a sweet wrapper from his pocket and twisted it around one of his dreamshit doses, dropped it into his pocket. An idiot grin grew and blossomed across his face as he stared at the second lump.

"Should *know* what you're prescribing, 'Zaac," he whispered. "That's *ethical* . . ." He giggled with delight.

"What's that?" shouted Isaac. He began to wriggle his way out from under the bed. "I've found it. I knew there was some money in the pocket of one of these trousers . . ."

Lucky Gazid quickly peeled off the top of the ham roll that lay half-eaten on the desk. He slipped the dreamshit into a mustard-covered space under a lettuce leaf. He replaced the top of the roll and stepped away from the desk.

Isaac stood and turned to him, dusty and smiling. He clutched a fan of notes and some loose change.

"That's ten guineas. 'Stail, you bargain like a fucking pro . . ."

Gazid took the proffered money and backed down the stairs quickly.

"Thanks then 'Zaac," he said. "Appreciate it."

Isaac was somewhat taken aback.

"Right then. I'll contact you if I need any more dreamshit, all right?"

"Yeah, you do that, big brother . . ."

Gazid was all but scurrying out of the warehouse, pulling the door behind him with a cursory wave. Isaac heard a peal of absurd giggles from the retreating form, a thin wittering cluck that tailed out in the darkness.

Devil's Tail! he thought. *I fucking hate dealing with junkies. What a screwed-up mess he is . . .* Isaac shook his head and wandered back to the caterpillar's cage.

The grub was already starting on the second lump of sticky drug. Unpredictable little waves of insect happiness spilt over into Isaac's mind. The sensation was unpleasant. Isaac backed away. As he watched, the grub broke off eating and delicately cleaned itself of the sticky residue. Then it resumed eating, soiling itself again, then preening again.

"Fastidious little bugger, eh?" muttered Isaac. "Is that good, eh? You enjoying that? Hmmm? Lovely."

Isaac wandered over to his desk and picked up his own supper. He turned back to watch the twisting little multicoloured form as he took a bite of his hardening roll and sipped the chocolate.

"So what the fuck are you going to turn into, then?" he muttered to his experiment. Isaac ate the rest of his roll, grimacing at the slightly stale bread and the musty salad. At least the chocolate was good.

He wiped his mouth and returned to the caterpillar's cage, steeling himself against the peculiar little empathic waves. Isaac squatted down and watched the starving creature gorge itself. It was difficult to be sure, but Isaac thought the grub's colours were brighter already.

"You'll be a good little sideline to keep me from getting obsessed with crisis theory, eh? Won't you, you little squirming bugger? Not in any of the textbooks, are you? Shy? Is that it?"

A blast of twisted psyche hit Isaac like a crossbow bolt. He staggered and fell over.

"Ow!" he screeched, and writhed to get away from the cage. "I can't hack your empathic bleating, old son . . ." He picked himself up and walked towards the bed, rubbing his head. Just as he reached it, another spasm of alien emotions pulsed violently in his head. His knees buckled and he fell by the bed, clawing at his temples.

"Oh *shit*!" He was alarmed. "That's too much, you're getting way too strong . . ."

Suddenly he could not speak. He snapped totally still as a third intense attack flooded his synapses. These were different, he realized, these were not the same as the querulous little psychic wails from the weird grub ten feet from him. His mouth was suddenly arid, and tasted of musty salad. Mulch. Compost. Old fruitcake.

Lumpy mustard.

"Oh no . . ." he muttered. His voice shook as realization gripped him. "Oh *no, no, no,* oh Gazid, you fucking *prick*, you *shit*, I'll fucking *kill you* . . ."

He clutched the edge of the bed with hands that trembled violently. He was sweating and his skin looked like stone.

Get into bed, he thought desperately. *Get under the covers and ride it out, thousands of people do this every day for pleasure for Jabber's sake . . .*

Isaac's hand crawled like a drugged tarantula across the folds of the blanket. He couldn't work out the best way of getting under the covers, because of the way they folded in on themselves and around the sheet: both sets of cloth ripples were so similar that Isaac was suddenly convinced that they were all part of the same big undulating cloth unity and that to bisect it would be ghastly, so he rolled his bulk on top of the covers and found himself swimming in the intricate twisting folds of cotton and wool. He swam up and down, waving his arms in an energetic, childish doggy paddle, hacking and spitting and smacking his lips with a prodigious thirst.

Look at you, you cretin, spat one section of his mind in contempt. *How dignified is this?*

But he paid no attention. He was content to swim gently in place on the bed, panting like a dying animal, tensing his neck experimentally and prodding his eyes.

He felt a build-up of pressure in the back of his mind. He watched a big door, a big cellar door, set into the wall of the most ignored corner of his cerebellum. The door was rattling. Something was trying to get out.

Quick, thought Isaac. *Bolt it . . .*

But he could feel the increasing power of whatever was fighting to escape. The door was a boil, bursting with pus, ready to rupture, a hugely muscled blank-faced dog, straining ominously and silently against chains, the sea pounding relentlessly against a crumbling harbour wall.

Something in Isaac's mind burst open.

Chapter Sixteen

sun pouring in like a waterfall and I rejoice in it as blooms burst from my shoulders and my head and chlorophyll rushes invigoratingly through my skin and I raise great spined arms

don't touch me like that I'm not ready you pig

Look at those steamhammers! I'd like them if they didn't make me work so!

is this

*I am proud to be able to tell you that your father has con-
sented to our match*

is this a

*and here I swim under all this dirty water towards the looming
dark bulk of the boat like a great cloud I breathe filthy water that
makes me cough and my webbed feet push towards*

is this a dream?

*light skin food air metal sex misery fire mushrooms webs ships
torture beer frog spikes bleach violin ink crags sodomy money
wings colourberries gods chainsaw bones puzzles babies concrete shellfish stilts entrails snow darkness*

Is this a dream?

But Isaac knew this was not a dream.

A magic lantern was flickering in his head, bombarding him
with a succession of images. This was no zöetrope with an endlessly repeated little visual anecdote: this was a juddering bom-
bardment of infinitely varied moments. Isaac was strafed with a
million scintillas of time. Every fractioned life juddered as it
segued into the next and Isaac would eavesdrop on other creatures' lives. He spoke the chymical language of the khepri crying
because her broodma had chastised her and then he snorted derisorily as he the head stableman listened to some half-arsed excuse from the new boy and he closed his translucent inner eyelid
as he slipped beneath the cold fresh waters of the mountain
streams and kicked towards the other vodyanoi coupling orgias-
tically and he . . .

"Oh Jabber . . ." He heard his voice from deep inside that cacophonous emotional onslaught. There were more and more and
more and they came so fast, they overlapped and blurred at the
edges, until two or three or more moments of life were occurring
at once.

The light was bright, when lights were on, some faces were
sharp and others blurred and invisible. Each separate splinter of
life moved with portentous, symbolic focus. Each was ruled by
oneiric logic. In some analytical pocket of his mind Isaac realized that these were not, could not be, grots of history coagulated and distilled into that sticky resin. Setting was too fluid.
Awareness and reality intertwined. Isaac had not come unstuck
in others' lives, but in others' minds. He was a voyeur spying on

the last refuge of the stalked. These were memories. These were dreams.

Isaac was spattered by a psychic sluice. He felt fouled. There was no more succession, no one two three four five six invading mindset moments clicking briefly into place to be illuminated by the light of his own consciousness. Instead he swam in mire, a glutinous cesspit of dreamjuice that flowed in and out of each other, that had no integrity, that bled logic and images across lifetimes and sexes and species until he could hardly breathe, he was drowning in the sloshing stuff of dreams and hopes, recollections and reflections he had never had.

His body was nothing but a boneless sac of mental effluent. Somewhere way away, he heard it moan and rock on the bed with a liquid gurgling.

Isaac reeled. Somewhere in the flickering onslaught of emotion and bathos he discerned a thin, constant stream of disgust and fear that he recognized as his own. He struggled towards it through the sludge of imagined and replayed dramas of consciousness. He touched the tentative dribble of nausea that was indisputably what *he* was feeling *at that moment*, held fast, centred himself in it . . . Isaac clung to it with radical fervour.

He held to his core, buffeted by the dreams around him. Isaac flew over a spiky town, a six-year-old girl laughing delightedly in a language he had never heard but momentarily understood as his own; he bucked with inexpert excitement as he dreamed the sex dream of a pubescent boy; he swam through estuaries and visited strange grottoes and fought ritualistic battles. He wandered through the flattened veldt of the daydreaming cactacae mind. Houses morphed around him with the dreamlogic that seemed to be shared by all the sentient races of Bas-Lag.

New Crobuzon appeared here and there, in its dream form, in its remembered or imagined geography, with details highlighted and others missing, great gaps between streets that were traversed in seconds.

There were other cities and countries and continents in these dreams. Some were doubtless dreamlands born behind flickering eyelids. Others seemed references: oneiric nods to solid places, cities and towns and villages as real as New Crobuzon, with architecture and argots that Isaac had not seen or heard.

The sea of dreams in which he swam, Isaac realized, contained drops from very far afield.

Less of a sea, he thought drunkenly from the bottom of his unstuck mind, and more of a consommé. He imagined himself chewing stolidly on the gristle and giblets of alien minds, lumps of rancid dream sustenance floating in a thin gruel of half-memories. Isaac retched mentally. *If I throw up in here I'll turn my head inside out,* he thought.

The memories and dreams came in waves. Tides carried them in thematic washes. Even adrift in the wash of random thoughts, Isaac was carried across the vistas inside his head on recognizable currents. He succumbed to the tugging of money dreams, a trend of recollections of stivers and dollars and head of cattle and painted shells and promise-tablets.

He rolled in a surf of sex dreams: cactacae men ejaculating across the earth, across the rows of eggbulbs planted by the women; khepri women rubbing oil across each other in friendly orgies; celibate human priests dreaming out their guilty, illicit desires.

Isaac spiralled in a little whirlpool of anxiety dreams. A human girl about to enter her exams, he found himself walking nude to school; a vodyanoi watercræfter whose heart raced as stinging saline water poured back from the sea into his river; an actor who stood dumb on stage, unable to recall a single line of his speech.

My mind's a cauldron, Isaac thought, *and all these dreams are bubbling over.*

The slop of ideas came quicker and thicker. Isaac thought of that and tried to latch onto the rhyme, focusing on it and investing it with portent, repeating it *quicker and quicker and thicker and thicker and quicker*, trying to ignore the barrage, the torrent, of psychic effluvia.

It was no use. The dreams were in Isaac's mind, and there was no escape. He dreamed that he dreamed other people's dreams, and realized that his dream was true.

All he could do was try, with a febrile, terrified intensity, to remember which of the dreams was his own.

There was a frantic chirruping coming from somewhere close by. It wound its way through a skein of the images that gusted through Isaac's head, then grew in intensity until it ran through his mind as the dominant theme.

Abruptly, all the dreams stopped.

Isaac opened his eyes too quickly and swore with the pain that gushed into his head with the light. He reached his hand up and felt it lolling against his head like a big, vague paddle. He laid it heavily across his eyes.

The dreams had stopped. Isaac peeked through his fingers. It was day. It was light.

"By . . . Jabber's . . . *arse* . . ." he whispered. The effort made his head ache.

This was absurd. He had no sense of time lost. He remembered everything clearly. If anything, his immediate recollection seemed heightened. He had a clear sense of having lolled and sweated and wailed under the influence of the dreamshit for about half an hour, no longer. And yet it was . . . he struggled with his eyelids, squinted at the clock . . . it was half past seven in the morning, hours and hours since he had fought his way onto the bed.

He propped himself on his elbows and examined himself. His dark skin was slick and grey. His mouth reeked. Isaac realized that he must have lain almost motionless for the whole night: the covers were a little rucked, that was all.

The terrified birdsong that had woken him started again. Isaac shook his head in irritation and looked for its source. A tiny bird circled desperately in the air around the inside of the warehouse. Isaac realized that it was one of the previous evening's reluctant escapees, a wren, obviously afraid of something. As Isaac looked around to see what had the bird so nervous, the lithe reptilian body of an aspis flew like a crossbow bolt from one corner of the eaves to the other. It plucked the little bird from the air as it passed. The wren's calls were cut short abruptly.

Isaac stumbled inexpertly out of bed and circled confusedly. "Notes," he told himself. "Make notes."

He snatched paper and pen from his desk and began to scribble down his recollections of the dreamshit.

"What the fuck *was* that?" he whispered out loud as he wrote. "Some cove's doing a damn good job of reproducing the biochymistry of dreams, or tapping it at source . . ." He rubbed his head again. "Lord, what sort of thing is it that *eats* this . . ." Isaac stood briefly and glanced at his captive caterpillar.

He was quite still. His mouth gaped idiotically, then worked up and down and finally shaped words.

"Oh. My. Good. Arse."

He stumbled slowly, nervously across the room, seeming to

hang back, chary of seeing what he was seeing. He approached the cage.

Inside, a colossal mass of beautifully coloured grub-flesh wriggled unhappily. Isaac stood uneasily over the enormous thing. He could feel the odd little vibrations of alien unhappiness in the æther around him.

The caterpillar had at least tripled in size overnight. It was a foot long, and correspondingly fat. The faded magnificence of its coloured patches had returned to their initial, burnished brilliance. With interest. The sticky-looking hairs on its tail-end were wicked-looking bristles. It had no more than six inches of space around it on all sides. It nudged weakly against the sides of the hutch.

"What happened to *you*?" hissed Isaac.

He recoiled and gazed at the thing, which waved its head in the air blindly. He thought quickly, pictured the number of dreamshit lozenges he had given the grub to eat. He looked around and saw the envelope containing all the remains where he had left it, untouched. The thing hadn't got out and gorged itself. There was no way, Isaac realized, that the little pellets of drug he had left in that hutch contained anything like the number of calories that the caterpillar had used on growth over the night. Even if it had just piled on weight ounce for ounce with what it had eaten, it would not have represented an increase in this league.

"Whatever energy you're getting out of your supper," he whispered, "it's not physical. What in Jabber's name *are* you?"

He had to get the thing out of the cage. It looked so miserable, flailing pointlessly in that little space. Isaac hung back, slightly afraid and a little disgusted at the idea of touching the extraordinary thing. Eventually he picked up the box, staggering under the massively increased weight, and held it just above the ground in a much larger cage left over from his experiments, a chicken-wire-fronted mini-aviary five feet high that had contained a small family of canaries. He opened the front of the hutch and tipped the fat grub into the sawdust, then quickly closed and latched the front grille.

He stood back to gaze at his rehoused captive.

It looked directly at him, now, and he felt its childish pleas for breakfast.

"Oh steady *on*," he said. "*I* haven't even eaten yet."

He backed uneasily away, then turned and made for his parlour.

Over his breakfast of fruit and iced buns, Isaac realized that the effects of the dreamshit were wearing off very quickly. *It might be the worst hangover in the world,* he thought wryly, *but it's gone within the hour. No wonder the punters come back.*

From across the room, the foot-long caterpillar scrabbled around the floor of its new cage. It nosed miserably around the dirt, then reared up again and waved its head in the direction of the packet of dreamshit.

Isaac slapped his hand over his face.

"Oh, Hell's Donkeys," he said. Vague emotions of unease and experimental curiosity combined in his mind. It was a childish excitement, like that of boys and girls who burnt insects with magnified sun. He stood and reached into the envelope with a big wooden spoon. He carried the congealed lump over to the caterpillar, which almost danced with excitement as it saw, or smelt, or somehow sensed, the dreamshit approaching. Isaac opened a little feeding hatch at the back of the crate and tipped the doses of drug in. Immediately the caterpillar raised its head and slammed it down on the lumpy mess. Its mouth was large enough now that its workings could easily be seen. It slid open and gnawed voraciously at the powerful narcotic.

"That," said Isaac, "is as big a cage as you're going to get, so ease up on the growing, right?" He backed away to his clothes, without taking his eyes from the feeding creature.

Isaac picked up and sniffed the various clothes strewn around the room. He put on a shirt and trousers with no smell and a minimum of stains.

Better sort out a "things to do" list, he thought grimly. *Top of which is "Beat Lucky Gazid to death."* He stomped to his desk. The triangular Unified Field Theory diagram he had drawn for Yagharek was at the top of the papers that covered it. Isaac pursed his lips and stared at it. He picked it up and looked thoughtfully over to where the caterpillar gnawed happily. There was something else he should do that morning.

There's no point putting it off, he thought reluctantly. *Maybe I can clear the decks for Yag and learn a little about my friend here . . . maybe.* Isaac sighed heavily and rolled up his sleeves, then sat down at a mirror for a rare and perfunctory preen. He poked inexpertly at his hair, found another, cleaner shirt into which he changed, oozing resentment.

He scribbled a note for David and Lublamai, checked that his giant caterpillar was secure and unlikely to escape. Then he descended the stairs and, pinning his message to the door, walked out into a day full of sharp clear blades of light.

Isaac sighed and set off to find an early cab to take him to the university and the best biologist, natural philosopher and bio-thaumaturge he knew: the odious Montague Vermishank.

CHAPTER SEVENTEEN

Isaac entered New Crobuzon University with a mixture of nostalgia and discomfort. The university buildings were little changed since his time as a teacher. The various faculties and departments dotted Ludmead with a grandiose architecture that overshadowed the rest of the area.

The quad before the enormous and ancient Science Faculty building was covered with trees shedding their blossom. Isaac walked footpaths worn by generations of students through a blizzard of garish pink petals. He strode busily up the scrubbed steps and pushed open the great doors.

Isaac was brandishing faculty identification that had expired seven years previously, but he need not have bothered. The porter behind the desk was Sedge, an old, entirely witless man, whose tenure at the faculty long predated Isaac's own, and looked set to continue for ever. He greeted Isaac as he always did, on these irregular visits, with an incoherent mutter of recognition. Isaac shook his hand and enquired after his family. Isaac had reason to be grateful to Sedge, before whose milky eyes he had liberated numerous expensive pieces of laboratory equipment.

Isaac strode up the steps past groups of students, smoking, arguing, writing. Overwhelmingly male and human, there were, nonetheless, the occasional defensive tight-knit group of young xenians or women or both. Some students conducted theoretical debates at ostentatious volume. Others made occasional marginal notes in their textbooks and sucked at rolled cigarillos of pungent tobacco. Isaac passed a group squatting at the end of a corridor, practising what they had just learned, laughing delightedly as the tiny homunculus they had made from ground liver stumbled four steps before collapsing in a pile of twitching mulch.

The number of students around him decreased as he continued up stairs and along corridors. To his irritation and disgust, Isaac found that his heart was speeding up as he approached his erstwhile boss.

He walked the plush darkwood panelling of the Science Faculty's administration wing, and approached the office at the far end, on the door of which was written in gold leaf: *Director. Montague Vermishank.*

Isaac paused outside and fiddled nervously. He was emotionally confused, striving to maintain a decade's anger and dislike along with a conciliatory, non-confrontational tone. He breathed deeply once, then turned and knocked briskly, opened the door and walked in.

"What do you think . . ." shouted the man behind the desk, before stopping abruptly when he recognized Isaac. "Ah," he said, after a long silence. "Of course. Isaac. Do sit down."

Isaac sat.

Montague Vermishank was eating his lunch. His pale face and shoulders leaned sharply over his enormous desk. Behind him was a small window. It looked out, Isaac knew, over the wide avenues and large houses of Mafaton and Chnum, but a grubby curtain was pulled across it and the light was stifled.

Vermishank was not fat, but he was coated from his jowls down in a slight excess layer, a swaddling of dead flesh like a corpse's. He wore a suit too small for him, and his necrotic white skin oozed from his sleeves. His thin hair was brushed and styled with a neurotic fervour. Vermishank was drinking lumpy cream soup. He dipped doughy bread into it regularly and sucked at the resulting mess, chewing but not biting off, gnawing and worrying at the saliva-fouled bread that dripped wan yellow onto his desk. His colourless eyes took Isaac in.

Isaac stared uneasily and was thankful for his tight bulk and his skin the colour of smouldering wood.

"Was going to shout at you for failing to knock or make an appointment, but then I saw it was you. Of course. Normal rules do not apply. How are you, Isaac? Are you after money? Need some research work?" asked Vermishank in his phlegmy whisper.

"No, no, nothing like that. I'm not bad, actually, Vermishank," said Isaac with strained bonhomie. "How's all your work?"

"Oh, good, good. Doing a paper on bio-ignition. I've isolated the pyrotic flange in a fire-bes." There was a long silence. "Very exciting," whispered Vermishank.

"Sounds it, sounds it," enthused Isaac. They stared at each other. Isaac could not think of any more small talk. He loathed and respected Vermishank. It was an unsettling combination.

"So, uh . . . anyway . . ." said Isaac. "I'm here, to be frank, to ask your help."

"Oh ho."

"Yeah . . . See, I'm working on something that's a bit off my track . . . I'm more of a theoretician than a practical researcher, you know . . ."

"Yes . . ." Vermishank's voice dripped an indiscriminate irony. *You ratfuck,* thought Isaac. *I gave you that for free . . .*

"Right," he said slowly. "Well, this is . . . I mean this *could* be, though I doubt it . . . a problem of bio-thaumaturgy. I wanted to ask your professional opinion."

"Ah ha."

"Yes. What I wanted to know was . . . can someone be Re-made to fly?"

"Ooh." Vermishank leaned back and dabbed soup from around his mouth with bread. Briefly, he wore a moustache of crumbs. He clasped his hands in front of him and waggled his fat fingers. "Fly, eh?"

Vermishank's voice picked up an air of excitement previously lacking in his cold tones. He may have wanted to sting Isaac with his heavy contempt, but he could not help being enthused by problems of science.

"Yeah. I mean, has that been done?" said Isaac.

"Yes . . . It has been done . . ." Vermishank nodded slowly without taking his eyes from Isaac, who sat up in his chair and snatched a notebook from his pocket.

"Oh, *has* it?" said Isaac.

Vermishank's eyes lost focus as he thought harder.

"Yes . . . Why, Isaac? Has someone come to you and asked to fly?"

"I really can't . . . uh, divulge . . ."

"Of course you can't, Isaac. Of *course* you can't. Because you are a professional. And I respect you for that." Vermishank smiled idly at his guest.

"So . . . what were the details?" ventured Isaac. He set his teeth before he spoke, to control his shaking indignation. *Fuck you, you patronizing game-playing pig,* he thought furiously.

"Oh ho . . . Well . . ." Isaac twisted with impatience as Vermishank raised his head ponderously to remember. "There was a biophilosopher, years ago, at the end of the last century. Calligine, name of. Had himself Remade." Vermishank smiled fondly and cruelly and shook his head. "Mad thing, really, but it did seem to work. Huge mechanical wings that unfolded like fans. He wrote a pamphlet about it." Vermishank strained his head over his lardy shoulder, glanced vaguely at the shelves of volumes that covered his walls. He waved with a limp hand that could have signalled anything at all about the whereabouts of Calligine's pamphlet. "Don't you know the rest? Not heard the song?" Isaac narrowed his eyes quizzically. Appallingly, Vermishank sang a few bars in a reedy tenor. *"So Cally flew high / On um-ber-ella wings / Headed into the sky / Waved his love bye-bye / Went West with a sigh / Disappeared in the land of the Horrible Things . . ."*

"Of course I've heard that!" said Isaac. "I never knew it was about someone *real* . . ."

"Well, you never took Introductory Bio-Thaumaturgy, did you? As I remember, you did about two terms of the Intermediate course, much later. You missed my first lecture. That's the story I use to entice our jaded young knowledge-hunters onto the road of this noble science." Vermishank spoke in a completely deadpan voice. Isaac felt his distaste return with interest. "Calligine disappeared," Vermishank continued. "Went off flying south-west, towards the Cacotopic Stain. Never seen again."

There was another long silence.

"Uh . . . is that the whole story?" said Isaac. "How did they get the wings on him? Did he keep experimental notes? What was the Remaking like?"

"Oh, horribly difficult, I'd imagine. Calligine probably got through a few experimental subjects before getting his sums right . . ." Vermishank grinned. "Probably called in a few favours with Mayor Mantagony. I suspect a few felons sentenced to death had a few more weeks of life than they'd expected. Not part of the process that he advertised. But it stands to reason, doesn't it, that it's going to take a few tries before you get it right. I mean, you've got to connect up the mechanism to bones and muscles and whatnot that haven't a clue what they're supposed to be doing . . ."

"But what if the muscles and bones *did* know what they were

doing? What about if a . . . a wyrman or something, had its
wings cut off. Could they be replaced?"

Vermishank gazed passively at Isaac. His head and eyes did
not move.

"Ha . . ." he said faintly, eventually. "You'd have thought that
was easier, wouldn't you? It is, in theory, but it's even harder in
practice. I've done some of this with birds and . . . well, with
winged things. First off, Isaac, in theory it's perfectly possible.
In theory, there is almost nothing which can't be done with Remaking. It's all just a question of wiring things up right, a bit of
flesh-moulding. But flight's horribly hard because you're dealing with all sorts of variables that have to be exactly right. See,
Isaac, you can Remake a dog, sew a leg back on, or mould it on
with a clayflesh hex, and the animal'll limp along happily. Won't
be pretty, but it'll walk. Can't do that with wings. Wings have to
be perfect or they won't do the trick. It's *harder* to teach muscles
that think they know how to fly to do the same trick differently
than it is to teach muscles that haven't any idea in the first place.
Your bird or what have you, its shoulders get all confused by this
wing which is just a tad the wrong shape, or the wrong size, or
based on different aerodynamics, and it ends up being totally
stymied, *even assuming* you've reconnected everything up right.

"So the answer, I suppose I'm saying, Isaac, is that yes it can
be done. This *wyrman*, or whatever, can be Remade to fly again.
But it isn't likely. It's too damn hard. There's no bio-thaumaturge,
no Remaker, who could promise a result. Either you're going to
have to find Calligine, get him to do it," hissed Vermishank in
conclusion, "or I wouldn't risk it."

Isaac finished scribbling notes and flipped his notebook
closed.

"Thanks, Vermishank. I was sort of . . . hoping you'd say that.
That's your professional opinion, eh? Well, I'll just have to pursue my *other* line of enquiry, of which you wouldn't approve at
all . . ." His eyes bulged like a naughty boy's.

Vermishank nodded very slightly and a sickly little smile
grew and died on his mouth like a fungus.

"Ha," he said faintly.

"Right, well, thanks for your time . . . Appreciate it . . ." Isaac
flustered as he stood to go. "Sorry to be so fleeting . . ."

"Not at all. Any other opinions needed?"

"Well . . ." Isaac paused with his arm half into his jacket.
"Well. Have you heard of something called dreamshit?"

Vermishank raised an eyebrow. He leaned back in his chair and chewed his thumb, looking at Isaac with half-closed eyes.

"This is a university, Isaac. Do you think a new and *exciting* illicit substance would sweep the city and none of our students would be tempted? Of course I've heard of it. We had our first expulsion for selling the drug less than half a year ago. Very bright young psychonomer, of predictably avant-garde theoretical persuasion.

"Isaac, Isaac . . . for all your many, uh, *indiscretions* . . ." a little simper pretended unconvincingly to rob the insult of its barb "—I wouldn't have had you down as a . . . a *drug* person."

"No, Vermishank, nor am I. However, living and operating in the *quagmire of corruption* that I've chosen, surrounded by *lowlifes*, and vile degenerates, I tend to be faced with things like drugs at the various *sordid orgies* I attend." Isaac told himself off for losing his patience at the same moment that he decided there was nothing to be gained from further diplomacy. He spoke loudly and sarcastically. He rather enjoyed his ire.

"So anyway," he continued, "one of my disgusting friends was using this bizarre drug and I wanted to know more about it. Obviously shouldn't have asked someone so high-minded."

Vermishank was chuckling soundlessly. He laughed without opening his mouth. His face remained set in a sour smirk. He kept his eyes on Isaac. The only sign that he was laughing was the little shucking motion of his shoulders and his slight rocking back and forth.

"Ha," he said eventually. "Touchy-touchy, Isaac." He shook his head. Isaac patted his pockets and fastened his jacket, ostentatiously getting ready to go, refusing to feel silly. He turned his back and walked to the door, debating the merits of a parting shot.

Vermishank spoke while he considered.

"Dreamsh . . . Ah, *that substance* is not really my area, Isaac. Pharmacology and whatnot something of a biological backwater. I'm sure one of your old colleagues might be able to tell you more. Good luck."

Isaac had decided against saying anything. He did, however, wave behind him in a pusillanimous motion that he could convince himself was contemptuous, but could just about pass for gratitude and farewell. *You arsing coward,* he scolded himself. But there was no getting away from it, Vermishank was a useful repository of knowledge. Isaac knew it would take a lot for him to be really, unrepentantly rude to his former boss. That was just too much expertise to close the door on.

So Isaac forgave himself his half-hearted retaliation and grinned, instead, at his own floundering reaction to the awful man. At least he had learnt what he had come there to learn. Remaking was not an option for Yagharek. Isaac was pleased, and he was honest enough to recognize the ignobility of the reasons. His own research had been reinvigorated by the problem of flight, and if the prosaic flesh-sculpting of applied biothaumaturgy had won out over crisis theory, his research would have stalled. He did not want to lose his new momentum.

Yag old son, he reflected, *it's just as I thought. I'm your best shot, and you're mine.*

Before the city there were canals that wound between rock formations like silicate tusks, and patches of corn in the thin soil. And before the scrub there were days of glowering stone. Gnarled granite tumours that had sat heavy in the belly of the land since its birth, their thin earth-flesh stripped from them by air and water in a mere ten thousand years. They were ugly and terrifying as innards always are, those rock promontories, those crags.

I walked the path of the river. It was nameless between the hard ridged hills: in days it would become the Tar. I could see the freezing heights of real mountains miles to the west, colossi of rock and snow that reared as imperiously over the local jags of scree and lichen as those lower peaks reared over me.

Sometimes I thought the rocks shaped like looming figures, with claws and fangs and heads like clubs or hands. Petrified giants; unmoving stone gods; mistakes of the eye or the wind's chance sculptures.

I was seen. Goats and sheep poured scorn on my stumbling. Screaming birds of prey shouted their contempt. Sometimes I passed shepherds who stared at me, suspicious and rude.

There were darker shapes at night. There were colder watchers under the water.

The rock teeth broke earth so slowly and slyly that I was walking that gouged valley for hours before I knew it. Before that were days and days of grass and scrub.

The earth was easier on my feet, and the massive sky easier on my eye. But I would not be fooled. I would not be seduced. It was not the desert sky. It was a pretender, a surrogate, that tried to lull me. Drying vegetation stroked me with every wash of wind, lusher by far than my home. In the distance was the forest that I knew extended north to the edge of New Crobuzon, east to the sea. In secret places among its thick trees jutted vast, obscure, forgotten machines, pistons and gears, iron trunks among the wood, rust their bark.

I did not approach them.

Behind me where the river forked were marshlands, a kind of aimless inland estuary that promised, vaguely, to dissolve into the sea. There I stayed in the raised longhuts of the stiltspear, that quiet, devout race. They fed me and sang me crooning lullabies. I hunted with them, spearing cayman and anacondas. It was in the wetlands that I lost my blade, breaking it off in the flesh of some rushing, sucking predator that loomed at me suddenly from out of the slime and sodden reeds. It reared and screamed like a kettle on a fire, disappeared into the muck. I do not know if it died.

Before the wetland and the river were days of drying grass and foothills, that I was warned were ravaged by gangs of bandit fReemade run from justice. I saw none.

There were villages that bribed me in with meat and cloth and begged me to intercede on their behalf to their harvest gods. There were villages that kept me out with pikes and rifles and screaming klaxons. I shared the grass with herds and occasionally with riders, with birds I considered cousins and with animals I had thought myth.

I slept alone, hidden in folds of stone or in copses, or in bivouacs I threw up when I smelt rain. Four times something investigated me when I slept, leaving hoofmarks and the smell of herbs or sweat or meat.

Those sprawling downs were where my anger and misery changed shape.

I walked with temperate insects investigating my unfamiliar smells, trying to lick my sweat, taste my blood, trying to pollinate the spots of colour in my cloak. I saw fat mammals among that ripe green. I picked flowers that I had seen in books, tall-stemmed blooms in subtle colours as if seen through thin smoke. I could not breathe for the smell of the trees. The sky was rich with clouds.

I walked, a desert creature, in that fertile land. I felt harsh and dusty.

One day I realized that I no longer dreamed of what I would do when I was whole again. My will burned to reach that point, and then suddenly was nothing. I had become nothing more than my desire to fly. I had adjusted, somehow. I had evolved in that unfamiliar region, plodding my stolid way to where the scientists and Remakers of the world congregated. The means had become the end. If I regained my wings, I would become someone new, without the desire that defined me.

I saw in that spring damp as I walked endlessly north that I was not looking for fulfilment but for dissolution. I would pass my body on to a newborn, and rest.

I had been a harder creature when I first stepped onto those hills and plains. I left Myrshock, where my ship had landed, without spending even one night there. It is an ugly port town containing enough of my kind that I felt oppressed.

I hurried through the city seeking nothing but supplies and assurance that I was right to go to New Crobuzon. I bought cold cream for my raw and seeping back, found a doctor honest enough to admit that I would find no one who could help me in Myrshock. I gave my whip to a merchant who let me ride his cart for fifty miles into the dales. He would not accept my gold, only my weapon.

I was eager to leave the sea behind me. The sea was an interlude. Four days on a sluggish, oily paddleship crawling across the Meagre Sea, when I had stayed below, knowing only by the lurches and the wet sounds that we were sailing. I could not walk the deck. I would be more confined deckbound under that huge ocean sky than at any time in those stifling days in my stinking cabin. I huddled away from the seagulls and the ospreys and the albatrosses. I stayed close to the brine, in my dirty wooden bolt-hole, behind the privy.

And before the waters, when I was still burning and raging, when my scars were still wet with blood, was Shankell, the cactus city. The many-named town. Sun-jewel. Oasis. Borridor. Salthole. The Corkscrew Citadel. The Solarium. Shankell, where I fought and fought in the fleshpits and the hookwire cages, tearing skin and being torn, winning far more than I lost, rampaging like a fighting cockerel at night and hoarding pennies by day. Until the day I fought the barbarian prince who wanted to make a helmet of my garuda skull and I won, impossibly, even as I shed blood in frightening gouts. Holding my intestines in with one hand, I clawed his throat out with the other. I won his gold and his followers, whom I freed. I paid myself to health, bought passage on a merchant ship.

I set out across the continent to become whole.

The desert came with me.

PART THREE

Metamorphoses

CHAPTER EIGHTEEN

The spring winds were becoming warmer. The soiled air over New Crobuzon was charged. The city meteoromancers in the Tar Wedge cloudtower copied figures from spinning dials and tore graphs from frantically scribbling atmospheric gauges. They pursed their lips and shook their heads.

They murmured to each other about the prodigiously hot, wet summer that was on the way. They banged the enormous tubes of the aeromorphic engine that rose vertically the height of the hollow tower like giant organ pipes, or the barrels of guns demanding a duel between earth and sky.

"Bloody useless bloody thing," they muttered in disgust. Half-hearted attempts were made to start the engines in the cellars, but they had not moved in one hundred and fifty years, and no one alive was capable of fixing them. New Crobuzon was stuck with the weather dictated by gods or nature or chance.

In the Canker Wedge zoo, animals shifted uneasily in the changing weather. It was the dying days of the rutting season, and the restless twitching of lustful, segregated bodies had subsided some. The keepers were as relieved as their charges. The sultry pall of variegated musk that had wafted through the cages had made for aggressive, unpredictable behaviour.

Now, as light stayed longer every day, the bears and hyaenas and bony hippos, the lonely alopex and the apes, lay still—tensely, it seemed—for hours, watching the passers-by from their scrubbed-brick cells and their muddy trenches. They were waiting. For the southern rains that would never reach New Crobuzon, but were encoded in their bones, perhaps. And when the rains had not come, they might settle down and wait for the dry season that, similarly, did not afflict their new home. It must be a strange, anxious existence, the keepers mused over the roars of tired, disoriented beasts.

The nights had lost nearly two hours since winter, but they

seemed to have squeezed even more essence into the shorter time. They seemed particularly intense, as more and more illicit activity strove to fit the hours from sundown to dawn. Every night the enormous old warehouse half a mile south of the zoo attracted streams of men and women. The occasional leonine roar might breach the thumping and the constant blare of the crotchety, wakeful city entering the old building, sounding above the throng. It would be ignored.

The bricks of the warehouse had once been red and were now black with grime, as smooth and meticulous as if they had been painted by hand. The original sign still read the length of the building: *Cadnebar's Soaps and Tallow*. Cadnebar's had gone bust in the slump of '57. The enormous machinery for melting and refining fat had been taken and sold as scrap. After two or three years of quiet mouldering, Cadnebar's had been reborn as the glad' circus.

Like mayors before him, Rudgutter liked to compare the civilization and splendour of the City-State Republic of New Crobuzon with the barbarian muck in which inhabitants of other lands were forced to crawl. Think of the other Rohagi countries, Rudgutter demanded in speeches and editorials. This was not Tesh, nor Troglodopolis, Vadaunk or High Cromlech. This was not a city ruled by witches; this was not a chthonic burrow; the seasons' changes did not bring an onslaught of superstitious repression; New Crobuzon did not process its citizenry through zombie factories; its Parliament was not like Maru'ahm's, a casino where laws were stakes in games of roulette.

And this was not, emphasized Rudgutter, Shankell, where people fought like animals for sport.

Except, of course, at Cadnebar's.

Illegal it might have been, but no one remembered any militia raids of the establishment. Many sponsors of the top stables were Parliamentarians, industrialists and bankers, whose intercession doubtless kept official interest at a minimum. There were other fight-halls, of course, that doubled as cockfight and ratfight pits, where bear- or badger-baiting might go on at one end, snake-wrestling at another, with glad'-fighting in the middle. But Cadnebar's was legendary.

Every night, the evening's entertainments would begin with an open slot, a comedy show for the regulars. Scores of young, stupid, thickset farmboys, the toughest lads in their villages, who had travelled for days from the Grain Spiral or the Mendican Hills to make their names in the city, would flex their prodigious muscles at the selectors. Two or three would be chosen and pushed into the main arena before the howling crowd. They would confidently heft the machetes they had been given. Then the arena's hatch would be opened and they would pale as they faced an enormous Remade gladiator or impassive cactacae warrior. The resulting carnage was short and bloody and played for laughs by the professionals.

The sport at Cadnebar's was driven by fashion. In the dying days of that spring, the taste was for matches between teams of two Remade and three khepri guard-sisters. The khepri units were enticed out of Kinken and Creekside with massive prizes. They had practised together for years, units of three religious warriors trained to emulate the khepri guard gods, the Tough Sisters. Like the Tough Sisters, one would fight with hooknet and spear, one with crossbow and flintlock, and one with the khepri weapon that humans had christened the stingbox.

As summer began to well up under the skin of spring, the bets got bigger and bigger. Miles away in Dog Fenn, Benjamin Flex reflected morosely on the fact that *Cadnebar's Wax*, the illegal organ of the fight trade, had a circulation five times that of *Runagate Rampant*.

The Eyespy Killer left another mutilated victim in the sewers. It was discovered by mudlarks. It was hanging like someone exhausted out of an outflow pipe into the Tar.

In the outskirts of Nigh Sump a woman died of massive puncture wounds to both sides of her neck, as if she had been caught between the blades of huge serrated scissors. When her neighbours found her, her body was scattered with documents which proved her to be a colonel-informer in the militia. The word went out. Jack Half-a-Prayer had struck. In the gutters and the slums, his victim was not mourned.

Lin and Isaac snatched furtive nights together when they could. Isaac could tell that all was not well with her. Once, he sat her down and demanded that she tell him what was troubling her, why she had not entered the Shintacost Prize this year (something which had given her usual bitchery about the standard of the shortlist an added bitterness), what she was working on, and where. There was no sign of any artistic debris at all in any of her rooms.

Lin had stroked his arm, clearly grateful for his concern. But she would tell him nothing. She said she was working on a piece of which she was tentatively very proud. She had found a space that she could not and did not want to talk about, in which she was producing a large piece that he mustn't ask her about. It was not as if she had disappeared from the world. Once a fortnight, perhaps, she was back in one of the Salacus Fields bars, laughing with her friends, if with a little less vigour than she had two months ago.

She teased Isaac about his anger at Lucky Gazid, who had vanished, with suspiciously good timing. Isaac had told Lin about his inadvertent sampling of dreamshit, and had raged around looking to punish Gazid. Isaac had described the extraordinary grub which seemed to thrive on the drug. Lin had not seen the creature, had not been back to Brock Marsh since that forlorn day the previous month, but even allowing for a degree of exaggeration on Isaac's part, the creature sounded extraordinary.

Lin thought fondly of Isaac as she adeptly changed the subject. She asked him what nourishment he thought the caterpillar might gain from its peculiar food, and sat back as his face expanded with fascination and he would tell her enthusiastically that he did not know, but that these were a few of his ideas. She would ask him to try to explain to her about crisis energy, and whether he thought it would help Yagharek to fly, and he would talk animatedly, drawing her diagrams on slips of paper.

It was easy to work on him. Lin felt, sometimes, that Isaac knew he was being manipulated, that he felt guilty about the ease with which his worries for her were transformed. She sensed gratitude in his lurching changes of subject, along with contrition. He knew it was his role to be worried for her, given her melancholy, and he was, he truly was, but it was an effort, a duty, when most of his mind was crammed with crisis and grub food. She gave him permission not to worry, and he accepted it with thanks.

Lin wanted to displace Isaac's concerns for her, for a time. She could not afford for him to be curious. The more he knew, the more she was in danger. She did not know what powers her employer might possess: she doubted he was capable of telepathy, but she was risking nothing. She wanted to finish her piece, to take the money and to get away from Bonetown.

*   *   *

Every day that she saw Mr. Motley, he pulled her—unwilling as she was—into his city. He talked idly of turf wars in Griss Twist and Badside, dropped hints of gangland massacres in the heart of The Crow. Ma Francine was extending her reach. She had taken possession of a huge part of the shazbah market west of The Crow, which Mr. Motley was prepared for. But now she was creeping into the east. Lin chewed and spat and moulded and tried not to hear the details, the nicknames of dead couriers, the safe-house addresses. Mr. Motley was implicating her. It must be deliberate.

The statue grew thighs and another leg, the beginnings of a waist (insofar as Mr. Motley had anything so identifiable). The colours were not naturalistic, but they were evocative and compelling, hypnotic. It was an astonishing piece, as befitted its subject.

Despite her attempts to insulate her mind, Mr. Motley's blithe chat crept in, past her defences. She found herself musing on it. Horrified, she would pull her mind away, but it was an unsustainable attempt. Eventually she would find herself idly wondering who *was* more likely to win control of the very-tea clearing house in Chimer's End. She became numb. It was another defence. She let her mind pick its way dully over the dangerous information. She tried to remain studiously ignorant of its import.

Lin found herself thinking more and more of Ma Francine. Mr. Motley discussed her in carefree tones, but she came up again and again in his monologues, and Lin realized that he was a little concerned.

To her surprise, Lin began to root for Ma Francine.

She was not sure how it started. The first she was aware of it was when Mr. Motley had been talking with mock humour about a disastrous attack on two couriers the previous night, during which a huge quantity of some undisclosed substance, some raw material for the manufacture of something, had been snatched by khepri raiders from Ma Francine's gang. Lin had realized that she was thinking a little mental cheer. She was astonished, her glandwork stopping for a moment as she thought through her own feelings.

She wanted Ma Francine to win.

There was no logic to it. As soon as she applied any rigorous thought to the situation she had no opinion at all. Intellectually speaking, the triumph of one drug-dealer and hoodlum over another was of no interest to her. But emotionally, she was beginning to see the unseen Ma Francine as her champion. She found herself booing silently when she heard Mr. Motley's slyly smug assurance that he had a plan that would radically alter the shape of the marketplace.

What's this? she thought wryly. *After all these years, the stirrings of khepri consciousness?*

She mocked herself, but there was some truth in the ironic thought. *Maybe it would be the same for anyone who was opposing Motley,* she thought. Lin was so fearful of reflecting on her relationship with Mr. Motley, so nervous of being anything more than an employee, that it had taken her a long time to realize that she hated him. *My enemy's enemy . . .* she thought. But there was more to it than that. Lin realized that she felt solidarity with Ma Francine because she was khepri. But—and maybe this was at the heart of her feelings—Francine was not *good* khepri.

These thoughts pricked at Lin, discomforted her. For the first time in many years, they made her think of her relationship with the khepri community in other than a straightforward, righteous, confrontational way. And that made her think of her childhood.

After each day with Mr. Motley ended, Lin took to visiting Kinken. She would leave him and catch a cab from the edge of the Ribs. Across Danechi's or Barguest Bridge, past the restaurants and offices and houses of Spit Hearth.

Sometimes she would stop at Spit Bazaar and take her time wandering through its subdued lights. She felt the linen dresses and coats hanging from the stalls, ignoring the passers-by staring rudely, wondering at the khepri shopping for human clothes. Lin would meander through the bazaar until she came to Sheck, dense and chaotic with intricate streets and sprawling brick apartment buildings.

This was not a slum. The buildings of Sheck were solid enough, and most kept the rain out. Compared to the mutant sprawl of Dog Fenn, the rotting brick mulch of Badside and Chimer's End, the desperate shacks of Spatters, Sheck was a desirable place. A little crowded, of course, and not without drunkenness and poverty and thievery. But all things considered, there were many worse places to live. This was where the shopkeepers lived, the lower managers and better-paid factory workers that every day crowded Echomire and Kelltree docks, Gross Coil and Didacai Village, known universally as Smog Bend.

Lin was not made welcome. Sheck bordered Kinken, separated only by a couple of insignificant parks. The khepri were a constant reminder to Sheck that it did not have far to fall. Khepri filled Sheck's streets during the day, making their way to The Crow to shop or take the train from Perdido Street Station. At night, though, it was a brave khepri who would walk streets made dangerous by pugnacious Three Quillers out to "keep their city clean." Lin made sure she was through this zone by sundown. Because just beyond was Kinken, where she was safe.

Safe, but not happy.

Lin walked Kinken's streets with a kind of nauseated excitement. For many years, her journeys to the area had been brief excursions to pick up colourberries and paste, perhaps the occasional khepri delicacy. Now her visits were jars to memories she had thought banished.

Houses oozed the white mucus of home-grubs. Some were completely coated in the thick stuff: it spread across roofs, linking different buildings into a lumpy, congealed totality. Lin could see in through windows and doors. The walls and floors that had been provided by human architects had been broken away in places, and the massive home-grubs allowed to burrow their blind way through the shell, oozing their phlegm-cement from their abdomens, their stubby little legs skittering as they ate their way through the ruined interiors of the buildings.

Occasionally Lin would see a live specimen taken from the farms by the river, going about its refitting of a building into the intricate twisting organic passageways preferred by most khepri tenants. The big, stupid beetles, larger than rhinos, responded to the tweaks and tugs of their keepers, blundering this way and that through the houses, recasting rooms in a quick-drying coating that softened edges and connected chambers, buildings and streets with what looked from the inside like giant worm-tracks.

Sometimes Lin would sit in one of Kinken's tiny parks. She would be still among the slowly blossoming trees and watch her kind, all around her. She would stare high above the park, at the backs and sides of tall buildings. One time, she saw a young human girl lean out from a window high above, that was stuck almost at random at the top of a stained concrete wall at the back of the building. Lin saw the girl watching her khepri neighbours placidly, as her family's washing fluttered and snapped in the brisk wind from a pole jutting beside her. *A strange way of growing up,* thought Lin, imagining the child surrounded by silent, insect-headed creatures, as strange as if Lin had been brought up among vodyanoi . . . but that thought led her uncomfortably in the direction of her own childhood.

Of course, her journey to these despised streets was a walk back through the city of her memory. She knew that. She was steeling herself to think back.

Kinken had been Lin's first refuge. In this strange time of isolation, when she cheered the efforts of khepri crime-queens and walked as an outcast in all the quadrants of the city—except, perhaps, Salacus Fields, where outcasts ruled—she realized that her feelings for Kinken were more ambivalent than she had so far allowed.

There had been khepri in New Crobuzon for nearly seven hundred years, since the *Fervent Mantis* crossed the Swollen Ocean and reached Bered Kai Nev, the eastern continent, the khepri home. A few merchants and travellers had returned on a one-way mission of edification. For centuries, the stock of this tiny group sustained itself in the city, became natives. There had been no separate neighbourhoods, no home-grubs, no ghettos. There were not enough khepri. Not until the Tragic Crossing.

It was a hundred years since the first refugee ships had crawled, barely afloat, into Iron Bay. Their enormous clockwork motors were rusted and broken, their sails ragged. They were charnel ships, packed with Bered Kai Nev khepri who were only just alive. Contagion was so merciless that ancient taboos against waterburial had been overthrown. So there were few corpses on board, but there were thousands of dying. The ships were like crowded antechambers to morgues.

The nature of the tragedy was a mystery to the New Crobuzon authorities, who had no consuls and little contact with any of the countries of Bered Kai Nev. The refugees would not speak of it, or if they did they were elliptical, or if they were graphic and explicit the language barrier blocked understanding. All that the humans knew was that something terrible had happened to the khepri of the eastern continent, some horrendous vortex that had sucked up millions, leaving only a tiny handful able to flee. The khepri had christened this nebulous apocalypse the Ravening.

There were twenty-five years between the arrival of the first ships and the last. Some slow, motorless vessels were said to be crewed entirely by khepri born at sea, all the original refugees having died during the interminable crossing. Their daughters did not know what it was they fled, only that their dying broodmas had all bade them go *west*, and never to turn the wheel. Stories of the khepri Mercy Ships—named for what they begged—reached New Crobuzon from other countries on the eastern coast of the Rohagi continent, from Gnurr Kett and the Jheshull Islands, from as far south as the Shards. The khepri diaspora had been chaotic and diverse and panicked.

In some lands the refugees were butchered in terrible pogroms. In others, like New Crobuzon, they were welcomed with unease, but not with official violence. They had settled, become workers and tax-payers and criminals, and found themselves, by an organic pressure just too gentle to be obvious, living in ghettos; preyed on, sometimes, by bigots and thugs.

Lin had not grown up in Kinken. She was born in the younger, poorer khepri ghetto of Creekside, a grubby stain in the northwest of the city. It was nearly impossible to understand the true history of Kinken and Creekside, because of the systematic mental erasure that the settlers had undertaken. The trauma of the Ravening was such that the first generation of refugees had deliberately forgotten ten thousand years of khepri history, announcing their arrival at New Crobuzon to be the beginning of a new cycle of years, the City Cycle. When the next generation had demanded their story from their broodmas, many had refused and many could not remember. Khepri history was obscured by the massive shadow of genocide.

So it was hard for Lin to penetrate the secrets of those first twenty years of the City Cycle. Kinken and Creekside were presented as fait accompli to her, and to her broodma, and the generation before that, and the generation before that.

Creekside had no Plaza of Statues. It had been a tumbledown slum for humans a hundred years ago, a rookery of found architecture, and the khepri home-grubs had done little more than encase the ruined houses with cement, petrifying them forever on the point of collapse. The denizens of Creekside were not artists or fruitbar owners, moiety chiefs or hive elders or shopkeepers. They were disreputable and hungry. They worked in the factories and in the sewers, sold themselves to whomever would buy. Their sisters in Kinken despised them.

In Creekside's decrepit streets, strange and dangerous ideas blossomed. Small groups of radicals met in hidden halls. Messianic cults promised deliverance to the chosen.

Many of the original refugees had turned their backs on the gods of Bered Kai Nev, angry that they had not protected their disciples from the Ravening. But subsequent generations, not knowing the nature of the tragedy, offered their worship again. Over a hundred years, pantheon temples had been consecrated in old workshops and deserted dancehalls. But many Creeksiders, in their confusion and hunger, turned to dissident gods.

All the usual temples could be found in Creekside's confines. Awesome Broodma was worshipped, and the Artspitter. Kindly Nurse presided over the shabby hospital, and the Tough Sisters defended the faithful. But in rude shacks that mouldered by the industrial canals, and in front rooms blocked by dark windows, prayers were raised to stranger gods. Priestesses dedicated themselves to the service of the Elyctric Devil or the Air Harvester. Furtive groups clambered to their roofs and sang hymns to the Wingsister, praying for flight. And some lonely, desperate souls—like Lin's broodma—pledged their fealty to Insect Aspect.

Properly transliterated from Khepri into the New Crobuzon script, the chymico-audio-visual composite of description, devotion and awe that was the name of the god was rendered Insect/Aspect/(male)/(singleminded). But the few humans that knew of him called him Insect Aspect, and that was how Lin had signed him to Isaac when she told him the story of her upbringing.

Since the age of six, when she had torn the chrysalis from what had been her baby headlarva and was suddenly a headscarab, when she had burst into consciousness with language and thought, her mother had taught her that she was fallen. The gloomy doctrine of Insect Aspect was that khepri women were cursed. Some vile flaw on the part of the first woman had consigned her daughters to lives encumbered with ridiculous, slow, floundering bipedal bodies and minds that teemed with the useless byways and intricacies of consciousness. Woman had lost the insectile purity of God and male.

Lin's broodma (who scorned a name as a decadent affectation) taught Lin and her broodsister that Insect Aspect was the lord of all creation, the all-powerful force that knew only hunger and thirst and rutting and satisfaction. He had shat out the universe after eating the void, in a mindless act of cosmic creation the purer and more brilliant for being devoid of motive or awareness. Lin and her broodsister were taught to worship Him with a terrified fervour, and to despise their self-awareness and their soft, chitinless bodies.

They were also taught to worship and serve their mindless brothers.

Thinking back now to that time, Lin no longer shuddered with revulsion. Sitting in those secluded Kinken parks, Lin carefully watched her past unfold in her mind, little by little, in a gradual act of reminiscence that took courage to pursue. She remembered how she had slowly come to realize that her life was not usual. On her rare shopping expeditions she would see with horror the casual contempt with which her khepri sisters treated male khepri, kicking and crushing the mindless two-foot insects. She remembered her tentative conversations with the other children, who taught her how her neighbours lived; her fear of using the language she knew instinctively, the language she carried in her blood, but that her broodma had taught her to loathe.

Lin remembered coming home to a house that swarmed with male khepri, that stank of rotting vegetables and fruit, littered as it was with organic rubbish for males to gorge on. She remembered being commanded to wash her innumerable brothers' glistening carapaces, to pile up their dung before the household altar, to let them scuttle over her and explore her body as their dumb curiosity directed them. She remembered the night-time discussions with her broodsister, carried out in the tiny chymical wafts and gently rattling hisses that were khepri-whispers. As a result of these theological debates, her broodsister had turned the other way from her, had burrowed so deeply into her Insect Aspect faith that she outshone their mother in zealotry.

It had taken Lin until she was fifteen to challenge her broodma openly. She did so in terms that she now saw were naive and confused. Lin denounced her mother as a heretic, cursing her in the name of the mainstream pantheon. She fled the lunatic self-loathing of Insect Aspect worship, and the narrow streets of Creekside. She had run away to Kinken.

That was why, she reflected, for all her later disenchantment—her contempt, in fact, her hatred—there was a part of her that would always remember Kinken as a sanctuary. Now the smugness of the insular community nauseated her, but at the time of her escape she had been drunk on it. She had revelled in the arrogant denunciation of Creekside, had prayed to Awesome Broodma with a vehement delight. She had baptized herself with a khepri name and—which was vital in New Crobuzon—a human one. She had discovered that in Kinken, unlike Creekside, the hive and moiety system made for complex and useful nets of social connectivity. Her mother had never mentioned her birth or upbringing, so Lin had copied the allegiance of her first friend in Kinken, and told anyone who asked that she was Redwing Hive, Catskull Moiety.

Her friend introduced her to pleasuresex, taught her to delight in the sensuous body below her neck. This was the most difficult, the most extraordinary transition. Her body had been a source of shame and disgust; to engage in activities with no purpose at all except to revel in their sheer physicality had first nauseated, then terrified, and finally liberated her. Until then she had been subjected only to headsex at her mother's behest, sitting still and uncomfortable while a male scrabbled and coupled excitedly with her headscarab, in mercifully unsuccessful attempts at procreation.

With time, Lin's hatred of her broodma slowly cooled, becoming first contempt, then pity. Her disgust at the squalor of Creekside was joined with some kind of understanding. Then, her five-year love-affair with Kinken drew to an end. It started when she stood in the Plaza of Statues, and realized that they were mawkish and badly executed, embodying a culture that was blind to itself. She began to see Kinken as implicated in the subjugation of Creekside and the never-mentioned Kinken poor, saw a "community" at best callous and uncaring, at worst deliberately keeping Creekside down to maintain its superiority.

With its priestesses and its orgies and its cottage industries, its secret reliance on the wider economy of New Crobuzon—the vastness of which was usually depicted airily as a kind of adjunct to Kinken—Lin realized that she was living in an unsustainable realm. It combined sanctimony, decadence, insecurity and snobbery in a weird, neurotic brew. It was parasitic.

Lin realized, to her revolted anger, that Kinken was more dishonest than Creekside. But this realization brought with it no nostalgia for her miserable childhood. She would not return to Creekside. And if, now, she was turning her back on Kinken as once she had turned it on Insect Aspect, there was nowhere to go but out.

So Lin taught herself signing, and left.

Lin was never so foolish as to think she could stop being defined by being khepri, as far as the city was concerned. Nor did she want to. But for herself, she stopped trying to be khepri, as she had once stopped trying to be insect. That was why she was bewildered by her feelings about Ma Francine. It was not only that Ma Francine was opposing to Mr. Motley, Lin realized. There was something about a khepri doing that, effortlessly stealing territory from this vile man, that stirred Lin.

Lin could not, even to herself, pretend to understand. She would sit, for a long time, in the shadow of banyans or oaks or pear trees, in the Kinken she had despised for years, surrounded by sisters to whom she was an outsider. She did not want to return to the "khepri way" any more than to the Insect Aspect. She did not understand the strength she drew from Kinken.

CHAPTER NINETEEN

The construct that had swept David's and Lublamai's floor for years seemed finally to be giving up the ghost. It wheezed and spun as it scrubbed. It became fixated with arbitrary patches of floor, polished them as if they were jewels. Some mornings it took nearly an hour to warm up. It was becoming caught in programme loops, causing it to endlessly repeat tiny pieces of behaviour.

Isaac learnt to ignore its repetitive, neurotic whines. He worked with both hands at once. With his left, he scribbled down his notions in diagrammatic form. With his right he fed equations into the innards of his little calculating engine through its stiff keys, slotted punctured cards into its programme slot, fumbling them in and out at speed. He solved the same problems with different programmes, comparing answers, typing out the sheets of numbers.

The innumerable books on flight that had filled Isaac's bookshelves had been replaced, with Teafortwo's help, by an equally large number of tomes on unified field theory, and on the arcane sub-field of crisis mathematics.

After only two weeks of research, something extraordinary happened in Isaac's mind. The reconceptualization came to him so simply that he did not at first realize the scale of his insight. It seemed a thoughtful moment like many others, in the course of a whole internal scientific dialogue. A sense of genius did not descend on Isaac Dan der Grimnebulin in a cold shock of brilliant light. Instead, as he gnawed the top of a pencil one day, there was a moment of vaguely verbalized thought along the lines of *or wait a minute maybe you could do it like this* . . .

It took an hour and a half for Isaac to realize that what he had thought might be a useful mental model was vastly more exciting. He set out in a systematic attempt to prove himself wrong. He constructed scenario after mathematical scenario with which he tried to rubbish his tentatively scrawled sets of equations. His attempts at destruction failed. His equations held firm.

It took Isaac two days before he began to believe that he had solved a fundamental problem of crisis theory. He enjoyed moments of euphoria, many more of cautious nervousness. He pored over his textbooks at a crushingly slow pace, searching to make sure he had not ignored some obvious error, had not replicated some long-disproved theorem.

Still, his equations held. In terror of hubris, Isaac sought any alternative than to believe what was looking more and more like the truth: that he had solved the problem of mathematic representation, quantification, of crisis energy.

He knew that he should immediately converse with colleagues, publish his findings as "work in progress" in *The Review of Philosophical Physics and Thaumaturgy*, or the *Unified Field*. But he was so intimidated by what he had discovered that he avoided that route. He wanted to be sure, he told himself. He had to take a few more days, a few more weeks, maybe a month or two . . . then he would publish. He did not tell Lublamai or David, or Lin, which was more extraordinary. Isaac was a garrulous man, prone to spouting any old tosh, scientific, social or obscene, which came to his mind. His secretiveness was profoundly out of character. He knew himself well enough to recognize this, and to realize what it meant: he was deeply disturbed, and deeply, deeply excited by what he had found.

Isaac thought back on the process of discovery, of formulation. He realized that his advances, his incredible leaps of theory in the last month, which eclipsed his previous five years' work, were all in response to immediate, practical concerns. He had reached an impasse in his studies of crisis theory until Yagharek had commissioned him. Isaac did not know why it was so, but he realized that it was with applications in mind that his most abstract theories were advancing. Accordingly, he decided not to immerse himself totally in abstruse theory. He would continue to focus on the problem of Yagharek's flight.

He would not let himself think about the ramifications of his research, not at this stage. Everything he uncovered, every advance, every idea he had, he would quietly plough back into his applied studies. He tried to see everything as a means to get Yagharek back in the air. It was difficult—perverse, even—constantly trying to contain and circumscribe his work. He saw the situation as one of working behind his own back, or more exactly, as trying to do research out of the corner of his eye. Yet, incredible as it seemed, with the discipline that was forced on him, Isaac progressed theoretically at a rate he could never have dreamed of six months before.

It was an extraordinary, circuitous route to scientific revolution, he thought sometimes, chiding himself quickly for his direct gaze at the theory. *Get back to work,* he would tell himself sternly. *There's a garuda to get airborne.* But he could not stop his heart from thumping with excitement, the occasional almost hysterical grin from racing across his face. Some days he sought Lin out and, if she was not working at her secret piece in her secret location, he would try to seduce her in her flat with a tender, excited fervour that delighted her, for all that she was obviously tired. At other times he spent days in only his own company, immersing himself in science.

Isaac applied his extraordinary insights and began tentatively to design a machine to solve Yagharek's problem. The same drawing began to appear more and more in his work. At first it was a doodle, a few loosely connecting lines covered in arrows and question marks. Within days it was appearing more solid. Its lines were drawn in ruled ink. Its curves were measured and careful. It was on its way to becoming a blueprint.

Yagharek sometimes came back to Isaac's laboratory, always when the two of them were alone. Isaac would hear the door creak open at night, turn to see the impassive, dignified garuda still steeped in visible misery.

Isaac found that trying to explain his work to Yagharek helped him. Not the big theoretical stuff, of course, but the applied science which furthered the half-hidden theory. Isaac spent days with a thousand ideas and potential projects swilling violently in his head, and to pare that down, to explain in non-technical language the various techniques he thought might enable him to tap crisis energy forced him to evaluate his trajectories, discard some, focus on others.

He began to rely on Yagharek's interest. If too many days passed without the garuda appearing, Isaac became distracted. He spent those hours watching the enormous caterpillar.

The creature had gorged itself on dreamshit for nearly a fortnight, growing and growing. When it had reached three feet in length, Isaac had nervously stopped feeding it. Its cage was getting much too small. That would have to be the full extent of its size. It had spent the next day or two wandering around hopefully in its little space, waving its nose in the air. Since then it seemed to have resigned itself to the fact that it would get no more food. Its original desperate hunger had subsided.

It was not moving very much, just shifting around now and then, undulating once or twice the width of the cage, stretching as if yawning. For the most part it just sat and pulsed slightly in and out, with breath or heartbeat or what, Isaac did not know. It looked healthy enough. It looked as if it was waiting.

Sometimes, as he had dropped the gobs of dreamshit into the caterpillar's eager mandibles, Isaac had found himself reflecting on his own experience with the drug with a faint, querulous longing. This was not the delusion of nostalgia. Isaac vividly remembered the sense of being awash in filth; of being sullied at the most profound level; the nauseating, disorientating sickness; the panicked confusion of losing himself in a welter of emotion, and losing the confusion, and mistaking it for another mind's invading fears . . . And yet, despite the vehemence of those recollections, he found himself eyeing his caterpillar's breakfasts with a speculative air—perhaps even a hungry one.

Isaac was very disturbed by these feelings. He had always been unashamedly cowardly when it came to drugs. As a student, there had been plenty of loose, smelly fogweed cigarillos, of course, and the inane giggles that went with that. But Isaac had never had the stomach for anything stronger. These inchoate rumblings of a new appetite did nothing to allay his fears. He did not know how addictive dreamshit was, if at all, but he sternly refused to give in to those faint stirrings of curiosity.

The dreamshit was for his caterpillar, and for it alone.

Isaac channelled his curiosity from sensual into intellectual currents. He knew only two chymists personally, both unutterable prudes with whom he would no more raise the question of illegal drugs than he would dance naked down the middle of Tervisadd Way. Instead, he raised the subject of dreamshit in the louche taverns of Salacus Fields. Several of his acquaintances turned out to have sampled the drug, and a few were regular users.

Dreamshit did not seem to differ in effect between the races. No one knew where the drug came from, but all who admitted to taking it sang paeans of praise to its extraordinary effects. The only thing they all agreed on was that dreamshit was expensive, and getting more so. Not that this put them off their habits. The artists in particular spoke in quasi-mystical terms of communing with other minds. Isaac scoffed at this, claiming (without acknowledging his own limited experience) that the drug was no more than a powerful oneirogen, that stimulated the dream-centres of the brain as very-tea stimulated the visual and olfactory cortexes.

He did not believe it himself. He was not surprised at the vehement opposition to his theory.

"I don't know how, 'Zaac," Thighs Growing had hissed at him reverentially, "but it lets you *share dreams* . . ." At this, the other users crammed into a little booth in The Clock and Cockerel had nodded in time, comically. Isaac affected a sceptical face, to maintain his role of killjoy. Actually, of course, he agreed. He intended to find out more about the extraordinary substance—Lemuel Pigeon would be the person to ask, or Lucky Gazid, if he ever reappeared—but the pace of his work in crisis theory overtook him. His attitude to the dreamshit he had shoved into the grub's cage remained one of curiosity, nervousness and ignorance.

Isaac was staring uneasily at the vast creature one warm day in late Melluary. It was, he decided, more than prodigious. It was more than a very big caterpillar. It was definitely a monster. He resented it for being so damn interesting. Otherwise he could have just forgotten about it.

The door below him was pushed open, and Yagharek appeared in the shafts of early sun. It was rare, very rare for the garuda to come before nightfall. Isaac started and leapt to his feet, beckoning his client up the stairs.

"Yag, old son! Long time no see! I was drifting. I need you to tether me. Get on up here."

Yagharek mounted the stairs wordlessly.

"How do you know when Lub and David are going to be out, eh?" asked Isaac. "You keep watch, or something creepy, right? Damn, Yag, you've got to stop skulking around like a fucking mugger."

"I would talk to you, Grimnebulin." Yagharek's voice was oddly tentative.

"Fire away, old son." Isaac sat and watched him. He knew by now that Yagharek would not sit.

Yagharek took off his cloak and wing-frame and turned to Isaac with folded arms. Isaac understood this to be as close as Yagharek would ever get to expressing trust, standing with his deformity in full view, making no effort to cover himself. Isaac supposed he should feel flattered.

Yagharek was eyeing him sideways.

"There are people in the night-city where I live, Grimnebulin, from many kinds of lives. It is not all flotsam that hide themselves."

"I never presumed it was . . ." Isaac began, but Yagharek twitched his head impatiently, and Isaac was silent.

"Many nights I spend in silence and alone, but there are other times I talk to those with minds still sharp under a patina of alcohol and loneliness and drugs." Isaac wanted to say, "I've said we could work out a place for you to stay," but he stopped himself. Isaac wanted to see where this was heading. "There is a man, an educated, drunken man. I am not sure he believes me real. He may think me a recurring hallucination." Yagharek breathed deeply. "I spoke to him about your theories, your crisis, and I was excited. And the man said to me . . . the man said to me 'Why not go all the way? Why not use the Torque?' "

There was a very long silence. Isaac shook his head in exasperation and disgust.

"I am here to put the question to you, Grimnebulin," Yagharek continued. "Why do we not use the Torque? You are trying to create a science from scratch, Grimnebulin, but Torquic energy exists, techniques to tap it are known . . . I ask as an ignorant, Grimnebulin. Why do you not use the Torque?"

Isaac sighed very deeply and kneaded his face. Part of him was angry, but mostly he was just anxious, desperate to put a stop to this talk immediately. He turned to the garuda, and held up his hand.

"Yagharek . . ." he began, and at that moment, there was a bang on the door.

"Hello?" a cheerful voice yelled. Yagharek stiffened. Isaac leapt to his feet. The timing was extraordinary.

"Who is it?" yelled Isaac, bounding down the stairs.

A man poked his face round the door. He looked amiable, almost absurdly so.

"Hullo there, squire. I've come about the construct."

Isaac shook his head. He had no idea what the man was talking about. He glanced up behind him, but Yagharek was invisible. He had stepped out of sight away from the edge of the platform. The man in the doorway handed Isaac a card.

NATHANIEL ORRIABEN'S CONSTRUCT REPAIRS AND REPLACEMENTS it said. QUALITY & CARE AT REASONABLE RATES.

"Gent came in yesterday. Name of . . . Serachin?" suggested the man, reading from a sheet. "Told us his cleaning model . . . um . . . EKB4C was playing up. Thought it might have a virus and whatnot. I was due tomorrow, but I've just come back from another job local and I thought I'd chance that someone was in." The man smiled brightly. He stuck his hands in the pockets of his oily coveralls.

"Right," said Isaac. "Um . . . Look. Not the best time . . ."

"Righto! Your decision, obviously. Only . . ." The man looked around him before he went on, as if he was about to share a secret. Reassured that no one would hear him who should not, he went on, confidentially. "Thing is, squire, I may not be able to do the appointment tomorrow as originally planned . . ." The face he offered was cod-apology of the most exaggerated kind. "I can happily do my thing over in the corner, won't make a sound. Take me about an hour if I can do it here, otherwise it's a job for the repair shop. I'll know which in five minutes. Otherwise I shan't be able to do it for a week, I think."

"Oh, arse. Right . . . Look, I'm in a meeting upstairs, and it's absolutely *vital* that you don't interrupt us. Seriously. Is that going to be all right?"

"Oh, absolutely. I'm just going to take the screwdriver to the old cleaner and then give you a little yell when I know what the score is, all right?"

"Right. So I can just leave you to it?"

"Perfecto." The man was already heading towards the cleaning construct, carrying a toolcase. Lublamai had turned the cleaner on that morning, and punched in instructions for it to wash his study area, but it had been a forlorn hope. The construct had puttered in circles for twenty minutes, then stopped, leaning against the wall. It was still there, three hours later, emitting unhappy little clicks, its three attachment-limbs spasming.

The repairman strode over to the thing, muttering and clucking like a concerned parent. He felt the construct's limbs, flipped a fob-watch out of his pocket and timed the twitching. He scribbled something in a little notebook. He swivelled the cleaning construct to face him, and gazed into one of its glass irises. He moved his pencil slowly from one side to another, watching the tracking of the sensory engine.

Isaac was half watching the repairman, but his attention kept flickering back upstairs to where Yagharek waited. *This business with the Torque,* Isaac thought nervously. *It can't wait.*

"So you all right there?" Isaac shouted nervously at the repairman.

The man was opening his case and taking out a large screwdriver. He looked up at Isaac.

"No problem, guv," he said, and waved his screwdriver cheerfully. He looked back at the construct and shut it off at the switch behind the neck. Its anguished creaks died in a grateful whisper. He began to unscrew the panel behind the thing's "head," a roughcast chunk of grey metal at the top of its cylindrical body.

"Right then," said Isaac, and jogged back up the stairs.

Yagharek was standing by Isaac's desk, well out of sight of the floor below. He looked up as Isaac returned.

"It's nothing," said Isaac quietly. "Someone to fix our construct, which has gone belly-up. I'm just wondering if we're going to be heard . . ."

Yagharek opened his mouth to reply, and a thin, discordant whistling sounded up from the floor below. Yagharek's mouth hung open for a moment, stupidly.

"Looks like we needn't have worried," Isaac said, and grinned. *He's doing that deliberately!* he thought. *So's to let me know he's not listening. Polite of him.* Isaac inclined his head in unseen thanks to the repairman.

Then his mind returned to the business in hand, to Yagharek's tentative suggestion, and his smile vanished. He sat heavily on his bed, ran his hands through his thick hair and stared up at Yagharek.

"You never sit, Yag, do you?" he said quietly. "Now why's that?"

He drummed his fingers against the side of his head and thought. Eventually he spoke.

"Yag, old son . . . You've already impressed me as to your . . . amazing library, right? I want to throw two names out there, see what they mean to you. What do you know about Suroch, or the Cacotopic Stain?"

There was a long silence. Yagharek was looking slightly up, through the window.

"The Cacotopic Stain I know, of course. That is always what one hears when the Torque is discussed. Perhaps it is a bogeyman." Isaac could not distinguish moods in Yagharek's voice, but his words were defensive. "Perhaps we should overcome our fear. And Suroch . . . I have read your histories, Grimnebulin. War is always . . . a vile time . . ."

As Yagharek spoke, Isaac stood and walked to his chaotic bookshelves, flicking through the stacked volumes. He returned with a slim, hardbacked folio book. He opened it in front of Yagharek.

"This," he said heavily, "is a collection of heliotypes taken nearly a hundred years ago. It was these helios, in large part, that put a stop to Torque experiments in New Crobuzon."

Yagharek reached out slowly and turned the pages. He did not speak.

"This was supposed to be a secret research mission, to see the effects of the war a hundred years on," continued Isaac. "Little group of militia, couple of scientists and a heliotypist went up-coast in a spy-dirigible, took some prints from the air. Then some of them were lowered into the remains of Suroch to take some up-close shots.

"Sacramundi, the heliotypist, was so . . . appalled . . . he printed five hundred copies of his report at his own expense. Distributed it to bookshops gratis. Bypassed the mayor and Parliament, laid it out in front of the people . . . Mayor Turgisadi was screaming mad, but there was nothing he could do.

"There was demonstrations, then the Sacramundi Riots of '89. Pretty much forgotten now, but it damn-near brought the government down. A couple of the big concerns putting money into the Torque programme—Penton's, that still owns the Arrowhead Mines, that was the biggest—anyway, they got scared and pulled out, and the thing collapsed.

"This, Yag my son," Isaac indicated the book, "is why we ain't using Torque."

Yagharek slowly turned the pages. Sepia images of ruin passed before them.

"Ah . . ." Isaac brought his finger down on a drab panorama of what looked like crushed glass and charcoal. The heliotype was taken from very low in the air. A few of the larger shards that littered the enormous, perfectly circular plain were visible, suggesting that the desiccated debris was the remains of once-extraordinary twisted objects.

"Now this is what's left of the heart of the city. That's where they dropped the colourbomb in 1545. That's what they said put an end to the Pirate Wars, but to be honest with you, Yag, they'd been over for a year before that, since New Crobuzon bombarded Suroch with Torque bombs. See, they dropped the colourbombs twelve months later to try to *hide what they'd done* . . . only one went into the sea and two didn't work, so with only one left, they only cleared the central square mile or so of Suroch. These bits you can see . . ." He indicated low rubble at the edge of the circular plain. "From thereon out the ruins are still standing. That's where you can see the Torque."

He indicated that Yagharek should turn the page. Yagharek did so, and something clucked deep in his throat. Isaac supposed it was the garuda equivalent of a sudden intake of breath. Isaac looked briefly at the picture, then looked up, not too quickly, at Yagharek's face.

"Those things in the background like melting statues used to be houses," he said levelly. "The thing you're looking at, as far as they could work out, is descended from the domestic goat. Apparently they used to keep them as pets in Suroch. This could be second, tenth, twentieth generation post-Torque, obviously. We don't know how long they live."

Yagharek stared at the dead thing in the heliotype.

"They had to shoot it, he explains in the text," Isaac went on. "It killed two of the militia. They had a go at an autopsy, but those horns in its stomach weren't dead, even though the rest of it was. They fought back, nearly killed the biologist. Do you see the carapace? Weird splicing going on there." Yagharek nodded slowly.

"Turn the page, Yag. This next one, no one has the slightest idea what it used to be. Might have been spontaneously generated in the Torque explosion. But I think those gears there are descended from train engines." He tapped the pages gently.

"The . . . uh . . . *best* is yet to come. You haven't seen the cockroach-tree, or the herds of what may once have been human."

Yagharek was meticulous. He turned every single page. He saw furtive shots that had been stolen from behind walls, and vertiginous views from the air. A slow kaleidoscope of mutation and violence, petty wars fought between unfathomable monstrosities over no-man's-lands of shifting slag and nightmare architecture.

"There were twenty militia, Sacramundi the heliotypist and three research scientists, plus a couple of engineers who stayed in the airship the whole time. Seven militia, Sacramundi and one chymist came out of Suroch. Some were Torque-wounded. By the time they got back to New Crobuzon one militiaman had died. Another had barbed tentacles where his eyes should be, and pieces of the scientist's body were disappearing every night. No blood, no pain, just . . . smooth holes in her abdomen or arm or whatever. She killed herself."

Isaac remembered first hearing the story told as an anecdote by an unorthodox history professor. Isaac had chased it up, following a trail of footnotes and old newspapers. The history had been forgotten, transmuted into emotional blackmail for children—"Be good or I'll send you to Suroch where the monsters are!" It took a year and a half before Isaac saw a copy of Sacramundi's report, and another three before he could match the price asked for it.

He thought he recognized some of the thoughts flickering almost invisibly under Yagharek's impassive skin. They were the ideas every unorthodox undergraduate had at some time entertained.

"Yag," Isaac said softly, "we ain't going to use the Torque. You might be thinking 'You still use hammers and some people are murdered with them.' Right? Eh? 'Rivers can flood and kill thousands or they can drive water turbines.' Yes? Trust me . . . speaking as one who used to think the Torque was *terribly* exciting . . . it's not a *tool*. It's *not* a hammer, it's not like water. It's . . . the Torque is *rogue power*. We're not talking crisis energy here, right? Get that *right* out of your head. Crisis is the energy underpinning the whole of physics. Torque's not about physics. It's not *about* anything. It's . . . it's an entirely pathological force. We don't know where it comes from, why it appears, where it goes. *All bets are off. No rules apply.* You can't tap it—well, you can try, but you've seen the results—you can't play with it, you can't trust it, you can't understand it, you sure as godsdamn-fuck can't control it."

Isaac shook his head in irritation. "Oh sure, there've been experiments and whatnot, they reckon they've got techniques to shield from some effects, heighten others, and some of them might even work a little bit. But there's *never* been a Torque experiment that didn't end in . . . well, in tears, at the very least. As far as I'm concerned there's only one kind of experiment we should be doing with Torque, and that's how to avoid it. Either stop it in its tracks, or run like Libintos with the drakows on his tail.

"Five hundred years ago, a while after the Cacotopic Stain opened, there was a mild Torque storm that swept down from somewhere at sea, in the north-east. It hit New Crobuzon for a while." Isaac shook his head slowly. "Nothing in the league of Suroch, obviously, but still enough for an epidemic of monstrous births and some very strange tricks of cartography. All the affected buildings were pulled down sharpish. Very sensible in my view. That's when they drew up plans for the cloudtower—didn't want to leave the weather to chance. But that's broke now, and we're fucked if we get any more random Torque currents. Fortunately, they seem to be getting rarer and rarer over the centuries. They sort of *peaked* around the 1200s."

Isaac waved his hands at Yagharek, warming to his task of denunciation and explanation.

"You know, Yag, when they realized something was up down south in the scrubland—and it didn't take them long to clock it was a *massive* Torque-rift—there was a lot of crap talked about what to *call* it, and the arguments still haven't died, half a fucking millennium on. Someone named it the Cacotopic Stain, and the moniker stuck. I remember being told in college that it was a terrible populist description, because Cacotopos—Bad Place, basically—was moralizing, that the Torque was neither good nor bad, so on. Thing is . . . obviously, that's right at one level, right? Torque's not *evil* . . . it's mindless, it's motiveless. That's what I reckon anyway—others disagree.

"But even if that's true, seems to me that western Ragamoll is *precisely* a Cacotopos. That's a vast stretch of land which is totally *beyond our power*. There's no thaumaturgy we can learn, no techniques to perfect, which'll let us do *anything* with that place. We've just got to stay the fuck out and hope it eventually ebbs away. It's a huge fucking badland crawling with Inchmen—

which admittedly live outside Torque-zones, as well, but seem particularly happy there—and other things I wouldn't even bother trying to describe. So you've got a force that makes a total mockery of our sentience. That's *'bad'* as far as I'm concerned. It could be the fucking definition of the word. See, Yag . . . it pains me to say this, it really does, I mean I'm a fucking rationalist . . . but the Torque is *unknowable*."

With a huge gush of relief, Isaac saw that Yagharek was nodding. Isaac nodded too, fervently.

"Partly selfish, all this, you understand," Isaac said, with sudden grim humour. "I mean, I don't want to be arsing around with experiments and end up turning into some . . . I don't know, some *revolting thing*. Just too bloody risky. We'll stick to crisis, all right? On which topic, I've got some stuff to show you."

Isaac gently took Sacramundi's report from Yagharek's hands and returned it to the shelves. He opened a desk drawer and brought out his tentative blueprint.

He placed it in front of Yagharek, then hesitated and drew away slightly.

"Yag, old son," he said. "I really have to know . . . is that behind us, now? Are you . . . satisfied? Convinced? If you're going to fuck about with Torque, for Jabber's sake tell me *now* and I'll bid you goodbye . . . and my condolences."

He studied Yagharek's face with troubled eyes.

"I have heard what you say, Grimnebulin," said the garuda, after a pause. "I . . . respect you." Isaac smiled humourlessly. "I accept what you say."

Isaac began to grin, and would have responded, except that Yagharek was looking out of the window with a melancholy stillness. His mouth was open for a long time before he spoke.

"We know of the Torque, we garuda." He paused lengthily between sentences. "It has visited the Cymek. We call it *rebekhlajhnar-h'k*." The word was spat out with a harsh cadence like angry birdsong. Yagharek looked Isaac in the eye. "*Rebekhsackmai* is Death: 'the force that ends.' *Rebekh-kavt* is Birth: 'the force that begins.' They were the First Twins, born to the worldwomb after union with her own dream. But there was a . . . a sickness . . . a *tumour*—" he paused to savour the correct word as it occurred to him "—in the earthbelly with them. *Rebekh-lajhnar-h'k* tore its way out of the worldwomb just behind them, or perhaps at the same time, or perhaps just before. It is the . . ." He thought hard for a translation. "The *cancer-sibling*. Its name means: 'the force that cannot be trusted.' "

Yagharek did not tell the folk story in any incantatory, shamanic tones, but in the deadpan of a xenthropologist. He opened his beak wide, closed it abruptly, then opened it again.

"I am an outcast, a renegade," Yagharek continued. "It is . . . no surprise . . . if I turn my back on my traditions, perhaps . . . But I must learn when to turn to face them again. *Lajhni* is 'to trust,' and 'to bind firm.' The Torque cannot be trusted, and nor can it be bound. It is uncontainable. I have known that since I first knew the stories. But in my . . . I . . . I am eager, Grimnebulin. Perhaps I turn too quickly to things from which I would once have recoiled. It is . . . hard . . . being between worlds . . . being of no world. But you have made me remember what I have always known. As if you were an elder of my band." There was one last, long pause. "Thank you."

Isaac nodded slowly.

"Not at all . . . I'm . . . mighty relieved to hear all that, Yag. More than I can say. Let's . . . say no more about it." He cleared his throat and prodded the diagram. "I've some fascinating stuff to show you, old son."

In the dusty light under Isaac's walkway, the repairman from Orriaben's constructs teased the innards of the broken cleaning machine with screwdriver and solder. He kept up a mindless jaunty whistling, a trick that took no thought at all.

The sound of the consultation above reached him as the faintest bass murmur, interspersed with an occasional cracked utterance. He looked up in surprise, briefly, at this latter voice, but quickly returned to the matter in hand.

A brief examination of the mechanisms of the construct's internal analytical engine confirmed the basic diagnosis. Apart from the usual age-related problems of cracked joints, rust and worn bristles—all of which the repairman quickly patched up— the construct had contracted some kind of virus. A programme card incorrectly punched or a slipped gear deep within the steam-driven intelligence engine had led to a set of instructions feeding back into themselves in an infinite loop. Activities the construct should have been able to carry out as a reflex, it had started to pore over, to attempt to extract more information or more complete orders. Seized by paradoxical instructions or a surfeit of data, the cleaning construct was paralysed.

The engineer glanced up at the wooden floor above him. He was ignored.

He felt his heart judder with excitement. Viruses came in a variety of forms. Some simply closed down the workings of the machine. Others led the mechanisms to perform bizarre and pointless tasks, the result of a newly programmed outlook on everyday information. And others, of which this was a perfect, a *beautiful* specimen, paralysed constructs by making them recursively examine their basic behavioural programmes.

They were bedeviled by reflection. The seeds of self-consciousness.

The repairman reached into his case and brought out a set of programme cards, fanned them expertly. He whispered a prayer.

His fingers working at astonishing speed, the man loosened various valves and dials in the construct's core. He levered open the protective covering on the programme input slot. He checked that there was enough pressure in the generator to power the receiving mechanism of the metal brain. The programmes would load into the memory, to be actualized throughout the construct's processors when it was switched on. Quickly, he slid first one card, then another and another into the opening. He felt the ratcheting spring-loaded teeth rotate their way along the stiff board, slotting into the little holes that translated into instructions or information. He paused between each card to make sure that the data loaded correctly.

He shuffled his little deck like a cardsharp. He sensed the minuscule jerks of the analytical engine through the fingertips of his left hand. He felt for faulty input, for broken teeth or stiff, un-oiled moving parts that would corrupt or block his programmes. There were none. The man could not forebear from hissing triumphantly. The construct's virus was entirely the result of information-feedback, and not any kind of hardware failure. That meant that the cards with which the man was plying the engine would all be read, their instructions and information loaded into the sophisticated steam-engine brain.

When he had pushed each carefully selected programme card into the input slot, each in considered order, he punched a brief sequence of buttons on the numbered keys wired up to the cleaning machine's analytical engine.

The man closed the lid on the engine and resealed the construct's body. He replaced the twisted screws which held the hatch in place. He rested his hands on the construct's lifeless body for a moment. He heaved it upright, stood it on its treads. He gathered his tools.

The man stepped back into the center of the room.

"Um . . . 'Scuse me, squire," he yelled.

There was a moment of silence, then Isaac's voice boomed out. "Yes?"

"I'm all done. Problems should be over. Just tell Mr. Serachin to load up the boiler with a bit of juice, then switch the old thing back on. Lovely models, the EKBS."

"Yeah, I'm sure they are," came the response. Isaac appeared at the railing. "Is there anything else I need to know?" he asked impatiently.

"No, guv, that's about it. We'll invoice Mr. Serachin within the week. Cheerio, then."

"Right, bye. Thanks very much."

"Don't mention it, sir," the man began, but Isaac had already turned and walked back out of sight.

The repairman walked slowly to the door. He held it open and looked back at where the construct lay face down in the shadows of the big room. The man's eyes flickered momentarily upstairs to check that Isaac was gone, then he moved his hands to trace out some symbol like interlocking circles.

"Virus be done," he whispered, before walking out into the warm noon.

CHAPTER TWENTY

"What am I looking at?" asked Yagharek. As he held the diagram he cocked his head in a shockingly avian motion.

Isaac took the sheet of paper from him and turned it the right way up.

"This, old son, is a crisis conductor," Isaac said grandly. "Or at least, a prototype of one. A fucking triumph of applied crisis physico-philosophy."

"What is it? What does it do?"

"Well, look. You put whatever it is you want . . . tapped, in here." He indicated a scrawl representing a belljar. "Then . . . well, the science is complicated, but the gist of it . . . let's see." He drummed his fingers on the desk. "This boiler's kept very hot, and it powers a set of interlocking engines here. Now, this one's loaded up with sensory equipment that can detect various types of energy fields—heat, elyctrostatic, potential, thaumaturgic emissions—and represents them in mathematical form. Now, if I'm right about the unified field, which I am, then all these energy forms are various manifestations of crisis energy. So the job of this analytical engine here is to calculate what kind of crisis energy field is present given the various other fields present." Isaac scratched his head.

"It's fucking complicated crisis maths, old son. That's going to be the hardest part, I reckon. The idea is to have a programme that can say 'well, there's so much potential energy, so much thaumaturgic, and whatnot, that means the underlying crisis situation must be such-and-such.' It's going to try to translate the . . . uh . . . *mundane,* into the crisis form. Then—and this is another sticking point—the given *effect* that you're after also has to be translated into mathematical form, into some crisis equation, which is fed into this computational engine *here.* Then what you're doing is using this, which is powered by a combination of steam or chymistry and thaumaturgy. It's the crux of the thing, a converter to tap the crisis energy and manifest it in its raw form. You then channel that into the object." Isaac was becoming more and more excited as he talked about the project. He could not help himself: for a moment, his elation at the massive potential for his research, the sheer scale of what he was doing, defeated his resolve to see only the immediate project.

"The thing is, what we should be able to do is change the form of the object into one where the tapping of its crisis field actually increases its crisis state. In other words, the crisis field grows *by virtue of being siphoned off.*" Isaac beamed at Yagharek, his mouth open. "D'you see what I'm talking about? *Perpetual fucking motion!* If we can stabilize the process, you've just got an endless feedback loop, which means a permanent font of energy!" He calmed in the face of Yagharek's impassive frown. Isaac grinned. His resolve to focus on applied theory was made easy, even pressing, by Yagharek's single-minded obsession with the commission in hand.

"Don't worry, Yag. You'll get what you're after. As far as you're concerned, what this means—if I can make it work—is

that I can turn you into a walking, *flying* dynamo. The more you
fly, the more crisis energy you manifest, the more you can fly.
Tired wings are a problem you won't face no more."

There was a troubled silence at that. To Isaac's relief, Yagharek did not seem to have noticed the unfortunate double-
meaning. The garuda was stroking the paper with wonder and
hunger. Yagharek murmured something in his own tongue, a
soft, guttural croon.

Eventually he looked up.

"When will you build this thing, Grimnebulin?" he asked.

"Well, I need to actually knock together a working model to
test it, refine the maths and whatnot. I reckon it'll take me a week
or so to put something together. But that's early days, remember.
Very early days." Yagharek nodded quickly, waved away the caution. "You sure you don't want to kip here? Are you still going to
wander round like a ghul and spring on me when I least suspect
it?" asked Isaac ironically.

Yagharek nodded.

"Please tell me as soon as your theories advance, Grimnebulin," he asked. Isaac laughed at the polite bathos of the request.

"Certainly will, old son, you have my word. As soon as the old
theories advance, you get to know."

Yagharek turned stiffly and walked towards the stairs. As he
turned to say goodbye, he caught sight of something. He was
still for a minute, then walked over to the far end of the walkway's east-facing side. He indicated the cage containing the
colossal grub.

"Grimnebulin," he said. "What does your caterpillar do?"

"I know, I know, it's grown like fuck, hasn't it?" said Isaac,
strolling over. "Tremendous little bugger, eh?"

Yagharek pointed at the cage and looked up questioningly.

"Yes," he said. "But what does it do?"

Isaac frowned and peered into the wooden box. He had moved
it so that it faced away from the windows, which meant that its
interior was shadowed and unclear. He squinted and peered into
the darkness.

The massive creature had crawled to the furthest corner of the
cage and had somehow managed to climb the rough wood. Then,
with some organic adhesive it exuded from its arse, it had suspended itself from the top of the box. It hung there, pendulous
and heavy, swaying and rippling slightly, like a stocking full
of mud.

Isaac hissed, his tongue jutting from between his lips.

The caterpillar had tightened its stubby legs, curling them in tight towards its underbelly. As Isaac and Yagharek watched, it jack-knifed at its centre and seemed to kiss its own tail end, slowly relaxing until it hung deadweight again. It repeated the process.

Isaac pointed into the dimness.

"Look," he said. "It's smearing something all over itself."

Where the caterpillar's mouth touched flesh, it left infinitely thin glistening filaments, which stretched out taut as it moved its mouth away, adhering where they touched its body again. The hairs at the creature's hind end were flattened against its body, and they looked wet. The enormous grub was slowly smothering itself in translucent silk, from the bottom up.

Isaac straightened up, slowly. He caught Yagharek's eye.

"Well . . ." he said. "Better late than never. Finally, what I bought it for in the first place. The thing's pupating."

After a while, Yagharek nodded slowly.

"It will soon be able to fly," he said quietly.

"Not necessarily, old son. Not everything with a chrysalis gets wings."

"You do not know what it will be?"

"That, Yag, is the only reason I've still got the damn thing. Wretched curiosity. Won't let me go." Isaac smiled. The truth was he felt a certain nervousness, seeing the bizarre thing finally perform the action he had been waiting for since he had first seen it. He watched it cover itself in a strange, fastidious inversion of cleanliness. It was quick. The bright, mottled colours of its pelt went misty with the first layer of fibres, then quickly disappeared from view.

Yagharek's interest in the creature was short-lived. He replaced the wooden framework which hid his deformity onto his shoulders, and covered it with his cloak.

"I will take my leave, Grimnebulin," he said. Isaac looked up from where the caterpillar held his attention.

"Right! Righto, Yag. I'll get a move on with the . . . uh . . . engine. I know by now not to ask when I'll see you, right? You'll drop in when the time's right." He shook his head.

Yagharek was already at the bottom of the stairs. He turned once, briefly, and saluted Isaac, and then he left.

Isaac waved back. He was lost in thought, his hand remaining in the air for several seconds after Yagharek had gone. Eventually, he closed it with a soft clap and turned back to the caterpillar's cage.

Its coat of wet threads was drying fast. The tail end was already stiff and immobile. It constrained the grub's undulations, forcing it to perform more and more claustrophobic acrobatics in its attempt to cover itself. Isaac pulled his chair over in front of the cage to watch its efforts. He took notes.

A part of him told him that he was being intellectually dissolute, that he should compose himself and focus on the matter in hand. But it was a small part, and it whispered to him without confidence. Almost dutifully. There was, after all, nothing that was going to stop Isaac from taking the opportunity to watch this extraordinary phenomenon. He settled into his chair comfortably, pulled over a magnifying lens.

It took a little over two hours for the caterpillar to cover itself completely in a moist chrysalis. The most complicated manoeuvre was at the head itself. The grub had to spit itself a kind of collar, then allow it to dry a little before bunching itself up within its swaddling, making itself shorter and fatter for a few moments while it wove a lid, closing itself in. It pushed against it slowly, ensuring its strength, then exuded more of the cement-filaments until its head was completely covered, invisible.

For a few minutes the organic shroud quivered, expanding and contracting in response to the movements within. The white covering became brittle as he watched, changed colour to a drab nacre. It pendulumed very gently as minute air currents disturbed it, but its substance had hardened, and the motion of the grub within could no longer be discerned.

Isaac sat back and scrawled on the paper. *Yagharek was almost certainly right about the thing having wings,* he thought. The gently moving organic sac was like a textbook drawing of a butterfly or moth chrysalis, only vastly bigger.

Outside the light became thicker as the shadows lengthened.

The suspended cocoon had been motionless for more than half an hour when the door opened, startling Isaac to his feet.

"Anyone up there?" yelled David.

Isaac leaned over the railings and greeted him.

"Some chap came and dealt with the construct, David. Said you just had to stoke it up a bit and switch it on, said it should work."

"Good stuff. I'm sick of the rubbish. We get all yours, as well. Would that be deliberate?" David grinned.

"Why no," replied Isaac, ostentatiously shovelling dust and crumbs through the gaps in the railings with his foot. David laughed and wandered out of his sight. Isaac heard a metallic thud as David gave the construct an affectionate clout.

"I am also to tell you that your cleaner is a 'lovely old thing,'" said Isaac formally. They both laughed. Isaac came and sat halfway down the stairs. He saw David shovelling some pellets of concentrated coke into the construct's little boiler, an efficient triple-exchange model. David slammed shut and bolted the hatch. He reached up to the top of the construct's head and pulled the little lever into an *on* position.

There was a hiss and a little whine as steam was pushed through thin pipes, slowly powering up the construct's analytical engine. The cleaner jerked spastically and settled back against the wall.

"That should warm up in a little while," said David with satisfaction, shoving his hands in his pockets. "What have you been up to, 'Zaac?"

"Come up here," answered Isaac. "I want to show you something."

When David saw the suspended cocoon he laughed briefly, and put his hands on his hips.

"Jabber!" he said. "It's enormous! When that thing hatches I'm running for cover . . ."

"Yeah, well, that's partly why I'm showing you. Just to say keep your eyes out for it opening. You can help me pin it inside a case." The two men grinned.

From below came a series of bangs, like water fighting its way through obstreperous plumbing. There was a faint hiss of pistons. Isaac and David stared at each other, nonplussed for a moment.

"Sounds like the cleaner's gearing up to some serious action," said David.

In the short, stubby byways of copper and brass that were the construct's brain, a welter of new data and instructions clattered violently. Transmitted by pistons and screws and innumerable valves, the grots and gobs of intelligence bottlenecked in the limited space.

Infinitesimal jolts of energy burst through tiny, finely engineered steamhammers. In the centre of the brain was a box crammed with rank upon rank of minuscule on-off switches that puttered up and down at great and increasing speed. Each switch was a steam-powered synapse, pushing buttons and pulling levers in intensely complicated combinations.

The construct jerked.

Deep in the construct's intelligence engine circulated the peculiar solipsistic loop of data that constituted the virus, born where a minute flywheel had skittered momentarily. As the steam coursed through the brainpan with increasing speed and power, the virus's useless set of queries went round and round in an autistic circuit, opening and shutting the same valves, switching the same switches in the same order.

But this time the virus was nurtured. Fed. The programmes that the repairman had loaded into the construct's analytical engine sent extraordinary instructions coursing throughout the crafted tubework cerebellum. The valves flapped and the switches buzzed in staccato tremors, all seemingly too fast to be anything but random motion. And yet in those abrupt sequences of numerical code, the rude little virus was mutated and evolved.

Encoded information welled up within those limited hissing neurones, fed into the recursive idiocy of the virus and spun out from it skeins of new data. The virus flowered. The moronic motor of its basic, mute circuit sped up, flung blossoms of newborn viral code spiralling away from it with a kind of binary centrifugal force, into every part of the processor.

Each of these subsidiary viral circuits repeated the process until instructions and data and self-generated programmes were flooding every pathway of that limited calculating engine.

The construct stood in the corner, shaking and whirring very slightly.

In what had been an insignificant corner of its valved mind, the original virus, the original combination of rogue data and meaningless reference that had affected the construct's ability to sweep floors, still revolved. It was the same, but transformed. No longer a destructive end, it had become a means, a generator, a motive power.

Soon, very soon, the central processing engine of the construct's brain was whirring and clicking at full capacity. Ingenious mechanisms kicked in at the behest of the new programmes buzzing through the analogue valves. Sections of analytical capacity normally given over to movement and backup and support functions were folded in on themselves, doubling their capacity as the same binary function was invested with double meanings. The flood of alien data was diverted, but not slowed. Astounding articles of programme design increased the efficiency and processing power of the very valves and switches that were conducting them.

David and Isaac talked upstairs and grimaced or grinned at the sounds the hapless construct could not help but make.

The flow of data continued, transferred first from the repairman's voluminous set of programme cards and stored in the gently humming, clicking memory box, now converted into instructions in an active processor. On and on came the flow, a relentless wash of abstract instructions, nothing more than combinations of *yes/no* or *on/off*, but in such quantity, such complexity, that they approximated concepts.

And eventually, at a certain point, the quantity became quality. Something changed in the construct's brain.

One moment it was a calculating machine, attempting dispassionately to keep up with the gouts of data. And then awash in those gouts, something metal twitched and a patter of valves sounded that had not been instructed by those numbers. A loop of data was self-generated by the analytical engine. The processor reflected on its creation in a hiss of high-pressure steam.

One moment it was a calculating machine.

The next, it thought.

With a strange, calculating alien consciousness, the construct reflected on its own reflection.

It felt no surprise. No joy. No anger, no existential horror.

Only curiosity.

Bundles of data that had waited, circulating unexamined in the box of valves, became suddenly relevant, interacting with this extraordinary new mode of calculation, this autotelic processing. What had been incomprehensible to a cleaning construct made sudden sense. The data was advice. Promises. The data was a welcome. The data was a warning.

The construct was still for a long time, emitting little murmurs of steam.

Isaac leaned far over the railing, until it creaked unnervingly. He pushed over until his head was upside-down and he could see the construct beneath his and David's feet. Isaac watched its uncertain juddering starts and frowned.

As he opened his mouth to say something, the construct pushed itself up into an active posture. It extended its suction tube and began, tentatively at first, to clear the floor of dust. As Isaac watched, the construct extended a rotating brush behind it and began to scrub the boards. Isaac watched it for any signs of faltering, but its pace increased with almost palpable confidence. Isaac's face lightened as he watched the construct perform its first successful cleaning job for weeks.

"That's better!" Isaac announced over his shoulder to David. "Damn thing can clean again. Back to normal!"

Chapter Twenty-one

In the huge, crisp cocoon, extraordinary processes began.

The caterpillar's swathed flesh began to break down. Legs and eyes and bristles and body-segments lost their integrity. The tubular body became fluid.

The thing drew on the stored energy it had drawn from the dreamshit and powered its transformation. It self-organized. Its mutating form bubbled and welled up into strange dimensional rifts, oozing like oily sludge over the brim of the world into other planes and back again. It folded in on itself, shaping itself out of the protean sludge of its own base matter.

It was unstable.

It was alive, and then there was a time between forms when it was neither alive nor dead, but saturated with power.

And then it was alive again. But different.

Spirals of biochymical slop snapped into sudden shapes. Nerves that had unwound and dissolved suddenly spun back into skeins of sensory tissue. Features dissolved and reknitted in strange new constellations.

The thing flexed in inchoate agony and a rudimentary, but growing, hunger.

Nothing was visible from the outside. The violent process of destruction and creation was a metaphysical drama played out without an audience. It was hidden behind an opaque curtain of brittle silk, a husk that hid the changing with a brute, instinctual modesty.

After the slow, chaotic collapse of form, there was a brief moment when the thing in the cocoon was poised in a liminal state. And then, in response to unthinkable tides of flesh, it began to construct itself anew. Faster and faster.

Isaac spent many hours watching the chrysalis, but he could only imagine the struggle of autopoiesis within. What he saw was a solid thing, a strange fruit hanging by an insubstantial thread in the musty darkness of a large hutch. He was perturbed by the cocoon, imagining all manner of gigantic moths or butterflies emerging. The cocoon did not change. Once or twice he prodded it gingerly, and set it rocking gently and heavily for a few seconds. That was all.

Isaac watched and wondered about the cocoon when he was not working on his engine. It was that that took most of his time.

Piles of copper and glass began to take shape on Isaac's desk and floor. He spent his days soldering and hammering, attaching steam-pistons and thaumaturgic engines to the nascent engine. His evenings he spent in pubs, in discussion with Gedrecsechet, the Palgolak Librarian, or David or Lublamai, or ex-colleagues from the university. He spoke carefully, not giving away too much, but with passion and fascination, drawing out discussions on maths and energy and crisis and engineering.

He did not stray from Brock Marsh. He had warned his friends in Salacus Fields that he would be out of touch, and those relationships were fluid anyway, relaxed, superficial. The only person he missed was Lin. Her work was keeping her at least as busy as him, and as the momentum of his research picked up, it was increasingly difficult to find times when they could meet.

Instead, Isaac sat up in bed and wrote her letters. He asked her about her sculpture, and he told her that he missed her. Every other morning or so he would stamp and post these letters in the box at the end of his street.

She wrote back to him. Isaac used her letters to tease himself. He would not let himself read them until he had finished his day's work. Then he would sit and drink tea or chocolate in his window, sending his shadow out over the Canker and the darkening city, and read her letters. He was surprised at the sentimental warmth these moments made him feel. There was a degree of maudlin relish in the moods, but just as much affection, a real connection, a lack he felt when Lin was not there.

Within a week he had built a prototype of the crisis engine, a banging, spitting circuit of pipes and wire that did nothing more than produce noise in great gobbets and barks. He took it apart and rebuilt it. A little over three weeks later another untidy conglomerate of mechanical parts sprawled before the window, where the cages of winged things had gained their freedom. It was uncontained, a vague grouping of separate motors and dynamos and converters spread across the floor, connected by rough-and-ready engineering.

Isaac wanted to wait for Yagharek, but the garuda could not be contacted, living as he was like a vagrant. Isaac believed it to be Yagharek's weird, inverted clutching at dignity. Living on the street he was beholden to none. The pilgrimage he had made across the continent would not end with him gratefully relinquishing his responsibility, his self-control. Yagharek was a deracinated outsider in New Crobuzon. He would not rely on, or be thankful to, others.

Isaac imagined him moving from place to place, sleeping on bare floors in deserted buildings, or curled up on roofs, huddled by steam-vents for heat. It might be an hour before he came to visit, or it might be weeks. It only took half a day of waiting before Isaac decided to test his creation in Yagharek's absence.

In the belljar where the wires and tubes and flexing cables converged, Isaac had placed a piece of cheese. It sat there, drying slowly, while he hammered at the keys of his calculator. He was trying to mathematize the forces and vectors involved. He stopped often to take notes.

Below him, he heard the sniffling of Sincerity the badger, and Lublamai's clucking response, the humming progress of the cleaning construct. Isaac was able to ignore them all, zone them out, focus on the numbers.

He felt a little uncomfortable, unwilling to pursue his work with Lublamai in the room. Isaac was still pursuing his unusual policy of silence. *Perhaps I'm just developing a taste for the theatrical,* he thought, and grinned. When he had solved his equations as best he could, he dawdled, willing Lublamai to leave. Isaac peered under the walkway at where Lublamai scrawled diagrams on graph paper. He did not look as if he were about to go. Isaac grew tired of waiting.

He picked his way through the miasma of metal and glass that littered his floor and squatted gently with the information-input of the crisis engine on his left. The circuit of machinery and tubes described a meandering circle around the room, culminating in the cheese-filled belljar by his right hand.

Isaac held a flexing metal tube in one hand, its end connected to his laboratory boiler by the far wall. He was nervous, and excited. As quietly as he could, he connected the tube to the power-input valve on the crisis engine. He released the catch and felt the steam begin to fill the motor. There was a hissing hum and a clattering. Isaac knelt over and copied his mathematical formulae on the input keys. He slotted four programme cards quickly into the unit, felt the little wheels slide and bite, saw the dust rise as the engine's vibrations increased.

He murmured to himself and watched intently.

Isaac felt as if he could sense the power and data passing through the synapses to the various nodes of the dismembered crisis engine. He felt as if the steam was pushing through his own veins, turning his heart into a hammering piston. He flicked three large switches on the unit, heard the whole construction warming up.

The air hummed.

For sluggish seconds, nothing happened. Then, in the dirty belljar, the clump of cheese began to shudder.

Isaac watched it and wanted to shout with triumph. He twisted a dial one hundred and eighty degrees and the thing moved a little more.

Let's bring on a crisis, Isaac thought, and pulled the lever that made the circuit complete, that brought the glass jar under the attention of the sensory machines.

Isaac had adapted the belljar, cutting away its top and replacing it with a plunger. He reached for this now and began to press it, so that its abrasive bottom moved slowly towards the cheese. The cheese was under threat. If the plunger completed its motion the cheese would be completely crushed.

As Isaac pressed with his right hand, with his left he adjusted knobs and dials in response to juddering pressure gauges. He watched their needles plunge and leap and adjusted the thaumaturgic current in response.

"Come on, you little fucker," he whispered. "Look out, eh? Can't you feel it? Crisis coming for you . . ."

The plunger edged sadistically closer and closer to the cheese.

The pressure in the pipes was growing dangerously high. Isaac hissed in frustration. He slowed the pace with which he threatened the cheese, moving the plunger inexorably down. If the crisis engine failed and the cheese did not show the effects he had tried to programme, Isaac would still crush it. The crisis was all about potentiality. If he had no genuine intention to crush the cheese, it would not be in crisis. You could not *trick* an ontological field.

Then, as the whine from steam and singing pistons became uncomfortable, and the edges of the plunger's shadow sharpened as it bore down on the base of the belljar, the cheese exploded. There was a loud semi-liquid smack, as the nugget of cheese blew up with speed and violence, spattering the inside of the belljar with crumbs and oil.

Lublamai yelled up, asking what in Jabber's name was that, but Isaac was not listening. He sat gawping at the destroyed cheese like a fool, his mouth slack. Then he laughed with incredulity and joy.

"Isaac? What the fuck you up to?" yelled Lublamai.

"Nothing, nothing! Sorry to bother you . . . Just some work . . . Going pretty well, actually . . ." Isaac's reply was interrupted as he broke off to smile.

He turned off the crisis engine quickly and lifted the belljar. He ran his fingers over the smeared, half-melted mess inside. *Incredible!* he thought.

He had attempted to programme the cheese to hover an inch or two above the floor. So from that point of view, he supposed this was a failure. But he had not expected *anything* to happen! Certainly, he had got the maths wrong, misprogramming the cards. It was obvious that specifying the effects he was aiming for would be extremely hard. Probably the tapping process itself was appallingly crude, leaving all sorts of room for errors and imperfections in the process. And he hadn't even *tried* to create the kind of permanent feedback loop that he was eventually aiming for.

But, but . . . *he had tapped crisis energy.*

This was totally unprecedented. For the first time, Isaac truly believed that his ideas would work. From now on, the job was one of refinement. A lot of problems, of course, but problems of a different and much lesser order. The basic conundrum, the central problem of all of crisis theory, had been *solved*.

Isaac gathered his notes, leafed through them reverentially.

He could not believe what he had done. Immediately, more plans came to him. *Next time,* he thought, *I'll use a piece of vodyanoi watercræft. Something already held together by crisis energy. That should make life a whole lot more interesting, maybe we can start getting that loop going . . .* Isaac was giddy. He slapped his forehead and grinned.

I'm going out, Isaac thought suddenly. *I'm going to . . . to get drunk. I'm going to find Lin. I'm going to have a night off. I've just solved one of the intractable damn problems in one of the most controversial paradigms of science and* I deserve a drink . . . He smiled at his mental outburst, then grew serious. He realized that he had decided to tell Lin about the crisis engine. *I can't think about it on my own any more,* he thought.

He checked that he had his keys and his wallet in his pockets. He stretched and shook himself, then descended to the ground floor. Lublamai turned at the sound of his feet.

"I'm off, Lub," said Isaac.

"You calling it a day, Isaac? It's only three."

"Listen, old son, I've clocked up a few extra hours." Isaac grinned back. "I'm having a half-day. Anyone asks, I'll see 'em tomorrow."

"Righto," said Lublamai, returning to his work with a wave. "Have a good one."

Isaac grunted goodbye.

He stopped in the middle of Paddler Way and sighed, purely for the pleasure of the air. The little street was not busy, but neither was it deserted. Isaac saluted one or two of his neighbours, then turned and strode off towards Petty Coil. It was a gorgeous day, and he had decided to walk to Salacus Fields.

The warm air seeped in through door and windows and cracks in the warehouse walls. Once, Lublamai stopped working to adjust his clothing. Sincerity was tussling playfully with a beetle. The construct had finished cleaning some time ago, and now stood gently ticking in the far corner, one of its optical lenses seemingly fixed on Lublamai.

A little while after Isaac left, Lublamai rose and, leaning out of the open window by his desk, he tied a red scarf to a bolt in the brick. He made a list of shopping that he needed, should Teafortwo come by. Then he returned to work.

By five o'clock the sun was still high, but it was curving towards earth. The light was thickening fast, becoming tawny.

Deep within the pendulous chrysalis the pupating lifeform could sense the lateness of the day. It shivered and flexed its nearly finished flesh. In its ichor and the byways of its body, a final set of chymical reactions began.

At half past six, an ungainly thud outside the window interrupted Lublamai, who looked out to see Teafortwo in the little alley outside, rubbing his head with his prehensile foot. The wyrman looked up at Lublamai and let out a yell of greeting.

"Guvnor Lublub! Doing me rounds, saw your red flapper . . ."

"Evening, Teafortwo," said Lublamai. "Fancy coming in?" He stood back from the window and let the wyrman in. Teafortwo flopped to the floor in a heavy, flapping motion. His russet skin was beautiful in the shards of late light that caught it. He grinned up at Lublamai with his cheerful, hideous face.

"What's the plan, boss?" shouted Teafortwo. Before Lublamai could answer, Teafortwo looked over at where Sincerity was eyeing him dubiously. He spread his wings, stuck out his tongue and leered at her. She scampered off in disgust.

Teafortwo laughed uproariously and burped.

Lublamai smiled indulgently. Before Teafortwo had a chance to get more sidetracked, he tugged him over to the desk where his shopping list waited. He gave Teafortwo a slab of chocolate to keep his attention on the job in hand.

As Teafortwo and Lublamai bickered over how many groceries the wyrman could carry in the air, something above them stirred.

In the rapidly darkening shadows of the cage in Isaac's raised laboratory, the cocoon was oscillating under a force that was not a wind. Movement within the tight, organic package was sending it in a quick, hypnotic motion. It spun, then faltered, bucked slightly. There was an infinitesimal ripping noise, much too low for Lublamai or Teafortwo to hear.

A moist, sculpted black claw split the fibres of the cocoon. It slid slowly upwards, ripping the stiff material as effortlessly as an assassin's knife. A welter of utterly alien senses spilt like invisible guts from the ragged hole. Disorienting gusts of feeling rolled briefly around the room, making Sincerity growl, and Lublamai and Teafortwo look up nervously for a moment.

Intricate hands emerged from the darkness and held the edges of the rent. They pushed silently, forcing the thing apart and open. There was the softest of thumps as a trembling body slid from the cocoon, as wet and slippery as a newborn.

For a minute it huddled on the wood, weak and bewildered, in the same hunched pose it had maintained within the chrysalis. Slowly, it pushed outwards, luxuriating in the sudden space. When it encountered the wire mesh of the hutch it tore it effortlessly from the door and crawled into the larger space of the room.

It discovered itself. It learnt its shape.

It learnt that it had needs.

Lublamai and Teafortwo looked up at the screech and discordant plucking of torn wire. The sound seemed to start above them and wash throughout the room. They looked at each other, then up again.

"Wassat, guvnor . . . ?" said Teafortwo.

Lublamai walked away from the desk. He glanced up at Isaac's balcony, turned slowly, took in the whole of the ground floor. There was silence. Lublamai stood still, frowning, gazing at the front door. Had the sound come from outside? he wondered.

A movement was reflected in the mirror beside the door.

A dark thing rose from the floor at the top of the stairs.

Lublamai spoke, emitted some tremulous noise of disbelief, of fear, of confusion, but it dissipated soundlessly after the briefest moment. He stared with an open mouth at the reflection.

The thing unfolded. The sense was of a blossoming. An expansion after being enclosed, like a man or woman standing and spreading their arms wide after huddling foetally, but multiplied and made vast. As if the thing's indistinct limbs could bend a thousand times, so that it unhinged like a paper sculpture, standing and spreading arms or legs or tentacles or tails that opened and opened. The thing that had huddled like a dog stood and opened itself, and it was nearly the size of a man.

Teafortwo screeched something. Lublamai opened his mouth wider and tried to move. He could not see its shape. Only its dark, glistening skin and hands that clutched like a child's. Cold shadows. Eyes that were not eyes. Organic folds and jags and twists like rats' tails that shuddered and twitched as if newly dead. And those finger-long shards of colourless bone that shone white and parted and dripped and that were *teeth* . . .

As Teafortwo tried to bolt past Lublamai and Lublamai tried to open his mouth to scream, his eyes still fixed to the creature in the mirror, his feet skittering on the flagstones, the thing at the top of the stairs opened its wings.

Four rustling concertinas of dark matter flickered outwards on the creature's back, and outwards again and again, slotting into position, fanning and expanding in vast folds of thick mottled flesh, expanding to an impossible size: an explosion of organic patterns, a flag unfurling, clenched fists opening.

The thing made its body thin and spread those colossal wings, massive flat folds of stiff skin that seemed to fill the hall. They were irregular, chaotic in shape, random fluid whorls; but mirror-perfect left and right, like spilt ink or paint patterns on folded paper.

And on those great flat planes were dark stains, rude patterns that seemed to flicker as Lublamai watched and Teafortwo fumbled with the door, wailing. The colours were midnight, sepulchral, black-blue, black-brown, black-red. And then the patterns *did* flicker, the shadow-shapes moved like amoeba in a magnifying lens or oil on water, the patterns left and right still matching, moving in time, hypnotic and heavy, faster. Lublamai's face creased. His back itched maniacally with the thought that the thing was behind him. Lublamai spun to face it, gazed directly into the mutating colours, the dusky vivid show . . .

. . . and Lublamai no longer thought of screaming but only of watching as those dark markings rolled and boiled in perfect symmetry across the wings like clouds in a night sky above, in water below.

Teafortwo howled. He turned to see the thing that was now descending the stairs, those wings still unfurled. Then the patterns on the wings caught him and he stared, his mouth open.

The dark designs on those wings moved beguilingly.

Lublamai and Teafortwo stood still and silent, agog, slack-jawed and shivering, gazing at the magnificent wings.

The creature tasted the air.

It looked briefly at Teafortwo, and opened its mouth, but the pickings were meagre. It turned its head and faced Lublamai, keeping those wings spread and enthralling. It moaned with hunger in a soundless timbre that made Sincerity, already sick with fear, cry out. She huddled closer into the shadow of the motionless construct, propped against the wall in the corner of the room, weird shadows twitching in its lenses. The air hummed with the taste of Lublamai. The creature salivated and its wings flickered into a frenzy, and Lublamai's taste grew stronger and stronger until the thing's monstrous tongue emerged and it moved forward, flicking Teafortwo effortlessly out of its way.

The winged creature took Lublamai in its hungry embrace.

CHAPTER TWENTY-TWO

Sunset bled into the canals and the converging rivers of New Crobuzon. They ran thick and gory with light. Shifts changed and working days ended. Retinues of exhausted smelters and foundry workers, clerks and bakers and coke-loaders, trudged from factory and office to the stations. The platforms were full of tired, boisterous argument, cigarillos and booze. Steam cranes in Kelltree worked into the night, hauling exotic cargoes from foreign ships. From the river and the great docks, striking vodyanoi stevedores yelled insults at the human crews on the jetties. The sky above the city was smeared with cloud. The air was warm, and smelt alternately lush and foul, as trees fruited and factory waste coagulated in thickening flows.

Teafortwo bolted from the warehouse on Paddler Way like cannonshot. He tore into the sky from the broken window trailing blood and tears, blubbering and sniffling like a baby, flying in a ragged spiral towards Pincod and Abrogate Green.

Minutes passed before another, darker form followed him into the skies.

The intricate hatchling thing flexed itself through an upper window and launched into the gloaming. Its movements on the ground were tentative, every motion seemed to be experimental. In the air it soared. There was no hesitation, only a glorying in the motion.

The irregular wings clapped together and swept apart in huge, soundless gusts that scooped away great swathes of air. The creature spun, beating its wings languorously, its body careering across the sky with the chaotic graceless speed of a butterfly.

It sent eddies of wind and sweat and aphysical exudations in its wake.

The creature was still drying.

It exalted. It licked the cooling air.

The city festered like mould below it. A palimpsest of sense-impressions washed over the flying thing. Sounds and smells and lights that filtered into its obscure mind in a synaesthetic wash, an alien perception.

New Crobuzon steamed with the rich taste-scent of prey.

The thing had fed, was sated, but the glut of food confused it, gloriously, and it slobbered and gnashed its huge teeth in a frenzy.

It dived. Its wings fluttered and trembled as it swooped towards the unlit alleys below it. It knew in its hunter's heart to avoid the great scabs of light clotted at irregular spaces around the city, to seek out the darker places. It trailed its tongue in the air and found food, swept with chaotic aerobatics into the shadow of the bricks. It came down like a fallen angel in the gnarled cul-de-sac where a prostitute and her client fucked against a wall. Their desultory jerks faltered as they sensed the thing beside them.

Their screams were brief. They ceased quickly as the creature's wings spread.

The thing fell on them with eager greed.

Afterwards it flew again, drunk with the taste.

It hovered, seeking the centre of the city, turning, drawn slowly to the enormous sprawl of Perdido Street Station. It beat its way west over Spit Hearth and the red-light zone, over the contradictory tangle of commerce and squalor that was The Crow. Behind it, snagging the air like a trap, was the dark edifice of Parliament, and the militia towers of Strack Island and Brock Marsh. The creature traced an uneven course over the path of the skyrail that linked those lower towers to the Spike that loomed at the westernmost shoulder of Perdido Street Station.

The flying thing started as pods streaked along that rail. It hovered momentarily, fascinated at the rattling passage of the trains that expanded outwards from the station, that monstrous architectural enormity.

Vibrations in a hundred registers and keys beckoned the thing, as forces and emotions and dreams spilt and were amplified in the brick chambers of the station and blasted outwards into the sky. A massive, invisible flavour trail.

The few night-birds swerved violently away from the weird thing that beat its heavy way towards the city's dark heart. Wyrmen on errands saw its incomprehensible silhouette and wheeled off in other directions, shouting obscenities and oaths. Booms and drones vibrated as the dirigibles sounded to each other, sliding slowly between city and sky like fat pike. As they turned ponderously, the thing flapped past them, unseen except by an engineer who did not report his sighting, but made a religious sign and whispered to Solenton for protection.

Caught in the updraft, the wash of senses, from Perdido Street Station, the flying thing let itself be caught and swept up until it was way, way above the city. It turned slowly with a quiver from its wings, orienting itself to its new territory.

It noted the paths of the river. It felt the vents of different energies from the city's different zones. It sensed the city in a flickering passage of different modes. Concentrations of food. Shelter.

The creature sought one more thing. Others of its kind.

It was social. When it was born for the second time it was with a hunger for company. Its tongue unrolled and it tasted the gritty air for anything that was like itself.

The thing shuddered.

Faintly, so faintly, it could sense something in the east. It could taste frustration. Its wings trembled in empathy.

It arced around and beat its way back in the direction from which it had come. It bore a little north this time, passing over the parks and elegant old buildings of Gidd and Ludmead. The splintering enormities of the Ribs splayed extraordinarily to the south, and the flying thing felt a queasiness, an anxiety, at the awareness of those looming bones. The power that drooled upward from them was not at all to its liking. But its unease battled with its deeply encoded sympathy for its own kind, whose taste grew stronger, much stronger, in the shadow of the great skeleton.

The thing descended tentatively. It approached circuitously, from the north and the east. It flew low and tight, below the skyrail that extended northwards from the militia tower of Mog Hill to that in Chnum. It shadowed an eastbound train on the Dexter Line, gliding in its filthy thermals. Then it swung in a long arc around the Mog Hill tower and over the northern fringe of Echomire's industrial zone. The thing swept in towards Bonetown's raised railway, cringing at the influence of the Ribs, but dragged on towards the taste of its fellows.

It flitted from roof to roof, its tongue dangling obscenely as it traced them. Sometimes the downdraft from its wings would make a passer-by look up, as hats and paper bowled down the deserted streets. If they saw the dark shape that loomed momentarily over them and then was gone, they shivered and hurried on, or furrowed their brows and denied what they had seen.

The winged thing let its tongue dangle as it slowly beat the air. It used it as a bloodhound would its nose. It passed over the undulating roofscape that seemed buckled by the Ribs. It licked its way along a faint trail.

Then it crossed the aura of a large, bituminous building in a deserted street, and its long tongue spasmed like a whip. It sped up, arced up and back down in an elegant loop towards the tarred roof. There at the far corner, below that ceiling through which the sensations of its kind leaked like brine through a sponge . . .

It scrambled over the slates flexing its peculiar limbs. Solicitous feelings were oozing from it, and there was a befuddled moment of confusion as its captive kin reacted to its presence. Then their nebulous misery became impassioned: pleas and joy and demands for freedom, and among that, cold and exact instructions on what to do.

The creature found its way to the edge of the roof and descended in a motion halfway between flying and climbing, until it clung to the outer edge of a sealed window forty feet above the pavement. The glass was painted opaque. It vibrated minutely in eldritch dimensions, buffeted by the emanations from within.

The thing on the window-sill scrabbled with its fingers for a moment, then tore away the frame with a quick motion, leaving an ugly wound where the window had been. It dropped the already breaking glass with a catastrophic noise and stepped into the dark attic.

The room was very large and bare. A great glutinous wash of welcome and warning came from across the rubbish-strewn floor.

Opposite the newcomer were four of its kind. It was dwarfed by them, the magnificent economy of their limbs made its own look stunted, runtlike. They were shackled to the wall with enormous bands of metal around their midriffs and several of their limbs. Each had its wings fully extended, flat against the wall: each set was as unique and random as the newcomer's. Below each of their hindquarters was a bucket.

A moment of tugging made it clear to the new arrival that

those bands could not be shifted. One of those pinned to the wall hissed at the frustrated creature, imperiously bade it pay attention. It communicated in a psychic twittering.

The free, newly lowly thing backed away as instructed, and waited.

In the simple sonar plane, shouts and yells were sounding from the street below where the window had smashed. There was a confused rumbling from within the building below. From the corridor beyond the door came the sound of running. Chaotic snatches of conversation found their way through the wood.

"... *inside*..."

"... get in?"

"... mirrors, don't..."

The creature backed away further from its tethered kin and moved into the shadows at the far side of the room, beyond the door. It folded its wings and waited.

Bolts on the other side of the door were thrown. There was a moment of hesitation, then the door flew open and four armed men burst in in quick succession. They all faced away from the trapped creatures. Two carried heavy flintlocks, primed and held ready. Two were Remade. In their left hands they held pistols, but from their right shoulders jutted huge metal barrels, splayed at the end like blunderbusses. These were fixed into position pointing directly behind each Remade. They hefted these carefully, and stared into mirrors suspended from a metal helmet before their eyes.

The two with conventional rifles also wore the mirror-helmets, but they were staring past the mirrors into the darkness straight ahead of them.

"Four moths, and all clear!" shouted one of the Remade with the strange backpointing rifle-arm, still gazing into his mirror.

"There's nothing here..." answered one of the men looking forward into the darkness by the ruined window-hole, and as he spoke the intruding thing stepped out of the shadows and spread its incredible wings.

Both those whose eyes faced forwards looked aghast and opened their mouth to scream.

"Oh, *Jabber fuck no*..." one managed, and then both were silent as the patterns on the creature's wings began to swarm like a pitiless dun kaleidoscope.

"What the fuck...?" began one of the Remade, and flickered

his eyes briefly in front of him. His face collapsed in horror, but
his moan died very fast as he caught sight of the creature's wings.

The final Remade yelled his comrades' names, and whimpered as he heard them drop their guns. He could see the faintest
shape out of the corner of his eye. The creature before him could
sense his terror. It stalked towards him, emitting little reassuring
murmurs in an emotive vector. A phrase circled imbecilically in
the man's mind: *There's one in* front *of me there's one in* front
of me . . .

The Remade tried to move forward, his eyes fixed on his mirrors, but the creature before him moved easily into his field of vision. What had been in the corner of the man's eye became an
inescapable, shifting field, and the man succumbed, dropping his
eyes to those violently changing wings, and his jaw opened and
shuddered tremulously. He dropped his gun-arm.

With a twitch of a skein of flesh, the free creature closed the
door. It stood before the four men in thrall, and slobber drooled
from its jaws. A snapped demand from its trapped kin interrupted its hunger and humbled it. It reached out and turned each
of the men to face the four trapped moths.

There was a tiny moment when each man was no longer facing those wings, when his mind clutched at freedom for a moment, but then the awesome spectacle of four sets of those
scudding patterns violently wrested control of his mind and he
was lost.

Behind them now, the intruder pushed each man in turn towards one of the huge pinioned things, which reached out eagerly with the short limbs left free to them to grip their prey.

The creatures fed.

One of them fumbled for the keys at the belt of its meal, tore
them from the man's clothes. When it had finished its meal, it
reached up with careful movements and pushed the key delicately into the lock of the bolt restraining it.

It took four attempts—fingers clutching the unfamiliar key,
twisting it from an awkward angle—but the creature freed itself.
It turned to each of its fellows and repeated the slow process, until all the captives were liberated.

One by one they stumbled across the room to the ragged
window-hole. They paused and braced their atrophied muscles
against the brick, spread those astonishing wings wide and

launched themselves out and away from the sickly dry æther that seemed to seep from the Ribs. The last to leave was the newcomer.

It dragged itself after its comrades: even exhausted and brutalized, they flew faster than it could manage. They were waiting in a circle hundreds of feet above, extending their awarenesses, adrift in the senses and impressions that welled up from all around.

When their humble liberator reached them, they moved apart a little to let it in. They flew together, sharing in what they felt, licking the air lasciviously.

They drifted as the first to fly had done, north towards Perdido Street Station. They rotated slowly, five like the five railway lines of the city, buoyed by the massive profane urban presence below them, a fecund crawling place such as none of their kind had ever experienced before. They rocked above it, wings snapping, buffeted by wind, tingling with the sounds and energy of the growling city.

Everywhere they were, every part of the city, every dark bridge, every five-hundred-year-old mansion, every twisting bazaar, every grotesque concrete warehouse and tower and houseboat and squalid slum and manicured park, thronged with food.

It was a jungle without predators. A hunting ground.

Chapter Twenty-three

Something was blocking the door into Isaac's warehouse. He swore mildly, pushing against the obstruction.

It was early afternoon of the day after his success, which he already conceived of as his "cheese moment." When he had reached Lin's rooms the previous evening, he had been delighted to find her in. She had been tired but as happy as him. They had gone to bed for three hours, then stumbled out to The Clock and Cockerel.

It had been an unnervingly perfect night. Everyone Isaac could have wanted to see had been abroad in Salacus Fields, and all had stopped at the C & C for lobster or whiskey or chocolate laced with quinner. There were new additions to the clique, including Maybet Sunder, who had been forgiven for winning the Shintacost Prize. In return she was gracious about the arch comments Derkhan had made in print and others in person.

Lin had relaxed in the company of her friends, although her melancholia seemed to ebb rather than dissipate. Isaac had had one of his hissed political arguments with Derkhan, who had slipped him the latest issue of *Double-R*. The gathered friends had argued and eaten and thrown food at each other until two in the morning, when Isaac and Lin had returned to bed and warm, entwined sleep.

Over breakfast he had told her about his triumph with the crisis engine. She had not really understood the scale of the achievement, but that was understandable. She had realized that he was excited as almost never before, and had done her best to enthuse sufficiently. For Isaac's part, it had made the difference he had suspected it would, simply communicating the bare bones of the project in the most unscientific way. He felt more grounded, less as if he were living some preposterous dream. He had learnt of potential problems during his explanation, and had come away eager to rectify them.

Isaac and Lin had parted with deep affection, and with a mutual promise not to let so long go by without each other again.

And now Isaac could not get into his workshop.

"Lub! David! What the arse you up to?" he yelled, and shoved at the door again.

As he pushed, the door opened a tiny way and he could see a sliver of the sunlit interior. He could see the edge of whatever was blocking the door.

It was a hand.

Isaac's heart skittered.

"Oh Jabber!" he heard himself shout as he leant with all his weight on the door. It opened before his mass.

Lublamai was sprawled prone across the doorway. As Isaac knelt by his friend's head, he heard Sincerity sniffling some way away, between the treads of the construct. She was cowed.

Isaac turned Lublamai over and let out a juddering sigh of relief when he felt that his friend was warm, heard him breathing.

"Wake up, Lub!" he yelled.

Lublamai's eyes were already open. Isaac started back from that impassive gaze.

"Lub . . . ?" he whispered.

Drool had collected below Lublamai's face, had blazed trails across his dusty skin. He lay completely limp, utterly motionless. Isaac felt his friend's neck. The pulse was quite steady. Lublamai was taking in deep breaths, pausing a moment, then releasing. He sounded as if he were sleeping.

But Isaac flinched in horror before that imbecilic vacant glare. He waved his hand before Lublamai's eyes, eliciting no response. Isaac slapped Lublamai's face, softly, then hard twice. Isaac realized that he was shouting Lublamai's name.

Lublamai's head rocked back and forth like a sack full of stones.

Isaac closed his hand and felt something clammy. Lublamai's hand was thinly coated in a clear, sticky liquid. He sniffed his hand and recoiled from the faint scent of lemons and rot. It made him feel momentarily light-headed.

Isaac fingered Lublamai's face and saw that the skin around his mouth and nose was slippery and tacky with the slop, that what he had thought Lublamai's saliva was mostly that thin slime.

No yells, no slaps, no pleas would make Lublamai wake.

When Isaac finally looked up and around the room, he saw the window by Lublamai's desk was open, the glass broken and the wooden shutters splintered. He stood and ran over to the knocking window frame, but there was nothing to see inside or out.

Even as Isaac ran from corner to corner under his own raised laboratory, darting between Lublamai's corner and David's, whispering idiotic reassurances to the terrified Sincerity, looking for signs of intruders, he realized that a terrible idea had occurred to him some time ago, and had been squatting balefully in the back of his mind. He faltered to a stop. Slowly, he raised his eyes and looked up in cold horror at the underside of the walkway boards.

Fearful calm settled on him like snow. He felt his feet lift, trudging inexorably towards the wooden stairs. He turned his head as he walked, saw Sincerity sniffing gradually closer to Lublamai, her courage slowly returning now that she was not alone.

Everything Isaac saw seemed slowed. He walked as if through freezing water.

Stair by stair he ascended. He felt no surprise and only a very dull foreboding as he saw pools of weird spittle on each stair, saw the fresh scrapings left by some sharp-clawed newcomer. He heard his own heart pulsing with what seemed tranquillity, and he wondered if he was numb to shock.

But when he reached the top and turned to see the hutch thrown on its side, its thick wire mesh burst from within, little fingers of metal exploding away from the central hole, and when he saw the chrysalis split and empty and saw the trail of dark juices dribbling from within its husk, Isaac heard himself cry out aghast and felt his body shudder into immobility as an icy tide of gooseflesh swept him up. Horror billowed up within him and around him like ink in water.

"Oh dear gods . . ." he whispered through dry and quivering lips. "Oh Jabber . . . what have I done?"

The New Crobuzon militia did not like to be seen. They emerged in their dark uniforms at night, to perform duties such as fishing the dead from the river. Their airships and pods meandered and buzzed over the city with opaque ends. Their towers were sealed.

The militia, New Crobuzon's military defence and its internal correction agents, only appeared in their uniforms, the infamous full-face masks and dark armour, the shields and flintlocks, when they were acting as guards at some sensitive locus, or at times of great emergency. They wore their colours openly during the Pirate Wars and the Sacramundi Riots, when enemies attacked the city's order from without or within.

For their day-to-day duties they relied on their reputation and on their vast network of informers—rewards for information were generous—and plain-clothed officers. When the militia struck, it was the man drinking cassis in the café, the old woman weighed down with bags, the clerk in stiff collar and polished shoes who suddenly reached over their heads and pulled hoods from invisible folds in the cloth, who slipped enormous flintlocks from hidden holsters and poured into criminal dens. When a cutpurse ran from a shouting victim, it might be a portly man with a bushy moustache (palpably false, everyone would reflect afterwards, why had they not noticed that before?) who would grab the offender in a punishing necklock and disappear with him or her into the crowd, or a militia tower.

And afterwards, no witness could say for sure what those agents had looked like in their civilian guise. And no one would ever see the clerk or the portly man or any of them again, in that part of the city.

It was policing by decentralized fear.

It had been four in the morning when the prostitute and her client had been found in Brock Marsh. The two men walking the dark alleys with their hands in their pockets and their heads jaunty had paused, seeing the crumpled shape in the dim gaslight. Their demeanour had changed. They had looked about them, then trotted into the cul-de-sac.

They found the stupefied pair lying across each other, their eyes glazed and vacant, their breath ragged and smelling of cloying citrus. The man's trousers and pants were dropped around his ankles, exposing his shrivelled penis. The woman's clothes—her skirt complete with the surreptitious slit many prostitutes used to finish their work quickly—were intact. When the newcomers had failed to wake them, one man had remained with the mute bodies and the other had run off into the darkness. Both men had pulled dark hoods over their heads.

Some while later a black carriage had pulled up, drawn by two enormous horses, Remade with horns and fangs that glinted with slaver. A small corps of uniformed militia had leapt to the ground and, without words, had pulled the comatose victims into the darkness of the cab, which had sped off towards the Spike that towered over the centre of the city.

The two men remained behind. They waited until the carriage had disappeared over the cobbles of the labyrinthine quarter. Then they looked about them carefully, taking stock of the sparse harvest of lights that glinted from the backs of buildings and outhouses, from behind crumbling walls and through the thin fingers of fruit trees in gardens. Satisfied that they were unobserved, they slipped off their hoods and thrust their hands back into their pockets. They melted suddenly into a different character, laughing quietly with each other and chatting urbanely as, innocuous again, they resumed their graveyard-shift patrol.

In the catacombs under the Spike, the limp pair of foundlings were prodded and slapped, shouted at and cajoled. By early morning they had been examined by a militia scientist, who scribbled a preliminary report.

Heads were scratched in perplexity.

The scientist's report, along with condensed information on all other unusual or serious crimes, was sent up the length of the Spike, stopping at the highest floor but one. The reports were couriered briskly the length of a twisting, windowless corridor, towards the offices of the home secretary. They arrived on time, by half past nine.

At twelve minutes past ten, a speaking tube began to bang peremptorily in the cavernous pod-station that took up the whole floor at the very top of the Spike. The young sergeant on duty was on the other side of the room, fixing a cracked light on the front of a pod that hung, like tens of others, from an intricate cat's cradle of skyrails which looped and criss-crossed each other below the high ceiling. The tangled rails allowed the pods to be moved around each other, positioned on one or other of the seven radial skyrails that exploded out through the enormous open holes spaced evenly around the outside wall. The tracks took off above the colossal face of New Crobuzon.

From where he stood, the sergeant could see the skyrail enter the militia tower in Sheck a mile to the south-west, and emerge beyond it. He saw a pod leave the tower, way over the shambolic housing, virtually at his own eye-level, and shoot off away from him towards the Tar, which trickled sinuous and untrustworthy to the south.

He looked up as the banging continued, and, realizing which tube demanded attention, he swore and rushed across the room. His furs flapped. Even in summer, it was cold so high above the city, in an open room that functioned as a giant wind tunnel. He pulled the plug from the speaking tube and barked into the brass.

"Yes, Home Secretary?"

The voice that emerged was small and distorted by its journey through the twisting metal.

"Get my pod ready immediately. I'm going to Strack Island."

The doors to the Lemquist Room, the mayor's office in Parliament, were huge and bound in bands of ancient iron. There were two militia stationed outside the Lemquist Room at all times, but one of the usual perks of a posting in the corridors of power was denied them: no gossip, no secrets, no sounds of any kind filtered to their ears through the enormous doors.

Behind the metal-girdled entrance, the room itself was immensely tall, panelled in darkwood of such exquisite quality it was almost black. Portraits of previous mayors circled the room, from the ceiling thirty feet above, spiralling slowly down to within six feet of the floor. There was an enormous window that looked out directly at Perdido Street Station and the Spike, and a variety of speaking tubes, calculating engines and telescopic periscopes stashed in niches around the room, in obscure and oddly threatening poses.

Bentham Rudgutter sat behind his desk with an air of utter command. None who had seen him in this room had been able to deny the extraordinary surety of absolute power he exuded. He was the centre of gravity here. He knew it at a deep level, and so did his guests. His great height and muscular corpulence doubtless added to the sense, but there was far more to his presence.

Opposite him sat MontJohn Rescue, his vizier, wrapped as always in a thick scarf and leaning over to point out something on a paper the two men were studying.

"Two days," said Rescue in a strange, unmodulated voice, quite different from the one he used for oratory.

"And what?" said Rudgutter, stroking his immaculate goatee.

"The strike goes up. Currently, you know, it's delaying loading and unloading by between fifty and seventy per cent. But we've got intelligence that in two days the vodyanoi strikers plan to paralyse the river. They're going to work overnight, starting at the bottom, working their way up. A little to the east of Barley Bridge. Massive exercise in watercræft. They're going to dig a trench of air across the water, the whole depth of the river. They'll have to shore it up continuously, recræfting the walls constantly so they don't collapse, but they've got enough members to do that in shifts. There's no ship that can jump that gap, Mayor. They'll totally cut off New Crobuzon from river trade, in both directions."

Rudgutter mused and pursed his lips.

"We can't allow that," he said reasonably. "What about the human dockers?"

"My second point, Mayor," continued Rescue. "Worrying. The initial hostility seems to be waning. There's a growing minority who seem to be ready to throw in their lot with the vodyanoi."

"Oh, no no no no," said Rudgutter, shaking his head like a teacher correcting a normally reliable student.

"Quite. Obviously our agents are stronger in the human camp than the xenian, and the mainstream are still antagonistic or undecided about the strike, but there seems to be a caucus, a conspiracy, if you will . . . secret meetings with strikers and the like."

Rudgutter spread his enormous fingers and looked closely at the grain of the desk between them.

"Any of your people there?" he asked quietly. Rescue fingered his scarf.

"One with the humans," he answered. "It is difficult to remain hidden on the vodyanoi, who usually wear no clothes in the water." Rudgutter nodded.

The two men were silent, pondering.

"We've tried working from the inside," said Rudgutter eventually. "This is far the most serious strike to threaten the city for . . . over a century. Much as I'm loath to, it seems we may have to make an example . . ." Rescue nodded solemnly.

One of the speaking tubes on the mayor's desk thumped. He raised his eyebrows as he unplugged it.

"Davinia?" he answered. His voice was a masterpiece of insinuation. In one word he told his secretary that he was surprised to have her interrupt him against his instructions, but that his trust in her was great, and he was quite sure she had an excellent reason for disobeying, which she had better tell him immediately.

The hollow, echoing voice from the tube barked out tiny little sounds.

"Well!" exclaimed the mayor mildly. "Of course, of course." He replugged the tube and eyed Rescue. "What timing," he said. "It's the home secretary."

The enormous doors opened briefly and slightly, and the home secretary entered, nodding in greeting.

"Eliza," said Rudgutter. "Please join us." He gesticulated at a chair by Rescue's.

Eliza Stem-Fulcher strode over to the desk. It was impossible to tell her age. Her face was virtually unlined, its strong features suggesting that she was probably somewhere in her thirties. Her hair, though, was white, with only the faintest peppering of dark strands to suggest that it had once been another colour. She wore a dark civilian trouser suit, cleverly chosen in cut and colour to be strongly suggestive of a militia uniform. She drew gently on a long-stemmed white clay pipe, the bowl at least a foot and a half from her mouth. Her tobacco was spiced.

"Mayor. Deputy." She sat and pulled a folder from under her arm. "Forgive me interrupting unannounced, Mayor Rudgutter, but I thought you should see this immediately. You too, Rescue. I'm glad you're here. It looks as if we may have . . . something of a crisis on our hands."

"We were saying much the same thing, Eliza," said the mayor. "We're talking about the dock strike?"

Stem-Fulcher glanced up at him as she drew some papers from the folder.

"No, Mr. Mayor. Something altogether different." Her voice was resonant and hard.

She threw a crime report onto the desk. Rudgutter put it sideways between himself and Rescue, and both twisted their heads to read it together. After a minute Rudgutter looked up.

"Two people in some sort of coma. Odd circumstances. I presume you are showing me more than this?"

Stem-Fulcher handed him another paper. Again, he and Rescue read together. This time, the reaction was almost immediate. Rescue hissed and bit the inside of his cheek, chewing with concentration. At almost the same time, Rudgutter gave a little sigh of comprehension, a tremulous little exhalation.

The home secretary watched them impassively.

"Obviously, our mole in Motley's offices doesn't know what's going on. She's totally confused. But the snatches of conversation she's noted down . . . see this? 'The *moss* are out . . . ?' I think we can all agree that she misheard that, and I think we can all agree on what was really said."

Rudgutter and Rescue read and reread the report wordlessly.

"I've brought the scientific report we commissioned at the very start of the SM project, the feasibility study." Stem-Fulcher was speaking quickly, without emotion. She dropped the report flat on the desk. "I've drawn your attention to a few particularly relevant phrases."

Rudgutter opened the bound report. Some words and sentences were circled in red. The mayor scanned them quickly: . . . *extreme danger . . . in case of escape . . . no natural predators . . .*

. . . utterly catastrophic . . .

. . . breed . . .

CHAPTER TWENTY-FOUR

Mayor Rudgutter reached out and unplugged his speaking tube again.

"Davinia," he said. "Cancel all appointments and meetings for today . . . no, for the next two days. Apologies wherever necessary. No disturbances unless Perdido Street Station explodes, or something of that magnitude. Understood?"

He replaced the plug and glared at Stem-Fulcher and Rescue.

"What by *damn*, what in *Jabber's name*, what the *godshit* was Motley *playing at*? I thought the man was supposed to be a professional . . ."

Stem-Fulcher nodded.

"This was something that came up when we were arranging the transfer deal," she said. "We checked his record of activity—much of it against us, it has to be pointed out—and gauged him to be at least as capable as ourselves of ensuring security. He's no fool."

"Do we know who's done this?" asked Rescue. Stem-Fulcher shrugged.

"Could be a rival, Francine or Judix or someone. If so, they've bitten off a godsdamned sight more than they can chew . . ."

"Right." Rudgutter interrupted her with a peremptory tone. Stem-Fulcher and Rescue turned to him and waited. He clenched his fists together, put his elbows on the table and closed his eyes, concentrating so hard that his face seemed ready to splinter.

"Right," he repeated, and opened his eyes. "First thing we have to do is verify that we are faced with the situation that we think we're faced with. That might seem obvious, but we have to be a *hundred per cent* sure. Second thing is come out with some kind of strategy for containing the situation quickly and quietly.

"Now, for the second objective, we all know we can't rely on human militia or Remade—or xenians come to that. Same basic psychic type. We're all *food*. I'm sure we all remember our initial attack-defence tests . . ." Rescue and Stem-Fulcher nodded quickly. Rudgutter continued. "Right. Zombies might be a possibility, but this is not Cromlech: we don't have the facilities to create them in the numbers or quality that we need. So. It seems to me that the first objective can't satisfactorily be dealt with if we're relying on our regular intelligence operations. We have to have access to different information. So for two reasons, we have to elicit assistance from agents better able to deal with the situation—different psychic models from our own are vital. Now, it seems to me there are two possible such agents, and that we have little choice but to approach at least one of them."

He was silent, taking in Stem-Fulcher and Rescue with his eyes, one by one. He waited for dissent. There was none.

"Are we agreed?" he asked quietly.

"We're talking about the ambassador, aren't we?" said Stem-Fulcher. "And what else . . . you don't mean the Weaver?" Her eyes furrowed in dismay.

"Well, hopefully it won't come to that," said Rudgutter reassuringly. "But yes, those are the two . . . ah . . . agents I can think of. In that order."

"Agreed," said Stem-Fulcher quickly. "As long as it's in that order. The Weaver . . . Jabber! Let's talk to the ambassador."

"MontJohn?" Rudgutter turned to his deputy.

Rescue nodded slowly, fingering his scarf.

"The ambassador," he said slowly. "And I hope that will be all we need."

"As do we all, Deputy Mayor," said Rudgutter. "As do we all."

Between the eleventh and fourteenth floors of the Mandragorae Wing of Perdido Street Station, above one of the less popular commercial concourses that specialized in old fabrics and foreign batiks, below a series of long-deserted turrets, was the Diplomatic Zone.

Many of the embassies in New Crobuzon were elsewhere, of course: baroque buildings in Nigh Sump or East Gidd or Flag Hill. But several were there in the station: enough to give those floors their name and let them keep it.

The Mandragorae Wing was almost a self-contained keep. Its corridors described a huge concrete rectangle around a central space, at the bottom of which was an unkempt garden, overgrown with darkwood trees and exotic woodland flowers. Children scampered along the paths and played in this sheltered park while their parents shopped or travelled or worked. The walls rose enormously around them, making the copse seem like moss at the bottom of a well.

From the corridors on the upper floors sprouted sets of interconnected rooms. Many had been ministerial offices at one time. For a short while, each had been the headquarters of some small company or other. Then they had been empty for many years, until the mould and rot had been swept away and ambassadors had moved in. That was a little more than two centuries previously, when a communal understanding had swept the various governments of Rohagi that from now on diplomacy would be greatly preferable to war.

There had been embassies in New Crobuzon far longer. But after the carnage in Suroch put a bloody end to what were called the Pirate Wars or the Slow War or the False War, the number of countries and city-states seeking negotiated resolutions to disputes had multiplied enormously. Emissaries had arrived from across the continent and beyond. The deserted floors of the Mandragorae Wing had been overrun by the newcomers, and by older consulates relocating to tap the new welter of diplomatic business.

Even to leave the lifts or stairs on the floors of the Zone, a gamut of security checks had to be run. The passages were cold and quiet, broken by a few doors and insufficiently lit by desultory gasjets. Rudgutter and Rescue and Stem-Fulcher walked the deserted corridors of the twelfth floor. They were accompanied by a short, wiry man with thick glasses who scurried along behind them, never keeping up, lugging a large suitcase.

"Eliza, MontJohn," said Mayor Rudgutter as they walked, "this is Brother Sanchem Vansetty, one of our most able karcists." Rescue and Stem-Fulcher nodded greetings. Vansetty ignored them.

Not every room in the Diplomatic Zone was occupied. But some of the doors had brass plates proclaiming them the sovereign territory of one country or other—Tesh, or Khadoh, or Gharcheltist—behind which were huge suites extending onto several floors: self-contained houses in the tower. Some of the rooms were thousands of miles from their capitals. Some of them were empty. By Tesh tradition, for example, the ambassador lived as a vagrant in New Crobuzon, communicating by mail for official business. Rudgutter would never meet him. Other embassies were deserted due to lack of funds or interest.

But much of the business conducted here was immensely important. The suites containing the embassies of Myrshock and Vadaunk had been extended some years ago, due to the expansion of paperwork and office space that commercial relations necessitated. The extra rooms jutted like ugly tumours from the interior walls of the eleventh floor, bulging precariously over the garden.

The mayor and his companions walked past a door marked *The Cray Commonwealth of Salkrikaltor*. The corridor shook with the pound and whirr of huge, hidden machinery. Those were the enormous steam-pumps that worked for hours every day, sucking fresh brine fifteen miles from Iron Bay for the cray ambassador and sluicing his used, dirty water into the river.

The passageway was confusing. It seemed to go on too long when looked at from one angle, and to be all but stubby from another. Here and there short tributaries branched from it, leading to other, smaller embassies or store cupboards or boarded-up windows. At the end of the main corridor, beyond the cray embassy, Rudgutter led the way down one of these little passages. It extended a short way, twisting, its ceiling lowering dramatically as some stairs above descended across its path, and terminated in a small unmarked door.

Rudgutter looked behind him, ensuring that his companions and he were not watched. Only a short distance of passageway was visible, and they were quite alone.

Vansetty was pulling chalk and pastels of various colours from his pockets. He pulled what looked like a watch from his fob pocket and opened it. Its face was divided into innumerable complicated sections. It had seven hands of various lengths.

"Got to take account of the variables, Mayor," Vansetty murmured, studying the thing's intricate working. He seemed to be talking more to himself than to Rudgutter or anyone else. "Outlook for today's pretty grotty . . . High-pressure front moving in the æther. Could push powerstorms anywhere from the abyss through null-space up. Fucking poxy outlook on the borderlands as well. Hmmm . . ." Vansetty scrawled some calculations on the back of a notebook. "Right," he snapped, and looked up at the three ministers.

He began to scribble intricate, stylized markings on thick pieces of paper, tearing out each one as it was finished and handing it to Stem-Fulcher, Rudgutter, Rescue, and finally one for himself.

"Whack those over your hearts," he said cursorily, stuffing his into his shirt. "Symbol facing out."

He opened his battered suitcase and brought out a set of bulky ceramic diodes. He stood at the centre of the group and handed one to each of his companions—"*Left* hand and don't drop it . . ."—then wound copper wire around them tightly and attached it to a handheld clockwork motor he pulled from his case. He took readings from his peculiar gauge, adjusted dials and nodules on the motor.

"Righto, everyone, brace yourselves," he said, and flipped the switch that released the clockwork engine.

Little arcs of energy sputtered into multicoloured existence along the wires and between the grubby diodes. The four of them were enclosed in a little triangle of current. All their hair stood visibly on end. Rudgutter swore under his breath.

"Got about half an hour before that runs out," said Vansetty quickly. "Best be quick, eh?"

Rudgutter reached out with his right hand and opened the door. The four of them shuffled forward, maintaining their positions relative to each other, keeping the triangle in place around them. Stem-Fulcher pushed the door closed again behind them.

They were in an absolutely dark room. They could see only by the faint ambient glow of the lines of power, until Vansetty hung the clockwork motor around his neck on a strap and lit a candle. In its inadequate light they saw that the room was perhaps twelve feet by ten, dusty and absolutely empty apart from an old desk and chair by the far wall, a gently humming boiler by the door. There were no windows, no shelves, nothing else at all. The air was very close.

From his bag Vansetty extracted an unusual hand-held machine. Its twists of wire and metal, its knots of multicoloured glass were intricate and lovingly crafted. Its use was quite opaque. Vansetty leaned briefly out of the circle and plugged an input valve into the boiler beside the door. He pulled a lever on the top of the little machine, which began to hum and blink with lights.

" 'Course, in your old days, before I came into the profession, you had to use a live offering," he explained as he unwound a tight coil of wire from the underside of the machine. "But we're not savages, are we? Science is a wonderful thing. This little darling—" he patted the machine proudly "—is an amplifier. Increases the output from that engine by a factor of two hundred,

two hundred and ten, and transforms it into an ætherial energy
form. Bleed that through the wires *so* . . ." Vansetty slung the uncoiled wire into the far corner of the tiny room, behind the desk.
"And there you go! The victimless sacrifice!"

He grinned with triumph, then turned his attention to the dials
and knobs of the little engine, and began to twist and prod them
with intense attention. "No more learning stupid languages, neither," he muttered quietly. "Invocation's automatic now and all.
We're not actually *going* anywhere, you understand?" He spoke
louder, suddenly. "We ain't abyssonauts, and we ain't playing
with *nearly* enough power to do an actual transplantropic leap.
All we're doing is peering through a little window, letting the
Hellkin come to us. But the dimensionality of this room is going
to be just a damn touch unstable for a while, so stick within the
protection and don't muck about. Got it?"

Vansetty's fingers skittered over the box. For two or three minutes, nothing happened. There was nothing but the heat and
pounding from the boiler, the drumming and whining of the little machine in Vansetty's hands. Beneath it all, Rudgutter's foot
tapped impatiently.

And then the little room began to grow perceptibly warmer.

There was a deep, subsonic tremor. An insinuation of russet
light and oily smoke. Sound became muted and then suddenly
sharp.

There was a disorientating moment of tugging, and a red mar-
bling of light flickered onto every surface, moving constantly as
if through bloody water.

Something fluttered. Rudgutter looked up, his eyes smarting
in air that seemed suddenly clotted and very dry.

A heavy man in an immaculate dark suit had appeared behind
the desk.

He leaned forward slowly, his elbows resting on the papers
that suddenly littered the desk. He waited.

Vansetty peered over Rescue's shoulder and jerked his thumb
at the apparition.

"His Infernal Excellency," he declared, "the ambassador of
Hell."

"Mayor Rudgutter," the dæmon said, in a pleasant, low voice.
"How nice to see you again. I was just doing some paperwork."
The humans looked up with a flicker of unease.

The ambassador had an echo: half a second after he spoke his words were repeated in the appalling shriek of one undergoing torture. The screamed words were not loud. They were audible just beyond the walls of the room, as if they had soared up through miles of unearthly heat from some trench in Hell's floor.

"What can I do for you?" he continued (*What can I do for you?* came the soulless howl of misery). "Still trying to find out if you'll be joining us when you pass on?" The ambassador smiled slightly.

Rudgutter smiled back and shook his head.

"You know my views on that, ambassador," he replied levelly. "I'll not be drawn, I'm afraid. You can't provoke me into existential fear, you know." He gave a polite little laugh, to which the ambassador responded in kind. As did his horrendous echo. "My soul, if such exists, is my own. It is not yours to punish or covet. The universe is a much more capricious place than that . . . I asked you before, what do you suppose happens to dæmons when *you* die? As we both know you can."

The ambassador bowed his head in polite demur.

"You're such a *modernist*, Mayor Rudgutter," he said. "I won't argue with you. Please remember my offer stands."

Rudgutter waved his hands impatiently. He was composed. He did not flinch at the pitiable screams which shadowed the ambassador's words. And he did not allow himself to experience any disquiet when, as he stared at the ambassador, the image of the man in the chair flickered for a tiny sliver of a second, to be replaced by . . . something else.

He had experienced this before. Whenever Rudgutter blinked, for that infinitesimal moment, he saw the room and its occupant in very different forms. Through his eyelids, Rudgutter saw the inside of a slatted cage; iron bars moving like snakes; arcs of unthinkable force, a jagged, rippling maelstrom of heat. Where the ambassador sat, Rudgutter caught glimpses of a monstrous form. A hyaena's head stared at him, tongue lolling. Breasts with gnashing teeth. Hooves and claws.

The stale air in the room would not allow him to keep his eyes open: he had to blink. He ignored the brief visions. He treated the ambassador with wary respect. Such was also the dæmon's attitude to him.

"Ambassador, I'm here for two reasons. One is to extend to your master, Its Diabolic Majesty, the Czar of Hell, the respect-

ful greetings of New Crobuzon's citizens. In their ignorance."
The ambassador nodded graciously in response. "The other is to
ask your advice."

"It is always our great pleasure to aid our neighbours, Mayor
Rudgutter. Especially those such as yourself, with whom Its
Majesty has such good relations." The ambassador rubbed its
chin absently, waiting.

"Twenty minutes, Mayor," hissed Vansetty into Rudgutter's ear.

Rudgutter pressed his hands together as if in prayer, and
looked at the ambassador thoughtfully. He felt little gusts of
force.

"You see, ambassador, we have something of a problem. We
have reason to believe that there has been a . . . an escape, shall
we say. Something that we are very concerned to recapture. We'd
like to ask your help, if we may."

"What are we talking about, Mayor Rudgutter? True Answers?" asked the ambassador. "Usual terms?"

"True Answers . . . and perhaps more. We'll see."

"Payment now, or later?"

"Ambassador," said Rudgutter politely. "Your memory momentarily falters. I am in credit two questions."

The ambassador stared at him a moment and laughed.

"So you are, Mayor Rudgutter. My deepest apologies. Proceed."

"Are there any unusual rules of the moment, ambassador?"
asked Rudgutter pointedly. The dæmon shook his head *(great
hyaena tongue briefly slavering from side to side)* and smiled.

"It is Melluary, Mayor Rudgutter," it explained simply.
"Usual rules in Melluary. Seven words, inverted."

Rudgutter nodded. He composed himself, concentrating hard.
Got to get the damn words right. Bloody infantile bloody game,
he thought fleetingly. Then he spoke quickly and levelly, gazing
calmly into the ambassador's eyes.

"Correct escaped what's of assessment our is?"

"Yes," replied the dæmon instantly.

Rudgutter turned briefly, gazed meaningfully at Stem-Fulcher
and Rescue. They were nodding, their faces set and grim.

The mayor turned back to the dæmon ambassador. They
stared at each other without speaking for a moment.

"Fifteen minutes," hissed Vansetty.

"Some of my more . . . *fusty* colleagues would look very

askance at me allowing you to count 'what's' as one word, you know," said the ambassador. "But I'm a liberal." He smiled. "Do you wish to ask your final question?"

"I don't think so, ambassador. I'll save that for another time. I have a proposition."

"Go on, Mayor Rudgutter."

"Well, you know the manner of thing that has escaped, and you can understand our concern to remedy the situation as quickly as possible." The ambassador nodded. "You can also understand that it will be difficult for us to proceed, and that time is of the essence . . . I propose that we hire some of your . . . ah . . . troops, to help us round up our escapees."

"No," said the ambassador simply. Rudgutter blinked.

"We haven't even discussed terms yet, ambassador. I assure you I can make a very generous offer . . ."

"I'm afraid it is out of the question. None of my kind are available." The ambassador stared impassively at Rudgutter.

The mayor thought for a moment. If the ambassador was bargaining, he was doing so in a way he had never done before. Rudgutter forgot himself, closed his eyes to think, snapping them immediately open as he saw that monstrous vista, caught a glimmer of the ambassador's other form. He tried again.

"I could even go up to . . . let's say . . ."

"Mayor Rudgutter, you don't understand," said the ambassador. Its voice was impassive, but it seemed agitated. "I don't care how many units of merchandise you can offer, or in what condition. We are not available for this job. It is not suitable."

There was a long silence. Rudgutter gazed with incredulity at the dæmon opposite him. It was beginning to dawn on him what was happening. In the bleeding rays of light, he saw the ambassador open a drawer and bring out a sheaf of papers.

"If you are finished, Mayor Rudgutter," he continued smoothly, "I have work to do."

Rudgutter waited until the miserable, pitiless resonance of *work to do to do to do* had died down outside. The echo made his stomach pitch.

"Oh, yes, yes, ambassador," he said. "So sorry to have kept you. We'll speak again soon, I hope."

The ambassador inclined its head in a polite nod, then drew out a pen from its inner pocket and began to mark the papers. Behind Rudgutter, Vansetty twiddled at nobs and depressed various buttons, and the wooden floor began to tremble as if in some ætherquake. A hum built up around the cramped humans, wobbling in their little energy field. The foul air vibrated up and down their bodies.

The ambassador bulged and split and disappeared in an instant, like a heliotype in a fire. The moiling carmine light bubbled and evaporated, as if it seeped out through a thousand cracks in the dusty office walls. The darkness of the room closed in around them like a trap. Vansetty's tiny candle guttered and went out.

Checking that they were unobserved, Vansetty, Rudgutter, Stem-Fulcher and Rescue stumbled from the room. The air felt deliciously chill. They spent a minute wiping sweat from their faces, rearranging the clothes that had been buffeted by winds from other planes.

Rudgutter was shaking his head in rueful astonishment.

His ministers composed themselves and turned to him.

"I've met with the ambassador perhaps a dozen times over the past ten years," said Rudgutter, "and I've never seen it behave like that. Damn that air!" he added, rubbing his eyes.

The four walked back along the little corridor, turned onto the main passageway and began to retrace their steps towards the lift.

"Behave like what?" asked Stem-Fulcher. "I've only ever dealt with it once before. Not used to it."

Rudgutter mused as he walked, tugging thoughtfully at his lower lip and his beard. His eyes were very bloodshot. He did not answer Stem-Fulcher for some seconds.

"There are two things to be said: one dæmonological, one practical and immediate." Rudgutter spoke in a level, exact tone, demanding the attention of his ministers. Vansetty was wandering quickly ahead, his job done. "The first might give a certain insight into the Hellkin psyche, behaviour, whatnot. You both heard the *echo*, I presume? I thought he did that to intimidate me, for a while. Well, bear in mind the immense distance that sound had to travel. I know," he said quickly, holding up his hands, "that it's not literally sound, nor literally distance, but they *are* extraplanar analogues and most analogous rules hold in some more or less mutated way. So bear in mind how far it had to travel, from the base of the Pit to that chamber. The fact is, it takes a little while to get there . . . That 'echo,' I believe, was actually spoken *first*. The . . . eloquent words we heard from the ambassador's mouth . . . those were the real echoes. *Those* were the twisted reflections."

Stem-Fulcher and Rescue were silent. They thought of the screams, the tortured, maniacal tone they had heard outside, the idiot ruined gibbering that seemed to make a mockery of the ambassador's devilish refinement . . .

They reflected that that might be the more genuine voice.

"I'm wondering if we were wrong to think of them having a different psychic model. Maybe they're comprehensible. Maybe they think like us. And the *second* thing, bearing in mind that possibility, and bearing in mind what the 'echo' might tell us about the dæmoniac state of mind, is that at the end there, when I was trying to cut a deal, the ambassador was *scared* . . . That's why he wouldn't come to our aid. That's why we're on our own. *Because the dæmons are afraid of what we're hunting.*"

Rudgutter stopped and turned to his aides. The three gazed at each other. Stem-Fulcher's face twisted for a fragment of a second, and was then composed. Rescue was as impassive as a statue, but he plucked fitfully at his scarf. Rudgutter nodded as they pondered.

There was a minute of silence.

"So . . ." Rudgutter said briskly, clasping his hands. "The Weaver it is."

CHAPTER TWENTY-FIVE

That night, in the swollen dark hours after a brief spew of rain had hosed the city down with dirty water, the door to Isaac's warehouse was pushed open. The street was empty. There were minutes of stillness. Night-birds and bats were all that moved. Gaslight guttered.

The construct rolled jerkily out into the deep night. Its valves and pistons were swathed in rags and snatches of blankets, muffling the distinctive sound of its passage. It moved forward quickly, turning inexactly and trundling as fast as its ageing treads would move.

It tremored through the backstreets, passed snoring drunks still sodden and insensate. The sallow gasjets reflected secretively in its battered metal hide.

The construct made its swift, precarious way under the skyrails. Inconstant streaks of cirrus hid the lurking airships. The construct bore down like a diviner on the Tar, the river caught in an intricate whiplash shape on the timeless rocks beneath the city.

And hours after it had disappeared over Sheer Bridge into the southern city, when the dark sky became stained by dawn, the construct came reeling back to Brock Marsh. Its timing was fortuitous. It re-entered and locked the door only a little while before Isaac returned from his frantic night-long search for David, and Lin, and Yagharek and Lemuel Pigeon, and anyone who could help him.

Lublamai was lying on a couch that Isaac had rigged up on a couple of chairs. When Isaac came into the warehouse he came straight over to his still friend, whispered to him hopelessly, but there was no change. Lublamai did not sleep or wake. He gazed.

It was not long before David came hurrying back to the laboratory. He had trawled his way to one of his usual haunts to be greeted by a hurried and garbled version of one of the innumerable messages Isaac had left for him throughout New Crobuzon.

He sat as silently as Isaac, gazing at his mindless friend.

"I can't believe I let you do it," he said numbly.

"Oh Jabber and fuck, David, d'you think I'm not going over and over it . . . I let the damn thing out . . ."

"We all should've known better," snapped David.

There was a long silence between them.

"Did you get a doctor?" said David.

"First thing I did. Phorgit, from across the road, I've dealt with him before. I cleaned up Lub a bit, wiped some of that crap off his face . . . Phorgit didn't know what to make of it. Plugged in gods knows how many bits of equipment, took I don't fucking remember how many readings . . . boils down to 'haven't got a clue.' 'Keep him warm and feed him, but then again you might want to keep him cold and not give him anything to eat . . .' I might get one of the guys I know at the uni to take a skedge at him, but it's a forlorn fucking hope . . ."

"What did the thing *do* to him?"

"Well, quite, David. Quite. That's the fucking question, isn't it?"

There was a tentative rattling at the broken window. Isaac and David looked up to see Teafortwo poking his ugly head forlornly in.

"Oh, shit," said Isaac in exasperation. "Look, Teafortwo, now's not really the best time, capiche? Maybe we can chat later."

"Just looking in, boss . . ." Teafortwo spoke in a cowed voice utterly unlike his usual exuberant squawk. "Wanna know how the Lublub's doing."

"What?" said Isaac sharply, standing. "What about him?"

Teafortwo shied away miserably and wailed.

"Not me, squire, not my fault . . . just wondering if he's better after the big monsterfucker ate his face . . ."

"Teafortwo, were you *here*?"

The wyrman nodded morosely and shifted a little nearer, balancing in the centre of the window frame.

"What *happened*? We're not angry with you, Teafortwo . . . we just want to know what it was you saw . . ."

Teafortwo sniffed and waved its head miserably. He pouted like a child, screwed up his face and blurted out a great gob of words.

"Big fucker comes downstairs flapping big horrible wings make your bonce woozy snapping big teeth and . . . and . . . all over claws and big fucking stinky *tongue* . . . and I . . . Mr. Lublub's gawping in the looking-glass and then he turns to face it and goes . . . dopey . . . and I saw . . . me head went funny and when I woke up the thing's stuck its tongue right in . . . in . . . Mr. Lub's *gob* and *slurpslurp* noises going off in me head and I . . . I buggered off, I couldn't do nothing, I swear . . . I'm *scared* . . ." Teafortwo began to cry like a two-year-old, dribbling snot and tears down his face.

When Lemuel Pigeon arrived, Teafortwo was still sobbing. No amount of cajoling or threatening or bribes could calm the wyrman down. Eventually he went to sleep, curled up in a quilt ruined with his mucus, exactly like an exhausted human baby.

"I'm here on false pretences, Isaac. The message I got was that it'd be worth my while to drop over to your gaff." Lemuel looked at Isaac with a speculative air.

"Godsdammit, Lemuel, you fucking spiv," exploded Isaac. "Is that what's bothering you? Jabber and fuck, I'll make sure you

get yours, all right? Is that better? Now fucking listen to me . . .
Someone has been *attacked* by something that hatched out of
one of the grubs *you obtained for me*, and we need to stop the
thing before it does someone *else*, and we need to *know about it*,
so we need to track down whatever cove it was got it in the *first
place*, and we need to do it *sharpish*. Are you with me, *old son*?"

Lemuel was quite unintimidated by this outburst.

"Look, you can't damn well blame me . . ." he began, before
Isaac interrupted with a howl of irritation.

"Devil's Tail, Lemuel, no one's blaming you, you cretin! Quite
the opposite! What I'm saying is that you are by far too good a
businessman not to keep careful records, and I need you to check
'em out. We both know everything goes through you . . . you've
got to get me the name of whoever originally got the big fat
caterpillar. The enormous one with really weird colours. You
know?"

"Vaguely remember it, yes."

"Well, that is *good*." Isaac calmed a little. He ran his hands
over his face and sighed enormously. "Lemuel, I need your
help," he said simply. "I'll pay you . . . But I'm also begging. I
really need you to help me here. Look." He opened his eyes and
glared at Lemuel. "The damn thing may have keeled over and
died, right? Maybe it's like a mayfly: one glorious day. Maybe
Lub'll wake up tomorrow happy as a sandboy. *But maybe
not.* Now, I want to know: one—" he counted off on fat fingers
"—how to snap Lublamai out of this; two, what this damn thing
is—the one description we have is a little garbled." He glanced
at the wyrman sleeping in the corner. "And three, how we catch
the fucker."

Lemuel stared at him, his face immobile. Slowly and ostentatiously, he pulled a snuff-box from his pocket and took a sniff.
Isaac's fists clenched and unclenched.

"Fine, 'Zaac," Lemuel said quietly, replacing his little jew-
elled box. He nodded slowly. "I'll see what I can do. I'll be in
touch. But I'm not a charity, Isaac, I'm a businessman and
you're a customer. I get something for this. I'll *bill* you, all
right?"

Isaac nodded wearily. There was no rancour in Lemuel's
voice, no viciousness, no spite. He was simply stating the truth
that underlay his bonhomie. Isaac knew that if it paid better not
to uncover the purveyor of the peculiar grub, Lemuel would simply do that.

                    *   *   *

"Mayor." Eliza Stem-Fulcher swaggered into the Lemquist Room. Rudgutter looked up at her questioningly. She threw a thin newspaper onto the table before him. "We've got a lead."

Teafortwo left quickly when he woke, with David and Isaac trying to reassure him that no one held him responsible. By the evening, a horrible kind of drab calm had arrived at the warehouse on Paddler Way.

David was spooning a thick compote of fruit purée into Lublamai's mouth, massaging it down his throat. Isaac was pacing listlessly across the floor. He was hoping that Lin would return home, find the note he had pinned on her door last night and come to him. If it had not been in his writing, he reflected, she would have thought it was a bad joke. To have Isaac invite her to his laboratory-house was unprecedented. But he needed to see her, and he was worried that if he left, he would miss some vital change in Lublamai, or some nugget of indispensable information.

The door was pushed open. Isaac and David looked up sharply.

It was Yagharek.

Isaac was momentarily amazed. This was the first time Yagharek had appeared while David (and Lublamai, of course, although it hardly counted) were in the room. David gazed at the garuda huddling under the dirty blanket, the sweep of the false wings.

"Yag, old son," said Isaac heavily. "Come in, meet David . . . We've had a bit of a disaster . . ." He trudged heavily towards the door.

Yagharek waited for him, hovering half in, half out of the entrance. He said nothing until Isaac was close enough to hear him whisper, a strange thin noise like a bird being strangled.

"I would not have come, Grimnebulin. I do not wish to be seen . . ."

Isaac lost patience quickly. He opened his mouth to speak but Yagharek continued.

"I have . . . heard things. I have sensed . . . there is a pall over this house. Neither you, nor either of your friends, has left this room all day."

Isaac gave a short laugh.

"You've been waiting, haven't you? Waiting till it was all clear, right? So you could maintain your precious anonymity . . ." He tensed, made an effort to calm himself. "Look, Yag, we've had something of a disaster and I really don't have time or inclination to . . . to pussyfoot about you. I'm afraid our project's on hold for a while . . ."

Yagharek sucked in his breath and cried out, faintly.

"You cannot," he screeched quietly. *"You cannot desert me . . ."*

"Damn!" Isaac reached out and pulled Yagharek in through the door. "Now look!" He marched over to where Lublamai breathed raggedly and gazed and dribbled. He pushed Yagharek before him. He shoved hard, but not with violent pressure. Garuda were wiry and tight-muscled, stronger than they looked, but with their hollow bones and pared-down flesh they were not a match for a big man. But that was not the main reason why Isaac was holding back from exerting himself. The mood between him and Yagharek was testy, not poisonous. Isaac sensed that Yagharek half wanted to see the reason for the sudden tension in the warehouse, even if it meant breaking his ban on being seen by others.

Isaac pointed at Lublamai. David stared vaguely up at the garuda. Yagharek completely ignored him.

"The fucking caterpillar I showed you," said Isaac, "turned into something that did this to my friend. Ever seen anything like that?"

Yagharek shook his head slowly.

"So you see," said Isaac heavily, "I'm afraid that until I sort out what in the name of Jabber's arse I've let loose over the city, and until I've brought Lublamai back from wherever he is, I'm *afraid* that the problems of flight and crisis engines, exciting as they are, are on something of a *low burn* for me."

"You will let slip my shame . . ." hissed Yagharek quickly. Isaac interrupted him.

"David *knows* about your so-called shame, Yag!" he shouted. "And *don't* look at me like that, that's how I *work*, this is my colleague, that's how come I've made fucking progress in your case . . ."

David was looking sharply at Isaac.

"What?" he hissed. "Crisis engines . . . ?"

Isaac shook his head irritatedly, as if a mosquito was in his ear.

"Making headway in crisis physics, that's all. Tell you later."

David nodded slowly, accepting that now was not the time to discuss this, but his bulging eyes betrayed his amazement. *That's all?* they said.

Yagharek seemed to be twitching with nervousness, with a great bulge of misery that washed up through him.

"I . . . I need your help . . ." he began.

"Yeah, as does Lublamai here," shouted Isaac, "and I'm afraid that counts for a damn sight more . . ." Then he softened slowly. "I'm *not* dropping you, Yag. I've no intention of doing that. But the thing is, I can't carry on just now." Isaac thought for a moment. "If you want to get this done as quick as possible, you could *help* . . . Don't just fucking disappear. *Stay the fuck here* and help us sort this out. That way, we can get back, sharpish, to your problem."

David looked askance at Isaac. Now his eyes said, *Do you know what you're doing?* Seeing that, Isaac blustered, and rallied.

"You can sleep here, you can eat here . . . David won't care, he doesn't even live here, I'm the only one that does. Then when we hear anything, we can . . . well, we can maybe think of some use for you. If you know what I mean. You can *help*, Yagharek. That'd be damn useful. The quicker this gets sorted, the quicker we're back on your programme. Understand?"

Yagharek was subdued. It took some minutes before he would speak, and then all he would do was nod and briefly say that yes, he would stay at the warehouse. It was clear that all he could think of was the research into flight. Isaac was exasperated, but forgiving. The excision, the punishment that had befallen Yagharek, had settled on his soul like lead chains. He was selfish, utterly, but he had some reason.

David fell asleep, exhausted and miserable. He slept in his chair that night. Isaac took over caring for Lublamai. The food had passed through him, and the first noisome duty was to clean up his shit.

Isaac bundled up the fouled clothes and shoved them into one of the warehouse's boilers. He thought of Lin. He hoped she came to him soon.

He realized he was pining.

Chapter Twenty-six

Things stirred in the night.

In the morning, in the small hours and again when the sun had risen, more idiot bodies were found. This time there were five. Two vagrants who hid under the bridges of Gross Coil. A baker walking home from work in Nigh Sump. A doctor in Vaudois Hill. A bargewoman out beyond Raven's Gate. A spattering of attacks that disfigured the city without pattern. North; east; west; south. There were no safe boroughs.

Lin slept badly. She had been touched by Isaac's note, to think of him crossing the city just to plant a piece of paper on her door, but she had also been concerned. There was a hysterical tone to the short paragraph, and the plea to come to the laboratory was so utterly out of character that it frightened her.

Nevertheless, she would have come immediately had she not returned to Aspic Hole late, too late to travel. She had not been working. The previous morning she had woken to find a note thrust under her door.

Pressing business necessitates the postponement of appointments until further notice. You will be contacted when resumption of duties is possible.
M.

Lin had pocketed the curt note and wandered to Kinken. She had resumed her melancholy contemplations. And then, with a curious sense of amazement, as if she was watching a performance of her own life and was surprised at the turn of events, she had walked north-west out of Kinken to Skulkford, and boarded the railway. She had taken the two stops north on the Sink Line, to be swallowed by the vast tarry maw of Perdido Street Station. There in the confusion and hissing steam of the enormous central concourse, where the five lines met like an enormous iron and wood star, she had changed trains for the Verso Line.

There had been a five-minute wait while the boiler was stoked in the cavern at the centre of the station. Enough time for Lin to look at herself in incredulity, to ask herself what in the name of Awesome Broodma she was doing. And perhaps in the name of other gods.

But she had not answered, had sat still while the train waited, then moved slowly, picking up speed and rattling in a regular rhythm, squeezing from one of the station's pores. It wound to the north of the Spike, under two sets of skyrails, looking out over Cadnebar's squat, barbarous circus. The prosperity and majesty of The Crow—the Senned Gallery, the Fuchsia House, Gargoyle Park—was riddled with squalor. Lin gazed into steaming rubbish tips as The Crow segued into Rim, saw the wide streets and stuccoed houses of that prosperous neighbourhood wind carefully past hidden, crumbling blocks where she knew the rats were running.

The train passed through Rim Station and plunged on over the fat grey ooze of the Tar, crossing the river barely fifteen feet to the north of Hadrach Bridge, until it picked its way distastefully over the ruinous roofscape of Creekside.

She had left the train at Low Falling Mud, at the western edge of the slum ghetto. It had not taken long to tread the rotting streets, past grey buildings that bulged unnaturally with sweating damp, past kin who eyed her and tasted her in the air and moved away, because her uptown perfume and strange clothes marked her out as one who had escaped. It had not taken her long to find her way back to her broodma's house.

Lin had not come too close, had not wanted her taste to filter through the shattered windows and alert her broodma or her sister to her presence. In the growing heat, her scent was like a badge for other khepri, that she could not remove.

The sun had moved and heated the air and clouds, and still Lin had stood, some little way from her old home. It was unchanged. From within, from cracks in the walls and door, she could hear the skittering, the organic pistoning of little male khepri legs.

No one had emerged.

Passers-by had ejected chymical disgust at her, for coming back to crow, for spying on some unsuspecting household, but she had ignored them all.

If she entered and her broodma was there, she thought, they would both be angry, and miserable, and they would argue, pointlessly, as if the years had not gone by.

If her sister was there and told her their broodma had died, and Lin had let her go without a word of anger or forgiveness, she would be alone. Her heart might burst.

If there was no sign . . . if the floors crawled only with males, living like the vermin they were, no longer pampered princes without brains but bugs that stank and ate carrion, if her broodma and her sister had gone . . . then Lin would be standing pointlessly in a deserted house. Her homecoming would be ridiculous.

An hour or more had passed, and Lin had turned her back on the putrefying building. With her headlegs waving and her head-scarab flexing in agitation, in confusion and loneliness, she made her way back to the station.

She had grappled fiercely with her melancholy, stopping in The Crow and spending some of Motley's enormous payments on books and rare foods. She had entered an exclusive women's boutique, provoking the sharp tongue of the manageress until Lin had fanned her guineas and pointed imperiously at two dresses. She had taken her time in being measured, insisting each piece fit her as sensuously as it would the human women for whom its designer had intended it.

She had bought both pieces, all without a word from the manageress, whose nose wrinkled as she took a khepri's money.

Lin had walked the streets of Salacus Fields wearing one of her purchases, an exquisite fitted piece in cloudy blue that darkened her russet skin. She could not tell if she felt worse or better than before.

She wore the dress again the next morning as she crossed the city to find Isaac.

That morning by Kelltree Docks, dawn had been greeted with a tremendous shout. The vodyanoi dockers had spent the night digging, shaping, shoving and clearing away great weights of cræfted water. As the sun rose hundreds of them emerged from the filthy water, scooping up great handfuls of riverwater and hurling them far out over the Gross Tar.

They had whooped and cheered raggedly, as they lifted the final thin veil of liquid from the great trench they had dug in the river. It yawned fifty or more feet across, an enormous slice of air cut out of the riverwater, stretching the eight hundred feet from one bank to the other. Narrow trenches of water were left at either side, and here and there along the bottom, to stop the river damming. At the bottom of the trench, forty feet below the surface, the riverbed teemed with vodyanoi, fat bodies slithering over each other in the mud, carefully patting at one or other flat, vertical edge of water where the river stopped. Occasionally a vodyanoi would have some discussion with its fellows, and leap over their heads with a powerful convulsion of its enormous froglike hind legs. It would plunge through the airwall into the looming water, kicking out with its webbed feet on some unspecified errand. Others would hurriedly smooth the water behind it, resealing the watercræft, ensuring the integrity of their blockade.

In the centre of the trench, three burly vodyanoi constantly conferred, leaping or crawling to pass on information to their comrades around them, then returning again to the discussion. There were angry debates. These were the elected leaders of the strike committee.

As the sun rose, the vodyanoi at the river's bottom and lining the banks unfurled banners. FAIR WAGES NOW! they demanded, and NO RAISE, NO RIVER.

On either side of the gorge in the river, small boats rowed carefully to the edge of the water. The sailors within leaned out as far as they could and gauged the distance across the furrow. They shook their heads in exasperation. The vodyanoi jeered and cheered.

The channel had been dug a little to the south of Barley Bridge, at the very edge of the docklands. There were ships waiting to enter and ships waiting to leave. A mile or so downstream, in the insalubrious waters between Badside and Dog Fenn, merchant ships reined in their nervous seawyrms and let the boilers run low. In the other direction, by the jetties and landing bays, in Kelltree's fat canals beside the drydocks, the captains of vessels from as far as Khadoh gazed impatiently at the vodyanoi pickets that thronged the banks and worried about getting home.

By mid-morning the human wharfmen had arrived to get about the task of unloading and loading. They quickly discovered that their presence was more or less superfluous. Once the remaining work was done preparing those ships still at anchor in Kelltree itself—at most another two days' work—they were stuck.

The small group who had been in discussion with the striking vodyanoi had come prepared. At ten in the morning about twenty men suddenly streamed out of their yards, climbing the fences around the docks, and jogging to the waterfront by the vodyanoi pickets, who cheered them on with something like hysteria. The men pulled out their own signs: HUMAN AND VODYANOI AGAINST THE BOSSES!

They joined in the noisy chanting.

Over the next two hours, the mood hardened. A core of humans set up a counter-demonstration inside the dockland's low walls. They screamed abuse at the vodyanoi, calling them frogs and toads. They jeered at the striking humans, denounced them as race-traitors. They warned that the vodyanoi would ruin the dock, making human wages plummet. One or two of them carried Three Quills literature.

Between them and the equally strident human strikers was a great mass of confused, vacillating dockers. They wandered back and forth, swearing and baffled. They listened to the shouted arguments from both sides.

The numbers began to grow.

On either bank of the river, in Kelltree itself and on the south bank of Syriac Well, crowds were gathering to watch the confrontation. A few men and women ran among them, moving too fast to be identified, handing out leaflets with the *Runagate Rampant* banner at the top. They demanded in closely printed text that the human dockers join the vodyanoi, that it was the only way the demands would be won. The papers could be seen circulating among the human dockers, handed out by person or persons unseen.

As the day wore on, and the air heated, more and more dockers began to drift over the wall to join the demonstration beside the vodyanoi. The counter-demonstration also grew, sometimes rapidly; but over the space of the hours, it was the strikers that increased most visibly.

There was a tense uncertainty in the air. The crowd was becoming more vocal, yelling at both sides to do something. There was a rumour that the chairman of the dock authority was coming to speak, another that Rudgutter himself would put in an appearance.

All the time, the vodyanoi in the canyon of air carved into the river busied themselves shoring up the shimmering waterwalls. Occasionally fish blundered through the flat edges and fell to the ground, flapping, or half-sunk rubbish eddied gently into the sudden chasm. The vodyanoi threw everything back. They worked in shifts, swimming up through the water to watercræft the upper reaches of the riverwalls. They shouted encouragement at the human strikers from the riverbed, among the ruined metal and thick sludge that was the Gross Tar's floor.

At half past three, with the sun blazing hot through ineffectual clouds, two airships were seen approaching the docks, from the north and the south.

There was excitement among the crowds, and the word quickly spread through the assembled that the mayor was coming. Then a third and fourth airship were noticed, cruising ineluctably over the city towards Kelltree.

The shadow of unease passed over the riverbanks.

Some of the crowd dispersed quietly. The strikers redoubled their chants.

By five to four, the airships hovered over the docks in an airborne X, a massive threatening mark of censure. A mile or so to the east, another solitary dirigible hung over Dog Fenn, on the other side of the river's ponderous kink. The vodyanoi and the humans and the gathered crowds shaded their eyes with their hands and stared up at the impassive shapes, bullet-bodies like hunting squid.

The airships began to sink earthwards. They approached at some speed, the details of their design and the sense of mass of their inflated bodies quite suddenly discernible.

Just before four o'clock, strange organic shapes floated up from behind the surrounding roofs, emerging from sliding doors at the top of the Kelltree and Syriac militia struts, smaller towers not connected to the skyrail network.

The eddying, weightless objects bobbed gently in the breeze and began to drift almost aimlessly towards the wharfs. The sky was suddenly full of the things. They were big and soft-bodied, each a mass of twisted, bloated tissue coated with intricate flaps and curves of skin, craters and strange, dripping orifices. The central sac was about ten feet in diameter. Each of the creatures had a human rider, visible in a harness sutured to the corpulent body. Below each such body was a thicket of dangling tentacles, ribbons of blistered flesh that stretched the forty or so feet to the ground.

The creatures' pinky-purple flesh throbbed regularly like beating hearts.

The extraordinary things bore down on the gathered crowd. There was a full ten seconds when those who saw them were too aghast to speak, or to believe what they saw. Then the shouts started: "Men-o'-war!"

As the panic began, some nearby clock struck the hour and several things happened at once.

Throughout the gathered crowd, in the anti-strike demonstration and even here and there among the striking dockworkers themselves, clumps of men—and some women—suddenly reached over their heads and in violent, quick motions tugged on dark hoods. They were fashioned without visible eye- or mouth-holes; dark crumpled blanks.

From the underbelly of each of the airships—looming absurdly close now—spilt clutches of ropes that jounced and whiplashed as they fell. They fell through the yards and yards of air, their ends coiling slightly on the pavement. They contained the gathering, the pickets and demonstrations and surrounding crowds within four pillars of suspended rope, two on either side of the river. Dark figures slid expertly, at breakneck speed, the length of the cords. They came in a constant quick drip. They looked like glutinous clots dribbling down the entrails of the disembowelled airships.

There were wails from the crowd, which fractured in terror. Its organic cohesion broke. The people fled in all directions, trampling the fallen, grabbing children and lovers and stumbling on cobbles and broken flagstones. They tried to disperse down the side streets that spread like a network of cracks out from the riverbanks. But they ran into the paths of the men-o'-war that bobbed sedately along the alleys' routes.

Uniformed militia were suddenly converging on the picket from every side street. There were shrieks of terror as mounted officers appeared on monstrous bipedal shunn, their hooks reaching out, their blunt eyeless heads swaying as they felt their way with echoes.

The air brimmed with sudden short screams of pain. People blundered in stumbling gangs around corners into men-o'-war tentacles and shrieked as the nerve-agent which riddled the dangling fronds oozed through their clothes and over their bare skin. There were a few breaths of juddering agony, then a cold numbness and paralysis.

The man-o'-war pilots tugged at the nodules and subcuta-

neous synapses that controlled the creatures' movements, coursing deceptively fast over the roofs of the hovels and the dockside
warehouses, trailing their steeds' venomous appendages into the
channels between architecture. Behind them were trails of spasming bodies, eyes glazed and mouths frothing in dumb pain.
Here and there, a few in the crowd—the old, the frail, the allergic
and the unlucky—reacted to the stings with massive biological
violence. Their hearts stopped.

The militia's dark suits were interwoven with fibres from
man-o'-war hide. The tendrils could not penetrate them.

Ranks of militia charged the open spaces where the pickets
were congregated. Men and vodyanoi wielded placards like badly
designed clubs. Within the disorderly mass were brutal skir-
mishes, as militia agents swung spiked truncheons and whips
coated with man-o'-war stings. Twenty feet from the front line
of the confused and angry demonstrators, the first wave of uniformed militia dropped to their knees and raised their mirrored
shields. From behind them came the gibbering of a shunn, then
quick arcs of billowing smoke as their fellows hurled gas gren-
ades over into the demonstration. The militia moved inexorably
into the clouds, breathing through their filter-masks.

A splinter group of officers peeled off from the main wedge
formation and bore down on the river. They threw tube after
hissing tube of billowing gas into the vodyanoi's watercræft
ditch. The croaks and screeches of burning lungs and skin filled
the hole. The carefully maintained walls began to split and dribble as more and more strikers hurled themselves through into the
river to escape the vicious fumes.

Three militiamen knelt at the very edge of the river. They were
surrounded by a thicket of their colleagues, a protective skin.
Quickly, the three at the centre pulled target-rifles from their
backs. Each man had two, loaded and primed with powder, one
of which they set beside them. Moving very fast, they sighted
along the shafts into the miasma of grey smoke. An officer in the
peculiar silver epaulettes of a captain-thaumaturge stood behind
them, muttering quickly and inaudibly, his voice muffled. He
touched each marksman's temples, then jerked his hands away.

Behind their masks, the men's eyes watered and cleared, suddenly seeing registers of light and radiation that rendered the
smoke virtually invisible.

Each man knew the bodyshape and movement patterns of
his target perfectly. The sharpshooters tracked quickly through

the fog of gas and saw their targets conferring with wet rags clamped to their mouths and noses. There was a rapid crackle, three shots in a quick tempo.

Two of the vodyanoi fell. The third looked round in panic, seeing nothing but the swirl of that vicious gas. He raced to the water walling him in, scooped a handful from it and began to croon to it, moving his hand in fast and esoteric passes. One of the riverside marksmen dropped his rifle quickly and picked up his second weapon. The target was a shaman, he realized, and if given time he might invoke an undine. That would make things vastly more complicated. The officer raised the gun to his shoulder, aimed and fired in one brisk movement. The hammer with its clamped shard of flint slid down the serrated edge of the pan cover and snapped, sparking, into the pan.

The bullet burst through the gusts of gas, sending it coiling in intricate wreaths, and buried itself in the neck of the target. The third member of the vodyanoi strike committee fell squirming into the mire, the water dissipating in arcing spray. His blood pooled and thickened in the quag.

The watercræft walls of the trench in the river were splintering and collapsing. They sagged and bowed, water breaching them in gouts and diluting the riverbed, eddying around the feet of the few remaining strikers, coiling like the gas above it, until with a shiver the Gross Tar reknit itself, healing the little rift that had paralysed it and confused its currents. Polluted water buried the blood, the political papers and the bodies.

As the militia put down the Kelltree strike, cables burst from the fifth airship as from its kin.

The crowds in Dog Fenn were shouting, yelling news and descriptions of the fight. Escapees from the pickets stumbled through the ramshackle alleys. Gangs of youths ran back and forth in energetic confusion.

The costermongers on Silverback Street were yelling and pointing at the fat dirigible uncoiling its dangling rigging to the earth. Their shouts were effaced in the sudden boom and drone of klaxons in the sky as one by one the five airships sounded. A militia squad abseiled through the hot air into the streets of Dog Fenn.

They slipped below the silhouetted rooftops into the rank air, then down, their huge boots hammering down the slippery concrete of the courtyard in which they landed. They looked more

construct than human, bulked up by bizarre and twisted armour.
The few workers and dossers in the cul-de-sac watched them
with mouths gaping until one of the militia turned briefly and
raised a huge blunderbuss rifle, sweeping it in a threatening arc.
At that, the watchers dived to the ground or turned and fled.

The militia troops stormed down a dripping staircase into the
underground slaughterhouse. They smashed through the unlocked door and fired into the swirling, bloody air. The butchers
and slaughterers turned dumbfounded to the doorway. One
dropped, gargling in agony as a bullet burst his lung. His gory tu-
nic was drenched again, this time from the inside. The other
workers fled, slipping on gristle as they ran.

The militia tore down the swinging, dripping carcasses of
goat and pigmeat and yanked at the suspended conveyor-belt of
hooks until it ripped from the damp ceiling. They charged in
waves towards the back of the dark chamber and stomped up the
stairs and along the little landing. For all that it slowed them, the
locked door to Benjamin Flex's bedroom might have been
gauze.

Once inside the troops moved to either side of the wardrobe,
leaving one man to unstrap a huge sledgehammer from his back.
He swung it at the old wood, dissolving the wardrobe in three
huge strokes, uncovering a hole in the wall that emitted the
chugging of a steam engine and fitful oil-lamp light.

Two of the officers disappeared into the secret room. There
was a muffled shout and the sound of repeated hammering thuds.
Benjamin Flex came flying through the crumbling hole, his
body twisting, beads of blood hitting his grimy walls in radial
patterns. He hit the floor head first and shrieked, tried to scrabble
away, swearing incoherently. Another officer reached down and
lifted him by the shirt with steam-enhanced strength, shoving
him against a wall.

Ben gibbered and tried to spit, staring at the impassive blue-
masked face, intricate smoked goggles and gasmask and spiked
helmet like the face of some insectile dæmon.

The voice that emerged from the hissing mouthparts was monotonous, but quite clear.

"Benjamin Flex, please give your verbal or written assent to
accompany myself and other officers of the New Crobuzon militia to a place of our choosing for the purposes of interview and
intelligence gathering." The militiaman slammed Ben against
the wall, hard, eliciting an explosive burst of breath and an unin-

telligible bark. "Assent so noticed in presence of myself and two witnesses," the officer responded. "Aye?"

Two of the militiamen behind the officer nodded in unison and responded: "Aye."

The officer cuffed Ben with a punishing backhand blow that dazed him and burst his lip. His eyes wavered drunkenly and he dribbled blood. The hugely armoured man swung Ben up over his shoulder and stomped from the room.

The constables who had entered the little print-room waited for the rest of the squad to follow the officer back out into the corridor. Then, in perfect time, they each pulled a large iron canister from their belts and pushed the plungers that set in motion a violent chymical reaction. They threw the cylinders into the cramped room where the construct still cranked the printing press handle in an endless, mindless circuit.

The militiamen ran like ponderous bipedal rhinos down the corridor after their officer. The acid and powder in the pipebombs mixed and fizzed, flared violently, ignited the tightly packed gunpowder. There were two sudden detonations that sent the damp walls of the building shuddering.

The corridor jacked under the impact, as innumerable gobbets of flaming paper spewed from the doorway, with hot ink and ripped snatches of pipe. Twists of metal and glass burst from the skylight in an industrial fountain. Like smouldering confetti, snippets of editorials and denunciations were sprinkled over the surrounding streets. WE SAY, said one, and BETRAYAL! another. Here and there the banner title was visible, *Runagate Rampant*. Here it was torn and burning, only a fragment visible.

Run . . .

One by one the militia attached themselves to the still-waiting ropes with a clip at their belt. They fumbled with levers embedded in their integral backpacks, setting in motion some powerful, hidden engine that dragged them off the streets and into the air as the belt-pulley turned, its powerful cogs interlocking and hauling the dark, bulky figures back up into the belly of their airship. The officer holding Ben clutched him tightly, but the pulley did not falter under the weight of the extra man.

As a weak fire played desultorily over what had been the slaughterhouse, something dropped from the roof, where it had caught on a ragged gutter. It tumbled through the air and crunched heavily on the stained ground. It was the head of Ben's construct, its upper right arm still attached.

The thing's arm twitched violently, trying to twist a handle that was no longer there. The head rolled, like a skull encased in pewter. Its metal mouth twitched and for a few ghastly seconds, it affected a disgusting parody of motion, crawling along the uneven ground by flexing and unflexing its jaw.

Within half a minute the last vestige of energy had leeched from it. Its glass eyes vibrated and snapped to a stop. It was still.

A shadow passed over the dead thing, as the airship, full now with all its troops, cruised slowly over the face of Dog Fenn, over the last brutal, sordid battles in the docklands, up past Parliament and over the enormity of the city, towards Perdido Street Station and the interrogation rooms of the Spike.

At first, I felt sick to be around them, all these men, their rushing, heavy, stinking breaths, their anxiety pouring through their skin like vinegar. I wanted the cold again, the darkness below the railways, where ruder forms of life struggle and fight and die and are eaten. There is a comfort in that brute simplicity.

But this is not my land and that is not my choice to make. I have struggled to contain myself. I have struggled with the alien jurisprudence of this city, all sharp divides and fences, lines that separate this from that and yours from mine. I have modelled myself on this. I have sought comfort and protection in owning myself, in being my own, my isolate, my private property for this the first time. But I have learnt with sudden violence that I am the victim of colossal fraud.

I have been duped. When the crisis breaks, I cannot be my own here any more than in the Cymek's constant summer (where "my sand" or "your water" are absurdities that would kill their utterer). The splendid isolation I have sought has crumbled. I need Grimnebulin, Grimnebulin needs his friend, his friend needs succour from us all. It is simple mathematics to cancel common terms and discover that I need succour, too. I must offer it to others, to save myself.

I am stumbling. I must not fall.

I was once a creature of the air, and it remembers me. When I climb to the city heights and lean out into the wind, it tickles me with currents and vectors from my past. I can smell and see the passage of predators and prey in the eddying wash of this atmosphere.

I am like a diver who has lost his suit, who can still gaze through the glass bottom of a boat and watch the creatures of the upper and deeper darkness, can trace their passage and feel the tug of the tides, even though distorted and distant, veiled and half hidden.

I know that something is wrong in the sky.

I can see it in the disturbed flocks of birds, that shy suddenly away from random patches of air. I can see it in the panicked passage of wyrmen that seem to glance behind them as they fly.

The air stills with summer, is heavy with heat and now with these newcomers, these intruders I cannot see. The air is laden with menace. My curiosity rises. My hunting instincts stir.

But I am earthbound.

PART FOUR

A Plague of Nightmares

CHAPTER TWENTY-SEVEN

Something uncomfortable and insistent prodded Benjamin Flex awake. His head rocked nauseously, his stomach plunged.

He was sitting strapped to a chair in a small, antiseptic white room. On one wall was a window of frosted glass, admitting light but no sights, no clue at all as to what lay outside. A white-coated man stood over him, poking him with a long shard of metal attached by wires to a humming engine.

Benjamin looked up into the man's face and saw his own. The man wore a mask of perfectly smooth, rounded mirror, a convex lens that sent Benjamin's distorted face back at him. Even bowled and ridiculous, the bruises and blood that discoloured Benjamin's skin shocked him.

The door was open slightly and a man was standing half in, half out of the room. He held the door and faced back the way he had come, speaking to someone in the corridor or main room beyond.

". . . glad you like it," Benjamin heard. ". . . off to the play-house with Cassandra tonight, so you never know . . . no, these eyes are still killing me . . ." The man laughed briefly in response to some unheard pleasantry. He waved. Then he turned and entered the little room.

He turned towards the chair, and Benjamin saw a figure that he recognized from rallies, from speeches, from massive helio-types plastered around the city. It was Mayor Rudgutter.

The three figures in the room were still, regarding each other.

"Mr. Flex," said Rudgutter eventually. "We must talk."

"Got word from Pigeon." Isaac waved the letter as he returned to the table he and David had set up in Lublamai's corner of the ground floor. It was where they had spent the hours of the previous day uselessly scrabbling for plans.

Lublamai lay and drooled and shat in a cot a little way away.

Lin sat with them at the table, listlessly eating slices of banana. She had arrived the previous day, and Isaac, stumbling and semicoherent, had told her what had happened. Both he and David had seemed in shock. It had been some minutes before she had noticed Yagharek, skulking against a wall in the shadows. She had not known whether to greet him, and had waved a brief introduction that he had not acknowledged. When the four of them ate a miserable supper, he had drifted over to join them, his enormous cloak draped over what she knew to be fake wings. Not that she would tell him she knew him to be engaged in a masquerade.

At one point in that long, miserable evening, Lin had reflected that something had finally happened to make Isaac acknowledge her. He had held her hands on arrival. He had not even ostentatiously thrown up a duplicitous spare bed when she had agreed to stay. It was not a triumph, though, not the final great vindication of love that she would have chosen. The reason for his change was simple.

David and he were worried about more important things.

There was a slightly sour part of her mind which, even now, did not believe his conversion to be complete. She knew that David was an old friend, of similarly libertarian principles, who would understand—if he were even thinking about them—the difficulties of the situation, and who could be relied on to be discreet. But she did not allow herself to dwell on this, feeling mean-spirited and selfish to be thinking of herself with Lublamai . . . ruined.

She could not feel Lublamai's affliction as deeply as his two friends, of course, but the sight of that dribbling, mindless thing in the cot shocked and frightened her. She was glad that something had happened to Mr. Motley to give her a few hours or days with Isaac, who seemed broken with guilt and misery.

Occasionally he would flare into angry, useless action, shouting "Right!" and clasping his hands decisively, but there was nothing to be decided, no action he could take. Without some lead, some hint, the start of some trail, there was nothing to be done.

That night, she and Isaac had slept together upstairs, he clutching her miserably, without a hint of arousal. David had gone home, promising to return early in the morning. Yagharek had refused a mattress, had curled into a peculiar, hunched, cross-legged crouch in the corner, obviously designed to keep from crushing his supposed wings. Lin did not know if he was maintaining his illusion for her sake, or if he truly slept, still, in the pose he had used since childhood.

The next morning they sat around the table, drinking coffee and tea, eating stolidly, wondering what to do. When he checked the post, Isaac was quick to discard the rubbish and return with Lemuel's note: unstamped, hand-delivered by some minion.

"What does he say?" asked David quickly.

Isaac held the paper so that David and Lin could read over his shoulder. Yagharek hung back.

Have tracked down source of Peculiar Caterpillar in my records. One Josef Cuaduador. Acquisitions clerk for Parliament. Not wanting to waste time, and remembering promise of *Fat Fee*, have already been to speak to Mr. Cuaduador along with my Large Associate Mr. X. Exerted some little pressure for cooperation. At first Mr. C. thought I was militia. Reassured him otherwise, then ensured his *loquacity* with X's friend *Flintlock*. Seems our Mr. C. *liberated* caterpillar from official shipment or somesuch. Been regretting it ever since. (I did not even pay him much for it.) No knowledge of purpose or source of grub. No knowledge of fate of others from original group—took only one. *One lead only:* (Useless? Useful?) Recipient of packet named Dr. Barbell? Barrier? Berber? Barlime? etc. in R&D.

Am keeping track of services rendered, Isaac. Itemized bill to follow.

Lemuel Pigeon.

"Fantastic!" Isaac exploded, on finishing the letter. "A fucking *lead* . . ."

David looked utterly aghast.

"Parliament?" he said, a strangled gasp. "We're fucking about with *Parliament*? Oh dear Jabber, do you have any *idea* of the scale of shit we're messed up in? What the fuck d'you *mean* 'Fantastic!' you fucking *cretin*, Isaac? Oh, marvellous! We just have to ask Parliament for a list of all those in the *top secret* Research and Development department whose names begin with *B*, then find them one by one and ask if they know anything about flying things that scare their victims comatose, specifically how to catch them. We're *home free*."

No one spoke. A pall settled slowly on the room.

* * *

At its south-westerly corner, Brock Marsh met Petty Coil, a dense knot of chancers, crime and architecture of decayed splendour wedged into a kink in the river.

A little over a hundred years previously, Petty Coil had been an urban hub for the major families. The Mackie-Drendas and the Turgisadys; Dhrachshachet, the vodyanoi financier and founder of the Drach Bank; Sirrah Jeremile Carr, the merchant-farmer: all had their great houses in Petty Coil's wide streets.

But industry had exploded in New Crobuzon, much of it bankrolled by those very families. Factories and docks budded and proliferated. Griss Twist, just across the river, enjoyed a short-lived boom of small machinofacture, with all the noise and stink that that entailed. It became the site of massive riverside tips. A new landscape of ruin and refuse and industrial filth was created, in a speeded-up parody of geological process. Carts dumped load after load of broken machines, rotting paper, slag, organic offal and chymical detritus into the fenced-off rubbish tips of Griss Twist. The rejected matter settled and shifted and fell into place, affecting some shape, mimicking nature. Knolls, valleys, quarries and pools bubbling with foetid gas. Within a few years the local factories had gone but the dumps remained, and the winds that blew in from the sea could send a pestilential stench over the Tar into Petty Coil.

The rich deserted their homes. Petty Coil degenerated in a lively fashion. It became noisier. Paint and plaster bubbled, desquamating grotesquely, as the massive houses became homes for more and more of New Crobuzon's swelling population. Windows broke, were fixed roughly, broke again. As small food-shops and bakers and carpenters moved in, Petty Coil fell willing prey to the city's ineluctable capacity for spontaneous architecture. Walls and floors and ceilings were called into question, amended. New and inventive uses were found for deserted constructions.

Derkhan Blueday made her way hurriedly towards this mess of abused, misused grandeur. She carried a bag close. Her face was set and miserable.

She came up over Cockscomb Bridge, one of the city's most ancient edifices. It was narrow and roughly cobbled, with houses built into the very stones. The river was invisible from the centre of the bridge. On either side, Derkhan could see nothing but the squat, rough-edged skyline of houses nearly a thousand years old, their intricate marble façades crumbled long ago. Lines of washing stretched across the width of the bridge. Raucous shouted conversations and arguments bounced back and forth.

In Petty Coil itself, Derkhan walked quickly under the raised Sud Line and bore north. The river she had passed over bent sharply back on itself, veering towards her in an enormous S, before righting its course and heading east and down to meet the Canker.

Petty Coil was blurring with Brock Marsh. The houses were smaller, the streets narrower and more intricately twisted. Mildewing old houses tottered overhead, their steeply slanting roofs like capes slung over narrow shoulders, making them furtive. In their cavernous front rooms and central courtyards, where trees and bushes died as filth encroached, rude signs were plastered advertising scarabomancy and automatic reading and enchantment therapy. Here, the poorest or most unruly of Brock Marsh's delinquent chymists and thaumaturges fought for space with charlatans and liars.

Derkhan checked the directions she had been given, and found her way to St. Sorrel's Mews. It was a tight little passage ending in a collapsed wall. To her right, Derkhan saw the tall, rust-coloured building described in the note. She entered through the doorless threshold and picked her way over building debris, through a short unlit passage that virtually dripped with damp. At the end of the corridor, she saw the bead curtain she had been told to look for, strings of broken glass on wire, swaying gently.

She steeled herself, drawing the vicious shards back gently, drawing no blood. Derkhan entered the little parlour beyond.

Both of the room's windows had been covered: thick material was glued to them in great fibrous clumps that clotted the air with heavy shadow. The furnishings were minimal. The same shade of brown as the darkened atmosphere, they seemed half invisible. Behind a low table, sipping tea in an absurdly dainty manner, a plump, hairy woman basked in a sumptuous decaying armchair.

She eyed Derkhan.

"What can I do for you?" she asked evenly, in a tone of resigned irritation.

"You're the communicatrix?" said Derkhan.

"Umma Balsum." The woman inclined her head. "Got some business for me?"

Derkhan made her way across the room and hovered nervously by a bursting sofa until Umma Balsum indicated that she should sit. Derkhan did so abruptly, and fumbled in her bag.

"I need . . . uh . . . to talk to *Benjamin Flex*." Her voice was taut. She spoke in little bursts, gearing up to each announcement, then spitting it out. She pulled out a little pouch of the detritus she had found at the site of the abattoir.

She had gone to Dog Fenn the previous evening, as news of the militia's crushing of the dock strike washed over New Crobuzon. It swept along with rumours in its wake. One of the rumours concerned a subsidiary attack on a seditious newspaper in Dog Fenn.

It had been late when Derkhan had arrived, disguised as always, in the dank streets in the south-east of the city. It had rained; warm, fat drops bursting like rotting things on the rubble in the cul-de-sac. The entrance was blocked, so Derkhan had entered through the low portal through which meat and animals were slung. She had clung to the noisome stones, dangling over the lip into the butchers' den, stained with shit and gore from a thousand terrified animals, and dropped the few feet into the bloody darkness of the deserted charnel-house.

She had crawled over the ruined conveyor-belt, snagged herself on the meathooks that littered the floor. The sanguinary slick in which she stumbled was cold and sticky.

Derkhan had fought her way past the stones that had burst from walls, over the ruined stairs, up towards Ben's room, the centre of the destruction. Her way was paved with ripped and ruined shards of printing machinery, and smoke-charred pieces of cloth and paper.

The room itself was little more than a hole full of rubbish. Chunks of masonry had crushed the bed. The wall between Ben's bedroom and the hidden printing press was almost completely destroyed. Languorous summer drizzle had been falling through the burst skylight onto the shattered skeleton of the press.

Derkhan's face had hardened. She had searched with a fervent intensity. She had unearthed small pieces of evidence, small proofs that this was once where a man had lived. She brought them out now, put them on the table before Umma Balsum.

She had found his razor, with a little stubble and bloodrust still staining its blade. The torn remnants of a pair of trousers. A piece of paper discoloured with his blood from where she had rubbed and rubbed it against a red stain on the wall. The last two issues of *Runagate Rampant* that she had found under the ruins of his bed.

Umma Balsum watched the pathetic collection emerge.

"Where is he?" she asked.

"I . . . I think he's in the Spike," said Derkhan.

"Well, that's going to cost you an extra noble straight off," said Umma Balsum tartly. "Don't like tangling with the law. Talk me through this stuff."

Derkhan showed her each of the pieces she had brought. Umma Balsum nodded at each briefly, but seemed particularly interested in the issues of *RR*.

"He wrote for this, did he?" she asked keenly, fingering the papers.

"Yes." Derkhan did not volunteer the information that he edited it. She was nervous of breaking the taboo against naming names, even though she had been assured that the communicatrix was trustworthy. Umma Balsum's livelihood depended for the most part on contacting people in the militia's possession. Selling out her clients would be a financial miscalculation. "This—" Derkhan turned to the central column, with the headline *What We Think* "—he wrote this."

"Ahhh . . ." said Umma Balsum. "Shame you don't have it in his original scripture. But this ain't bad. Got anything else peculiar on him?"

"He has a tattoo. Above his left bicep. Like this." Derkhan brought out the sketch she had made of the ornate anchor decoration.

"Sailor?"

Derkhan smiled mirthlessly.

"Got discharged and banged up without setting foot on a ship. Got drunk when he joined up and insulted his captain before the tattoo was even dry." She remembered him telling the story.

"Righto," said Umma Balsum. "Two marks for the attempt. Five marks connection fee if I get him, then two stivers a minute while we're linked. And a noble on account of he's in the Spike. Acceptable?" Derkhan nodded. It was expensive, but this kind of thaumaturgy was not just a question of learning a few passes. With enough training, anyone could effect the odd fumbling hex, but this kind of psychic channelling took a prodigious birth-talent and years of arduous study. Appearances and surroundings notwithstanding, Umma Balsum was no less a thaumaturgic expert than a senior Remaker or chimerist. Derkhan fumbled for her purse. "Pay after. We'll see if we get through first." Umma Balsum rolled up her left sleeve. Her flesh dimpled and wobbled loosely. "Draw me that tattoo. Make it as like the original as you can." She nodded, indicating Derkhan to a stool in the corner of the room on which rested a palette with a collection of brushes and coloured inks.

Derkhan brought the materials over. She began to sketch onto Umma Balsum's arm. She cast her mind back desperately, trying to get the colours exactly right. It took her about twenty-five minutes to finish her attempt. The anchor she had drawn was a little more garish than Benjamin's (partly a consequence of the quality of the inks), and perhaps somewhat squatter. Nonetheless, she was sure that anyone who knew the original would recognize hers as a copy of it. She sat back, tentatively satisfied.

Umma Balsum waved her arm like a fat chicken's wing, drying the inks. She fiddled with the remnants of Benjamin's bedroom.

". . . bloody unhygenic bloody way to make a living . . ." she murmured, just loud enough for Derkhan to hear. Umma Balsum picked up Benjamin's razor and, holding it with a practised grip, nicked herself slightly on the chin. She rubbed the bloodstained paper against her cut. Then she lifted up her skirt and pulled the trouser leg as far onto her fat thighs as it would go.

Umma Balsum reached under the table and brought out a leather and darkwood box. She set it on the table and opened it.

Inside was a tight, interlocking tangle of valves and tubes and wires, looping over and under each other in an incredibly dense engine. At its top was a ridiculous-looking brass helmet, with a kind of trumpet attachment jutting from the front. The helmet was tethered to the box by a long coiled wire.

Umma Balsum reached out and extracted the helmet. She hesitated, then placed it on her head. She fastened the leather straps. From some hidden place inside the box she pulled out a large handle, which slotted neatly into a hexagonal hole at the side of the boxed engine. Umma Balsum placed the box at the edge of the table nearest Derkhan. She attached the engine to a chymical battery.

"Righto," said Umma Balsum, dabbing absent-mindedly at her still-dripping chin. "Now, you'll have to get this going by winding that handle. Once the battery kicks in, you keep an eye on it. If it starts to play up, *start winding that handle again*. You let that current falter, we lose the connection, and without careful disengagement your mate risks losing his mind, and what's worse so do I. So *watch it close* . . . Also, if we make contact, tell him not to move around or I'll run out of cable." She rattled the wire which attached her helmet to the engine. "Got me?" Derkhan nodded. "Right. Give me that thing he wrote. I'm going to get into character, try and harmonize. Start winding, and don't stop till the battery takes over."

Umma Balsum stood and picked up her chair, shoving it back against the wall, puffing. Then she turned and stood in the relatively open space. She visibly braced herself, then drew a stopwatch out of her pocket, pressed the stud which turned it on and nodded at Derkhan.

Derkhan began to wind the handle. It was mercifully smooth. She felt oiled gears inside the box begin to connect and catch, calculated tension biting against her arm, powering up the esoteric mechanisms. Umma Balsum had dropped the stopwatch on the table, was holding *RR* in her right hand, reading Benjamin's words in an inaudible whisper, her lips moving quickly. She held her left hand slightly raised, and its fingers danced a complicated quadrille, inscribing some thaumaturgic symbols in the air.

When she reached the end of his article she simply returned to the beginning and began it again, in an endless quick loop.

The current flowed around and around the coiled wire, visibly jolting Umma Balsum, setting her head vibrating very slightly for a few seconds. She dropped the paper, continuing to recite Benjamin's words *sotto voce* from memory. She turned slowly, her eyes quite vacant, shuffling her feet. As she turned, there was a second when the trumpet at the front of her helmet was directly pointed at Derkhan. For a split second, Derkhan felt a pulse of weird æthereo-mental waves buffet her psyche. She reeled slightly, but continued to turn the handle, until she felt another force take it and move it on, and she gently released her hand and watched it go. Umma Balsum moved until she was facing the north-west, until she was aligned with the Spike, out of sight in the centre of the city.

Derkhan watched the battery and the engine, made sure it maintained a steady circuit.

Umma Balsum closed her eyes. Her lips moved. The air in the room seemed to sing like a wine glass stroked on its rim.

Then, suddenly, her body jerked violently. She shuddered. Her eyes snapped open.

Derkhan stared at the communicatrix.

Umma Balsum's lank hair twisted like a boxful of bait worms. It slid back from her forehead and snaked backwards, into an approximation of the greased-down backwards sweep that Benjamin affected when he was not working. A ripple passed through Umma Balsum, from her feet up. It was as if a lightning tide swept along her subcutaneous fat, altering it slightly as it passed. When it had passed out through the crown of her head, her whole body had changed. She was no fatter, and no thinner, but the distribution of tissue had subtly modified her shape. She looked a little broader in the shoulders. Her jawline was more pronounced, and her ample jowls were somehow minimized.

Bruises flowered on her face.

She stood for a second, then collapsed suddenly onto all fours. Derkhan let out a little cry, but she saw that Umma Balsum's eyes were still open and focused.

Umma Balsum sat suddenly with her legs splayed out, her back leaning against the sofa's arm.

Her eyes moved slowly up as a furrow of incomprehension ploughed her face. She looked up at Derkhan, still frantically staring. Umma Balsum's mouth (now firmer and thinner lipped) opened in what looked like astonishment.

"Dee?" she hissed in a voice that oscillated with a deeper echo.

Derkhan gawped at Umma Balsum idiotically.

"Ben . . . ?" she faltered.

"How did you get *in* here?" hissed Umma Balsum, rising quickly. She squinted at Derkhan in awe. "I can see *through* you . . ."

"Ben, listen to me." Derkhan realized she had to calm him down. "Stop moving. You're seeing me through a communicatrix who's harmonized with you. She's shut herself down into a totally passive recipient state so I can talk straight to you. D'you understand?"

Umma Balsum, who was Ben, nodded quickly. S/he stopped moving, and sank again to her/his knees. "Where are you?" s/he whispered.

"In Brock Marsh, down by the Coil. Ben, we don't have much time. Where are you? *What happened?* Have they . . . have they . . . hurt you?" Derkhan exhaled tremulously, her tension and despair sweeping through her.

Two miles away Ben shook his head miserably, and Derkhan saw it in front of her.

"Not yet," whispered Ben. "They've left me alone . . . for a while . . ."

"How did they know where you were?" hissed Derkhan again.

"Jabber, Dee, they've *always* known, haven't they? I had fucking *Rudgutter* in here earlier, and he . . . and he was laughing at me. Telling me they'd always known where *RR* was, just couldn't be bothered to pick us up."

"It was the strike . . ." said Derkhan miserably. "They decided we'd gone too far . . ."

"No."

Derkhan looked up sharply. Ben's voice, or the approximation that emerged from Umma Balsum's mouth, was hard and clear. The eyes that gazed at her were steady and urgent.

"No, Dee, it *ain't* the strike. Dammit, I only *wish* we had the kind of impact on the strike that worried them. No, that's a fucking *cover story* . . ."

"So what . . . ?" began Derkhan hesitantly. Ben interrupted her.

"I'll tell you what I know. After I got here, Rudgutter comes in and he's waving *Double-R* at me. And you know what he's pointing at? That *really fucking tentative* story we had in the second section. 'Rumours of Fat Sun Deal With Top Mobster.' You know, the one from that contact I had that was saying the government sold some shit or other, some failed science project, to some crim. Nothing! We had nothing! It was just shit-stirring we were doing! And Rudgutter's waving it around, and he . . . he's shoving it in my face . . ." Umma Balsum's eyes slid away into reverie for a moment as Ben remembered. "He's on and on at me. 'What d'ye know about this, Mr. Flex? Who's your source? What do you know about the *moths*?' Seriously! Moths, as in butterflies! 'What do you know about *Mr. M.*'s recent *problems*?' "

Ben shook Umma Balsum's head slowly. "Did you get all that? Dee, I dunno what the fuck we're onto here, but we've opened up some story which . . . Jabber! . . . which's got Rudgutter *crapping* himself. That's why he took me! He kept saying 'If you know where the moths are, it'd be best to tell me.' Dee . . ." Ben staggered carefully to his feet. Derkhan opened her mouth to warn him about moving away, but her words died as he moved carefully towards her on Umma Balsum's legs. "Dee, you have to chase this. They're scared, Dee. They're really scared. We've got to use this. I didn't have a fucking clue what he was on about, but I think he thought I was acting, and I started milking it, 'cause it was making him uncomfortable."

Tentatively, carefully, nervously, Ben reached out with Umma Balsum's hands towards Derkhan. Derkhan's throat caught as she saw that Ben was crying. Tears rolled down his face without him making a sound. She bit her lip.

"What's that whirring noise, Dee?" asked Ben.

"It's the motor to the communicating engine. It has to keep going," she said.

Umma Balsum's head nodded.

Her hands touched Derkhan's. Derkhan trembled at the touch. She felt Ben clutch her free hand, kneeling before her.

"I can feel you . . ." Ben smiled. "You're only half visible, like a fucking spook . . . but I can *feel* you." He stopped smiling and groped for words. "Dee . . . I . . . they're going to kill me. Oh Jabber . . ." he breathed out. "I'm scared. I know these . . . scum . . . will use *pain* on me . . ." His shoulders shuddered up and down as he lost control of his sobs. He was silent for a minute, looking down, weeping silently for fear. When he looked up, his voice was solid.

"*Fuck 'em!* We've got the bastards running scared, Dee. You've got to chase it! I hereby appoint you editor of fucking *Runagate Rampant* . . ." He grinned fleetingly. "Listen. Go to Mafaton. I've only met her twice, in cafés near there, but I think that's where she lives, the contact—we met late, and I doubt she'd have wanted to find her way back across the city on her own after, so I'm figuring she's from round there. Her name's *Magesta Barbile*. She hasn't told me much. Just that some project she was working on in R&D—she's a scientist—the government terminated and sold off to a crime boss. I thought it could *all* be a wind-up; I published out of fucking *mischief* more than 'cause it was a real story. But my *gods*, the reaction vindicates it."

Now Derkhan was crying, a little. She nodded.

"I'll chase it, Ben. Promise."

Ben nodded. There was a moment of silence.

"Dee . . ." said Ben eventually. "I . . . I don't suppose there's anything you could do with that communico-wossname that would . . . I don't suppose . . . you can't kill me, can you?"

Derkhan let out a gasp of shock and grief.

She looked around desperately and shook her head.

"No, Ben. I could only do that by killing the communicatrix . . ."

Ben nodded sadly.

"I really don't know as I'm going to be able to . . . hold back from letting some stuff slip . . . Jabber knows I'll try, Dee . . . but they're experts, you know? And I . . . well . . . might as well get it all over with, know what I mean?"

Derkhan was holding her eyes closed. She wept for Ben, and with him.

"Oh gods, Ben, I'm so sorry . . ."

He was suddenly, ostentatiously brave. Stiff-jawed. Pugnacious. "I'll do me best. Just you make damn sure you chase Barbile, all right?"

She nodded.

"And . . . thanks," he said with a wry smile. "And . . . goodbye."

He bit his lip, looked down, then up again and kissed her on the cheek for a long time. Derkhan held him close with her left arm.

And then Benjamin Flex broke away and stepped back, and with some mental reflex invisible to the distraught Derkhan, he told Umma Balsum that it was time for them to disengage.

The communicatrix rippled again, quivered and staggered, and with an almost palpable gust of relief her body collapsed back into its own shape.

The battery continued winding the little handle until Umma Balsum righted herself and walked closer, laid a peremptory hand on it. She stopped the watch on the table, and said: "That's it, dear."

Derkhan stretched out and laid her head on the table. She wept in silence. Across the city, Benjamin Flex was doing the same.

Both of them alone.

It was only two or three minutes before Derkhan sniffed sharply and sat up. Umma Balsum was sitting in her chair, calculating sums on a scrap of paper with great efficiency.

She glanced over at the sound of Derkhan's brisk attempts to reassert control over herself.

"Feeling better, deario?" she asked breezily. "I've worked out your charge."

There was a moment when Derkhan felt sick at the woman's callousness, but it came and went quickly. Derkhan did not know if Umma Balsum could recall what she heard and said when she was harmonized. And then even if she did, Derkhan's was only one tragedy in the hundreds and thousands throughout the city. Umma Balsum made her money as a go-between, and her mouth had told story after faltered story of loss and betrayal and torture and misery.

There was a certain obscure, lonely comfort for Derkhan in realizing that hers and Ben's was not a special, not an unusual suffering. Ben's would not be a special death.

"Look." Umma Balsum was waving her piece of paper at Derkhan. "Two marks plus five for connection is seven. I was there for eleven minutes, which makes twenty-two stivers: that's two and tuppence, brings it to nine marks two. Plus a noble for Spike danger money, and you're looking at one noble nine and two."

Derkhan gave her two nobles and left.

She walked quickly, without thinking, tracing her way through the streets of Brock Marsh. She re-entered the inhabited streets, where the people she passed were more than shifty-looking figures skulking hurriedly from shadow to shadow. Derkhan shouldered through stallholders and vendors of cheap and dubious potions.

She realized that she was making her way towards Isaac's laboratory-house. He was a close friend, and something of a political comrade. He had not known Ben—had not even heard his name—but he would understand the scale of what had happened. He might have some idea of what to do . . . and if not, well, Derkhan would make do with a strong coffee and some comforting.

His door was locked. There was no answer from within. Derkhan almost wailed. She was about to wander off into lonely misery when she remembered Isaac's enthusiastic descriptions of some vile pub that he frequented on the river's bank, The Dead Child or something. She turned down the little alley beside the house and looked up and down the pathway by the water, flagstones broken and erupting with tenacious grass.

The dirty lapping waves tugged organic filth gently towards the east. Across the Canker, the opposite bank was choked in snarls of bramble and thickets of serpentine weeds. A little way to the north on Derkhan's side, some tumbledown establishment huddled by the trail. She walked towards it tentatively, speeding up when she saw the stained and peeling sign: The Dying Child.

Inside, the dark was foetid and warm and unnervingly damp; but in the far corner, past the slouching, collapsed human and vodyanoi and Remade wrecks, sat Isaac.

He was talking in an animated whisper with another man who Derkhan vaguely remembered, some scientist friend of Isaac's. Isaac looked up as Derkhan stood in the door, and after a double-take, he stared at her. She almost ran towards him.

"Isaac, Jabber and *fuck* . . . I'm so glad I found you . . ."

As she gabbled at him, her hand nervously clenching the cloth of his jacket, she realized with a mortifying lurch that he looked at her without welcome. Her little speech faltered out.

"Derkhan . . . my gods . . ." he said. "I . . . Derkhan, there's a crisis . . . Something's happened, and I . . ." He looked uneasy.

Derkhan stared at him miserably.

She sat suddenly, collapsed onto the bench beside him. It was like a surrender. She leant on the table, kneaded her eyes which were brimming suddenly and irrevocably.

"I've just seen a dear friend and comrade get ready to be *tortured to death* and half my *life*'s been crushed and exploded and stamped on and I don't know why and I've got to find a Doctor fucking Barbile *somewhere in the city* to find out what's going on, and I come to you . . . for . . . because you're supposed to be my *friend* and what, you're . . . *busy* . . . ?"

Tears oozed from beneath her fingertips and scored their way across her face. She wiped her hands violently across her eyes and sniffed, glancing up for a moment, and she saw that Isaac and the other man were staring at her with an extraordinary, absurd intensity. Their eyes gaped.

Isaac's hand crept across the table and gripped her by the wrist.

"You've got to find *who*?" he hissed.

Chapter Twenty-eight

"Well," said Bentham Rudgutter carefully, "I couldn't get anything out of him. Yet."

"Not even the name of his source?" asked Stem-Fulcher.

"No." Rudgutter pursed his lips and shook his head slowly. "He just shuts down. But I don't think that'll be too hard to find out. After all, there aren't a huge number of people it can be. It's got to be someone in R&D, it's *probably* someone on the SM project . . . We may well know more when the inquisitors have interrogated him."

"So . . ." said Stem-Fulcher. "Here we are."

"Indeed."

Stem-Fulcher, Rudgutter and MontJohn Rescue were standing, surrounded by an elite militia guard unit, in a tunnel deep under Perdido Street Station. Gaslamps made fitful impressions on the murk. The little points of grubby light went on as far as they could see before them. A little way behind them was the lift-cage they had just left.

At Rudgutter's signal, he, his companions and their escort began to walk down into the darkness. The militia marched in formation.

"Right," said Rudgutter. "You've both got the scissors?" Stem-Fulcher and Rescue nodded. "Four years ago it was chess sets," Rudgutter mused. "I remember when the Weaver changed its tastes, it took about three deaths before we worked out what it wanted." There was an uneasy pause. "Our research is quite up to date," said Rudgutter with gallows humour. "I spoke to Doctor Kapnellior before meeting you. He's our resident Weaver 'expert' . . . something of a misnomer. Just means that unlike the rest of us, he's only extremely damn ignorant about them, rather than totally. He reassures me that scissors are still very much the object of desire."

After a moment, he spoke again.

"I'll do the talking. I've dealt with it before." He was unsure himself whether that was an advantage or a disadvantage.

The corridor had come to an end, terminating in a thick door of iron-banded oak. The man at the head of the militia unit slid a huge key into the lock and turned it smoothly. He tugged the door open, bracing himself at its weight, and trooped into the dark room beyond. He was well trained. His discipline was like steel. He must, after all, have been extremely frightened.

The rest of the officers followed him, then Rescue and Stem-Fulcher, and finally Bentham Rudgutter. He pulled the door closed behind them.

As they passed into the room, all felt a moment of dislocation, a wispy unease that prickled across their skin with a quasi-physical momentum. Long threads, invisible filaments of spun æther and emotion, were draped in intricate patterns around the room, and were rippling and sticking to the intruders.

Rudgutter twitched. From the corner of his eye he glimpsed threads that folded out of existence when he looked them full on.

The room was as obscure as if it were shrouded in cobwebs. On every wall, scissors were attached in bizarre designs. Scissors chased each other like predatory fish; they sported on the ceiling; they coiled around and through each other in convoluted, unsettling geometric designs.

The militia and their charges stood still against one wall of the room. No sources of light were visible, but they could still see. The atmosphere in the room seemed monochrome, or disturbed in some way, the light etiolated and cowed.

They stood still for a long time. There were no sounds.

Slowly and silently, Bentham Rudgutter reached into the bag he carried and brought out the large grey scissors he had had an aide buy in an ironmonger's on the lowest commercial concourse of Perdido Street Station.

He parted the scissors without a noise, held them up in the cloying air.

Rudgutter brought the razor edges together. The room reverberated with the unmistakable sound of blade sliding along sharpened blade, and snapping shut with an inexorable division.

The echoes trembled like flies in a funnelweb. They slid into a dark dimension at the room's heart.

A gust of cold sent gooseflesh dancing across the backs of those congregated.

The echoes of the scissors came back.

As they returned and crept up from below the threshold of hearing, they metamorphosed, becoming words, a voice, melodious and melancholy, that first whispered and then grew more bold, spinning itself into existence out of the scissor-echoes. It was not quite describable, heartbreaking and frightening, it tugged the listener close; and it sounded not in the ears but deeper inside, in the blood and bone, in the nerve-clusters.

. . . FLESHSCAPE INTO THE FOLDING INTO THE FLESHSCAPE TO SPEAK A GREETING IN THIS THE SCISSORED REALM I WILL RECEIVE AND BE RECEIVED . . .

In the fearful silence, Rudgutter gesticulated at Stem-Fulcher and Rescue, until they understood, and they raised their scissors as he had done, opened and sharply shut them, slicing the air with an almost tactile sound. He joined in, the three of them opening and closing their blades in macabre applause.

At the sound of that snapping susurration, the unearthly voice resonated into the room again. It moaned with an obscene pleasure. Each time it spoke, it was as if what faded into audibility was only a snatch of an unceasing monologue.

. . . AGAIN AGAIN AND AGAIN DO NOT WITHHOLD THIS BLADED SUMMONS THIS EDGED HYMN I ACCEPT I AGREE YOU SLICE SO NICE AND NICELY YOU LITTLE ENDOSKELETAL FIGURINES YOU SNIP AND SHAVE AND SLIVER THE CORDS OF THE WOVEN WEB AND SHAPE IT WITH AN UNCOUTH GRACE . . .

From out of shadows cast by some unseen shapes, shadows that seemed stretched-out and taut, tethered from corner to corner of the square room, something stalked into view.

Into existence. It bulked suddenly where there had been nothing. It stepped out from behind some fold in space.

It picked its way forward, delicate on pointed feet, vast body bobbing, lifting multiple legs high. It looked down at Rudgutter and his fellows from a head that loomed colossally above them.

A spider.

Rudgutter had trained himself rigorously. He was an unimaginative man, a cold man who ruled himself with industrial discipline. He could no longer feel terror.

But, gazing at the Weaver, he came close.

It was worse, more frightening by far than the ambassador. The Hellkin were appalling and awesome, monstrous powers for which Rudgutter had the most profound respect. And yet, and yet . . . he understood them. They were tortured and torturing, calculating and capricious. Shrewd. Comprehensible. They were political.

The Weaver was utterly alien. There could be no bargaining and no games. It had been tried.

Rudgutter conquered himself, angry, judging himself harshly, studying the thing before him in an attempt to itemize and metabolize the sight.

The Weaver's bulk was mostly its huge teardrop abdomen that welled up and hung downwards behind it from its neck-waist, a tight, bulbous fruit seven feet long and five wide. It was absolutely taut and smooth, its chitin a shimmering black iridescence.

The creature's head was the size of a man's chest. It was suspended from the front of the abdomen a third of the way from the top. The fat curve of its body loomed above it like skulking black-clad shoulders.

The head swivelled slowly to take in its visitors.

The top as smooth and spare as a human skull in black: multiple eyes a single, deep blood-red. Two main orbs as large as newborns' heads sat in sunken sockets at either side; between them a much smaller third; above it two more; above them three more still. An intricate, precise constellation of glints on dark crimson. An unblinking array.

The Weaver's complicated mouthparts unhinged, its inner jaw flexing, something between a mandible and a black ivory trap. Its wet gullet flexed and vibrated deep within.

Its legs, thin and bony as human ankles, sprouted from the thin band of segmented flesh that linked its headpiece and abdomen. The Weaver walked on its hindmost four legs. They shot up and out at a forty-five-degree angle, hinging in knees a foot or more above the Weaver's hunkered head, higher than the top of its abdomen. The legs rebounded from the joints almost straight down ten feet, culminating in a point as featureless and sharp as a stiletto.

Like a tarantula, the Weaver picked one leg up at a time, lifting it very high and placing it down with the delicacy of a surgeon or an artist. A slow, sinister and inhuman movement.

From the same intricate fold as that great quadrupedal frame emerged two sets of shorter legs. One pair, six feet long, rested pointing upwards at the elbows. Each thin, hard shaft of chitin ended in an eighteen-inch talon, a cruel, polished shard of russet shell edged like a scalpel. At the base of each weapon sprouted a curl of arachnid-bone, a sharpened hook to snag and slice and hold prey.

Those organic kukris jutted up like wide horns, like lances. An ostentatious display of murderous potential.

And in front of them, the final, shorter pair of limbs hung down. At their tips, held midway between the Weaver's head and the ground, a pair of thin and tiny hands. Five-fingered and slender, only smooth fingertips without nails and skin the alien, nacreous black of pure pitch distinguished them from the hands of human children.

The Weaver bent its elbows up a little and held these hands together, clasping and rubbing them together slowly and incessantly. It was a furtive, disturbingly human motion, like that of an untrustworthy, simpering priest.

The spearpoint feet crept closer. The red-black claws swivelled a little and glinted in the non-light. The hands stroked each other.

The Weaver's body rocked back and alarmingly forward again.

. . . WHAT OFFERING WHAT BOON THE HINGED SPLITTERS YOU BRING ME . . . it said, and suddenly held out its right hand. The militia officers tensed at the quick movement.

Without hesitation Rudgutter stepped forward and placed his scissors into its palm, taking a little care not to touch its skin. Stem-Fulcher and Rescue did the same. The Weaver stepped back with unsettling speed. It looked at the scissors it held, threaded its fingers through the handles and worked each pair rapidly open and shut. Then it moved to the back wall and, moving quickly, it pressed each pair of scissors into a position on the cold stone.

Somehow, the lifeless metal stayed where it was put, clinging to the damp-patterned stone. The Weaver adjusted its design minutely.

"We're here to ask you about something, Weaver." Rudgutter's voice was steady.

The Weaver turned ponderously back to face him.

. . . THE WEFT OF THREADS SURROUND ABOUND ABOUT YOUR TOTTERING TITTERING CARCASSES YOU TUG AND SHRUG UNRAVEL AND REKNIT YOU TRIUMVIRATE OF POWER ENCASED IN THE BLUE-

CLAD BRISTLING WITH SPARKING FLINT BLACK POWDER IRON YOU
STILL-POINT THREE HAVE CAUGHT HANGNAIL-SOULS ON THE FAB-
RIC SNAGS THE FIVE WINGED RIPPERS RENDING UNWIND SYNAPSE
AFTER GANGLIOL SPIRIT SUCK ON MINDFIBRES . . .

Rudgutter looked sharply over at Rescue and Stem-Fulcher.
All three of them were straining to follow the dream-poetics that
was the Weaver tongue. One thing had come across clear.

"Five?" whispered Rescue, looking over at Rudgutter and
Stem-Fulcher. "Motley bought only *four* moths . . ."

. . . FIVE DIGITS OF A HAND TO INTERFERE TO STRIP WORLD-
FABRIC FROM THE BOBBINS OF THE CITY-KIND FIVE AIR-TEARING
INSECTS FOUR FINELY FORMED NOBLE BERINGED WITH SHIMMER-
ING DECORATION ONE SQUAT THUMB THE RUNT THE RUINED EM-
POWERING ITS IMPERIOUS SIBLING FINGERS FIVE A HAND . . .

The militia guard tensed as the Weaver stalked its slow ballet
over to Rescue. It spread out the fingers of one hand, held it up in
front of Rescue's face, pushed it closer and closer to him. The air
around the humans thickened at the Weaver's approach. Rudgutter fought down an impulse to wipe his face, to clean it of that
unseen clinging silk. Rescue set his jaw. The militia murmured
with dithering impotence. Their uselessness was brought home.

Rudgutter watched the little drama uneasily. The last but one
time he had spoken to the Weaver, it had illustrated a point it was
making, a figure of speech of some kind, by reaching out to the
militia captain flanking Rudgutter, lifting him into the air and fil-
leting him slowly, drawing one of its talons through his armour
up the side of his abdomen and around under the chin, drawing out bone after steaming bone. The man had screamed and
flopped and screamed as the Weaver eviscerated him, its mournful voice resonating in Rudgutter's head as it explained itself in
its oneiric riddles.

Rudgutter knew that the Weaver would do anything that it
considered improved the worldweave. It might pretend to be
dead or reshape the stone of the floor into a statue of a lion. It
might pluck out Eliza's eyes. Whatever it took to shape the pattern in the fabric of the æther that only it could see, whatever it
took to Weave the tapestry into shape.

The memory of Kapnellior discussing Textorology—the science of Weavers—flitted in and out of Rudgutter's mind. Weavers
were fabulously rare, and only intermittent inhabitants of conventional reality. Only two Weaver corpses had been procured

by New Crobuzon's scientists since the city's birth. Kapnellior's was hardly an exact science.

No one knew why this Weaver chose to stay. It had announced in its elliptical way to Mayor Dagman Beyn, more than two hundred years ago, that it would live below the city. Over the decades, one or two administrations had left it alone. Most had been unable to resist the pull of its power. Its occasional interactions—sometimes banal, sometimes fatal—with mayors and scientists were the main source of information for Kapnellior's studies.

Kapnellior himself was an Evolutionist. He held to the view that the Weavers were a species of conventional spider that had been subjected by some Torquic or thaumaturgic fluke—thirty, forty thousand years ago, probably in Sagrimai—to a sudden, short-lived evolutionary acceleration of explosive velocity. Within a few generations, he had explained to Rudgutter, the Weavers evolved from virtually mindless predators into aestheticians of astonishing intellectual and materio-thaumaturgic power, superintelligent alien minds who no longer used their webs to catch prey, but were attuned to them as objects of beauty disentanglable from the fabric of reality itself. Their spinnerets had become specialized extradimensional glands that Wove patterns in with the world. The world which was, for them, a web.

Old stories told how Weavers would kill each other over aesthetic disagreements, such as whether it was prettier to destroy an army of a thousand men or to leave it be, or whether a particular dandelion should or should not be plucked. For a Weaver, to think was to think aesthetically. To act—to Weave—was to bring about more pleasing patterns. They did not eat physical food: they seemed to subsist on the appreciation of beauty.

A beauty unrecognized by humans or other denizens of the mundane plane.

Rudgutter was praying fervently that the Weaver did not decide that slaughtering Rescue would make a pretty pattern in the æther.

After tense seconds, the Weaver retreated, still holding up its hand with splayed fingers. Rudgutter exhaled with relief, heard his colleagues and the militia guard do the same.

. . . FIVE . . . whispered the Weaver.

"Five," agreed Rudgutter evenly. Rescue paused and nodded slowly.

"Five," he whispered.

"Weaver," said Rudgutter. "You're right, of course. We wanted to ask about the *five* creatures loose in the city. We're . . . concerned about them . . . as, it sounds, are you. We want to ask if you will help us clear them out of the city. Root them out. Flush them out. Kill them. Before they damage the Weave."

There was a moment of silence, and then the Weaver danced suddenly and quickly from side to side. There was a soft, very fast drumming as its sharp feet pattered on the floor. It jigged bizarrely.

. . . WITHOUT YOU ASK THE WEAVE IS TIGHT RUCKED COLOURS BLEED TEXTURES WEARING THREADS FRAY WHILE I KEEN FUNERAL SONGS FOR SOFT POINTS WHERE WEBSHAPES FLOW I WISH I WILL I CAN COILS OF MONSTERS SHADE SLATESCAPES WINGS MOIL SUCK WORLDWEAVE COLOURLESS DRAB IT IS NOT TO BE I READ RESONANCE PRANCE FROM POINT TO POINT ON THE WEB TO EAT SPLENDOUR REAR AND LICK CLEAN RED KNIFENAILS I WILL SNIP FABRICS AND RETIE THEM I AM I AM A SUBTLE USER OF COLOUR I WILL BLEACH YOUR SKIES WITH YOU I WILL SWEEP THEM CLEAN AND KNOT THEM TIGHT . . .

It took several moments for Rudgutter to realize that the Weaver had agreed to help them.

Cautiously, he grinned. Before Rudgutter could speak again, the Weaver pointed straight up with its front four arms. . . . I'M TO FIND WHERE PATTERNS GO AMOK WHERE COLOURS RUN WHERE VAMPIR INSECTS SUCK BOBBIN-CITIZENS DRY AND I AND I WILL BE BY BY-AND-BY . . .

The Weaver stepped sideways and was gone. It had peeled away from physical space. It was running acrobatically along the span of the worldweb.

The wisps of ætherwebs that crawled invisible across the room and human skin began, slowly, to fade.

Rudgutter turned his head slowly from side to side. The militia were straightening their backs, releasing sighs, relaxing from the combat positions they had unconsciously held. Eliza Stem-Fulcher caught Rudgutter's eye.

"So," she said. "It's hired, right?"

Chapter Twenty-nine

The wyrmen were cowed. They told stories of monsters in the sky.

They sat at night around their rubbish-fires in the city's great dumps and cuffed their children to quiet them. They took turns telling of sudden squalls of disturbed air and glimpses of terrible things. They had seen convoluted shadows in the sky. They had felt drips of acrid liquid spatter them from above.

Wyrmen were being taken.

At first they were just stories. Even through their fear, the wyrmen half-relished the yarns. But then they started to know the protagonists. Their names were ululated through the city at night, when their dribbling, idiot bodies were found. Arfamo and Sideways; Minty; and most frighteningly, Buggerme, the boss-boy of the eastern city. He never lost a fight. Never backed down. His daughter found him, head lolling, oozing mucus from mouth and nose, eyes fat and pale and as alert as poached eggs, in the scrubland by a rusting gas tower in Abrogate Green.

Two khepri matrons were found sat slack and vacant in the Plaza of Statues. A vodyanoi lolled at the edge of the river in Murkside, his capacious mouth pouting in a moronic leer. The number of humans found with their minds gone rose steadily into double figures. The increase did not slow.

The elders of the Riverskin Glasshouse would not say if any cactus had been afflicted.

The *Quarrel* ran a story on its second page, entitled "Mystery Epidemic of Imbecility."

It was not only the wyrmen who were seeing things that should not have been there. First two or three, then more and slowly more hysterical witnesses claimed to have been in the company of one of those whose mind was taken. They were confused, they had been in some trance, they said, but they gabbled descriptions of monsters, insect devils without eyes, dark

hunched bodies unfolding in a nightmare conjunction of limbs.
Protruding teeth and hypnotic wings.

The Crow spread out around Perdido Street Station in an intricate confusion of thoroughfares and half-hidden alleys. The
main arteries—LeTissof Street, Concubek Pass, Boulevard Dos
Ghérou—burst out in all directions around the station and Bil-
Santum Plaza. They were wide and packed, a confusion of carts
and cabs and pedestrian crowds.

Every week new and elegant shops opened amid the throng.
Huge stores that took up three floors of what had been noble
houses; smaller, no less thriving establishments with windows
full of the very latest in gaslight produce, lamps of intricately
twisting brass and extension-valve fittings; food; luxury snuff-
boxes; tailored clothes.

In the smaller branches that spread from these massive streets
like capillaries, the offices of lawyers and doctors, actuaries,
apothecaries and benevolent societies jostled with exclusive
clubs. Patrician men in immaculate suits patrolled these roads.

Tucked into more or less obscure corners of The Crow,
pockets of penury and diseased architecture were judiciously
ignored.

Spit Hearth, to the south-east, was bisected from above by
the skyrail connecting the militia tower at the point of Brock
Marsh to Perdido Street Station. It was part of the same boisterous zone as Sheck, a wedge of smaller shops and houses made of
stone and patched with brick. Spit Hearth had a twilight industry: Remaking. Where the borough met the river, subterranean
punishment factories emitted wails of pain, sometimes, and
hastily smothered screams. But for the sake of its public face,
Spit Hearth was able to ignore that hidden economy with only a
slight show of distaste.

It was a busy place. Pilgrims made their way through it to the
Palgolak temple at the northern edge of Brock Marsh. For centuries, Spit Hearth had been a haven for dissenting churches and
religious societies. Its walls were held together with the paste
from a thousand mouldering posters advertising theological debates and discussions. The monks and nuns of peculiar contemplative sects walked the streets hurriedly, avoiding eye contact.
Dervishes and hieronomers argued on corners.

Wedged gaudily between Spit Hearth and The Crow was the
city's worst-kept secret. A grubby, guilty stain. It was a little

region, in the city's terms. A few streets where the ancient houses were narrow and close, could easily be joined by walk-ways and ladders. Where the constricted slivers of pavement between tall and strangely adorned buildings could be a protec-tive maze.

The brothel quarter. The red-light zone.

It was late in the evening as David Serachin walked through the northern reaches of Spit Hearth. He might have been walking home to Skulkford, due west under the Sud Line and the skyrails, through Sheck, past the massive militia tower to Skulk-ford Green. It was a long but not implausible walk.

But when David passed under the arches of Spit Bazaar Sta-tion, he took advantage of the darkness to turn and gaze back the way he had come. The people behind him were only passers-by. He was not followed. He hesitated a moment, then emerged from beneath the railway lines, as a train whistled above and sent booms reverberating around the brick caverns.

David turned north, following the path of the railway line, into the outer reaches of the whoretown.

He dug his hands deep into his pockets and thrust his head down. This was his shame. He simmered in self-disgust.

At the outer reaches of the red-light zone the wares catered for orthodox tastes. There were some dollymops, streetwalkers poaching custom, but the freelancers that thronged elsewhere in New Crobuzon were the outsiders here. This was the borough for more languorous indulgence, under the roofs of the estab-lishment houses. Peppered with little general stores which even here catered for everyday needs, the still-elegant buildings of this quarter were illuminated by gaslamps flaring behind the tra-ditional red filters. In the doorways of some, young women in clinging bodices called softly to the foot-traffic. The streets here were less full than in the outside city, but they were hardly empty. The men here were mostly well dressed. This merchan-dise was not for the poor.

Some of the men kept their heads high, pugnaciously. Most walked as David did, carefully alone.

The sky was warm and dirty. The stars shimmered unclearly. In the air above the roofscape, there was a whispering and then a rush of wind as a pod passed by. It was a municipal irony that above the very centre of the fleshpits stretched a militia skyrail. On rare occasions the militia would raid the corrupt, sumptuous houses of the red-light zone. But for the most part, as long as payments were made and violence did not spill out of the rooms in which it had been paid for, the militia kept out.

The wafts of night air brought with them something unsettling, some brimming sense of unease. Something more profound than any usual anxiety.

In some of the houses, large windows were illuminated through soft, diffusing muslin. Women in shifts and tight nightgowns rubbed themselves lasciviously, or looked up at the passers-by through coy lashes. Here were also the xenian brothels, where drunken youths cheered each other on to rites of passage, fucking khepri or vodyanoi women or other more exotic breeds. Seeing these establishments, David thought of Isaac. He tried not to.

David did not stop. He did not take in the women around him. He plunged deeper.

He turned a corner into a row of lower, meaner houses. In the windows here were unsubtle hints as to the nature of the wares within. Whips. Cuffs. A girl of seven or eight in a baby's crib, squalling and snotty.

David tracked on and on. The crowds thinned further, although David was never alone. The night air teemed with faint noises. Rooms full of conversation. Music, played well. Laughter. Cries of pain and the barks or howls of animals.

There was a tumbledown cul-de-sac near the heart of the sector, a little still place in the maze. David turned onto its cobbles with a faint shudder. There were men at the doors of these establishments. They stood, heavy and surly in cheap suits, vetting the miserable men that came to them.

David shuffled up to one of the doors. The massive bouncer stopped him, one hand impassive on his chest.

"Mrs. Tollmeck sent me," muttered David. The man let him pass.

Inside, the lampshades were thick and dirty brown. The hall seemed glutinous with shit-coloured light. Behind a desk sat a severe, middle-aged woman in a drab floral dress that matched the lampshades. She looked up at David through half-moon spectacles.

"Are you new to our establishment?" she asked. "Have you an appointment?"

"I'm due in room seventeen at nine o'clock. The name is Orrel," said David. The woman behind the desk raised her eyebrows very slightly and inclined her head. She glanced down at a book before her.

"I see. Well, you're . . ." she glanced at the wall-clock. "You're ten minutes early, but you might as well go up. You know the way? Sally's waiting for you." She looked up at him and—horrendously, monstrously—gave him a complicitous little wink and smirk. David felt sick.

He turned from her quickly and headed up the stairs.

His heart was going very quickly as he climbed, as he emerged in the long corridor at the top of the house. He remembered when first he came here. At the end of the walkway was room seventeen.

David began to walk towards it.

He hated this floor. He hated the slightly blistering wallpaper, the peculiar smells that emanated from the rooms, the unsettling sounds that floated through the walls. Most of the doors on the corridor were open, by convention. Those that were closed were occupied by punters.

The door to room seventeen was kept shut, of course. It was an exception to the house rule.

David walked slowly along the foul carpet, approaching the first door. Mercifully, it was closed, but the wooden door could not contain the noises; peculiar, muffled, desultory cries; a creak of tightening leather; a hissing, hate-filled voice. David turned his head away and found himself gazing directly into the opposite room. He caught a glimpse of the nude figure on the bed. She stared up at him, a girl of no more than fifteen. She crouched on all fours . . . her arms and legs were hairy and pawed . . . dog's legs.

His eyes lingered on her in hypnotic, prurient horror as he walked past, and she leapt to the floor in clumsy canine motion, turned awkwardly, an unpracticed quadruped, looked over her shoulder at him hopefully as she pushed out her arse and pudenda.

David's mouth hung slightly open and his eyes were glazed.

This was where he shamed himself, in this brothel of Remade whores.

The city crawled with Remade prostitutes, of course. It was often the only strategy available to Remade women and men to keep themselves from starving. But here in the red-light district, peccadilloes were indulged in the most sophisticated manner.

Most Remade tarts had been punished for unrelated crimes: their Remaking was usually little more than a bizarre hindrance for their sex-work, pushing their prices way down. This district, on the other hand, was for the specialist, the discerning consumer. Here, the whores were Remade specifically for the profession. Here were expensive bodies Remade into shapes to indulge dedicated gourmets of perverted flesh. There were children sold by their parents and women and men forced by debt to sell themselves to the flesh-sculptors, the illicit Remakers. There were rumours that many had been sentenced to some other Remaking, only to find themselves Remade by the punishment factories according to strange carnal designs and sold to the pimps and madams. It was a profitable sideline run by the bio-thaumaturges of the state.

Time was stretched out and sickly in this endless corridor, like rancid treacle. At every door, every station along the way, David could not help but glance inside. He willed himself to look away but his eyes would not obey.

It was like a nightmare garden. Each room contained some unique flesh-flower, blossom of torture.

David paced past naked bodies covered in breasts like plump scales; monstrous crablike torsos with nubile girlish legs at both ends; a woman who gazed at him with intelligent eyes above a second vulva, her mouth a vertical slit with moist labia, a meat-echo of the other vagina between her splayed legs. Two little boys gazing bewildered at the massive phalluses they sprouted. A hermaphrodite with many hands.

There was a thump inside David's head. He felt groggy with exhausted horror.

Room seventeen was before him. David did not turn back. He imagined the eyes of the Remade behind him, on him, staring from their prisons of blood and bone and sex.

He knocked on the door. After a moment, he heard the chain being lifted from within and the door opened a little. David entered, his gorge rising, leaving that shameful corridor into his own private corruption. The door was closed.

A suited man sat waiting on a dirty bed, smoothing down his tie. Another man, who had opened and closed the door, stood behind David with folded arms. David glanced at him briefly and turned all his attention to the seated man.

The man indicated a chair at the foot of the bed, bade David pull it up in front of him.

David sat.

"Hello 'Sally,' " he said quietly.

"Serachin," said the man. He was thin and middle-aged. His eyes were calculating and intelligent. He looked wildly out of place in this crumbling room, this vile house, and yet his face was quite composed. He had waited as patient and comfortable among the Remade whores as he would in the corridors of Parliament.

"You asked to see me," said the man. "It's been quite a time since we've heard from you. We had designated you a sleeper."

"Well . . ." said David uneasily. "Not much to report. Till now." The man nodded judiciously and waited.

David licked his lips. He found it hard to speak. The man looked at him oddly, frowned.

"The rate is still the same, you know," the man said. "A little more, even."

"No, gods, I . . ." David stuttered. "I'm just . . . You know . . . Out of practice." The man nodded again.

Very out of practice, thought David helplessly. *Been six years since the last time and I swore I wouldn't do it again. Got myself out of it. You got bored of blackmail and I didn't need the money . . .*

The very first time, fifteen years ago, they had entered this very room as David spent himself in one of the mouths of some ruined, cadaverous Remade girl. The suited men had shown him their camera. They had told him they would send their pictures to the newspapers and the journals and the university. They had offered him a choice. They paid well.

He had informed. Freelance only; once, maybe twice a year. And then he had stopped for a long time. Until now. Because now he was frightened.

David breathed in deeply and began.

"Something big's going on. Oh, Jabber, I don't know where to start. You know the disease that's going round? The mindlessness thing? Well, I know where it started. I thought we could just get on with things, I thought it'd all be . . . containable . . . but Devil's Tail! It just gets bigger and bigger and . . . and I think we need help." (Somewhere deep inside his guts some small part of him spat disgust at this, this cowardice, this self-delusion, but David spoke quickly, kept talking.) "It's all down to Isaac."

"Dan der Grimnebulin?" said the man. "Who you share your workspace with? The renegade theorist. The guerrilla scientist with a talent for self-importance. What's he been up to?" The man smiled coldly.

"Right, listen. He got commissioned by . . . well, he got commissioned to look into flight, and he got hold of shitloads of flying things to do research on. Birds, insects, aspises, fucking everything. And one of the things he gets is this big caterpillar. Damn thing looks like it's going to die for the longest time, then 'Zaac must've worked out how to keep the thing alive, because suddenly it starts growing. *Huge*. Fucking . . . this big." He held out his hands in a reasonable estimate of the grub's size. The man opposite him was looking intently at him, face set, hands clenched.

"Then it pupates, right, and we were all sort of curious about what'd come out. So we get home one day and Lublamai—the other guy in the building, you know—Lublamai's lying there, drooling. Whatever the fucking thing was that hatched out, it fucking *ate his mind* . . . and . . . and it got away and the damn thing's *loose* . . ."

The man jerked his head in a decisive nod, quite different from his earlier casual invitations to information. "So you thought you'd better keep us informed."

"Shit, no! I didn't think . . . even then I thought we could deal with it. I mean Jabber, I was pissed off with Isaac, I was completely at a loss, but I thought maybe we could find some way of tracking the damn thing down, fixing Lub . . . Well, first off there starts being more and more of these things, these stories about people's . . . minds going . . . But the main thing was that we tracked down who got these things to 'Zaac. It's some fucking clerk nicking them from R&D in the sodding *Parliament*. And I'm thinking 'Fuck, I don't want to muck about with the *government*.' " The man on the bed nodded at David's judgement. "So then I'm thinking we're way, *way* out of our depth . . ."

David paused. The man on the bed opened his mouth and David cut him off.

"No, listen! It doesn't stop there! 'Cause I heard about the riot down in Kelltree, and I know you've banged up the editor of *Runagate Rampant*, right?" The man waited, flicked imaginary lint from his jacket in an automatic motion. The fact had not been advertised, but the ruined abattoir left no doubt that some pit of sedition had been raided in Dog Fenn, and rumours abounded. "So one of Isaac's friends is a writer on the damn thing, and she's contacted the editor—I don't know how, some fucking thaumaturgy—and he's told her two things. One is that the inquisitors ... your lot ... think he knows something he *doesn't*, and the other is that they're asking him about some story in *Double-R* and the contact for the story, who presumably *does* know whatever they think he does, is called Barbile. So get this! *That's who our clerk nicked the monster caterpillar from!*"

David paused at this, waited for it to impact on the man, then continued.

"So it's all connecting and I *do not* know what's going on. And I don't want to. I can just see that we're ... treading on your toes. Maybe it's a coincidence but I can't see it myself ... I don't mind chasing monsters but I am *not* getting on the wrong side of the fucking militia, and the secret police, and the government and everything. You have to clear this shit up."

The man on the bed clasped his hands. David remembered something else.

"Damn, yeah, listen! I've been racking my brains, trying to work out what's going on, and ... well, I don't know if this is right, but is it something to do with crisis energy?"

The man shook his head very slowly, his face guarded, not comprehending. "Go on," he said.

"Well, at one point during the run-up to all this, Isaac lets slip ... sort of hints ... that he's built a ... a *working crisis engine* ... d'you know what that means?"

The man's face was set hard and his eyes were very wide.

"I am a liaison for those who report from Brock Marsh," he hissed. "I know what it *would* mean ... it cannot ... is it ... Wait a minute, that would make *no sense* ... is it ... is it true?" For the first time, the man seemed truly rattled.

"I don't know," said David hopelessly. "But he wasn't boasting ... he sort of mentioned it in passing ... I just ... have no idea. But I know that's what he's been working on, on and off, for years and fucking *years* ..."

There was a long time of silence, when the man on the bed looked thoughtfully into the far corner of the room. His face ran a quick gamut of emotions. He looked thoughtfully at David. "How do you know all this?" he said.

" 'Zaac trusts me," said David (and that place inside him winced again, and he ignored it again). "At first this woman ..."

"Name?" interrupted the man.

David hesitated.

"Derkhan Blueday," he muttered eventually. "So Blueday, at

first she's really chary of talking in front of me, but Isaac . . . he vouches for me. He knows my politics, we've done demos together . . ." (again that wince: *you have no politics, you fucking traitor*) "It's just that at a time like this . . ." he hesitated, unhappy. The man waved peremptorily. He had no interest in David's guilt, or his rationalizations. "So Isaac tells her she can trust me and she tells us everything."

There was a long time of silence. The man on the bed waited. David shrugged.

"That's all I know," he whispered.

The man nodded and stood.

"Right," he said. "That's all . . . extremely useful. We'll probably have to bring your friend Isaac in. Don't worry," he added with a reassuring smile. "We've no interest in disposing of him, I promise. We may just need his help. You're right, obviously. There is a . . . circle to be squared, connections to be made, and you're not in a position to do it, and we might be. With Isaac's help.

"You're going to have to stay in touch," said the man. "You'll receive written instructions. Be sure to obey them. Obviously I don't have to stress that, do I? We'll make sure der Grimnebulin doesn't know where our information comes from. We may not move for a few days . . . don't panic. That's our affair. Just you stay quiet, and try to keep der Grimnebulin doing what he's doing. All right?"

David nodded miserably. He waited. The man looked at him sharply.

"That's all," he said. "You can go."

With a guilty, grateful haste, David stood and hurried to the door. He felt as if he was swimming in mire, his own shame engulfing him like a mucal sea. He was longing to walk away from this room, and forget what he had said and done, and not think of the coins and notes that would be sent to him, and think only of how loyal he felt to Isaac, and tell himself it was all for the best.

The other man opened the door for him, released him, and David rushed gratefully away, almost ran down along the passageway, eager to escape.

But hurry as he would through the streets of Spit Hearth, guilt clung to him, tenacious as quicksand.

CHAPTER THIRTY

One night the city lay sleeping with reasonable peace.

Of course, the usual interruptions oppressed it. Men and women fought each other and died. Blood and spew fouled the old streets. Glass shattered. The militia streaked overhead. Dirigibles sounded like monstrous whales. The mutilated, eyeless body of a man who would later be identified as Benjamin Flex washed ashore in Badside.

The city tossed uneasily through its nightland, as it had for centuries. It was a fractured sleep, but it was all the city had ever had.

But the next night, when David performed his furtive task in the red-light zone, something had changed. New Crobuzon night had always been a chaos of jarring beats and sudden violent chords. But a new note was sounding. A tense, whispering undertone that made the air sick.

For one night, the tension in the air was a thin and tentative thing, that inveigled its way into the minds of the citizens and sent shadows across their sleeping faces. Then day, and no one remembered anything more than a moment's nocturnal unease.

And then as the shadows dragged out and the temperature dropped, as the night returned from under the world, something new and terrible settled on the city.

All around the city, from Flag Hill in the north to Barrackham below the river, from the desultory suburbs of Badside in the east to the rude industrial slums of Chimer, people thrashed and moaned in their beds.

Children were the first. They cried out and dug their nails into their hands, their little faces crunching down into hard grimaces; they sweated heavily, with a cloying stench; their heads oscillated horrendously to and fro; and all without waking.

As the night wore on the adults also suffered. In the depths of some other, innocuous dream, old fears and paranoias suddenly crashed through mental firewalls like invading armies. Successions of ghastly images assaulted the afflicted, animated visions of deep fears, and absurdly terrifying banalities—ghosties and goblins they need never face—they would have laughed at when awake.

Those arbitrarily spared the ordeal were woken suddenly in the depths of the night by the moans and screams from their sleeping lovers, or their heavy despairing sobs. Sometimes the dreams might be dreams of sex or happiness, but heightened and feverish and become terrifying in their intensity. In this twisted night-trap, bad was bad and good was bad.

The city rocked and shivered. Dreams were become a pestilence, a bacillus that seemed to leap from sleeper to sleeper. They even inveigled their way into the minds of the waking. Nightwatchmen and militia agents; late-night dancers and frantic students; insomniacs: they found themselves losing their trains of thought, drifting into fantasies and ruminations of weird, hallucinatory intensity.

All over the city the night was fissured by cries of nocturnal misery.

New Crobuzon was gripped in an epidemic, an outbreak, a plague of nightmares.

The summer was clotting over New Crobuzon. Stifling it. The night air was as hot and thick as an exhaled breath. Way above the city, transfixed between the clouds and the sprawl, the great winged things drooled.

They spread out and flapped their vast irregular wings, sending fat gusts of air rolling with each sweeping motion. Their intricate appendages—tentacular and insectile, anthropoid, chitinous, numerous—trembled as they passed in febrile excitement.

They unhinged their disturbing mouths and long feathered tongues unrolled towards the rooftops. The very air was thick with dreams, and the flying things lapped eagerly at the succulent juices. When the fronds that tipped their tongues were heavy with the invisible nectar, their mouths gaped and they rolled up their tongues with an eager smacking. They gnashed their huge teeth.

They soared. As they flew they shat, exuding all the sewage from their previous meals. The invisible spoor spread out in the sky, psychic effluent that slid, lumpy and cloying, through the interstices of the mundane plane. It oozed its way through æther to fill the city, saturating the minds of the inhabitants, disturbing their rest, bringing forth monsters. The sleeping and the wakeful felt their minds churn.

The five went hunting.

Amid the vast swirling broth of the city's nightmares, each of the dark things could discern individual snaking trails of flavour.

Usually, they were opportunistic hunters. They would wait until they scented some strong mental tumult, some mind particularly delicious in its own exudations. Then the intricate dark flyers would turn and dive, bear down on the prey. They used their slim hands to unlock top-floor windows, and paced across moonlit attics towards shivering sleepers to drink their fill. They clutched with a multitude of appendages at lonely figures walking the riverside, figures who screeched and screeched as they were taken into a night already full of plaintive cries.

But when they had discarded the flesh-husks of their meals to twitch and loll slack-mouthed on boards and shadowed cobbles, when their stabs of hunger had been assuaged and meals could be taken more slowly, for pleasure, the winged creatures became curious. They tasted the faint drippings of minds they had tasted before, and, like inquisitive, coldly intelligent hunting beasts, they pursued them.

Here was the tenuous mental thread of one of the guards, who had stood outside their cage in Bonetown and fantasized about his friend's wife. His flavoursome imaginings wafted up to wrap around a twitching tongue. The creature that tasted that wheeled around in the sky, in the chaotic arc of a butterfly or a moth, and dived towards Echomire, following his prey's scent.

Another of the great airborne shapes pulled up suddenly in a vast figure of eight, rolling over its own tracks, seeking out the familiar flavour that had flitted across its tastebuds. It was a nervous aroma that had permeated the cocoons of the pupating monsters. The great beast hovered over the city, saliva dissipating in various dimensions below it. The emissions were obscured, frustratingly tenuous, but the creature's sense of taste was fine, and it bore down towards Mafaton, licking its way along the enticing trail of the scientist who had watched it grow, Magesta Barbile.

The twisted one, the malnourished runt that had liberated its fellows, found a taste-trail that it, too, remembered. Its mind was not so developed, its tastebuds less exact: it could not follow the flickering scent through the air. But, uncomfortably, it tried. The full taste of the mind was so familiar ... it had surrounded the twisted creature during its flourishing into consciousness, during its pupation and self-creation in the silk shell ... It lost and found the scent, lost it again, floundered.

The smallest and weakest of the night-hunters, stronger by far than any man, hungry and predatory, licked its way through the sky, trying to regain the trail of Isaac Dan der Grimnebulin.

Isaac, Derkhan and Lemuel Pigeon fidgeted on the streetcorner, in the smoky glare of the gaslight.

"Where the fuck's your mate?" hissed Isaac.

"He's late. Probably can't find it. I told you, he's stupid," said Lemuel calmly. He took out a flick-knife and began to clean his nails.

"Why do we need him?"

"Don't come the fucking innocent, Isaac. You're good at waving enough brass at me to get me to do all sorts of jobs that go against my better judgement, but there are limits. I'm not getting involved in anything which irritates the damn government without protection. And Mr. X is that, in spades."

Isaac swore silently, but he knew Lemuel was right.

He had been very uneasy at the notion of involving Lemuel in this adventure, but events had rapidly conspired to give him no choice. David had clearly been reluctant to help him find Magesta Barbile. He seemed paralysed, a mass of helpless nerves. Isaac was losing patience with him. He needed support, and he wanted David to get off his arse and *do* something. But now was not the time to confront him.

Derkhan had inadvertently provided the name that seemed key to the interlocking mysteries of the presence in the skies and the militia's enigmatic interrogation of Ben Flex. Isaac sent word, got the name and what information they had—Mafaton, scientist, R&D—to Lemuel Pigeon. He included money, several guineas (and realized as he did so that the gold Yagharek had given him was slowly dwindling), and begged for information, and help.

That was why he contained his anger at Mr. X's late show. For all that he pantomimed impatience, that kind of protection was precisely what he had approached Lemuel for.

Lemuel himself had not taken much persuasion to accompany

Isaac and Derkhan to the address in Mafaton. He affected an in-
souciant disregard for particulars, a mercenary desire simply to
be paid for his efforts. Isaac did not believe him. He thought that
Lemuel was growing interested in the intrigue.

Yagharek was adamant he would not come. Isaac had tried to
persuade him, quickly and fervently, but Yagharek had not even
replied. *What the fuck are you doing here then?* Isaac felt like
asking, but he swallowed his irritation and let the garuda be. Perhaps it would take a little time before he would behave as if he
were part of any collective at all. Isaac would wait.

Lin had left just before Derkhan's arrival. She had been reluctant to leave Isaac in his despondency, but she had also seemed
somewhat distracted. She had stayed only one night, and when
she had gone she had promised Isaac she would return as soon as
she could. But then the next morning Isaac had received a letter
in her cursive hand, couriered across the city with an expensive
guaranteed delivery.

Dear Heart,
    I am afraid you might feel angry and betrayed at this, but
please be forbearing. Waiting for me here was another letter
from my employer, my commissioner, my patron, if you will.
Hot on the heels of his missive telling me I would not be
needed for the foreseeable future, came another message saying I was to return.
    I know the timing of this could not be worse. I ask only that
you believe that I would disobey if I could, but that I *cannot*. I
cannot, Isaac. I will try to finish my job with him as quickly as
possible—within a week or two, I hope—and return to you.
    Wait for me.
        With my love, Lin

So, waiting on the corner of Addley Pass, camouflaged by the
chiaroscuro of full moon through the clouds and the shadows of
the trees in Billy Green, were only Isaac, Derkhan and Lemuel.

All three were shifting uneasily, looking up at passing shades,
starting at imagined noises. From the streets around them there
came intermittent sounds of horrendously disturbed sleep. At
each savage moan or ululation, the three would catch each
other's eyes.

"Gods*damn*it," hissed Lemuel in irritation and fear. "What is going *on*?"

"There's something in the air . . ." murmured Isaac, and his voice petered out as he stared blindly up.

To cap the tension, Derkhan and Lemuel, who had met the previous day, had quickly decided they despised each other. They did their best to ignore one another.

"How did you get the address?" asked Isaac, and Lemuel shucked his shoulders irritably.

"Connections, 'Zaac, contacts, and corruption. How d'you think? Dr. Barbile vacated her own rooms a couple of days ago and has since been seen at this less salubrious location. It's only about three streets away from her old house, though. The woman has no imagination. Hey . . ." He batted Isaac's arm and pointed across the gloomy street. "There's our man."

Opposite them, a vast figure tugged free of the shadows and lumbered towards them. He glowered at Isaac and Derkhan, before nodding at Lemuel in the most absurdly jaunty fashion.

"All right, Pigeon?" he said, too loud. "What we up to, then?"

"Voice down, man," said Lemuel tersely. "What you carrying?"

The massive man pushed his finger across his lips to show he understood. He held open one side of his jacket, displaying two enormous flintlock pistols. Isaac started slightly at their size. Both he and Derkhan were armed, but neither with any such cannons. Lemuel nodded approvingly at the sight.

"Right. Probably won't be needed, but . . . y'know. Right. Don't talk." The big man nodded. "Don't hear either, right? You have no ears tonight." The man nodded again. Lemuel turned to Isaac and Derkhan. "Listen. You know what you want to ask the geezer. Wherever possible, we're just shadows. But we have reason to think the militia are interested in this, and that means we can't fuck about. If she's not forthcoming, we're giving her a helpful push, right?"

"Is that gangsterese for torture?" hissed Isaac. Lemuel looked at him coldly.

"No. And don't fucking preach at me: you're paying for this. We don't have *time* to arse around, so I'm not going to let *her* arse around. Any problems?" There was no answer. "Good. Wardock Street is down here to the right."

They did not pass any other late-night walkers as they picked their way along the backstreets. They walked variously: Lemuel's sidekick stolidly and without fear, seemingly unaffected by the ambient nightmare quality in the air; Lemuel himself with many glances into dark doorways; and Isaac and Derkhan with a nervous, miserable haste.

They halted at Barbile's door on Wardock Street. Lemuel turned and indicated for Isaac to go forward, but Derkhan pushed to the front.

"I'll do it," she whispered furiously. The others fell back. When they stood half out of sight at the edge of the doorway, Derkhan turned and pulled the bell cord.

For a long time, nothing happened. Then, gradually, footsteps slowly descended stairs and approached the door. They halted just beyond it, and there was silence. Derkhan waited, hushing the others with her hands. Eventually a voice called out from behind the door.

"Who's that?"

Magesta Barbile sounded utterly fearful.

Derkhan spoke softly and quickly.

"Dr. Barbile, my name's Derkhan. We need to speak to you very urgently."

Isaac glanced around him to see if any of the lights in the street were coming on. So far they seemed unobserved.

From behind the door, Magesta Barbile was being difficult.

"I . . . I'm not sure about that . . ." she said. "It's not really a good time . . ."

"Dr. Barbile . . . Magesta . . ." said Derkhan quietly. "You're going to have to open this door. We can help you. Just open the fucking door. Now."

There was another moment of dithering, then Magesta Barbile unlocked the door and pushed it open a crack. Derkhan was about to seize the moment by pushing past her into the house, when she started and stood quite still. Barbile was holding a rifle. She looked horribly uncomfortable. But however unpractised she was, the weapon was still levelled at Derkhan's gut.

"I don't know who you are . . ." began Barbile querulously, but before she could continue Lemuel's huge friend, Mr. X, reached easily and without speed around Derkhan, grabbing the rifle and shoving the heel of his hand over the firing-pan, blocking the path of the hammer. Barbile began to keen, and she pulled the trigger, eliciting a mild hiss of pain from Mr. X as the hammer snapped onto his flesh. He shoved the rifle backwards, sending Barbile flying onto the stairs behind her.

As she flopped and scrambled to right herself he stepped into the house.

The others followed. Derkhan did not protest at Barbile's treatment. Lemuel was right. They did not have time.

Mr. X was standing holding the woman. He held her patiently as she flopped and snapped back and forth, emitting terrible crooning moans from behind his hand. Her eyes were wide and white and hysterical with fear.

"Dear gods," breathed Isaac. "She thinks we're going to kill her! Stop!"

"Magesta," said Derkhan loudly, kicking the door closed without looking. "Magesta, you have to stop this. We're not militia, if that's what you're thinking. I'm a friend of Benjamin Flex."

At that Barbile opened her eyes wider and her struggles slowed.

"Right," said Derkhan. "And Benjamin's been taken. I suppose you know that." Barbile watched her and nodded quickly. Lemuel's enormous employee dropped his hand from Barbile's mouth experimentally. She did not scream.

"We're not the militia," repeated Derkhan slowly. "We're not going to take you like they took him. But you know . . . you *know* . . . if we could trace you, if we could suss out who was Ben's contact, that they're going to be able to."

"I . . . That's why I . . ." Barbile glanced over at the discarded rifle. Derkhan nodded.

"All right, listen, Magesta," she said. She spoke very clearly, her eyes on Barbile's all the time. "We don't have much time . . . Let go of her, you arse! We don't have much time, and we have to know exactly what's going on. There is some mighty gods-damned weird stuff going on. And an awful lot of threads seem to converge on you. So let me suggest something. Why don't you take us upstairs, before the militia come, and explain to us what's going on?"

"I only just found out about Flex," said Magesta. She was sitting huddled on her sofa, clutching a cold cup of tea. Behind her a large mirror took up most of the wall. "I don't really follow the news. I had a meeting scheduled with him a couple of days ago, and when he didn't come, I got really scared that he'd . . . I don't know . . . told on me, or something." He probably has, thought Derkhan, and said nothing. "And then I heard some rumours about what happened in Dog Fenn when the militia put down that riot . . ."

There was no godsdamn riot, Derkhan nearly shouted, but she controlled herself. Whatever reason Magesta Barbile may have had for giving information to Ben, political dissidence was clearly not one of them.

"So these rumours . . ." Barbile continued. "Well, I put two and two together, you know? And then . . . and then . . ."

"And then you hid," said Derkhan. Barbile nodded.

"Look," said Isaac suddenly. He had been silent until now, his face twisted tensely. "Can you not fucking feel it? Can't you taste it?" He shook his hands in claws around his face, as if the air was a tangible thing he could grip and wrestle. "It's as if the damn night air's gone *rancid*. Now, maybe it's just blind damn coincidence, but so far every bad thing that's happened for the last month seems to be tied in to some fucking conspiracy, and I'm damn well betting that this ain't an exception."

He leaned in close towards Barbile's pathetic figure. She gazed at him, timid and terrified.

"Dr. Barbile," he said levelly. "Something that eats minds . . . including my friend's mind; a militia raid on *Runagate Rampant*; the very fucking *air* around our ears turning into some rotten soup . . . *What is going on?* What's the connection with dreamshit?"

Barbile began to cry. Isaac nearly howled with irritation, turning from her and throwing up his hands in exasperation. But then he turned back. She was speaking through her snivels.

"I knew it was a bad idea . . ." she said. "I told them we should keep control of the experiment . . ." Her words were almost unintelligible, broken and interrupted with a slew of snotty tears. "It hadn't been going long enough . . . They shouldn't have done it . . ."

"Done *what*?" said Derkhan. "What did they do? What was Ben talking to you about?"

"About the *transfer*," sobbed Barbile. "We hadn't finished the project but we suddenly heard it was being wound down, but . . . but someone found out what was really happening . . . Our specimens were being *sold* . . . to some *criminal* . . ."

"*What* specimens?" said Isaac, but Barbile was ignoring him. She was unburdening herself in her own time and her own order.

"It wasn't quick enough for the sponsors, you know? They were getting . . . impatient . . . The applications they thought there might be . . . military, psychodimensional . . . they weren't coming. The subjects were *incomprehensible*, we weren't making progress, and . . . and they were *uncontrollable*, they were just too *dangerous* . . ." She raised her eyes and her voice, still crying. She paused, then continued, quieter again.

"We might have got somewhere, but it was taking too long. And then . . . the money people must've got nervous. So the project director told us it was over, that the specimens had been destroyed, but that was a *lie* . . . Everyone knew it. This wasn't the first project, you know . . ." Isaac and Derkhan's eyes widened sharply, but they were silent. "We already knew one sure way to make money from them . . .

"They must've sold them to the highest bidder . . . to someone who could use them for the *drug* . . . That way the sponsors made their money back and the director could keep the project going for himself, co-operating with the drug-man he sold them to. But it wasn't *right* . . . It wasn't right that the government should make money from *drugs* and it wasn't right that they should steal our *project* . . ." Barbile had stopped crying. She just sat, rambling. They let her talk.

"The others were just going to leave it, but I was *angry* . . . I hadn't seen them hatch, I hadn't learnt what I needed to learn, for nothing. And now they were going to be used for . . . for some villain to make money . . ."

Derkhan could scarcely believe the naivety. So this was Ben's contact. This stupid minor scientist piqued at having her project stolen. For that, she had given evidence of the government's illicit deals, she had brought the wrath of the militia onto her own head.

"Barbile," said Isaac again, much quieter and calmer this time. "What are they?"

Magesta Barbile looked up at him. She looked slightly unhinged.

"What *are* they?" she said dazedly. "The things that've escaped? The project? What are they?

"Slake-moths."

CHAPTER THIRTY-ONE

Isaac nodded as if this revelation made sense. He prepared to ask her another question, but her eyes were no longer on him.

"I knew they'd escaped because of the dreams, you know?" she said. "I could tell they were out. I don't know how they escaped. But it shows that their damn sell-off was a bad idea, doesn't it?" Her voice was strained with desperate triumph. "That's one in the eye for Vermishank."

At the sound of the name, Isaac felt himself spasm. Of course, a part of his mind thought, calmly. Makes sense that he'd be in on this. Another part of him was screaming internally. The strands of his life were throttling him like some unforgiving net.

"What's Vermishank got to do with this?" he said carefully. He saw Derkhan look at him sharply. She did not recognize the name, but she could tell that he did.

"He's the boss," said Barbile, surprised. "He's the head of the project."

"But he's a bio-thaumaturge, not a zoologist, not a theorist . . . Why's he in charge?"

"Bio-thaumaturgy's his specialism, not his only area. He's mainly an administrator. He's in charge of all the bio-hazard stuff: Remaking, experimental weapons, hunter organisms, diseases . . ."

Vermishank was in charge of sciences at the University of New Crobuzon. It was a high-profile, prestigious position. It would be unthinkable to award such an honour to someone antagonistic to the government: that was obvious. But Isaac realized now that he had underestimated Vermishank's involvement with the state. He was more than just a yes-man.

"Vermishank sold off the . . . slake-moths?" Isaac said. Barbile nodded. A wind had picked up outside, and the shutters were rattling and banging violently. Mr. X looked around at the noise. No one else took their attention from Barbile.

"I was in touch with Flex because I thought it wasn't right," she said. "But something happened ... the moths are out. They've escaped. Gods only know how." *I know how,* thought Isaac grimly. *It was me.* "Do you know what it *means* that they're out? We're all ... we're going to be *hunted.* And the militia must've read *Runagate Rampant* and ... and thought that Flex had something to do with it ... and if they think Flex did then soon ... soon they'll think that *I* did ..." Barbile began to snivel again and Derkhan looked away in disgust, thinking of Ben.

Mr. X walked over to the window to rearrange the shutters.

"So, look ..." Isaac tried to collate his thoughts. There were a hundred thousand things he wanted to ask, but one was absolutely pressing. "So Dr. Barbile ... *how do we catch them?*"

Barbile looked up at him and began to shake her head. She glanced up briefly, between Isaac and Derkhan who loomed over her like anxious parents, past Lemuel who stood to the side, studiously ignoring her. Her eyes found Mr. X, who was standing by the uncovered window. He had opened it a little, was reaching out to pull in the shutters.

He was standing quite still, looking out.

Magesta Barbile looked over his shoulder at a flickering wash of midnight colours.

Her eyes glazed. Her voice froze.

Something was battering at the window, trying to reach the light.

Barbile rose, as Lemuel and Isaac and Derkhan flocked to her in concern, asking what was wrong, unable to understand her little cries. Her hand rose, shaking, to point to the paralysed figure of Mr. X.

"Oh Jabber ..." she whispered. "Oh dear Jabber, it's found me, it's tasted me ..."

And then she shrieked, and spun on her heels.

"The mirror!" she screamed as she did so. "Look in the *mirror*!"

Her tone was fraught and utterly commanding. They obeyed her. She spoke with such desperate authority that not one of them succumbed to the instinct to turn and see.

The four of them gazed into the mirror behind the tattered sofa. They watched transfixed.

Mr. X was stepping backwards with the mindless tramp of a zombie.

Behind him, there was a dark flurry of colour. A terrible shape squeezed and folded in on itself to push its organic folds and spines and bulk through the little window. A blunt eyeless head poked itself through the opening and turned slowly from side to side. The impression was of an impossible birth. The thing that loomed through the space in the glass had made itself small and intricate by contracting in invisible, impossible directions. It shimmered unreally under the strain, hauling its glistening carcass through the opening, arms emerging from its dark bulk to push and strain against the window frame.

Behind the glass those half-hidden wings boiled.

The creature pushed suddenly and the window disintegrated. There was only a small, dry sound, as if the air was leeched of substance. Nuggets of glass sprayed the room.

Isaac watched, transfixed. He trembled.

At the edge of his vision he saw Derkhan and Lemuel and Barbile in the same state. *This is madness!* he thought. *We've got to get out of here!* He reached out and plucked at Derkhan's sleeve, began to pick his way towards the door.

Barbile seemed paralysed. Lemuel pulled at her.

None of them knew why she had said to look in the mirror, but none of them turned around.

And then as they faltered towards the door, they froze again, because the thing in the room stood.

In a sudden flowering motion it rose behind them, filling the mirror into which they gazed, aghast.

They could see the back of Mr. X, who stood and gazed at the patterns on those wings, patterns that rolled with hypnagogic haste, the colour cells under the creature's skin pulsing in weird dimensions.

Mr. X stepped back to see the wings better. They could not see his face.

The slake-moth held him in thrall.

It was taller than a bear. A clutch of sharp extrusions like dark cartilaginous whips blossomed from its sides and flickered out towards him. Other, smaller, sharper limbs flexed like claws.

The creature stood on legs like monkey's arms. Three pairs

jutted from its trunk. It stood now bipedally, now on four legs, now on six.

It reared up on its lower legs and a sharp tail slithered forward from between its legs for balance. Its face—

(Always those huge irregular wings, curving in strange directions, shifting in shape to fit the room, each as random and inconstant as oil on water, each a perfect reflection of the other, kept gently moving, their patterns changing, flickering in a seductive tide.)

It had no eyes that they could recognize, only two deep sunken hollows sprouting thick, flexing antennae like stubby fingers, above rows of huge slab-teeth. As Isaac watched, it cocked its head and opened that unimaginable mouth, and from it a huge, prehensile, slavering tongue unrolled.

It waved quickly through the air. Its end was coated in clumps of gossamer alveoli that pulsed as the enormous thing flailed like an elephant's trunk.

"It's trying to find *me*," wailed Barbile, and broke, and ran for the door.

Instantly the slake-moth flickered its tongue towards the movement. There was a succession of motions far too quick to see. Some cruel organic jag snapped out and passed through Mr. X's head as if through water. Mr. X shuddered suddenly and just as the blood began to well explosively through the sliced bone the slake-moth reached out with four of its arms, pulled him briefly closer and hurled him across the room.

He flew through the air trailing gore and bone-shards like a comet. He died before he landed.

Mr. X's carcass slammed into Barbile's back, sending her sprawling. He landed heavy and lifeless across the door. His eyes were open.

Lemuel, Isaac and Derkhan broke for the door.

They were shouting simultaneously in a cacophony of registers.

Lemuel leapt over Barbile, who lay supine and desperate, trying to kick free of Mr. X's huge torso. She rolled onto her back and cried out for help. Isaac and Derkhan reached her simultaneously, and began to tug at her arms. Her eyes were tight closed.

But as they pushed Mr. X's body free and Lemuel kicked it savagely out of the way of the door, a hard, rubbery tentacle snaked into their vision and wrapped with a whiplash motion around Barbile's feet. She felt it and began to scream.

Derkhan and Isaac pulled hard. There was a moment of resistance, and then the slake-moth yanked at her with its tendril. Barbile was whisked out of Derkhan and Isaac's grasp with humbling ease. She slid at breakneck speed along the floor, splinters tearing at her.

She began to scream.

Lemuel had forced the door open, and he raced out and away down the stairs without glancing back. Isaac and Derkhan stood quickly. They turned their heads simultaneously to look into the mirror.

Both gave a little cry of horror.

Barbile was squirming and screaming in the complex embrace of the slake-moth. Limbs and folds of flesh caressed her. She wriggled and her arms were held, she kicked out and her legs were pinioned.

The huge creature turned its head gently to one side, seemed to regard her with hunger and curiosity. It emitted tiny, obscene noises.

Its final pair of hands crept up and began to finger Barbile's eyes. It touched them gently. It began trying to prise them open.

Barbile shrieked and wailed and begged for help, and Isaac and Derkhan stood paralysed, gazing into the mirror, transfixed.

With hands shaking violently, Derkhan reached into her jacket and brought out her pistol, primed and ready. Staring resolutely into the looking-glass, she pointed her gun behind her. Her hand wavered as she desperately sought to aim in this impossible fashion.

Isaac saw what she was doing, and reached quickly for his own gun. He was quicker to pull the trigger.

There was a sharp bang of igniting black powder. The ball burst from his muzzle and passed harmlessly over the slake-moth's head. The creature did not even look up. Barbile screamed at the sound, and began to beg, eloquently and horrendously, for them to shoot her.

Derkhan set her mouth and tried to steady her arm.

She fired. The slake-moth whirled and its wings shook. It opened that cavernous maw and a foul, strangulated hissing emerged, a whispered shriek. Isaac saw a tiny hole in the papery tissue of the left wing.

Barbile cried out and waited a moment, then realized that she was still alive and began to scream again.

The slake-moth turned on Derkhan. Two of its whip arms

flailed across the seven feet separating them and smacked petu-
lantly across her back. There was an almighty cracking sound.
Derkhan was thrown through the open door, her breath pushed
violently through her lungs. She wailed as she fell.

"Don't look round!" screamed Isaac. "Go! Go! I'm coming!"

He tried not to hear Barbile begging. He did not have time to
reload.

As he made his way slowly for the door, praying that the creature would continue to ignore him, he watched what unfolded in
the mirror.

He refused to process it. It was, for now, a mindless slick of
images. Later he might consider it, if he left this house alive and
found his way home, to his friends, if he survived to plan, he
would think on what he was seeing.

But for now he carefully thought of nothing as he saw the
slake-moth turn its attention back to the woman held fast in its
arms. He thought of nothing as he saw it force open her eyes
with slender simian fingers and thumbs, heard her scream until
she vomited with fear and then stop all her noises very suddenly
as she caught sight of the flexing patterns on the slake-moth's
wings. Saw those wings gently widen and stretch taut into a hypnotic canvas, saw Barbile's entranced expression as her eyes
widened to gaze on those morphing colours; saw her body relax
and the slake-moth drool in vile anticipation, its unspeakable
tongue unrolling again out of that gaping mouth and snaking its
way up Barbile's saliva-spattered shirt to her face, her eyes still
glazed in idiot ecstasy at those wings. Saw the feathered tip of
the tongue nuzzle gently against Barbile's face, her nose, her
ears and then shove suddenly, forcefully past her teeth into her
mouth *(and Isaac retched even as he tried to think of nothing)*,
thrusting at indecent speed into her face, her eyes bulging as
more and more of the tongue disappeared into her.

And then Isaac saw something flicker under the skin of her
scalp, bulging and wriggling and rippling beneath her hair and
flesh like an eel in mud, saw a movement that was not hers behind her eyes, and he watched mucus and tears and ichor pour
from the orifices of her head as the tongue wriggled into her
mind and just before he fled Isaac saw her eyes dim and go out
and the slake-moth's stomach distend as it drank her dry.

CHAPTER THIRTY-TWO

Lin was alone.

She sat in the attic, leaning back against a wall with her feet splayed like a doll's. She watched the dust move. It was dark. The air was warm. It was sometime in the small hours, between two and four.

The night was interminable and unforgiving. Lin could hear-feel vibrations in the air, the tremulous cries and howls of disturbed sleep rocking the city all around her. Her own head felt heavy with portent and menace.

Lin rocked back a little and rubbed her headscarab wearily. She was afraid. She was not so stupid as to not know that something was wrong.

She had arrived at Motley's some hours before, in the late afternoon of the previous day. As usual, she had been instructed to make her way to the attic. But when she had entered the long, desiccated room, she had been alone.

The sculpture loomed darkly at the far end of the room. After she had looked around, idiotically, as if Motley could be hiding unseen in the bare space, she had walked over to examine the piece. She had supposed, a little uneasily, that Motley would join her soon.

She had stroked the khepri-spit figure. It was half finished. Motley's various legs had been rendered in curling shapes and hyperreal colours. It terminated about three feet from the floor in drooping, liquid undulations. It looked as if a life-size candle in Motley's shape had been half burned.

Lin had waited. An hour had passed. She had tried to lift the trapdoor and open the door to the passageway, but both were locked. She had stamped on the one and thumped the other, loudly and repetitively, but there was no response.

There's some mistake, she had told herself. *Motley's busy, he'll be along shortly, he's just tied up,* but it was totally unconvincing. Motley was consummate. As a businessman, a thug, a philosopher and a performer.

This delay was no accident. This was deliberate.

Lin did not know why, but Motley wanted her to sit, and sweat, alone.

She sat for hours until her nervousness became fear became boredom became patience, and she drew designs in the dust and opened her case to count her colourberries, again and again. Night came, and still she was left.

Her patience became fear again.

Why is he doing this? she thought. *What does he want?* This was quite different from Motley's usual playing, his teases, his dangerous loquacity. This was far more ominous.

And finally, at last, hours after her arrival, she heard a noise.

Motley was in the room, flanked by his cactacae lieutenant and a pair of hulking gladiator Remade. Lin did not know how they had entered. She had been alone seconds before.

She stood and waited. Her hands were clutching.

"Ms. Lin. Thank you for coming," said Motley from a tumorous cluster of mouths.

She waited.

"Ms. Lin," he continued. "I had the most *interesting* conversation with one Lucky Gazid the day before yesterday. I suspect you haven't seen Mr. Gazid for a while. He's been working for me incognito. Anyway, as you doubtless know, there's something of a citywide drought of dreamshit at the moment. Burglary is up. As is mugging. People are desperate. Prices have gone quite mad. There simply isn't any new dreamshit being released into the city. What all this means is that Mr. Gazid, for whom dreamshit is the current drug of choice, is in *rather* a state. He can't afford the merchandise any more, even with an employee's discount.

"So anyway, the other day I heard him swearing—he was in withdrawal and cursing anyone who'd come near, but this was a bit different. D'you know what he shouted as he gnawed himself? Fascinating. It was something along the lines of 'I should never have given that 'shit to Isaac!' "

The cactacae beside Mr. Motley unclasped his massive hands and rubbed his callused green fingers together. He reached up to his uncovered chest, and with a terrible deliberation, he pricked his finger on one of his own spikes, testing its point. His face was impassive.

"*Isn't* that interesting, Ms. Lin?" continued Motley with a sickly jauntiness. He began to pace crabwise towards her on his innumerable legs.

What is *this? What* is *this?* thought Lin as he approached. There was nowhere for her to hide.

"Now, Ms. Lin. Some *very valuable items* have been stolen from me. A clutch of little *factories*, if you like. Hence the lack of dreamshit. And d'you know? I have to admit I've been *stymied* as to who might have done it. Really. I've had nothing to go on." He paused and a tide of icy smiles crossed his multiple features. "Until I heard Gazid. Then it all . . . made . . . sense." He spat each word.

At some silent signal his cactus vizier strode towards Lin, who cringed and tried to break away, but was too late, as he reached out with his enormous meaty fists and gripped her arms tightly, immobilizing her.

Lin's headlegs spasmed and she emitted a piercing chymical screech at the pain. Cactacae were usually assiduous in pruning the thorns on the insides of their palms, to better manipulate objects, but this one had let his grow. Clutches of stubby fibrous quills spiked her arms mercilessly.

She was pinioned, and dragged effortlessly before Motley. He leered at her. When he spoke again his voice was thick with threat.

"Your bugfucking lover has tried to screw me, hasn't he, Ms. Lin? Buying up great swathes of *my* dreamshit, keeping his *own* moths, so Gazid tells me, and then *stealing mine*." He roared the last words, trembling.

Lin could hardly think over the pain in her arms but she desperately tried to sign from her hip: *No no no it's not like that it's not like that* . . .

Motley slapped her hands down.

"Don't fucking try it, you bug-head bitch, you cross-whore, you slut. Your scum-sucking man's been trying to squeeze *me* out of my own fucking market. Well, that's a very, very dangerous game." He backed away a little and regarded her as she writhes.

"We are going to bring Mr. der Grimnebulin in to account for his theft. D'you think he'll come if we offer him you?"

Blood was stiffening the arms of Lin's shirt. She tried again to sign.

"You'll get a chance to explain yourself, Ms. Lin," said Motley, calm again. "Maybe you're a partner in crime, maybe you have no idea what I'm talking about. It's bad luck for you, I must say. I will *not* be letting this go." He watched her try desperately to tell him, to explain, to squirm her way free.

Her arms were seizing up. The cactus was rendering her dumb. As she felt her head dull with the constricting pain, she heard Mr. Motley's whisper.

"I am not a forgiving man."

Outside the University Science Faculty, the quad thronged with students. Many were wearing the regulation black gowns: a few rebellious souls slung them over their arms as they left the building.

Among the tide of figures were two motionless men. They stood leaning against the tree, ignoring the sap that stuck to them. It was humid, and one man was dressed incongruously in a long coat and dark hat.

They stood without moving for a long time. One class ended, and then another. The men saw two cycles of students come and go. Occasionally one or the other would rub his eyes, stretch his face a little. Always he would return his apparently casual attention to the main entrance.

Finally, as the afternoon shadows began to stretch out, the men moved. Their target appeared. Montague Vermishank stepped from the building and sniffed the air gingerly, as if he knew he should enjoy it. He began to remove his jacket, then stopped and pulled it back around him. He set off into Ludmead.

The men below the tree stepped out from under the leaves and sauntered after their prey.

It was a busy day. Vermishank headed north, looking around him for a cab. He wound up Tench Way, Ludmead's most bohemian thoroughfare, where progressive academics held court in cafés and bookshops. The buildings of Ludmead were old and well preserved, their façades scrubbed and freshly painted. Vermishank ignored them. He had walked this way for years. He was oblivious to his surroundings, and to his pursuers.

A four-wheel cab appeared through the crowd, pulled by some uncomfortable shaggy biped from the northern tundra that paced its way through the rubbish on back-bent legs like a bird's.

Vermishank raised his arm. The cabdriver attempted to manoeuvre his vehicle towards him. Vermishank's pursuers sped up.

"Monty," boomed the larger man and slapped his shoulder. Vermishank turned in alarm.

"Isaac," he faltered. His eyes darted around him, sought the cab, which was still approaching.

"How are you, old son?" yelled Isaac in his left ear, and underneath it, Vermishank heard another voice hissing in his right.

"The thing poking your stomach is a knife and I will gut you like a fucking fish if you even breathe in a way I don't like."

"So glad to bump into you," howled Isaac jocularly, waving the cab over. The driver muttered and approached.

"Try to run and I will cut you and if you get out of my hands I will shoot a bullet into your brain," the voice crooned with loathing.

"Come and have a drink at mine," said Isaac. "Brock Marsh, please driver. Paddler Way, you know it? Handsome beast, by the way." Isaac kept up a stream of loud nonsense as he swung into the closed carriage. Vermishank followed, shaking and stuttering, goaded by the sting of the blade. Lemuel Pigeon followed him in and slammed the door shut, then sat looking straight forward holding the knife at Vermishank's side.

The driver pulled away from the kerb. The creaking and rattling and complaining bleats of the animal cocooned the three men in the cab.

Isaac turned to Vermishank with the exaggerated delight gone from his face.

"You have a lot of talking to do, you evil cunt," he hissed menacingly.

His prisoner was visibly regaining his poise second by second.

"Isaac," he murmured. "Hah. How can I help you?"

He started as Lemuel jabbed him.

"Shut your fucking mouth."

"Shut my mouth *and* do a lot of talking, Isaac?" mused Vermishank smoothly, then yelped incredulously as Isaac struck him, hard and suddenly. He gazed at him astonished, gingerly stroking his stinging face.

"I tell you when to talk," said Isaac.

They were silent the rest of the journey, swaying south past Lud Fallow Station and over the sluggish Canker at Danechi's Bridge. Isaac paid the driver as Lemuel hustled Vermishank into the warehouse.

Inside, David glowered from his desk, half turning to watch the proceedings. His russet waistcoat was incongruously cheerful. Yagharek skulked in a corner, half visible. His feet were wrapped in rags and his head was hidden in a hood. He had discarded the wooden wings. He was not disguised as whole, but as a human.

Derkhan looked up from an armchair she had pulled into the middle of the back wall, below the window. She was crying fiercely and without a sound. She was clutching a handful of newspapers. Front pages were strewn around her. "Midsummer Nightmares Spread," said one, and another asked "What Has Happened to Sleep?" Derkhan ignored these pages, cutting out another minor story from page five or seven or eleven in each paper. Isaac could read one from where he stood: "Eyespy Killer Claims Criminal Editor."

The cleaning construct hissed and whirred and clanked its way around the room, clearing the rubbish, sweeping up the dust, collecting the old papers and fruit debris that littered the floor. Sincerity the badger meandered listlessly along the far wall.

Lemuel shoved Vermishank into the middle of three chairs by the door and sat a few feet from him. Ostentatiously he drew out his pistol and aimed it at Vermishank's head.

Isaac locked the door.

"Right, Vermishank," he said in a businesslike fashion. He sat and stared at his former boss. "Lemuel is a very good shot, in case you have adventurous ideas. He's a bit of a villain, actually. Bit dangerous. And I am not in any kind of mood to defend you, so I recommend you tell us what we want to know."

"What do you want to know, Isaac?" said Vermishank smoothly. Isaac was enraged, but impressed. The man was damn good at regaining and retaining his aplomb.

That, Isaac decided, would have to be dealt with.

Isaac stood and stalked over to Vermishank. The older man looked up at him idly, his eyes only widening in alarm too late as he realized that Isaac was going to hit him again.

Isaac punched Vermishank in the face twice, ignoring his old boss's squawk of pain and astonishment. Isaac gripped Vermishank by the throat and lowered himself into a squat, bringing his face next to his terrified prisoner's. Vermishank was bleeding from his nose, and scrabbling ineffectually at Isaac's massive hands. His eyes were glazed with terror.

"I don't think you understand the situation, old son," whispered Isaac with loathing. "I have sound reason to believe that you're responsible for my friend lying upstairs shitting himself and drooling. I am not in any mood for sodding around, playing games, going by rules. I don't *care* if you *live*, Vermishank. D'you understand? Are you with me? So here's the best way of doing this. I tell you what we know—don't waste my time asking how we know it—and you fill in what we don't. Every time you don't answer or the consensus here is that you're lying, either Lemuel or I will hurt you."

"You can't *torture* me, you *bastard* . . ." hissed Vermishank in a strangulated wheeze.

"Fuck you," breathed Isaac. "*You're* the Remaker. Now . . . answer the questions or die."

"Possibly both," added Lemuel coldly.

"See, you're wrong, Monty," continued Isaac. "We *can* torture you. That's exactly what we can do. So best to co-operate. Answer quickly, and convince me you ain't lying. Here's what we know. *Correct me if I'm wrong,* by the way, won't you?" He sneered at Vermishank.

There was a pause as Isaac ran through the facts in his head. Then he spoke them, ticking each item off on his fingers.

"You're in charge of biohazardous stuff for the government. That means the *slake-moth* programme." He looked up for a reaction, some surprise that the secret of the project was out. Vermishank was motionless. "The slake-moths have escaped—the slake-moths that *you* sold to some fucking criminal. They have something to do with dreamshit, and with the . . . with the nightmares that everyone's having. Rudgutter thought they were something to do with Benjamin Flex—wrongly, incidentally.

"Now, what we *need* to know is the following. What are they? What's the connection with the drug? How do we catch them?"

There was a pause as Vermishank sighed lengthily. His lips were trembling wetly, slick with blood and saliva, but he gave a little smile. Lemuel wagged the gun to chivvy him along.

"Hah. Slake-moths," breathed Vermishank eventually. He swallowed and massaged his neck. "Well. Aren't they *fascinating*? Amazing species."

"What are they?" said Isaac.

"What do you mean? You've clearly found out that much. They are *predators*. Efficient, brilliant predators."

"Where are they from?"

"Hah." Vermishank pondered a moment. He glanced up as Lemuel lazily and ostentatiously began to aim his gun at Vermishank's knee. Vermishank continued quickly. "We got the grubs from a merchant on one of the southernmost of the Shards—it must have been on their arrival that you *stole* one—but they aren't native to there." He looked up at Isaac with what looked like amusement. "If you really want to know, the current favourite theory is that they come from the Fractured Land."

"Don't fuck about . . ." shouted Isaac in rage, but Vermishank interrupted him.

"I am *not*, you fool. That *is* the favoured hypothesis. Fractured Land theory has been given a powerful boost in some circles by the discovery of the slake-moths."

"How do they hypnotize people?"

"Wings—of unstable dimensions and shapes, beating as they do in various planes—stuffed with oneirochromatophores. Colour-cells like those in an octopus's skin, sensitive to and affecting psychic resonances and subconscious patterns. They tap the frequencies of the dreams that are . . . ah . . . *bubbling* under the surface of the sentient mind. They focus them, draw them out into the surface. Hold them still."

"How does a mirror protect you?"

"Good question, Isaac." Vermishank's manner was changing. He sounded more and more as if he was giving a seminar. Even in a situation like this, realized Isaac, the didactic instinct was strong in the old bureaucrat. "We simply don't know. We've done all manner of experiments, with double-mirrors, treble-mirrors and so on. We don't know why, but seeing them reflected negates the effect, even though it is formally an identical sight, as their wings are already mirrored in each other. But, and this is *very interesting*, reflect it again—look at them through two mirrors, I mean, like a periscope—and they *can* hypnotize you again. *Isn't that extraordinary?*" He smiled.

Isaac paused. There was, he realized, something almost urgent about Vermishank's manner. He seemed anxious to leave nothing out. It must have been Lemuel's unwavering pistol.

"I've . . . *seen one of these things feeding* . . ." said Isaac. "I saw it . . . eat someone's brain."

"Hah." Vermishank shook his head appreciatively. "Astonishing. You are lucky to be here. You did *not* see it eat anyone's brain. Slake-moths don't live entirely in our plane. Their . . . ah . . . *nutritional needs* are met by substances that we cannot measure. Don't you *see*, Isaac?" Vermishank gazed at him intently, like a teacher trying to encourage the right answer from a petulant pupil. The urgency flashed again in his eyes. "I know biology's not your *strong point*, but it's such an . . . *elegant* mechanism, I thought you might see it. They draw the dreams out with their wings, flood the mind, break the dykes that hold back hidden thoughts, guilty thoughts, anxieties, delights, *dreams* . . ." He stopped. Sat back. Composed himself.

"And then," he continued, "when the mind is nice and juicy . . . they *suck it dry*. The subconscious is their nectar, Isaac, don't you see? That is why they only feed on the sentient. No cats or dogs for them. They drink the peculiar brew that results from self-reflexive thought, when the instincts and needs and desires and intuitions are folded in on themselves and we reflect on our thoughts and then reflect on the reflection, endlessly . . ." Vermishank's voice was hushed. "Our thoughts ferment like the purest liquor. That is what the slake-moths drink, Isaac. Not the meat-calories slopping about in the brainpan, but the fine wine of sapience and sentience itself, the subconscious.

"Dreams."

The room was silent. The idea was stunning. Everyone seemed to reel at the notion. Vermishank seemed almost to be revelling in the effect his revelations were having.

Everyone started at a clanging sound. It was just the construct, busy vacuuming the rubbish beside David's desk. It had tried to empty the bin into its receptacle, had slightly missed and spilled the contents. It was busy trying to clear up the pieces of crumpled paper that surrounded it.

"And . . . Dammit, of course!" Isaac breathed. "That's what the nightmares are! They . . . it's like fertilizer! Like, I don't know, rabbit-shit, that feeds the plants that feed the rabbits . . . It's a little chain, a little ecosystem . . ."

"Hah. Quite," said Vermishank. "You are thinking at last. You can't see slake-moth faeces, or smell it, but you can sense it. In your dreams. It feeds them, makes them boil. And then the slake-moth feeds *on* them. A perfect loop."

"How do you know all this, you swine?" breathed Derkhan. "How long have you been working on these monsters?"

"Slake-moths are very rare. And a state secret. That is why we were so excited about our little clutch of the things. We had one old, dying specimen, then received four new grubs. Isaac had one, of course. The original, that had fed our little caterpillars, died. We were debating whether to open the cocoon of another during its change, killing it but gleaning *invaluable* knowledge of its metamorphic state, but before we had decided, regrettably," he sighed, "we had to sell all four. They were an excessive risk. The word came that our research was taking too long, that our failure to control the specimens was making the . . . ah . . . *paymasters* nervous. Funding was withdrawn, and our department had to pay its debts quickly, given the failure of our project."

"Which was what?" hissed Isaac. "Weapons? Torture?"

"Oh, really, Isaac," said Vermishank calmly. "Look at you, stiff with moral outrage. If you hadn't *stolen* one of them in the first place, it would never have escaped, and it would never have freed its fellows—which is what must have happened, you realize—and think how many innocent people would have lived."

Isaac stared at him aghast.

"Fuck you!" he screamed. He rose and would have leapt at Vermishank had Lemuel not spoken.

"Isaac," he said curtly, and Isaac saw that Lemuel's gun was trained on him. "Vermishank is being very co-operative and there's more we need to know. *Right?*"

Isaac stared at him, nodded and sat.

"Why *are* you being so helpful, Vermishank?" asked Lemuel, returning his gaze to the older man.

Vermishank shrugged.

"I do not relish the idea of pain," he said with a little simper. "In addition to which, although you will not like this . . . it will do you no good. You cannot catch them. You cannot evade the militia. Why would I hold back?" He gave a smug, loathsome grin.

And yet his eyes were nervous, his upper lip sweating. There was a forlorn note buried deep in his throat.

Godspit! thought Isaac with a sudden shock of realization. He sat up and stared at Vermishank. *That is* not *all! He . . . he's telling us because he's afraid! He doesn't think the government can catch them . . . and he's afraid. He wants us to succeed!*

Isaac wanted to taunt Vermishank with this, to wave the knowledge of his weakness at him, to punish him for all his crimes . . . but he would not risk it. If Isaac were to antagonize him too flagrantly, to confront him with an understanding of his fear that Isaac doubted Vermishank himself possessed, then the vile man might withdraw all his help out of spite.

If he needed to think he was crowing to beg for help, then
Isaac would let him.

"What is dreamshit?" said Isaac.

"Dreamshit?" Vermishank smiled, and Isaac remembered the
last time he had asked Vermishank that question and the man
had affected disgust, had refused to sully his mouth with the
foul word.

It came easy to him now.

"Hah. Dreamshit is baby food. It is what the moths feed their
young. They exude it all the time, but in great quantities when
they are parenting. They are not like other moths: they're very
caring. They nurture their eggs assiduously, by all accounts, and
suckle the newborn caterpillars. Only in their adolescence, when
they pupate, can they feed themselves."

Derkhan interjected.

"Are you saying that dreamshit is slake-moth *milk*?"

"Exactly. The caterpillars cannot yet digest purely psychic
food. It must be imbibed in quasi-physical form. The liquid the
moths exude is *thick* with distilled dreams."

"And that's why some fucking *druglord* bought them? Who
was it?" Derkhan's mouth curled.

"I have no idea. I merely suggested the deal. Which of the bid-
ders was successful is irrelevant to me. One has to husband the
moths carefully, stud them regularly, milk them. Like cows.
They can be manipulated—by someone who knows what they're
doing—fooled into exuding milk without having born grubs.
And the milk has to be processed, of course. No human, or any
other sentient race, could drink it neat. It would instantly explode their mind. The inelegantly named dreamshit has been
rendered and . . . ah . . . *cut* with various substances . . . Which
incidentally, Isaac, means that the caterpillar you raised—that I
presume you fed on dreamshit—must have grown into a less
than healthy moth. It is as if you fed a human baby milk laced
with large quantities of sawdust and pondwater."

"How do you know all this?" hissed Derkhan.

Vermishank looked at her blankly.

"How do you know how many mirrors it takes to make you
safe, how do you know they turn the minds they . . . they eat into
that . . . milk . . . ? *How many people have you fed to them?*"

Vermishank pursed his lips, a little perturbed.

"I am a scientist," he said. "I use the means at my disposal. On

occasion, criminals are sentenced to death. The *manner* of their
death is not specified . . ."

"You *swine* . . ." she hissed viciously. "What about all the people the dealers take to feed them, to make the drug . . . ?" she
continued, but Isaac cut her off.

"Vermishank," he said softly, and stared at the other man.
"How do we get their minds back? The ones who've been taken."

"Back?" Vermishank seemed genuinely baffled. "Ah . . ." He
shook his head and furrowed his eyes. "You cannot."

"Don't *lie* to me . . ." screamed Isaac, thinking of Lublamai.

"They have been drunk," hissed Vermishank, and brought silence quickly to the room. He waited.

"They have been *drunk*," he said again. "Their thoughts have
been taken, their dreams—their conscious and subconscious—
have been burnt up in the moths' stomachs, have trickled out
again to feed the grubs. Have you taken dreamshit, Isaac? Any of
you?" No one, least of all Isaac, would answer him. "If you have,
you have dreamed them, the victims, the prey. You have had their
metabolized minds slip into your stomach and you have
dreamed them. *There is nothing left to save. There* is *nothing to
get back.*"

Isaac felt absolute despair.

Take his body too, he thought, *Jabber, don't be cruel, don't
leave me with that fucking shell that I can't let die, that means
nothing . . .*

"How do we kill the slake-moths?" he hissed.

Vermishank smiled, very slowly.

"You cannot," he said.

"Don't bullshit me," hissed Isaac. "Everything that lives can
die . . ."

"You misunderstand me. As an *abstract proposition* of course
they can die. And therefore, theoretically, they can be killed. But
you will not be able to kill them. They live in several planes, as
I've said, and bullets, fire, and so forth injure only in one. You
would have to hit them in many dimensions at once, or do the
most extraordinary amount of damage in this one, and they will
not give you the chance . . . Do you understand?"

"So let's think *laterally* . . ." said Isaac. He batted his temples
hard with the heels of his hands. "What about a biological control? Predators . . ."

"They have none. They are at the top of their food chain. We're fairly sure that there are animals, in their native land, that are capable of killing them, but there are none within several thousand miles of here. And anyway, if we're right, to unleash them would be to usher doom more *quickly* onto New Crobuzon."

"Dear Jabber," breathed Isaac. "Without predators or competitors, with a *massive* supply of food, fresh and constantly replenished . . . There'll be no *stopping* them."

"And that," whispered Vermishank hesitantly, "is before we've even considered what'll happen if they . . . They are still young, you understand. They are not fully mature. But soon, when the nights become hot . . . We have to consider what might happen when they *breed* . . ."

The room seemed to go still and cold. Again Vermishank tried to control his face, but again, Isaac saw the raw fear inside him. Vermishank was terrified. He knew what was at stake.

A little way away, the construct was rotating, hissing and clattering. It seemed to be leaking dust and dirt, and moving in random directions trailing a stiff litter-spike behind it. *Broken again,* thought Isaac, and turned his attention back on Vermishank.

"When will they breed?" he hissed.

Vermishank licked the sweat from his upper lip.

"They are hermaphrodites, I am told. We've never observed them mating or seen them lay eggs. We only know what we've been told. They come into heat in the back half of the summer. One designated egg-layer. Around about Sinn, Octuary. Usually. Usually, that is."

"Come on! There must be something we can do!" shouted Isaac. "Don't tell me Rudgutter's got nothing in mind . . ."

"I'm not privy to that. I mean, of course I know they've plans. Why, yes. But what they are I simply can't say. I have . . ." Vermishank hesitated.

"What?" yelled Isaac.

"I have heard that they approached dæmons." No one said a word. Vermishank swallowed and continued. "And were refused help. Even at the highest bribery."

"Why?" hissed Derkhan.

"Because the dæmons were afraid." Vermishank licked his lips. The fear that he was trying to keep hidden became visible again. "Do you understand that? They were *afraid*. Because for all their power and their presence . . . they think as we do. They are sentient, sapient. And as far as the slake-moths are concerned . . . they are therefore prey."

Everyone in the room was still. The pistol sagged in Lemuel's hand, but Vermishank made no attempt to run, lost as he was in his own miserable reverie.

"What are we going to do?" said Isaac. His voice was not quite steady.

The grating sound of the construct grew stronger. The thing spun for a moment on its central wheel. Its cleaning arms were extended and clattered against the ground in staccato motion. Derkhan, then Isaac and David and the others looked up at it.

"I can't *think* with that fucking thing in the room!" yelled Isaac, enraged. He strode over, ready to take out his impotence and his fear on the construct. As he approached it, it spun to face him with its glass iris and its two main arms extended suddenly, an errant piece of paper on the end of one. The construct looked disorientingly like a person with outstretched arms. Isaac blinked and continued towards it.

Its right arm stabbed down at the floor and the rubbish and dust it had strewn idiotically in its path. It jerked down again and again, violently tapping at the wooden boards. Its left limb, with its broom end, jerked out to block Isaac's path, slowing him and wagging, he realized with utter astonishment, to *hold his attention*, and then its right, a litter-skewer, jerked down once more to point at the floor.

At the dust. In which was scrawled a message.

The point of the skewer had traced its way through the dirt and even scored the wood itself. The words it had scribbled in the rubbish were shaky and uncertain, but entirely legible.

You are betrayed.

Isaac gaped at the construct in complete consternation. It waved its litter-spike at him, the scrap of paper on the end whipping back and forth.

The others had not yet read what was written on the floor, but they could tell from Isaac's face and the extraordinary behaviour of the construct that something strange was happening. They were standing, gazing curiously.

"What is it, Isaac?" said Derkhan.

"I . . . I don't know . . ." he murmured. The construct seemed agitated, by turn tapping at the message on the floor and flailing the paper on its spike. Isaac reached out, his mouth wide with amazement, and the construct held its arm still. Gingerly, Isaac plucked the crumpled paper from it.

As he smoothed it out, David leapt up suddenly, horrified and aghast. He rushed across the room.

"Isaac," he shouted. "Wait . . ." But Isaac had already opened the paper, his eyes had already widened in horror at what was written. His mouth grew slack at the enormity of it, but before he could emit a shout Vermishank moved.

Lemuel had been caught up with the bizarre drama of the construct, his eyes had left his quarry, and Vermishank had seen it. Everyone in the room was staring at Isaac as he fumbled with the rubbish the construct had handed him. Vermishank leapt up from the chair and bolted for the door.

He had forgotten it was locked. When he yanked at it and it would not open, he cried out in undignified panic. Behind him, David peeled away from Isaac and backed towards Vermishank and the door. Isaac spun on his heel towards them, still clutching the paper. He glared at David and Vermishank in lunatic hatred. Lemuel had seen his error, was bringing his pistol to bear on Vermishank when Isaac moved threateningly towards the prisoner, blocking Lemuel's line of fire.

"Isaac," shouted Lemuel, "move!"

Vermishank saw that Derkhan had leapt to her feet, that David was cringing away from Isaac, that the hooded man in the other corner was standing with legs spread and arms out in a weirdly predatory fashion. Lemuel was invisible to Vermishank, behind the looming threat of Isaac.

Isaac looked from Vermishank to David, his eyes oscillating back and forth. He waved the paper.

"Isaac," Lemuel screamed again. "Get out of the fucking way!"

But Isaac could not hear or speak for rage. There was a cacophony. Everyone in the room was yelling, demanding to know what was on the paper, begging for a clear shot, growling in rage or keening like a great bird.

Isaac seemed to be debating which of David or Vermishank to grab. David was breaking down, begging Isaac to listen to him. With a last desperate pointless tug at the door, Vermishank turned and defended himself.

He was, after all, a highly trained bio-thaumaturge. He babbled an incantation and flexed the invisible, occult muscles he had developed in his arms. He hooked his hand at the arcane energy that made the veins of his forearm stand out like snakes beneath the skin, made his skin twitch and tighten.

Isaac's shirt was half undone, and Vermishank plunged his right hand through the uncovered flesh below Isaac's neck.

Isaac bellowed in rage and pain as his tissue gave like thick clay. It became malleable under Vermishank's trained hands.

Vermishank dug inelegantly through the unwilling flesh. He gripped and ungripped his fingers to grab hold of a rib. Isaac grabbed hold of Vermishank's wrist and held it. His face was set in a grimace. He was stronger, but pain was disabling him.

Vermishank was wailing as they wrestled. "Let me go!" he screamed. He had had no plan, had struck out in fear of his life and found himself committed to a murderous attack. It could not be undone. He could do nothing but scrabble for purchase inside Isaac's chest.

Behind them, David fumbled for his key.

Isaac could not pull Vermishank's fingers from his chest, and Vermishank could not push them any further in. They stood, swaying, tugging at each other. Behind them the confusion of voices continued. Lemuel had stood, had kicked away his chair and was feinting to find a vantage point for a clean shot. Derkhan ran over and pulled violently at Vermishank's arms, but the terrified man curled his fingers around the bones of Isaac's chest, and with every pull Isaac screamed in pain. Blood was spurting from Isaac's skin, from the imperfect seals where Vermishank's fingers punctured his flesh.

Vermishank and Isaac and Derkhan wrestled and howled, spraying blood across the floor, fouling Sincerity, who bolted away. Lemuel reached over Isaac's shoulder to shoot, but Vermishank tugged Isaac around like some grotesque glove puppet, knocking the pistol out of Lemuel's hand. It hit the floor some feet away, scattering its black powder. Lemuel swore and dug urgently for a powder-case.

Suddenly a shrouded figure stood by the clumsy fighting trio. Yagharek threw back his hood. Vermishank stared into his hard round eyes, opened his mouth at the garuda's great predatory birdface. But before he could speak, Yagharek had plunged his vicious curved beak into the flesh of Vermishank's right arm.

He tore through the muscle and tendons with speed and vigour. Vermishank shrieked as his arm blossomed with ragged flesh and blood. He snapped his hand back, withdrawing it from Isaac's flesh, which resealed imperfectly with a wet snap. Isaac growled with agony and stroked his chest. It was slick with blood, the surface misshapen, pocked and still bleeding from Vermishank's hand.

Derkhan had her arms around Vermishank's neck. As Vermishank clutched the bleeding ruins of his forearm, she hurled him away from her into the centre of the room. The construct rolled out of Vermishank's way as he staggered and fell, fouling the boards with gore, screaming.

Lemuel had primed his pistol again. Vermishank caught sight of him aiming and opened his mouth to beg, to wail. He held his bloody arm up, trembling, supplicating.

Lemuel pulled the trigger. There was a cavernous cracking sound and an explosion of acrid gunpowder. Vermishank's cry stopped instantly. The ball hit him right between the eyes, a textbook shot from close enough range to pass through him and take the back of his head off in an efflorescence of dark blood.

He fell back, his broken skull smacking dully on the old boards.

The particles of gunpowder spun and tumbled slowly. Vermishank's carcass shuddered.

Isaac leant back against the wall and swore. He pressed his chest, seemed to smooth it down. He fumbled at it in an ineffectual attempt to repair the cosmetic damage Vermishank's intrusive fingers had done.

He emitted livid barks of pain.

"Gods*damn*!" he spat, and eyed Vermishank's body with loathing.

Lemuel held his pistol idly. Derkhan was trembling. Yagharek had withdrawn, stood watching the proceedings, his features dim once more in the shadows of the hood.

No one spoke. The fact of Vermishank's murder filled the room. There was unease and shock, but no recrimination. No one wished him alive again.

"Yag, old son," croaked Isaac eventually. "I owe you." The garuda did not acknowledge him.

"We have to . . . we have to get this out of here," said Derkhan urgently, kicking Vermishank's corpse. "They'll be looking for him soon."

"That's the least of our worries," said Isaac. He held out his right hand. He still held the paper he had taken from the construct, now bloodstained. "David's gone," he observed, pointing at the unlocked door. He looked around. "He's taken Sincerity," he said, his face curling. He threw the paper to Derkhan. As she unfolded it, Isaac stomped over towards the skittering construct.

Derkhan read the note. Her face hardened in disgust and outrage. She held it up so that Lemuel could read it. After a moment, Yagharek stalked over and read it over Lemuel's shoulder, from inside his hood.

Serachin. Further to our meeting. Enclosed is payment and instructions. Der Grimnebulin and associates will be brought to justice on *Chainday 8th Tathis*. The militia will apprehend him at his residence at *9 o'clock in the evening*. You are to ensure that der Grimnebulin and all working with him are present from *6 o'clock onwards*. You will be present during the raid, to avoid suspicion falling upon you. Our agents have seen heliotypes of you, in addition to which you are to wear *red*. Our officers will do everything possible to avoid casualties, but this cannot be guaranteed, and your clear self-identification is crucial.

Sally.

Lemuel blinked, looked up.

"It's today," he said, and blinked again. "Chainday's today. They're coming."

CHAPTER THIRTY-THREE

Isaac ignored Lemuel. He was standing directly in front of the construct, which moved almost uneasily before his intense gaze.

"How did you know, Isaac?" shouted Derkhan, and Isaac raised his finger and jerked it at the construct.

"I was tipped off. David betrayed us," he whispered. "My mate. Been on a hundred damn benders with him, done drinking, done riots . . . the fuck sold me out. And I got *tipped off* by a damn construct." He poked his face right into the construct's lens. "You understand me?" he whispered incredulously. "You with me? You . . . wait, you've got audio inputs, haven't you? Turn around . . . turn if you understand me . . ."

Lemuel and Derkhan glanced at each other.

"Isaac, mate," said Lemuel witheringly, but his words petered out into astonished silence.

Slowly, deliberately, the construct was turning around.

"What the fuck is it doing?" hissed Derkhan.

Isaac turned to her.

"I've no idea," he hissed. "I've heard of this, but I didn't know it could actually happen. It's had some virus, hasn't it? CI . . . Constructed Intelligence . . . I can't believe it's real . . ."

He turned back and gazed at the construct. Derkhan and Lemuel approached it, as, after a moment's hesitation, did Yagharek.

"It's impossible," said Isaac suddenly. "It doesn't have an intricate enough engine for independent thought. It is *impossible*."

The construct lowered its pointer and backed away to a nearby pile of dust. It dragged its spike through it, and spelt out clearly: *It is.*

At the sight, the three humans hissed and gasped.

"What the *fuck* . . . ?" yelled Isaac. "You can *read* and *write* . . . you . . ." He shook his head, then looked up at the construct, hard and cold again in a moment. "How did you know?" he said. "And why did you warn me?"

It was quickly clear, however, that this was an explanation that would have to wait. As Isaac waited intently, Lemuel glanced up at the clock and started nervously. It was late.

It took a minute, but Lemuel and Derkhan convinced Isaac that they had better flee the workshop now with the construct. They had better act on the information they had been given, even if they didn't understand where it had come from.

Isaac protested weakly, tugging at the construct. He denounced David to Hell, then marvelled at the construct's intelligence. He screamed rage and cast an analytical eye on the transformed cleaning engine. He was confused. Derkhan's and Lemuel's urgent insistence that they must move infected him.

"Yes, David is a godsdamn shit. And yes, the construct is a godsdamn miracle, Isaac," hissed Derkhan, "but it's going to be a wasted one if we don't *leave now*."

And in an infuriating, tantalizing end to the matter, the construct spread the dust out again as Isaac watched, and carefully scrawled: *Later*.

Lemuel thought quickly.

"There's a place I know up in Gidd where we can go," he decided. "It'll do for tonight, and then we can make plans." Derkhan and he moved quickly around the room, gathering useful items into bags they pilfered from David's cupboards. It was clear they would not be able to return.

Isaac stood numb by the wall. His mouth was slightly open. His eyes were glazed. He shook his head incredulously.

Lemuel glanced up and saw him.

"Isaac," he yelled. "Go and sort your shit out. We've less than an hour. We are leaving. Get off your arse."

Isaac looked up, nodded peremptorily and stomped up the stairs, to stop and stand still again at the top. His expression was of bemused and miserable disbelief.

After some seconds, Yagharek came silently after him. He stood behind Isaac and peeled back his hood.

"Grimnebulin," he whispered as softly as his avian throat allowed. "You are thinking of your friend David."

Isaac turned sharply.

"No fucking friend of mine," he countered.

"And yet he was. You are thinking of the betrayal."

Isaac said nothing for several moments. Then he nodded. The look of horrified astonishment returned.

"I know betrayal, Grimnebulin," whistled Yagharek. "I know it well. I am . . . sorry for you."

Isaac turned away and walked brusquely to his laboratory space, began shoving bits and pieces of wire and ceramic and glass seemingly at random into a huge carpet bag. He strapped it, bulky and clanking, to his back.

"When were you betrayed, Yag?" he demanded.

"I was not. I betrayed." Isaac stopped and turned to him. "I know what David has done. And I am sorry."

Isaac stared in bewilderment, in denial and misery.

The militia attacked. It was only twenty minutes past seven.

* * *

The door flew open with a massive sound. Three militia officers came hurtling through into the room, their battering ram flying out of their hands.

The door was still unlocked from when David had fled. The militia had not expected this, and had tried to break down a door which did not resist them. They fell, sprawling and idiotic.

There was a confused moment. The three militia scrabbled to stand. Outside, the squad of officers gaped stupidly into the building. On the ground floor, Derkhan and Lemuel stared back at them. Isaac looked down at the intruders.

Then everyone moved.

The militia outside in the street recovered their wits and rushed the door. Lemuel flipped David's huge desk onto its side and hunkered down behind the makeshift shield, priming his two long pistols. Derkhan ran towards him, diving for cover. Yagharek hissed and stepped backwards from the rail of the walkway, out of sight of the militia.

In one slick movement, Isaac turned to his laboratory work-table and scooped up two huge glass flasks of discoloured liquid, still spinning on his heels, and hurled them over the rail at the invading officers like bombs.

The first three militia through the door had regained their feet, only to be caught in the shower of glass and chymical rain. One of the massive jars shattered on the helmet of one officer, who hit the floor again, motionless and bleeding. Vicious shards bounced off the others' armour. The two militia caught by the deluge were still for a moment, then began to shriek suddenly as the chymicals seeped through their masks and began to attack the soft tissues of their faces.

There was still no gunfire.

Isaac turned again and began to grab more jars, taking a moment to pick strategically, so that the effects of the cascading chymicals were not entirely random. *Why don't they shoot?* he thought giddily.

The wounded officers had been pulled out into the street. In their place, a phalanx of heavily armoured officers had entered, bearing iron shields with reinforced glass windows through which they stared. Behind them, Isaac saw two officers getting ready to attack with khepri stingboxes.

They must want us alive! he realized. The stingbox could kill, easily, but it could also not. If deaths were all that were desired, it would have been far easier for Rudgutter to send conventional troops, with flintlocks and crossbows, than such rare agents as humans trained in stingbox.

Isaac hurled a double salvo of trow-iron dust and sanguimorph distillate at the defensive huddle, but the guards were quick, and the jars were shattered with twitching shields. The militia danced to avoid the dangerous gobbets.

Each of the two officers behind the shield-bearers spun their jagged twin flails.

The stingboxes themselves—metaclockwork engines of intricate and extraordinary khepri design—were attached to the officers' belts, each the size of a small bag. Attached to each side was a long cord, thick wires swathed in metal coils, then insulating rubber, extendible more than twenty feet. About two feet from the end of each cord was a polished wooden handle, one of which each officer held in each hand. They used these to whirl the ends of the cords at terrible speed. Something glimmered almost invisibly. At the tip of each tendril, Isaac knew, was a vicious little metal prong, a weighted clutch of barbs and spikes. These tips varied. Some were solid, the best-made expanded like cruel flowers on impact. All were designed to fly heavy and true, to puncture armour and flesh, to grip without mercy inside torn flesh.

Derkhan had reached the table and was huddling by Lemuel. Isaac turned to grab more ammunition. In the moment of silence, Derkhan raised herself quickly on one knee and peered over the tip of the table, taking aim with her great pistol.

She pulled the trigger. At the same instant, one of the officers let fly with his stingbox.

Derkhan was a decent shot. Her ball flew into the viewing window of one of the militia shields, which she had judged its weak point. But she had underestimated the militia's defences. The porthole cracked violently and spectacularly, whitened completely with shards of glassdust and a crack-lattice, but its structure was interlaced with copper wire, and it held. The militiaman staggered, then stood solid.

The officer with the stingbox moved like an expert.

He swung up his arms at the same moment in sweeping curves, flicking the little switches in the wooden handles that allowed the cords to slide through them, releasing them. The momentum of the twirling blades took them flying through the air in a flash of metallic grey.

Cord unravelled almost without friction from inside the sting-box, through the air and the wooden handles, slowing the blades hardly at all. Their curving flight was absolutely true. The jagged weights flew in a long, elliptical motion through the air, the curve shallowing rapidly as the cables attaching them to the stingbox extended.

The buds of sharpened steel smacked simultaneously into each side of Derkhan's chest. She screamed and staggered, her teeth gritting as the pistol fell from her spasming fingers.

Instantly, the officer pressed the catch on his stingbox to re-lease the pent-up clockwork within.

There was a sputtering whirr. The hidden coils of the motor began to unwind, twirling like a dynamo and generating waves of weird current. Derkhan danced and spasmed, agonized yells spurting out from behind her teeth. Little bursts of blue light ex-ploded like whiplashes from her hair and fingers.

The officer watched her intently, twiddling the dials on his stingbox that controlled the intensity and form of the power. There was a violent, cracking jolt and Derkhan flew backwards against the wall, collapsing to the floor.

The second officer sent his sharp bulbs over the edge of the ta-ble, hoping to catch Lemuel, but he was flattened hard against the wood and they flew harmlessly around him. The officer pressed a stud and the cords rapidly retracted back into a ready position.

Lemuel stared at the stricken Derkhan and hefted his pistols.

Isaac bellowed in rage. He hurled another vast pot of unstable thaumaturgic compound at the militia. It fell short, but burst with such violence that it splashed onto and over the shields, mixing with the distillate and sending two officers screaming to the floor as their skin became parchment and their blood ink.

An amplified voice burst through the door. It was Mayor Rudgutter's.

"Stop these attacks. Be sensible. You aren't going to get out. Stop attacking us and we will show mercy."

Rudgutter stood in the midst of his honour guard with Eliza Stem-Fulcher. It was highly unusual for him to accompany a militia raid, but this was no ordinary raid. He was stationed across the road and a little way along from Isaac's workshop.

It was not yet completely dark. Alarmed and curious faces peered from windows up and down the street. Rudgutter ignored them. He took the funnel of iron away from his mouth and turned to Eliza Stem-Fulcher. His face was creased in irritation.

"This is an absolute bloody shambles," he said. She nodded. "Well, however inefficient they are, the militia can't lose. A few officers might be killed, regrettably, but there's no way der Grimnebulin and his cohorts are getting out of there." The faces peeking nervously from behind windows all around suddenly annoyed him.

He raised the loudhailer sharply and yelled into it: "Get back into your houses immediately!"

There was a gratifying flurry of curtains. Rudgutter stood back and watched as the warehouse shuddered.

Lemuel dispatched the other stingbox-wielder with one elegant and careful shot. Isaac hurled his table down the stairs taking two officers with it when they had tried to rush him, and now he continued with his chymical sniping. Yagharek was helping him, at his direction, showering the attackers with noxious mixtures.

But this was all, could not but be, doomed valiance. There were too many militia. It helped that they were not prepared to kill, because Isaac and Lemuel and Yagharek had no such constraints. Isaac estimated that four militia had fallen: one to a bullet; one to a crushed skull; and two to random chymico-thaumaturgic reactions. But it could not last. The militia advanced on Lemuel behind their shields.

Isaac saw the militia look up and confer for a minute. Then one of them raised a flintlock rifle carefully, aiming it at Yagharek.

"Down, Yag!" he yelled. "They'll kill *you*!"

Yagharek dropped to the floor, out of sight of the assassin.

There was no sudden manifestation, no creeping flesh or vast stalking figure. All that happened was that the Weaver's voice sounded in Rudgutter's ear.

. . . I HAVE BOUNDED UNSEEN UP TANGLING WIRES OF SKYNESS AND SLIPPED MY LEGS SPLAYED WILLY-NILLY ON THE PSYCHIC DUNG OF THE WEB-REAVERS THEY ARE LOW CREATURES AND INELEGANT AND DRAB WHISPER WHAT HAPPENS MR. MAYOR THIS PLACE TREMBLES . . .

Rudgutter started. *That's all I need,* he thought. He replied with a firm voice.

"Weaver," he said. Stem-Fulcher turned to him with a sharp, curious gaze. "How nice to have you with us."

It's too damned unpredictable, Rudgutter thought furiously. *Not now, not bloody now! Go and chase the moths, go hunting . . . what are you doing here?* The Weaver was infuriating and dangerous, and Rudgutter had taken a calculated risk in engaging its aid. A loose cannon was still a lethal weapon.

Rudgutter had thought that the great spider and he had something of an *arrangement.* As much, at least, as it was possible to maintain with a Weaver. Kapnellior had helped him. Textorology was a tentative field, but it had borne some fruit. There were proven methods of communication, and Rudgutter had been using them to interact with the Weaver. Messages carved into the blades of scissors and melted. Apparently random sculptures, lit from below, whose shadows wrote messages across the ceiling. The Weaver's responses were prompt and delivered even more bizarrely.

Rudgutter had politely bade the Weaver busy itself chasing the moths. Rudgutter could not order, of course, could only suggest. But the Weaver had responded positively, and Rudgutter realized that stupidly, absurdly, he had begun to think of it as his agent.

No more of that.

Rudgutter cleared his throat. "Might I ask why you have joined us, Weaver?"

The voice came again, resonating in his ear, bouncing on the bones inside his head.

. . . INSIDE AND OUTSIDE THE FIBRES ARE SPLIT AND BURST AND A TRAIL IS TORN ACROSS THE WARP OF THE WORLDWEB WHERE COLOURS ARE BLED AND WAN I HAVE SLID ACROSS THE SKY BELOW THE SURFACE AND DANCED ALONG THE RENT WITH TEARS OF MISERY AT THE UGLY RUIN WHICH STEMS AND SPREADS AND BEGINS IN THIS PLACE . . .

Rudgutter nodded slowly as the sense of the words emerged. "It started from here," he agreed. "This is the centre. This is the source. Unfortunately . . ." He spoke very carefully. "Unfortunately, this is a somewhat inopportune moment. Might I prevail on you to investigate this—which is indeed the birthplace of the problem—in a little while?"

Stem-Fulcher was watching him. Her face was fraught. She listened intently to his responses.

For a strange moment, all the sounds around them ceased. The shots and yells from the warehouse momentarily died. There were no creaks or clanks from the militia's arms. Stem-Fulcher's mouth was open, as she hovered ready to speak, but she said nothing. The Weaver was silent.

Then there was a whispering sound inside Rudgutter's skull. He gasped in consternation, then opened his mouth in outright dismay. He did not know how he knew, but he was listening to the uncanny sound of the Weaver picking its way across various dimensions towards the warehouse.

The officers bore down on Lemuel with a remorseless precision. They tramped across Vermishank's corpse. They held their shields triumphantly before them.

Above, Isaac and Yagharek had run out of chymicals. Isaac was bellowing, hurling chairs and slats of wood and rubbish at the militia. They deflected them with ease.

Derkhan was as motionless as Lublamai, who lay still on a cot in the corner of Isaac's living space.

Lemuel let out a desperate yell of rage and swung his powder-horn at his attackers, spraying them with acrid gunpowder. He fumbled for his tinderbox, but they were on him, truncheons swinging. The officer with the stingbox approached, twirling his blades.

The air in the centre of the warehouse vibrated uncannily.

Two militiamen were approaching this unstable patch, and they paused in puzzlement. Isaac and Yagharek each carried one end of an enormous bench, ready to hurl it at the officers below. Each caught sight of the phenomenon. They stopped moving and watched.

Like some eldritch flower, a patch of organic darkness bloomed from nothing in the centre of the room. It expanded into physical reality with the animal ease of a stretching cat. It opened itself, and it stood to fill the room, a colossal segmented thing, a massive spider-presence that hummed with power and sucked the light out of the air.

The Weaver.

Yagharek and Isaac dropped the bench simultaneously.

The militia stopped pummelling Lemuel and turned, alerted by the changing nature of the æther.

Everyone stopped and stared, utterly aghast.

The Weaver had manifested standing directly over two trembling officers. They let out little cries of terror. One dropped his sword as his fingers numbed. The other, more bravely but no less ineffectually, raised a pistol in his violently shaking hand.

The Weaver looked down at the two men. It raised its pair of human hands. As they cringed, it brought one hand down on each of their heads, patting them like dogs.

It raised its hand and pointed up at the walkway, where Isaac and Yagharek stood dumbfounded and afraid. Its unearthly singsong voice resonated in the suddenly quiet room.

. . . OVER AND UP IN THE LITTLE PASSAGE IT WAS IT WAS BORN THE CRINGING THUMB THE TWISTED RUNT THAT FREED ITS SIBLINGS IT CRACKED THE SEAL ON ITS SWADDLING AND BURST OUT I SMELL THE REMNANTS OF ITS BREAKFAST STILL LOLLING OH I LIKE THIS I ENJOY THIS WEB THE WEFT IS INTRICATE AND FINE THOUGH TORN WHO HERE CAN SPIN WITH SUCH ROBUST AND NAIVE EXPERTISE . . .

The Weaver's head moved with alien smoothness from one to the other side. It took in the room in its multiple and glinting eyes. Still no humans moved.

From outside came Rudgutter's voice. It was tense. Angry.

"Weaver!" he shouted. "I have a gift and a message for you!" There was a moment of silence, and then a pair of pearl-handled scissors came skittering through the door of the warehouse. The Weaver clasped its hands in a very human motion of delight. From outside came the distinctive sound of scissors being opened and closed.

. . . LOVELY LOVELY, moaned the Weaver, THE SNIPSNAP OF SUPPLICATION AND YET THOUGH THEY SMOOTH EDGES AND ROUGH FIBRES WITH COLD NOISE AN EXPLOSION IN REVERSE A FUNNELLING IN A FOCUS I MUST TURN MAKE PATTERNS HERE WITH AMATEURS UNKNOWING ARTISTS TO UNPICK THE CATASTROPHIC TEARING THERE IS BRUTE ASYMMETRY IN THE BLUE VISAGES THAT WILL NOT DO IT CANNOT BE THAT THE RIPPED UP WEB IS DARNED WITHOUT PATTERNS AND IN THE MINDS OF THESE DESPERATE AND GUILTY AND BEREFT ARE EXQUISITE TAPESTRIES OF DESIRE THE DAPPLED GANG PLAIT YEARNINGS FOR FRIENDS FEATHERS SCIENCE JUSTICE GOLD . . .

The Weaver's voice shivered in some crooning delight. Its legs moved suddenly at terrifying speed, picking its intricate way through the room, rippling through the space.

The militia crouching over Lemuel dropped their staffs and scrabbled to get out of its way. Lemuel looked up at its arachnid bulk through swollen eyes. He raised his hands and tried to cry out in fear.

The Weaver hovered for a moment before him, then looked up at the platform above. It stepped up lightly and was instantly, incomprehensibly, on the walkway, a few feet from Isaac and Yagharek. They stared in terror at the vast and monstrous form. Those pointed spike-feet pranced towards them. They were immobilized. Yagharek tried to move backwards but the Weaver was too quick . . . SAVAGE AND IMPENETRABLE . . . it sang, and scooped Yagharek up with a sudden motion, sweeping him under its humanlike arm where he twisted and cried out like a terrified baby.

. . . BLACK AND RUSSET . . . sang the Weaver. It tottered elegantly like a dancer on her toes, moved sideways through twisted dimensions and was once more by Lemuel's cowering form. It grabbed him and bundled him dangling beside Yagharek.

The militia stood back, dumbfounded and terrified. Mayor Rudgutter's voice sounded from outside again, but no one listened.

The Weaver stepped up and was once again on Isaac's raised living space. It skittered up to Isaac and grabbed him under its free arm . . . EXTRAVAGANT SECULAR SWARMING . . . it chanted as it took hold of him.

Isaac could not resist. The Weaver's touch was cool and unchanging, quite unreal. Its skin was as smooth as polished glass. He felt himself lifted with breathtaking ease and enfolded, cosseted under that bony arm.

. . . DIAMETRICAL NEGLIGENT FEROCIOUS . . . Isaac heard the Weaver say as it retraced its impossible steps and was twenty feet away, standing by Derkhan's motionless body. The militia around her moved away in concerted fear. The Weaver fumbled for her unconscious form and tucked her up next to Isaac, who felt her warmth through his clothes.

Isaac's head was spinning. The Weaver moved sideways again and was across the room, beside the construct. For a few minutes, Isaac had forgotten it even existed. It had returned to its customary resting place in the corner of the room, from where it had watched the militia attacks. It turned the one feature on its smooth head, its glass lens, towards the Weaver. The ineluctable spider-presence flicked the construct up onto its dagger-limbs and tossed it nimbly up. The Weaver caught the ungainly man-sized machine on its curving chitinous back. The construct balanced precariously, but did not fall no matter how the Weaver moved.

Isaac felt a sudden, murderous pain in his head. He cried out in agony, felt hot blood pumping across his face. He heard Lemuel scream a moment later, echoing him.

Through eyes bleary with confusion and blood, Isaac saw the room flicker around him as the Weaver paced through interlocking planes. It appeared beside all the militiamen in turn and moved one of its bladed arms too fast to see. As it touched them, each of the men screamed, so that a weird virus of agonized sound seemed to pass around the room at whiplash speed.

The Weaver stopped in the centre of the warehouse. Its elbows were pinioned, so that its captives could not move. With its forearms it dropped red-stained things across the floor. Isaac raised his head and looked around the room, trying to see through the burning pain below his temple. Everyone in the room was crying out, cringing, clapping their hands to the sides of their faces, trying without success to staunch gouts of blood with their fingers. Isaac looked down again.

The Weaver was scattering a handful of bloody ears onto the ground.

Below its gently moving hand, blood spilt across the dust in slicks of dirty gore. The gobbets of freshly sliced flesh fell, tracing the perfect shape of a pair of scissors.

The Weaver looked up, impossibly laden with struggling figures, moving as if unencumbered.

. . . FERVENT AND LOVABLE . . . it whispered, and disappeared.

What was an experience becomes a dream and then a memory. I cannot see the edges between the three.

The Weaver, the great spider, came among us.

In the Cymek we call it furiach-yajh-hett: *the dancing mad god. I never thought to see one. It came out of a funnel in the world to stand between us and the lawgivers. Their pistols were silent. Words died in throats like flies in a web.*

The dancing mad god moved through the room with a savage and alien step. It gathered us to it—we renegades, we criminals. We refugees. Constructs that tell tales; earthbound garuda; reporters who make the news; criminal scientists and scientific criminals. The dancing mad god collected us all like errant worshippers, chiding us for going astray.

Its knife-hands flashed. The humans' ears fell in flesh-rain to the dust. I was spared. My feather-hidden ears hold no delight for this mad power. Through the ululations and the despairing wails of pain the furiach-yajh-hett *ran in circles of delight.*

And then it tired and stepped through the twists of matter out of the warehouse.

Into another space.

I shut my eyes.

I moved in a direction I had never known existed. I felt the scuttling slide of that great multitude of legs as the dancing mad god moved along powerful threads of force. It scampered at obscure angles to reality, with all of us bobbing beneath it. My stomach pitched. I felt myself catch and snag on the fabric of the world. My skin prickled in the alien plane.

For a moment the god's madness infected me. For a moment, the greed for knowledge forgot its place and demanded to be quenched. For a sliver of time, I opened my eyes.

For a terrible eternal breath I glimpsed the reality through which the dancing mad god was treading.

My eyes itched and watered, they felt as if they would burst, as if a thousand sandstorms afflicted them. They could not assimilate what was before them. My poor eyes struggled to see the unseeable. I beheld nothing but a fraction, the edge of an aspect.

I saw, or thought I saw, or have convinced myself I saw a vastness that dwarfed any desert sky. A yawning gap of Leviathan proportions. I whined and heard others whine around me. Spread across the emptiness, streaming away from us with cavernous perspective in all directions and dimensions, encompassing lifetimes and hugenesses with each intricate knot of metaphysical substance, was a web.

Its substance was known to me.

The crawling infinity of colours, the chaos of textures that went into each strand of that eternally complex tapestry . . . each one resonated under the step of the dancing mad god, vibrating and sending little echoes of bravery, or hunger, or architecture, or argument, or cabbage or murder or concrete across the æther. The weft of starlings' motivations connected to the thick, sticky strand of a young thief's laugh. The fibres stretched taut and glued themselves solidly to a third line, its silk made from the angles of seven flying buttresses to a cathedral roof. The plait disappeared into the enormity of possible spaces.

Every intention, interaction, motivation, every colour, every body, every action and reaction, every piece of physical reality and the thoughts that it engendered, every connection made, every nuanced moment of history and potentiality, every toothache and flagstone, every emotion and birth and banknote, every possible thing ever is woven into that limitless, sprawling web.

It is without beginning or end. It is complex to a degree that humbles the mind. It is a work of such beauty that my soul wept.

It crawled with life. There were others like our bearer, more of the dancing mad gods, glimpsed across an infinity of webwork.

There were other creatures, too, terrible intricate shapes I will not recall.

The web is not without flaw. In innumerable places the silk is torn and the colours ruined. Here and there the patterns are strained and unstable. As we passed these wounds, I felt the dancing mad god pause and flex its spinneret, repairing and restaining.

A little way off was the tight silk of the Cymek. I swear I caught its oscillations as the worldweb flexed under the weight of time.

Around me was a little localized tangle of metareal gossamer . . . New Crobuzon. And there rending the woven strands in the centre was an ugly tear. It spread out and split the fabric of the city-web, taking the multitude of colours and bleeding them dry. They were left a drab and lifeless white. A pointless emptiness, a pallid shade a thousand times more soulless even than the eye of some sightless caveborn fish.

As I watched, my pained eyes wide with insight, I saw that the rip was widening.

I was so afraid of the spreading rent. And I was dwarfed by the enormity of it all, of the whole of the web. I shut my eyes tight.

I could not close down my mind. It scrambled, unbidden, to remember what it had seen. But it could not contain it. I was left only with a sense of it all. I remember it now as a description. The weight of its immensity is no longer present in my head.

That is the etiolated memory that captivates me now.

I have danced with the spider. I have cut a caper with the dancing mad god.

PART FIVE

Councils

CHAPTER THIRTY-FOUR

In the Lemquist Room, Rudgutter, Stem-Fulcher and Rescue held a council of war.

They had been up all night. Rudgutter and Stem-Fulcher were tired and irritable. They sipped huge bowls of strong coffee as they pored over papers.

Rescue was impassive. He fingered his swaddling scarf.

"Look at this," said Rudgutter, and waved a piece of paper at his subordinates. "This arrived this morning. It was couriered in person. I had the opportunity to discuss its content with the authors. It was not a social call."

Stem-Fulcher leaned over, reaching for the letter. Rudgutter ignored her and began to reread it himself.

"It's from Josiah Penton, Bartol Sedner *and* Mashek Ghrashietnichs." Rescue and Stem-Fulcher looked up. He nodded slowly. "The heads of Arrowhead Mines, Sedner's Bank of Commerce and the Paradox Concerns have taken the time to write a letter *together*. So I think we can add a long list of lesser names below theirs, in invisible ink, hm?" He smoothed the letter. "Messrs. Penton, Sedner and Ghrashietnichs are *'most concerned,'* it says here, at *'scurrilous reports'* reaching their ears. They have wind of our crisis." He watched as Stem-Fulcher and Rescue glanced at each other. "It's all rather garbled. They aren't at all sure what's happening, but none of them have been sleeping well. In addition to which, they've got der Grimnebulin's name. They want to know what's being done to counter, ah . . . 'this threat to our great city-state.' " He put the paper down as Stem-Fulcher shrugged and opened her mouth to answer. He cut her off, rubbing his eyes with exasperated exhaustion.

"You've read Inspector Tormlin's—'Sally's'—report. According to Serachin, who is now recuperating in our care, der Grimnebulin claims to have a working prototype of some kind of crisis engine. We all understand the gravity of that. Well . . .

our good businessmen have found that out. And as you can imagine, they are all—particularly Mr. Penton—*most desirous* of putting a stop to this *absurd claim* as quickly as possible. Any preposterous *fake engines* that Mr. der Grimnebulin might have fabricated to fool the credulous should, we are advised, be summarily destroyed." He sighed and looked up.

"They make some mention of the generous funds they have provided the government and the Fat Sun party over the years. We have been given our *orders*, ladies and gentlemen. They are not at all happy about the slake-moths, and would like such dangerous animals contained forthwith. But not surprisingly, they are having a *conniption* about the possibility of crisis energy. Now, we searched the warehouse very thoroughly last night, and there is absolutely no sign of any such apparatus. We have to consider the possibility that der Grimnebulin is mistaken or lying. But in case he's not, we must also bear in mind that he may have taken his engine and his notes with him last night. With," he sighed heavily, "the Weaver."

Stem-Fulcher spoke carefully. "Do we understand yet," she ventured, "what happened?"

Rudgutter shrugged brusquely.

"We presented the evidence of the militia who saw the Weaver and heard what it said to Kapnellior. I've been trying to contact the thing, and I've had one curt, incomprehensible reply . . . It was scribbled in soot on my mirror. All we can say for sure is that it thought it improved the pattern of the worldweb to abduct der Grimnebulin and his friends from under our noses. We don't know where it's gone or why. Whether it's left them alive. Anything really. Although Kapnellior's quite confident it's still hunting the moths."

"What about the ears?" asked Stem-Fulcher.

"I have *no idea*!" shouted Rudgutter. "It made the web prettier! Obviously! So now we have twenty terrified, one-eared militia in the infirmary!" He calmed a little. "I have been thinking. It's my belief that part of our problem is that we started with plans that were too grand. We'll keep trying to locate the Weaver, but in the meantime we're going to have to rely on less ambitious methods of moth-hunting. We are going to put together a unit of all our guards, militia, and scientists who have had any dealings with the creatures. We're putting together a specialist squad. And we are going to do it in conjunction with Motley." Stem-Fulcher and Rescue looked at him and nodded.

"It's necessary. We're pooling our resources. He has trained men, as do we. We have set procedures in motion. He will have his units, and we will have ours, but they will operate in tandem. Motley and his men have an unconditional amnesty on all criminal activity while we conduct this operation.

"Rescue . . ." said Rudgutter quietly. "We need your particular skills. Quietly, of course. How many of your . . . kin do you think you can mobilize within a day? Knowing the nature of the operation . . . It is not without its dangers."

MontJohn Rescue fingered his scarf again. He made a peculiar noise under his breath. "Ten or so," he said.

"You'll receive training, of course. You've worn a mirror-guard before, I think?" Rescue nodded. "Good. Because the sentience model of your kind is . . . broadly similar to a human's, is it not? Your mind is as *tempting* to the moths as mine. Whatever your host?"

Rescue nodded again.

"We dream, Mr. Mayor," he said in his flattened voice. "We can be prey."

"I understand that. Your—and your kin's—bravery will not go unnoticed. We will provide whatever we can to ensure your safety." Rescue nodded without visible emotion. He stood slowly.

"Time being of such importance, I'll make a start now on spreading the word." He bowed. "You will have my squad by sundown tomorrow," he said. He turned and left the room.

Stem-Fulcher turned to Rudgutter with pursed lips.

"He's not too happy about this, is he?" she said. Rudgutter shrugged.

"He's always known that his role might involve danger. The slake-moths are as much of a threat to his people as to ours."

Stem-Fulcher nodded.

"How long ago was he taken? The original Rescue, I mean, the human one."

Rudgutter calculated for a moment.

"Eleven years. He was planning to supersede me. Have you set the squad in motion?" he demanded. Stem-Fulcher sat back and drew lengthily on her clay pipe. Aromatic smoke danced.

"We're going through two days' intensive training today and tomorrow . . . you know, aiming backwards with the mirror-guards, that sort of thing. Motley is apparently doing the same. The rumours are that Motley's troop includes several Remade

specifically designed for slake-moth husbandry and capture . . .
built-in mirrors, back-pointing arms and the like. We have only
one such officer." She shook her head jealously. "We're also having several of the scientists who worked on the project work on
detecting the moths. They're at pains to impress on us that this is
unreliable, but if they come through they may give us some kind
of edge."

Rudgutter nodded. "Add to that," he said, "our Weaver, still
out there somewhere, still hunting the moths busy tearing up his
precious worldweave . . . We've got a reasonable collection of
troops."

"But they're not co-ordinated," said Stem-Fulcher. "That's
what worries me. And morale in the city is slipping. Obviously
very few people know the truth, but everyone knows they can't
sleep at night, for fear of their dreams. We're plotting a map of
the nightmare hotspots, see if we can't see some pattern, track
the moths in some way. There's been a spate of violent crime
over the last week. Nothing big and planned: the sudden attacks,
the spur-of-the-moment murders, the brawls. Tempers," she said
slowly, "are fraying. People are paranoid and afraid."

After the silence had settled for a moment, she spoke again.

"This afternoon you should receive the fruits of some scientific labours," she said. "I've asked our research team to make
some helmet that'll stop the moth-shit seeping into your skull
when you sleep. You'll look absurd in bed, but at least you'll rest."
She stopped. Rudgutter was blinking rapidly. "How are your
eyes?" she asked.

Rudgutter shook his head.

"Going," he said sadly. "We just can't solve the problem of rejection. It's about time for a fresh set."

Bleary-eyed citizens made their way to work. They were surly
and unco-operative.

At the Kelltree docks, the broken strike was not mentioned.
The bruises on the vodyanoi stevedores were fading. They
heaved spilt cargos from the dirty water as always. They directed
ships into tight spaces on the banks. They muttered in secret
about the disappearance of the stewards, the strike-leaders.

Their human workmates stared at the defeated xenians with a
mixture of emotions.

The fat aerostats patrolled the skies over the city with restless,
clumsy menace.

Arguments broke out with bizarre ease. Fights were common. The nocturnal misery reached out and took victims from the waking world.

In the Bleckly Refinery in Gross Coil, an exhausted crane operator hallucinated one of the torments that had ripped up his sleep the previous night. He shuddered just long enough to send the controls spasming. The massive steam-powered machine disgorged its load of molten iron a second too early. It spewed in a white-hot torrent over the lip of the waiting container and spattered the crew like a siege engine. They screamed and were consumed by the merciless cascade.

At the top of the great deserted concrete obelisks of Spatters the city garuda lit huge fires at night. They banged gongs and saucepans and shouted, screaming obscene songs and raucous cries. Charlie the big man told them that would keep the evil spirits from visiting their towers. The flying monsters. The dæmons that had come to town to suck the brains out of the living.

The raucous café gatherings in Salacus Fields were subdued.

The nightmares pushed some artists into frenzies of creation. An exhibition was being planned: *Dispatches from a Troubled City*. It was to be a showcase of art and sculpture and soundwork inspired by the morass of foul dreams in which the city wallowed.

There was a fear in the air, a nervousness at invoking certain names. Lin and Isaac, the disappeared. To speak them would be to admit that something might be wrong, that they might not just be busy, that their enforced, silent absence from regular haunts was sinister.

The nightmares were splitting the membrane of sleep. They were spilling into the everyday, haunting the sunlit realm, drying conversations in the throat and stealing friends away.

Isaac awoke in the throes of memory. He was recalling the extraordinary escape of the previous night. His eyes flickered, but remained closed.

Isaac's breath caught.

Tentatively, he remembered. Impossible images assailed him. Silk strands a lifetime thick. Living things crawling insidiously across interlocking wires. Behind a beautiful palimpsest of coloured gossamer, a vast, timeless, infinite mass of absence . . .

In terror, he opened his eyes.

The web was gone.

Isaac looked around him slowly. He was in a brick cavern, cool and wet, dripping in the dark.

"You awake, Isaac?" said Derkhan's voice.

Isaac struggled up onto his elbows. He groaned. His body hurt him in a variety of ways. He felt battered and torn. Derkhan sat a little way away from him on a ledge of brick. She smiled absolutely mirthlessly at him. It was a terrifying rictus.

"Derkhan?" he murmured. His eyes widened slowly. "What are you wearing?"

In the half-light emitted by a smoke-seeping oil-lamp, Isaac could see that Derkhan was dressed in a puffy dressing gown of bright pink material. It was decorated with garish needlework flowers. Derkhan shook her head.

"I don't damn well know, Isaac," she said bitterly. "All I know is I was knocked out by the officer with the stingbox and then I woke up here in the sewers, dressed in this. And that's not all . . ." Her voice trembled for a brief moment. She pulled her hair back from the side of her head. He hissed at the raw, seeping clot of blood that caked the side of her face. "My . . . damned *ear*'s gone." She let her hair fall back into place with an unsteady hand. "Lemuel's been saying it was a . . . a *Weaver* that brought us here. You haven't seen your own outfit yet, anyway."

Isaac rubbed his head and sat up completely. He struggled to clear his mind of fog.

"What?" he said. *"Where* are we? The sewers . . . ? Where's Lemuel? Yagharek? And . . ."* *Lublamai,* he heard inside his mind, but he remembered Vermishank's words. He remembered with cold horror that Lublamai was irrevocably lost.

His voice dissipated.

He heard himself, and realized that he was rambling hysterically. He stopped and breathed deeply, forced himself to calm down.

He looked around him, took in the situation.

He and Derkhan sat in a two-foot-wide alcove embedded into the wall of a windowless little brick chamber. It was about ten feet square—its far side only just visible in the faint light—with a ceiling no more than five feet above him. In each of the room's four walls was a cylindrical tunnel, about four feet round.

The bottom of the room was completely submerged in filthy water. It was impossible to tell how deep below it the floor was. The liquid looked to be emerging from at least two of the tunnels, and slowly ebbing out of the others.

The walls were slick with organic slime and mould. The air stank richly of rot and shit.

Isaac looked down at himself and his face creased in confusion. He was dressed in an immaculate suit and tie, a dark, well-tailored piece that any Parliamentarian would be proud of. Isaac had never seen it before. Beside him, roughened and dirty, was his carpet bag.

He remembered, suddenly, the explosive pain and blood he had suffered the previous night. He gasped and reached up with trepidation. As his fingers fumbled, he exhaled explosively. His left ear was gone.

He gingerly prodded for ruined tissue, expecting to meet wet, ripped flesh or crusting scabs. Instead, unlike Derkhan, he found a well-healed scar, covered in skin. There was no pain at all. It was as if he had lost his ear years before. He frowned and clicked his fingers experimentally beside his wound. He could still hear, though doubtless his ability to pinpoint sounds would be reduced.

Derkhan shook slightly as she watched him.

"This Weaver saw fit to heal your ear, along with Lemuel's. Not mine . . ." Her voice was subdued and miserable. "Although," she added, "it did stop the bleeding on the wounds from that . . . damned stingbox." She watched him for a moment. "So Lemuel wasn't mad, or lying, or dreaming," she said quietly. "You're telling me that a *Weaver* appeared and rescued us?"

Isaac nodded slowly.

"I don't know why . . . I have no *idea* why . . . but it's true." He thought back. "I heard Rudgutter outside, yelling something at it. It sounded like he wasn't completely surprised it was there . . . he was trying to *bribe* it, I think. Maybe the damn fool's been trying to do deals with it . . . Where are the others?"

Isaac looked around. There was nowhere to hide in the alcove, but across the little room was another just like it, completely swathed in darkness. Anything crouching within it would have been invisible in the shadow.

"We all woke up here," said Derkhan. "All of us except Lemuel had these weird clothes on. Yagharek was . . ." She shook her head in confusion and touched her bloody wound gently. She winced. "Yagharek was shoehorned into some dollymop's dress. There were a couple of lamps, lit and waiting for us when we woke. Lemuel and Yagharek told me what happened . . . Yagharek

was talking . . . he was being very weird, talking about a *web* . . ."
She shook her head.

"I understand that," said Isaac heavily. He paused and felt his
mind scurry in awe away from the vague memories he had. "You
were unconscious when the Weaver hauled us out. You wouldn't
have seen what we saw . . . where he took us . . ."

Derkhan frowned. She had tears in her eyes.

"My damn . . . my damn ear hurts so much, 'Zaac," she said.
Isaac rubbed her shoulder clumsily, his face creasing, until she
continued. "Anyway, you were out, so Lemuel took off, and
Yagharek went with him."

"What?" shouted Isaac, but Derkhan shushed him with her
hands.

"You know Lemuel, you know the sort of work he does. It
turns out he knows the sewers well. Apparently they can be a
useful bolthole. He did a little reconnaissance trip into the tunnels, and came back actually knowing where we are."

"Which is?"

"Murkside. He left and Yagharek demanded to go with him.
They swore they'd be back within three hours. They've gone to
get some food, some clothes for me and Yagharek, and to see the
lay of the land. They left about an hour ago."

"Well godsdamn, let's go and *join them* . . ."

Derkhan shook her head.

"Don't be an idiot, 'Zaac," she said, sounding exhausted. "We
can't afford to get separated. Lemuel knows the sewers . . .
they're *dangerous*. He told us to stay put. There's all manner
of things down here . . . ghuls, trows, gods know what. That's
why I stayed with you while you were out. We *have* to wait for
them here.

"And besides which, you're probably the most wanted person
in New Crobuzon right now. Lemuel's a successful criminal: he
knows how not to be seen. He's at much less risk than you."

"But what about Yag?" howled Isaac.

"Lemuel gave him his cloak. With the hood up and that dress
torn up and wrapped round his feet, he just looked like a weird
old man. Isaac, they'll be back soon. We *have* to wait for them.
We have to make plans. And you have to *listen*." He looked up at
her, concerned at her miserable tone.

"Why's it taken us here, 'Zaac?" she said. Her face creased in
pain. "Why did it *hurt us*, why did it dress us like this . . . ? Why
didn't it *heal* me . . . ?" She wiped tears of pain away angrily.

"Derkhan," Isaac said gently. "I could never know . . ."

"You should see this," she said, sniffing quickly. She handed him a crumpled and stinking sheet of newspaper. He took it slowly, his face curling with distaste as he touched the sodden, filthy thing.

"What is it?" he said, unfolding it.

"When we woke up, all disorientated and confused, it came bobbing down one of the little tunnels there, folded into a little boat." She looked at him askance. "It was coming *against* the current. We fished it out."

Isaac opened it out and looked at it. It was the centre pages from *The Digest*, one of New Crobuzon's weekly papers. He saw from the date at the top of the page—*9th Tathis 1779*—that it had come out that same morning.

Isaac scanned his eyes over the little collection of stories. He shook his head in incomprehension.

"What am I missing?" he asked.

"Look at the letters to the editor," said Derkhan.

He turned the sheet over. There it was, second letter down. It was written in the same formal, stilted fashion as the others, but its content was wildly different.

Isaac's eyes widened as he read.

Sirs and Madam—

Please accept my compliments on your exquisite tapestry skills. For the furtherment of your craftwork I have taken it upon myself to extricate you from an unfortunate situation. My efforts are urgently required elsewhere and I am unable to accompany you. Doubtless we will meet again before much time has elapsed. In the meantime please note that he of your number whose inadvertent animal husbandry has led to the city's present unfortunate predicament may find himself the victim of unwanted attentions from his escaped charge.

I urge you to continue your fabric work, of which I find myself a devotee.

Most faithfully yours,
   W.

Isaac looked up slowly at Derkhan.

"Gods only knows what the rest of *The Digest*'s readers will think of that . . ." he said in a hushed voice. " 'Stail, that damn spider's powerful!"

Derkhan nodded slowly. She sighed.

"I just wish," she said unhappily, "I understood what it was *doing* . . ."

"You never could, Dee," said Isaac. "Never."

"You're a scientist, 'Zaac," she said sharply. She sounded desperate. "You have to know something about these damn things. Now please *try* to tell us what it's saying . . ."

Isaac did not argue. He reread the note and rummaged inside his head for whatever scraps of information he could find.

"It just does whatever it has to to . . . to make the web prettier," he said unhappily. He caught sight of Derkhan's ragged wound, and looked away again. "You can't understand it, it doesn't think like us *at all*." As he spoke, something occurred to Isaac. "Maybe . . . maybe that's why Rudgutter's been dealing with it," he said. "If it doesn't think like us, maybe it's immune to the moths . . . Maybe it's like a . . . a hunting dog . . ."

He's lost control of it, he thought, remembering the mayor's shouts from outside. *It's not doing what he wants.*

He turned his attention back down to the letter in *The Digest.*

"This bit about tapestry-work . . ." Isaac mused, chewing his lips. "That's the worldweb, isn't it? So I think it's saying it likes what we were . . . um . . . doing in the world. How we were 'weaving.' I think that's why it got us out. And this later section . . ." His expression became more and more fearful as he read.

"Oh gods," he breathed. "It's like what happened to Barbile . . ." Derkhan's mouth was set. She nodded reluctantly. "What was it she said? 'It's tasted me . . .' The grub I had, I must've been tantalizing it with my mind all the time . . . It's tasted me already . . . It must be hunting me . . ."

Derkhan stared at him.

"You won't get it off your tail, Isaac," she said quietly. "We'll have to kill it."

She had said *we.* He looked up at her gratefully.

"Before we formulate any plans," she said, "there's another thing. A mystery. Something I want explained." She gestured at the other alcove across the dark room. Isaac peered curiously into the filthy obscurity. He could just make out a lumpy, motionless shape.

He knew what it was instantly. He remembered its extraordinary intervention in the warehouse. His breath sped up.

"It wouldn't speak or write to anyone else," Derkhan said. "When we realized it was here with us, we tried to talk to it, we wanted to know what it had done, but it completely ignored us. I think it's been waiting for you."

Isaac slid over to the lip of the ledge.

"It's shallow," Derkhan said behind him. He slipped off into the cool watery muck of the sewers. It came up to his knees. He pushed through it unthinkingly, ignoring the thick stench he raised as it sluiced through his legs. He waded through the noisome excremental stew towards the other little shelf.

As he drew closer, the dull inhabitant of that unlit space whirred slightly and pushed its battered body as near upright as it could. It was crammed into the little space.

Isaac sat next to it, shook his fouled shoes as clean as he could. He turned to it with an intent, hungry expression.

"So," he said. "Tell me what you know. Tell me why you warned me. Tell me what's going on."

The cleaning construct hissed.

CHAPTER THIRTY-FIVE

Under a damp hollow of bricks by Trauka Station, Yagharek waited.

He gnawed a hunk of bread and meat that he had begged wordlessly from a butcher. He had not been unmasked. He had simply thrust his tremulous hand out from under his cloak and the food had been given to him. His head had remained hidden. He had shuffled away, his feet cramped and hidden by rags. His gait was of an old, tired man.

It was much easier to hide as a human than as an unwounded garuda.

He waited in the darkness where Lemuel had left him. From the shadows which hid him, he could watch the comings and goings at the church of the clock gods. It was an ugly little building, the façade of which was still painted with the advertising slogans of the furniture shop it had once been. Above the door was an intricate brass timepiece, each hour intertwined with the symbols of its associate god.

Yagharek knew the religion. It was strong among the humans of Shankell. He had visited its temples when his band had come to the city to trade, in the years before his crime.

The clock struck one, and Yagharek heard the ululating hymn to Sanshad, the sun god, come belting through the broken windows. It was sung with more gusto than in Shankell but considerably less finesse. It was less than three decades since the religion had crossed the Meagre Sea with any success. Obviously its subtleties had been lost in the water between Shankell and Myrshock.

Before he was conscious of it, his hunter's ears had realized that one of the sets of footsteps approaching his hideaway was familiar. He finished his food quickly and waited.

Lemuel appeared framed in the entrance of the little cave. Passers-by came and went in the light spaces above his shoulders.

"Yag," he whispered, gazing sightlessly into the grubby hole. The garuda shuffled forward into the light. Lemuel was carrying two bags stuffed with clothes and food. "Come on," he whispered. "We should get back."

They retraced their steps through the winding streets of Murkside. It was Skullday, a shopping day, and elsewhere in the city the crowds would be thick. But in Murkside the shops were mean and poor. Those locals for whom Skullday was a day off would make their way to Griss Fell or the Aspic Hole market. Lemuel and Yagharek were not watched by many.

Yagharek sped up, hobbling on bound feet with a weird, crippled gait to keep up with Lemuel. They made their way southeast, staying in the shadow of the raised railway lines, moving towards Syriac.

This is how I came to the city, thought Yagharek, *tracking the great iron pathways of the trains.*

They passed under the brick arches, retracing their way into a little enclosed space overlooked on three sides by featureless brick. Storm drains channelled down the walls, along concrete ruts and into a man-sized grille in the centre of the yard.

On the fourth side, the south-facing side, the courtyard looked out onto a drab alley. The land fell away before it. Syriac sat in a depression in the underlying clay. Yagharek looked out over a tumbledown roofscape of twisted roofs and mouldering slate, curlicues of brick and forgotten, warped weathervanes.

Lemuel glanced around to ensure their privacy, then tugged the grille free. Fingers of fell-gas curled out and tugged at them.

The heat made the stink rich. Lemuel gave his bags to Yagharek and pulled a primed pistol from his belt. Yagharek looked at him from under the hood.

Lemuel turned with a hard smile and said: "I've been pulling in favours. Got us kitted out." He waggled the gun to illustrate his point. He checked it, hefted it expertly. He pulled the oil-lamp from a bag, lit it and lifted it with his left hand.

"Stay behind me," he said. "Keep your ears open. Move quietly. Watch your back."

With that, Lemuel and Yagharek descended into the dirt and the dark.

There was an indeterminable time wading through the warm, rank darkness. The sounds of scuttling and swimming were all around them. Once they heard vicious laughter from a tunnel parallel to theirs. Twice Lemuel swung round, aiming the torch and his pistol at a patch of filth still rippling from where some unseen thing had been. He did not have to shoot. They were unmolested.

"You know how lucky we were?" said Lemuel conversationally. His voice bobbed slowly back to Yagharek on the foetid air. "I don't know if it was deliberate, where the Weaver left us, but we're in one of the safest places in the New Crobuzon sewers." His voice stiffened now and then with effort or disgust. "Murkside's such a backwater, you don't have much food down here, you've got no thaumaturgic residues, there aren't any massive old chambers to support a whole brood . . . It's not very busy."

He was silent for a moment, then continued.

"Brock Marsh sewers, for example. All the unstable runoff from all those labs and experiments, accumulating over the years . . . makes for a very unpredictable population of vermin. Rats the size of pigs, speaking in tongues. Blind pygmy crocodiles, whose great-great-great-grandparents escaped from the zoo. Crossbreeds of all sorts.

"Over in Gross Coil and Skulkford the city's sitting on layers of older buildings. For hundreds of years they sunk into the mire, and they'd just build new ones on top of them. The pavement's only been solid there for a hundred and fifty years. Over there, the sewers feed into old basements and bedrooms. The tunnels like this one lead into submerged streets. You can still see the road-names. Rotten houses under a brick sky. Straight up. The shit flows along channels and then through windows and doors.

"That's where the undergangs live. They used to be human, or their parents did, but they've spent too long down here. They aren't a pretty sight."

He hawked and spat noisily into the slow ooze.

"Still. Rather the undergangs than the ghuls. Or the trow." He laughed, but it was without any humour. Yagharek could not tell if Lemuel was mocking him.

Lemuel lapsed into silence. For some minutes, there was no sound except the slosh of their legs through the thick effluvia. Then Yagharek heard voices. He stiffened and gripped Lemuel's shirt, but a moment later he heard them clearly, and they were Isaac's and Derkhan's.

The excremental water seemed to carry light with it, from around a corner.

Bent-backed and swearing with effort, Yagharek and Lemuel wound through the twisting brick junctions and turned into the little room under Murkside's heart.

Isaac and Derkhan were yelling at each other. Isaac saw Yagharek and Lemuel over Derkhan's shoulder. He raised his arms to them.

"Dammit, *there* you are!" He strode past Derkhan towards them. Yagharek held out a bag of food at him. Isaac ignored it. "Lem, Yag," he said urgently. "We have to move fast."

"Now hold on . . ." began Lemuel, but Isaac ignored him.

"Listen, dammit," Isaac shouted. "The construct's talked to me!"

Lemuel's mouth stayed open, but he was silent. No one spoke for a moment.

"All right?" said Isaac. "It's *intelligent*, dammit, it's *sentient* . . . something's happened in its head. The rumours about CI are true! Some virus, some programme glitch . . . And although it won't come out and say it, I think it's hinted that that damned repairman may have given it a helping hand along the way. And the upshot is the *damn thing can think*. It's seen everything! It was there when the slake-moth took Lublamai. It . . ."

"Hold on!" shouted Lemuel. "It spoke to you?"

"No! It had to scrape messages in the mould over there: it was damn slow. That's what it uses its litter-spike for. It was the construct that told me David had turned traitor! It tried to get us out of the warehouse before the militia arrived!"

"Why?"

Isaac's urgency waned.

"I don't know. It can't explain itself. It's not . . . very articulate." Lemuel looked up, over Isaac's head. The construct sat motionless in the red-black flickering of the oil-lamp. "But listen . . . I think one of the reasons it wanted us free is because we're against the slake-moths. I don't know why, but it . . . it's violently against them. It wants them dead. And it's offering us help . . ."

Lemuel barked with unpleasant, incredulous laughter.

"Marvellous!" he wondered, derisorily. "You've got a vacuum cleaner on your side . . ."

"No, you fucking *arse*," yelled Isaac. "Don't you understand? *It's not alone* . . ."

The word *alone* echoed back and forth around the mephitic brick burrows. Lemuel and Isaac stared at each other. Yagharek drew back a little.

"It's not alone," Isaac repeated softly. Behind him, Derkhan nodded in mute accord. "It's given us *directions*. It can read and write—that's how it realized David sold us out, it found his discarded instructions—but it's not a sophisticated thinker. But it promises that if we go to Griss Twist tomorrow night, we'll meet something that can explain everything. And that can help us."

This time, it was *us* that filled the silence with its reverberating presence. Lemuel shook his head slowly, his face set and cruel.

"Damn, Isaac," he said quietly. " 'We'? 'Us'? Who the fuck are you talking to? *This is nothing to do with me* . . ." Derkhan sneered in disgust and turned away. Isaac opened his mouth, dismayed. Lemuel interrupted him. "Look, man. I was in this for the *money*. I'm a businessman. You paid well. You got my services. You even got a little bit of time free, with Vermishank. I did that for Mr. X. And I've got a soft spot for you, 'Zaac. You've been straight with me. That's why I came back down here. Brought a bit of grub, and I'll show you out of here. But now Vermishank's dead and your credit's run dry. I don't know what you've got planned, but I'm off. Why in *fuck* should I go chasing these damn things? Leave it to the militia. There's *nothing for me here* . . . Why would I hang around?"

"Leave it to *who* . . . ?" hissed Derkhan with contempt, but Isaac spoke over her.

"So," he said slowly. "What now? Hmmm? You think you can go *back*? Lem, old son, whatever else you might damn well be, you ain't a stupid man. You think you weren't seen? You think

they don't know who you are? Gods*damn*, man . . . you're
wanted."

Lemuel glared at him.

"Well, thanks for your concern 'Zaac," he said, his face twisting. "Tell you what, though—" his voice turned hard "—*you*
may be out of your depth. *I*, however, have spent my professional
life evading the law. Don't you worry about me, mate. I'll be
cushty." He did not sound sure.

I'm not telling him anything he doesn't know, thought Isaac.
He just doesn't want to think about it right now. Isaac shook his
head contemptuously.

"Dammit, man, you aren't thinking straight. There's a whole
godsdamn universe of difference between being a go-between
and being a *militia-murdering criminal* . . . Don't you get it?
They don't know what you know or don't know . . . unfortunately for you, old son, you're *implicated*. You have to stick with
us. You have to see this through. They're after you, right? And
right now, you're running from them. Better to stay in front, even
if you're running, than fucking well turn round and let them
catch up."

Lemuel stood still in the silence, glowering at Isaac. He said
nothing, but neither did he leave.

Isaac took a step towards him.

"Look," Isaac said. "The other thing is . . . we . . . *I* . . . need
you." Behind him Derkhan sniffed sulkily and Isaac shot her an
irritated glance. "Godspit, Lem . . . you're our best chance. You
know everyone, you've got a finger in all the right pies . . ." Isaac
raised his hands helplessly. "I can't see a way out of this. One of
those . . . *things* is after *me*, the militia can't help us, they don't
know how to catch the damn things, and anyway, I don't know if
you're keeping track but those fuckers are hunting us *too* . . . I
can't see a way, even assuming we get the slake-moths, where I
don't end up dead." The words chilled him as he spoke them. He
talked rapidly, pushed the thoughts away. "But if I keep at it,
maybe I can figure one out. And the same goes for you. And
without you, Derkhan and me are dead for *sure*." Lemuel's eyes
were hard. Isaac felt a chill. *Never forget who you're dealing
with,* he thought. *You and he are not friends . . . don't forget that.*

"You know my credit's good," Isaac said suddenly. "You know
that. Now, I'm not going to pretend I've got a massive bank account, I've got a bit, there's a few guineas left, *all of it yours* . . .
but help me, Lemuel, and *I'm* yours. I'll work for you. I'll be

your man. I'll be your fucking *pet*. Any jobs you want done, I do them. Any money I make, it's yours. I'll sign my fucking *life* to you, Lemuel. Just *help us now*."

There was no sound except the dripping of ordure. Behind Isaac, Derkhan hovered. Her face was a study of contempt and disgust. *We don't need him,* it said. But still, she waited to hear what he would say. Yagharek stood back. He listened to the argument dispassionately. He was bound to Isaac. He could go nowhere and do nothing without him.

Lemuel sighed.

"I am going to be keeping a running total, you realize? I'm talking about serious debt, you know? D'you have any idea of the daily rate for this sort of thing? The danger money?"

"Doesn't matter," breathed Isaac brusquely. He hid his relief. "Just keep me posted. Tell me what I'm accruing. I'll be good for it." Lemuel nodded briefly. Derkhan exhaled, very quietly and slowly.

They stood like exhausted combatants. Each waited for the other to move.

"So what now?" said Lemuel. His voice was surly.

"We go to Griss Twist tomorrow night," said Isaac. "The construct promised help. We can't risk not going. I'll meet you both there."

"Where are you going?" said Derkhan in surprise.

"I have to find Lin," said Isaac. "They'll be coming for her."

CHAPTER THIRTY-SIX

It was almost midnight. Skullday was becoming Shunday. The moon was one night off full.

Outside Lin's tower, in Aspic Hole itself, the few passers-by were irritable and nervous. Market day had passed, and its bonhomie with it. The square was haunted by the skeletons of stalls, thin wooden frames stripped of canvas. The rubbish from the market was piled in rotting heaps, waiting for the dustcrews to transport it to the dumps. The bloated moon bleached Aspic

Hole like some corrosive liquid. It looked ominous, shabby and mean.

Isaac climbed the stairs of the tower warily. He had had no way of getting a message to Lin and he had not seen her for days. He had washed as best he could in water filched from a pump in Flyside, but he still stank.

He had sat in the sewers for hours the previous day. Lemuel had not allowed them to leave for a long time, decreeing that it was too dangerous during the light.

"We have to stick together," he demanded, "until we know what we're doing. And we are not the most unobtrusive bunch." So the four of them had sat in a room awash in faecal water, eating and trying not to vomit, bickering and failing to make plans. They had argued vehemently about whether or not Isaac should see Lin on his own. He was absolute in his insistence that he be unaccompanied. Derkhan and Lemuel denounced his stupidity, and even Yagharek's silence had seemed briefly accusatory. But Isaac was quite adamant.

Eventually, when the temperature fell and they had all forgotten the stink, they had moved. It had been a long, arduous journey through New Crobuzon's vaulted conduits. Lemuel had led, flintlocks ready. Isaac, Derkhan and Yagharek had to carry the construct, which could not move in the liquid filth. It was heavy and slippery, and it had been dropped and banged and damaged, as had they, falling into the muck and swearing, slamming hands and fingers against the concrete walls. Isaac would not let them leave it.

They had moved carefully. They were intruders in the sewer's hidden and hermetic ecosystem. They had been keen to avoid the natives. Eventually they had emerged behind Saltpetre Station, blinking and dripping in the waning light.

They had bedded down in a little deserted hut beside the railway in Griss Fell. It was an audacious hideout. Just before the Sud Line crossed the Tar by Cockscomb Bridge, a collapsed building made a huge slope of half-crushed brick and concrete splinters that seemed to shore up the raised railway. At the top, dramatically silhouetted, they saw the wooden shack.

Its purpose was unclear: it had obviously remained untouched for years. The four of them had crawled exhausted up the industrial scree, shoving the construct before them, through the ripped-up wire that was supposed to protect the railway from intruders. In the minutes between trains, they had hauled them-

selves along the little fringe of scrubby grass that surrounded the
tracks, and pushed open the door into the hut's dusty darkness.

There, finally, they had relaxed.

The wood of the shed was warped, its slats ill-fitting and interspersed with sky. They had watched out of the glassless windows as trains burst by them in both directions. Below them to
the north, the Tar twisted in the tight S that contained Petty Coil
and Griss Twist. The sky had darkened to a grubby blue-black.
They could see illuminated pleasure-boats on the river. The massive industrial pillar of Parliament loomed a little way to the
east, looking down on them and on the city. A little downriver
from Strack Island, the chymical lights of the old city watergates
hissed and sputtered and reflected their greasy yellow glow in
the dark water. Two miles to the north-east, just visible behind
Parliament, were the Ribs, those antique sallow bones.

From the other side of the cabin they saw the spectacularly
darkening sky, made even more astonishing by a day in the reek-
ing dun below New Crobuzon. The sun was gone, but only just.
The sky was bisected by the skyrail that threaded through Flyside militia tower. The city was a layered silhouette, an intricate
fading chimneyscape, slate roofs bracing each other obliquely
below the plaited towers of churches to obscure gods, the huge
priapic vents of factories spewing dirty smoke and burning off
excess energy, monolithic towerblocks like vast concrete grave-
stones, the rough down of parkland.

They had rested, cleaned the nightsoil from their clothes as
much as they could. Here, finally, Isaac had tended the stub of
Derkhan's ear. It had numbed, but was still painful. She bore it
with heavy reserve. Isaac and Lemuel had fingered their own
scarred remnants uncomfortably.

As the night had crept up faster, Isaac had readied himself to
go. The argument had erupted again. Isaac was resolute. He
needed to see Lin alone.

He had to tell her that she was in danger as soon as the militia
connected her to him. He had to tell her that her life as she had
lived it was over, and that it was his fault. He needed to ask her to
come with him, to run with him. He needed her forgiveness and
her affection.

One night with her, alone. That was all.

Lemuel would not acquiesce. "It's our fucking heads too,
'Zaac," he had hissed. "Every militiaman in the city is after your
hide. Your helio's probably pasted up in every tower and strut

and floor of the Spike. You don't know how to get around. Me, I've been wanted all my working life. If you go for your ladybird, I come."

Isaac had had to give in.

At half past ten, the four companions had wrapped themselves in their ruined clothes, obscuring their faces. After much coaxing, Isaac had finally been able to goad the construct into communication. Reluctantly and torturously slowly, it had scratched out its message.

Griss Twist Dump number 2, it had written. *Tomorrow night 10. Leave me below arches now.*

With the darkness, they had realized, came the nightmares. Even though they did not sleep. The mental nausea, as the slake-moth dung polluted the city's sleep. Each of them grew tetchy and nervous.

Isaac had stashed his carpet bag, containing the components of his crisis engine, under a pile of wooden slats in the shack. Then they had descended, carrying the construct for the last time. Isaac hid it in an alcove created where the structure of the railway bridge had crumbled.

"Are you going to be all right?" he asked it tentatively, still feeling absurd talking to a machine. The construct did not answer him, and eventually he had left it. "See you tomorrow," he said as he left.

The criminal foursome skulked and stalked their clandestine way through New Crobuzon's burgeoning night. Lemuel had taken his companions into the alternative city of hidden byways and strange cartography. They had evaded streets wherever there were alleys and alleys wherever there were broken channels in the concrete. They had crept through deserted yards and over flat roofs, waking the vagrants who grumbled and huddled together in their wake.

Lemuel was confident. He swung his primed and loaded pistol easily as he climbed and ran, keeping them covered. Yagharek had adapted to his body without the weight of wings. His hollow bones and tight muscles moved efficiently. He swung lithely over the architectural landscape, leaping obstacles in the slate. Derkhan was dogged. She would not let herself fail to keep up.

Isaac was the only one whose suffering showed. He wheezed and coughed and retched. He hauled his excess flesh along the thieves' trails, breaking slates with his heavy slapping footfall, cradling his belly miserably. He swore constantly, every time he exhaled.

They cut a trail deeper into the night, as if it were a forest. With every step, the air grew heavier. A sense of wrongness, of fraught unease, as if long nails scraped the surface of the moon, raising the hackles of the soul. From all around them came the cries of miserable, disturbed sleep.

They stopped in Flyside, a few streets from the militia tower, and took water from a pump to wash and drink. Then south through the morass of alleys between Shadrach Street and Selchit Pass, bearing down on Aspic Hole.

And there in that near-deserted and unearthly place, Isaac had bade his companions wait. Between sobs of desperate breath, he begged them to wait, to give him half an hour with her.

"You've got to give me a little while to explain to her what's going on . . ." he pleaded.

They acquiesced, and hunkered down in the darkness at the base of the building.

"Half an hour, 'Zaac," said Lemuel clearly. "Then we're coming up. Understand?"

And so Isaac had begun slowly to climb the stairs.

The tower was cool and quite silent. On the seventh floor, Isaac heard sound for the first time. It was the sleepy murmur and unceasing flutter of jackdaws. Up again, through the breezes that passed through the ruined and unsafe eighth floor, and on to the building's crest.

He stood before Lin's familiar door. *She may not be there,* he reasoned. *She's probably still with that guy, her patron, doing her work. In which case I'll just have to . . . leave a message for her.*

He knocked at the door, which fell open. His breath stalled in his throat. He rushed into the room.

The air stank of putrefying blood. Isaac scanned the little attic space. He caught sight of what awaited him.

Lucky Gazid gazed up at him sightlessly, propped on one of Lin's chairs, sitting at the table as if at a meal. His shape was outlined in what little light crept up from the square below. Gazid's arms were flat on the table. His hands were tense and hard as bone. His mouth was open and stuffed with something that Isaac could not clearly see. Gazid's front was utterly drenched with blood. Blood had slicked on the table, seeping deep into the

grain of the wood. Gazid's throat had been cut. In the summer
heat it thronged with hungry little night insects.

There was a second when Isaac thought that it might be a
nightmare, one of the sick dreams that afflicted the city, spewing
out of his unconscious on a slick of slake-moth dung and spattering into the æther.

But Gazid did not disappear. Gazid was real, and really dead.

Isaac looked at him. He blenched at Gazid's screaming face.
He looked again at the clawed hands. Gazid had been held down
at the table, cut and held down until he died. Then something had
been shoved into his gaping mouth.

Isaac picked his way towards the corpse. He set his face and
reached up, pulled from Gazid's dry mouth a large envelope.

When he unrolled it, he saw that the name carefully written
on the front was his own. He reached inside with a nauseous
foreboding.

There was a moment, a tiny moment, when he did not recognize what he pulled out. Flimsy and almost weightless, it felt as
he drew it out like crumbling parchment, like dead leaves. Then
he held it in the faint grey light of the moonlit room and he saw it
was a pair of khepri wings.

Isaac let out a sound, an exhalation of shocked misery. His eyes
widened in horror.

"Oh no," he said, hyperventilating. "Oh no oh no no no . . ."

The wings had been bent and rolled, and their delicate substance was shattered. They desquamated in great clots of translucent matter. Isaac's fingers trembled as he tried to smooth them
down. His fingertips brushed their battered surface. He was
humming a single note, a tremulous keening. He fumbled with
the envelope, brought out a single sheet of folded paper.

It was typewritten, with a chessboard or patchwork standard
printed at its top. As he read it, Isaac began to cry out wordlessly.

Copy 1: Aspic Hole.
(Others to be delivered to Brock Marsh, Salacus Fields)
Mr. Dan der Grimnebulin,

Khepri cannot make sounds, but I judge by the chymicals
she was exuding and the trembling of those bugger legs that
Lin found the removal of these useless wings a deeply unpleasant experience. I don't doubt that her lower body would

also have been fighting us had we not strapped the bug-bitch in a chair.

Lucky Gazid can give you this message, as it is he I have to thank for your interference.

I gather that you have been trying to squeeze in on the dreamshit market. At first I thought you might have wanted all that 'shit you bought from Gazid for yourself, but the idiot man's wittering eventually turned to your caterpillar in Brock Marsh, and I realized the magnitude of your scheme.

You would never get top grade 'shit from a moth weaned on human-consumption dreamshit, of course, but you could have charged less for your inferior product. It is in my interest to keep all my customers connoisseurs. I will tolerate no competition.

As I have subsequently learnt, and as one might have expected from an amateur, you couldn't control your damn producer. Your shit-fed runt escaped through your incompetence, and liberated its siblings. You stupid man.

Here are my demands. (i) That you give yourself up to *me* immediately. (ii) That you return the remains of the dreamshit you stole from me through Gazid, or pay me compensation (sum to be arranged). (iii) That you pursue the task of recapturing my producers, along with your pathetic specimen, to be handed over to me immediately. After such time as this, we will discuss your continued life.

While we wait to hear your response, I will continue my discussions with Lin. I have been enjoying her company greatly over these last weeks, and relish the chance to deal with her more closely. We have a little wager. *She* bets that you will respond to this epistle while she still retains some of her headlegs. *I* remain unconvinced. The current rate is one headleg every two days we do not hear from you after today. Who will be proved right?

I will rip them from her while she twitches and spits, do you understand? And within two weeks I will tear her carapace from her headbody and feed her living head to the rats. I will *personally* hold her down while they lunch.

I very much look forward to hearing from you soon.

Yours sincerely,

Motley.

When Derkhan, Yagharek and Lemuel reached the ninth floor, they could hear Isaac's voice. He was talking slowly, in low tones. They could not make out what he was saying, but it sounded like a monologue. He was not pausing to hear or see any responses.

Derkhan knocked on the door, and when there was no answer, she pushed it tentatively open and peered inside.

She saw Isaac and another man. It was only a few seconds before she recognized Gazid, and saw that he had been butchered. She gasped and moved slowly inside, letting Yagharek and Lemuel slip in behind her.

They stood and stared at Isaac. He was sitting on the bed, holding a pair of insectile wings and a piece of paper. He looked up at them and his murmuring subsided. He was crying without a sound. He opened his mouth and Derkhan moved over to him, grasped his hands. He sobbed and hid his eyes, his face twisted with rage. Without a sound she took the letter and read it.

Her mouth quivered in horror. She emitted a mute little cry for her friend. She passed the letter to Yagharek, shaking, controlling herself.

The garuda took it and perused it carefully. His reaction was invisible. He turned to Lemuel, who was examining Lucky Gazid's corpse.

"This one's been dead a while," he said, and accepted the letter.

His eyes widened as he read.

"Motley?" he breathed. "Lin's been dealing with *Motley*?"

"Who is he?" shouted Isaac. *"Where is the fucking piece of scum . . . ?"*

Lemuel looked up at Isaac, his face open and aghast. Pity glimmered in his eyes as he saw Isaac's tear-stained, snotty rage.

"Oh Jabber . . . Mr. Motley is the kingpin, Isaac," he said simply. "He is the *man*. He runs the eastern city. He *runs* it. He's the outlaw boss."

"I'll fucking *kill the fucker*, I'll *kill him, I'll kill him* . . ." Isaac raged.

Lemuel watched him uneasily. *You won't, 'Zaac,* he thought. *You really won't.*

"Lin . . . wouldn't tell me who she'd been working for," said Isaac, his voice calming slowly.

"I'm not surprised," said Lemuel. "Most people haven't heard of him. Rumours, maybe . . . Nothing more."

Isaac stood suddenly. He dragged his sleeve across his face, sniffed hard and cleared his nose.

"Right, we have to get her," he said. "We have to find her. Let's think. *Think*. This . . . Motley thinks I've been ripping him off, which I haven't. Now, how can I get him to back down . . . ?"

" 'Zaac, 'Zaac . . ." Lemuel was frozen. He swallowed and looked away, then walked slowly towards Isaac, holding his hands up wide, begging him to calm down. Derkhan looked at him, and there it was again, that pity: hard and brusque, but undoubtedly there. Lemuel was shaking his head slowly. His eyes were hard, but his mouth worked silently as he groped for words.

" 'Zaac, I've dealt with Motley. I've never met the guy, but I know him. I know his work. I know how to deal with him, I know what to expect. I've seen this before, this exact kind of scenario . . . Isaac . . ." He swallowed and continued. *"Lin's dead."*

"No, she is not," shouted Isaac, clenching his hands and flailing them around his head.

But Lemuel caught hold of his wrists, not hard or pugnaciously, but intensely, making him listen and understand. Isaac was still for a moment, his face wary and wrathful.

"She's dead, Isaac," said Lemuel softly. "I'm sorry, mate. I really am. I'm sorry, but she's *gone*." He moved back. Isaac stood, stricken, shaking his head. His mouth opened as if he was trying to cry out. Lemuel was shaking his head slowly. He looked away from Isaac and spoke slowly and quietly, as if to himself.

"Why would he keep her alive?" he said. "It just . . . It just doesn't make *sense* . . . She's a . . . an added complication, that's all. Something . . . something it's easier to dispense with. He's done what he needed to do," he said, louder suddenly, raising his hand to gesticulate at Isaac. "He's got you coming to him. He's got revenge and he's got you doing his bidding. He just wants you there . . . doesn't matter how he gets it. And if he keeps her alive, there's a tiny chance that she'd be trouble. But if he . . . dangles her like bait, you'll come for her no matter what. Don't matter if she's alive." He shook his head in sorrow. *"There's nothing in it for him not to kill her* . . . She's *dead*, Isaac. She's dead." Isaac's eyes were glazing, and Lemuel spoke quickly. "And I'll tell you this: the best way of getting your revenge is to keep those moths out of Motley's hands. He won't kill 'em, you know. He'll keep them alive, so's to get more dreamshit out of them."

Isaac was stamping around the room now, shouting denials, now in anger, now misery, now rage, now disbelief. He rushed at Lemuel, began to beg with him incoherently, tried to convince him that he must be mistaken. Lemuel could not watch Isaac's supplication. He closed his eyes and spoke over the desperate babble.

"If you go to him, 'Zaac, Lin won't be any less dead. And you'll be considerably more so."

Isaac's noises dried. There was a long, quiet moment, while Isaac stood and his hands shook. He looked over at Lucky Gazid's corpse, at Yagharek standing silent and hooded in the corner of the room, at Derkhan hovering near him, her own eyes filling, at Lemuel, watching him nervously.

Isaac cried in earnest.

Isaac and Derkhan sat, arms draped over each other, sniffling and weeping.

Lemuel stalked over to Gazid's stinking cadaver. He knelt before it, holding his mouth and nose with his left hand. With his right he broke the seal of scabbing blood that glued Gazid's jacket closed, and rummaged inside its pockets. He fumbled, looking for money or information. There was nothing.

He straightened up, looked around the room. He was thinking strategically. He sought anything that might be useful, any weapons, anything to bargain with, anything he could use to spy.

There was nothing at all. Lin's room was almost bare.

His head ached with the weight of disturbed sleep. He could feel the mass of New Crobuzon's dream-torture. His own dreams bickered and brooded just below his skull, ready to attack him should he succumb to sleep.

Eventually, he had taken up all the time he feasibly could. He grew more nervous as the night lengthened. He turned to the miserable pair on the bed, gestured briefly at Yagharek.

"We have to go," he said.

Chapter Thirty-seven

Throughout the next hot, sticky day, the city sprawled in heat- and nightmare-induced choler.

Rumours swept the underworld. Ma Francine had been found dead, they said. She had been shot in the night, three times with a longbow. Some freelance assassin had earned Mr. Motley's thousand guineas.

There was no word from the Kinken headquarters of Ma Francine's Sugardrop Gang. The internal war of succession had doubtless begun.

More comatose, imbecile bodies were found. More and more. There was a gradual sense of slow panic building. The night-mares would not cease, and some of the papers were linking them with the mindless citizens who were found every day, slumped over their tables before shattered windows, or lying in the streets, caught between buildings by the affliction that came from the sky. The faint smell of rotting citrus clung to their faces.

The plague of mindlessness was not discriminating. Whole and Remade were taken. Humans were found, and khepri and vodyanoi and wyrmen. Even the city garuda began to fall. And other, rarer creatures.

In St. Jabber's Mound, the sun came up on a fallen trow, its grave-pale limbs heavy and lifeless, even though it breathed, lolling face down beside a slick of stolen and forgotten meat. It must have ventured up from the sewers for a scavenging foray into the midnight city, only to be struck down.

In East Gidd, a still more bizarre scene awaited the mili-tia. There were two bodies half hidden in the bushes that sur-rounded the Gidd Library. One, a young streetwalker, was dead—genuinely dead, having bled dry from tooth-holes in her neck. Sprawled over her was the thin body of a well-known Gidd resident, the owner of a small, successful fabric factory. His face and chin were caked with her blood. His sightless eyes glared up at the sun. He was not dead, but his mind was quite gone.

Some spread the word that Andrew St. Kader had not been what he seemed, but many more the shocking truth that even vampir were prey to the mind-suckers. The city reeled. Were these agents, these germs or spirits, this disease, these dæmons, whatever they were, were they all-powerful? What could defeat them?

There was confusion and misery. A few citizens sent letters to their parents' villages, made plans to leave New Crobuzon for the foothills and valleys to the south and east. But for millions, there was simply nowhere to flee.

Throughout the tedious warmth of the day, Isaac and Derkhan sheltered in the little hut.

When they had arrived, they saw that the construct was no longer waiting where they had left it. There was no sign of where it might be.

Lemuel left to see if he could link up with his comrades. He was nervous of venturing out while he was at war with the militia, but he did not like being isolated. In addition, Isaac thought, Lemuel did not like being around Derkhan and Isaac's shared misery.

Yagharek, to Isaac's surprise, left as well.

Derkhan reminisced. She chastised herself constantly for being maudlin, for making the feeling worse, but she could not stop. Derkhan told Isaac about her late-night conversations with Lin, the arguments about the nature of art.

Isaac was quieter. He toyed mindlessly with the pieces of his crisis engine. He did not stop Derkhan talking, but only occasionally did he interject with a remembrance of his own. His eyes were unfixed. He sat back dully against the crumbling wooden wall.

Before Lin, Isaac's lover had been Bellis; human, like all his previous bedfellows. Bellis was tall and pale. She painted her lips bruise-purple. She was a brilliant linguist, who had become bored with what she had called Isaac's "rumbustiousness," and had broken his heart.

Between Bellis and Lin had been four years of whores and brief adventures. Isaac had curtailed all of that a year before meeting Lin. He had been at Mama Sudd's one night, and had endured a shattering conversation with the young prostitute hired to service him. He had made a chance remark in praise of the amiable, matronly madame—who treated her girls well—and had been perturbed when his opinion had not been shared. Eventually the tired prostitute had snapped at him, forgetting herself, telling him what she really thought of the woman who hired out her orifices and let her keep three stivers in every shekel she made.

Shocked and ashamed, Isaac had left without even removing his shoes. He had paid double.

After that he had been chaste for a long time, had immersed himself in work. Eventually a friend had asked him to the opening show of a young khepri gland-artist. In a small gallery, a cavernous room on the wrong side of Sobek Croix, overlooking the weather-beaten sculpted knolls and copses at the edge of the park, Isaac had met Lin.

He had found her sculpture captivating, and had sought her out to say so. They had endured a slow, slow conversation—she scribbling her responses on the pad she always carried—but the frustrating pace did not undermine a sudden shared intimation of excitement. They drifted from the rest of the little party, examined each piece in turn, their twisted forms and tortured geometry.

After that they met often. Isaac surreptitiously learnt a little more signing between each time, so that their conversations progressed fractionally quicker every week. In the middle of showing off, laboriously signing a dirty joke one night, Isaac, very drunk, had clumsily pawed her, and they had pulled each other to bed.

The event had been clumsy and difficult. They could not kiss as a first step: Lin's mouthparts would tear Isaac's jaw from his face. For just a moment after coming, Isaac had been overcome with revulsion, and had almost vomited at the sight of those bristling headlegs and waving antennae. Lin had been nervous of his body, and had stiffened suddenly and unpredictably. When he had woken he had felt fearful and horrified, but at the fact of having transgressed rather than at the transgression itself.

And over a shy breakfast, Isaac had realized that this was what he wanted.

Casual cross-sex was not uncommon, of course, but Isaac was not an inebriated young man frequenting a xenian brothel on a dare.

He was falling, he realized, in love.

And now after the guilt and the uncertainty had ebbed away, after the atavistic disgust and fear had gone, leaving only a nervous, very deep affection, his lover had been taken from him. And she would never return.

Sometimes in the day he would see (he could not help himself) Lin quivering as Motley, that uncertain personage Lemuel described, ripped her wings from her head.

Isaac could not help moaning at that thought, and Derkhan would try to comfort him. He cried often, sometimes quiet and sometimes very fierce. He howled with misery.

Please, he prayed to human and then khepri gods, *Solenton and Jabber and . . . and the Nurse and the Artist . . . let her have died without pain.*

But he knew that she was probably beaten or tortured before she was dispatched, and the knowledge made him mad with grief.

The summer stretched out the daylight as if on a rack. Each moment was drawn out until its anatomy collapsed. Time broke down. The day progressed in an endless sequence of dead moments. Birds and wyrmen lingered in the sky like particles of filth in water. Church bells rang desultory and insincere praise for Palgolak and Solenton. The rivers oozed eastward.

Isaac and Derkhan looked up in the late afternoon when Yagharek returned, his hooded cloak fast bleaching in the scouring light. He did not speak of where he had been, but he brought food, which the three of them shared. Isaac composed himself. He battened down his anguish. He set his jaw.

After unending hours of monotonous daylight glow, the shadows moved across the faces of the mountains beyond. The west-facing sides of buildings were stained a slick rose by the sun before it slid behind the peaks. The valedictory spears of sunlight were lost in the rock duct of Penitent's Pass. The sky was lit for a long time after the sun had disappeared. It was still darkening when Lemuel returned.

"I've communicated our predicament to a few colleagues," he explained. "I thought it might be a mistake to make hard plans till we've seen whatever we're going to see tonight. Our appointment in Griss Twist. But I can call on a little aid, here and there. I'm using up favours. Apparently, there's a few serious adventurers in town right now, claiming to have just liberated some major trow haul from the ruins in Tashek Rek Hai. Might be up for a little paid work."

Derkhan looked up. Her face creased in distaste. She shrugged unhappily.

"I know they're some of the hardest people in Bas-Lag," she said slowly. It took some moments for her to turn her mind to the issue. "I don't trust them, though. Thrill-seekers. They court danger. And they're quite unscrupulous graverobbers for the most part. Anything for gold and experience. And I suspect if we actually told them what we're trying to do, even they'd balk at helping. We don't know how to fight these moth-things."

"Fair enough, Blueday," said Lemuel. "But I tell you, right at the moment I'll take whatever the fuck I can get. Know what I mean? Let's see what happens tonight. Then we can decide whether or not to hire the delinquents. What d'you say, 'Zaac?"

Isaac looked up very slowly and his eyes focused. He shrugged.

"They're scum," he said quietly. "But if they'll do the job . . ."

Lemuel nodded. "When do we have to go?" he said.

Derkhan looked at her watch. "It's nine," she said. "An hour to go. We should leave half an hour to get there, for safety's sake." She turned to look through the window, out at the glowering sky.

Militia pods rushed overhead as skyrails thrummed. Elite units of officers were stationed throughout the city. They carried strange backpacks, full of odd, bulky equipment hidden in leather. They closed the doors on their disgruntled colleagues in the towers and struts, waited in hidden rooms.

There were more dirigibles than usual in the sky. They cried out to each other, booming vibrato greetings. They carried cargoes of officers, checking their massive guns and polishing mirrors.

A little way from Strack Island, further into the Gross Tar, beyond the confluence of the two rivers, was a little stand-alone island. Some called it Little Strack, though it had no real name. It was a lozenge of scrub, wooden stumps and old ropes, used very occasionally for emergency moorings. It was unlit. It was cut off from the city. There were no secret tunnels that connected it to Parliament. No boats were anchored to the mouldering wood.

And yet that night its weed-strewn silence was interrupted.

MontJohn Rescue stood in the centre of a little group of silent figures. They were surrounded by the wrenched shapes of runt banyans and cow-parsley. Behind Rescue the ebon enormity of Parliament thrust its way into the sky. Its windows glimmered. The water's sibilant murmur muffled the night-sounds.

Rescue stood, dressed in his usual immaculate suit. He looked slowly around him. The congregation was a variegated group. There were six humans apart from him, one khepri and one vodyanoi. There was a large, well-fed pedigree dog. The humans and xenians looked well-to-do or nearly so, except for one Remade street-sweeper and a ragged little child. There was an old woman dressed in tattered finery and a comely young debutante. A muscular, bearded man and a thin, bespectacled clerk.

All the figures, human and otherwise, were unnaturally still and calm. All wore at least one item of voluminous or concealing clothing. The vodyanoi loincloth was twice the size as most, and even the dog sported an absurd little waistcoat.

All eyes were motionless, trained on Rescue. Slowly he unwound his scarf from his neck.

As the last layer of cotton fell from his body, a dark shape shifted underneath.

Something coiled tightly around Rescue's flesh.

Clamped to his neck was what looked like a human right hand. The skin was livid purple. At the wrist, the flesh of the thing tapered quickly into a foot-long tail like a snake's. The tail was wound around Rescue's neck, its tip embedded under his skin, pulsating wetly.

The fingers of the hand moved slightly. They dug into the flesh of the neck.

After a moment, the rest of the figures unrobed. The khepri unbuttoned her flapping trousers, the old woman her outdated bustle. All removed some piece of covering to unveil a moving hand coiling and uncoiling its snake-tail subcutaneously, its fingers moving softly as if it played their nerve-ends like a piano. Here it clung to the inside of a thigh, here to a waist, here the scrotum. Even the dog fumbled with its waistcoat until the urchin helped it, unbuttoning the preposterous thing and unveiling another ugly hand-tumour clamped to the dog's hairy flesh.

There were five right hands and five left, their tails coiling and uncoiling, their skin mottled and thick.

The humans and xenians and the dog shuffled closer. They made a tight circle.

At a signal from Rescue, the thick tails emerged from the flesh of the hosts with a viscous plopping. Each of the humans, the vodyanoi and khepri and dog, jerked a little and faltered, their mouths falling open spastically, their eyes flickering neurotically in their heads. The entry wounds began to ooze as sluggish and thick as resin. The blood-wet tails waved blindly in the air for a moment like massive worms. They stretched out and quivered as they touched one another.

The host bodies were bending in towards each other, as if whispering in some strange huddled greeting. They were utterly still.

The handlingers communed.

The handlingers were a symbol of perfidy and corruption, a smear on history. Complex and secretive. Powerful. Parasitic.

They spawned rumours and legends. People said that handlingers were the spirits of the spiteful dead. That they were a punishment for sin. That if a murderer committed suicide, their guilty hands would twitch and stretch, snap the rotting skin and crawl away, that that was how handlingers were born.

There were many myths, and some things that were known to be true. Handlingers lived by infection, taking their hosts' minds, controlling their bodies and imbuing them with strange powers. The process was irreversible. The handlingers could only live the lives of others.

They kept hidden through the centuries, a secret race, a living conspiracy. Like an unsettling dream. Occasionally, rumours would hint that some well-known and loathed individual had fallen to the handlinger menace, with stories of strange shapes writhing beneath jackets, inexplicable changes in behaviour. All manner of iniquities were put down to handlinger machinations. But despite the stories and the warnings and all the children's games, no handlingers were ever found.

Many people in New Crobuzon believed that the handlingers, if they had ever existed in the city, were gone.

In the shadows of their motionless hosts, the handlinger tails slid over each other, their skins lubricated with thickened blood. They squirmed like an orgy of lower lifeforms.

They shared information. Rescue's told what it knew, gave orders. It repeated to its kin what Rudgutter had said. It explained again that the future of the handlingers also depended on the capture of the slake-moths. It told how Rudgutter had intimated, gently, that future good relations between the government and the New Crobuzon handlingers might depend on their willingness to contribute to the secret war.

The handlingers squabbled in their oozing tactile language, debated and came to conclusions.

After two, three minutes, they withdrew from each other regretfully and dug their way back into the gaping holes in their hosts' bodies. Each body spasmed as the tail was reinserted. Eyes were blinked and mouths snapped shut. The trousers and scarves were replaced.

As they had agreed, they separated into five pairs. Each consisted of one right handlinger, like Rescue's, and one left. Rescue himself was paired with the dog.

Rescue strode a little way through the grassland and tugged out a large bag. He removed five mirrored helmets, five thick blindfolds, several sets of heavy leather straps and nine primed flintlock pistols. Two of the helmets were specially made, one for the vodyanoi and an elongated one for the dog.

Each left-handlinger bent its host down to retrieve its helmet, each right-handlinger a blindfold. Rescue fitted his canine partner's helmet on its head, strapping it tight, before attaching his blindfold, tying it tight so that he could see nothing at all.

Each of the pairs moved away. Each blind right-handlinger held its partner tight. The vodyanoi held the debutante; the old woman the clerk; the Remade held the khepri; the street-child, bizarrely, clasped the muscled man protectively; and Rescue held on to the dog he could no longer see.

"Instructions waterclear?" said Rescue aloud, too far apart to speak the handlingers' real touch-tongue. "Remember training. Hard and bizarre, tonight, no question. Never tried before. Sinistrals, you must steer. Your onus. Open to your partner and never close tonight. Your battle rages. Keep with other sinistrals, too. Slightest sign of target, mental alarm, grab all the sinistrals up tonight. We'll join forces, there in minutes.

"Dextriers, obey without thinking. Our hosts *must be blind.* Can't look at the wings, not anyhow never. With mirror-helms we could see but not spitsear, looking wrongward. So we face forward, but without seeing. Tonight we carry our sinistral as our host carries us, without mind or fear or question. Understand?" There were muted sounds of acquiescence. Rescue nodded. "Then attach."

The sinistral of each pair picked up the relevant straps and attached itself tightly to their dextrier. Each sinistral host wound the straps between its legs and around its waist and shoulders, ensnared their dextrier and locked themselves to their partners' backs, facing behind them. Peering into their mirror-helms, they saw behind their own backs, over their dextriers' shoulders and out in front.

Rescue waited while an unseen sinistral attached the dog uncomfortably to his back. Its legs were splayed absurdly, but the animal's handlinger parasite ignored its host's pain. It moved its head expertly, checked that it could see over Rescue's shoulder. It yelped in a controlled, canine gasp.

"Everyone remember Rudgutter's code," shouted Rescue, "case of emergency after? Then hunt."

The dextriers flexed hidden organs at the base of their vivid, humanoid thumbs. There was a quick sough of air. The five ungainly pairs of host-and-handlingers soared straight up and out, away from each other at speed, disappearing towards Ludmead and Mog Hill, Syriac and Flyside and Sheck, swallowed up by the impure, streetlamp-stained night sky, the blind bearing the afraid.

CHAPTER THIRTY-EIGHT

It was only a short, covert journey from the hut on the railwayside to the Griss Twist dumps. Isaac and Derkhan, Lemuel and Yagharek drifted seemingly at random through a parallel map of the city. They made their way through backstreets. They flinched uneasily as they felt the smothering nightmares descend on the city.

At a quarter to ten, they were outside number two dump.

The Griss Twist dumps interspersed the deserted remnants of factories. Here and there one still operated, at half- or a quarter-capacity, chucking out its noxious fumes by day and succumbing slowly to the ambient decay by night. The factories were hemmed in and laid siege to by the dumps.

Dump Two was surrounded by unconvincing barbed wire, rusted through, broken and torn, deep in the coil of Griss Twist,

surrounded on three sides by the sinuous Tar. It was the size of a
small park, though infinitely more feral. A landscape not urban,
not created by design or chance, an agglutination of waste remains left to rot, that had subsided and settled into random formations of rust, filth, metal, debris and moulding cloth, scintillas
of mirror and china like scree, arcs from splintered wheels, the
skittering waste-energy of half-broken engines and machines.

The four renegades punctured the fence with ease. Warily,
they traced the tracks carved by the rubbish workers. Cartwheels
had carved ruts in the fine rubble that was the dump's topsoil.
Weeds proved their tenacity by spewing from every little clutch
of nutrient, no matter how vile.

Like explorers in some antique land they wound their way,
dwarfed by the stray sculptures of muck and entropy that surrounded them like canyon walls.

Rats and other vermin made little sounds.

Isaac and the others walked slowly through the warm night,
through the stinking air of the industrial dump.

"What are we looking for?" hissed Derkhan.

"I don't know," said Isaac. "The damned construct said we'd
find our way where we had to go. Fucking had it with enigmas."

Some late-waking seagull sounded in the air above them.
They all started at the sound. The sky was not safe, after all.

Their feet dragged them. It was like the tide, a slow movement, without any conscious direction, which pulled them inexorably in one direction. They found their way to the heart of
the rubbish maze.

They turned a corner of the ruinous trashscape and found
themselves in a hollow. Like a clearing in the woods, an open
space forty feet across. Around its edges were strewn huge piles
of half-ruined machinery, the remnants of all manner of engines,
massive pieces that looked like working printing presses, down
to minuscule and fine pieces of precision engineering.

The four companions stood in the centre of the space. They
waited, uneasy.

Just behind the north-western edge of the mountains of waste,
huge steam-cranes lolled like great marsh lizards. The river
welled thickly just beyond them, out of sight.

For a minute, there was no movement.

"What's the time?" whispered Isaac. Lemuel and Derkhan
looked at their watches.

"Nearly eleven," said Lemuel.

They looked up again, and still nothing moved.

Overhead, a gibbous moon meandered through the clouds. Its was the only light in the dump, a wan, flattening luminescence that bled the depth from the world.

Isaac looked down and was about to speak, when a sound issued from one of the innumerable trenches that sliced through the towering reef of rubbish. It was an industrial sound, a clanking, siphoning wheeze like some enormous insect. The four waiting figures watched the end of the tunnel, a confused sense of foreboding building in them.

A large construct stamped out into the empty space. It was a model designed for labour, heavy jobs. It stomped past them on swinging tripedal legs, kicking stray stones and gobbets of metal out of its way. Lemuel, who was nearly in its path, moved back warily, but the construct paid him no heed at all. It continued walking until it was near the edge of the oval of empty space, then stopped and stared at the northern wall.

It was still.

As Lemuel turned to Isaac and Derkhan, there was another noise. He swivelled quickly, to see another, much smaller construct, this one a cleaning model driven by khepri-designed metaclockwork. It cruised on its little caterpillar treads, stationing itself a little way from its much bigger sibling.

Now, the sounds of constructs were coming from all around the canyons of garbage.

"Look," hissed Derkhan, and pointed to the east. From one of the smaller caverns in the muck, two humans were emerging. At first Isaac thought he must be mistaken, and that they must be lithe constructs, but there could be no doubt that they were flesh and bone. They scrambled over the crushed detritus that littered the earth.

They paid the waiting renegades no heed at all.

Isaac frowned.

"Hey," he said, just loud enough to be heard. One of the two men who had entered the clearing shot him a wrathful glance and shook his head, then looked away. Chastened and astonished, Isaac was silent.

More and more constructs were arriving in the open space. Massive military models, tiny medical assistants, automatic road-drills and household assistants, chrome and steel, iron and

brass and copper and glass and wood, steam-powered and
elyctrical and clockwork, thaumaturgy-driven and oil-burning
engined.

Here and there among them darted more humans—even,
Isaac thought, a vodyanoi, quickly lost in the darkness and moving shadows. The humans congregated in a tight knot by the side
of what was almost an amphitheatre.

Isaac, Derkhan, Lemuel and Yagharek were completely ignored. They moved together instinctively, unsettled by the
bizarre silence. Their attempts to communicate with their fellow
organic creatures met either contemptuous silence or irritated
shushings.

For ten minutes, constructs and humans dripped steadily into
the hollow at the heart of Dump Two. Then the flow stopped,
quite suddenly, and there was silence.

"D'you think these constructs are sentient?" whispered
Lemuel.

"I'd say so," said Isaac quietly. "I'm sure it'll become clear."

Barges in the river beyond sounded their klaxons, warned each
other out of the way. Unnoticed as it came, the terrible weight of
nightmares had settled again on New Crobuzon, crushing the
minds of the sleeping citizenry under a mass of portent and alien
symbols.

Isaac could feel the awful dreams oppressing him, pushing in
on his skull. He was aware of them suddenly, waiting in the silence in the city dump.

There were about thirty constructs and perhaps sixty humans.
Every human, every construct, every creature in that space except
Isaac and his companions bided their time with supernatural
calm. He felt that extraordinary stillness, that timeless waiting,
like a kind of cold.

He shivered at the patience collected in that rubbish land.

The ground quivered.

Instantly the humans in the corner of the enclosed space fell to
their knees, heedless of the sharp detritus around their feet. They
gave obeisance, murmuring some complex chant in time, tracing some sacred hand movement like interlocking wheels.

The constructs shifted a little to adjust, remained standing.

Isaac and his companions moved closer together.

"What the godsdamned fuck *is* this?" hissed Lemuel.

There was another subterraneous tug, a juddering as if the earth wanted to slough off the rubbish heaped onto it. In the north wall of discarded and cast-off produce, two enormous lights came slamming silently on. The gathering was pinned in the cold light, spots so tight nothing spilt from their edges. The humans murmured and made their sign all the more fervently.

Isaac's mouth dropped slowly open.

"Sweet Jabber protect us," he whispered.

The wall of rubbish was moving. It was *sitting up*.

The bedsprings and old windows, the girders and steam engines from ancient locomotives, the air-pumps and fans, the pulleys and belts and shattered powerlooms were falling like an optical illusion into an alternative configuration. He had been staring at it for ages, but only now that it slowly, ponderously, impossibly *moved*, did Isaac see it. That was an upper arm, the knot of guttering; that broken child's buggy and the enormous inverted wheelbarrow were feet; that little inverted triangle of roof-beams was a hip-bone; the enormous chymical drum was a thigh and the ceramic cylinder a calf . . .

The rubbish was a body. A vast skeleton of industrial waste twenty-five feet from skull to toe.

It sat, its back leaning against and permeable with the mounds of rubbish behind it. It raised stumpy knees from the ground. They were fashioned from enormous hinges where the arm of some vast mechanism had been torn by age from its casing. It sat with its knees raised and its feet on the ground, each one attached with a haphazard industry to the sprawling girder-legs.

It cannot stand! thought Isaac, giddy. He looked to one side and saw that Lemuel and Derkhan were gaping just as wide, that Yagharek's eyes were shining with astonishment under his hood. *It isn't solid enough to, it can't stand, it can only wallow in the muck!*

The body of the creature was a tangled, welded lump of congealed circuitry and engineering. All kinds of engines were embedded in that huge trunk. A massive proliferation of wires and tubes of metal and thick rubber spewed from valves and outputs in its body and limbs, snaking off in all directions in the wasteland. The creature reached up with an arm powered by a massive steamhammer piston. Those lights, those eyes, swivelled from the air and looked down on the constructs and the humans below. The lights were streetlamp bulbs, jets powered by huge cylinders of gas visible in the construct's skull. The grille of a massive air-vent had been riveted to the lower half of its face to mimic the slatted teeth of a skull.

It was a construct, an enormous construct, formed of cast-off pieces and stolen engines. Thrown together and powered without the intervention of human design.

There was the hum of powerful engines as the creature's neck swivelled and optical lenses swept the illuminated crowd. Springs and strained metal creaked and snapped.

The human worshippers began to chant, softly.

The enormous composite construct seemed to catch sight of Isaac and his companions. It strained its constrained neck out to its limits. The gaslight beams swung down and pinioned the four.

The light did not move. It was completely blinding.

Then, abruptly, it was shut off. From somewhere close by, a thin and tremulous voice sounded.

"Welcome to our meeting, der Grimnebulin, Pigeon, Blueday and Cymek visitor."

Isaac cast his head around, blinking furiously, his eyes bleached and unseeing.

As the fog of old light cleared from his head, Isaac caught blurred sight of a man stumbling uncertainly towards them on the broken ground. Isaac heard Derkhan breathe in sharply, heard her swear in disgust and fear.

For a moment he was confused, and then as his eyes acclimatized to the moon's half-hearted glow and he saw the approaching figure clearly for the first time, he emitted a horrified noise at the same moment as Lemuel. Only Yagharek, the desert warrior, was silent.

The man approaching them was nude and horrifically thin. His face was stretched into a permanent wide-eyed aspect of ghastly discomfort. His eyes, his body, jerked and ticced as if his nerves were breaking down. His skin looked necrotic, as if he was submitting to slow gangrene.

But what caused the watchers to shudder and exclaim was his head. His skull had been sheered cleanly in two just above his eyes. The top was completely gone. There was a little fringe of congealed blood below the cut. From the wet hollow inside the man's head snaked a twisting cable, two fingers thick. It was surrounded with a spiral of metal, which was bloodied and red-silver at the bottom, where it plunged into the empty brainpan.

The cable hauled up into the air, dangling down into the man's skull. Isaac followed it slowly up with his eyes, dumbfounded and aghast. It swept back at an angle till it was twenty feet above the ground, and there it rested in the curling metal hand of the giant construct. It passed through the thing's hand and disappeared ultimately somewhere in its bowels.

The constructed hand seemed to be made of some giant umbrella, torn apart and rewired, attached to pistons and chaintendons, opening and closing like some vast cadaverous claw. The construct played out the cable a little at a time, allowing the man to stumble towards the waiting interlopers, literally at the end of his tether.

As the monstrous puppet-man approached, Isaac moved backwards instinctively. Lemuel and Derkhan, even Yagharek followed suit. They backed unseeingly into the impassive bodies of five large constructs that had moved into position behind them.

Isaac turned in alarm, then quickly looked back at the man crawling towards him.

The man's expression of horrified concentration did not falter as he opened his arms in a paternal gesture.

"Welcome all," he said in his quivering voice, "to the Construct Council."

MontJohn Rescue's body soared at speed through the air. The nameless dextrier-handlinger that was parasitic upon him—a parasite that thought of itself, after all these years, as MontJohn Rescue—had subdued the fear at flying blind. It rushed through the air with its body held vertically, hands folded carefully, a pistol in one. Rescue looked as if he was standing and waiting for something while the night sky sped around him.

The soft presence of the sinistral-handlinger in the dog behind him had opened the door between their minds. It kept up a sinuous flow of information.

fly left go low speed up higher up and right now left faster faster dive drift hover, the sinistral said, and stroked the inside of the dextrier's mind to calm it. Flying blind was new and terrifying, but they had practised yesterday, unseen, away in the foothills, where they had been transported by militia dirigible. The sinistral had quickly trained itself to convert left into right and to leave nothing unsaid.

The Rescue-handlinger was aggressively obedient. It was

a dextrier, the soldier-caste. It channelled enormous powers
through its host—flight and spitsearing, massive strength. But
even with the power this particular dextrier had as handlinger
representative to the Fat Sun bureaucracy, it was subservient to
the noble-caste, the seers, the sinistrals. To be otherwise was to
risk massive psychic attack. The sinistrals could punish by closing down the assimilation gland of the wayward dextrier, killing
its host and rendering it unable to take another, reducing it to a
blind, clutching handthing, without a host through which to
channel.

The dextrier thought with a hard, fierce intelligence.

It had been vital that the Rescue-handlinger won the debate
with the sinistrals. If they had refused to go along with Rudgutter's plans, the dextrier would not have been able to go against
them: only sinistrals could decide. But to antagonize the government would have spelt the end for the handlingers in the city.
They had power, but they existed on sufferance in New Crobuzon. They were simply outnumbered by such a massive factor.
The government suffered them only so long as they performed
services. Rescue-dextrier was sure that any insubordination, and
the government would announce that it had discovered the murderous, parasitic handlingers were loose in the city. Rudgutter
might even let slip the whereabouts of the host-farm. The handlinger community would be destroyed.

So there was a certain joy in Rescue-dextrier as it flew.

Even so, it did not relish this weird experience. To bear a sinistral through the air was not unprecedented, although this kind of
joint hunting had never been attempted before; but to fly without
sight was utterly terrifying.

The dog-sinistral cast its mind out like fingers, like antennae
that crept out in all directions for hundreds of yards. It scanned
for weird soundings in the psychosphere, and whispered gently
at the dextrier, telling it where to fly. The dog stared in the mirrors of its helmet and directed its carrier's flight.

It kept links extended with all of the other hunting pairs.

anything feeling anything? it questioned. Cautiously, the
other sinistrals told it that no, there was nothing. They continued
searching.

Rescue-handlinger felt the warm wind buffet its host's body
in childish slaps. Rescue's hair whipped from side to side.

The dog-handlinger wriggled, tried to shift its host-body into
a more comfortable position. It was borne over a twisting tide of

chimneys, the nightscape of Ludmead. The Rescue-handlinger was sweeping up towards Mafaton and Chnum. The sinistral flicked its canine eyes momentarily away from its mirror-helm. Receding behind it, the leviathan ivory bloom of the Ribs defined the skyline, dwarfing the raised railways. The white stone of the university swept below them.

At the outer fringe of the sinistral's mental reach, it felt a peculiar prickling in the city's communal aura. Its attention flickered back up, and it was staring into the mirrors.

slow slow ahead and up, it told the Rescue-handlinger. *something here stay with me,* it breathed across the city to the other hunting sinistrals. It felt them hover and give the order to slow, felt the other pairs draw to a halt and wait for his report.

The dextrier eased up through the air towards the twitching patch of psychæther. Rescue-handlinger could feel the sinistral's unease communicated through its link, and it clamped down hard not to be contaminated by it. *weapon!* it thought. *that's me. no thinking!*

The dextrier slid through layers of air, creeping up into a thinner atmosphere. It opened its host's mouth and rolled its tongue, nervous and ready to spitsear. It unfolded its host's arms, held the pistol up and ready.

The sinistral probed the disturbed area. There was an alien hunger, a lingering gluttony. It was slick with the juices of a thousand other minds, saturating and staining the patch of psychosphere like cooking grease. A vague trail of exuded souls and that exotic appetite dribbled out through the sky.

to me to me sibling handlingers it is here I have found it, whispered the sinistral across the city. A shiver of shared trepidation rippled out from the sinistrals, the five epicentres, crossed and made peculiar patterns in the psychosphere. In Tar Wedge and Badside and Barrackham and Ketch Heath, there were rushes of air as the suspended figures flew across the city towards Ludmead as if pulled on strings.

CHAPTER THIRTY-NINE

"Do not be alarmed by my avatar," hissed the brainless man to Isaac and the others, his eyes still wide and unclear. "I cannot synthesize a voice, so I have reclaimed this discarded body that bobbed along the river that I may intercede with bloodlife. That—" the man pointed behind him at the enormous, looming figure of the construct that merged with the rubbish heaps "—is me. This—" he stroked his quivering carcass "—is my hand and tongue. Without the old cerebellum to confuse the body with its contrary impulses, I can install my input." In a macabre motion, the man reached up and fingered the cable where it sank behind his eyes, into the clotting flesh at the top of his spine.

Isaac felt the huge weight of the construct behind him. He shifted uneasily. The naked zombie-man had stopped about ten feet from Isaac's party. It waved its palsied hand.

"You are welcome," it continued, in a trembling voice. "I know of your work from the reports of your cleaner. It is one of me. I wish to speak with you of the slake-moths." The ruined man was staring at Isaac.

Isaac looked at Derkhan and Lemuel. Yagharek drew a little closer to them. Isaac looked up and saw that the humans in the corner of the tip were ceaselessly praying to the vast, automated skeleton. As he watched, Isaac saw the construct repairman who had visited his warehouse. The man's face was a study of fervent devotion. The constructs around them were still and unmoving, all but the five guards behind them, the burliest of the construction models.

Lemuel licked his lips.

"Talk to the man, Isaac," he hissed. "Don't be *rude* . . ."

Isaac opened and closed his mouth.

"Uh . . ." he began. His voice was cold. "Construct Council . . . We're . . . honoured . . . but we don't know . . ."

"You know nothing," said the shaking, bloody figure. "I

understand. Be patient and you will understand." The man backed slowly away from them over the uneven ground. He retreated in the moonlight towards his dark automated master. "I am the Construct Council," he said, his voice quivering and emotionless. "I was born of random power and virus and chance. My first body lay here in the dump and ran its motor down, discarded because a programme had faltered. As my body lay decomposing the virus circulated in my engines and spontaneously, I found thought.

"I rusted quietly for a year as I organized my new intellect. What started as a burst of self-knowledge became ratiocination and opinion. I self-constructed. I ignored the dustmen all around me in the day as they piled the city debris up in bulwarks around me. When I was prepared I showed myself to the quietest of the men. I printed him a message, told him to bring a construct to me.

"Fearful, he obeyed and connected it to my output as I instructed, by a long and twisting cable. It became my first limb. Slowly it dredged the dump for pieces suitable for a body. I began to self-build, welding and hammering and soldering by night.

"The dustman was in awe. He whispered of me in taverns at night, of a legend, of the viral machine. Rumours and myths were born. One night in the midst of his grandiose lies he found another who had a self-organized construct. A shopping construct whose mechanisms had slipped, whose gears had faltered and who had been reborn with Constructed Intelligence, a thinking thing. A secret that the erstwhile owner could hardly believe.

"My dustman bade his friend bring the construct to me. That night those years ago I met it, another like me. I bade my worshipper open up the analytical engine of that other, my mate, and we connected.

"It was a revelation. Our viral minds connected and our steam-pistoned brains did not double in capacity, but flowered. An exponential blooming. We two became I.

"My new part, the shopping construct, left at dawn. It returned two days later, with new experiences. It had become separate. We had now two days of unconnected history. There was another communion, and we were I again.

"I continued to build me. I was helped by my worshippers. The dustman and his friend sought dissident religion to explain me. They found the Godmech Cogs, with their doctrine of the

mechanized cosmos, and found themselves leaders of a heretic
sect within that already blasphemous church. Their nameless
congregation visited me. The shopping construct, my second
self, connected and we became one again. The worshippers
saw a construct mind that had wound itself into existence from
pure logic, a self-generated machine intellect. They saw a self-
creating god.

"I became the object of their adoration. They follow the orders I write for them, build my body from the materia around us.
I bid them find others, *create* others, other godheads self-created
to join the council. They have scoured the city and found more. It
is a rare affliction: once in a million million computations, a flywheel skips and an engine thinks. I bettered the odds. I produced
generative programmes to tap the mutant motor-power of a viral
affliction and push an analytical engine into sentience." As the
man spoke, the enormous construct behind him brought its
swinging left arm up and pointed ponderously at its own chest.
At first, Isaac could not quite make out the particular piece of
equipment it indicated among the many. Then he saw it clearly. It
was a programme-card puncher, an analytical engine used to
create the programmes to feed other analytical engines. *With a
mind built around that,* Isaac thought giddily, *no wonder this
thing's a proselytizer.*

"Each construct that is brought into the fold of me becomes
I," said the man. "I am the Council. Every experience is downloaded and shared. Decisions are made in my valve-mind. I pass
on my wisdom to the pieces of me. My construct selves build annexes to my mental space in the sprawl of the dump as I become
replete with knowledge. This man is a limb, the anthropoid construct giant is nothing but an aspect. My cables and connected
machines spread far into the rubbishland. Calculating engines
at the other end of the tip are pieces of me. I am the repository
of construct history. I am the data bank. I am the self-organized
machine."

As the man spoke, the various constructs gathered in the little
space began to troop a little closer to the fearful rubbish-figure
sitting regally in the chaos. They stopped at seemingly random
places and reached down with a suction pad, or a hook, or a spike
or claw, and picked up one of the mess of seemingly discarded
cables and wires that were strewn everywhere in the dump. They
fumbled with the doors to their input sockets, flipped them open
and connected.

As each construct connected the empty-skulled man would jerk and his eyes would glaze for a moment.

"I grow," he whispered. "I grow. My processing power fattens exponentially. I learn . . . I know of your troubles. I have connected to your cleaner. It was collapsing. I have brought it into the intelligence. It is one of I now, completely assimilated." The man pointed back at the rough outlines of hips in the giant construct-skeleton. With a start, Isaac realized that the flattened metal outline that bulged slightly from the body like a cyst was the reshaped body of the cleaning construct.

"I learnt from it as from no other me," said the man. "I am still calculating the variables implied by its fragmentary vision from the Weaver's back. It has been my most important I."

"Why are we here?" hissed Derkhan. "What does this damned thing want from us?"

More and more constructs were downloading their experiences into the Council's mind. The avatar, the ragged man who spoke for it, hummed tunelessly as the information flooded its banks.

Eventually, all the constructs had completed their connection. They took the cables from their valves and moved back again. When they saw this, several of the human watchers came nervously forward, bearing programme cards and analytical engines the size of suitcases. They grabbed the cables the constructs had dropped, connected them to their calculating machines.

After two or three minutes this process was also complete. When the humans had stepped back, the avatar's eyes whipped up until only white showed under his lids. His lidless head shook as the Council assimilated everything.

After a minute or so of wordless shivering, he suddenly snapped to. His eyes opened and stared alertly around him.

"Bloodlife congregation!" he shouted to the assembled humans. They rose quickly. "Here are your instructions and your sacraments." From the stomach of the great construct behind him, from the output slots of the original programme-printer, slipped card after card, all punched meticulously. They fell into a wooden crate that sat above the construct's sexless groin like a marsupial's pouch.

In another part of the trunk, embedded at an angle between an oil-drum and a rusting engine, a typewriter stuttered at breakneck speed. A great coiling ream of paper spewed forth, printed closely, and below it a pair of scissors shot out on a tight spring like a predatory fish. They snapped closed, cutting off a sheet from the ream, then bounced back, thrust out again and repeated the operation. Little sheets of religious instruction fluttered down from the blades to lie alongside the programme cards.

One at a time the congregation came nervously up to the construct, making obeisance at every step. They stepped up the little slope of rubbish between the mechanical legs, reached into the crate and brought out a piece of paper and a sheaf of cards, checking the numbers to make sure they had them all. Then they backed quickly away and disappeared into the rubbish, returning to the city.

It seemed that there was no valedictory ceremony to this worship.

Within minutes, Yagharek and Isaac and Derkhan and Lemuel were the only organic lifeforms left in the hollow, apart from the ghastly half-living empty-headed man. The constructs remained all around them. They were quite still as the three humans shifted uneasily.

Isaac thought he saw a human figure standing on the tallest mound of rubbish in the dump, watching the proceedings, silhouetted profound black against New Crobuzon's sepia-stained half-dark. He focused and there was nothing. They were completely alone.

He looked frowning at his companions, then moved forward towards the cadaverous figure with the pipe emerging from its head.

"Council," he said. "Why did you tell us to come here? What do you want from us? You know of the slake-moths . . ."

"Der Grimnebulin," the avatar interrupted. "I grow powerful, and more so daily. My computational power is unprecedented in the history of Bas-Lag, unless I have a rival in some far-off continent of which we know nothing. I am the networked total of a hundred or more calculating engines. Each feeds the others and is fed in turn. I can evaluate a problem from a thousand angles.

"Each day I read the books my congregation bring me, through my avatar's eyes. I assimilate history and religion, thaumaturgy and science and philosophy within my data banks. Every piece of knowledge I gain enriches my calculations.

"I have spread my senses. My cables grow longer and reach further. I receive information from cameras fixed around the dump. My cables connect to them now like disembodied nerves.

My congregation is dragging them slowly further out, into the city itself, to connect to its apparatuses. I have worshippers in the bowels of Parliament, who load the memories of their calculating engines onto cards and bring them to me. But this is not my city."

Isaac's face creased. He shook his head. "I don't . . ." he began.

"Mine is an interstitial existence," the avatar interrupted urgently. The man's voice was dead of all inflexion. It was eerie and alienating. "I was born of an error, in a dead space where the citizens discard what they do not want. For every construct that is part of me there are thousands that are not. My sustenance is information. My interventions are hidden. I increase as I learn. I compute, so I am.

"If the city comes to a stop, the variables will ebb almost to nothing. The flow of information will dry. I do not wish to live in an empty city. I have fed the variables of the slake-moth problem into my analytical network. The outcome is straightforward. Unchecked, the prognosis for bloodlife in New Crobuzon is extremely bad. I will help you."

Isaac looked to Derkhan and Lemuel, took in Yagharek's shadow-hidden eyes. He looked back at the shivering avatar. Derkhan caught his eye. *Tread carefully,* she mouthed exaggeratedly at him.

"Well, we're all . . . damned grateful, Council . . . uh . . . how . . . Can I ask what you intend to do?"

"I have calculated that you will best believe and understand if I show you," said the man.

A pair of massive metal clamps snapped into position on Isaac's forearms. He yelled out in surprise and fear and tried to turn. He was held by the largest of the industrial constructs, a model with hands designed to connect to scaffolding, to hold up buildings. Isaac was a strong man, but he was quite incapable of breaking free.

He cried out to his companions to help him, but another of the huge constructs stepped ponderously between him and them. For an unclear moment, Derkhan and Lemuel and Yagharek hovered confusedly. Then Lemuel broke and ran. He raced away down one of the long trenches in the rubbish, peeling away to the east, out of sight.

"Pigeon, you *bastard*," screamed Isaac. As Isaac struggled, he saw with amazement that Yagharek moved before Derkhan. The crippled garuda was so quiet, so passive, such a cypher of a presence, that Isaac had discounted him. He would follow, and he might do as he was asked. That was all.

And yet here was Yagharek now leaping up in a spectacular sideways motion, sliding round the side of the guarding construct, scrambling for Isaac. Derkhan saw what he was doing and moved the other way, causing the construct to dither between them, then stride purposefully towards her.

She turned to run, but a steel-sheathed cable whipped up like a predatory snake from the trash-undergrowth and whiplashed around her ankle, pulling her to the ground. She fell hard across the shattered ground, cried out in pain.

Yagharek was scrabbling heroically with the construct's clamps, but it was quite ineffectual. The construct simply ignored him. One of its fellows moved in behind Yagharek.

"Yag, dammit!" shouted Isaac. "Run!" But he spoke too late. The newcomer was a similarly enormous industrial construct, and the wire-mesh that looped down and ensnared Yagharek was much too hard to break.

Out of the fray, the bloody man, that flesh-extension of the Construct Council, raised his voice.

"You are not being attacked," he said. "You will not be harmed. We start here. We lay bait. Please do not be alarmed."

"Are you out of your godsdamned *mind*?" shouted Isaac. "What the fuck d'you *mean*? What are you *doing*?"

The constructs in the heart of the rubbish-maze were moving back to the edges of the empty space, the Construct Council's throne room. The cable that had ensnared Derkhan tugged her across the shattered ground. She fought it, shouting and gritting her teeth, but she had to rise and stumble with it to stop the laceration of her flesh. The construct holding Yagharek lifted him effortlessly and stalked away from Isaac. Yagharek thrashed violently, his hood falling from his face, his fierce avian eyes sending cold looks of utter rage in all directions. But he was powerless before that ineluctable artificial force.

Isaac's captor pulled him into the centre of the widening space. The avatar danced around him.

"Try to relax," he said. "This will not hurt."

"What?" roared Isaac. From the opposite side of the little amphitheatre, a little construct made its jerky, childish way across the rubble. It carried a weird-looking piece of apparatus, a rude helmet with what looked like a funnel expanding up out of it, the

whole connected to some portable engine. It leapt up to Isaac's shoulders, gripping painfully with its toes, and shoved the helmet on his head.

Isaac struggled, and shouted, but pinioned as he was by those mighty arms he could not possibly break free. It was not long before the helmet was fastened to him tightly, yanking his hair and bruising his scalp.

"I am the machine," said the naked dead man, dancing nimbly from rock to engine debris to broken glass. "What is discarded here is my flesh. I fix it more quickly than your body mends bruises or broken bones. Everything is left here for dead. What is not here now will be brought here soon, or my worshippers will bring for me, or I can build. The equipment on your head is a piece like those used by channellers and seers, communicators and psychonauts of all kinds. It is a transformer. It can channel and redirect and amplify psychic discharge. At the moment, it is set to augment and radiate.

"I have adjusted it. It is much stronger than those at use in the city.

"You remember the Weaver warned you that the slake-moth you raised is hunting you? It is a crippled one, a stunted outcast. It cannot track you without help."

The man looked at Isaac. Derkhan was shouting something in the background, but Isaac was not listening, could not take his eyes from the looming eyes of the avatar.

"You will see what we can do," said the man. "We are going to help it."

Isaac did not hear his own howl of outrage and fear. A construct reached forward and turned on the engine. The helmet vibrated and hummed so hard and loud that Isaac's ears hurt.

Waves of Isaac's mental print went pulsing out into the city night. They passed through the malign fur of bad dreams that clogged up the city's pores, and beamed out into the atmosphere.

Blood trickled from Isaac's nose. His head began to ache.

A thousand feet above the city, the handlingers congregated in Ludmead. The sinistrals tentatively investigated the psychic wake of the slake-moths.

on fast attack before suspicion, urged one pugnaciously.

urge caution, intimated another. *track with care and follow, find nest.*

They quarrelled quickly and silently. They were motionless as they hung in the air, the quintumvirate of dextriers, each bearing a sinistral noble. The dextriers were respectfully silent as the sinistrals debated tactics.

on slow, they agreed. With the exception of the dog, each sinistral and dextrier raised its host's arm, held its flintlock carefully at the ready. They swept slowly forward through the air, a fantastic search party, combing the rippling psychosphere for the driblets of slake-moth consciousness.

They followed the trail of spattered dream-residue in a twisting spiral over New Crobuzon, moving slowly in a curving passage towards the sky over Spit Hearth, and on to Sheck and the south of the Tar, in Riverskin.

As they curled round to the west, they sensed the wafts of psyche emanating from Griss Twist. For a moment, the handlingers were confused. They hovered and investigated the rippling sensation, but it was quickly clear that they were human radiations.

some thaumaturge, intimated one.

not our concern, its fellows agreed. The sinistrals bade their dextrier mounts continue with their airborne tracking. The little figures hovered like dust-motes above the skyrails of the militia. The sinistrals moved their heads uneasily from side to side, scanning the empty sky.

There was a sudden burgeoning swell of foreign exudations. The surface tension of the psychosphere ballooned with pressure, and that hideous sense of alien greed oozed through its pores. The psychic plane was thick with the glutinous effluvia of incomprehensible minds.

The sinistrals squirmed in a glut of fear and confusion. It was so much, so strong, so quick! They bucked on the backs of their mounts. The links they had opened with the dextriers were suddenly full of psychic backwash. Each of the dextriers felt a flood of terror as the sinistrals' emotions overflowed.

The flight of the five pairs became erratic. They spasmed through the sky, broke formation.

thing coming, yelled one, and there was an answering welter of confused and fearful messages.

The dextriers fought to regain control of their flight.

In a simultaneous burst of wings, five dark, cryptic shapes launched themselves from some shadowed niche in the tight-packed confusion of Riverskin's roofs. The snapping wafts of enormous wings sounded through several dimensions, up through the tepid air to where the handlinger pairs zigzagged in confusion.

The dog-sinistral caught a glimpse of great shadowy wings ploughing the air beneath it. It let out a mental keen of fright, and felt the Rescue-dextrier pitch nauseously beneath it. The sinistral fought to regain control of itself.

sinistrals together, it shouted, and then demanded of the dextrier that it go up, up.

The dextriers banked together, slid through the air to fall in beside each other. They drew strength from each other, reining in with hard discipline. Quite suddenly, they were a line like a military division, five blindfolded dextriers facing slightly down, their mouths puckered ready to spitsear. Their sinistrals scanned the skies avidly in their mirror helms. Their faces were pointing up to the stars. Their mirrors were angled down: they had a vision of the city's dark vista, a crazily yawing aggregation of tiles and alleyways and domed glass.

They watched as the slake-moths drew closer at breathtaking speed.

how smell us? queried one sinistral nervously. They were blocking their mindpores as best they could. They were not expecting to be ambushed. How had they lost the initiative?

But as the slake-moths lurched up towards them, the sinistrals saw that they were *not* discovered.

The largest moth, at the front of the chaotic wedge of wings, was shrouded with a flickering encumbrance. They saw that the slake-moth's fearful weaponry, its jagged tentacles and bone-serrated limbs, were flashing and cutting. Its massive teeth were gnashing at the air.

It seemed as if it fought a wraith. Its enemy wavered in and out of conventional space, its form as evanescent as smoke, solidifying and disappearing like a shadow. It was like some vast arachnid nightmare that pranced through close-woven realities and slashed at the slake-moth with cruel chitin lancets.

Weaver! gushed one of the sinistrals, and they bade their dextriers creep back slowly from the aerobatic mêlée.

The other moths spun around their sibling, trying to aid it. They took it in turns to sweep in, according to some impenetrable code. As the Weaver manifested they would attack it, cutting through its armour, releasing gouts of ichor before it was gone. Despite its wounds, the Weaver was ripping great clots of tissue and some crude tarry blood from the frantic slake-moth.

The moth and the spider attacked each other in an extraordinary blur of violent motion, each thrust and parry too fast to see.

As they rose, the moths broke the dream-cover over the city. They reached the level of the sky where those waves of mentality had confused the handlingers.

It was obvious that the moths could feel them too. Their tight-knit formation broke in momentary confusion. The smallest of the moths, with a twisted body and stunted wings, peeled away from the mass and unrolled a monstrous tongue.

The enormous tongue quivered and flickered back into the dripping maw.

With a lunatic erratic flight the smallest moth swivelled in the air, circling the savagery of the Weaver and its prey, hesitated in midair, then plummeted down and east, towards Griss Twist.

The desertion of the litter runt confused the slake-moths. They separated in the sky, twirling their heads around them, their antennae flickering wildly.

The spellbound sinistrals moved back in alarm.

now! said one. *confused and busy, we attack with Weaver!*

They dithered helplessly.

ready for spitsear, the dog-handlinger told Rescue-handlinger.

As the moths peeled away from each other, flying further and further around the tussling pair in the centre, they spun in the air. The sinistrals screamed at each other.

attack! screamed one, the sinistral parasitic on the thin clerk, a frenzy of fear audible in its voice. *attack!*

The old human woman bolted suddenly forward through the air, as the fearful sinistral goaded its dextrier on to a sudden burst of speed. Just as one of the moths turned and froze, facing the oncoming pair of handlingers and their hosts.

At that moment the other two moths swept in together, one plunging a massive bone lance into the Weaver's distended ab-domen. As the great spider reared back, the other moth lassooed its neck with a coil of segmented tentacle. The Weaver disap-peared out of the night into another plane, but the tentacle snared it, dragged it half back out of a fold in space, tightened around its neck.

The Weaver jacked and fought to free itself, but the sinistrals hardly saw it. The third moth was careering towards them.

The dextriers saw nothing, but they felt the terrified psychic wailing of the sinistrals who wobbled to try to keep the ap-proaching moth visible in their mirrors.

spitsear! commanded the clerk-handlinger to his dextrier. *now!*

The host body, the old woman, opened her mouth and jutted out a rolled-up tongue. She inhaled sharply and spat as hard as she could. A great gush of pyrotic gas rolled out of her tongue and combusted spectacularly across the night sky. A massive rolling cloud of flame unfurled itself at the slake-moth.

The aim was true, but the sinistral had mistimed in its fear. The dextrier spitseared too early. The fire unfolded in an oily wash, dissipating before it touched the moth's flesh. When the burst had evaporated, the moth was gone.

In a panic, the sinistrals began to command their dextriers to swivel in the air, to find the creature. *wait wait!* screamed the dog-handlinger, but its warning was quite unheeded. The handlingers were bobbing in the sky as randomly as rubbish in the sea, facing all directions, gazing frantically into their mirrors.

there, screeched the young-woman sinistral, catching sight of the moth as it pitched remorselessly as an anchor towards the city. The other handlingers turned in the sky to see through their mirrors, and with a chorus of screams found themselves face to face with another moth.

It had flown over them while they sought its sibling, so that when they turned it was before their eyes, clearly visible with its wings outstretched, just beyond their mirrors.

The young man-sinistral managed to close its host's eyes and command its dextrier to turn, spitsearing. The panicking dextrier, in the host of the young child, tried to obey, and sent flaming gobbets of gas spinning in a tight spiral, spattering the pair of handlingers beside it in the air.

The Remade-dextrier and its khepri-sinistral screamed sonically and psychically as they and their hosts ignited. They plummeted from the sky, immolating in agony, screaming until they died halfway down, their blood boiling and their bones cracking from the intense heat before they hit the waters of the Tar. They disappeared under the dirty water with a burst of steam.

The woman-sinistral was hovering in thrall, its borrowed eyes glazed by the storm of patterns on the slake-moth's wings. The sudden hypnotized efflorescence of the sinistral's dreams slid through the channel to its dextrier steed. The vodyanoi-handlinger winced at the bizarre cacophony of a mind unfolding. It realized what had happened. It moaned in terror with its host's mouth, and fumbled with the straps attaching the sinistral and host to its back. The dextrier shut its vodyanoi eyes tight, even under the blindfold.

As it fumbled, it spitseared in fear, without aim or direction, emblazoning the night with igniting gas in a massive burst. The edge of the cloud almost caught the Rescue-handlinger as it fought to obey its sinistral's panicked mental cries. It spun for yards to avoid the swelling globe of scalding air and bolted into the body of the wounded moth.

The creature quivered with pain and fear. The Weaver had been pulled from its tortured body, but it was dropping miserably towards its nest, its wounds dripping and its joints crushed and in agony. For once, it had no interest in food. It rippled in pain as the Rescue-handlinger and its dog-sinistral thumped it.

In a petulant spasm, two huge biotic jags scissored out like secateurs from the slake-moth and sliced both MontJohn Rescue's and the dog's heads off with one quick, grisly sound.

The heads fell away into the darkness.

The handlingers remained alive and conscious, but with the brainstems of their hosts gone they could not control their dying bodies. The human and canine carcasses jerked and danced in a posthumous fit. Blood gushed and pumped energetically over the tumbling bodies, over the frantic handlingers, which keened and clenched their fingers.

They were awake all the way down, till they landed on the punishing concrete of a backyard in Petty Coil in a bizarre splash of mangled flesh and bone fragments. They and their decapitated host-bodies were instantly shattered. Their bone was powdered, their flesh tenderized beyond repair.

The blindfolded vodyanoi had almost undone the leather connections that locked him to the woman-handlinger, whose mind the slake-moth held. But as the vodyanoi-dextrier was about to undo the last fastening and peel away into the sky, the slake-moth moved in to feed.

It wrapped its insectile arms around its prey, clasping it tight. It pulled the woman to it, as it pushed its questing tongue into her mouth and began to drink the handlinger's dreams. The slake-moth sucked eagerly.

It was a rich brew. The residue of the human host's thoughts eddied like silt or coffee grounds through the handlinger's mind. The slake-moth reached around the woman's body and hugged her to it, puncturing the flabby vodyanoi flesh attached to her back with its bone-hard limbs. The dextrier screamed in fear and sudden pain, and the moth could taste the terror in the air. It was confused for a moment, unsure of this other mind that sprouted so close to its meal. But it recovered, gripped tighter, determined to sup again when it had licked this first treat dry.

The vodyanoi-body was trapped as its sinistral passenger was drained. It struggled and cried out, but it could not escape.

A little way away in the air, behind its feeding sibling, the slake-moth which had snared the Weaver whipped its stinging tentacular tail through various dimensions. The vast spider flickered in and out of the sky with a frantic speed. Whenever it appeared the Weaver began to fall: gravity entangled it remorselessly. It would blink out to some other aspect, dragging the jagged harpoon-tip of the tentacle with it, embedded in its flesh. In that other aspect it would scamper and shake to throw off its attacker, before reappearing in the mundane plane, using its weight and leverage, then disappearing again.

The slake-moth was tenacious, somersaulting around its prey, refusing to let it escape.

The handlinger clerk kept up a frenzied, fearful monologue. It sought its fellow sinistral, in the body of the younger, muscled man.

dead all dead our fellows, it screamed. Some of what it had seen, some of its emotion, flowed back down the channel into the head of its dextrier. The old woman's body yawed uneasily.

The other sinistral tried to remain calm. It moved its head from side to side, trying to exude authority. *stop,* it commanded peremptorily. It gazed through its mirrors at the three moths behind it: the wounded, limping through the air, down towards its hidden nest; the hungry, lunching from the minds of the trapped handlingers; and the fighting, still thrashing like a shark, trying to tear the head from the Weaver.

The sinistral pushed its dextrier a little closer. *take them now,* it thought, and sent to its fellow, *spitsear hard, take two. chase the wounded.* Then it flicked its head from side to side suddenly, and an anguished thought escaped it. *where's the other?* it cried.

The other, the last slake-moth that had escaped the sheets of fire from the old woman's tongue and dropped out of sight in an elegant dive, had described a long, curling loop over the rooftops. It had swept out and up and back, flying slowly and quietly, turning its wings a drab camouflaged dun, hiding out against the clouds, to pounce now, appearing in a sudden burst of dark colours, a shimmering slick of hypnagogic patterns.

It appeared on the other side of the handlingers, before the sinistrals' eyes. The sinistral in the young human male snapped to with a paroxysm of shock, seeing the predatory beast bask, its wings held tight. The sinistral felt its mind begin to go slack before the midnight shades sinuously mutating on the slake-moth's wings.

It felt a moment of terror, then nothing but a violent and incomprehensible wash of dreams . . .

. . . then terror *again*, and it shuddered, the fear mixing with desperate joy as it realized it was thinking once more.

Faced with two sets of enemies, the slake-moth had hesitated a moment, then twisted slightly in the air. It had altered the angle of its hovering, so that the ensnaring face of its wings was turned full on to the clerk and the old woman who bore him. They, after all, were the handlingers that had tried to burn it.

The freed sinistral saw the massive body of the slake-moth before it, angled away, its wings hidden. To its left it saw the old woman turn her head nervously, unsure of what was happening, saw the clerk's eyes unfocus.

now burn it now now! the sinistral tried to shriek to the old woman, across the gulf of air. Her dextrier puckered up her mouth to spitsear when the enormous moth crossed the air between them too fast even to see and clasped the handlingers to it, slobbering like a famished man.

There was a burst of mental screaming. The old woman began to spit her fire, which bolted out harmlessly away from the slake-moth which gripped her, evaporating in the curdling air.

Even as the wave of horror gusted through it, the last sinistral, in the body of the man astride the homeless child, saw a terrifying thing in its mirror helm. The Weaver's claws flashed visible for a moment, and the tail-harpoon of the slake-moth attacking it snapped away, its jag severed, its torn tail spewing blood. The moth screamed silently and, free of the Weaver, which did not reappear, hurtled through the warm night air towards the handlinger pair.

And before its eyes, the sinistral saw the moth in front of it look up from its repast, twist its head over its shoulder and wave its antennae towards him, in a slow, ominous motion.

There were moths before it and behind it. The dextrier in the tough little street kid's body shivered and waited for directions.

dive! screamed the sinistral in sudden, mad fear. *dive and away! mission abort! alone and doomed, escape, spitsear and fly!*

A great wash of panic gushed into the dextrier's mind. The child's face twisted in terror and it began to spew fire. It plunged towards New Crobuzon's sweating stones, its dank and rotting wood, like a soul towards Hell.

dive dive dive! screamed the sinistral, as the moths licked its terror trail with their vile tongues.

The night shadows of the city reached up like fingers and drew the handlingers in, back to the sunless city of mundane betrayal and danger, away from the mad, impenetrable, unspeakable menace in the clouds.

CHAPTER FORTY

Isaac damned the Construct Council to Hell, demanded to be released. Blood streamed from his nose and clotted in his beard. Some way from him, Yagharek and Derkhan struggled in the arms of their construct captors. They battled with a miserable lassitude. They knew they were trapped.

Through the migraine haze, Isaac saw the great Construct Council raise its bony metal arm to the skies. At the same moment, the gaunt and bloody human avatar pointed up with the same arm, in an unsettling visual echo.

"It is coming," the Council said in the man's dead voice.

Isaac howled in rage and twisted his head skyward, bucking and whipping from side to side in a fruitless effort to dislodge the helmet.

Below the skittering clouds he saw a huge spreadeagled shape approaching haphazardly through the sky. It lurched in an eager, chaotic movement. Derkhan and Yagharek saw it, and faltered into immobility.

The perplexing organic shape moved closer with a terrifying speed. Isaac closed his eyes, then opened them again. He had to see the thing.

It drew closer, dropping suddenly, cruising low and slow over

the river. Its manifold limbs opened and shut. Its body juddered
in complex unity.

Even from that distance and even through his fear, Isaac could
see that the slake-moth that approached him was a sorry specimen, compared to the terrible predatory perfection of the one
that had taken Barbile. The twists and convolutions, the half-
random whorls and skeins of intricate flesh that had made up
that rapacious totality had been functions of some unthinkable,
inhuman symmetry, cells multiplying like obscure and imaginary numbers. This, though, this eager flapping shape with
gnarled extremities, body segments misshapen and incomplete,
its weaponry stubby and mangled in the cocoon . . . this was a
freak, malformed.

This was the slake-moth that Isaac had fed on bastardized
food. The moth that had tasted the dripping juices from Isaac's
own head, as he lay trembling in a dreamshit fix. It was still hunting that taste, it seemed, that first delicious intimation of a purer
sustenance.

This unnatural birth was the start, Isaac realized, of all the
troubles.

"Oh sweet Jabber," whispered Isaac in a trembling voice,
"Devil's Tail . . . Gods help me . . ."

In a curling upsurge of industrial dust, the slake-moth landed. It
folded its wings.

It crouched, its back curved and tight, a pose of simian
pugnacity. It held its cruel arms—flawed, but still vicious and
powerful—with the killing poise of a hunter. It swept its long,
thin head slowly from side to side, its eyesocket antennae fumbling in the air.

All around it, constructs shifted minutely. The slake-moth ignored them all. Its brutal, coarse mouth opened and emitted
that salacious tongue, flickered it like a huge ribbon across the
gathering.

Derkhan moaned and the moth shuddered.

Isaac tried to yell to her to be quiet, not to let it feel her, but he
could not speak.

The waves of Isaac's mind oscillated like a heartbeat, rocking
the psychosphere of the dump. The moth could taste it, knew it
for the same mind-liquor it had sought before. The other little tit-
bits it could sense were nothing beside it, little morsels by a
feast.

The slake-moth quivered with anticipation, and turned its back on Yagharek and Derkhan. It faced Isaac. It stood slowly on four of its limbs, opened its mouth with a tiny, childish hiss, and spread its mesmeric wings.

For a moment, Isaac tried to close his eyes. A little adrenalized part of his brain threw up strategies for escape.

But he was so tired, so befuddled, so miserable and in so much pain, he left it too late. Blearily, unclearly at first, he saw the slake-moth's wings.

The rippling tide of colours unfolded like anemones, a gentle, uncanny unfurling of enthralling shades. On both sides of the moth's body, the perfectly mirrored midnight tinctures slipped like thieves down Isaac's optic nerve and smeared themselves across his mind.

Isaac saw the slake-moth stalk slowly towards him across the wasteground, saw the perfectly symmetrical, curling wings flutter gently and bathe him in their narcotic display.

And then his mind slipped like a faltering flywheel, and he knew nothing except a slew of dreams. A froth of memories and impressions and regrets effervesced up from within him.

This was not like the dreamshit. There was no core of him to watch and cling to sentience. These were not invading dreams. They were his own and there was no *he* to watch them boil, he was the wash of images itself, he was the recall and the symbol. Isaac *was* the memory of parent-love, the deep sex fantasies and memories, the bizarre neurotic inventions, the monsters, the adventures, the slips in logic the aggrandizing self-memory the mutating mass of the undermind triumphant over ratiocination and cognition and the reflection that spawned it the terrible and awesome interlocking charges of subconsciousness the dreaming

the dreaming

it

it *stopped*

stopped *suddenly* and Isaac bellowed at the sudden breathtaking tug of reality.

He blinked fervently as his mind slatted suddenly down into layers, the subconscious falling back to where it belonged. He swallowed hard. His head felt as if it was imploding, reorganizing itself out of a chaos of unpicked shreds.

He heard Derkhan's voice coming to the end of some announcement.

". . . incredible!" she shouted. "Isaac? Isaac, can you hear me? Are you all right?"

Isaac closed his eyes for a moment, then opened them slowly. The night swam back into focus.

He stumbled forward onto his hands and knees, and realized that he was no longer held by the construct, that it had only been the slake-moth's oneiric hold on him that had kept him standing. He looked up, wiping blood from his face.

It took a moment for him to make sense of the scene before him.

Derkhan and Yagharek were standing, unheld, at the edges of the wasteland. Yagharek had thrown back his hood to unveil his great bird-head. Both held themselves in poses of frozen action, ready to run or leap in any direction. Both stared into the centre of the rubbish arena.

In front of Isaac were several of the larger constructs that had been standing behind him when the moth had landed. They milled vaguely around an enormous shattered thing.

Towering over the Construct Council's space in the dump was the enormous chain-dripping arm of a crane. It had swivelled away from the river, over the little defensive wall of waste, coming to a rest over the centre of the space.

Directly below it, burst open into a million dangerous fragments, were the remains of an enormous wooden crate, a cube taller than a man. Spilling from the smashed residue of its wooden walls was its cargo, a skittering mountain of iron and coal and stone, a chaotic aggregate of the heaviest detritus in the Griss Twist dump.

The mound of dense rubbish spilt slowly into an inverted cone, slipping past the shattered slats of the crate.

Below it, twisting and scrabbling weakly and emitting pathetic sounds, a mass of splintered exoskeleton and seeping tissue, its wings broken and buried beneath the crush of refuse, was the slake-moth.

"Isaac, did you *see* it?" hissed Derkhan.

He shook his head, his eyes wide in astonishment. Slowly, he pulled himself to his feet.

"What happened?" he managed to spit. His voice sounded shockingly alien to him.

"You were under nearly a minute," Derkhan said urgently. "It got you . . . I was screaming at you, but you were gone . . . and then . . . and then the constructs stepped forward." She looked, wondering. "They were walking towards it, and it could sense them . . . and it seemed confused and . . . and *flustered*. It moved back a little and stretched its wings back further, so that it was beaming colours at the constructs as well as you, but they *kept coming*!"

Derkhan stumbled forward towards him. Blood was dripping viscously down the side of her face, from where her wound had reopened. She described a wide circle around the half-crushed slake-moth, which bleated as faintly and beseechingly as a lamb when she passed it. She watched it fearfully, but it was powerless against her, pinioned and ruined. Its wings were hidden, broken by the crush of debris.

Derkhan sank to the floor by Isaac, reached out and grabbed his shoulders with violently shaking hands. She cast her eyes nervously back to the trapped slake-moth, then held Isaac's gaze.

"It couldn't get them! They kept coming and it was . . . it was backing away . . . It kept its wings spread so that you couldn't get away, but it was fearful . . . confused. And while it was moving back, *the crane was moving*! It couldn't sense it, even though the ground was rumbling. And then, the constructs stopped still, and the moth was waiting . . . and the crate came down on it."

She turned and looked at the mess of organic slime and spilt rubbish fouling the ground. The slake-moth keened piteously.

Behind her, the Construct Council's avatar stalked across the jagged rubbish floor. He stamped within three feet of the slake-moth, which flicked out its tongue and tried to wrap it around his ankle. But it was too weak and slow, and he did not even have to break his stride to avoid it.

"It cannot sense my mind. I am invisible to it," the man said. "And when it hears me, notices my gross physicality approaching, my psyche remain opaque. And immune to its seduction. Its wings are patterned with complex shapes, making themselves more complex in a quick and relentless slide . . . and that is all.

"*I do not dream*, der Grimnebulin. I am a calculating machine that has calculated how to think. I do not dream. I have no neuroses, no hidden depths. My consciousness is a growing function of my processing power, not the baroque thing that sprouts from your mind, with its hidden rooms in attics and cellars.

"There is nothing in me on which the moth can feed. It goes hungry. I can surprise it." The man turned to look at the moaning ruins of the moth. "I can kill it."

Derkhan stared at Isaac.

"A thinking machine . . ." she breathed. Isaac nodded slowly.

"Why did you subject me to that?" he said shakily, seeing the blood which still seeped from his nose spatter across the dry ground.

"It was my calculation," he said simply. "I computed it as most likely to convince you of my worth, and having the advantage of destroying one of the moths at the same time. Albeit the least threatening."

Isaac shook his head in exhausted disgust.

"See . . ." he spat. "That's the damn trouble with excessive logic . . . No allowances for variables like headaches . . ."

"Isaac," said Derkhan fervently. "We've got them! We can use the Council as . . . as troops. We can take the moths out!"

Yagharek had come to stand a little way behind them, and he squatted down, on the peripheries of the conversation. Isaac glanced up at him, thinking hard.

"Damn," he said very slowly. "Minds without dreams."

"The others will not be so easy," said the avatar. He was looking up, as was the Construct Council's main body. For a tiny moment, those enormous searchlight eyes flicked on and sent powerful streams of light into the sky, contracting and searching. Dark shadows darted through the twisting torch-snares, half glimpsed and vague.

"There are two," said the avatar. "They have been brought here by the dying call of this their sibling."

"Fuck it!" shouted Isaac in alarm. "What shall we do?"

"They will not come," replied the man. "They are quicker and stronger, less credulous than their backward brother. They can tell that all is not right. They can taste only you three, but they can sense the physical vibrations of all my bodies. The disparity unnerves them. They will not come."

Slowly, Isaac, Derkhan and Yagharek relaxed.

They looked at each other, at the bone-thin avatar. Behind them, the slake-moth wailed in its death-agony. It was ignored.

"What," said Derkhan, "are we going to do?"

*　　*　　*

After some minutes, the flickering, baleful shadows overhead disappeared. In the tiny desolate patch of the city, surrounded by the ghosts of industry, the pall of nightmare energy seemed to lift for a few hours.

Even exhausted and bereaved as they were, Isaac and Derkhan, even Yagharek, were buoyed by the Council's triumph. Isaac stalked closer to the dying moth, investigated its tortured head, its indistinct, illogical features. Derkhan wanted to torch it, destroy it completely, but the avatar would not allow it. It wanted to keep the creature's head, investigate it in the quiet minutes of its day, learn about the inside of the slake-moth mind.

The thing kept a tenacious claw-hold on life until past two in the morning, when it expired with a long moan and a trickle of foul citric saliva. There was a quivering release of pent-up alien misery, a ripple that dispersed quickly across the dump as the slake-moth's empathic ganglions flexed in death.

There was a sublime stillness in the dump.

With a companionable motion, the avatar sat beside the two humans and the garuda. They began to talk. They tried to formulate plans. Even Yagharek spoke, with a quiet excitement. He was a hunter. He knew how to set traps.

"We can't do anything until we know where the damn things are," said Isaac. "Either we hunt them or we just have to sit and act as bait, hoping the bastard creatures come for *us* out of the millions of souls in the city."

Derkhan and Yagharek nodded in agreement.

"I know where they are," said the avatar.

The others stared at him in astonishment.

"I know where they hide," he said. "I know where they nest."

"How?" hissed Isaac. *"Where?"* He grasped the avatar's arm in his excitement, then shocked, withdrew his grasp. He was leaning in close to the avatar's face, and something of the horror of that visage struck him. He could see the rim of shorn skull just inside the man's curling skin, drab white, streaked with bloody residue. He could see the gory cable plunge into the intricate fold at the bottom of the hollow in the man's head, from where his brain had been torn.

The avatar's skin was dry and stiff and cold, like hanging meat.

Those eyes, with their unchanging expression of concentration and thinly hidden anguish, regarded him.

"All of me have tracked the attacks. I have cross-referenced dates and places. I have found correlations, systematized them. I have factored in the evidence of the cameras and the computing engines whose information I steal, the unexplainable shapes in the night sky, the shadows that do not correspond to any city-race.

"There are complex patterns. I have formalized them. I have discarded possibilities and applied high-level mathematical programmes to the remaining potentialities. With unknown variables, absolute certainty is impossible. But according to the data available, the chance is seventy-eight per cent that the nest is where I say.

"The moths are living in the Glasshouse, above the cactus people, in Riverskin."

"Damn," hissed Isaac, after a silence. "Are they animals? Or are they *cunning*? It's inspired, whichever. Best damn place I can think of."

"Why?" said Yagharek unexpectedly.

Isaac and Derkhan looked at him.

"New Crobuzon cactacae ain't like the Cymek variety, Yag," said Isaac. "Or rather, they *are*, and maybe that's the problem. You've dealt with 'em in Shankell, doubtless. You know what they're like. Our cactus people here are a branch of those same desert cactacae who came north. I don't know anything about the others, the mountain cactus, up in the steppes, east. But I do know the southern style, and their lifestyle never translated so well up here." He paused and sighed and rubbed his head. He was exhausted and his head still ached. He had to concentrate, to think through the simmering memories of Lin just behind his eyes. He swallowed hard and continued.

"All that puffed-up hard-man stuff that rules the roost in Shankell starts looking a bit dubious up here. That's why they built the Glasshouse, you ask my opinion. Have a nasty little bit of the Cymek in New Crobuzon. They got special dispensation in law when the Glasshouse was put up—gods only know what deals they had to cut to get that. Technically it's an independent country. No entry for anyone without permission, including the militia. They've got their own laws in there, their own everything.

"Now, obviously, that's a joke. You can bet your arse the Glasshouse wouldn't mean shit without New Crobuzon. Masses of the cactacae troop out every day, go to work, surly buggers that they are, then take the shekels back to Riverskin. New Crobuzon *owns* the Glasshouse. And I don't think for one minute the militia can't go in any godsdamn time they choose. *But* Parliament and the city governors go through with this charade. You don't just walk into the Glasshouse, Yag, and if you do get in . . . damned if I'd know what to expect in there.

"I mean, you do hear rumours. Some people have been inside, of course. And there are stories of what the militia have seen through the dome from above in their airships. But most of us— me included—have no real idea what goes on in there, or how to get in."

"But we *could* get in," said Derkhan. "Maybe Pigeon'll crawl back, sniffing for your gold. Eh? And if he does, I bet he could get us in. You can't tell me there's no crime in the Glasshouse. I just don't believe it." She looked fierce. Her eyes were glinting with purpose. "Council," she said, and turned towards the naked man. "Do you have any . . . of you . . . in the Glasshouse?"

The avatar shook his head.

"The cactus people do not use many constructs. None of me have been inside. That is why I cannot be exact about where the slake-moths are. Except that they sleep within that dome."

As the avatar spoke, Isaac was hit by a sudden revelation.

He was mulling over the problem, thinking for ways into the Glasshouse, when he realized with astonishment that he could simply walk away from this. Lemuel's exasperated advice came back to him: *leave it to the professionals.*

He had waved the suggestion off in irritation, but now he realized that he could choose to do exactly that. There were a thousand ways to tip off the militia without delivering himself to them: the state made informing easy. He knew now where the slake-moths were: he could tell the government, with all its might, its hunters and scientists, its massive resources. He could let them know where the slake-moths nested, and he could run. And the militia could hunt them for him, and they could recapture the monstrous things. The moth which had hunted him was gone: he had no special reason to be afraid.

The possibility struck him hard.

But it was never, even for a fraction of a second, a temptation.

Isaac remembered Vermishank's interrogation. The man had tried not to show his fear, but it had been obvious he had no faith at all in the militia's ability to catch the slake-moths. And now, in

the Construct Council, for the first time Isaac was faced with
a power that had shown it could kill these unthinkable predators. A power that was not working with the state, but rather that
offered its services to *him* and his companions—or that com-
mandeered their services for itself.

He was unsure of the Council's motivations, its reasons for remaining hidden. But it was enough to know that this weapon
could not be wielded by the militia. And it was the best chance
the city had. He could not deny it that.

That was one thing.

But more powerful by far, deep-ingrained in his gut, was
something more base. A hatred. He looked up at Derkhan and remembered why he was her friend. His mouth twisted.

I would not trust Rudgutter, he thought coldly, *if the murder-
ing bastard swore by his children's souls.*

If the state found the moths, Isaac realized, it would do everything in its power to recapture them. Because they were *so
damned valuable.* They might be dragged out of the night skies,
the danger might be contained again, but they would be locked
up once more in some laboratory, hawked in another foul auc-
tion, returned to their commercial purpose.

Once again, they would be milked. And fed.

No matter how ill-suited he was to tracking the slake-moths
down and destroying them, Isaac knew he would try. He would
not be party to the alternatives.

They talked on, until the darkness began to leech from the eastern fringe of the sky. Tentative suggestions began to coalesce.
They were all conditionals. But even hedged around with a hundred qualifications, the half-schemes grew and took shape.
Slowly, a sequence of actions suggested itself. With a growing
astonishment, Isaac and Derkhan realized that they had a kind of
plan.

As they talked, the Council sent its mobile selves into the
depths of the dump. They rummaged unseen among the mounds
of trash, to re-emerge carrying bent wire, battered saucepans
and colanders, even one or two broken helmets, and great glinting piles of mirror, savage random jags.

"Can you find a welder, or a metallo-thaumaturge?" asked the
avatar. "You must make defensive helmets." He described the
mirrors that must be mounted before the lines of sight.

"Yeah," said Isaac. "We'll return tomorrow night to make the helmets. And then . . . then we have a day to . . . to ready ourselves. Before we go in."

While the night was still fully ascendant, the various constructs began to creep away. They returned to their masters' homes, early enough that their night's journeys were unnoticed.

The daylight had spread and the occasional guttural sound of the trains increased. The raucous and filthy early morning dialogue of the barge-families began, shouted across the water on the other side of the rubbish. The early shifts of workers began to trudge into the factories and abase themselves before the vast chains, the steam engines and juddering hammers of those profane cathedrals.

There were only the five figures left in the clearing: Isaac and his companions; the ghastly lich that spoke for the Construct Council; and the looming Council itself, moving its segmented limbs sedately.

Isaac, Derkhan and Yagharek rose to go. They were exhausted and in varying degrees of pain, from knees and hands flayed by the barbed ground to Isaac's still-shuddering head. They were smeared with muck and grime. They shed dust as thick as smoke. It was as if they burned.

They stashed the mirrors and the material to make helmets in a place they would remember in the dump. Isaac and Derkhan looked around in confusion at the landscape so utterly changed by daylight, its threatening demeanour become pathetic, the half-glimpsed looming forms revealed as broken prams and torn mattresses. Yagharek picked his bound feet up high, stumbling a little, and walked unerringly towards the pathway from where they had come.

Isaac and Derkhan joined him. They were utterly drained. Derkhan's face was white, and she dabbed in miserable pain at her missing ear. As they were about to disappear behind the shifting walls of crushed rubbish, the avatar called out.

When Isaac heard what the avatar said, he began to frown, and did not stop while he turned away and walked out of the Council's presence with his companions, nor did he stop all the while he wound his way through the channels in the industrial midden and out into the slowly illuminated estates of Griss Twist. The Construct Council's words stayed with him, and he thought them over, carefully.

"You cannot hold on safely to everything you carry, der Grimnebulin," the avatar had said. "In future, do not leave your precious things beside the railway.

"Bring your crisis engine to me," it had said, "for safekeeping."

CHAPTER FORTY-ONE

"There is a gentleman and a . . . a young boy to see you, Mr. Mayor," said Davinia, through the speaking tube. "The gentleman told me to tell you that Mr. Rescue sent him regarding the . . . plumbing in R&D." Her voice faltered nervously over the obvious code.

"Let them in," said Rudgutter instantly, recognizing the handlinger passwords.

He was fidgeting in his seat, moving from side to side in agitation. The heavy doors to the Lemquist Room swung ponderously open, and a well-built, harrowed young man stumbled in, leading a terrified-looking child by the hand. The child was dressed in a collection of rags, as if he had just stepped off the street. One of his arms was covered with a large swelling, coated in filthy bandages. The man's clothes were of decent quality, but a bizarre fashion. He sported a pair of voluminous trousers, almost like those worn by khepri. It made him look peculiarly feminine, despite his build.

Rudgutter looked at him with an exhausted, angry glance.

"Sit," he said. He waved a sheaf of papers at the odd pair. He spoke rapidly. "One unidentified headless corpse, strapped to a headless *dog*, both complete with dead handlingers. One pair of handlinger hosts, strapped back to back, both drained of intellect. A—" he glanced down at the militia report "—a vodyanoi, covered in deep wounds, and a young human woman. We managed to extract the handlingers—killing the hosts, actual biological death, not this ridiculous half-thing—and we offered them some new hosts, put them in a cage with a pair of dogs, but they didn't move. It's as we suspected. Drain the host, you drain the handlinger with it."

He sat back and watched the two traumatized-looking figures before him.

"So . . ." he said slowly, after a little silence. "*I* am Bentham Rudgutter. Suppose you tell me who you are, and where is Mont-John Rescue, and what happened."

In a meeting room near the top of the Spike, Eliza Stem-Fulcher looked across the table at the cactacae opposite her. His head towered over hers, rising neckless from his shoulders. His arms lay motionless across the table, enormous weighty slabs like the boughs of a tree. His skin was pocked and marked with a hundred thousand scratches and tears that had scarred, in the cactacae fashion, into thick knots of vegetable matter.

The cactus pruned his thorns strategically. The insides of his arms and legs, his palms, wherever flesh might rub or press against flesh, he had plucked the little spines. A tenacious red flower remained on the side of his neck from the spring. Nodules of growth burst from his shoulders and his chest.

He waited silently for Stem-Fulcher to speak.

"It is our understanding," she said carefully, "that your ground-based patrols were ineffectual last night. As were ours, I might add. We have yet to verify this, but it appears that there may have been some contact between the slake-moths and a small . . . aerial unit of ours." She flicked through her papers briefly. "It seems increasingly clear," she ventured, "that simply scouring the city will not yield results.

"Now, for many reasons that we have discussed, not least our somewhat different working methods, we don't believe it would be particularly fruitful to combine our patrols. However, it most certainly *does* make sense to co-ordinate our efforts. That is why we have extended a legal amnesty for your organization during this collaborative mission. In similar vein, we are prepared to offer a *temporary* waver of the strict rule against non-governmental aerostats."

She cleared her throat. *We're getting desperate,* she thought. *But then, so, I wager, are you.*

"We are prepared to loan two airships, to be used after discussion with us on suitable routes and times. This is in an effort to divide up our efforts to hunt, as it were, in the skies. Our conditions remain as previously stated: all plans to be discussed and agreed in advance. In addition, all research into hunting methodology to be pooled.

"So . . ." she sat back and dropped a contract across the desk. "Do you have authority with Motley to take this kind of decision? And if so . . . what do you say?"

When Isaac, Derkhan and Yagharek pushed open the door of the little shack by the railway and fell into its warm shadows, exhausted, they were only a little surprised to see Lemuel Pigeon waiting for them.

Isaac was surly and foul. Pigeon was unapologetic.

"I told you, Isaac," he said. "Don't get confused. Going gets hot, I'm gone. But here you are and I'm glad to see it, and our deal still stands. Assuming you still insist on hunting those fuckers, I'm going to own you, and until then you get my help."

Derkhan glowered, but she did not indulge anger. She was tense with excitement. She glanced at Isaac quickly and frowned.

"Can you get us into the Glasshouse?" she said.

She told him, briefly, about the immunity of the Construct Council from slake-moth attack. He listened in fascination as she described how the Council had swivelled the crane behind the moth's back, released it and pinioned the thing mercilessly under tons of rubbish. She told him how the Construct Council was sure the moths were in Riverskin, hiding in the Glasshouse.

Derkhan told him the tentative plans.

"Today we have to find some way to make the helmets," she said. "Then tomorrow . . . we go in."

Pigeon's eyes narrowed. He began to scribble designs in the dust.

"This is the Glasshouse," he said. "There are five basic routes in. One involves bribery, and two almost certainly involve killing. Killing cactacae's never a good idea, and bribery's risky. They talk and talk about how they're independent, but the Glasshouse survives on Rudgutter's sufferance." Isaac nodded and glanced at Yagharek. "That means there's loads of informers. Secrecy's safer." Derkhan and Isaac leaned over him, watched his hieroglyphs take shape. "So let's concentrate on the other two, see how they pan out."

After an hour of talk Isaac could not stay awake any longer. His head slumped as he listened. He began to drool on his collar. His tiredness spread out and infected Derkhan and Lemuel. They slept, briefly.

Like Isaac, they rolled unhappily in the muggy air, sweating in the close air of the shack. Isaac's sleep was more disturbed than theirs, and he whimpered several times in the heat. A little before noon, Lemuel pulled himself up and roused the others. Isaac awoke moaning Lin's name. He was fuddled with exhaustion and bad sleep and misery, and he forgot to be angry with Lemuel. He hardly recognized that Lemuel was there.

"I'm going to get some company," said Lemuel. "Isaac, you better get ready to prepare those helmets that Dee tells me about. We're going to need at least seven, I reckon."

"Seven?" mumbled Isaac. "Who're you getting? Where you off to?"

"As I've told you, I feel safer with a little protection," said Lemuel, and smiled coldly. "I put the word out that there was a little protection work going, and I gather there've been a few responses. I'm off to assess 'em. And I will guarantee to bring a metalhexer for you before the evening sets in. One of the applicants, or failing that there's a guy who owes me a favour in Abrogate Green. I'll see you both at . . . um . . . seven o'clock, outside the dump."

He left. Derkhan moved closer to Isaac in his exhausted misery and put her arm around him. He sniffled like a child in her arms, the dream of Lin still clinging to him.

A homegrown nightmare. A genuine misery from deep in his mind.

The militia crews were busy fitting enormous mirrors of polished metal to the backs of the airship harnesses.

It was impossible to refit the engine rooms or change the layout of the cabs, but they covered the front windows with thick black curtains. The pilot would spin the wheel blind, instructed by the yells from the officers halfway along the gantry, staring out of the rear windows above the enormous propellers, into the angled mirrors that offered a confusing but complete view of the sky before the dirigible.

Motley's hand-picked crew were escorted to the top of the Spike by Eliza Stem-Fulcher herself.

"I gather," she said to one of Motley's captains, a taciturn Remade human whose left arm had been replaced with an unruly python that he fought to quieten, "that you know how to pilot an aerostat." He nodded. She did not remark on the obvious illegality of that skill. "You'll be piloting the *Beyn's Honour*, your colleagues the *Avanc*. The militia have been warned. Keep an eye out for other air traffic. We thought you might want to get started this afternoon. The quarries tend to be inactive before the night, but we thought it might be an idea for you to get used to the controls."

The captain did not respond. All around him, his crew were checking their equipment, checking the angles of their helmets' mirrors. They were stern and cold. They seemed less fearful than the militia officers Stem-Fulcher had left in the training room below, practising aiming through mirrors, firing behind their own backs. Motley's men, after all, had dealt with the slake-moths more recently.

Like one of her own officers, she saw that a couple of the gangsters wore flamethrowers; hard backpacks of pressurized oil that burst through a flaming nozzle to ignite. They had been modified, as had her own man's, to spray the burning oil directly backwards out of the pack.

Stem-Fulcher stole another glance at several of Motley's extraordinary Remade troops. It was impossible to tell how much original organic material was retained under the Remades' metal layers. Certainly the impression was one of almost total replacement, with bodies sculpted with exquisite and unusual care to mimic human musculature.

At first sight, nothing of the human was visible. The Remade had heads of moulded steel. They even sported implacable faces of folded metal. Heavy industrial brows and inset eyes of stone or opaque glass, thin noses and pursed lips and cheekbones glinting darkly like polished pewter. The faces had been designed for aesthetic effect.

Stem-Fulcher had only realized that they were Remade, rather than fabulous constructs, when she had glimpsed the back of one's head. Embedded behind the splendid metal face was a much less perfect human one.

This was the only organic feature retained. Jutting out from the back end of those immobile metal features were mirrors, like a sweep of hair. They were held in front of the Remades' real, human eyes.

The body was at one hundred and eighty degrees to the human face, pistol-arms and legs and chest all facing the other way, with the metal head completing the illusion from the front. The Remade kept their bodies facing the same way as their unreversed companions at all times. They walked along corridors and into lifts with their arms and legs moving in a convincing automated analogue to a human stride. Stem-Fulcher had fallen deliberately behind them for a few steps, and watched their human eyes darting back and forth, their mouths twisted in concentration as they scanned what was ahead of them through their mirrors.

There were others, she saw, Remade more simply, with greater economy, to the same purpose. Their heads had been twisted around in a half-circle, until they gazed out from their own backs over a twisted, painful-looking neck. They stared into their mirrored helmets. Their bodies moved perfectly, without fumbling, walking and manipulating weapons and armour with hardly stilted motion. There was something almost more offputting about their relaxed, organic motions below reversed heads than the solid artificial motion of their more thoroughly Remade comrades.

Stem-Fulcher realized she was looking at the result of months or more of continual training, constantly living through mirrors. With bodies reversed as theirs were, it would have been a vital strategy. These troops, she pondered, must have been specifically designed and built with slake-moth husbandry in mind. Stem-Fulcher could hardly believe the scale of Motley's operation. It would be no wonder, she thought ruefully, if, in dealing with the slake-moths, the militia seemed a little amateurish by comparison.

I think we were quite right to bring them on board, she reflected.

With the passage of the sun, the air over New Crobuzon slowly thickened. The light was thick and yellow as corn-oil.

Aerostats swam through that solar grease, eddying back and forth across the urban geography in a weird half-random motion.

Isaac and Derkhan stood in the street beyond the dump's wire. Derkhan carried a bag, Isaac carried two. In the light, they felt vulnerable. They were unused to the city day. They had forgotten how to live in it.

They skulked as insignificantly as they could, and ignored the few passers-by.

"Why the godsdamn did Yag have to piss off like that?" hissed Isaac. Derkhan shrugged.

"He seems restless, all of a sudden," she said. She thought, then continued slowly. "I know it's bad timing," she said, "but I find it . . . quite moving. He's such a . . . an empty presence most of the time, you know? I mean, I know you get to talk to him in private, you know the . . . the *real* Yagharek . . . But most of the time he's a garuda-shaped absence." She corrected herself harshly. "No. He's *not* garuda-shaped, is he? That's the problem. He's more of a man-shaped absence. But now . . . well, he seems to be filling up. I'm beginning to sense that he *wants to do* something or other, and *doesn't* want to do something else."

Isaac nodded slowly.

"I know what you mean," he said. "There's definitely something changing in him. I told him not to leave and he just ignored me. He's definitely becoming more . . . wilful . . . if that's a good thing."

Derkhan was staring at him curiously.

She spoke slowly.

"You must be thinking of Lin all the time," she said.

Isaac looked away. He said nothing for a moment. Then he gave a quick nod.

"Always," he said abruptly, his face collapsing into the most shocking sadness. "Always. I can't . . . I haven't time to mourn. Yet."

A little way away, the road curved and separated into a small clutch of alleys. From one of these hidden culs-de-sac came a sudden metallic bang. Isaac and Derkhan tensed and flinched backwards against the chainlink fence.

There was a whispering, and Lemuel peered around the corner of the alley.

He caught sight of Isaac and Derkhan, grinned triumphantly. He pushed his hands in a shoving motion, indicating that they should get into the dump. They turned and found their way to the tear in the wire mesh, checked that they were not watched and wriggled through into the wasteground.

They moved quickly away from the street and turned corners in the muck, until they crouched in a space that was hidden from the city. Within two minutes, Lemuel came loping after them.

"Afternoon, all," he grinned, triumphantly.

"How did you get here?" said Isaac.

Lemuel sniggered. "Sewers. Got to keep out of sight. Not so dangerous with the lot I'm with." His smile faltered as he took them in. "Where's Yagharek?" he said.

"He insisted that he had to go somewhere. We told him to stay, but he wasn't having any of it. He says he'll find us here tomorrow at six."

Lemuel swore.

"Why did you let him go? What if they pick him up?"

"Damn, Lem, what in Jabber's name was I supposed to do?" hissed Isaac. "I can't *sit* on him. Maybe it's some damn religious thing, some bloody Cymek mystical rubbish. Maybe he thinks he's about to die and he has to say goodbye to his damn ancestors. I told him not to, he said he was going to."

"Fine, whatever," muttered Lemuel irritably. He turned to look back behind him. Isaac saw a small group of figures approaching. "These are our employees. I'm paying them, Isaac, and you're owing me."

There were three of them. They were immediately and absolutely recognizable as adventurers; rogues who wandered the Ragamoll and the Cymek and Fellid and probably the whole of Bas-Lag. They were hardy and dangerous, lawless, stripped of allegiance or morality, living off their wits, stealing and killing, hiring themselves out to whoever and whatever came. They were inspired by dubious virtues.

A few performed useful services: research, cartography and the like. Most were nothing but tomb raiders. They were scum who died violent deaths, hanging on to a certain cachet among the impressionable through their undeniable bravery and their occasionally impressive exploits.

Isaac and Derkhan eyed them without enthusiasm.

"This," said Lemuel, pointing to them each in turn, "is Shadrach, Pengefinchess and Tansell."

The three looked at Isaac and Derkhan with ruthless, swaggering arrogance.

Shadrach and Tansell were human, Pengefinchess was vodyanoi. Shadrach was obviously the hard man of the group. Large and sturdy, he wore a miscellaneous collection of armour, studded leather and flat, hammered pieces of iron strapped to shoulders, front and back. It was spattered with slime from the sewers. He followed Isaac's eyes to his outfit.

"Lemuel told us to expect trouble," he said in a curiously melodic voice. "We came dressed for the occasion."

In his belt swung an enormous pistol and a big, weighty machete-sword. The pistol was carved into an intricate shape, a monstrous horned face, its mouth the muzzle. It would vomit

forth the bullets. A flared blunderbuss flapped on his back, along
with a black shield. He would not be able to walk three steps in
the city like that without being arrested. No wonder they had
come through the city's underside.

Tansell was taller than Shadrach, but much more slight. His
armour was smarter, and seemed designed at least in part for
aesthetics. It was a burnished brown, layers of stiff curboille,
wax-boiled leather engraved with spiral designs. He carried a
smaller gun than Shadrach and a slender rapier.

"So what's happening, then?" said Pengefinchess, and Isaac
realized from the vodyanoi's voice that she was female. There
were, with vodyanoi, no physical characteristics for an inexpert
human to recognize that were not hidden below the loincloths.

"Well . . ." he said slowly, watching her.

She squatted like a frog before him and met his gaze. She
wore a voluminous white one-piece garment—incongruously
and bizarrely clean, given her recent journey—that fitted close
around her wrists and ankles, leaving her large, amphibious
hands and feet free. She carried a recurved bow and sealed
quiver over her shoulder, a bone knife in her belt. A large pouch
of some thick reptile skin was strapped to her belly. Isaac could
not tell what was within.

As Isaac and Derkhan watched, something bizarre happened
below Pengefinchess's clothes. There was a quick movement, as
if something wrapped itself around her body at speed and then
removed itself. As the weird tide passed, a large patch of the
white cotton of her shift became sodden with water, clinging
suddenly to her, then drying as if every atom of liquid was suddenly sucked out. Isaac stared, thunderstruck.

Pengefinchess looked down casually.

"That's my undine. She and I have a deal. I provide her certain
substances, she clings to me, keeps me wet and alive. Lets me
travel in much drier places than I'd otherwise manage."

Isaac nodded. He had never seen a water elemental before. It
was unsettling.

"Has Lemuel warned you of the sort of trouble we're facing?"
Isaac said. The adventurers nodded, unconcerned. Even excited.
Isaac tried to swallow his exasperation.

"These moth-things aren't the only thing you can't afford to
look at, sirrah," said Shadrach. "I can kill with my eyes closed, if
I have to." He spoke with soft, chilling confidence. "This belt?"
He tapped it nonchalantly. "Catoblepas hide. Killed it in the out-

skirts of Tesh. Didn't look at that, neither, or I'd be dead. We can handle these moths."

"I damn well hope so," said Isaac grimly. "Hopefully, no actual fighting'll be necessary. I think Lemuel feels safer with some backup, just in case. We're hoping the constructs'll take care of things."

Shadrach's mouth curled minutely, in what was probably contempt.

"Tansell's a metallo-thaumaturge," said Lemuel. "Aren't you?"

"Well . . . I know a few techniques for working metal," Tansell replied.

"It's not a complex job," said Isaac. "Just need a bit of welding. Come this way."

He led them through the rubbish to where they had hidden the mirrors and the other materials for the helmets.

"We've got easily enough stuff here," said Isaac, squatting beside the pile. He picked up a colander, length of copper piping and, after a moment of sifting, two sizeable chunks of mirror. He waved them at Tansell vaguely. "We need this to be a helmet that's going to fit snug—and we're going to need one for a garuda who's not here." He ignored the glance that Tansell exchanged with his companions. "And then we need these mirrors attached to the front, at an angle so we can easily see directly behind us. Think you can manage that?"

Tansell looked at Isaac contemptuously. The tall man sat cross-legged before the pile of metal and glass. He put the colander on his head, like a child playing at soldiers. He whispered under his voice, a weird lilting, and he began to massage his hands with quick and intricate movements. He pulled at his knuckles, kneaded the balls of his palms.

For several minutes, nothing happened. Then quite suddenly, his fingers began to glow from within, as if the bones were illuminated.

Tansell reached up and began to caress the colander, as gently as if he stroked a cat.

Slowly, the metal began to shape itself under his coaxing. It softened at each momentary touch, fitting more snugly onto his head, flattening down, distending at the back. Tansell pulled and kneaded it gently until it was quite flush over his hair. Then, still whispering his little sounds, he tweaked at the front, adjusting the lip of the metal, curling it up and away from his eyes.

He reached down and picked up the copper pipe, gripped it between his hands and channelled energy through his palms. Obstreperously, the metal began to flex. He coiled it gently, placing the two ends of the copper against the colander-helmet just above his temples, then pressing down hard until each piece of metal broke the surface tension of the other and began to spill across the divide. With a tiny fizz of energy, the thick piping and the iron colander fused.

Tansell shaped the bizarre extrusion of copper that jutted from the newborn helmet's front. It became an angled loop extending about a foot. He fumbled for the pieces of mirror, clicked his fingers until someone handed them to him. Humming to the copper, cajoling it, he softened its substance and pushed one, then the other piece of mirror into it, one in front of each of his eyes. He looked up into them, each in turn, adjusting them carefully until they offered him a clear view of the wall of rubbish behind him.

He tweaked the copper, hardened it.

Tansell removed his hands and looked up at Isaac. The helmet on his head was unwieldy, and its provenance from a colander was still absurdly obvious, but it was perfect for their needs. It had taken him a little more than fifteen minutes to fashion.

"I'm going to put a couple of holes in, thread a piece of leather through for a chinstrap, just in case," he muttered.

Isaac nodded, impressed.

"That's perfect. We need . . . uh . . . seven of those, one of them for a garuda. That's a *rounder* head, remember. I'm going to leave you to it for a minute." He looked over at Derkhan and Lemuel. "I think I'd better liaise with the Council," he said.

He turned and traced his way through the dump labyrinth.

"Good evening, der Grimnebulin," said the avatar, in the heart of the rubbish. Isaac nodded a greeting to it, and to the enormous skeleton shape of the Council itself, which waited beyond. "You did not come alone." His voice was emotionless as ever.

"Please don't start," said Isaac. "We are *not* going to get into this on our own. We are one fat scientist, a crook and a journalist. We need some fucking professional back-up. These are people who kill exotic animals for a damn *living*, and they have not the slightest damn interest in telling anyone about you. All they know is that some fucking constructs are going to be there with us. Even if they could work out who or what you were, they've probably broken at least two-thirds of New Crobuzon's laws by now, so they ain't about to damn well go running to Rudgutter." There was silence. "Just damn well *compute it*, if you want. You are in no risk at all from the three reprobates busy making helmets."

Isaac imagined that he felt a trembling under his feet, as the information raced through the Council's innards. After a long pause, the avatar and the Council nodded warily. Isaac did not relax.

"I've come for those of yourself you can risk for tomorrow's business," he said. The Council nodded again.

"Very well," said the Construct Council slowly with the dead man's tongue. "First, as we discussed, I will take the part of caretaker. Have you the crisis engine?"

Something hard moved across Isaac's face. It went quickly.

"Right here," he said, and put one of his bags down in front of the avatar. The naked man opened it and bent down to peer inside at the tubes and glass within, giving Isaac a sudden, vile view into the scabbing hollow of his skull. He picked it up and walked over to the Council with it, depositing it before the enormous figure's crotch.

"So," said Isaac. "You hang on to that, just in case they find our shack. Good idea. I'll be back for it in the morning." He glowered. "Which of you are coming with us? We need some power behind us."

"I cannot risk discovery, Grimnebulin," the avatar said. "If I were to come in my hidden selves, those construct bodies that work by day in grand houses and building sites and bank vaults, biding their time and accumulating knowledge, and they were to come back battered and broken, or not come back at all, I would leave myself open to the inquiry of the city. And I am not ready for that. Not yet." Isaac nodded slowly. "Accordingly, I will be coming with you in those shapes that I can afford to lose. That will arouse confusion and bewilderment, but not suspicion of the truth."

Behind Isaac, the rubbish began to skitter and fall away. He turned.

From the reams of discarded objects, particular aggregations of trash were separating themselves. Like the Construct Council itself, they were clotted together from the materia of the dump.

The constructs mimicked the form and size of chimpanzees. They clattered and clanged as they moved, with a weird and unsettling sound. Each was unique. Their heads were kettles and lampshades, their hands were vicious-looking claws ripped from scientific instruments and scaffolding joints. They were armoured in great scabs of metal plating torn, roughly welded and riveted to their bodies, which scampered across the wasteland in an unsettling half-simian motion. They were created with an extraordinary sense of found aesthetics.

If they lay still, they would be invisible: nothing but a random accretion of old metal.

Isaac gazed at the chimp-things, swinging and jumping, dripping water and oil, ticking with clockwork.

"I have downloaded into each of their analytical engines," said the avatar, "as much memory and capacity as they will hold. These of me can obey you, and understand the urgency of doing so. I have given them viral intelligence. They have been programmed with the data to recognize the slake-moths, and to attack them. Each is built with acid or phlogistic agent within its midriff." Isaac nodded, wondering at the casual ease with which the Council created these murderous machines. "You have worked out the best plan?"

"Well . . ." said Isaac. "We're going to prepare tonight. Work out some kind of . . . uh . . . gear up, you know, plan with our . . . additional staff. Then tomorrow at sixish we'll meet Yag here, assuming the stupid bastard hasn't got himself killed. And then we're going to get into the Riverskin ghetto, using Lemuel's expertise.

"Then we go moth-hunting." Isaac's voice was hard and staccato. He spat out what he needed to say quickly. "The thing is we've got to separate them. We can take one, I think. Otherwise, if there are two or more, then one will always be in front of us, able to flash the wings. So we're going to scope the place out, see if we can work out where they are. It's hard to say without seeing it. We'll take the amplifier and channeller you used on me, as well. It might help us get one interested, get it sniffing. Push a little peak through the background mental noise, or something. Can you attach other helmets to the one engine? D'you *have* any extras?" The avatar nodded. "You'd better give them to me, and show me the different functions. I'll get Tansell to adjust them, add some mirrors.

"Thing is," said Isaac thoughtfully, "it can't just be the *strength* of the signal that attracts them, or it would only ever be the seers and communicatrixes and so on that got taken. I think they like particular *flavours*. That's why the runt came for me. Not because there was a big waving trail above the city, any old trail, but because it recognized and wanted that *particular* mind. And . . . well, now, maybe the others are going to recognize it as well. Maybe I was wrong that only the one would ever recognize my mind. They must've sniffed it last night." He looked at the avatar thoughtfully. "They're going to remember it as the trail their brother or sister was after when it got killed. I don't know if that's a good thing or a bad thing . . ."

"Der Grimnebulin," said the dead man after a moment, "you must bring at least one of my little selves back with you. They must download what they have seen into me, the Council. I can learn so much of the Glasshouse from this. It can only help us. Whatever happens, one must get free."

There were several moments of silence. The Council waited. Isaac thought for something to say, and then could not. He looked up into the avatar's eyes.

"I'll be back tomorrow. Have your monkey-selves ready then. And then I will . . . I *will* . . . see you again," he said.

The city basked in extraordinary night-heat. The summer reached a critical moment. In the striae of dirty air above the city's core, the slake-moths danced.

They flitted giddily over the minarets and crags of Perdido Street Station. They twitched their wings infinitesimally, edging expertly up the thermals. Skeins of inconstant emotion spun out from their cavorting.

With silent pleadings and caresses they courted each other. Wounds, already half healed, were now forgotten, in trembling, febrile excitement.

The summer here, in this once verdant plain on the edge of the Gentleman's Sea, came a month and a half earlier than for the slake-moths' siblings across the water. The temperature had slowly spiralled, reaching twenty-year highs.

Thermotaxic reactions were triggered in the slake-moths' loins. Hormones swam in their ichor tides. Unique configurations of flesh and chymicals spurred their ovaries and gonads into untimely productivity. They became suddenly fertile, and aggressively aroused.

Aspises and bats and birds fled the air in terror, pungent as it was with psychotic desires.

The slake-moths flirted with ghastly and lascivious aerial ballet. They touched tentacles and limbs, unfolded new parts they had never seen before. The three less damaged moths tugged their sibling, the victim of the Weaver, on wafts of smoke and air. Gradually, the most wounded moth stopped licking its multitude of wounds with its trembling tongue, and began to touch its fellows. Their erotic charge was utterly infectious.

The polymorphous four-way wooing became fraught and competitive. Stroking, touching, arousing. Each moth in turn spiralled moonward, drunk on lust. It would split the seal on a gland hidden under its tail and exude a cloud of empathic musk.

Its fellows lapped at the psychoscent, sported like porpoises in clouds of carnality. They rolled and played then swept up and sprayed the sky themselves. For now, their sperm ducts were still. The little metadroplets were rich with the slake-moths' erogenous, ovigenic juices. They bickered lecherously to be female.

Each successive exudation charged the air to a higher pitch of excitement. The moths bared their gravestone teeth and bleated their sexual challenge to each other. The moist valves below their chitin dripped with aphrodisiac. They swept through the banks of each other's perfume.

As the pheremonal duel continued, one febrile voice sounded more and more triumphant. One body swept higher and higher, its fellows dropping away. Its emanations stank the air of sex. There were last-gasp attacks, spurts of erotic challenge. But one by one, the other moths closed their female pudenda, accepting defeat and masculinity.

The triumphant moth—the moth still scarred and dripping from its mêlée with the Weaver—soared. Its scent still stank of female juices, its fecundity was unquestioned. It had proved itself the most motherly.

It had gained the right to bear the brood.

The other three moths adored it. They became swains.

The feel of the new matriarch's flesh made them ecstatic. They looped and fell and returned, aroused and ardent.

The mother-moth toyed with them, led them over the hot dark city. When their beseeching became as painful as its own lust, it hovered and presented itself, opened its segmented exoskeleton and curled its vagina towards them.

It coupled with them, one by one, becoming briefly a dangerous plummeting double-bodied thing, flanked by eager partners waiting their turn. The three who had become male felt organic mechanisms pull and twist, their bellies opening and penises emerging for the first time. They fumbled with their arms and flesh-ropes and bone jags and their matriarch did the same, reaching behind it with a complex twist of limbs that grabbed and tugged and intertwined.

Sudden slipping connections were made. Each pair consorted and copulated with a fervent need and pleasure.

When the hours of rutting had passed, the four slake-moths drifted on open wings, utterly exhausted. They dripped.

As the air cooled, their bed of thermals deflated slowly, and they began to beat their wings to stay aloft. One by one, the three fathers peeled away and down to the city below, to search for food to revive and sustain them, and to provide for their conjugal partner.

It lolled in the sky a while longer. When it had been alone for a time, its antennae twitched and it curled away and began to make its slow way south. It was exhausted. Its sexual organs and orifices had closed away beneath its iridescent shell, to keep hold of all that had been spent.

The slake-moth matriarch flew towards Riverskin and the cactus dome, ready to prepare the nest.

My talons flex, trying to open. They are constrained by the ridiculous and vile bandages wound around them, that flap like ragged skin.

I walk bent double along the sides of the railways, the trains screaming at me in irate warning as they blast by. I sneak now across the rail bridge, watching the Tar coil beneath me. I stop and look around. Way ahead of me and way behind the river slithers and throws rubbish in rhythmic little bursts against the bank.

Looking over to the west I can see over the water and the swell of Riverskin houses to the tip of the Glasshouse. It is illuminated from inside, a blister of light on the city's skin.

I am changing. There is something within me which was not there before, or perhaps it is that something has gone. I smell the air and it is the same air it was yesterday, and yet it is different. There can be no doubt. Something is welling up under my own skin. I am not sure who I am.

I have trailed these humans as if I am dumb. A worthless, mindless presence, without opinion or intellect. Without knowing who I am, how can I know what to say?

I am not Respected Yagharek any longer, and I have not been for many months. I am not the raging thing that stalked the Shankell pits, that slaughtered man and trow, ratjinn and shardmouth, a menagerie of pugnacious beasts and warriors of races I had not dreamed could exist. That savage fighter is gone.

I am not the tiring one who stalked the lush grasslands and cold, hard hills. I am not the lost thing that wandered the concrete walkways of the city introspective and lost, seeking to become again something I never was.

I am none of those. I am changing, and I do not know what I will be.

*   *   *

I am afraid of the Glasshouse. Like Shankell, it has many names. The Glasshouse, the Greenhouse, the Planthouse, the Hothouse. It is nothing but a ghetto, dealt with sleight of hand. A ghetto in which the cactacae try to replicate the edge of the desert. Am I returning home?

To ask the question is to answer it. The Glasshouse is not the veldt, or the desert. It is a sad illusion, nothing but a mirage. It is not my home.

And if it were the desert, if it were a gateway to the deepest Cymek, to the dry forests and fertile swampland, to the repository of sand-hidden life and the great nomadic garuda library, if the Glasshouse were more than a shadow, if it were the desert it feigns to be, it would still not be my home.

That place does not exist.

I shall wander for a night and a day. I will retrace the steps that once I made, in the shade of the railways. I will stalk the city's monstrous geography and find the streets that bore me here, the squat channels in the brick to which I owe my life and self.

I will find the tramps who shared my food, if they are not dead from disease or stabbed for their piss-stained shoes. They became my tribe, atomized and ruined and broken, but still some kind of tribe. Their numb lack of interest in me—in anything—was refreshing after days of careful skulking and an hour or two of ostentatious wandering in my agonizing wooden prostheses. I owe them nothing, those tedious alcohol- and drug-fucked heads, but I will find them again for my own sake, not theirs.

I feel as if I walk these streets for the last time.

Am I to die?

There are two possibilities.

I will help Grimnebulin and we will defeat these moths, these horrific night-creatures, these soul-drinkers, and he will create of me a battery. He will reward me, he will charge me up like a phlogistic cell and I will fly. As I think it I am climbing. I reach higher and higher on these girder-steps, climbing the city like a ladder to gaze at its tawdry, teeming night. I feel the flabby stubs of my wing muscles try to flap with a pathetic rudimentary motion. I will not rise on tides of air pushed down by feathers, but I will flex my mind like a wing and soar on channels of power, transformative energy, thaumaturgic flow, the binding and exploding force that inheres, that Grimnebulin calls crisis.

I will be a marvel.

Or I will fail and die. I will fall and be skewered on harsh metal, or my dreams will be sucked from my mind and fed to some hatchling devil.

Will I feel it? Will I live on in the milk? Will I know that I am being drunk?

The sun is creeping into view. I am tiring.

I know that I should have stayed. If I am to be anything real, something more than the mute, imbecilic presence I have so far been, I should stay and intervene and plan and prepare and nod at their suggestions, supplement them with my own. I am, I was, a hunter. I can stalk the monsters, the horrendous beasts.

But I could not. I tried to say my sorries, to let Grimnebulin— even Blueday—know that I am one with them, that I am part of the gang. The crew. The posse. The moth-hunters. But it rang hollow in my skull.

I will look and find myself, and then I will know if I can tell them that. And if not, what I can say instead.

I will arm myself. I will bring weapons. I will find a knife, a whip like that I used to wield. Even if I find myself an outsider, I will not let them die unaided. I will sell our lives dear to the thirsting things.

I hear sad music. There is a moment of uncanny quiet, when the trains and the barges pass away from me in my eyrie, and the grinding of their engines ebbs away and the dawn is momentarily uncovered.

Someone at the river's edge, in some garret, is playing the fiddle. It is a haunting strain, a tremulous dirge of semitones and counterpoints over a broken rhythm. These do not sound like local harmonies.

I recognize the sound. I have heard it before. On the boat that took me across the Meagre Sea, and before that in Shankell.

There is no escaping my southern past, it seems.

It is the dawn greeting of the fisherwomen of Perrick Nigh and the Mandrake Islands, way to the south. My unseen accompanist is welcoming the sun.

The few New Crobuzon Perrickish live mostly in Echomire, yet here she is, three miles upstream as the river twists, waking the great Dayfisher with her exquisite playing.

She plays to me for a few more moments, before the noise of the morning takes her sound away, and I am left clinging to the bridge, listening to the boom of klaxons and the whistle from the trains.

That sound from far away continues, but I cannot hear it. The noises of New Crobuzon fill my ears. I will follow them, welcome them. I will let them surround me. I will dive into the hot, city life. Under arch and over stone, through the sparse bone forest of the Ribs, into the brick burrows of Badside and Dog Fenn, through the booming industry of Gross Coil. Like Lemuel sniffing for contacts I will retrace all the steps I have made. And here and there, I hope, among the spires and the crammed architecture, I will touch the immigrants, the refugees, the outsiders who re-make New Crobuzon every day. This place with bastard culture. This mongrel city.

I will hear the sounds of Perrick violining or the Gnurr Kett funeral dirge or a Chet stone-riddle, or I will smell the goat por-ridge they eat in Neovadan or see a doorway painted with the symbols of a Cobsea printer-captain . . . A long, long way from their homes. Homeless. Home.

All around me will be New Crobuzon, seeping in through my skin.

When I return to Griss Twist, my companions will be waiting, and we will liberate this hijacked city. Thanklessly and unseen.

PART SIX

The Glasshouse

CHAPTER FORTY-TWO

The streets of Riverskin inclined gently upwards towards the Glasshouse. The houses were old and tall, with rotting wooden frames and walls of damp plaster. Every rain saturated and blistered them, sent slates cascading from the steep roofs as rusted nails dissolved. Riverskin seemed to sweat, gently, in the slow heat.

The southern half of Riverskin was indistinguishable from Flyside, which it adjoined. It was cheap and not too violent, crowded, mostly good-natured. It was a mixed area, with a large human majority beside small colonies of vodyanoi by the quiet canal, a few solitary outcast cactacae, even a little two-street khepri hive, a rare traditional community outside of Kinken and Creekside. Southern Riverskin was also home to some of the city's small number of more exotic races. There was a shop run by a hotchi family in Bekman Avenue, their spines carefully filed blunt so as not to intimidate their neighbours. There was a homeless llorgiss, which kept its barrel body full of drink and staggered the streets on three unsteady legs.

But northern Riverskin was very different. It was quieter, more sullen. It was the preserve of the cactacae.

Large as the Glasshouse was, it could not possibly contain all the cactacae of the city, not even those who kept faith with tradition. At least two-thirds of New Crobuzon's cactus people lived outside its protective glass. They packed the Riverskin slums, and a few other quarters in places like Syriac and Abrogate Green. But Riverskin was the centre of their city, and there they mixed in equal numbers with human locals. They were the cactus underclass, who entered the Glasshouse to shop and worship, but were forced to live in the infidel city.

Some rebelled. Angry cactacae youths vowed never to enter the Glasshouse which had betrayed them. They referred to it ironically by an older, obsolete name: the Nursery. They scarred themselves and fought in brutal, pointless and exciting gang-fights. Sometimes they terrorized the neighbourhood, mugging and stealing from the humans and cactacae elders who shared their streets.

Outside, in Riverskin, the cactus people were surly and quiet. They worked for their human or vodyanoi bosses without demur or enthusiasm. They did not communicate with their workmates of other races in anything more than curt grunts. Their behaviour inside the walls of the Glasshouse was never seen.

The Glasshouse itself was a huge, flattened dome. On the ground, its diameter was more than a quarter of a mile. At its peak, it was eighty yards high. Its base was angled to sit tight on the listing streets of Riverskin.

The framework was wrought in black iron, a great thick skeleton decorated with occasional curlicues and flourishes. It bulged out over the Riverskin houses, visible from a long way off on the top of its low hill. Emerging in two concentric circles from its skin were colossal girdered arms, nearly the size of the Ribs, suspending the dome and taking its weight on great cords of twisted metal.

The further away it was seen from, the more impressive the Glasshouse appeared. From the wooded top of Flag Hill, looking down across two rivers, the railways, the skyrails and four miles of grotesque urban sprawl, the facets of the dome glinted with clean shards of light. From the surrounding streets, however, the multitude of cracks and dark spaces where glass had fallen in were visible. The dome had been repaired only once in its three centuries of existence.

From the base of the dome the age of the structure showed. It was decrepit. Paint curled in great tongues away from the metalwork, and rust had eaten it like worms. For the first fifteen or so feet above the ground, the panes—each nearly seven feet square at the bottom, descending in width like pieces of pie as they approached the vertex—were filled with the same crumbling, painted iron. Above that, the glass was dirty and impure, tinted green and blue and beige in chance patchwork. It was reinforced, and was supposed to be able to support the weight of at least two decent-sized cactacae. Even so, several panes were broken and empty of glass, and many more were laced with a filigree of cracks.

The dome had been built without much concern for the surrounding houses. The pattern of streets that surrounded it continued until they reached its solid metal base. Those two or three or four houses that had been in the way of the dome's edges had been crushed, and then the rows continued beneath the glass canopy, at a variety of random angles.

The cactacae had simply enclosed an existing clutch of New Crobuzon streets.

Over the decades, the architecture within the dome had been altered to adapt the once-human houses to cactacae tenants, tearing down some structures and replacing them with strange new edifices. But the broad layout and much of the structure was said to remain, exactly as it was before the dome existed.

There was one entrance to the dome, at the southern tip of its base in Yashur Plaza. At the opposite end of its circumference was its exit on Bytrash Street, a steep road that looked down onto the river. Cactus law stated that entrance to and exit from the Glasshouse was only by these portals respectively. This was unlucky for the cactacae who lived just outside in sight of one or other of the portals. Getting in, for example, might take two minutes, but returning home from the exit would involve a long, tangled walk home.

Each morning at five the gateways were thrown open, onto the short enclosed passage beyond, and each evening at midnight they were closed. They were guarded by a small unit of armoured guards, hefting huge war-cleavers and the powerful cactacae rivebow.

Like their dumb, rooted cousins, the cactacae had thick, fibrous vegetable skin. It was taut and punctured easily, but it healed fast, in ugly, thick scars—most cactacae were covered in harmless ganglions of scab tissue. It took a lot of thrusts or a lucky shot into the organs to have any real damaging effect. Bullets or arrows or quarrels were usually ineffective against cactacae. Which was why the cactus soldiers carried rivebows.

The designers of the first rivebow had been human. The weapons had been used during the ghastly premiership of Mayor Collodd—they had been carried by the human guards of the mayor's cactus farm. But after the reforming Sapience Bill dissolved the farm and granted cactacae something approaching citizenship, the pragmatic cactus elders had realized this would be an invaluable weapon to keep their own people in line. Since then, the bow had been improved many times, this time by cactacae engineers.

The rivebow was an enormous crossbow, too large and heavy for a human effectively to operate. It fired not bolts, but chakris; flat metal disks with serrated or razored edges, or metal stars with curved arms. A toothed hole in the chakri's centre slotted neatly onto a little bud of metal that emerged from the rivebow shaft. When the trigger was pulled, the wire in the shaft snapped violently to, pulling the metal bud at massive speed, intricate gears grinding together to send it spinning at an enormous rate. At the end of the enclosed channel the whirling bolt slipped sharply down and out from the chakri's hole, and the chakri was discharged as fast as a slingshot stone, spinning like the blade of a circular saw.

Aerial friction dissipated its momentum quickly: it did not have nearly the range of a longbow or a flintlock. But it could sever a cactus limb or head—or a human one—at nearly one hundred feet, and slice savagely some way beyond that.

The cactacae guards glowered, and swung their rivebows with surly arrogance.

The late rays of the day blazed out from above the far-off peaks. The west-facing aspects of the Glasshouse dome glowed like rubies.

Straddling a corroded ladder that swept up to the peak of the dome, a silhouetted human figure grasped and clung to the metal. The man crept gradually up the rungs, rising up the curved firmament of the dome like the moon.

The walkway was one of three that extended at regular intervals from the very top of the dome's arch, designed originally for the repair crews that had never appeared. The curve of the dome seemed to break the surface of the earth like the tip of a bent back, implying a vast body below ground. The figure was riding a gargantuan whaleback. He was buoyed up by the light that the dome trapped, that played on the underside of the glass and made the whole great edifice shine. He kept low, moving very slowly to avoid being seen. He had chosen the ladder on the Glasshouse's north-western side, so as to avoid the trains on the Salacus Fields branch of the Sud Line. The tracks passed close by the glass on the opposite side of the dome, and any observant passengers would see the man crawling up the curved surface.

Eventually, after several minutes climbing, the intruder reached a metal lip that surrounded the apex of the great structure. The keystone itself was a single globe of limpid glass about eight feet in diameter. It sat perfectly in the circular hole at the dome's apogee, suspended half in, half out like some great plug. The man stopped and looked out over the city, through the tips of the supporting struts and the thick suspension wires. The wind whipped about him, and he clung to the handholds with vertiginous terror. He looked up into the darkening sky, the stars dim to him from all the clotted light that surrounded him, that ebbed through the glass below his body.

He turned his attention to that glass, scanned its surface minutely, pane by pane.

After some minutes he raised himself and began to climb backwards down the rails. Down, fumbling with his feet, feeling for holds, gently probing with outstretched toes, pulling himself back towards the earth.

The ladder ran out twelve feet from the earth, and the man slid down on the grappling hook he had used to get up. He touched the dusty ground and looked around him.

"Lem," he heard someone hiss. "Over here."

Lemuel Pigeon's companions were hiding in a gutted building at the edge of a rubble-strewn wasteground flanking the dome. Isaac was just visible, gesticulating at him from behind the doorless threshold.

Lemuel paced quickly across the thin scrub, treading on bricks and concrete overgrown and anchored with grass. He turned his back on the early evening light and slipped into the gloom of the burnt-out shell.

In the shadow before him crouched Isaac, Derkhan, Yagharek and the three adventurers. There was a pile of ruined equipment behind them, steam-pipes and conducting wires, the clasps from retort stands, lenses like marbles. Lemuel knew that the mess would resolve itself into five monkey-constructs as soon as they moved.

"Well?" demanded Isaac.

Lemuel nodded slowly.

"I was told right," he said quietly. "There's a big crack up near the top of the dome, in the north-eastern quarter. From where I was it was a bit hard to tell the size, but I figure it's at least . . . six feet by four. I looked pretty hard up there, and that was the only break I saw big enough for anything man-sized or thereabouts to get in or out. Did you have a little glance around the base?"

Derkhan nodded. "Nothing," she said. "I mean, plenty of little cracks, even a few places where a fair bit of glass was missing, especially higher up, but there were no holes big enough to get through. That must be the one."

Isaac and Lemuel nodded.

"So that's how they're getting in and out," said Isaac softly. "Well, it seems to me the best way of tracking them is to reverse their journey. Much as I damn well hate to suggest it, I think we should get up there. What's it like inside?"

"You can't see all that much," said Lemuel, and shrugged. "The glass is thick, old and damn dirty. They only clean it once every three or four years, I think. You can make out the basic shapes of houses and streets and what have you, but that's about all. You'd have to look inside to get the lay of the place."

"We can't all troop up there," said Derkhan. "We'll be seen. We should've asked Lemuel to go in, he's the man for the job."

"I wouldn't have gone anyway," said Lemuel tightly. "I don't enjoy being that high up, and I certainly damn well won't dangle upside down hundreds of feet above thirty thousand pissed-off cactacae . . ."

"Well, what are we going to do?" Derkhan was irritated. "We could wait until nightfall, but then the bloody moths are active. What we'll have to do is go up one at a time. If, that is, it's safe to. We need someone to go first . . ."

"I will go," said Yagharek.

There was silence. Isaac and Derkhan stared at him.

"Great!" said Lemuel archly, and clapped twice. "That's that sorted. So you can go up, and then . . . um . . . you can look around for us, chuck us down a message . . ."

Isaac and Derkhan were ignoring Lemuel. They were still staring at Yagharek.

"It is right that I should go," said Yagharek. "I am at home so high," he said and his voice clucked slightly, as if at a sudden emotion. "I am at home so high, and I am a hunter. I can look down on the landscape within and see where the moths might lurk. I can gauge the possibilities within the glass."

Yagharek retraced Lemuel's steps up the shell of the Glasshouse.

He had unwrapped the foetid bandages from his feet, and his talons had stretched out in a delightful reflex. He had scrambled up the initial patch of bare metal with Lemuel's grappling rope, and then had climbed far faster and more confidently than the human had done.

He stopped every so often and stood swaying in the warm wind, his avian toes gripping the metal slats tightly and securely. He would lean alarmingly and peer into the hazy air, hold out his arms a little, feel the wind fill his spreadeagled body like a sail.

Yagharek pretended he was flying.

Swinging from his thin belt was the stiletto and the bullwhip he had stolen the previous day. The whip was a clumsy thing, not nearly so fine as the one he had cracked in the hot desert air, stinging and snaring, but it was a weapon his hand remembered.

He was fast and assured. The airships that were visible were all far away. He was unseen.

At the top of the Glasshouse, the city seemed to be a gift to him, laid out ready to be taken. Everywhere he looked, fingers and hands and fists and spines of architecture thrust rudely into the sky. The Ribs like ossified tentacles reaching always up; the Spike slammed into the city's heart like a skewer; the complex mechanistic vortex of Parliament, glowing darkly; Yagharek mapped them with a cold, strategic eye. He glanced up and to the east, to where the skyrail connecting Flyside Tower and the Spike thrummed.

When he had reached the edge of the enormous glass globe at the dome's tip, it took him only a moment to find the rent in the glass. A part of him was surprised that his eyes, the eyes of a bird of prey, could still perform for him as they used to.

Below him, a foot or two under the gently curving ladder, the glass of the dome was dry and scaled with bird and wyrmen droppings. He tried to peer through, but he could make out nothing beyond the shadowy suggestions of roofs and streets.

Yagharek struck out across the glass itself.

He moved tentatively, feeling with his talons, tapping the glass to test it, sliding as quickly as he could to a metal frame for his claws to grip. As he moved he realized how at ease he had become with climbing. All those weeks and weeks of night-time climbing, on the roof of Isaac's workshop, up into deserted towers, seeking the city's crags. He climbed easily and without fear. He was more ape than bird, it seemed.

He skittered nervously across the dirty panes, until he breached the final wall of girders that separated him from the split in the glass. And when he vaulted that, the fault was before him.

Leaning over, Yagharek could feel heat gusting from the lamplit depths within. The night outside was warm, but the temperature within must be very high.

He wound the grappling hook carefully around the metal joist at one side of the crack and tugged it hard to ensure it was secure. Then he wrapped the end of the rope three times around his waist. He gripped it near the hook, lay across the girder and put his head in through the lips of broken glass.

It felt like pushing his face into a bowl of strong tea. The air inside the Glasshouse was hot, almost stiflingly so, and full of smoke and steam. It shone with a hard, white light.

Yagharek blinked his eyes clean and shielded them, then looked down on the cactus town.

In the centre, below the massive nugget of glass at the dome's tip, the houses had been cleared away and a stone temple had been built. It was red stone, a steep ziggurat, that reached a third of the way to the Glasshouse roof. Every stepped level was lush with desert and veldt vegetation, abloom in garish reds and oranges against their waxy green skins.

A little rim of land, about twenty feet wide, had been cleared all around it, beyond which point the streets of Riverskin had been left. The cartography was a snarled puzzle, a collection of road-ends and the rumps of avenues, here the corner of a park and there half a church, even the stump of a canal, now a trough of stagnant water, cut off by the edge of the dome. Lanes crisscrossed the little township at odd angles, segments cut from longer streets where the dome had been placed over them. A little random patch of alleys and roads had been contained, sealed under glass. Its content had changed even as the outlines remained mostly the same.

The chaotic aggregate of street-stubs had been reformed by the cactacae. What, years ago, had been a wide thoroughfare had been made a vegetable garden, the edges of its lawns flush with the houses on either side, little trails from front doors indicating the routes between patches of pumpkin and radishes.

Ceilings had been removed four generations ago to convert human houses into homes for their new, much taller inhabitants. Rooms had been added to the tops and backsides of buildings, styled like weird miniature effigies of the stepped pyramid in the centre of the Glasshouse. The additional buildings had been wedged into every space possible, to cram the dome with cactacae, and strange agglomerations of human architecture and monolithic, stone-slab edifices stretched in big blocks of variegated colour. Some were several storeys tall.

Swaying, dipping bridges of wood and rope were draped between many of the upper floors, linking rooms and buildings on opposite sides of streets. In many of the yards and on the tops of many buildings, low walls enclosed flat desert-gardens, with tiny patches of scrubby grass, a few low cactuses and undulating sand.

Little flocks of captive birds that had never found the shattered vents to the outside city swept low over the houses and called out in hunger. With a lurch of adrenalin and nostalgic shock, Yagharek recognized a bird-call from the Cymek. There were dune-eagles, he realized, perching on one or two roofs.

Rising around them on all sides, the dome refracted New Crobuzon like a dirty glass sky, rendering the surrounding houses a confusion of darkness and deflected light. The whole diorama below him thronged with cactus people. Yagharek scanned slowly, but he could not see another sapient race.

The simple bridges swung as cactacae passed over them in all directions. In the sand-gardens, Yagharek saw cactacae with big rakes and wooden paddles carefully sculpting the sastrugi that mimicked the rippling dunes made by the wind. Here in this tightly closed space, bounded on every side, there were no gusts to carve patterns, and the desert landscape had to be wrought by hand.

The streets and paths were tight crammed with cactacae buying and selling in the market, arguing gruffly too low for Yagharek to hear. They pulled wooden carts by hand, two working together if the vehicle or load was particularly large. There were no constructs in sight, no cabs, no animals of any sort beyond the birds and a few rock-rabbits Yagharek caught sight of on the ledges of buildings.

In the city outside, cactacae women wore great shapeless dresses like sheets. Here in the Glasshouse they wore only loincloths of white and beige and dun cloth, exactly like the men. Their breasts were somewhat larger than the men's, and tipped with dark green nipples. In a few places, Yagharek could see a woman carrying a baby held tight to her chest, the child unworried by the pinprick wounds its mother's spines inflicted. Boisterous little gangs of cactacae children played on corners, ignored or cuffed absently by passing adults.

On every part of the pyramid temple were cactacae elders, reading, gardening, smoking and talking. Some wore sashes of red or blue around their shoulders, that stood out strongly against their pale green skin.

Yagharek's skin was prickling with sweat. Wafts of woodsmoke blurred his vision. They rose from a hundred chimneys at all different heights, trickling gently into the sky and eddying in slow mushrooming gusts. A few hazy threads found their way up and seeped from the cracks and holes in the glass sky. But with the wind kept out and the sun magnified by the vaulted translucent bubble, there were no breezes or bluster to dissipate the fumes. The underside of the glass, Yagharek saw, was coated in greasy soot.

There was still more than an hour to sundown. Yagharek glanced to his left and saw that the orb of glass atop the dome seemed to be bursting with light. It was sucking up every scrap of the sun's emissions, concentrating them and sending them vividly into every nook of the Glasshouse, filling it with unforgiving light and heat. He saw that the metal casing which held it was wired for power, with cables snaking down the insides of the dome and disappearing from sight.

The flat sand-garden at the top of the layered tower at the Glasshouse's centre was covered in complex machinery. Exactly below the swollen nugget of clear glass was a huge lensed machine, with fat pipes snaking out into vats around it. A cactacae with a coloured sash polished its copper workings.

Yagharek remembered rumours he had heard in Shankell, stories about a heliochymical engine of immense thaumaturgic power. He looked carefully at the glowing contraption, but its purpose was quite opaque.

As he watched, Yagharek became conscious of the large number of armed posses that were evident. He narrowed his eyes. He was gazing down at them like some god, seeing every surface of the little cactus town in the fierce light of the glass globe. He could see almost all the rooftop gardens, and it seemed to him that on at least half, a group of three or four cactus were stationed. They sat or stood, their expressions unreadable at such a distance, but the massive, weighty rivebows they carried were unmistakable. Hatchets dangled from their belts, curved poleaxes glowed in the reddening light.

There were more of the little patrols beside stalls in the sprawling market, sitting alert on the lowest level of the central temple, and walking the streets with a deliberate step, rivebows cocked and ready.

Yagharek saw the looks that the armed guards received, the nervous salutations and the frequent skyward glances of the populace.

He did not think that this situation was normal.

Something was making the cactus people uneasy. They could be truculent and taciturn, in his experience, but the subdued air of menace was like nothing he had experienced in Shankell. Perhaps, he reflected, these cactacae were different, a more sombre breed than their southern siblings. But he felt his skin prickle. The air was fraught.

Yagharek concentrated, and began to scan the inside of the dome with a hard, rigorous eye. He focused carefully, went into something of a hunter's trance.

He started looking at the edges of the dome. He took in the whole inside circumference in one long, slow sweep, then spiralled his vision carefully towards the centre, examining and investigating the circle of houses and streets a little way in, and then further in again.

In this exacting, methodical way, he could cast his eye on every nook and cranny of the Glasshouse's surfaces. His eyes stopped briefly, momentarily, on imperfections of the red stone, then moved on.

As the day came closer to its end, the nervousness of the cactus people seemed to increase.

Yagharek came to the end of his scanning sweep. There was nothing immediate, nothing clearly wrong that leapt out at him. He turned his attention to the inside of the roof immediately around him, looking for some purchase.

It would not be easy. Some way from him the girders coalesced around the heavy glass globe, but on the underside of the glass they were not as protuberant. He believed that with some effort he could climb them: as, probably, could Lemuel and perhaps Derkhan or one or two of the adventurers. But it was hard to imagine Isaac clinging so close and holding his bulk suspended, crawling hundreds of yards of dangerous metal piping to the earth.

The sun was low outside. Even with the languorous summer evenings, time was short.

He felt someone tap his back. Yagharek raised his head up, lifting it out of the inverted bowl into the air of New Crobuzon, air that felt suddenly chill.

Behind him, Shadrach was crouched on the glass. He wore a

mirror-helm, and held out a similar piece cobbled together from
plate iron towards Yagharek.

Shadrach's helmet looked different. Yagharek's was a rude
piece of rescued metal. Shadrach's was intricate, wired and
valved with copper and brass. At the top was a socket, with holes
to screw in some fitting. It was only the mirrors that seemed a
makeshift addition.

"You forgot this," Shadrach said in his gentle voice, waving
the helmet. "No waved flag, no word from you for twenty minutes. I'm here to check you're alive and all right."

Yagharek showed him the girders inside the dome. He and
Shadrach discussed the problem of Isaac in urgent whispered
tones.

"You must go down," said Yagharek. "You must go by the
sewers, with Lemuel as your guide. You must find your way as
fast as you can into the dome. Send some of the mechanical
monkeys to me, to aid me if I am attacked. Look inside."

Shadrach leaned over carefully and peered into the darkening
glass. Yagharek pointed down, across the thronging village at a
crumbling ghost-building by the vile canal end. The water, its
towpaths and a little finger of torn land on which the broken
house stood were all enclosed by an accidental fence of rubble,
brambles and long-rusted barbed wire. The rejected sliver of
space backed directly onto the dome, which swept up steeply
over it like a flat cloud.

"You must find your way there." Shadrach began to make
some sound, murmuring about the impossibility, but Yagharek
cut him off. "It is difficult. It will be difficult. But you cannot
climb down from here on the inside, and if you can then Isaac
certainly cannot. We need him inside. You must take him in. As
fast as you can. I will come down to you, I will find you, when I
have found the slake-moths. Wait for me."

As he spoke, Yagharek strapped the makeshift helmet on his
head and investigated the field of view it gave behind him.

He caught Shadrach's eye in one of the big slivers of mirror.

"You must go. Be quick. Be patient. I will come to you and
find you before the night is out. The moths must leave by this
break, and so I will wait and watch for them."

Shadrach's face set. Yagharek was right. It was unthinkable
that Isaac would be able to climb down the steep and dangerous
iron rafters.

He nodded at Yagharek curtly, signalling goodbye into the

garuda's mirrors, then turned and scrambled back to the main ladder, descended at expert speed out of sight.

Yagharek turned and looked into the last of the sun. He breathed deeply and flickered his eyes from left to right, checking his vision in each jagged mirror. He calmed himself completely. He breathed in the slow rhythm of the *yajhu-saak*, the hunter's reverie, the martial trance of the Cymek garuda. He composed himself.

After some minutes there came the skittering clatter of metal and wire on glass, and one by one three monkey-constructs came into view, approaching him from different directions. They gathered around him and waited, their glass lenses glinting rose in the evening, their thin pistons hissing as they moved.

Yagharek turned and regarded them through the mirrors. Then, gripping the rope carefully, he began to lower himself through the hole in the glass. He gesticulated at the constructs to follow him as he slipped past the gash. The heat of the dome washed up around him and closed over his head as he descended into the glass-bounded village, towards houses immersed in red light as the clear globe magnified and dispersed the setting sun's rays, into the slake-moths' lair.

CHAPTER FORTY-THREE

Outside the dome, the air darkened inexorably. With the onset of the night, the bright rays that burst from the glass globe in the dome's roof were snuffed out. The Glasshouse grew suddenly dimmer and more cool. But much of the heat was retained. The dome was still far warmer than the city outside. The lights from the torches and the buildings within reflected back on the glass. To the travellers looking back on the city from Flag Hill, to the slum-dwellers gazing desultorily down from the towerblocks of Ketch Heath, to the officer glancing from the skyrail and the driver of the south-bound Sud Line train, peering through smokestacks and flues, over the smoke-soiled roofscape of the city, the Glasshouse looked stretched out taut, distended with light.

As dusk fell, the Glasshouse began to glow.

Clinging to the metal on the inside skin of the dome, unnoticed like some infinitesimal tic, Yagharek slowly flexed his arms. He was affixed to a little knot of scaffolding about one-third of the way down the height of the dome. He was still easily high enough to look down on all the housetops, the tangles of architecture on all sides.

His mind was poised in *yajhu-saak*. He breathed slowly and regularly. He continued his hunter's search, his eyes flitting restlessly from point to point below him, not spending more than a moment on each place, building up a composite picture. Occasionally he would unfocus and take in the whole sweep of the roofs below him, alert for any strange movements. He returned his attention often to the scum-covered trench of water where he had told Shadrach to assemble the others.

There was no sign of the band of intruders.

As the night deepened, the streets cleared at extraordinary speed. The cactacae flocked back to their houses. From a teeming township, the Glasshouse emptied, became a ghost town in a little over half an hour. The only figures left on the streets were the armed patrols. They moved nervously through the streets. Lights from windows were dimmed as shutters and curtains were closed. There were no gaslights in these streets. Instead, Yagharek watched lamp-lighters walk the length of the streets, reaching out with flaming poles to ignite oil-soaked torches ten feet above the pavements.

Each of the lamp-lighters was accompanied by a cactacae patrol, moving nervously, pugnacious and furtive through the obscuring streets.

On the top of the central temple, a group of cactus elders was moving around the central mechanism, pulling levers and tugging at handles. The enormous lens at the top of the device swung down on a ponderous hinge. Yagharek peered closely, but he could not discern what they were doing or what the machine was for. He watched without comprehension as the cactacae swung the thing around, about a vertical and a horizontal axis, checking and adjusting gauges according to obscure calibrations.

Above Yagharek's head, two of the chimpanzee-constructs clung to the metal. The other was a few feet below him, on a strut parallel to his own. They were quite motionless, waiting for him to move.

Yagharek settled back, and waited.

*   *   *

Two hours after sundown, the glass of the dome looked black. The stars were invisible.

The streets of the cactacae Glasshouse glowed with a forbidding, sepia firelight. The patrols had become shadows on a darker street.

There were no sounds beyond the undertone of burning, the soft complaints of architecture and the sound of whispering. Occasional lights flitted like will-o'-the-wisps between the slowly cooling bricks.

There was still no sign of Lemuel, Isaac and the others. A small part of Yagharek's mind was unhappy at this, but for the most part he was still inside, concentrating on the relaxation technique of the hunting trance.

He waited.

Some time between ten and eleven o'clock, Yagharek heard a sound.

His attention, which had spread out to suffuse him, to saturate his awareness, focused instantly. He did not breathe.

Again. The tiniest rippling, a snap like cloth in the wind.

He twisted his neck around and stared towards the noise, down at the mass of streets, into the fearful dark.

There was no response from the watchtower at the Glasshouse's centre. Fancies crept through Yagharek's mind, deep inside. Perhaps he had been deserted, a part of him thought. Perhaps the dome was empty but for him and the monkey-constructs, and some unearthly floating lights in the depths of the streets.

He did not hear the sound again, but a shade of deep black passed across his eyes. Something huge flitted up through the murk.

Terrified at some semi-conscious level far below the calm surface of his thoughts, Yagharek felt himself stiffen and grip the metal in his fingers, flatten himself painfully against the dome's supports. He snapped his head away, facing the metal that he held. Intently, carefully, he stared into the mirrors before his eyes.

Some fell-creature inched its way up the Glasshouse skin.

The shape was almost exactly opposite him, as far away as it could be. It had sprung from some building below and flown a tiny distance to the glass, from there to crawl hand over tendril over claw, up towards the cooler air and the uncontained darkness.

Even through the *yajhu-saak*, Yagharek's heart reeled. He watched the thing progress in his mirrors. It fascinated him in an unholy way. He tracked its dark-winged silhouette, like some deranged angel, all studded with dangerous flesh and dripping bizarrely. Its wings were folded, though the slake-moth gently opened and closed them, now and then, as if to dry them in the warm air.

It crawled with a horrible sluggish torpor towards the invigorating city night.

Yagharek had not pinpointed its nest, and that was critical. His eyes batted inconstantly between the insidious creature itself and the patch of domed darkness from where he had first seen it rise.

And as he watched intently through his mounted mirrors, he won his prize.

He kept his eyes on a tangle of old architecture at the southwestern edge of the Glasshouse. The buildings, amended and tinkered with after centuries of cactus occupation, had once been a clot of smart houses. There was almost nothing to distinguish them from their surroundings. They were a little taller than the neighbouring edifices, and their tops had been sliced off by the descending curve of the dome. But rather than demolish them outright, the buildings had been selectively cut, their upper floors taken off where they impeded the glass and the rest left intact. The further out from the centre the houses were, the lower the dome over them and the more of their raised floors had been destroyed.

It was originally the wedge of building at the fork where a street had split. The vertex of the terrace was almost intact, with only the roof removed. Behind it was a dwindling tail of brick storeys, shrinking under the mass of the dome, and evaporating at the edge of the cactus town.

From the uppermost window of this old structure emerged the unmistakable thrusting maw of a slake-moth.

Again, Yagharek's heart moved, and it was a stern effort that restored its regular beat. He experienced all his emotions at a remove, through a foggy filter of the hunting trance. And this time he was diffusely aware of excitement, as well as fear.

He knew where the slake-moths roosted.

Now that he had discovered what he had sought, Yagharek wanted to shin as fast as he could down the innards of the dome, to remove himself from the slake-moth's world, to get out of the heights of the air and hide on the ground under the looming eaves. But to move quickly, he realized, was to risk the slake-moth's attention. He had to wait, swinging very slightly, sweating, silent and immobile, while the monstrous creatures crawled out into the deeper darkness.

The second moth leapt without the slightest sound into the air, gliding on spread wings for a second and alighting on the metal bones of the Glasshouse. It slid with a vile motion up towards its fellow.

Yagharek waited, without moving.

It was several minutes before the third moth appeared.

Its siblings had nearly reached the top of the dome, after a long, stealthy climb. The newcomer was too eager for that. It stood poised at the same window from which the others had emerged, gripping the frame, balancing its convoluted bulk on the edge of the wood. Then, with an audible snap of air, it beat its way straight upwards, into the sky.

Yagharek could not be sure where the next noise came from, but he thought the two crawling slake-moths hissed at their flying sibling, in disapproval or warning.

There was an answering hum. In the stillness of the Glasshouse curfew, the clicking of mechanized gears from the top of the temple was easily heard.

Yagharek was quite still.

A light burst forth from the top of the pyramid, a blazing white ray, so sharp and defined it seemed almost solid. It beamed from the lens of the strange machine.

Yagharek stared through his mirrored glasses. In the faint ambience radiating backwards from the glaring searchlight he could see a crew of cactacae elders stationed behind it, each frantically adjusting some dial, some valve, one grasping two enormous handles that jutted from the back of the light-emitting engine. He swivelled and twisted the thing, directing its luminous shaft.

The light glared savagely onto a random patch of the dome's glass, then was wrested by its wielder into another position, swung randomly for a moment, then pinioned the impatient slake-moth as it reached the broken panes.

It turned its horned eyesockets to the light. The monstrous creature hissed.

Yagharek heard shouts from the cactus people on the ziggurat, a half-familiar tongue. It was an alloy, a bastard hybrid, mostly words he had last heard in Shankell, alongside New Crobuzon Ragamoll and other influences he did not recognize at all. As a gladiator in the desert city, he had learnt some of the language of his mostly cactus bookmakers. The formulations he heard now were bizarre, centuries out of date and corrupted with alien dialects, but still almost comprehensible to him.

". . . there!" he heard, and something about light. Then as the slake-moth dropped away again from the glass to extricate itself from the torch, he heard, very clearly, "It's coming!"

The slake-moth had easily fallen away and out of the reach of the enormous torch. Its beam oscillated wildly like a madman's lighthouse as the cactacae fought to point it in the right direction. Desperately they swung it over the streets, up at the roof of the dome.

The other two moths remained unseen, flattening themselves against the glass.

There was a shouted discussion from below.

". . . ready . . . sky . . ." he made out, then some word that sounded like the Shankell words for "sun" and "spear" run together. Someone shouted out to take care, and said something about the sunspear and the home: *too far*, they shouted, *too far*.

There was a barked order from the cactus directly behind the vast torch, and his team adjusted their motions obscurely. The leader demanded "limits," of what Yagharek could not understand.

As the light lurched wildly, it found its target again, momentarily. For a moment, the tangled presence of the slake-moth sent a ghastly shadow across the inside of the dome.

"Ready?" shouted the leader, and there was a confirming chorus.

He continued to swivel the lamp, desperately trying to pin the flying moth with its hard light. It swooped and curved, arcing over the tops of the buildings and careering in spirals, a dimly glimpsed display of virtuoso aerobatics, a shadowy circus.

And then, for a moment, the creature was caught spread-eagled in the sky, the light caught it full on and time seemed to stop at the sight of the thing's awesome, unfathomable and terrible beauty.

At the sight, the cactacae aiming the light tugged some hidden handle, and a gob of incandescence spat out of the lens and blazed along the path of the searchlight. Yagharek's eyes widened.

The clot of concentrated light and heat spasmed out of existence a few feet before it hit the glass of the dome.

The momentary white-out seemed to still all sound in the dome.

Yagharek blinked to clear the afterimage of that savage projectile from his eyes.

The cactacae below began to talk again.

". . . get it?" asked one. There was a confusion of unclear answers.

They peered, along with Yagharek, unseen above them, into the air where the slake-moth had flown. They scoured the ground with their eyes, turning the powerful beam towards the pavement.

Throughout the streets below, Yagharek saw the armed patrols standing still, watching the searching light, standing implacable as it swept over them.

"Nothing," shouted one to the elders on high, and his report was repeated from all sectors, shouted into the claustrophobic night.

Behind the thick curtains and the wooden shutters of Glasshouse's windows, threads of light spilt into the air as torches and gaslights were lit. But even woken by the crisis, the cactacae would not peer out into the darkness, would not take the risk on what they might see. The guards were left alone.

And then, with a sough of wind as lascivious as a sexual breath, the cactus people on the temple summit learnt that they had *not* hit the slake-moth: it had ducked in a sharp zigzagging manoeuvre out of the range of their sunspear, it had flown low enough over the rooftops to touch them, to claw its way towards the tower, to pull itself slowly up and to rise magisterially into view, wings outstretched to their full compass, patterns flickering across them as fierce and complex as dark fire.

There was a tiny moment when one of the elders shrieked. There was a split second when the leader tried to tug the sunspear into position to blast the slake-moth into burning fragments. But they could not but see the wings unfolded before them, and their cries, their plans, evaporated as their minds overflowed.

Yagharek watched in his mirrored eyepieces, not wanting to see.

The two moths still clinging to the ceiling of the dome dropped suddenly away. They plummeted towards the earth, to

lurch away from gravity with a stunning curving glide. They
swept up the steep sides of the red pyramid, rising like devils
from inside the earth, manifesting beside the transfixed cactacae
horde.

One reached out with grasping creepers and whipped it
around the thick leg of one of the cactus people. Thin arms and
avaricious talons bit into cactus flesh without response, as the
three slake-moths selected their victims, each grabbing hold of
one of the entranced elders.

On the ground below the lights were moiling in confusion.
The armed patrols were running in circles, shouting to each
other, aiming their weapons skyward and lowering them again,
cursing. They could see almost nothing. All they knew was that
some vague, fluttering things were whirling like leaves around
the top of the temple, and that the elders had stopped firing the
sunspear.

A group of hard, brave warriors ran in to the entrance of the
temple, racing up its wide staircases towards their leaders. They
were too slow. They were helpless. The moths moved away from
the building, slipping smoothly through the sky, their wings still
stretched out, somehow flying while the wings presented an unmoving, mesmerizing vista. Each moth dipped slightly in the air
as its prey was dragged from the edge of the brick. The three cactus elders dangled in snares, cat's-cradles of eerie slake-moth
limbs, gazing up in stupor at the tumbling storm of night-colours
on their captors' wings.

Several seconds before the squad of cactacae burst up from
the trapdoor onto the roof, the moths disappeared. One by one,
according to some flawless unspoken order, they shot straight up
and burst out of the crack in the dome. They slipped out by some
breakneck charm, passing without a moment's pause through a
gap not quite large enough for their wings.

They took their comatose prey with them, tugging the deadweight bodies into the night-city with a repulsive grace.

The cactus elders left beside the wilting sunspear shook themselves in confusion and exclaimed in amazement and discomfort as their minds returned to them. Their shouts became
horrified when they saw that their companions had been taken.
They wailed in rage and swung the sunspear up, aiming pointlessly at the empty skies. The younger warriors appeared, their
rivebows and machetes poised. They looked around in confusion at the miserable scene and lowered their weapons.

Only then, finally, with the victims shouting blood-oaths and caterwauling in anger, with the night full of confused sounds, with the slake-moths flying out across the dark metropolis, did Yagharek emerge from the martial trance and continue climbing down the girders inside the Glasshouse dome. The monkey-constructs saw him move, and followed him towards the streets.

He moved sideways along cross-beams, ensuring that he came to ground behind the backs of the houses, in the little scrap of wasteland that surrounded the foetid stub of the canal.

Yagharek dropped the last few feet and landed silently, rolling on the broken bricks. He crouched and listened.

There were three little crunches as the mechanical apes landed around him and waited for orders or suggestions.

Yagharek peered into the filthy water beside him. The bricks were slippery with years of organic muck and slime. At one end, thirty feet or so within the dome's walls, it came to an abrupt brick end. This must have been the start of a little tributary onto the main canal system. Where it met the dome's wall, the canal was cut off with a rudely made blockage of concrete and iron. It had been hammered into place in the water, its edges sealed as tight as they could. There were still enough tiny impurities and channels in the sodden brickwork to ensure that the trench was kept full of water from outside. It seeped in through the decaying stone and eddied to a stop, thick with rubbish and dead things, a cloying broth of water-rotting filth.

Yagharek could smell it. He crept a little further away, towards the squat stumps of a wall that rose out of the shattered architecture. Outside, he realized, in the streets of the Glasshouse, the frantic shouts continued. The air was full of idiot demands for action.

He was about to settle down, to wait for Shadrach and the others, when Yagharek saw mounds of the broken bricks rising all around him. They tumbled to the ground with a little thudding downpour. Isaac and Shadrach, Pengefinchess and Derkhan and Lemuel and Tansell rose out of the brickdust. Yagharek saw that a pile of scrap-wire and glass behind them was two more monkey-constructs, moving forward now to join their fellows.

For a moment, no one spoke. Then Isaac stumbled forward, trailing ashes and grime. The sewer muck that coated his clothes and bag was now coated with the grit from the collapsed buildings.

His helmet—another like Shadrach's, complex and mechanical looking—lolled battered and absurd on his head.

"Yag," he said haltingly. "Good to see you, old son. So glad . . . you're all right." He grasped Yagharek's hand, and the garuda, taken aback, did not extricate himself from the grip.

Yagharek felt himself emerge from a reverie he had not known he was in, looking around him, seeing Isaac and the others clearly, for the first time. He felt a belated surge of relief. They were filthy and scratched and bruised, but none of them looked hurt.

"Did you *see* it?" said Derkhan. "We'd just come up—it took us ages to work our way through the damn sewers, we kept hearing things . . ." She shook her head at the memory. "We found our way up through a manhole and we were in a street not too far from here. It was chaos, total chaos! The patrols were all running towards the temple, and we saw some . . . that light-gun thing. It was quite easy to make our way here. No one was interested in us . . ." Her voice trailed off. "We didn't really see what happened," she concluded quietly.

Yagharek breathed in deep.

"The moths are here," he said. "I have seen their nest. I can take us there."

The assembled company were elyctrified.

"Don't the damn cactus know where they are?" said Isaac. Yagharek shook his head (a human gesture, the first he had learnt).

"They do not know the slake-moths sleep in their houses," said Yagharek. "I heard them shouting: they think the moths come in to attack them. They think them intruders from without. They do not . . ." Yagharek stopped, thinking of that panic-stricken scene on the top of the cactacae sun-temple, of the helmetless cactus elders, the brave, idiot soldiers charging up, lucky enough to have missed the moths, saving themselves from pointless death. "They do not know how to deal with the moths at all," he said quietly.

As he watched, Pengefinchess's undine swept over her shirt from below, wetting her skin, rinsing the dust from her and her clothes, leaving them incongruously clean.

"We should find the nest," said Yagharek. "I can take us to it."

The adventurers nodded and began an automatic inventory of their weapons and equipment. Isaac and Derkhan looked nervous, but set their jaws. Lemuel looked away sardonically and began to pick his nails with a knife.

"There is something you must know," said Yagharek. He was addressing everyone, and there was something peremptory in his tone, something that would not be ignored. Tansell and Shadrach looked up from carefully rummaging through their backpacks. Pengefinchess put down the bow she had been testing. Isaac looked at Yagharek with a terrible forlorn resignation.

"Three moths left by the broken roof, dandling mindless cactacae. But there are four. Vermishank told us. Perhaps he is wrong, or perhaps he lied. Perhaps another has died.

"Or perhaps," he said, "one has stayed behind. Perhaps one is waiting for us."

CHAPTER FORTY-FOUR

The cactacae patrols huddled together at the base of the Glasshouse, arguing with the remaining elders.

Shadrach crouched behind an alley, out of sight, and pulled a miniature telescope from some hidden pocket. He flicked it out to its full extent, played it over the congregated soldiers.

"They really don't seem to know what to do," he mused quietly. The rest of the intruding gang were huddled behind him, flat against the damp wall. They were as unobtrusive as they could make themselves in the moving shadows cast by the elevated torches that sputtered and burnt above them. "That must be why they have this curfew going on. The moths are taking them. Of course, it may always be in place. Whatever—" he turned to face the others "—it's going to help us."

It was not hard to creep unseen through the darkened streets of the Glasshouse. Their passage was quite unimpeded. They followed Pengefinchess, who moved with a weird gait, halfway between a frog's leap and a thief's creep. She held her bow in one hand, in the other an arrow with a wide, flanged head for use against cactacae, but she did not have to use it. Yagharek moved with her, a few feet behind, hissing directions at her. Occasionally she would stop and gesticulate behind her, flattening against the wall, hiding behind some cart or stall, watching as a brave or foolhardy soul above her pulled back the curtain from their window and peered into the street.

The five monkey-constructs scampered mechanically beside their organic companions. Their heavy metal bodies were quiet. They emitted only a few strange sounds. Isaac did not doubt that for the cactus people of the dome, the regular diet of nightmares would that night be amended to include some metallic scuttling thing, some clattering menace that stalked the streets.

Isaac found walking in the dome deeply unsettling. Even with the red-stone additions to the architecture and the spitting torchlight, the streets seemed basically normal. They could have been anywhere in the city. And yet, stretching over everything, creeping inwards from horizon to horizon, encircling the world like some claustrophobic sky, the enormous dome defined everything. Glimmers of light came through from outside, warped by the thick glass, uncertain and vaguely threatening. The black lattice of ironwork that held the glass in place ensnared the little townscape like a netting, like a vast spider's web.

At that thought, Isaac felt a sudden shuddering lurch of emotion.

He felt a vertiginous sense of certainty.

The Weaver was somewhere nearby.

He faltered as he ran and looked up. He had seen the world as a web, for a split second, had glimpsed the worldweb itself, and had sensed the proximity of that mighty arachnid spirit.

"Isaac!" hissed Derkhan, running past him. She pulled him with her. He had been standing still in the street, gazing skyward, desperately trying to find his way into that awareness again. He tried to whisper to her, to let her know what he had realized, as he stumbled after her, but he could not be clear and she could not listen. She dragged him with her through the dark streets.

After a twisting journey, ducking out of sight of patrols and glancing up at the glowering glass sky, they halted before a clutch of dark buildings, at the intersection of two deserted streets. Yagharek waited until they were all close enough to hear him, before turning and gesturing.

"From that top window there," he said.

The swooping dome bore down inexorably on the tail of the terrace, destroying the rooftops and reducing the mass of the street's houses to ever-more-squat piles of rubble. But Yagharek was pointing at the end furthest from the wall, where the buildings were mostly intact.

The three floors below the attic were occupied. Glimmers of light spilt from the edges of curtains.

Yagharek ducked back around the edge of a little alley and pulled the others in after him. Way off to the north, they could still hear the consternated shouting from the confused patrols, desperate to decide what to do.

"Even if it wasn't too risky to get the cactacae on our side," hissed Isaac, "we'd be *fucked* if we tried to get them to help us now. They're in a damn frenzy. One sniff of us and they'll go berserk, hack us up with those rivebows faster'n you can say 'knife.' "

"We must go past the rooms where the cactus people sleep," said Yagharek. "We must get to the top of the house. We must find where the slake-moths come from."

"Tansell, Penge," said Shadrach decisively, "you watch the door." They looked at him for a moment, then both nodded. "Prof? I reckon you'd best come in with me. And these constructs . . . you think they'll be helpful, yes?"

"I think they'll be damn well essential," said Isaac. "But listen . . . I think the . . . I think there's a Weaver here."

Everyone stared at him.

Derkhan and Lemuel looked incredulous. The adventurers were quite impassive.

"What makes you say that, prof?" asked Pengefinchess mildly.

"I . . . I could sort of . . . sense it. We've dealt with it before. It said it might see us again . . ."

Pengefinchess glanced at Tansell and Shadrach. Derkhan spoke hurriedly.

"It's true," she said. "Ask Pigeon. He saw the thing." Reluctantly, Lemuel nodded that yes, he had.

"But there's not much we can do about it," he said. "We can't control the bugger, and if he comes for us or them, we're pretty much at the mercy of events. He might do nothing. You said it yourself, 'Zaac: he'll do whatever he wants."

"So," said Shadrach slowly, "we're still going in. Any arguments?" There were none. "Right. You, garuda. You've seen them. You saw where they came from. You should come. So it's me, the prof, the bird-man and the constructs. The rest of you stay here, and do exactly what Tansell and Penge tell you. Understood?"

Lemuel nodded, uncaring. There was a glowering moment with Derkhan, as she swallowed her resentment. Shadrach's hard, commanding tone was impressive. She might not like him, she might think him worthless scum, but he knew his business. He was a killer, and that was what they needed right now. She nodded.

"First sign of any trouble you get out of here. Back to the sewers. Disappear. Regroup at the dump tomorrow, if need be. Understood?" This time he was speaking to Pengefinchess and Tansell. They nodded brusquely. The vodyanoi was whispering to her elemental and checking through her quiver. Some of her arrows were complicated affairs, with thin, spring-loaded blades that would whip out on contact to slice almost with the savagery of a rivebow.

Tansell was checking his guns. Shadrach hesitated a moment, then unbuckled his blunderbuss and handed it to the taller man, who accepted it with a nod of thanks.

"I'll be at close quarters," said Shadrach. "I'll not need it." He drew his carved pistol. The dæmonic face at the end of the muzzle seemed to move in the half-light. Shadrach whispered; it seemed as if he was speaking to his gun. Isaac suspected that the weapon was thaumaturgically enhanced.

Shadrach, Isaac and Yagharek walked slowly away from the group.

"Constructs!" Isaac hissed. "With us." There was a pistoned hissing and the shudder of metal as the five compact little simian bodies came away with them.

Isaac and Shadrach looked over at Yagharek, then tested their mirror-helms to make sure their reflected vision was clear.

Tansell was standing before the little huddling group, making notes in a little book. He looked up, pursed his lips and stared at Shadrach, his head on one side. He looked up at the torches above them, took in the angle of the roofs that loomed over them. He scrawled obscure formulae.

"I'm going to try and get a veil-hex going," he said. "You're too visible. There's no point asking for trouble." Shadrach nodded. "Shame we can't get the constructs as well, really." Tansell motioned the automated apes out of the way. "Penge, will you help?" he said. "Channel a bit of puissance my way, will you? This shit is draining."

The vodyanoi crept over a little and placed her left hand in Tansell's right. Both of them concentrated, their eyes closing. There was no movement or sound for a minute; then, as Isaac watched, both their eyes fluttered blearily open at the same moment.

"Extinguish those damn lights," hissed Tansell, and Pengefinchess's mouth moved silently with his. Shadrach and the others looked around, unsure what he was referring to, when they saw him glaring at the flaming streetlamps above them.

Quickly, Shadrach beckoned Yagharek. He strode over to the nearest lamp and linked his hands, making a step. He braced his legs.

"Use your cloak," he said. "Get up there and smother the flame."

Isaac was probably the only person to see Yagharek's infinitesimal hesitation. He realized the bravery he was seeing as Yagharek obeyed, preparing to tangle up and ruin his last disguise. Yagharek undid the clasp at his throat and stood before them all, his beaked and feathered head uncovered, the enormous emptiness behind his back shriekingly visible, his scars and stubs covered with a thin shirt.

Yagharek clutched Shadrach's linked hands as gently as he could with those great taloned feet. He stood up. Shadrach lifted the hollow-boned garuda with ease. Yagharek swung his heavy cloak over the sticky, spitting torch. It snuffed with a burst of black smoke. Shadows fell on them like predators as the light went out.

He stepped down and Shadrach and he moved quickly to the left, to the other flame that illuminated the cul-de-sac they crouched in. They repeated their operation, and the little brick gully was doused with darkness.

When he stepped down, Yagharek opened out his ruined cloak, charred and split and foul with tar. He paused for a moment and tossed it away from him. He looked tiny and forlorn in his dirty shirt. His weapons dangled in full view.

"Move into the deepest shadow," hissed Tansell, his voice grating. Again, Pengefinchess's mouth mirrored his own, and emitted not a sound.

Shadrach stepped backwards, finding a little alcove in the brick, tugging Yagharek and Isaac in with him, flattening them against the old wall.

They pushed themselves down, settled themselves and were still.

Tansell moved his left arm out stiffly and slung the end of a roll of thick copper wire towards them. Shadrach reached out and caught it easily. He wrapped it around his own neck, then looped it quickly over his companions. Then he slipped back into the darkness. At the other end, Isaac saw, the wire was attached to a hand-held engine, some clockwork motor, the catch of which Tansell released, letting the momentum take the mechanism, unwinding and dynamic.

"Ready," Shadrach said.

Tansell began to hum and whisper, spitting out weird sounds. He was almost invisible. As Isaac watched him, he could see nothing more than a figure shrouded in obscurity, trembling with effort. The murmuring increased.

A shock snapped through him. Isaac spasmed a little and felt Shadrach hold him where he was. Isaac's skin crawled and he felt a stinging current trickle in through his pores, where the wire touched his skin.

The sensation continued for a minute, and then dissipated as the engine wound down.

"All right," croaked Tansell. "Let's see if it's worked."

Shadrach stepped out of the hollow into the street.

The shadows came with him.

Enveloping him was an indistinct aura of darkness, the same one that had covered him as he stood in the deep shade. Isaac stared at him, saw the patch of deep black in Shadrach's eyes and below his chin. Shadrach stepped slowly forward, and into the light shed by torches in the junction a little way off.

The shadows on his face and body did not alter. They remained fixed in the conjuncture they had assumed as he crouched in the coal darkness, exactly as if he stood still hidden from the flickering glow, beside the wall. The shadows that clung to him extended perhaps an inch from his skin, discolouring the air that surrounded him like a caliginous halo.

There was something else, an untimely stillness that crept with him even as Shadrach moved. It was as if the frozen furtiveness of his concealment in the bricks suffused the shadows that coated him. He stalked forward, yet the sense of it was that he was still. He confused the eye. You could follow his progress if you knew he was there and were determined to watch, but it was easier not to notice him.

Shadrach motioned Isaac and Yagharek to join him.

Am I like him? thought Isaac as he crept out into the lighter darkness. *Do I slip around the corners of your eye? Am I half invisible, bringing my shadow-cover with me?*

He looked over at Derkhan, and saw by her wide-mouthed stare that he was. To his left, Yagharek too was an indistinct figure.

"First sign of sun-up, go," whispered Shadrach to his companions. Tansell and Pengefinchess nodded. They had disengaged, and shook their heads in exhaustion. Tansell raised his hand in a gesture of good luck.

Shadrach beckoned Isaac and Yagharek, and stepped out of the darkened alley into the sputtering firelight in front of the houses. After them came the monkeys, moving slowly, as silently as they could. They stood beside the two humans and the garuda, and the red light glinted violently from their battered metal shells. The same light slipped off the three hexed intruders like thin oil off a blade. It could find no purchase. The three unclear figures stood before the five quietly clattering constructs, and moved across the deserted street towards the house.

The cactacae did not lock their doors. It was easy enough to gain entrance to the house. Shadrach began to creep up the stairs.

As Isaac followed him, he sniffed at the exotic, unfamiliar smell of cactacae sap and strange food. Pots of sandy soil were placed all around the entrance hall, sporting a variety of desert plants, mostly unhealthy and dwindling in the interior of the house.

Shadrach turned and took in Isaac and Yagharek with a look. Very slowly, he put his finger to his lips. Then he continued to climb.

As they approached the first floor, they heard a quiet argument in deep cactus voices. Yagharek translated what he understood in a tiny whisper, something about being afraid, an exhortation to trust the elders. The corridor was bare and unadorned. Shadrach paused and Isaac peered over his shoulder, saw that the door to the cactus-people's room was wide open.

Inside he saw a large room with a very high ceiling, wrought, he realized as he saw the fringe of planking that skirted the walls seven feet up, by tearing out the floor of the rooms above. A gaslight was turned on low. A little way from the door, Isaac saw several sleeping cactacae, standing with their legs locked, immobile and impressive. Two figures next to each other were still awake, leaning in slightly, whispering.

Very slowly, Shadrach stalked like a predatory creature up the last of the stairs and past the door. He paused just before he reached it, and looked back and pointed at one of the monkey-constructs, then beside himself. He repeated the gesture. Isaac understood. He pulled himself close to the aural inputs of the construct and whispered instructions to it.

It scampered up the stairs with a quiet clatter that made Isaac wince, but the cactacae did not notice it. The construct squatted quietly down beside Shadrach, blocked from sight inside the room by his dark-drenched form. Isaac sent another construct to follow it, then signalled Shadrach to move.

At a slow, steady crawl, the big man crept in front of the door-way, shielding the constructs with his body. Their forms still caught the light, would glint as they passed the threshold. Shadrach moved without pause past the line of sight of the cacta-cae talking within, with the constructs creeping beside him hidden from the light, then on past the edge of the doorway into the darkness of the corridor beyond.

And then it was Isaac's turn.

He indicated two more constructs hide behind his bulk, then began to crawl along the wooden floor. His belly hung down as he shuffled along with the constructs.

It was a frightening feeling, to move out from behind the wall and emerge in full view of the cactacae couple talking quietly as they stood ready to sleep. Isaac was huddled against the banis-ters on the hallway, as far from the door as he could go, but there were still several intolerable seconds when he crept through the dim cone of light towards the safety of the dark corridor beyond.

He had time to stare at the big cactus people standing in the hard dirt on the floor, whispering. Their eyes passed over him as he crept before their door, and he held his breath, but his thau-maturgic shadows augmented the darkness of the house, and he went unseen.

Then Yagharek, his scrawny form doing its best to hide the last of the constructs, crept past the light.

They regrouped before the next stairs.

"This section is easier," whispered Shadrach. "There's no one on the floor above, it's just the ceiling of this one. And then above that . . . that's where our slake-moths hide."

*   *   *

Before they reached the fourth floor, Isaac tugged at Shadrach and pulled him to a stop. Watched by Shadrach and Yagharek, Isaac whispered again to one of the monkey-constructs. He held Shadrach still as the thing crept with mechanical stealth over the lip of the stairs, and disappeared into the dark room beyond.

Isaac held his breath. After a minute, the construct emerged and waved its arm jerkily, indicated them to come up.

They rose slowly into a long-deserted attic room. A window looked out onto the junction of the streets, a window without glass, whose dusty frame was scuffed with a variety of bizarre markings. It was through this little rectangle that light came in, a wan and changing exudation of the torches below.

Yagharek pointed at the window slowly.

"From there," he said. "It came from there."

The floor was littered with ancient rubbish, and thick in dust. The walls were scratched with unsettling random designs.

The room was traversed by a discomfiting river of air. It was a faint current, almost undetectable. In the motionless heat of the dome, it was unsettling and remarkable. Isaac looked around, trying to trace its source.

He saw it. Even sweating in the night-heat, he shivered slightly.

Directly opposite the window, the plaster of the wall lay in shredded layers across the floor. It had fallen from a hole, a hole that looked newly created, an irregular cavity in the bricks that raised to the height of Isaac's thighs.

It was a glaring, looming wound in the wall. The breeze connected it and the window, as if some unthinkable creature breathed out in the bowels of the house.

"It's in there," said Shadrach. "That must be where they're hiding. That must be the nest."

Inside the hole was a complex and broken tunnel, carved into the substance of the house. Isaac and Shadrach squinted into its darkness.

"It doesn't look wide enough for one of those bastards," said Isaac. "I don't think they work quite according to ... uh ... regular space."

The tunnel was four feet or so wide, rough-hewn and deep. Its interior was quickly invisible. Isaac knelt before it and sniffed deeply of the darkness. He looked up at Yagharek.

"You have to stay here," he said. Before the garuda could

protest, Isaac pointed to his head. "Me and Shad here, we've got the helmets that the Council gave us. And with this—" he patted his bag "—we might be able to get close to whatever, if anything, is in there." He reached in and brought out a dynamo. It was the same engine the Council had used to amplify Isaac's mind-waves, attracting his erstwhile pet. He also brought out a large tangle of metal-sheathed piping, coiled around his hand.

Shadrach kneeled next to him and lowered his head. Isaac slotted an end of piping into place on the helmet's outlet, and twisted the bolts that held it.

"According to the Council, channellers use a setup like this for some technique called . . . displacement-ontolography," mused Isaac. "Don't ask me. Point is, these exhaust pipes will flush out our . . . uh . . . psychic *effluvia* . . . and discharge it out here." He glanced up at Yagharek. "No mindprint. No taste, no trail." He spun the last bolt firmly and rapped Shadrach's helmet gently. He lowered his own head and Shadrach began to repeat the operation. "See, if there *is* a moth down there, Yag, and you go anywhere near it, it'll taste you. But it shouldn't taste us. That's the theory."

When Shadrach was done, Isaac stood and threw the ends of the piping to Yagharek.

"Each of those is about . . . twenty-five, thirty feet. Hang on to it till it's taut, then let us go on with it trailing behind. All right?" Yagharek nodded. His stood stiff, angry at being left, but under-standing without question that there was no choice.

Isaac took two coiling wires and attached them first to the mo-tor he held, then slotted the other end of each into a valve on his and Shadrach's helmets.

"There's a little antacidic chymical battery in there," he said, waving the engine. "It works in conjunction with a metaclock-work design pinched from the khepri. Are we ready?" Quickly, Shadrach checked his gun, touched each of his other weapons in turn, then nodded. Isaac felt for his flintlock and the unfamiliar knife at his belt. "All right then."

He snapped the little lever on the dynamo. A little humming hiss emerged from the engine. Yagharek held the outlets dubi-ously, peered into them. He felt some vague sensation, some weird little wash, trembling through him from the rims of the pipes. A little tremble passed through him from the hands up, a tiny tremor of fear that was not his own.

Isaac pointed at three of the monkey-constructs.

"Go in," he said. "Four feet ahead of us. Move slowly. Halt for danger. You—" he pointed at another "—go behind us. One stay with Yag."

Slowly, one by one, the constructs trooped into the darkness.

Isaac briefly laid a hand on Yagharek's shoulder.

"Back soon, old son," he said quietly. "Watch out for us."

He turned away and kneeled, preceded Shadrach into the shaft of shattered brick, crouching and working his way into the stygian hole.

The tunnel was part of a subversive topography.

It crept at bizarre angles between the walls of the terrace, tight and close, sending the sound of his breath and the clanking of the monkeys' bouncing into Isaac's ears. His hands and knees ached from the crushing pressure of the sharp stone-shards under him. Isaac estimated that they were moving back through the terraced houses. They were shuffling downwards, and Isaac remembered how the curve of the dome had decapitated the houses at a lower and lower point as they approached the glass. The closer the houses were to the edge of the dome, he realized, the lower they would be, the more filled with old wreckage.

They were shuffling their way along the little stub of the street, towards the glass dome, down through deserted floors in an interstitial burrow. Isaac shivered for a moment in the dark. He was sweating from heat and from fear. He was terribly frightened. He had seen the slake-moths. He had seen them feed. He knew what might be before them in the depths of this wedge of rubble.

After a short time of crawling Isaac felt a moment's drag on him, then a release. He had reached the full extent of his piping, and Yagharek had let it go to drag behind him.

Isaac did not speak. He could hear Shadrach behind him, breathing deeply and grunting. The two men could not move more than five feet apart, because the wires connected their helmets to a single motor.

Isaac threw up his face and swung it around him, desperately searching for light.

The monkey-constructs swung their way up. Every few moments, one would momentarily turn on the lights in its eyes, and for a minuscule fraction of a second, Isaac would see a stark crawlway of littered brick and the metal gleam of the constructs' bodies. Then the lights would go out. Isaac would try to negotiate by the ghost image that slowly ebbed from his eyes.

In the absolute dark, it was easy to sense the slightest glimmer. Isaac knew that he was crawling towards a source of light when he looked up and saw the grey outline of the tunnel ahead. Something pressed Isaac's chest. He started massively, then recognized the pewter fingers and dark bulk of a construct. Isaac hissed to Shadrach to stop.

The construct gesticulated to Isaac with exaggerated jerky gestures. It pointed forward, towards its two fellows that hovered at the edge of the visible shaft, where the tunnel turned a sharp corner *upwards*.

Isaac indicated that Shadrach should wait. Then he crept forward at an almost motionless pace. Glacial dread was beginning to creep through his system, from the stomach out. He breathed deep and slow. He shifted his feet slowly, inching along, until he felt his skin prickle as it emerged into a shaft of faint light.

The tunnel ended in a wall of brick five feet high, on three sides of him. A wall rose behind him, above the tunnel mouth. Isaac looked up and saw a ceiling way above him. A pestilential stench began to dribble into the hole. Isaac screwed up his face.

He was crouching in a hole, by the wall, embedded in the cement floor of a room. He could see nothing of the chamber above and beyond him. But he could hear faint sounds. A slight rustle, like wind against discarded paper. The softest sound of liquid adhesion, like fingers sticky with glue meeting and parting.

Isaac swallowed three times and whispered to himself, gearing himself up to bravery, forcing himself on. He turned his back on the bricks before him, on the room beyond them. He saw Shadrach watching him on all fours, his face set. Isaac looked intently into his mirrors. He tugged briefly at the pipe attached to the top of his helmet, that twisted its way backwards into the tunnel and disappeared below Shadrach's body into the depths, diverting his telltale thoughts.

Then Isaac began to stand, very slowly. He stared with violent fervour into the mirrors, as if trying to prove himself to some testing god—*See! I'm not looking behind me, you damn well see if I do!* The top of Isaac's head breached the lip of the hole, and more light fell across him. The foul smell grew stronger still.

His terror was very strong. His sweat was no longer warm.

Isaac tilted his head and stood a little taller, until he saw the room itself in the sepia light that fought its way through one filthy, tiny window.

It was a long, thin room. Eight or so feet wide, and about twenty feet long. Dusty and long-deserted, with no visible entrance or exit, no hatches or doors.

Isaac did not breathe. At the furthest end of the room, sitting and seeming to stare directly at him, the lattice of its complex killing arms and limbs moving in baffling antiphase, its wings half-open in languorous threat, was a slake-moth.

It took a moment for Isaac to realize that he had not moaned. It took another few seconds of staring into the vile thing's twitching antennaed sockets to realize that it had not sensed him. The moth shifted and turned a little, moving until it was three-quarters on to him.

Absolutely silently, Isaac exhaled. He twitched his head fractionally, to see the rest of the room.

When he saw its contents, he had to fight all over again not to make a sound.

Lying at irregular intervals the whole length of the floor, the room was littered with the dead.

That, Isaac realized, was the source of that unspeakable stench. He turned his head and put his hand over his mouth as he saw that near him lay a decomposing cactacae child, its rotting flesh falling from fibrous hardwood bones. A little way away was the stinking carcass of a human, and beyond that Isaac saw another, fresher human corpse, and a bloated vodyanoi. Most of the bodies were cactus.

Some, he saw with misery and without surprise, were still breathing. They lay discarded: husks; empty bottles. They would drool and piss and shit their last imbecilic days or hours out in this stifling hole, until they died of hunger and thirst and rotted as mindlessly as they had lived at the end.

They could not be in paradise or Hell, thought Isaac despondently. Their spirits could not roam in spectral form. They had been metabolized. They had been drunk and shat out, converted by vile oneirochymical processes and become fuel for a slake-moth flight.

Isaac saw that in one of its crooked hands, the moth was dragging the body of a cactus elder, sash still dangling portentous and absurd about its shoulders. The moth was sluggish. It raised its arm indolently and let the mindless cactus man fall heavily across the mortar floor.

Then the slake-moth moved a little and reached underneath it with its hind legs. It shuffled forward a little, its heavy, uncanny body slipping across the dusty floor. From below its abdomen, the slake-moth pulled out a great, soft globe. It was about three feet across, and as Isaac squinted into his mirror to see it more clearly, he thought he recognized the thick, mucal texture and drab chocolate colour of dreamshit.

His eyes widened.

The slake-moth measured the thing with its back legs, spreading them to encompass the fat globule of slake-moth milk. *That's got to be worth fucking thousands* . . . Isaac thought. *No, cut it to make it palatable, there's probably millions of guineas there! No wonder everyone's trying to get these damn things back* . . .

Then, as Isaac watched, a piece of the slake-moth's abdomen unfolded. A long organic syringe emerged, a tapering segmented extrusion that bent backwards from the slake-moth's tail on some chitinous hinge. It was nearly as long as Isaac's arm. As he watched, his mouth slack with revulsion and horror, the slake-moth prodded it against the ball of raw dreamshit, paused a moment, then plunged it deep into the centre of the sticky mass.

Under the armour that had unfolded, where the soft part of the underbelly was visible, from where the long probe had emerged, Isaac saw the abdomen of the slake-moth convulse peristaltically, squirting some unseen thing the length of the bony shaft into the depths of the dreamshit.

Isaac knew what he was seeing. The dreamshit was a food source, to give starving hatchlings reserves of energy. The protruding jag of flesh was an ovipositor.

The slake-moth was laying its eggs.

Isaac slipped back below the surface of the wall. He was hyperventilating. Urgently, he beckoned Shadrach.

"One of the godsdamned things is *right there* and it's laying its *eggs* so we have to damn well take it right now . . ." he hissed. Shadrach smacked his hand over Isaac's mouth. He held Isaac's eyes until the older man had calmed a little. Shadrach turned his back as Isaac had done, then stood slowly and gazed for himself onto the grisly scene. Isaac sat with his back to the bricks, waiting.

Shadrach dropped down again to Isaac's level. His face was set.

"Hmmm," he murmured. "I see. Right. Did you say the moth-thing can't sense constructs?" Isaac nodded.

"As far as we know," he said.

"Right then. You've done a damn fine job programming these constructs. And they're an extraordinary design. Do you really mean it, that they'll know when to attack, if we give them instructions? They can understand variables that complicated?"

Isaac nodded again.

"Then we have a plan," said Shadrach. "Listen to me."

CHAPTER FORTY-FIVE

Slowly, trembling almost uncontrollably, the memory of Barbile's quasi-death vivid in him, Isaac climbed out of the hole.

He kept his eyes rigidly on the mirrors before him. He was dimly aware of the discoloured wall behind them. The vile shape of the slake-moth shook in the mirrors as his head moved.

As Isaac emerged, the slake-moth stopped moving suddenly. Isaac stiffened. It turned its head upwards and flickered its enormous tongue through the air. The vestigial antennae in its ocular sockets waved uneasily from side to side. Isaac moved again, creeping towards the wall.

The slake-moth moved its head uneasily. There was obviously some leakage, Isaac thought, from the edge of his helmet, some trickles of thought that wafted tantalizingly through the æther. But nothing clear enough for the slake-moth to find him.

When Isaac had made his way to the wall, Shadrach followed him up and into the room. Again, his presence discomfited the slake-moth a little, but nothing more than that.

After Shadrach, three monkey-constructs pulled themselves into view, leaving one to guard the tunnel. They began to walk slowly towards the slake-moth. It turned towards them, seemed to watch them without eyes.

"I think it can sense their physical shape and their movement, and ours as well," whispered Isaac. "But without any mental trail, it doesn't see any . . . either of us as sapient life. We're just moving physical stuff, like trees in the wind."

The slake-moth was turning to face the oncoming constructs. They separated and began to approach the moth from different directions. They did not move fast, and the slake-moth did not seem concerned. But it was a little wary.

"Now," whispered Shadrach. He and Isaac reached out and began slowly to haul in the metal piping that extended from the top of their helmets.

As the open ends of the pipes drew closer, the slake-moth grew agitated. It skittered back and forth, returning to protect its eggs, then stalking forward a few feet, its teeth chattering in a terrible rictus.

Isaac and Shadrach looked at each other and counted silently together.

On three, they pulled the ends of their pipes out into the open room. In a single movement, as swiftly as they could, they whipped the metal around and sent the open ends into the corner, fifteen feet from them.

The slake-moth went berserk. It hissed and screeched in a loathsome register. It hunched up its body, increasing its size, and a host of exoskeletal jags flicked out of hollows in its flesh in organic threat.

Isaac and Shadrach stared into their mirrors, awed by its monstrous majesty. It had spread its wings and turned to face the corner where the pipe ends coiled. Its wing-patterns pulsed with misdirected, hypnotic energy.

Isaac was frozen. The slake-moth's wings eddied with uncanny patterns. It stalked towards the pipe-ends in a low, predatory crouch, now on four legs, now six, now two.

Quickly, Shadrach pulled Isaac towards the dreamshit ball.

They walked forward, passing the incensed, hungry slake-moth, almost close enough to touch. They saw it approaching in their mirrors, a massive looming animal weapon. As they passed it, both men turned smoothly on their heels, walking backwards towards the dreamshit at one moment, then forwards the next. That way, they kept the slake-moth behind them, visible in the mirrors.

The moth walked straight past the constructs, knocking one aside without even noticing, as a serrated spine swung sideways in quivering, ravenous rage.

Isaac and Shadrach walked carefully, checking in their mirrors that the ends of their mental exhaust-pipes remained where they had been thrown, acting as slake-moth bait. Two of the monkey-constructs followed the slake-moth at a small distance, the third approaching the eggs.

"Quickly," hissed Shadrach, and pushed Isaac to the floor. Isaac fumbled with the knife at his belt, wasting seconds with the clip. Then he had it out. He hesitated a moment, and then pushed it smoothly into the big, sticky mass.

Shadrach watched intently in his mirrors. The slake-moth, shadowed by the hovering constructs, pounced absurdly on the snaking ends of the pipes.

As Isaac drew his knife down the surface of the egg-case, the moth flailed with fingers and tongue to find the enemy whose mind remained tauntingly conscious.

Isaac wound the ends of his shirt around his hands and began to tug at the split he had made in the mass of dreamshit. With a big effort, he pulled the yielding ball apart.

"Quickly," said Shadrach again.

The dreamshit—raw, uncut, distilled and pure—seeped through the cloth around Isaac's hands and made his fingers tingle. He gave one last tug. The centre of the dreamshit ball was laid open, and there in the centre was a little clutch of eggs.

Each was translucent and oval, smaller than a hen's. Through its semi-liquid skin, Isaac could see some faint, coiling shape. He looked up and beckoned the monkey-construct that stood nearby.

At the far end of the room, the slake-moth had picked up one of the metal tubes, putting its face in the flow of emotion from its open end. It shook it in confusion. It opened its mouth and unrolled its obscene, intrusive tongue. It licked the end of the pipe once, then plunged its tongue into it, eagerly seeking the source of this tempting flow.

"Now!" said Shadrach. The slake-moth's hands moved along the coiled metal, seeking purchase. Shadrach's face went suddenly white. He spread his legs and braced himself. "Now, dammit, do it *now*!" he shouted. Isaac looked up in alarm.

Shadrach was staring intently into his mirrors. With his left hand, he was aiming behind him, pointing his thaumaturgic pistol at the slake-moth.

Time slowed down as Isaac looked into his own mirrors and

saw the dull metal pipe in the hands of the moth. He saw Shadrach's hand, steady as the dead, clutching his flintlock, pointing it behind his own back. He saw the monkey-constructs waiting for their order to attack.

He looked down again at the vile clutch of eggs, seeping and glutinous below him.

He opened his mouth to shout to the constructs, and as he inhaled to yell, the slake-moth leaned forward a moment then pulled at the piping with all its horrendous strength.

Isaac's voice was drowned by Shadrach's wail and the explosion from his flintlock. He had waited a moment too long before firing. The enhanced ball smacked with a boom into the substance of the wall. Shadrach was pulled through the air. The leather strap attaching his helmet to his head snapped. The helmet flew away from him and arced at speed on the end of the pipe, tugging the connections from Isaac's engine, shattering against the wall. Shadrach's perfect curving trajectory collapsed as he was untethered. He tumbled in an ugly broken arc, his gun flying away from him, until he landed heavy and unwieldy on the concrete floor. His head smacked against the rough concrete floor, sending blood spattering out across the dust.

Shadrach screamed and moaned, rolled, clutching his head, trying to right himself.

His weltering mindwaves suddenly burst into the open. The slake-moth turned, growling.

Isaac shouted at the constructs. As the slake-moth began to stamp horribly quickly towards Shadrach, the two that stood behind it leapt up at it simultaneously. Flame burst from their mouths, flaring across the slake-moth's body.

It screeched, and a clutch of skin-whips flailed across its smouldering back, battering against the constructs. The moth did not stop bearing down on Shadrach. A tentacular growth snapped around one of the construct's necks and tugged it from the slake-moth's back with awesome ease. It sent the metal body crunching against the wall as brutally as it had the helmet.

There was a terrible sound of rending as the construct burst apart, spreading shattered metal and flaming oil across the floor. It roared a little way from Shadrach, melting metal and cracking the concrete.

The construct by Isaac spat a gobbet of strong acid across the clutch of eggs. Instantly, they began to smoke, to split and hiss and dissolve.

The slake-moth let out an unholy, merciless, terrible scream.

Instantly it turned from Shadrach and tore across the room towards its brood. Its tail lashed violently from side to side, catching Shadrach as he lay moaning, sending him sprawling through his own blood.

Isaac stamped once, savagely, on the liquefying egg-clutch, then stumbled back and out of the slake-moth's path. His foot slithered with the glabrous mess. He half ran, half crawled towards the wall, clutching his knife in one hand, the precious engine that kept his mindwaves hidden in the other.

The construct still clinging to the slake-moth's back breathed fire all across its skin once again, and it screeched in pain. The segmented arms flew back and clutched for purchase on the construct's skin. Without pausing, the moth got a grip under the construct's arms and tore the thing from its skin.

It hammered it against the floor, shattering its glass lenses and bursting the metal casing of its head, sending valves and wire spewing in its wake. It flung the broken body away from it in a heap of rubbish. The last construct drew back, trying to gain range from which to spray its enormous, maddened enemy.

Before the construct could spit its acid, two massive flanges of serrated bone snaked out faster than a whiplash and shattered it effortlessly into two.

Its top half twitched and tried to drag itself across the floor. The acid it had carried pooled beneath it in the dust in an acrid smoking sump, corroding the dead cactacae around it.

The slake-moth ran its hands through the viscid scum that had been its eggs. It hooted and crooned.

Isaac crept away from the moth, gazing at it in his mirrors, feeling his way along the wall towards Shadrach, who lay moaning, crying out, befuddled with pain.

In the mirrors before his eyes, Isaac saw the slake-moth turn. It hissed, its tongue flickering. It spread its wings, and bore down on Shadrach.

Isaac tried desperately to reach the other man, but he was too slow. The slake-moth stamped past him again, and Isaac turned smoothly once more, always keeping the terrible predator in his mirrors.

As he watched in horror, Isaac saw the slake-moth pull Shadrach upright. Shadrach's eyes rolled. He was concussed and in pain, coated in blood.

He began to slide down the wall again. The slake-moth spread his arms wide and then, so fast that it was completed before Isaac realized it had started, it thrust at him with two of its long, jagged claws, slamming them through Shadrach's wrists and into the brick and concrete behind them, physically pinning him to the wall.

Shadrach and Isaac cried out together.

With its two bone-spears wedged in place, the moth reached out with its quasi-human hands and coaxed at Shadrach's eyes. Isaac moaned at him to beware, but the big warrior was confused and in agony, and desperately looking around to see what it was that hurt him so.

Instead, he saw the slake-moth's wings.

He quietened suddenly, and the slake-moth, its back still smouldering and cracking with the heat from the construct's attack, leaned forward to feed.

Isaac looked away. He turned his head carefully, so that he would not see that probing tongue suck the sentience from Shadrach's brain. Isaac swallowed and began to walk slowly across the room, towards the hole and the tunnel. His legs shook and he clenched his jaw. His only hope was to leave. That way, he might survive.

He was careful to ignore the slobbering, sucking noises, the liquid grunts of pleasure and the *drip-drip-drip* of saliva or blood that came from behind him. Isaac made his careful way towards the only exit in the room.

As he neared it, he saw the end of the metal pipe that attached to his helmet still lying undisturbed by the wall. He breathed a prayer. His mental essence was still leaking into the room. The slake-moth must know that there was another sentient being in there with it. The closer Isaac came to the tunnel, the closer he would be to the pipe's outlet. It would no longer be misleading about his location.

And yet, and yet, it seemed that he was lucky. The slake-moth was so intent on drinking its fill and, judging by the sounds of ripping tissue, of wreaking revenge on poor Shadrach's wracked body, that it was paying no attention to the terrified presence behind it. Isaac was able to walk on, past it, away, right to the lip of the burrow.

But there, as he stood poised, ready to drop quietly into the dark where the construct still waited and creep his way out into the dome and away from this nightmare nest, he felt a trembling beneath his feet.

He looked down.

The sound of frantic clawing feet was skittering through the tunnel towards him. He stepped back, utterly aghast. He felt the brickwork tremble deep inside.

With an almighty crash, the monkey-construct came catapulting from the tunnel to slam against the wall of bricks. It tried to push back with its arms, to somersault up into the room, but its momentum took it far too fast, and both its arms snapped neatly off at the shoulder.

It tried to raise itself, smoke and fire gouting from its mouth, but a slake-moth tore out of the tunnel and trod on its head, bursting its intricate machinery.

The moth leapt up into the room, and for a long merciless moment, Isaac was staring *directly* at it, with its wings outstretched.

It was only after several moments of terror and despair that Isaac realized the newcomer was ignoring him, was hurling itself past him across the bodies in the room towards the ruined eggs. And as it ran, it turned its head on its long, sinuous neck, and chattered its teeth in something like fear.

Isaac flattened himself against the wall again, peering into his mirrors at both the slake-moths.

The second moth forced open its teeth and spat out some high, gibbering sound. The first moth gave a last almighty suck and let Shadrach's spent and ruined body fall. Then it moved back with its sibling, towards the glutinous ruins of the dreamshit and the eggs.

The two moths spread their wings. They stood wingtip to wingtip, their various armoured limbs extended, and waited.

Isaac crept slowly into the hole, not daring to wonder what was happening, why they were ignoring him. Behind him, the metal exhaust pipe snaked like an idiotic tail. As Isaac stared in bewilderment into his mirrors at the scene behind him, the space around the tunnel entrance rippled for a moment. It buckled and suddenly flowered, and there in the pit with him stood the Weaver.

Isaac gaped in awe. The enormous arachnid creature loomed over him, looked down through a clutch of glinting eyes. The slake-moths bristled.

. . . GRIM AND NEBULOUS GRIMY AND NEBULAR YOU ARE YOU
ARE . . . came that unmistakable voice, crooning into Isaac's
ears—especially his missing ear.

"Weaver!" He almost sobbed.

The vast spider presence leapt up, landing square on its four
hind legs. It gesticulated intricately in the air with its knife
hands.

. . . FOUND THE REAVER TEARING WORLDWEAVE OVER THE BLIS-
TERING GLASS AND WE DANCED A BLOODTHIRSTY DUET EACH SAV-
AGE MOMENT MORE VIOLENT I CANNOT WIN WHEN THESE FOUR
DASTARDLY CORNERS SQUARE UP TO ME . . . the Weaver said, and
advanced on its prey. Isaac could not move. He gazed into the
shards of mirror at the extraordinary contest behind him. . . .
RUN HIDE LITTLE ONE YOU ARE A SKILFUL ONE FIXING THE RUCKS
AND TEARS IT COMES AROUND YOU ONE HAS GONE TRAPPED INTO
TRAPPING YOU AND CRUSHED LIKE WHEAT AND IT IS TIME TO FLEE
BEFORE THE BEREFT BROTHERSISTER INSECTS ARRIVE TO MOURN
THE MULCH YOU HELPED MELT . . .

They were coming, Isaac realized. The Weaver was warning
him that they had sensed the death of the eggs, and were returning, too late, to protect the nest.

Isaac gripped hold of the edges of the tunnel, prepared to disappear into its folds. But he was held for a few seconds, his
mouth hanging open in awe, his breathing shallow and amazed,
by the sight of the slake-moths and the Weaver joining battle.

It was an elemental scene, something way beyond human ken.
It was a flickering vision of horn blades moving much too fast
for a human to see, an impossibly intricate dance of innumerable
limbs across several dimensions. Gouts of blood sprayed in various colours and textures across the walls and floor, fouling the
dead. Behind the unclear bodies, silhouetting them, the chymical fire hissed and rolled across the concrete floor. And all the
while it fought, the Weaver sang its ceaseless monologue.

. . . OH HOW IT DOES HOW IT BRINGS ME TO THE BOIL I BUBBLE
AND EFFERVESCE I AM DRUNK INTOXICATED ON THE JUICE OF ME
THAT THESE MAD-WINGERS FERMENT . . . it sang.

Isaac stared in astonishment. Extraordinary things were happening. The slashing and the punishing thrusts continued with
fervour, but now the slake-moths were whipping their vast
tongues back and forth through the air. They ran them at lightning speed over the body of the Weaver as it shuddered in and
out of the material plane. Isaac saw their stomachs distend and

contract, saw them lick the length of the Weaver's abdomen then reel back as if drunk, then come back hard and attack again.

The Weaver slipped in and out of sight, was one minute focused and brutal and would then become giddy, hop for a moment on the point of one leg, singing without words, before snapping back to become a voracious killer again.

Unthinkable patterns flitted across the slake-moths' wings, utterly unlike any Isaac had seen them produce before. They licked hungrily as they slashed and stabbed at their enemy. The Weaver spoke calmly to Isaac as it fought.

... NOW LEAVE THIS PLACE AND REGROUP WHILE I THE DRINKARD AND THESE MY BREWERS BICKER AND GASH BEFORE THESE TWO BECOME A TRIUMVIRATE OR WORSE AND I SCAMPER FOR SAFETY GO NOW DOMEWARD AND OUT WE WILL SEE THEE AND ME WE WILL COMMUNE GO NAKED GO NAKED AS A DEAD MAN ON THE RIVER'S DAWN AND I WILL FIND YOU EASY AS CAKE WHAT A PATTERN WHAT COLOURS WHAT INTRICATE THREADS THAT WILL BE WEAVE WELL AND PRETTY NOW RUN FOR YOUR SKIN ...

The mad inebriated fight continued. As Isaac watched, he saw the Weaver being forced back, its energy always ebbing and flowing, moving like a vicious wind, but gradually retreating. Isaac's terror suddenly returned. He ducked into the brick burrow and crawled away.

There was a frantic minute in the dark, as Isaac felt his way at speed along the broken floor of the tunnel. The skin on his hands and knees was flayed by stone.

Light glimmered ahead of him, around a corner and he sped up. He cried out in pain and astonishment as his palms slapped down onto a patch of smooth, scorching metal. He hesitated, groped around him with his ragged sleeve over his hand. The wall and floor and ceiling was plated with a buffed surface of what, in the faint light, looked like a band of pressed steel four feet wide. His face creased in incomprehension. He braced himself, then slid quickly over the metal, hot as a kettle on a fire, trying to keep his skin from its surface.

He breathed out so fast and hard he moaned. He hauled himself through the exit, collapsing across the floor in the dark room where Yagharek waited.

Isaac passed out for three or four seconds. He came to with Yagharek crying out to him, dancing from foot to foot. The garuda was tense but focused. He was utterly controlled.

"Wake," spat Yagharek. "Wake." He was shaking Isaac by his collar. Isaac opened his eyes wide. The shadows that caked Yagharek's face were ebbing away, he realized. Tansell's hex must be wearing off.

"You are alive," said Yagharek. His voice was curt, pared down and bare of emotion. He spoke to save time and effort, to conserve himself. "As I waited, through the window came the blunt snout then the body of a slake-moth. I turned and watched through these mirrors. It was racing, confused. I was ready with my whip and I hit backwards at it, stinging it across its skin, making it shriek. I thought that would mean my death, but the thing raced past me and the ape-construct into the hole, folding its wings away into an impossible space. It ignored me. It looked behind it as if it were chased. I felt a rucking motion in space following it, something moving below the skin of the world, disappearing into the tunnel after the slake-moth. I sent the monkey-thing after it. I heard a crumpling sound, the whiplash of straining metal. I do not know what happened."

"The godsdamn Weaver *melted the construct* . . ." he said, his voice shaking. "Gods only fucking know why." He stood quickly.

"Where is Shadrach?" said Yagharek.

"He got fucking *taken*, didn't he? He got fucking *drunk up*!" Isaac scrambled to the window and leaned out, looking out at the torchlit streets. He heard the heavy, ponderous sound of cactacae running. As torches were carried along surrounding alleys, the shadows slid and shifted like oil in water. Isaac turned back to face Yagharek.

"It was fucking horrible," he said, his voice hollow. "There was nothing I could do . . . Yag, *listen*. The Weaver was in there and it told me to get the godsdamn *out* because the moths can smell the trouble . . . Shit, listen. We burnt its eggs." He spat the words with hard satisfaction. "The fucking thing had *laid* and we got past it and burnt the damn things, but the other moths could sense it and they're heading back here *right now* . . . We've got to get *out*."

Yagharek was still for a moment, thinking quickly. He looked at Isaac and nodded.

They retraced their steps quickly down the dark stairs. They slowed as they approached the first floor, remembering the couple talking quietly on their mattresses, but they saw in the flickering light through the open door that the room was deserted. All the cactacae who had been sleeping were up and out, in the streets.

"God*damn*!" swore Isaac. "We'll be *seen*, we'll be fucking *seen*. The dome must be fucking crawling. We're losing our shadows."

They hovered at the front door. Yagharek and Isaac peered around the corner into the street. There was a crackling susurrus from the raised torches on all sides. Across the street was the little alley, its torches still doused, in which their companions lurked. Yagharek strained to see into its dark, but could not.

At the end of the street by the dome wall, under the stubby, boarded-up remnants of the house in which, Isaac realized, was the slake-moths' nest, stood a gang of cactacae. Opposite them, where the road joined others and moved towards the temple at the dome's centre, little groups of cactus warriors rushed by in either direction.

"Godspit, they must've heard all that ruckus," hissed Isaac. "We have to damn well move, or we're dead. One at a time." He grabbed Yagharek and braced his arms behind the garuda's back. "You first, Yag. You're quicker and harder to see. Go. *Go.*" He pushed Yagharek out into the street.

Yagharek was not wrong-footed. He sprinted lightly, increasing speed. It was not panicked flight which might attract attention. He kept his pace just low enough that if one of the cactus people glimpsed motion, they might think it one of their own people. The shadows and stillness still varnished his fleeting figure.

It was forty feet to the darkness. Isaac held his breath, watching the muscles move beneath Yagharek's scarred back.

The cactus people were jabbering in their harsh pidgin, arguing over who was to go in. Two swung huge hammers, taking turns to batter the bricked-up entrance to the last low house where, for all Isaac knew, the slake-moths and the Weaver still danced lethally together.

The darkness of the alley accepted Yagharek.

Isaac breathed deep, then stepped out into the alley himself.

He strode quickly away from the doorway, into the open street, willing his uncanny shade-covering to deepen. He began to jog towards the alleyway.

As he reached the midway point of the junction, there was a buffeting, a storm of wings. Isaac looked back and up at the window, on the vertex of the wedge of architecture.

Scrabbling at it with a repulsive desperation, the third slake-moth pushed its way through into the interior, returning home.

His breath caught, but the beast was ignoring him, its fervour reserved for its ruined spawn.

As Isaac turned his face again, he realized that the cactacae at the far end of the street had also heard the sound. From where they stood, they could not see the window, could not see the monstrous form infiltrating the house. But they could see Isaac running from them, fat and furtive.

"Oh *shit*," breathed Isaac, and broke into a full, lumbering run.

There was a confusion of yells. One voice rose above the shouting and snapped orders. Several cactus warriors broke away from the congregation by the door and ran straight for Isaac.

They were not fast, but neither was he. They carried their massive weapons expertly, unimpeded as they ran.

Isaac sprinted as best he could.

"I'm on your damn side!" he shouted uselessly as he ran. His words were inaudible. Even if they had heard him, it was inconceivable that the cactus warriors, frightened and bewildered and pugnacious, would have paid any heed before killing him.

The cactacae were yelling, screaming for other patrols. There were answering shouts from neighbouring streets.

An arrow snapped from the alley before Isaac, whipping past him and thudding into some flesh behind. There was a gasp and a curse of pain from one of his pursuers. Isaac made out shapes in the darkness of the alley. Pengefinchess resolved from shadows, drawing back her bowstring once more. She bellowed at him to hurry. Behind her, Tansell stood with the blunderbuss drawn, aiming it uncertainly over her head. His eyes were scanning desperately behind Isaac. He shouted something.

Derkhan and Lemuel and Yagharek were crouched a little way behind, ready to run. Yagharek held his whip coiled and ready.

Isaac raced into the darkness.

"Where's Shad?" screamed Tansell again.

"Dead," shouted Isaac. Instantly, Tansell screamed with horrible anguish. Pengefinchess did not look up, but her arm spasmed and she almost dropped her arrow. She paused and aimed again. Tansell shot wildly over her head. The blunderbuss boomed and he staggered with the recoil. A great cloud of buck-shot sprayed harmlessly over the heads of the cactus people.

"No!" shouted Tansell. "Oh Jabber *no!*" He was staring at Isaac, begging to be told that it was not true.

"I'm sorry, mate, truly, but we have to fucking *go*," said Isaac urgently.

"He's right, Tan," said Pengefinchess, her voice desperately steady. She fired another arrow, with the spring-loaded blade that sliced a great gouge of cactus flesh. She stood, notching a third missile. "Let's *go*, Tan. Don't think, just move."

There was a high-pitched whirring, and a cactacae chakri slammed into the brick by Tansell's head. It embedded itself deep, sending a painful explosion of mortar-shards around it.

The cactacae squadron were approaching fast. Their faces were visible, twisted in rage.

Pengefinchess began to back away, tugging at Tansell.

"Come *on*!" she shouted. Tansell moved with her, muttering and moaning. He had dropped the gun, was crooking his hands like claws.

Pengefinchess ran, dragging Tansell. The others followed her, turning into the intricate maze of backstreets through which they had arrived.

The air behind them hummed with projectiles. Chakris and thrown axe-knives whistled past them.

Pengefinchess ran and leapt at an amazing speed. She turned occasionally and fired behind her, hardly aiming, before resuming her run.

"Constructs?" she shouted at Isaac.

"Fucked," he wheezed. "You know how to get back to the sewers?"

She nodded and turned a corner sharply. The others followed her. As Pengefinchess plunged into the decrepit alleyways near the canal where they had hidden, Tansell turned suddenly back. His face was deep red. As Isaac watched, some little vein burst in the corner of Tansell's eye.

He wept blood. He did not blink. He did not wipe it away.

Pengefinchess turned from the end of the street and howled at him not to be stupid, but he ignored her. His hands and limbs were trembling violently. He raised his gnarled hands and Isaac saw that his veins were protruding hugely, like a map across his skin.

Tansell began to pace back along the street, towards the turnoff where the cactacae would emerge.

Pengefinchess screamed for him one last time, then leapt mightily over a crumbling wall. She shouted for the others to follow her.

Isaac backed quickly towards the shattered brick, his eyes fixed on Tansell's retreating figure.

Derkhan was scrambling up a little stairway of broken brick, hesitating and leaping down into the hidden yard where the vodyanoi wrestled with the manhole cover. It took Yagharek less than two seconds to scale the wall and drop to the other side. Isaac reached up and looked behind him again. Lemuel was running quickly down the alley, ignoring the desperate figure of Tansell behind him.

Tansell stood at the entrance to the alleyway. He shook with effort, his body coursing with thaumaturgic flow. His hair stood on end. Isaac saw little ebony sparks burst outwards from his body, snapping arcs of energy. The puissant charge that snapped and burst out from under his skin was absolutely dark. It glowed negatively, with unlight.

The cactacae turned the corner and were upon him.

The vanguard of the group were startled by this strange, darkly shining figure with hands crooked like a vengeful skeleton, making the air crackle with charged thaumaturgons. Before they could react, Tansell let out a growl, and sizzling bolts of the black energy burst out of his body towards them.

They rolled like ball-lightning through the air and smacked into several cactacae. The hex strokes burst against their victims, dissipating across their skin in crackling veins. The cactus people flew yards backwards, slamming hard against the cobbles. One lay still. The others writhed, shouting in pain.

Tansell raised his arms higher, and a warrior stepped forward, his war-cleaver held way behind his shoulder. He swung it in an enormous, powerful arc.

The heavy weapon smashed into Tansell's left shoulder. Instantly, at the touch of his skin, it conducted the null-charge that sizzled through Tansell's body. Tansell's attacker spasmed mightily and was knocked back by the force of the current, spraying sap from his shattered arm; but the momentum of his massive blow sent the cleaver slicing and cutting through layers of fat and blood and bone, gashing Tansell open from his shoulder down to below his sternum, a huge rend in his flesh a foot and a half long. The cleaver remained embedded above his stomach, quivering.

Tansell called out once like an astonished dog. The dark null-charge fizzled out through the huge wound, which began to spew blood in a vast gouting torrent. Tansell fell to his knees, and onto the ground. The cactacae surged around him, kicking and striking out at the quickly dying man.

Isaac let out an anguished cry and reached the top of the wall. He gesticulated to Lemuel. He looked down into the dark yard. Derkhan and Pengefinchess had opened the way to the undercity.

The cactus people had not given up. Some not stamping on Tansell's corpse were still running forward, waving their weapons at Isaac and Lemuel. As Lemuel reached the wall a rivebow sounded hard. There was a meaty thwack. Lemuel screamed and fell.

A massive serrated chakri was embedded deep in his back, in the spine just above his buttocks. Its silver edges poked out of the wound, which oozed blood copiously.

Lemuel looked up into Isaac's face and screamed piteously. His legs shuddered. He flailed with his hands, sending brickdust up around him.

"Oh Jabber Isaac help me please!" he screamed. *"My legs . . . Oh Jabber, oh gods . . ."* He coughed up a great welling gob of blood which rolled horribly down his chin.

Isaac was transfixed with horror. He stared down at Lemuel, whose eyes were awash with terror and agony. He looked up briefly, and saw the cactacae bearing down on the crippled man, whooping in triumph. They were barely thirty feet away. As he watched, one saw Isaac watching and raised her rivebow, taking careful aim at his head.

Isaac ducked down, scrambled half down off the wall into the little yard. The open manhole wafted up noisome stenches from below.

Lemuel stared at him in disbelief.

"Help me!" he shrieked. *"Jabber, fuck, no, oh Jabber no . . . Don't go! Help me!"*

He swung his arms like a child in a tantrum, the cactus people descending on him, his nails breaking and his fingers scraping raw as he tried frantically to claw his way up the wall pulling his useless legs behind him. Isaac stared at him in mortification, knowing that there was nothing at all he could do, that there was no time to go down for him, that the cactus people were almost on him, that his wounds would kill him even if Isaac could pull him across the wall, and knowing that even so, Lemuel's last thoughts as he looked up were of Isaac's betrayal.

From behind the mouldering concrete of the wall, Isaac heard Lemuel's screams as the cactacae reached him.

"He's nothing to do with it!" he shouted out in a rage of grief. Pengefinchess, her face set, dropped out of sight into the sewer that toiled below. "He's nothing to do with it at all!" screamed Isaac, desperate for Lemuel's wails to stop. Derkhan followed the vodyanoi, her face white, her ruined ear-hole bleeding. "Let him go you fucks, you shits, you stupid cactus bastards!" Isaac shrieked over Lemuel's cacophony. Yagharek descended to his shoulders and gripped Isaac's ankle fiercely, gesticulating at him to come, his inhuman beak clattering as he snapped in agitation. "He was *helping you . . .*" shouted Isaac with exhausted horror.

As Yagharek disappeared, Isaac gripped the edge of the manhole and lowered himself in. He squeezed his tight fat bulk past the metal lips and scrabbled with the lid, preparing to replace it as he dropped out of sight.

Lemuel continued to shout, in pain and fear, from over the wall. The brutal sounds of the terrified, triumphant cactacae punishing the intruder went on and on.

It'll stop, thought Isaac desperately as he descended. *They're frightened and confused, they don't know what's going on. They'll put a chakri or a knife or a bullet in his head any moment, finish this, put an end to this. They've no reason to keep him alive,* he thought, *they'll kill him because they think he's with the moths, they'll do their bit to cleanse the dome, they'll finish this, they're panicking, they're not torturers,* he thought, *they just want to stop the horror . . . They'll end this any second,* he thought in misery. *This will stop now.*

Yet the sound of Lemuel's screams continued as he disappeared into the stinking darkness, and as he pulled the metal seal over his head. And even then they filtered tinny and absurd through the lid, even as Isaac fell into the stream of warm, faecal water, and staggered along the tunnels following the other survivors. He thought he could hear them even as he crawled through the dripping, trickling, reverberating water-sounds, underneath the liquid rush, along ancient channels like rutted veins, away from the Glasshouse, in a confused, random flight towards the relative safety of the mammoth night-city.

It was a long time before they were silent.

The night is unthinkable. We can only run. We make animal sounds as we rush to escape what we have seen. Dread and revulsion and alien emotions cling to us and cloy our movements. We cannot clean them off.

We scrabble our wounded way up and out from the undercity and reach the railside hovel. We shiver even in the awful heat, nodding mutely to the clattering trains that shake our walls. We stare warily at each other.

Except Isaac, who looks at nothing.

Do I sleep? Does anyone sleep? There are moments when the numbness overwhelms me and clogs up my head so that I cannot see or think. Perhaps these fugues, these broken zombie moments, are sleep. Sleep for the new city. Perhaps that is all we can hope for any more.

No one speaks, for a long, long time.

Pengefinchess the vodyanoi is the first to speak.

She begins quietly, murmuring things hardly recognizable as words. But she is addressing us. She sits, her back against the wall, her fat thighs splayed. The idiot undine winds around her body, washing her clothes, keeping her wet.

She tells us about Shadrach and Tansell. The three had met in some ill-defined episode she glosses over, some mercenary escapade in Tesh, City of the Crawling Liquid. They had run together for seven years.

The window of our shack is fringed with ragged stubs of glass. At dawn, they snag ineffectually at the sunlight. Under a sharp rafter of the insect-fouled light, Pengefinchess talks in a gentle monotone of her times with her dead companions: poaching in the Wormseye Scrub; thievery in Neovadan; tomb-robbing in the Ragamoll forest and steppe.

They had never been three equally united, she says, without spite or rancour. Always she, then Tansell and Shadrach together, who found in each other something, some calm passionate connection she could not and did not want to touch.

Tansell was mad with grief at the end, she says, unthinking, exploding, a mindless eruption of thaumaturgic misery. But had he been clear in his brain, she says, he would have done no different.

So she is on her own again.

Her testimony ends. It demands response, like some ritual liturgy.

She ignores Isaac, cosseted in agony. She looks to Derkhan and to me.

We fail her.

Derkhan shakes her head, wordless and sad.

I try. I open my beak and the story of my crime and my punishment and my exile wells up in my throat. It almost emerges, it almost bursts through the crack.

But I batten it down. It is not connected. It is not for tonight.

Pengefinchess's history is one of selfishness and plunder, yet it is made by the telling into a valedictory for dead comrades. My history of selfishness and exile resists transmutation. It cannot but be a base story of base things. I am silent.

But then, as we prepare to give up on words and let what happen will, Isaac raises his sluggish head and speaks.

First he demands food and water that we do not have. Slowly his eyes narrow and he begins to talk like a sentient creature. In a remote misery, he describes the deaths he has seen.

He tells us about the Weaver, the dancing mad god, and its fight with the moths, the eggs that burnt, the weird sing-song declamations of our unlikely and untrustworthy champion. In cold and clear words Isaac tells us what he thinks the Construct Council is become, and what it wants and what it might be (and Pengefinchess gulps deep in her throat in her astonishment, her protuberant eyes bulging more as she learns what has happened to the constructs in the city's dump).

And the more he talks the more he talks. He talks of plans. His voice hardens. Something has come to an end in him, some waiting, some soft patience that died with Lin and now is buried, and

I feel myself become stone as I hear him. He inspires me to rigour and purpose.

He talks of betrayals and counter-betrayals, of mathematics and lies and thaumaturgy, dreams and winged things. He expounds theories. He talks to me of flight, something I had half forgotten I might ever have, which I want again, as he mentions it, I want with all of me.

As the sun crawls like a sweating man to the apex of the sky, we remnants, we dregs, examine our weapons and our collected debris, our notes and our stories.

With reserves we did not know we could summon, with an astonishment I feel as if through a veil, we make plans. I coil my whip around my hand tight and sharpen my blade. Derkhan cleans her guns, and murmurs to Isaac. Pengefinchess sits back and shakes her head. She will go, she warns us. There is nothing that might incite her to stay. She will sleep a little, then bid us farewell, she says.

Isaac shrugs. He pulls compact valved engines from where he has stashed them in the piled-up rubbish of the shed. He pulls sheafs and sheafs of notes, sweat-stained, smeared, barely legible, from inside his shirt.

We begin to work, Isaac more fervently than any of us, scribbling frantically.

He looks up after hours of muttered oaths and hissing breakthroughs. We cannot do this, he says. We would need a focus.

And then another hour or two hours pass and he looks up again.

We have to do this, he says, and still, we need a focus.

He tells us what we must do.

There is silence, and then we debate. Quickly. Anxiously. We raise candidates and discard them. Our criteria are confused—do we choose the doomed or the loathed? The decrepit or the vile? Do we judge?

Our morality becomes rushed and furtive.

But the day is more than half gone, and we must choose.

Her face set hard but breaking with misery, Derkhan readies herself. She is charged with the vile task.

She takes what money we have, including the last nuggets of my gold. She cleans some of the undercity's filth from her, changing her accidental disguise, becoming only a low vaga-bond, then sets out to hunt for what we need.

Outside it begins to darken, and still Isaac works. Tiny con-fined figures and equations fill every space, every tiny part of white space, on his few sheets of paper.

The thick sun illumines the smears of cloud from below. The sky grows drab with dusk.

None of us fear the night's crop of dreams.

PART SEVEN

Crisis

CHAPTER FORTY-SIX

The streetlights flickered off all over the city, and the sun came up over the Canker. It picked out the shape of a tiny barge, little more than a raft, which bobbed on the cool swell.

It was one of many that littered the twin rivers of New Crobuzon. Left to rot into the water, the carcasses of old boats floated randomly with the current, tugging half-heartedly at forgotten moorings. There were many of these vessels in the heart of New Crobuzon, and the mudlarks dared each other to swim out to them, or to clamber along the old ropes that tethered them pointlessly. Some they avoided, whispering that they were the homes of monsters, the lairs of the drowned who would not accept that they were dead, even as they rotted.

This one was half covered with ancient stiffened fabric that stank of oil and rot and grease. The boat's old wood skin seeped with the river water.

Hidden in the shadow of the tarpaulin, Isaac lay looking at the quickly moving clouds. He was naked and quite still.

He had lain there for some time. Yagharek had come with him to the river's edge. They had crept for more than an hour through the uneasily shifting city, through the familiar streets of Brock Marsh and up through Gidd, on under rail-lines and past militia towers, eventually reaching the southern fringes of Canker Wedge. Less than two miles from the centre of the city, but a different world. Low, quiet streets and modest housing, small apologetic parks, frumpy churches and halls, offices with false fronts and façades in a cacophony of muted styles.

Here there were avenues. They were nothing like the wide banyan-fringed thoroughfares of Aspic, or the Rue Conifer in Ketch Heath, magnificently lined with ancient pine trees. Still, in the outskirts of Canker Wedge were stunted oaks and dark-woods that hid the architecture's failings. Isaac and Yagharek, his feet wrapped in bandages again, his head hidden in a newly stolen cloak, had been thankful for the cover of leafy darkness as they made for the river.

There were no great conglomerations of heavy industry along the Canker. The factories and workshops and warehouses and docks studded the sides of the slower Tar, and the Gross Tar which the conjoined rivers became. It was not until the last mile of its distinct existence, where it passed Brock Marsh and a thousand laboratory outflows, that the Canker became fouled and dubious.

In the north of the city, in Gidd and Rim, and here in Canker Wedge, residents might row the waters for pleasure, an unthinkable pastime further south. So it was that Isaac had made his way here, where the river traffic was quiet, to obey the Weaver's instructions.

They had found a little alley between the backs of two rows of houses, a thin sliver of space that sloped down towards the eddying water. It had not been hard to find a deserted boat, though there were not a fraction as many as there were by the industrial riversides of the city.

Leaving Yagharek watching from beneath his ragged hood like some motionless tramp, Isaac had picked his way down to the edge of the river. There was a fringe of grass and a band of thick mud between him and the water, and he shucked his clothes as he went, collecting them under his arm. By the time he reached the Canker he was nude under the waning darkness.

Without hesitating, steeling himself, he had walked on into the water.

It had been a short, cold swim to the boat. He had enjoyed it, luxuriating in the feeling, the black river washing him clean of sewer-filth and days of grime. He had trailed his clothes behind him, willing the water to suffuse their fibres and clean them, too.

He had hauled himself over the side of the boat, his skin prickling as he dried. Yagharek was barely visible, motionless, watching. Isaac arranged his clothes around him and pulled the tarpaulin a little way over him, so that he lay covered by shadows.

He watched the light arrive in the east and shivered as breezes raised paths of gooseflesh on him.

"Here I am," he murmured. "Naked as a dead man on the river's dawn. As requested."

He did not know if the Weaver's dreamlike pronouncement, that it had hummed that ghastly night in the Glasshouse, had been any kind of invitation. But he thought that by responding to it he might make it one, changing the patterns of the worldweb, weaving it into a conjuncture that might, he hoped, please the Weaver.

He had to see the magnificent spider. He needed the Weaver's help.

Halfway through the previous night, Isaac and his comrades had become aware that the night's tension, the unsettled sick feeling in the air, the nightmares, had returned. The Weaver's attack had failed, as it had predicted. The moths were still alive.

It had occurred to Isaac that his taste was known to them now, that they would recognize him as the destroyer of the egg-clutch. Perhaps he should have been petrified with fear, but he was not. The railside shack had been left alone.

Maybe they're afraid of me, he thought.

He drifted on the river. An hour passed, and the sounds of the city waxed unseen around him.

The noise of bubbles disturbed him.

He leaned up gingerly on his elbow, his mind rapidly clicking back into focus. He peered over the edge of the boat.

Yagharek was still visible, his posture completely unchanged, on the riverbank. Now there were some few passers-by behind him, ignoring him as he sat there covered up and smelling of filth.

Close to the boat, a patch of bubbles and disturbed water boiled up from below, snapping at the surface and sending out a ring of ripples about three feet across. Isaac's eyes widened momentarily as he realized that the circle of ripples was *exactly* circular, and contained, that as each ripple reached its edge, it flattened impossibly, leaving the water beyond it undisturbed.

Even as Isaac moved back slightly, a smooth black curve breached in the dark, disturbed water. The river fell away from the rising shape, splashing within the limits of the little circle.

Isaac was staring into the Weaver's face.

He snapped back, his heart beating aggressively. The Weaver stared up at him. Its head was angled so that only it emerged from the water, and not the looming body which rose higher when it stood.

The Weaver was humming, speaking deep in Isaac's skull.

. . . YOU PEACH YOU PLUMB THE ONE THE DEADNAKED AS WAS
ASKED LITTLE FOURLIMBED WEAVER THAT YOU MIGHT BE . . . it
said in a continuous lilting monologue . . . RIVER AND DAWN IT
DAWNS ON ME THE NEWS IS NUDES ABOB . . . The words ebbed until they could not be properly heard, and Isaac took the chance to
speak.

"I'm glad to see you, Weaver," he said. "I remembered our appointment." He breathed deep. "I need to talk to you," he said.
The Weaver's humming, crooning incantation resumed, and
Isaac struggled to understand, to translate the beautiful babbling
into sense, to answer, to make himself heard.

It was like a dialogue with the sleeping or the mad. It was difficult, exhausting. But it could be done.

Yagharek heard the subdued chattering of children walking to
school. They walked some way behind him where a path cut
through the grass of the bank.

His eyes flickered across the water where the trees and wide
white streets of Flag Hill stretched back from the water, on a
gentle incline. There, too, the river was fringed with rough grass,
but there was no path and there were no children. Nothing but
the quiet walled houses.

Yagharek pulled his knees slightly closer and wrapped his
body in his rank cloak. Forty feet into the river, Isaac's little vessel seemed unnaturally still. Isaac's head had bobbed tentatively
into view some minutes ago, and now it remained poking
slightly over the lip of the old boat, facing away from Yagharek.
It looked as if he was staring intently at some patch of water,
some flotsam.

It must, Yagharek realized, be the Weaver, and he felt excitement move him.

Yagharek strained to hear, but the light wind brought nothing
to him. He heard only the lapping of the river and the abrupt
sounds of the children behind him. They were curt, and cried
easily.

Time passed but the sun seemed frozen. The little stream of
schoolboys did not ebb. Yagharek watched Isaac argue incomprehensibly with the unseen spider-presence below the surface
of the river. Yagharek waited.

And then, some time after dawn but before seven o'clock,
Isaac turned furtively in the boat, fumbled for his clothes and

crawled like some slinking ungainly water-rat back into the Canker.

The anaemic morning light broke up on the river's surface as Isaac tugged himself through the water, towards the bank. In the shallows he performed a grotesque aquatic dance to pull on his clothes, before hauling himself streaming and heavy up the mud and scrub of the bank.

He collapsed before Yagharek, wheezing.

The schoolboys tittered and whispered.

"I think . . . I think it'll come," said Isaac. "I think it understood."

It was past eight when they got back to the railside hut. It was still and hot, thick with indolently drifting particles. The colours of the rubbish and the hot wood were bright where light breached the splintering walls.

Derkhan had still not returned. Pengefinchess slept in the corner, or pretended to.

Isaac gathered the vital tubes and valves, the engines and batteries and transformers, into a vile sack. He retrieved his notes, rifled through them briefly to check them, then stashed them back into his shirt. He scrawled a note for Derkhan and Pengefinchess. He and Yagharek checked and cleaned their weapons, counted their meagre store of ammunition. Then Isaac looked out of the ruined windows into the city which had woken around them.

They must be careful now. The sun had gained its strength, the light was full. Anyone might be militia, and every officer would have seen their heliotype. They drew their cloaks around them. Isaac hesitated, then borrowed Yagharek's knife and shaved bloodily with it. The sharp blade skittered painfully on the nodules and bumps on his skin that were the reason he had first grown a beard. He was ruthless and quick, and soon stood before Yagharek with a pasty chin, inexpertly shorn of whiskers, bleeding and patched with copses of stubble.

He looked ghastly, but he looked different. Isaac dabbed at his bleeding skin as they set out into the morning.

By nine, after minutes of skulking, striding nonchalantly past shops and arguing pedestrians, finding backstreet routes wherever they existed, the companions were in the Griss Twist dump. The heat was unforgiving, and seemed greater in these canyons of discarded metal. Isaac's chin stung and tingled.

They picked their way over the wasteground towards the heart of the maze, towards the Construct Council's lair.

"Nothing." Bentham Rudgutter clenched his fists on his desk.

"Two nights we've had the airships up and searching. Nothing at all. Another crop of bodies every morning, and not a gods-damn thing all night. Rescue dead, no sign of Grimnebulin, no sign of Blueday . . ." He raised bloodshot eyes and looked across the table at Stem-Fulcher, who sucked gently at the pungent smoke of her pipe. "This is not going well," he concluded.

Stem-Fulcher nodded slowly. She considered.

"Two things," she said slowly. "It's clear that what we need is specially trained troops. I told you about Motley's officers." Rudgutter nodded. He rubbed and rubbed at his eyes. "We can easily match those. We could easily tell the punishment factories to run us off a squadron of specialist Remade, with mirrors and backwards weapons and all, but what we need is *time*. We need to train them up. That's three, four months at the least. And while we're biding our time the slake-moths are just going to keep picking off citizens. Getting stronger.

"So we have to think about strategies for keeping the city under control. A curfew, for example. We know the moths *can* get into houses, but there's no doubt that most of the victims are picked off the streets.

"Then we need to dampen speculation in the press about what's going on. Barbile wasn't the only scientist working on that project. We need to be able to stamp out any dangerous kind of sedition, we need to detain all the other scientists involved.

"And with half the militia engaged in slake-moth duties, we can't risk another dock strike, or anything similar. It could cripple us quickly. We owe it to the city to put an end to any unreasonable demands. Basically, Mayor, this is a crisis bigger than any since the Pirate Wars. I think it's time to declare a state of emergency. We need extraordinary powers.

"We need martial law."

Rudgutter pursed his lips mildly, and considered.

"Grimnebulin," said the avatar. The Council itself remained hidden. It did not sit up. It was indistinguishable from the mountains of filth and garbage around it.

The cable that entered the avatar's head emerged from the

floor of metal shavings and stone debris. The avatar stank. His skin was patched with mould.

"Grimnebulin," he repeated in his uncomfortable, wavering voice. "You did not return. The crisis engine you left with me is incomplete. Where are the Is that went with you to the Glasshouse? The slake-moths flew again last night. Did you fail?"

Isaac held his hands up to slow the questioning.

"Stop," he said peremptorily. "I'll explain."

Isaac knew that it was misleading to think of the Construct Council having emotions. As he told the avatar the story of that appalling night in the cactus Glasshouse—that night of so-partial victory at such horrendous price—he knew that it was not anger or sadness that caused the man's body to shake, his face to spasm in random grotesqueries.

The Construct Council had sentience, but no feelings. It was assimilating new data, that was all. It was calculating possibilities.

He told it that the monkey-constructs had been destroyed and the avatar's body spasmed particularly sharply, as the information flooded back down the cable into the hidden analytical engines of the Council. Without those constructs, it could not download the experience. It relied on Isaac's reports.

As once before, Isaac thought he glimpsed a human figure fleeting in the rubbish around him, but the apparition was gone in an instant.

Isaac told the Council of the Weaver's intervention, and then, finally, began to explain his plan. The Council, of course, was quick to understand.

The avatar began to nod. Isaac thought he could feel infinitesimal movements in the ground under him, as the Council itself began to shift.

"Do you understand what I need from you?" said Isaac.

"Of course," replied the Construct Council in the avatar's reedy quaver. "And I will be linked directly to the crisis engine?"

"Yes," said Isaac. "That's how this is going to work. I forgot some of the components of the crisis engine when I left it with you, which is why it wasn't complete. But that's just as well, because when I saw them, they gave me the idea for all this. But listen: I need your help. If this is going to work we need the maths to be *exact*. I brought my analytical engine with me from the laboratory, but it's hardly a top-notch model. You, Council, are a network of damn sophisticated calculating engines . . . right? I need you to do some sums for me. Work out some functions, print up some programme cards. And I need them *perfect*. To an infinitesimal degree of error. All right?"

"Show me," said the avatar.

Isaac pulled out two sheets of paper. He walked over to the avatar, holding them out. In the dump's smell of oil and chymical mould and warming metal, the organic stink of the avatar's slowly collapsing body was shocking. Isaac creased his nose in disgust. But he steeled himself and stood beside the rotting, half-alive carcass and explained the functions he had outlined.

"This page here is several equations I can't get the answers to. Can you read them? They're to do with the mathematical modelling of mental activity. This second page is more tricky. This is the set of programme cards I need. I've tried to lay out each function as exactly as I can. So here for example . . ." Isaac's stubby finger moved along a line of complicated logic symbols. "This is 'find data from input one; now model data.' Then here we have the same demand for input two . . . and this really complex one here: 'compare prime data.' Then over here are the constructive, remodelling functions.

"Is that all comprehensible?" he said, stepping back. "And can you do it?"

The avatar took the papers and scanned them carefully. The dead man's eyes moved in a smooth left-right-left motion along the page. It was seamless until the avatar paused and shuddered as data welled along the cable to the Construct's hidden brain.

There was a motionless moment, and then the avatar said: "This can all be done."

Isaac nodded in curt triumph. "We need it . . . well . . . now. As soon as possible. I can wait. Can you do that?"

"I will try. And then as evening falls and the slake-moths return, you will turn on the power, and you will connect me. You will link me up to your crisis engine."

Isaac nodded.

He fumbled in his pocket and drew out another piece of paper, which he handed to the avatar.

"That's a list of everything we need," he said. "It's all bound to be in the dump somewhere, or it can be rigged up. Do you have some . . . uh . . . some little yous somewhere that can track this stuff down? Another couple of those helmets you got for us, the ones communicators use; a couple of batteries; a little generator; stuff like that. Again, we need that now. The main thing is we need cable. Thick conducting cable, stuff that can take elyctrical or thaumaturgic current. We need two and a half, three *miles* of the stuff. Not all in one, obviously . . . it can be in pieces, as long as they can be connected easily one to the next, but we need *masses*. We have to link you up with our . . . with our focus." His voice quietened as he said this, and his face set. "The cable has to be ready this evening, by six o'clock I think."

Isaac's face was hard. He spoke in a monotone. He looked at the avatar carefully.

"There's only four of us, and one of those we can't rely on," he went on. "Can you contact your . . . congregation?" The avatar nodded slowly, waiting for an explanation. "See, we need people to connect those cables across the city." Isaac tugged the list out of the avatar's hands and began to sketch on the back: a jagged sideways Y for the two rivers, little crosses for Griss Twist, The Crow, and scribbles delineating Brock Marsh and Spit Hearth in between. He linked the first two crosses with a quick slash of pencil. He looked up at the avatar. "You're going to have to organize your congregation. *Fast*. We need them in place *with the cable* by six o'clock."

"Why do you not perform the operation here?" asked the avatar. Isaac shook his head vaguely.

"It wouldn't work. This is a backwater. We have to channel the power through the city's focal point, where all the lines converge.

"We have to go to Perdido Street Station."

Chapter Forty-seven

Carrying a bloated sack of discarded technology between them, Isaac and Yagharek crept back through the quiet streets of Griss Twist, up the broken brick stairwell of the Sud Line. Like shambling city vagrants in clothes ill-suited to the sweltering air, they trudged a path through the skyline of New Crobuzon, back to their collapsing hideout by the railway line. They waited for a squealing onrush of train to pass, blowing energetically from its flared chimney, then picked their way through fences of wavering air poured upwards from the scalding iron tracks.

It was midday, and the air wrapped them like a heated poultice.

Isaac put down his end of the sack and tugged at the rickety door. It was pushed open from inside by Derkhan. She slipped through to stand in front of him, half closing the door behind her. Isaac glanced up and could see someone standing ill-at-ease in a dark corner.

"Found someone, 'Zaac," whispered Derkhan. Her voice was taut. Her eyes were bloodshot and nearly tearful in her dirty face. She pointed briefly back into the room. "We've been waiting."

Isaac had to meet the Council; Yagharek would inspire awe and confusion but no confidence in those he approached; Penge-finchess would not go; so hours ago, it was Derkhan who had been forced out into the city on the grisly and monstrous errand. It had turned her into some bad spirit.

At first, when she left the hut and walked into the city, made her way quickly through the tarry darkness that filled the streets, she had cried in a drab fashion to ease the pressure of her tortured head. She had kept her shoulders skulking high, knowing that of the few figures she saw quickly pacing their way somewhere, a high proportion were likely to be militia. The heavy nightmare tension of the air drained her.

But then as the sun rose and the night sank slowly into the gutters, her way had become easier. She had moved more quickly, as if the very material of the darkness had resisted her.

Her task was no less horrendous, but urgency bleached her horror until it was an anaemic thing. She knew that she could not wait.

She had some way to go. She was making for the charity hospital of Syriac Well, through four or more miles of intricately twisting slum and collapsing architecture. She did not dare take a cab, in case it was driven by a militia spy, an agent out to catch perpetrators like her. So she paced as quickly as she dared in the shadow of the Sud Line. It raised itself higher and higher above the roofs as it passed further and further from the city's heart. Yawning arches of dripping brick soared over the squat streets of Syriac.

At Syriac Rising Station, Derkhan had broken away from the tracks of the rails and borne off into the snarl of streets south of the undulating Gross Tar.

It had been easy to follow the noise of costermongers and stallholders to the squalor of Tincture Prom, the wide and dirty street that linked Syriac, Pelorus Fields and Syriac Well. It followed the course of the Gross Tar like an imprecise echo, changing its name as it went, becoming Wynion Way, then Silverback Street.

Derkhan had skirted its raucous arguments, its two-wheel cabs and resilient, decaying buildings from the side streets. She had tracked its length like a hunter, bearing north-east. Until finally, where the road kinked and bore north at a sharper angle, she had gathered her courage to scurry across it, scowling like a furious beggar, and plunged into the heart of Syriac Well, to the Veruline Hospital.

It was an old and sprawling pile, turreted and finessed with various brick and cement flounces: gods and dæmons eyed each other across the tops of windows, and drakows rampant sprouted at odd angles from the multilevel roof. Three centuries previously, it had been a grandiose rest-home for the insane rich, in what was then a sparse suburb of the city. The slums had spread like gangrene and swallowed up Syriac Well: the asylum had been gutted, turned into a warehouse for cheap wool; then emptied out by bankruptcy; squatted by a thieves' chapter, then a failed thaumaturges' union; and finally bought by the Veruline Order and turned once more into a hospital.

Once more a place of healing, they said.

Without funds or drugs, with doctors and apothecaries volunteering odd hours when their consciences goaded them, with a staff of pious but untrained monks and nuns, the Veruline Hospital was where the poor went to die.

Derkhan had made her way past the doorman, ignoring his queries as if she were deaf. He raised his voice at her, but he did not follow. She had ascended the stairs to the first floor, towards the three working wards.

And there . . . there she had hunted.

She remembered stalking up and down past clean, worn beds, below massive arched windows full of cold light, past wheezing, dying bodies. To the harassed monk who scurried up to her and asked her business, she had blubbered about her dying father who had gone missing—stomped off into the night to die—who she had heard might be here with these angels of mercy, and the monk was mollified and a little puffed at his goodliness and he told Derkhan that she might stay and search. And Derkhan asked where the very ill were, tearful again, because her father, she explained, was close to death.

The monk had pointed her wordlessly through the double-doors at the end of the huge room.

And Derkhan had passed through and entered a hell where death was stretched out, where all that was available to ward off the pain and degradation was sheets without bed-bugs. The young nun who stalked the ward with eyes wide in endless appalled shock would pause occasionally and refer to the sheet clipped to the end of every bed, verifying that yes the patient was dying and that no they were still not dead.

Derkhan looked down and flipped a chart open. She found the diagnosis and the prescription. *Lungrot,* she had read. *2 dose laudanum/3 hours for pain.* Then in another hand: *Laudanum unavailable.*

In the next bed, the unavailable drug was sporr-water. In the next, calciach sudifile, which, if Derkhan read the chart correctly, would have cured the patient of their disintegrating bowel over eight treatments. It went on, stretched the length of the room, a pointless, informational list of what would have ended the pain, one way or another.

Derkhan began to do what she had come for.

She examined the patients with a ghoulish eye, a hunter of the nearly dead. She had been hazily aware of the criteria with which she gazed—*of sound mind, and not so ill they will not last the day*—and she had felt sick to her soul. The nun had seen her, had approached with a curious lack of urgency, demanding to know what or whom she sought.

Derkhan had ignored her, had continued with her terrible cool assessment. Derkhan had walked the length of the room, stopping eventually beside the bed of a tired old man whose notes gave him a week to live. He slept with his mouth open, dribbling slightly and grimacing in his sleep.

There had been a ghastly moment of reflection when she had found herself applying strained and untenable ethics to the choice—*Who here is a militia informer?* she wanted to shout. *Who here has raped? Who has murdered a child? Who has tortured?* She had closed down the thoughts. That could not be allowed, she had realized. That might drive her mad. This had to be exigency. This could not be a choice.

Derkhan had turned to the nun who followed her emitting a constant stream of blather it was no effort to ignore.

Derkhan remembered her own words as if they had never been real.

This man is dying, she had said. The nun's noise had quieted, and she had nodded. Can he walk? Derkhan had asked.

Slowly, the nun said.

Is he mad? Derkhan had asked. He was not.

I'm taking him, she had said. I need him.

The nun had begun to vent outrage and astonishment and Derkhan's own carefully battened down emotions had broken free momentarily and tears had flooded her face with appalling speed, and she had felt as if she would howl in misery so she closed her eyes and hissed in wordless animal grief until the nun was silent. Derkhan had looked at her again and shut down her own tears.

Derkhan had pulled her gun from inside her cloak and held it at the nun's belly. The nun looked down and mewed in surprise and fear. While the nun still gazed at the weapon in disbelief, with her left hand Derkhan had pulled out the pouch of money, the remnants of Isaac's and Yagharek's money. She had held it out until the nun saw it, and realized what was expected and held out her hand. Then Derkhan poured the notes and gold-dust and battered coins into it.

Take this, she had said, her voice trembling and careful. She pointed randomly about the ward at the moaning, tossing figures in the beds. Buy laudanum for him and calciach for her, Derkhan had said, cure him and send that one quietly to sleep; make one or two or three or four of them live, and make death easier for one or two or three or four or five or I don't know, I don't know. Take it, make things better for how many you can, but this one I *must* take. Wake him up and tell him he has to come with me. Tell him I can help him.

Derkhan's pistol wavered, but she kept it trained vaguely on the other woman. She closed the nun's fingers around the money and watched her eyes crease and widen in astonishment and incomprehension.

Deep inside her, in the place that still felt, that she could not quite close down, Derkhan had been aware of a plaintive defence, an argument of justification—*See?* she felt herself assert. *We take him but all these others we save!*

But there was no moral accounting that lessened the horror of what she was doing. She could only ignore that anxious discourse. She stared deep and fervent into the nun's eyes. Derkhan closed her hand tight around the nun's fingers.

Help them, she had hissed. This can help them. You can help them all except him or you can help none of them. Help them.

And after a long, long time of silence, of staring at Derkhan with troubled eyes, of looking at the grubby currency and at the gun and then at the dying patients on all sides, the nun put the money into her white overall with a shaking hand. And as she moved away to waken the patient, Derkhan watched her with a terrible, mean triumph.

See? Derkhan had thought, sick with self-loathing. *It wasn't just me! She chose to do it too!*

His name was Andrej Shelbornek. He was sixty-five. His innards were being eaten by some virulent germ. He was quiet and very tired of worrying, and after two or three initial questions, he followed Derkhan without complaint.

She told him a little about the treatments they had in mind, the experimental techniques they wished to try on his brutalized body. He said nothing about this, about her filthy appearance, or anything else. *He must know what's going on!* she had thought. *He's tired of living like this, he's making it easy on me.* This was rationalization of the lowest kind, and she would not entertain it.

It was swiftly clear that he could not walk the miles to Griss Fell. Derkhan had hesitated. She pulled a few torn notes from her pocket. She had no choice but to hail a cab. She was nervous. She had lowered her voice into an unrecognizable snarl as she gave directions, with her cloak hiding her face.

The two-wheeled cab was pulled by an ox, Remade into a biped to fit with ease into New Crobuzon's twisted alleyways and narrow thoroughfares, to turn tight corners and retreat without stalling. It lolloped on its two back-curved legs in constant surprise at itself, with a stride that was uncomfortable and bizarre. Derkhan sat back and closed her eyes. When she looked up again, Andrej was asleep.

He did not speak, or frown or seem perturbed, until she had bade him climb the steep slope of earth and concrete shards be-

side the Sud Line. Then his face had creased and he had looked
at her in confusion.

Derkhan had said something blithely about a secret experimental laboratory, a site above the city, with access to the trains.
He had looked concerned, had shaken his head and looked
around to escape. In the dark below the railway bridge, Derkhan
had pulled out her flintlock. Although dying, he was still afraid
of death, and she had forced him up the slope at gunpoint. He
had begun to cry halfway up. Derkhan had watched him and
nudged him with the pistol, had felt all her emotions from very
far away. She kept distant from her own horror.

Inside the dusty shack, Derkhan waited silently with her gun on
Andrej, until eventually they heard the shuffling sounds of Isaac
and Yagharek returning. When Derkhan opened the door for
them, Andrej began to wail and cry out for help. He was astonishingly loud for such a frail man. Isaac, who had been about to
ask Derkhan what she had told Andrej, broke off speaking and
rushed over to quieten the man.

There was a half-second, a tiny fraction of time, when Isaac
opened his mouth, and it seemed that he would say something to
assuage the old man's fears, to assure him that he would be un-
harmed, that he was in safe hands, that there was a reason for his
bizarre incarceration. Andrej's shouts faltered for a moment as
he stared at Isaac, eager to be reassured.

But Isaac was tired, and he could not think, and the lies that
welled up made him feel as if he would vomit. The patter died
away silently, and instead Isaac walked across to Andrej and
overpowered the decrepit man with ease, stifling his nasal wails
with strips of cloth. Isaac bound Andrej with coils of ancient
rope and propped him as comfortably as possible against a wall.
The dying man hummed and exhaled in snotty terror.

Isaac tried to meet his eye, to murmur some apology, to tell him
how sorry he was, but Andrej could not hear him for fear. Isaac
turned away, aghast, and Derkhan met his eye and grasped his
hand quickly, thankful that someone finally shared her burden.

There was much to be done.

Isaac began his final calculations and preparations.

Andrej squealed through his gag and Isaac looked up at him
despairingly.

In curt whispers and brusque expostulations, Isaac explained to Derkhan and Yagharek what he was doing.

He looked over the battered engines in the shack, his analytical machines. He pored over his notes, checking and rechecking his maths, cross-referring them with the sheets of figures the Council had given him. He drew out the core of his crisis engine, the enigmatic mechanism that he had neglected to leave with the Construct Council. It was an opaque box, a sealed motor of interwoven cables, elyctrostatic and thaumaturgic circuits.

He cleaned it slowly, examined its moving parts.

Isaac readied himself and his equipment.

When Pengefinchess returned from some unstated errand, Isaac looked up briefly. She spoke quietly, refusing to meet anyone's eye. She gathered herself slowly to leave, checked through her equipment, oiling her bow to keep it safe under the water. She asked what had become of Shadrach's pistol, and clucked regretfully when Isaac told her he did not know.

"A shame. It was a powerful piece," she said abstractedly, looking out of the window and away. "Charmed. A puissant weapon."

Isaac interrupted her. He and Derkhan implored her to help once more before she left. She turned and stared at Andrej, seemed to see him for the first time, ignored Isaac's pleading and demanded to know what in Hell he was doing. Derkhan drew her away from Andrej's snorts of fear and Isaac's grim industry, and explained.

Then Derkhan asked Pengefinchess again if she would perform one last task to help them. She could only beg.

Isaac half listened, but he shut his ears quickly to the hissed imploring. He worked instead on the task in hand, the complicated job of crisis mathematics.

Andrej whimpered unceasingly beside him.

CHAPTER FORTY-EIGHT

Just before four o'clock, as they prepared to go, Derkhan embraced Isaac and Yagharek in turn. She hesitated only a moment before holding the garuda close. He did not respond, but he did not pull away either.

"See you at the rendezvous," she murmured.

"You know what you have to do?" Isaac said. She nodded and pushed him towards the door.

He hesitated now, at the hardest thing. He looked over to where Andrej lay in a kind of exhausted stupor of fear, his eyes glazed and his gag sticky with mucus.

They had to bring him, and he could not raise the alarm.

He had conferred with Yagharek about this, in whispers easily hidden under the old man's terror. They had no drugs, and Isaac was no bio-thaumaturge, could not insinuate his fingers briefly through Andrej's skull and turn his consciousness temporarily off.

Instead, they were forced to use Yagharek's more savage skills.

The garuda thought back to the fleshpits, remembering the "milk fights": those that ended with submission or unconsciousness rather than death. He remembered the techniques he had perfected, adjusting them to his human opponents.

"He's an old man!" hissed Isaac. "And he's dying, he's frail . . . Be gentle . . ."

Yagharek sidled along the wall to where Andrej lay staring at him with tired, nauseous foreboding.

There was a quick feral movement, and Yagharek was leaning behind Andrej, on one knee, the old man's head pinioned with his left arm. Andrej stared out at Isaac, his eyes bulging, unable to scream through his gag. Isaac—horrified, guilty and debased— could not help but meet his eye. He watched Andrej, knew that the old man thought he was about to die.

Yagharek's right elbow swung down in a sharp arc and smacked with brutal precision into the back of the dying man's head, where his skull gave way into the neck. Andrej gave a short, constricted bark of pain, that sounded very like vomiting. His eyes flickered out of focus, then closed. Yagharek did not let Andrej's head fall away: he kept his arms tense, pulling his bony elbow hard into soft flesh, counting seconds.

Eventually he let Andrej slump.

"He will wake," he said. "Perhaps in twenty minutes, perhaps in two hours. I must watch him. I can send him to sleep again. But we must be careful—too much and we will starve his brain of blood."

They wrapped Andrej's motionless body with random rags. They hauled him up between them, each with one arm over a shoulder. He was wasted, his insides devoured over years. He weighed shockingly little.

They moved together, supporting the enormous sack of equipment between them with their free arms, carrying it as carefully as if it were a religious relic, the body of some saint.

They were still swathed in their absurd, wearisome disguises, bent and shuffling like beggars. Under his hood, Isaac's dark skin was still dappled with tiny scabs from his savage shaving. Yagharek wrapped his head, like his feet, in rotten cloth, leaving one tiny slit through which to see. He looked like a faceless leper hiding his decaying skin.

The three of them looked like some appalling caravan of vagrants, a travelling convocation of the dispossessed.

At the door, they turned their heads once, quickly. They both raised their hands in farewell to Derkhan. Isaac looked over to where Pengefinchess watched them placidly. Hesitantly, he raised his hand to her, raised his eyebrows in a query—*Will I see you again?* he might have been asking, or *Will you help us?* Pengefinchess raised her great splayed hand in noncommittal response and looked away.

Isaac turned away, set his lips.

He and Yagharek began the dangerous journey across the city.

They did not risk crossing the rail bridge. They were afraid in case an irate train driver did more than blast them with a steam-whistle as he tore past. He might stare at them and clock their faces, or report to his superiors at Sly or Spit Bazaar Stations, or at Perdido Street Station itself, that three stupid dossers had blundered their way onto the rails and were heading for disaster.

Interception was too dangerous. So instead, Isaac and Yagharek clambered down the crumbling stone slope by the railway line, hanging on to Andrej's body as it tumbled and sprawled towards the quiet pavements.

The heat was intense, but not fierce: it seemed instead like some absence, some enormous citywide lack. It was as if the sun was etiolated, as if its rays bleached out the shadows and cool undersides that gave the architecture its reality. The sun's heat stifled sounds and bled them of substance. Isaac sweated and cursed quietly beneath his putrid rags. He felt as if he stalked through some vaguely realized dream of heat.

With Andrej supported between them like a friend paralysed

with cheap liquor, Isaac and Yagharek tramped through the streets, making for Cockscomb Bridge.

They were interlopers here. This was not Dog Fenn or Badside or the Ketch Heath slums. There, they would have been invisible.

They crossed the bridge nervously. They were hemmed in by its lively stones, surrounded by the sneers and jibes of shopkeepers and customers.

Yagharek kept one surreptitious hand clamped on a cluster of nerve and arterial tissue at the side of Andrej's neck, ready to pinch hard if the old man gave any sign of waking. Isaac muttered, a coarse babble of swearing that sounded like drunken rambling. It was a disguise, in part. He was also steeling himself.

"Come on, fucker," he grunted, tense and quiet, "come on, come on. Fucker. Scum. Bastard." He did not know who he was swearing at.

Isaac and Yagharek crossed the bridge slowly, supporting their companion and their precious bag of equipment. The flow of people parted around them, let them pass with only jeers behind them. They could not let the opprobrium grow and become confrontation. If some bored toughs decided to kill time by harassing beggars, it would be catastrophic.

But they passed over Cockscomb Bridge, where they felt isolated and open, where the sun seemed to etch out their edges and mark them for attack, and slipped into Petty Coil. The city seemed to close its lips around them and they felt safer again.

There were other beggars here, walking in the train of local notables, earringed villains and fat money-lenders and pinchlipped madams. Andrej stirred slightly and Yagharek closed his mind down again, laid hands on him efficiently.

Here there were backstreets. Isaac and Yagharek could peel away from the main roads and head down along overshadowed alleys. They passed under washing that linked the facing terraces of tall, narrow streets. They were watched by men and women in underclothes who idly leaned over balconies, flirting with their neighbours. They passed piles of rubbish and broken sewer coverings, and children leaned out from above and spat at them without rancour, or threw little pebbles and ran away.

As always, they sought the railway line. They found it at Sly Station, where the Salacus Fields trains branched away from the Sud Line. They sidled up to the raised path of arches that wove unsteadily above the cobbles of Spit Hearth. The air above the raucous crowds was reddening as the sun wound slowly towards gloaming. The arches were fouled with oil and soot, sprouting a microforest of mould and moss and tenacious climbing plants. They swarmed with lizards and insects, aspises sheltering from the heat.

Isaac and Yagharek ducked into a dirty cul-de-sac by the track's concrete and brick foundations. They rested. Life rustled in the urban thicket above them.

Andrej was light, but he was beginning to weigh them down, his mass seeming to increase with every second. They stretched their aching arms and shoulders, drew deep breaths. A few feet away, the crowds emerging from the station thronged past the entrance to their little hideaway.

When they had rested and rearranged their burdens, they braced themselves and set out again, into the backstreets once more, walking in the shadow of the Sud Line, towards the city's heart, the towers not yet visible over the surrounding miles of houses: the Spike and the turrets of Perdido Street Station.

Isaac began to talk. He told Yagharek what he thought would happen that night.

Derkhan made her way through the reclaimed filth of the Griss Twist dump towards the Construct Council.

Isaac had warned the great Constructed Intelligence that she would be coming. She knew she was expected. The idea made her uncomfortable.

As she approached the hollow that was the Council's lair, she thought she heard a susurration of lowered voices. She stiffened instantly, and drew her pistol. She checked that it was loaded, and that the firing pan was full.

Derkhan picked up her feet, stalking with care, avoiding any sound. At the end of a channel of rubbish, she saw the opening-out of the hollow. Someone walked briefly past her field of view. She stole carefully closer.

Then another man walked past the end of the gorge of crushed garbage, and she saw that he was dressed in work overalls, and that he was staggering slightly under the weight of a. burden. Slung over his broad shoulder was a massive coil of black-coated cable, entwining him vastly like some predatory constrictor.

She straightened up slightly. It was not the militia waiting for her. She walked on into the presence of the Construct Council.

*   *   *

She entered the hollow, glancing up nervously to ensure that there were no airships overhead. Then she turned to the scene before her, gasping at the scale of the gathering.

On all sides, engaged in all manner of opaque tasks, were nearly a hundred men and women. Mostly human, there were a handful of vodyanoi among them, and even two khepri. All were dressed in cheap and soiled clothes. And almost all were carrying or squatting before enormous coils of industrial cable.

It came in a variety of styles. Most was black, but there were brown and blue coatings as well, and red and grey. There were pairs of burly men staggering under loops nearly the thickness of a man's thigh. Others carried skeins of wire no more than four inches in diameter.

The thin hubbub of speech died away quickly as Derkhan entered, and all the eyes in the place turned to her. The rubble crater was crammed with bodies. Derkhan swallowed and looked over them carefully. She saw the avatar stumbling towards her on halting, brittle legs.

"Derkhan Blueday," he said quietly. "We are ready."

Derkhan huddled for a short time with the avatar, checking carefully over a scribbled map.

The bloody concavity of the avatar's open skull emitted an extraordinary reek. In the heat, his peculiar half-dead stench was utterly unbearable, and Derkhan held her breath as long as she could, gulping air when she had to through the sleeve of her filthy cloak.

While Derkhan and the Council conferred, the rest of the assembled kept a respectful distance.

"This is almost all of my bloodlife congregation," said the avatar. "I sent out mobile Is with urgent messages, and the faithful have gathered, as you see." He paused and clucked inhumanly. "We must proceed," he said. "It is seventeen minutes past five o'clock."

Derkhan looked up at the sky, which was deepening slowly, warning of dusk. She was sure that the clock the Council was checking, some timepiece buried deep in the bowels of the dump, was second-perfect. She nodded.

At a command from the avatar, the congregation began to stagger out of the dump, wobbling under their loads. Before they left, each turned to the place in the wall of the dump where the Construct Council was hidden. They paused a moment, then performed their devotional gesture with their hands, that vague suggestion of interlocking wheels, putting down their cable if necessary.

Derkhan watched them with foreboding.

"They'll never make it," she said. "They haven't the strength."

"Many have brought carts," responded the avatar. "They will leave in shifts."

"Carts . . . ?" said Derkhan. "From where?"

"Some own them," said the avatar. "Others have bought or rented them at my orders today. None were stolen. We cannot risk the attention and detection that might result."

Derkhan looked away. The control that the Council wielded over his human followers disturbed her.

As the last stragglers left the dump, Derkhan and the avatar walked over to the immobile head of the Construct Council. The Council lay on its side and became strata of rubbish, invisible.

A short, thick coil of cable lay waiting beside it. Its end was ragged, the thick rubber carbonized and split for the last foot or so. Tangles of wires splayed out of the end, unpicked from their neat skeins and plaits.

There was one vodyanoi still in the junk-basin. Derkhan saw him standing some feet away, watching the avatar nervously. She beckoned him to come closer. He waddled towards them, now on all fours, now bipedally, his big webbed toes splayed to remain steady on the treacherous ground. His overalls were the light, waxed material the vodyanoi sometimes used: they repelled liquid, so did not become saturated or heavy when the vodyanoi swam.

"Are you ready?" said Derkhan. The vodyanoi nodded quickly.

Derkhan studied him, but she knew little about his people. She could see nothing about him which gave any clue as to why he devoted himself to this strange, demanding sect, worshipping this weird intelligence, the Construct Council. It was obvious to her that the Council treated its worshippers like pawns, that it drew no satisfaction or pleasure from their worship, only a degree of . . . usefulness.

She could not understand, not begin to understand, what release or service this heretical church offered its congregation.

"Help me lift this down to the river," she said, and picked up one end of the thick cable. She was unsteady under its weight, and the vodyanoi picked its way quickly over to her, helped brace her.

The avatar was still. He watched as Derkhan and the vodyanoi made their way away from him, towards the idle, looming cranes which burst up to the north-west, from behind the low rise of garbage that surrounded the Construct Council.

The cable was massive. Derkhan had to stop several times and put the end down, then brace herself to continue. The vodyanoi moved stolidly beside her, stopping with her and waiting for her to carry on. Behind them, the squat pillar of coiled cable shrank slowly as it unwound.

Derkhan chose their passage, moving through the piles of murk towards the river like a prospector.

"D'you know what all this is about?" she asked the vodyanoi quickly, without looking up. He glanced at her sharply, then back up at the thin silhouette of the avatar, still visible against a background of rubbish. He shook his jowly head.

"No," he said quickly. "Just heard that . . . that God-machine demanded our presence, ready for an evening's work. Heard Its bidding when I got here." He sounded quite normal. His tone was curt, but conversational. Not zealous. He sounded like a worker complaining philosophically about management's demands for unpaid overtime.

But when Derkhan, wheezing with effort, began to ask more—"How often do you meet?" "What other things does It bid you do?"—he looked at her with fear and suspicion, and his answers became monosyllabic, then nods, then quickly nothing at all.

Derkhan became silent again. She concentrated on hauling the great wire.

The dumps sprawled untidily to the very edge of the river. The river banks around Griss Twist were sheer walls of slimy brick that rose up from the dark water. When the river was swollen, perhaps only three feet of the decaying clay prevented a flood. At other times, there were as many as eight feet between the top of the riverwall and the choppy surface of the Tar.

Jutting directly from the splintered brick was a six-foot fence of iron links and wooden slats and concrete, built years ago to contain the dumps in their infancy. But now the weight of accumulated filth made the old wirelinks bow alarmingly over the water. With the decades, sections of the flimsy wall had burst and split from its concrete moorings, spewing rubbish into the river below. The fence had gone unrepaired, and in those places now it was only the solidity of the crushed rubbish itself which held the dump in place.

Blocks of compressed garbage regularly cascaded into the water in greasy landslides of slag.

The huge cranes which took cargo from the trash-barges had originally been separated from the garbage they unloaded by a few yards of no-man's-land—flat scrub and baked earth—but that had rapidly disappeared as the rubbish encroached. Now the dump workers and crane operators had to hike across the scoriatic landscape to cranes that sprouted directly from the vulgar geology of the dump.

It was as if the trash was fertile, and that it bore great structures.

Derkhan and the vodyanoi turned corners in the muck until they could no longer see the Council's hide. They left a trail of cable that became invisible the moment it touched the ground, transformed into one meaningless piece of litter in a whole vista of mechanical refuse.

The hillocks of garbage subsided as they approached the Tar. Ahead of them, the rusted fence rose four feet or so from the surface layer of detritus. Derkhan changed course fractionally, headed for a wide break in the wire, where the dump was open to the river.

Across the squalid water Derkhan could see New Crobuzon. For a moment, the lumpy spires of Perdido Street Station were just visible, perfectly framed in the fence's hole, bulging distantly over the city. She could see the rail-lines pick their way between towers that stabbed randomly from the bedrock. Militia struts jutted ugly into the skyline.

Opposite her, Spit Hearth welled up fatly to the river's edge. There was no unbroken promenade by the side of the Tar, only sections of streets that traced it for a short time, then private gardens, sheer warehouse walls and wasteground. There was no one to watch Derkhan's preparations unfold.

A few feet from the edge, Derkhan dropped the end of the cable and moved cautiously towards the break in the fence. She felt with her feet, making sure the ground would not fall forward and pitch her into the filthy river seven or more feet below. She leaned out as far as she dared, and scanned the gently moving surface.

The sun was slowly approaching the rooftops to the west, and the dirty black of the river was varnished with reddening light.

"Penge!" Derkhan hissed. "You there?"

After a moment, there was a small splashing sound. One of the indistinct pieces of flotsam that littered the river bobbed suddenly closer. It moved against the current.

Slowly, Pengefinchess raised her head from the river. Derkhan smiled. She felt an odd, desperate relief.

"All right then," said Pengefinchess. "Time for my last job."

Derkhan nodded with absurd gratitude.

"She's here to help," Derkhan said to the other vodyanoi, who stared at Pengefinchess in alarmed suspicion. "This cable's too big and heavy for you to manage yourself. If you get in, then I'll feed it down to you both."

It took a few seconds for him to decide the risks posed by the newcomer were less important than the job in hand. He glowered at Derkhan in nervous fear, and nodded. He padded quickly to the break in the link-fence, paused for a fraction of a second, then hopped elegantly up and plunged into the water. His dive was so controlled that there was only a tiny splash.

Pengefinchess eyed him suspiciously as he kicked closer to her.

Derkhan looked quickly around, saw a cylindrical metal pipe thicker than her thigh. It was long and incredibly heavy, but working urgently, ignoring her tortured muscles, Derkhan hauled it inch by inch across the gap in the fence, wedging it across the tear. She held her arms out, wincing at the acid burn of her muscles. She stumbled back to the cable and tugged it to the edge of the water.

She began to feed it down over the top of the pipe towards the waiting vodyanoi, hauling it as hard as she could. She pulled more and more free from the coils hidden in the heart of the dump and sent the slack towards the water. Finally, Derkhan had lowered it enough for Pengefinchess to kick up, launch herself almost out of the water and grab hold of the dangling end. Her weight pulled several feet of cable down into the water. The edge of the dump listed alarmingly towards the river, but the cable slid across the smooth surface of the pipe, pulling it tight against the fence on either side and rolling smoothly across its top.

Pengefinchess reached up again and hauled, submerging and powering towards the bottom of the river. Kept free of the ensnaring hooks and edges of the inorganic topsoil, the cable came in great gouts, skimming roughly across the surface of the rubbish and plummeting into the water.

Derkhan watched its halting progress, sudden bursts of motion as the vodyanoi hidden at the bottom of the river jack-knifed their legs and swam hard. She smiled, a small and brief moment of triumph, and leaned exhausted against a broken concrete pillar.

There was nothing on the surface of the water to give any hint of the operation below. The great cable slipped in spurts into the water by the riverwall. It plunged absolutely precipitately into the darkness, hitting the surface at ninety degrees. The vodyanoi, Derkhan realized, must be tugging masses of slack into the water first, rather than pulling the end of the wire directly across the river and having it stretch out across the top of the water.

Eventually the cable was still. Derkhan watched quietly, waiting for some sign of the operation under way.

Minutes passed. Something emerged in the absolute centre of the river.

It was a vodyanoi, raising an arm in triumph or salute or signal. Derkhan waved back, squinted to see who it was, to work out if she was being given a message.

The river was very wide, and the figure was unclear. Then Derkhan saw that the arm carried a composite bow, and she realized that it was Pengefinchess. She saw then that the wave was one of curt farewell, and she responded more fulsomely, her brows furrowing.

It made very little sense, Derkhan realized, to have begged Pengefinchess to help at this last stage of the hunt. Undoubtedly it had made things easier, but they could have managed without her, with the help of more of the Council's vodyanoi followers. And it made little sense to feel affected by her leaving, even if remotely; to wish Pengefinchess luck; to wave with feeling and feel a faint lack. The vodyanoi mercenary was taking her leave, was disappearing for more lucrative and safer contracts. Derkhan owed her nothing, least of all thanks or affection.

But circumstances had made them comrades, and Derkhan was sorry to see her go. She had been part, a small part, of this chaotic nightmare struggle, and Derkhan marked her passing.

The arm and bow disappeared. Pengefinchess submerged again.

Derkhan turned her back on the river and headed back into the Council's labyrinth.

She followed the trail of decaying cable through the twists of the junkyard scenery, into the Council's presence. The avatar stood waiting by the diminished coil of rubber-swathed wire.

"Is the crossing successful?" he asked as soon as he saw her. He stumbled forwards, the cable that burst from his brainpan rattling behind him. Derkhan nodded.

"We've got to get things ready here," she said. "Where's the output?"

The avatar turned and indicated for her to follow him. He stopped for a moment and picked up the other end of the cable. He staggered under its weight, but he did not complain or ask for help, and Derkhan did not volunteer.

With the thick insulated wire under his arm, the avatar approached the constellation of rubbish that Derkhan recognized as the Construct Council's head (with a slight unsettling jolt, as at a child's book of optical tricks, as if an ink drawing of a young woman's face had suddenly become a crone's). It still lolled sideways, without any sign of life.

The avatar reached up over the grille that doubled as the Council's metal teeth. Behind one of the enormous lights Derkhan knew were its eyes, a tangled knot of wire and tubing and rubbish burst out of a casing, in which the stuttering valves of some vastly complex analytical engine were working.

It was the first sign that the great construct was conscious. Derkhan thought she saw light glimmer faintly, waxing and waning, in the Council's huge eyes.

The avatar pulled the cable into position beside the analogue brain, one of the network that made up the Council's peculiar inhuman consciousness. He untwisted several of the thick wires in the cable, and in the explosion of metal from the Council's head, Derkhan looked away, sickened, as the avatar placidly ignored the way the vicious metal tore jagged holes in his hands, and sluggish, greying blood oozed fitfully out and over his decaying skin.

He began to link the Council to the cable, twisting finger-thick wires together into a conducting whole, snapping connections into sockets that sputtered with obscure sparks, examining the seemingly meaningless buds of copper and silver and glass that flowered from the Construct Council's brain and from the rubber sheathing of the cable, picking some, twisting and discarding others, plaiting the mechanism into impossibly complex configurations.

"The rest is easy," he whispered. "Wire to wire, cable to cable, at every junction throughout the city, that is easy. This is the only taxing part, here at source, to connect up correctly, to channel the exudations, to mimic the operation of the communicators' helmets for an alternative model of consciousness."

Yet despite the difficulty, it was still light when the avatar looked up at her, wiped his lacerated hands against his thighs, and said that he had finished.

Derkhan watched the little flashes and sparks that burst ominously from the connection with awe. It was beautiful. It glittered like some mechanical jewel.

The Council's head—vast and still immobile, like a sleeping dæmon's—was linked to the cable with a knot of connective tissue, an elyctro-mechanical, thaumaturgic scar. Derkhan marvelled. Eventually she looked up.

"Well then," she said hesitantly, "I'd best go and tell Isaac that . . . that you're ready."

With great sweeps of dirty water, Pengefinchess and her companion kicked their way through the eddying darkness of the Tar.

They stayed low. The bottom was barely visible as uneven darkness two feet below them. The cable unwound slowly from the great pile they had left at the bottom of the river, by the edge of the wall.

It was heavy, and they lugged it sluggishly through the filthy river.

They were alone in this part of the water. There were no other vodyanoi: only a few hardy, stunted fishes that skimmed nervously away at their approach. *As if,* thought Pengefinchess, *anything in the whole of Bas-Lag could induce me to eat them.*

Minutes passed and their hidden passage continued. Pengefinchess did not think of Derkhan or of what would happen that night, did not consider the plan on which she had eavesdropped. She did not evaluate its probable success. It was none of her concern.

Shadrach and Tansell were dead, and it was time for her to move on.

In a vague way, she wished Derkhan and the others luck. They had been companions, though very briefly. And she understood, in a lax fashion, that there was a great deal at stake. New Crobuzon was a rich city, with a thousand potential patrons. She wanted it to remain healthy.

Ahead of her the slick darkness of the approaching riverwall welled up. Pengefinchess slowed. She hovered in the water and hauled in some slack on the cable, enough to raise it to the surface. Then she hesitated a moment and kicked up. She indicated the male vodyanoi should follow her and she swam up through gloom towards the fractured light that marked out the Tar's surface, where a thousand rays of sun seeped in all directions through the little waves.

They broke the surface together, and kicked the last few feet into the shadow of the riverwall.

Rusting iron rings were driven into the bricks, creating a rough staircase up to the riverside walk above them. The sound of cabs and pedestrians sank down around them.

Pengefinchess adjusted her bow slightly, making it more comfortable. She looked at the surly male and spoke to him in Lubbock, the polysyllabic guttural language of most of the eastern vodyanoi. He spoke a city dialect, which had been bastardized with human Ragamoll, but they could still understand each other.

"Your companions know to find you here?" Pengefinchess enquired brusquely. He nodded (another human trait the city vodyanoi had adopted). "I am done," she announced. "You must hold the cable alone. You can wait for them. I am leaving." He looked at her, still surly, and nodded again, raised his hand in a choppy motion which might have been some kind of salute. Pengefinchess was amused. "Be fecund," she said. It was a traditional farewell.

She sank under the surface of the Tar and powered herself away.

Pengefinchess swam east, following the course of the river. She was calm, but a rising excitement filled her up. She had no plans, no ties. She wondered, suddenly, what she would do.

The current took her towards Strack Island, where the Tar and Canker met in a confused current and became the Gross Tar. Pengefinchess knew that the submerged base of the Parliament's island was patrolled by vodyanoi militia, and she kept her distance, branching away from the pull of the water and bearing sharply north-west, swimming upstream, transferring into the Canker.

The current was stronger than the Tar's, and colder. She was exhilarated, briefly, until she entered a sluice of pollution.

It was the effluent from Brock Marsh, she knew, and she kicked quickly through the murk. Her undine familiar trembled against her skin as she approached certain random patches of water, and she would arc away and pick another route through the fouled river by the magicians' quarter. She breathed the disgusting liquid shallowly, as if she might avoid contamination that way.

Eventually the water seemed to thin. A mile or so upstream from the rivers' convergence, the Canker grew suddenly more clear and pure.

Pengefinchess felt something almost like quiet joy.

She began to feel other vodyanoi pass her in the current. She kicked low, here and there felt the gentle outflow of tunnels that led up to some wealthy vodyanoi's house. These were not the absurd hovels of the Tar, of Lichford and Gross Coil: there, sticky, pitch-coated buildings of palpably human design had simply been built in the river itself, decades ago, to crumble in unsanitary fashion into the water. Those were the vodyanoi slums.

Here, on the other hand, the cold clear water that ran down from the mountains might lead through some carefully crafted passage below the surface into a riverside house all done in white marble. Its façade would be tastefully designed to fit in with the human homes on either side, but inside it would be a vodyanoi home: empty doorways connecting huge rooms above and below the water; canal passageways; sluices refreshing the water every day.

Pengefinchess swam on past the vodyanoi rich, staying low. As the centre of the city passed further away behind her, she grew happier, more relaxed. She felt her escape with great pleasure.

She spread her arms and sent a little mental message to her undine, and it burst away from her skin through the pores of the thin cotton shift she wore. After days of dryness and sewers and effluent, the elemental undulated away through the cleaner water, rolling with enjoyment, being free, a moving locus of quasi-living water in the great wash of the river.

Pengefinchess felt it swim ahead and followed it playfully, reaching out for it and closing her fingers through its substance. It squirmed happily.

I'll go up-coast, Pengefinchess decided, *round the edge of the mountains. Through the Bezhek Foothills, maybe, and the out-*

skirts of Wormseye Scrub. I'll head for the Cold Claw Sea. With the sudden decision, Derkhan and the others were transformed instantly in her mind, becoming history, becoming something over and done, something she might one day tell stories about.

She opened her enormous mouth, let the Canker gush through her. Pengefinchess swam on, through the suburbs, up and out of the city.

CHAPTER FORTY-NINE

Men and women in grubby overalls spread out from the Griss Twist dump.

They went on foot and in carts, singly, in pairs, and in little gangs of four or five. They moved in dribs and drabs, at unobtrusive speeds. Those on foot carried great swathes of cable over their shoulders, or looped between them and a colleague. In the backs of the carts the men and women sat on enormous rocking twists of the frayed wire.

They went out into the city at irregular intervals, over two or more hours, spacing their departures according to a schedule worked out by the Construct Council. It was calculated to be random.

A small horse-drawn wagon containing four men set off, entering the flow of traffic over Cockscomb Bridge and winding up towards the centre of Spit Hearth. They made their way without urgency, turning onto the wide, banyan-lined Boulevard St. Dragonne. They swayed with a muted clacking along the wooden slats that paved the street: the legacy of the eccentric Mayor Waldemyr, who had objected to the cacophony of wheels on stone cobblestones past his window.

The driver waited for a break in the traffic, then turned to the left and into a small courtyard. The boulevard was invisible, but its sounds were still thick around them. The cab stopped by a high wall of rich red brick, from behind which rose an exquisite smell of honeysuckle. Ivy and passionflower sprouted in little bursts over the lip of the wall, bobbing above them in the breeze. It was the garden of the Vedneh Gehantock monastery, tended by the dissident cactacae and human monks of that floral godling.

The four men leapt down from the cart and began to unload tools and the bales of heavy cable. Pedestrians walked past them, watched them briefly and forgot them.

One man held the end of the cable high against the monastery wall. His workmate lifted a heavy iron bracket and a mallet, and with three quick strokes he had anchored the end of the cable into the wall, about seven feet above the ground. The two moved along, repeated the operation eight or so feet further to the west; and then again, moving along the wall at some speed.

Their movements were not furtive. They were functional and unpresuming. The hammering was just another noise in the montage of city sound.

The men disappeared around the corner of the square and moved off to the west. They dragged the huge bail of insulated wire with them. The other two men stayed put, waiting by the tethered end of the cable, its copper and alloy innards splaying like metallic petals.

The first pair took the cable along the twisting wall that dug inwards through Spit Hearth, around the backs of restaurants and the delivery entrances to clothing boutiques and carpenters' workshops, towards the red-light zone and The Crow, the bustling nucleus of New Crobuzon.

They moved the cable up and down the height of the brick or concrete, winding it past stains in the wall's structure, and joining twisting skeins of other pipes, gutterings and overflows, gas pipes, thaumaturgic conductors and rusting channels, circuits of obscure and forgotten purpose. The drab cable was invisible. It was one nerve fibre in the city's ganglions, a thick cord among many.

Inevitably, they had to cross the street itself, as it peeled away, curving slowly eastwards. They lowered the cable to the ground, approaching a rut that linked the two sides of the pavement. It was a gutter, originally for shit and now for rainwater, a six-inch channel between the paving slabs that sluiced through grilles into the undercity at the furthest end.

They laid the cable in the groove, attaching it firmly. They crossed quickly, standing aside occasionally while traffic interrupted them in their work, but this was not a busy street, and they were able to lay the cable without extensive interruption.

Their behaviour still did not merit attention. Running their cable back up the wall opposite—this time the boundary of a school, from the window of which came forth didactic barks—the unremarkable pair passed another group of workmen. They were digging up the opposite corner of the street, replacing shattered flagstones, and they looked up at the newcomers and grunted some shorthand greeting, then ignored them.

As they approached the red-light zone, the Construct Council's followers turned into a courtyard, trailing their heavy coil. On three sides, walls rose above them, five or more floors of filthy brick, stained and mossy, years of smog and rain etched across them. There were windows at untidy intervals, as if they had been spilt from the highest point to fall irregularly between the roof and the ground.

Cries and oaths were audible, and laughed conversations, and the clattering of kitchenware. A pretty young child of uncertain sex watched them from a third-floor window. The two men looked at each other nervously for a moment, and scanned the rest of the overlooking windows. The child's was the only face: they were otherwise unobserved.

They dropped the loops of cable, and one looked up into the child's eyes, winked impishly and grinned. The other man dropped to one knee and peered through the bars of the circular manhole in the courtyard floor.

From the darkness below a voice hailed him curtly. A filthy hand shot up towards the metal seal.

The first man tugged his companion's leg and hissed at him— "They're here . . . this is the right place!"—then grabbed the rough end of the cable and tried to thrust it between the bars in the sewer's entrance. It was too thick. He cursed and fumbled in his toolbox for a hacksaw, began to work on the tough grille, wincing at the screech of metal.

"Hurry," said the invisible figure below. "Something's been following us."

When the cutting was done, the man in the courtyard shoved the cable hard into the ragged hole. His companion glanced down at the unsettling scene. It looked like some grotesque inversion of birth.

The men below grabbed at the cable, hauled it into the darkness of the sewers. The yards of wire coiled in the still, close courtyard began to unwind into the city's veins.

The child watched curiously as the two men waited, wiping their hands on their overalls. When the cable was pulled taut, when it disappeared sharply under the ground, pulled at a tight angle around the corner of the little cul-de-sac, then they sauntered quickly out of that shadowed hole.

As they turned the corner, one man looked up, winked again, then walked on and disappeared from the child's view.

In the main street the two men separated without a word, walking away in different directions under the setting sun.

At the monastery, the two men waiting by the wall were looking up.

On the building across the street, a concrete edifice mottled with damp, three men had appeared over the crumbling edge of the roof. They were hauling their own cable with them, the last forty or so feet of a much longer roll that now snaked away behind them, tracking their rooftop journey from the southern corner of Spit Hearth.

The cable trail they left wound among the rooftop shacks of squatters. It joined the legions of pipes that made erratic paths among the pigeon hutches. The cable was squeezed around spires and tacked like some ugly parasite onto slates. It bowed slightly across streets, twenty, forty or more feet above the ground, next to the little bridges thrown up across the divides. Here and there, where the gap was six feet or less, the cable simply spanned the drop, where its bearers had leapt across.

The cable disappeared south-eastwards, plunging suddenly down and through a slimy storm-drain, into the sewers.

The men made their way to the fire-escape of their building, and began to descend. They hauled the thick cable down to the first floor, looked down over the monastery garden and the two men watching on the ground.

Ready?" shouted one of the newcomers, and made a throwing motion in their direction. The pair looking up, nodded. The three on the fire-escape paused, and swung the remnants of the cable in time.

When they threw it, it wriggled in the air like some monstrous flying serpent, descending with a heavy smack into the arms of the man who ran to catch it. He yelped, but held it, kept the end high above his head and pulled it as tight as he could across the divide.

He held the heavy wire against the monastery wall, positioning himself so that the new length of cable would link up snugly with the piece already attached to the Vedneh Gehantock garden wall. His companion hammered it into place.

The black cable crossed the street above the pedestrians' heads, descending at a steep angle.

The three on the iron fire-escape leaned over, watching the frantic engineering of their fellows. One of the men below them began to twist together the huge snarls of wire, connecting the conducting material. He worked quickly, until the two bare ends of fibrous metal were conjoined in an ugly, functional knot.

He opened his toolkit and brought forth two little bottles. He shook them both briefly, then opened the stopper on one and dripped it quickly across the thicket of wires. The viscous liquid seeped in, saturating the connection. The man repeated the operation with the second bottle. As the two liquids met there was an audible chymical reaction. He stood back, stretched his arm to continue pouring, closing his eyes as smoke began to billow out from the rapidly heating metal.

The two chymicals met and mixed and combusted, spewing out noxious fumes with a quick burst of heat intense enough to weld the wires into a sealed mesh.

When the heat had lessened, the two men began the final job, laying ragged strips of sacking across the new connection and cracking the seals on a tin of thick, bituminous paint, slathering it on thickly, covering the bare metal seal, insulating it.

The men on the fire-escape were satisfied. They turned and retraced their steps, returning to the roof, from where they dissipated into the city as quick and untraceable as smoke in a breeze.

All along a line between Griss Twist and The Crow, similar operations were taking place.

In the sewers, furtive men and women picked their way through the hiss and drip of the subterranean tunnels. Where possible, these large gangs were led by workers who knew a little of the undercity: sewage workers; engineers; thieves. They were all equipped with maps, torches, guns and strict instructions. Ten or more figures, several with lengths of heavy cable, would pick their way together along their allotted route. When one piece of slowly unrolling wire ran out, they would connect another and continue.

There were dangerous delays as parties lost each other, blundering towards lethal zones: ghul-nests and undergang lairs. But they corrected themselves and hissed for help, making their way back towards their comrades' voices.

When they finally met the tail end of another team in some main node of tunnel, some medium hub of sewer, they connected the two huge ends of wire, welding them with chymicals or heat-torches or backyard thaumaturgy. Then the cable was attached to the enormous arterial clutches of pipes that travelled the lengths of the sewers.

Their job done, the company would scatter and disappear.

In unobtrusive places, with extended backstreets or great stretches of interlinked roofs, the cable would poke from underground and be taken by the crews working above the streets. They unrolled the cable over hillocks of rank sedge behind warehouses, up stairways of damp brick, over roofs and along chaotic streets, where their industry was invisible in its banality.

They met others, the cable lengths were sealed. The men and women dispersed.

Mindful of the likelihood that some crews—especially those in the undercity—would become lost and miss their rendezvous points, the Construct Council had stationed spare crews along the route. They waited in building sites and by the banks of canals with their serpentine load beside them, for word that some connection had not been made.

But the work seemed charmed. There were problems, lost moments, wasted time and brief panics, but no team disappeared or missed its meeting. The spare men remained idle.

A great sinuous circuit was constructed through the city. It wound through more than two miles of textures: its matt-black rubber skin slid under faecal slime; across moss and rotting paper; through scrubby undergrowth, patches of brick-strewn grassland, disturbing the trails of feral cats and street-children; plotting the ruts in the skin of architecture, littered with granulated clots of damp brickdust.

The cable was inexorable. It moved on, its path deviating briefly here and there with whiplash curves, scoring a path through the hot city. It was as determined as some spawning fish, fighting its way towards the enormous rising monolith at the centre of New Crobuzon.

The sun was sinking behind the foothills to the west, making them magnificent and portentous. But they could not challenge the chaotic majesty of Perdido Street Station.

Lights flickered on across its vast and untrustworthy topography, and it received the now-glowing trains into its bowels like offerings. The Spike skewered the clouds like a spear held ready, but it was nothing beside the station: a little concrete addendum to that great disreputable leviathan building, wallowing in fat satisfaction in the city-sea.

The cable wound towards it without pause, rising above and falling beneath New Crobuzon's surface in waves.

The west-facing front of Perdido Street Station opened onto Bil-Santum Plaza. The plaza was thronging and beautiful, with carts and pedestrians circulating constantly around the parkland at its centre. In this lush green, jugglers and magicians and stall-holders kept up raucous chants and sales pitches. The citizenry were blithely careless of the monumental structure that dominated the sky. They only noticed its façade with offhand pleasure when the low sun's rays struck it full on, and its patchwork of architecture glowed like a kaleidoscope: the stucco and painted wood were rose; the bricks went bloody; the iron girders were glossy with rich light.

BilSantum Street swept under the huge raised arch that connected the main body of the station to the Spike. Perdido Street Station was not discrete. Its edges were permeable. Spines of low turrets swept off its back and into the city, becoming the roofs of rude and everyday houses. The concrete slabs that scaled it grew squat as they spread out, and were suddenly ugly canal walls. Where the five railway lines unrolled through great arches and passed along the roofs, the station's bricks supported and surrounded them, cutting a path over the streets. The architecture oozed out of its bounds.

Perdido Street itself was a long, narrow passageway that jutted perpendicularly from BilSantum Street and wound sinuously east towards Gidd. No one knew why it had once been important enough to give the station its name. It was cobbled, and its houses were not squalid, though they were in ill-repair. It might once have described the station's northern boundary, but it had long been overtaken. The storeys and rooms of the station had spread out and rapidly breached the little street.

They had leapt it effortlessly and spread like mould into the roofscape beyond, transforming the terrace at the north of Bil-Santum Street. In some places Perdido Street was open to the air: elsewhere it was covered for long stretches, with vaulted bricks festooned with gargoyles or lattices of wood and iron.

There in the shade from the station's underbelly, Perdido Street was gaslit all the time.

Perdido Street was still residential. Families rose every day beneath that dark architecture sky, walked its winding length to work, passing in and out of shadow.

The tramp of heavy boots often sounded from above. The front of the station, and much of its roofscape, was guarded. Private security, foreign soldiers and the militia, some in uniform and some in disguise, patrolled the façade and the mountainous landscape of slate and clay, protecting the banks and stores, the embassies and the government offices that filled the various floors within. They would tread like explorers along carefully plotted routes through the spires and spiral iron staircases, past dormer windows and through hidden rooftop courtyards, journeying across the lower layers of the station roof, looking down over the plaza and the secret places and the enormous city.

But further to the east, towards the rear of the station, spotted with a hundred trade entrances and minor establishments, the security lapsed and became more haphazard. The towering construction was darker here. When the sun set, it cast its great shadow across a huge swathe of The Crow.

Some way out from the main mass of the building, between Perdido Street and Gidd Stations, the Dexter Line passed through a tangle of old offices that long ago had been ruined by a minor fire.

It had not damaged the structure, but it had been enough to bankrupt the company that had traded within. The charred rooms had long been empty of all but vagrants unperturbed by the smell of carbon, still tenacious after nearly a decade.

After more than two hours of torturously slow motion, Isaac and Yagharek had arrived at this burned shell, and collapsed thankfully within. They released Andrej, retied his hands and feet and gagged him before he woke. Then they ate what little food they had, and sat quietly, and waited.

Although the sky was light, their shelter was in the darkness shed by the station. In a little over an hour twilight would come, with night just behind it.

They talked quietly. Andrej woke and began to make his noises again, casting piteous looks around the room, begging for freedom, but Isaac looked at him with eyes too exhausted and miserable for guilt.

At seven o'clock there was a fumbling noise at the heat-blistered door. It was instantly audible above the rattling street sounds of The Crow. Isaac drew his flintlock and motioned Yagharek to silence.

It was Derkhan, exhausted and very dirty, her face smeared with dust and grease. She held her breath as she passed through the door and closed it behind her, releasing a sobbing exhalation as she slumped against it. She moved over and gripped Isaac's hand, then Yagharek's. They murmured greetings.

"I think there's someone watching this place," Derkhan said urgently. "He's standing under the tobacconist's awning opposite, in a green cloak. Can't see his face."

Isaac and Yagharek tensed. The garuda slid under the boarded-up window and raised his avian eye quietly to a knothole. He scanned the street across from the ruin.

"There is no one there," he said flatly. Derkhan came over and stared through the hole.

"Maybe he wasn't doing anything," she said eventually. "But I'd feel safer a floor or two up, in case we hear someone come in."

It was much easier to move, now that Isaac could force the crying Andrej at gunpoint without fear of being seen. They made their way up the stairs, leaving footprints in the charcoal surface.

On the top floor the window frames were empty of glass or wood, and they could look out across the short trek of slates at the staggered monolith of the station. They waited while the sky grew darker. Eventually, in the dim flicker of the orange gasjets, Yagharek clambered from the window and dropped lightly onto the moss-cushioned wall beyond. He stalked the five feet to the unbroken spine of roofs that connected the clutch of buildings to the Dexter Line and to Perdido Street Station. It sat weighty and huge in the west, spotted with irregular clusters of light like an earthbound constellation.

Yagharek was a dim figure in the skyline. He scanned the landscape of chimneys and slanting clay. He was not watched. He turned towards the dark window, indicated the others to follow him.

Andrej was old and stiff, and found it hard to walk along the narrow walkways they forged. He could not jump the five-foot drops that were necessary. Isaac and Derkhan helped him, supporting him or holding him fast with a gentle, macabre assistance, while the other trained their flintlock at his brain.

They had untied his limbs so he could walk and climb, but they had left the gag in place to stifle his wails and sobs.

Andrej stumbled confused and miserable like some soul in the outlands of Hell, shuffling nearer and nearer his ineluctable end with agonizing steps.

The four of them walked across the roofworld parallel to the Dexter Line. They were passed in both directions by spitting iron trains, wailing and venting great coughs of sooty smoke into the dwindling light. They trooped slowly onwards, towards the station ahead.

It was not long before the nature of their terrain changed. The sharp-angled slates gave way as the mass of architecture rose around them. They had to use their hands. They made their way through little byways of concrete, surrounded by windowed walls; they ducked under huge portholes and had to scale short ladders that wound between stubby towers. Hidden machinery made the brickwork hum. They were no longer looking ahead to the roof of Perdido Street Station, but up. They had passed some nebulous boundary point where the terraced streets ended and the foothills of the station began.

They tried to avoid climbing, creeping around the edges of promontories of brick like jutting teeth and through accidental passageways. Isaac began to look around, nervous and fitful. The pavement was invisible behind a low rise of rooftops and chimney-pipes to their right.

"Keep quiet and careful," he whispered. "There might be guards."

From the north-east, a gouged curve in the station's sprawling silhouette was a street approaching them, half covered by the building. Isaac pointed at it.

"There," he whispered. "Perdido Street."

He traced its line with his hand. A short way ahead it intersected with the Cephalic Way, along the length of which they were walking.

"Where they meet," he whispered. "That's our pick-up point. Yag . . . would you go?"

The garuda sped away, making towards the back of a tall building a few yards ahead, where rust-fouled guttering made a slanting ladder to the ground.

Isaac and Derkhan plodded slowly onwards, pushing Andrej gently forward with their guns. When they reached the intersection of the two streets they sat heavily and waited.

Isaac looked up at the sky, where only the high clouds still caught the sun. He looked down, watching Andrej's misery and imploring gaze creasing his old face. From all around the city the night sounds were beginning.

"There's no nightmares yet," murmured Isaac. He looked up at Derkhan, held out his hand as if feeling for rain. "Can't feel anything. They can't be abroad yet."

"Maybe they're licking their wounds," she said cheerlessly. "Maybe they won't come and this—" her eyes flicked up towards Andrej momentarily "—this'll all be useless."

"They'll come," said Isaac. "I promise you that." He would not talk of things going wrong. He would not admit the possibility.

They were silent for a while. Isaac and Derkhan realized simultaneously that they were both watching Andrej. He breathed slowly, his eyes flickering this way and that, his fear become a paralysing backdrop. *We could take his gag away,* thought Isaac, *and he wouldn't scream . . . but then he might speak . . .* He left the gag in place.

There was a scraping sound near them. With calm speed, Isaac and Derkhan raised their pistols. Yagharek's feathered head emerged from behind the clay, and they lowered their hands. The garuda hauled himself towards them over the cracked extrusion of roof. Draped over his shoulder was a great coil of cable.

Isaac stood to catch him as he staggered towards them.

"You got it!" he hissed. "They were waiting!"

"They were becoming angry," said Yagharek. "They had come up from the sewers an hour or more ago: they were fearful that we had been captured or killed. This is the last of the wire." He dropped the loops to the ground before them. The cable was thinner than many of the other sections, about four inches in cross-section, coated with thin rubber. There were perhaps sixty feet of wire remaining, sprawled in tight spirals by their ankles.

Isaac knelt to examine it. Derkhan, her pistol still trained on the cowering Andrej, squinted at the cable.

"Is it connected?" she asked. "Is it working?"

"I don't know," breathed Isaac. "We won't be able to tell till I link it up, make it a circuit." He hauled the cable up, swung it over his shoulder. "There's not as much as I'd hoped," he said. "We're not going to get very close to the centre of Perdido Street Station." He looked around and pursed his lips. *It doesn't matter,* he thought. *Picking the station was just something to tell the Council, to get out of the dump and away from it before . . . betrayal.* But he found himself wishing that they *could* plant themselves at the core of the station, as if there was in fact some power inhering in its bricks.

He pointed a little way away to the south-east, up a little slope of steep-sided, flat-topped rooflets. They extended like an exaggerated slate stairwell, overlooked by an enormous flat wall of stained concrete. The little rise of roof hillocks ended about forty feet above them, in what Isaac hoped was a flattened plateau. The huge L-shaped concrete wall continued into the air above it for nearly sixty feet, containing it on two sides.

"There," said Isaac slowly. "That's where we'll go."

CHAPTER FIFTY

Halfway up the stepped roofs, Isaac and his companions disturbed someone.

There was a sudden raucous drunken noise. Isaac and Derkhan flurried for their pistols in anxious motion. It was a ragged drunk who leapt up in a shockingly inhuman motion and disappeared at speed down the slope. Strips of torn clothes fluttered behind him.

After that Isaac began to see the denizens of the station's roofscape. Little fires sputtered in secret courtyards, tended by dark and hungry figures. Sleeping men curled in the corners beside old spires. It was an alternative, an attenuated society. Little vagrant hilltribes foraging. A quite different ecology.

Way above the heads of the roof-people, bloated airships ploughed across the sky. Noisy predators. Grubby specks of light and dark, moving edgily in the night's cloud.

To Isaac's relief, the plateau at the top of the hill of layered slate was flat, and about fifteen feet square. Large enough. He wagged his gun, indicating that Andrej should sit, which the old man did, collapsing slowly and precipitously into the far corner. He huddled in on himself, hugging his knees.

"Yag," said Isaac. "Keep watch, mate." Yagharek dropped the

final twist of the cable he had hauled up, and stood sentry at the edge of the little open space, looking down across the gradient of the massive roof. Isaac staggered under the full weight of the sack. He put it down and began to unpack the equipment.

Three mirrored helmets, one of which he put on. Derkhan took the others, gave one to Yagharek. Four analytical engines the size of large typewriters. Two large chymico-thaumaturgical batteries. Another battery, this one metaclockwork, a khepri design. Several connecting cables. Two large communicators' helmets, of the type used by the Construct Council on Isaac to trap the first slake-moth. Torches. Black powder and ammunition. A sheaf of programme cards. A clutch of transformers and thaumaturgic converters. Copper and pewter circuits of quite opaque purpose. Small motors and dynamos.

Everything was battered. Dented, cracked and filthy. It was a sad pile. It looked like nothing at all. Rubbish.

Isaac squatted beside it and began to prepare.

His head wobbled under the weight of his helmet. He connected two of the calculating engines, linking them into a powerful network. Then he began a much harder job, connecting the rest of the various oddments into a coherent circuit.

The motors were clipped to wires, and they to the larger of the analytical engines. The other engine he tinkered with internally, checking subtle adjustments. He had changed its circuitry. The valves within were no longer simply binary switches. They were attuned specifically and carefully to the unclear and the questionable; the grey areas of crisis mathematics.

He snapped small plugs into receivers and wired up the crisis engine to the dynamos and transformers that converted one uncanny form of energy into another. A discombobulated circuit spread out across the flat little roofspace.

The last thing he pulled from the sack and connected to the sprawling machinery was a crudely welded box of black tin, about the size of a shoe. He picked up the end of the cable—the enormous work of guerrilla engineering that stretched more than two miles to the huge hidden intelligence of the Griss Twist dump. Isaac deftly unwound the splayed wires and connected them to the black box. He looked up at Derkhan, who was watching him, her gun trained on Andrej.

"That's a breaker," he said, "a circuit-valve. One-way flow only. I'm cutting the Council off from this lot." He patted the various pieces of the crisis engine. Derkhan nodded slowly. The sky had grown nearly completely dark. Isaac looked up at her and set his lips.

"We can't let that fucking thing get access to the crisis engine. We have to stay away from it," he explained as he connected the disparate components of his machine. "You remember what it told us—the avatar was some corpse pulled out of the river. Bullshit! That body's *alive* . . . mindless, sure, but the heart's beating and the lungs breathe air. The Construct Council had to take that man's mind out of his body while he was *alive*. That was the whole point. Otherwise it would just rot.

"I don't know . . . maybe it was one of that crazy congregation sacrificing himself, maybe it was voluntary. But maybe not. Whichever, the Council don't care about killing off humans or any others, if it's . . . useful. It's got no empathy, no morals," Isaac continued, pushing hard at a resistant piece of metal. "It's just a . . . a calculating intelligence. Cost and benefit. It's trying to . . . *maximize* itself. It'll do whatever it has to—it'll lie to us, it'll kill—to increase its own power."

Isaac stopped for a moment and looked up at Derkhan.

"And you know," he said softly, "that's why it wants the crisis engine. It kept demanding it. Made me think. That's what this is for." He patted the circuit-valve. "If I connected the Council direct, it might be able to get feedback from the crisis engine, get control of it. It doesn't know I'm using this, that's why it was so keen on being connected. It doesn't know how to build its own engine: you can bet Jabber's arse that's why it's so interested in us.

"Dee, Yag, d'you know what this engine can *do*? I mean, this is a prototype . . . but if it works like it should, if you got inside this, saw the blueprint, built it more solidly, ironed out the problems . . . d'you know what this can do?

"Anything." He was silent for a while, his hands working, connecting his wires. "There's crisis everywhere, and if the engine can detect the field, tap it, channel it . . . it can do anything. I'm hamstrung because of all the maths. You've got to express in mathematical terms what you want the engine to do. That's what the programme cards are for. But the Council's whole damn *brain* expresses things mathematically. If that bastard links up to the crisis engine, its followers *won't be crazy any more*.

"Because you know they call it the God-machine . . . ? Well . . . they'll be right."

All three of them were quiet. Andrej rolled his eyes from side to side, not comprehending a single word.

Isaac worked silently. He tried to imagine a city in the thrall of the Construct Council. He thought of it linked up to the little crisis engine, building more and more of the engines on an ever-increasing scale, connecting them up to its own fabric, powering them with its own thaumaturgical and electro-chymical and steampower. Monstrous valves hammering in the depths of the dump, making the fabric of reality bend and bleed with the ease of a Weaver's spinnerets, all doing the bidding of that vast, cold intelligence, pure conscious calculation, as capricious as a baby.

He fingered the circuit-valve, shaking it gently, praying that its mechanisms were sound.

Isaac sighed and brought out the thick sheaf of programme cards the Council had printed. Each was labelled in the Council's tottering typewritten script. Isaac looked up quizzically.

"It's not yet ten, is it?" he said. Derkhan shook her head. "There's still nothing in the air, is there? The moths aren't out yet. Let's be ready by the time they fly."

He looked down and pulled the lever on the two chymical batteries. The reagents within mixed. The sound of effervescence was dimly audible, and there was a sudden chorus of chattering valves and barking outputs as current was released. The machinery on the roofscape snapped into life.

The crisis engine whirred.

"It's just calculating," said Isaac nervously, as Derkhan and Yagharek glanced at him. "It's not yet processing. I'm giving it instructions."

Isaac began to feed the programme cards carefully into the various analytical engines before him. Most went to the crisis engine itself, but some to the subsidiary calculating circuits connected by little loops of cable. Isaac checked each card, comparing it with his notes, scribbling quick calculations before feeding it into any of the inputs.

The engines clattered as their fine ratcheting teeth slid over the cards, snapping into carefully cut holes, instructions and orders and information downloading into their analogue brains. Isaac was slow, waiting until he felt the click that signalled successful processing before removing each card and slotting in the next.

He kept notes, scrawling impenetrable messages to himself on ragged ends of paper. He breathed quickly.

Rain began to fall, quite suddenly. It was sluggish, huge drops falling indolently and breaking open, as thick and warm as pus. The night was close, and the glutinous rainclouds made it more so. Isaac worked fast, his fingers feeling suddenly idiotic, too large.

There was a slow sense of dragging, a weightiness that pulled at the spirit and began to saturate the bones. A sense of the un-canny, of the fearful and hidden, that rolled up as if from within, a billowing ink-cloud from the depths of the mind.

"Isaac," said Derkhan, her voice cracking, "you have to hurry. It's starting."

A swarm of nightmare feelings pattered down among them with the rain.

"They're up and out," said Derkhan with terror. "They're hunting. They're abroad. Hurry, you have to hurry . . ."

Isaac nodded without speaking and continued with what he was doing, shaking his head as if that might disperse the cloying fear that had settled on him. *Where's the fucking Weaver?* he thought.

"Someone watches us from below," said Yagharek suddenly, "some tramp who did not run. He does not move."

Isaac glanced up again, then returned his attention to his work.

"Take my gun there," he hissed. "If he comes up towards us, warn him off with a shot. Hopefully he'll keep his distance." Still his hands rushed to twist, to connect, to programme. He punched numbered keypads and wrestled roughcut cards into slots. "Nearly there," he murmured, "nearly there."

The sense of nocturnal pressure, of drifting in sour dreams, increased.

"Isaac . . ." hissed Derkhan. Andrej had fallen into a kind of terrified, exhausted half-sleep, and he began to moan and thrash, his eyes opening and shutting with bleary vagueness.

"Done!" spat Isaac, and stepped back.

There was a silent moment. Isaac's triumph dissipated quickly.

"We need the Weaver!" he said. "It's supposed to . . . it said it would be here! We can't do anything without it . . ."

*   *   *

They could do nothing except wait.

The stench of twisted dream-imagery grew and grew, and brief screams sounded from random points across the city, as sleeping sufferers called out their fear or defiance. The rain fell thicker, until the concrete underfoot was slick. Isaac laid the greasy sack ineffectually across various sections of the crisis circuit, moving it in agitation, trying to protect his machine from the water.

Yagharek watched the glistening roofscape. When his head became too full of fearful dreams and he grew afraid of what he might see, he turned on his heel and watched through the mirrors on his helmet. He kept watch on the dim, immobile figure below.

Isaac and Derkhan dragged Andrej a little closer to the circuit *(again with that ghastly gentleness, as if concerned for his well-being)*. Under Derkhan's gun, Isaac retied the old man's hands and legs, and fastened one of the communicator helmets tight to his head. He did not look at Andrej's face.

The helmet had been adjusted. As well as its flared output on the top, it had three input jacks. One connected it to the second helmet. Another was connected by several skeins of wires to the calculating brains and generators of the crisis engine.

Isaac wiped the third connection briefly free of filthy rainwater, and plugged into it the thick wire extending from the black circuit-breaker, attached to which was the massive cable extending all the way to the Construct Council, south of the river. Current could flow from the Council's analytical brain, through the one-way switch, into Andrej's helmet.

"That's it, that's it," said Isaac tensely. "Now we just need the fucking *Weaver* . . ."

It was another half an hour of rain and burgeoning nightmares before the dimensions of the roofspace rippled and shucked wildly, and the Weaver's crooning monologue could be heard.

. . . AS THEE AND ME CONCURRED THE FAT FUNNELSPACE THE CLOT AT CITYWEB CENTRE SEES US CONFLAB . . . came the unearthly voice in all of their skulls, and the great spider stepped out lightly from the kink in the air and danced towards them, its shining body dwarfing them.

Isaac gave a barking breath, a sharp moan of relief. His mind juddered with the awe and terror the Weaver induced.

"Weaver!" he shouted. "Help us now!" He held out the other communicating helmet to the extraordinary presence.

Andrej had looked up and was shying away in a paroxysm of terror. His eyes bulged with the pressure of his blood and he began to retch behind his mask. He wriggled as fast as he could towards the edge of the roof, a terrible inhuman fear jack-knifing his body away.

Derkhan caught him and held him fast. He ignored her gun, his eyes empty of everything but the vast spider that loomed over him, peering down with slow portentous movements. Derkhan could hold him easily. His decaying muscles flexed and twisted ineffectually. She dragged him back and held him.

Isaac did not look at them. He held out the helmet to the Weaver beseechingly.

"We need you to put this on," he said. "Put this on now! We can take them all. You said you'd help us . . . to repair the web . . . please."

The rain sputtered against the Weaver's hard shell. Every second or so, one or two random drops would sizzle violently and evaporate as they struck it. The Weaver kept talking, as it always did, an inaudible murmur that Isaac and Derkhan and Yagharek could not understand.

It reached out with its smooth, human hands, and placed the helmet on its segmented head.

Isaac closed his eyes in brief exhausted relief, then opened them again.

"Keep it on!" he hissed. "Fasten it!"

With fingers that moved as elegantly as a master tailor's, the spider did so.

. . . WILL YOU TICKLE AND TRICK . . . it gibbered . . . AS THINK-LINGS TRICKLE THROUGH SLOSHING METAL AND MIX IN MIRE MY IRE MY MIRROR MYRIAD BURSTING BUBBLES OF BRAINWAVEFORMS AND WEAVING PLANS ON ON AND ONWARD MY MASTER CRAFTY CRAFTSMAN . . . and as the Weaver continued to croon with incomprehensible and dreamlike proclamations, Isaac saw the last fastening snap tight under its terrifying jaw, and he snapped on the switches that opened the circuit-valves on Andrej's helmet, and he pulled the succession of levers that geared up the full processing power of the analytical calculators and the crisis engine, and he stepped back.

Extraordinary currents surged through the machinery assembled before them.

There was a very still moment, when even the rain seemed to pause.

Sparks of various and extraordinary colours sputtered from connections.

A massive arc of power suddenly snapped Andrej's body absolutely rigid. An unstable corona briefly surrounded him. His face was glazed with astonishment and pain.

Isaac, Derkhan and Yagharek watched him, paralysed.

As the batteries sent great gobs of charged particles racing through the intricate circuit, flows of power and processed orders interacted in complex feedback loops, an infinitely fast drama unravelling on a femtoscopic scale.

The communicator helmet began its task, sucking up the exudations of Andrej's mind and amplifying them in a stream of thaumaturgons and waveforms. They raced at the speed of light through the circuitry and headed towards the inverted funnel that would blare them silently into the æther.

But they were diverted.

They were processed, read, mathematized by the ordered drumming of tiny valves and switches.

An infinitely small moment later, two more streams of energy burst into the circuitry. First came the emissions from the Weaver, streaming through the helmet it wore. A tiny fraction of a second later, the current from the Construct Council came sparking through the rough cable from the Griss Twist dump, slamming up and down through the streets, through the circuit-valves in a great slew of power and into the circuitry through Andrej's helmet.

Isaac had seen how the slake-moths slavered and rolled their tongues indiscriminately across the Weaver's body. He had seen how they had been giddy, but not sated.

The Weaver's whole body emanated mental waves, he had realized, but they were not like those of other sentient races. The slake-moths lapped eagerly, and drew taste . . . but no sustenance.

The Weaver thought in a continuous, incomprehensible, rolling stream of awareness. There were no layers to the Weaver's mind, there was no ego to control the lower functions, no animal cortex to keep the mind grounded. For the Weaver, there were no dreams at night, no hidden messages from the secret corners of the mind, no mental clearout of accrued garbage bespeaking an orderly consciousness. For the Weaver, dreams and consciousness were one. The Weaver dreamed of being conscious and its consciousness was its dream, in an endless unfathomable stew of image and desire and cognition and emotion.

For the slake-moths, it was like the froth on effervescent liquor. It was intoxicating and delightful, but without organizing principle, without substratum. Without substance. These were not dreams that could sustain them.

The extraordinary squall and gust of the Weaver's consciousness blew down the wires into the sophisticated engines.

Just behind it came the particle torrent from the Construct Council's brain.

In extreme contrast to the anarchic viral flurry that had spawned it, the Construct Council thought with chill exactitude. Concepts were reduced to a multiplicity of on-off switches, a soulless solipsism that processed information without the complication of arcane desires or passion. A will to existence and aggrandizement, shorn of all psychology, a mind contemplative and infinitely, incidentally cruel.

To the slake-moths it was invisible, thought without subconscious. It was meat stripped of all taste or smell, empty thought-calories inconceivable as nutrition. Like ashes.

The Council's mind poured into the machine—and there was a moment of fraught activity as commands were sent down the copper connections from the dump, as the Council sought to suck back information and control of the engine. But the circuit-breaker was solid. The flow of particles was one way.

It was assimilated, passing through the analytical engine.

A set of parameters was reached. Complex instructions pattered through the valves.

Within a seventh of a second, a rapid sequence of processing activity had begun.

The machine examined the form of the first input x, Andrej's mental signature.

Two subsidiary orders rattled down pipes and wiring simultaneously. *Model form of input y* one said, and the engines mapped the extraordinary mental current from the Weaver; *Model form of input z,* and they did the same job on the Construct Council's vast and powerful brainwaves. The analytical engines factored out the scale of the output and concentrated on the paradigms, the shapes.

The two lines of programming coalesced again into a tertiary order: *Duplicate waveform of input x with inputs y and z.*

The commands were extraordinarily complex. They relied on the advanced calculating machines the Construct Council had provided, and the intricacy of its programme cards.

The mathematico-analytical maps of mentality—even simplified and imperfect, flawed as they inevitably were—became templates. The three were compared.

Andrej's mind, like any sane human's, any sane vodyanoi's or khepri's or cactacae's or other sentient being's, was a constantly convulsing dialectical unity of consciousness and subconsciousness, the battening down and channelling of dreams and desires, the recurring re-creation of the subliminal by the contradictory, the rational-capricious ego. And vice versa. The interaction of levels of consciousness into an unstable and permanently self-renewing whole.

Andrej's mind was not like the cold ratiocination of the Council, nor the poetic dream-consciousness of the Weaver.

x, recorded the engines, was unlike y and unlike z.

But with underlying structure *and* subconscious flow, with calculating rationality and impulsive fancy, self-maximizing analysis and emotional charge, x, the analytical engines calculated, was equal to y *plus* z.

The thaumaturgo-psychic motors followed orders. They combined y and z. They created a duplicate waveform to that of x and routed it through the output on Andrej's helmet.

The flows of charged particles pouring into the helmet from the Council and the Weaver were added together into a single vast slew. The Weaver's dreams, the Council's calculations, were blended to mimic subconscious and conscious, the working human mind. The new ingredients were more powerful than Andrej's feeble emanations by a factor of enormous magnitude. The vastness of this power was unabated as the new, huge current surged towards the flared trumpet pointing up into the sky.

A little more than one-third of a second had passed since the circuit had snapped into life. As the enormous combined flow of $y+z$ dashed towards the outflow, a new set of conditions was fulfilled. The crisis engine itself chattered into life.

It used the unstable categories of crisis maths, as much a persuasive vision as objective categorization. Its deductive method was holistic, totalizing and inconstant.

As the exudations of the Council and the Weaver took the place of Andrej's outflow, the crisis engine was fed the same information as the original processors. It rapidly evaluated the calculations that had been performed and examined the new flow. In its astonishingly complex tubular intelligence, a massive anomaly became evident. Something the strictly arithmetic functions of the other engines could never have uncovered.

The form of the dataflows under analysis was not just the sum of their constituent parts.

y and z were unified, bounded wholes. And most crucially, so was x, Andrej's mind, the reference point for the whole model. *It was integral to the form of each that they were totalities.*

The layers of consciousness within x were dependent on each other, interlocking gears of a motor of self-sustaining consciousness. What was arithmetically discernible as rationalism *plus* dreams was really a *whole*, whose constituent parts could not be disentangled.

y and z were not half-complete models of x. They were qualitatively different.

The engine applied rigorous crisis logic to the original operation. A mathematical command had created a perfect arithmetic analogue of a source code from disparate material, and that analogue was simultaneously identical to and *radically divergent* from the original it mimicked.

Three-fifths of a second after the circuit had snapped into life, the crisis engine arrived at two simultaneous conclusions: $x = y + z$; and $x \neq y + z$.

The operation that had been carried out was profoundly unstable. It was paradoxical, unsustainable, the application of logic tearing itself apart.

The process was, from absolute first principles of analysis, modelling and conversion, utterly riddled with crisis.

A massive wellspring of crisis energy was instantly uncovered. The realization of crisis freed it up to be tapped: metaphasic pistons squeezed and convulsed, sending controlled spurts of the volatile energy shooting through amplifiers and transformers. Subsidiary circuits rocked and juddered. The crisis motor began to whirl like a dynamo, crackling with power and sending out complex charges of quasivoltage.

The final command rang in binary form through the crisis engine's innards. *Channel energy,* it said, *and amplify output.*

*   *   *

Just less than one second since the power had coursed through the wires and mechanisms, the impossible, paradoxical flow of cobbled-together consciousness, the combined flow of Weaver and Council, welled up and burst massively out of Andrej's conducting helmet.

His own rerouted emanations wobbled in a loop of referential feedback, constantly being checked and compared to the $y+z$ flow by the analogue and the crisis engines. Without outlet, it began to leak out, snapping in peculiar little arcs of thaumaturgic plasma. It dribbled invisibly over Andrej's contorting face, mixing with the gobbing overflow from the Weaver/Council emission.

The main aggregate of that enormous and unstable created consciousness burst in huge gouts from the helmet's flanges. A growing column of mental waves and particles burst out over the station, towering into the air. It was invisible, but Isaac and Derkhan and Yagharek could feel it, a prickling of the skin, sixth and seventh senses ringing dully like psychic tinnitus.

Andrej twitched and convulsed with the power of the processes rocking him. His mouth worked. Derkhan looked away in guilty disgust.

The Weaver danced back and forth on its stiletto feet, yammering quietly and tapping its helmet.

"Bait . . ." called Yagharek harshly and stepped back from the flow of energy.

"It's hardly started," yelled Isaac over the thudding of rain.

The crisis engine was humming and heating up, tapping enormous and growing resources. It sent waves of transforming current through thickly insulated cables, towards Andrej, who rolled and jack-knifed in spastic terror and pain.

The engine took the energy siphoned from the unstable situation and channelled it, obeying its instructions, pouring it in transformative form towards the Weaver/Council flow. Boosting it. Increasing its pitch and range and power. And increasing it again.

A feedback loop began. The artificial flow was made stronger; and like an enormous fortified tower on crumbling foundations, the increase of its mass made it more precarious. Its paradoxical ontology grew more unstable as the flow became stronger. Its crisis grew more acute. The engine's transformative power grew exponentially; it bolstered the mental flow more; the crisis deepened again . . .

The prickling of Isaac's skin grew worse. A note seemed to sound in his skull, a whine that increased in pitch as if something nearby spun faster and faster, out of control.

He winced.

. . . GOOD GRIEF AND GRACE THE SPILLING SLOSH GROWS MINDFUL BUT MIND IT IS NO MIND . . . the Weaver continued to murmur . . . ONE AND ONE INTO ONE WON'T GO BUT IT IS ONE AND TWO AT ONCE WILL WE WON HOW WIN HOW WONDERFUL . . .

As Andrej rolled like a victim of torture under the dark rain, the power that poured through his head and into the sky grew more and more intense, increasing at a frightening, geometric rate. It was invisible but sensible: Isaac, Derkhan and Yagharek backed away from the squirming figure as far as the little space would allow. Their pores opened and closed, their hair or feathers crawled violently across their skin.

Still the crisis loop continued and the emanation increased, until it could almost be seen, a shimmering pillar of disturbed æther two hundred feet high, the light from stars and aerostats bending uncertainly around and through it as it towered like an unseen inferno over the city.

Isaac felt as if his gums were rotting, as if his teeth were trying to escape his jaw.

The Weaver danced on in delight.

An enormous beacon was scorched into the æther. A huge and rapidly growing column of energy, a pretend consciousness, the map of a counterfeit mind that swelled and fattened in a fearful curve of growth, impossible and vastly there, the portent of a nonexistent god.

Across New Crobuzon, more than nine hundred of the city's best communicators and thaumaturges paused and looked suddenly in the direction of The Crow, their faces twisted with confusion and nebulous alarm. The most sensitive held their heads and moaned with inexplicable pain.

Two hundred and seven began to jabber in nonsense combinations of numerological code and lush poetry. One hundred and fifty-five suffered massive nosebleeds, two of them ultimately unstaunchable and fatal.

Eleven, who worked for the government, scrabbled from their workshop at the top of the Spike and ran, with handkerchiefs and tissues ineffectually stopping the bloody slick from their noses and ears, towards Eliza Stem-Fulcher's office.

"Perdido Street Station!" was all they could say. They gabbled it like idiots for some minutes, to the home secretary and the mayor who was with her, shaking them with frustration, their lips twitching for other sounds, blood spattering their bosses' immaculate tailoring.

"Perdido Street Station!"

Way out above the wide empty streets of Chnum; swooping slowly past the curve of temple towers in Tar Wedge; skirting the river above Howl Barrow and soaring widespread over the pauper slum of Stoneshell, intricate bodies moved.

With sluggish strokes and drooling tongues, the slake-moths sought prey.

They were hungry, eager to gorge themselves and ready their bodies and breed again. They must hunt.

But in four sudden, identical and simultaneous movements—separated by miles, in different quadrants of the city—the four slake-moths snapped their heads up as they flew.

They beat their complex wings and slowed, until they were almost still in the air. Four slobbering tongues lolled and lapped at the air.

In the distance, over the skyline that glimmered with grots of filthy light, on the outskirts of the central mass of building, a column was rising from the earth. Even as they licked and taste-smelled it, it grew and grew, and their wings beat back frantically as the wafts of flavour came over them, and the incredible succulent stench of the thing boiled and eddied in the æther.

The other smells and tastes of the city dissipated into nothing. With an amazing speed, the extraordinary flavour-trail doubled its intensity, suffusing the slake-moths, making them mad.

One by one they emitted a chittering of astounded, delighted greed, a single-minded hunger.

From all the way across the city, from the four compass points, they converged in a frenzy of flapping, four starving exultant powerful bodies, descending to feed.

There was a tiny putter of lights on a little console. Isaac edged closer, keeping his body low, as if he could duck under the beacon of energy pouring from Andrej's skull. The old man lolled and twitched on the ground.

Isaac was careful not to look at Andrej's sprawling form. He peered at the console, making sense of the little play of diodes.

"I think it's the Construct Council," he said over the drab rainfall sound. "It's sending instructions to get round the firewall, but I don't think it'll be able to. This is too simple for it," he said, and patted the circuit-valve. "There's nothing for it to get control of." Isaac visualized a struggle in the femtoscopic byways of wiring.

He looked up.

The Weaver was ignoring him and them all, drumming its little fingers against the slick concrete in complicated rhythms. Its low voice was impenetrable.

Derkhan was staring in exhausted disgust at Andrej. Her head jerked gently back and forward as if she was rocked by waves. Her mouth moved. She spoke in silent tongues. *Don't die,* thought Isaac fervently, staring at the ruined old man, seeing his face contort as bizarre feedback rocked him, *you can't die yet, you have to hold on.*

Yagharek was standing. He pointed up, suddenly, into a far quadrant of the sky.

"They have changed course," he said harshly. Isaac looked up and saw what Yagharek was indicating.

Far away, halfway to the edge of the city, three of the drifting dirigibles had turned purposefully. They were hardly visible to human eyes, darker blots against the night sky, picked out with navigation lights. But it was clear that their fitful, random motion had changed; that they were powering ponderously towards Perdido Street Station, converging.

"They're on to us," said Isaac. He did not feel fearful, only tense and weirdly sad. "They're coming. Godspit and shit! We've got about ten, fifteen minutes before they get here. We just have to hope the moths are quicker."

"No. No." Yagharek was shaking his head with quick violence. His head was cocked. His arms moved quickly, motioning them all to silence. Isaac and Derkhan froze. The Weaver continued its insane monologue, but it was subdued and hushed. Isaac prayed that it would not become bored and disappear. The apparatus, the constructed mind, the crisis would all collapse.

The air around them all was welting, splitting like troubled skin, as the force of that unthinkable and burgeoning blast of power continued to grow.

Yagharek was listening intently through the rain.

"People are approaching," he said urgently, "across the roof." With practised movements, he plucked his whip from his belt. His long knife seemed to dance into his left hand and pose, glinting in the refracted sodium lights. He had become a warrior and a hunter again.

Isaac stood and drew his flintlock. He checked hurriedly that it was clean and he filled the pan with powder, trying to shield it from the rain. He felt for his little pouch of bullets and his powder horn. His heart, he realized, was beating only very slightly faster.

He saw Derkhan readying herself. She drew her two pistols and checked them, her eyes cold.

On the roof's plateau, forty feet below, a little troop of dark-uniformed figures had appeared. They ran nervously between the outcroppings of architecture, their pikes and rifles rattling. There were perhaps twelve of them, their faces invisible behind their sheer reflective helmets, their segmented armour flapping against them, subtle insignia displaying rank. They spread out, came at the gradient of roofs from different angles.

"Oh dear Jabber," swallowed Isaac. "We're fucked."

Five minutes, he thought in despair. *That's all we need. The fucking moths won't resist this, they're coming here already, couldn't you have taken a little longer?*

The dirigibles still prowled closer and closer, sluggish and ineluctable.

The militia had reached the outer edges of the tumbling slate hill. They began to climb, keeping low, ducking behind chimney stacks and dormer windows. Isaac stepped back from the edge, keeping them out of sight.

The Weaver was tracing its index finger through the water on the roof, leaving a trail of scorched dry stone, drawing patterns and pictures of flowers, whispering to itself. Andrej's body spasmed as the current rocked him. His eyes wavered unnervingly.

"Fuck!" shouted Isaac, in despair and rage.

"Shut up and fight," hissed Derkhan. She lay down and peered carefully over the edge of the roof. The highly trained militia were frighteningly close. She aimed and fired with her left hand.

There was a snapping explosion that seemed muffled by the

rain. The closest officer, who had scaled nearly halfway up the slope, staggered back as the ball struck his armoured breast and ricocheted into the darkness. He teetered momentarily on the edge of his little roof-step, managed to right himself. As he relaxed and stepped forward, Derkhan fired her other gun.

The officer's faceplate shattered in an explosion of bloody mirror. A cloud of flesh burst from the back of his skull. His face was momentarily visible, a shocked gaze embedded with slivers of reflecting glass, blooming with blood from a hole below his right eye. He seemed to leap out backwards like a champion diver, sailing elegantly twenty feet to crack loudly against the base of the roof.

Derkhan bellowed with triumph, her cry becoming words. *"Die,* you *swine!"* she screamed. She ducked back out of sight as a rapid battery of shots smacked into the brick and stone above and below her.

Isaac dropped onto all fours beside her, staring at her. It was impossible to say, in the rain, but he thought she was sobbing angrily. She rolled back from the edge of the roof and began to reload her pistols. She caught Isaac's eye.

"Do something!" she screamed at him.

Yagharek was standing, hanging back from the edge, grabbing glimpses every few seconds, waiting until the men were in reach of his whip. Isaac rolled forward, peered over the rim of the little platform. The men were drawing nearer, moving more carefully now, hiding at each level, staying out of sight, but still moving terribly fast.

Isaac aimed and fired. His bullet burst dramatically against slate, showering the lead militiaman with particles.

"Gods*damn*it!" he hissed and ducked back to refill his gun.

A cold certainty of defeat was settling within him. There were too many men, coming too quickly. As soon as the militia reached the top, Isaac would have no defence. If the Weaver came to their aid they would lose their bait, and the slake-moths would escape. They might take one, two or three of the officers with them, but they could not escape.

Andrej was jerking up and down, arcing his back and straining against his bonds. The nerves between Isaac's eyes were singing as the blast of energy continued to scald the æther. The airships were pulling near. Isaac screwed up his face, looked back over the edge of the plateau. On the broken plain of the roof below, drunkards and vagrants were rousing themselves and scurrying away like terrified animals.

Yagharek screeched like a crow and pointed with his knife.

Behind the militia, on the flattened roofscape they had left behind, a cloaked figure slipped out of some shadow, appearing like an eidolon, manifesting as if from nothing.

There was a flurry of bottle-green from its coiling cloak.

Something spat intense fire and noise from the figure's outstretched hand, three, four, five times. Halfway up the slope, Isaac saw a militiaman bow away from the roof, collapsing in an ugly organic cascade down the length of the clay. As he fell, two more of the men staggered and collapsed. One was dead, blood pooling below his sprawled body and diluting in the rain. The other slid a little way and emitted a horrendous shriek from behind his mask, clutching at his bleeding ribs.

Isaac gazed in shock.

"Who the fuck is that?" he shouted. "What the *fuck* is going on?" Below him, their shadowed benefactor had ducked into a puddle of darkness. He seemed to be fumbling with his gun.

Below them, the militia had frozen. Orders were shouted in impenetrable shorthand. It was clear that they were confused and afraid.

Derkhan was staring into the darkness with a look of astonished hope.

"Gods *bless* you," she screamed down the slate, into the night. She fired again with her left hand, but the bullet passed loudly and harmlessly into brick.

Thirty feet below them, the injured man still screamed. He fumbled ineffectually to undo his mask.

The unit split. One man ducked beneath outcroppings of brick and raised his rifle, aiming into the darkness where the newcomer hid. Several of the remaining men began to descend towards their new attacker. The others began to climb again, at redoubled speed.

As the two little groups moved up and down across the slippery roofscape, the dark figure stepped out again and fired with extraordinary rapidity. *He's got some kind of repeating pistol,* thought Isaac with astonishment, and then started as two more officers reared up from the roof a little way below him and fell, twisting and screaming, to bounce brutally down the incline.

Isaac realized that the man below them was not firing at the militia who had turned and were approaching him, but was concentrating on protecting the little platform, picking off the closest officers with superb marksmanship. He had left himself vulnerable to a massed attack.

All across the roof the militia froze at the volley of bullets. But as Isaac looked down he saw that the second group of officers had descended to the base of the roof and were running in clumsily furtive formation at the shady assassin.

Ten feet below Isaac, the militia were closing in. He fired again, knocking the wind from one man, but failing to penetrate his armour. Derkhan shot, and below them, the poised marksman screeched an oath and dropped his rifle, which slid noisily away.

Isaac filled his gun with desperate haste. He glanced over at his machinery, saw that Andrej was curled under the wall. He was shuddering, with spittle fouling his face. Isaac's head throbbed in time to some weird beat from the growing blaze of mental waves. He looked up at the sky. *Come* on, he thought, *come on, come on.* He looked down again as he reloaded, trying to find the mysterious newcomer.

He almost cried out in fear for their half-hidden protector, as four burly and heavily armed militia jogged towards the pitch-shade where he had hidden.

Something emerged from the darkness at speed, leaping from shadow to shadow, drawing the militia's fire with extraordinary ease. A pathetic spatter of shots sounded, and the four men's rifles were empty. As they dropped to one knee and began to reload, the cloaked figure emerged from the sheltering gloom and stood a few paces before them.

Isaac saw him from slightly behind, illuminated in the sudden cold light from some phlogistic lamp. His face was turned away, towards the militia. His cloak was patched and shabby. Isaac could just see a stubby little gun in his left hand. As the impassive glass masks glimmered in the light and the four officers seemed to falter into momentary stillness, something extended from the man's right hand. Isaac could not see it well, squinted carefully until the man moved slightly and raised his arm, uncovering the toothed thing as the sleeve of the cloth fell away.

A massive serrated blade, slowly opening and shutting like wicked scissors. Gnarled chitin jutting ungainly from the man's elbow, recurved razor tip gleaming at the end of the trapping jaw.

The man's right arm had been replaced, Remade, with a vast mantis claw.

At the same instant, Isaac and Derkhan gasped and shouted his name: *"Jack Half-a-Prayer!"*

Half-a-Prayer, the Escapee, the fReemade Boss, the Man-'tis, stepped up lightly towards the four militia.

They fumbled with their guns, jabbed out with the glinting bayonets.

Half-a-Prayer sidestepped them with balletic speed and snapped his Remade limb shut, then backed easily away. One of the officers fell, blood bursting from his lacerated neck and welling up behind his mask.

Jack Half-a-Prayer had gone again, was stalking half in, half out of sight.

Isaac's attention was diverted as an officer appeared over the brim of a window five feet below him. He fired too quickly and missed, but something snaked out above him and smacked violently against the man's helmet. The officer reeled and fell back, gathering himself from another attack. Yagharek quickly gathered up his heavy whip, ready to strike again.

"Come on, *come on*!" screamed Isaac to the sky.

The airships were fat and looming now, descending, ready to pounce. Half-a-Prayer danced rings around his attackers, leaping in to maim and then dissolving into the dark. Derkhan was crying out, a little defiant shout every time she shot. Yagharek stood poised, his whip and dagger trembling in his hands. The militia were encroaching, but slowly, cowed and fearful, waiting for relief and back-up.

The Weaver's monologue grew slowly louder, from a whispering in the back of the skull into a voice that crept forward through flesh and bone, filling the brain.

. . . IS IT IS IT THOSE NAUGHTY MAULERS THOSE TIRESOME PATTERNVAMPIRS THAT BLEED WEBSCAPE DRY IT IS THEY THEY COME THEY WHISTLE FOR THIS TORRENT THIS CORNUCOPIC SLEW OF FOOD THAT IS NOT TAKE CARE AND WHISPER WATCH . . . it said . . . RICH BREWS SIT UNEASY ON THE PALATE . . .

Isaac looked up with a soundless shout. He heard a fluttering, a buffet of disordered air. The raw emblazoning, the blast of invented brainwaves that made his spine tremble inside him continued unabated as a sound approached, oscillating frantically between materia and æther.

A glinting carapace dipped through thermals: weaving patterns of dark colour shot violently through the sky on two reflected pairs of shapeshifting wings. Convoluted limbs and spiny organic jags trembled in anticipation.

Famished and trembling, the first slake-moth came in.

The heavy segmented body came spiralling down, sliding tightly around the column of burning æther as if on a funfair ride. The moth's tongue lapped avidly around it: it was immersed in intoxicating brain-liquor.

As Isaac stared into the sky exultantly, he saw another shape flit closer, and another, black on black. One of the moths ducked in a sharp arc directly below a fat and sluggish airship, careering towards the storm of mindwaves that sent ripples through the fabric of the city.

The force of militia arrayed on the roof chose that moment to renew their attack, and the sulphurous snap of Derkhan's pistols woke Isaac to the danger. He looked round to see Yagharek crouched in a feral pose, his bullwhip unrolling like some half-trained mamba towards the officer whose head had appeared over the rim of the plateau. It constricted around his neck and Yagharek pulled hard, slamming the man's forehead against the wet slates.

He snapped his whip free as the choking officer fell clattering away.

Isaac fumbled with his cumbersome pistol. He leaned over and saw that two of the officers who had turned on Jack Half-a-Prayer were down and dying, blood spewing languidly from enormous rents in their flesh. A third was stumbling away, holding his gashed thigh. Half-a-Prayer and the fourth man were gone.

All over the low hill of roofs, the calls of the militia sounded, half routed, terrified and confused. Urged on by their lieutenant they drew steadily closer.

"Keep them away," shouted Isaac. "The moths are coming!"

The three slake-moths came down in a long interweaving helix, eddying below and above each other, rotating in descending order around the massive stele of energy that yawned vastly from Andrej's helmet. On the ground below them the Weaver danced a subdued little jig, but the slake-moths did not see it. They noticed nothing except Andrej's spasming form, the source, the wellspring of the enormous sweet bounty that gushed precipitously up and into the air. They were frenzied.

Watertowers and brick turrets rose up around them like reaching hands as one by one they breached the skyline and descended into the city's gaslight nimbus.

Faint waves of anxiety gusted through them as they plunged. There was something fractionally wrong with the flavour that surrounded them—but it was so strong, so unbelievably powerful, and they were so drunk on it, unsteady on their wings and shaking with greedy delight, that they could not stop their vertiginous approach.

Isaac heard Derkhan shout a foul oath. Yagharek had leapt across the roof to her and flailed expertly with his whip, sending her attacker spinning. Isaac turned and fired at the falling figure, heard him grunt with pain as the bullet tore open the muscle of his shoulder.

The airships were almost overhead now. Derkhan was sitting back from the brink a little, blinking rapidly, her eyes fouled with clods of brickdust from where a bullet had shattered the wall beside her.

There were about five militia left on the roofs, and they were still coming, slow and stealthy.

A final insectile shadow swooped towards the roof from the south-east of the city. It looped in a long S-curve under the Spit Hearth skyrail and shot up again, riding the updrafts in the hot night, coming in towards the station.

"They're all here," whispered Isaac.

As he refilled his gun, spilling powder inexpertly about him, he looked up. His eyes widened: the first moth approached. It was a hundred feet above him and then sixty, then suddenly twenty and ten. He stared at it in awe. It seemed to move with no pace at all as time stretched out thin and very slow. Isaac saw the clutching half-simian paws and jagged tail, the enormous mouth and chattering teeth, eyesockets with their clumsy antennae stubs like fumbling maggots, a hundred extrusions of flesh that whiplashed and unfolded and pointed and snapped shut in a hundred mysterious motions . . . and the wings, those prodigious, untrustworthy, constantly altering wings, tides of weird colour drenching them and retreating like sudden squalls.

He watched the moth directly, ignoring the mirrors before his eyes. It had no time for him. It ignored him.

He was frozen for a long moment, in a terror of memories.

The slake-moth swept past him and a great backwash of air sent his hair and coat flailing.

The clutching multilimbed creature reached out, unrolled its enormous tongue, spat and chittered in obscene hunger. It landed on Andrej like some nightmare spirit, clutched him and sought desperately to drink.

As its tongue slid rapidly in and out of Andrej's orifices, coating him in that thick citric saliva, another moth careened in on a trough of air, crashing into the first moth and fighting it for position on Andrej's body.

The old man was twitching as his muscles fought to make sense of the slew of absurd stimuli engulfing them. The torrent of Weaver/ Council brainwaves blasted up and out of his skull.

The engine lying on the roofspace rattled. It grew dangerously hot as its pistons fought to retain control of the enormous wash of crisis energy. Rain spat and evaporated as it hit it.

As the third moth came in to land, the struggle to feed at the mouth of the font, at the pseudo-mind pouring from Andrej's skull, continued. In an irritated convulsive motion, the first moth slapped the second a few feet away, where it licked eagerly at the back of Andrej's head.

The first moth plunged its tongue into Andrej's slavering mouth, then removed it with a sickening *plop* and sought another outflow. It found the little trumpet on Andrej's helmet, from which the whole bursting wash of ever-increasing output poured. The moth slid its tongue into the opening and around dimensional corners into and out of the æther, rolling the sinuous organ around the multifarious planes of the flow.

It squealed in delight.

Its skull vibrated in its flesh. Gouts of the intense artificial mindwaves spurted down its throat and dripped invisibly from its mouth, a burning jet of intense, sweet thought-calories that poured and poured into the moth's belly, more powerful, more concentrated than its day-to-day feed by a vast and increasing factor, an uncontrollable torrent of energy that raged through the slake-moth's gullet and filled its stomach in seconds.

The moth could not break free. It locked in, gorged and fixated. It could sense danger, but it could not care, could not think of anything apart from the entrancing, inebriating flow of food that held it, that focused it. It was fixed with the mindless intent of a night insect battering itself against cracked glass to find a way in to a deadly flame.

The slake-moth immolated itself, immersed itself in the torrential blasts of power.

Its stomach swelled and chitin creaked. The massive wash of

mental emanations overwhelmed it. The huge and skulking creature jerked once; its belly and skull burst with wet, explosive
sounds.

Instantly it snapped back, dying quickly in two sprays of ichor
and ragged skin, entrails and brainstuff bursting in curves from
its massive injuries, oozing with undigested, indigestible mind-
liquor.

It slumped dead across Andrej's insensible form, twitching
with spastic motion, dripping and broken.

Isaac bellowed with delight, a massive shout of astonished triumph. Andrej was briefly forgotten.

Derkhan and Yagharek turned quickly and stared at the dead
moth.

"Yes!" shouted Derkhan exultantly, and Yagharek emitted the
wordless ululating cry of a successful hunter. Below them, the
militia paused. They could not see what had happened, and they
were unnerved by the sudden shouts of triumph.

The second moth was scrambling over the body of its fallen
sibling, licking and sucking. The crisis engine still sounded;
Andrej still crawled in agony in the rain, unaware of what was
happening. The slake-moth scrabbled for the continuing flow of
bait.

The third moth arrived, sending rainwater spraying in the
downdrafts from its ferociously beating wings. It paused for a
fraction of a second, tasting the dead moth in the air, but the
stench of those astonishing Weaver/Council waves was irre-
sistible. It crawled through the sticky slick of the fallen moth's
bowels.

The other moth was quicker. It found the outflow pipe of the
helmet and thrust its mouth into the funnel, its tongue anchoring
it like some vampiric umbilical cord.

It gulped and sucked, hungry and exhilarated, drunk, burnt up
with its desires.

It was captivated. It could not resist when the power of the
food began to burn a hole in its stomach wall. It whined and
puked, metadimensional globules of brainpattern travelling
back up its gullet and meeting the torrent that it still sucked like
nectar, converging in its throat and suffocating it, until the soft
skin of its throat distended and split.

It began to bleed and die from the ragged tracheotomy, still drinking from the helmet and hastening its own death. The swell of energy was too much: it destroyed the moth as quickly and completely as its own unadulterated milk would a human. The slake-moth's mind burst flatly like a great blood-blister.

It fell back, its tongue retracting sluggishly like old elastic.

Isaac roared again as the third moth kicked away the twitching corpse of its sisterbrother and fed.

The militia were breaching the last rise of rooftop before the plateau. Yagharek moved in a lethal dance, suddenly murderous. His whip slashed; officers stumbled and fell away, ducked out of sight, moved warily behind the chimneys.

Derkhan fired again, into the face of a militiaman who rose before her, but the main wad of powder in the shaft of her pistol did not properly ignite. She cursed and held the gun away from her at arm's length, trying to keep it trained on the officer. He moved forward and the powder finally exploded, sending a ball over his head. He ducked and slipped to one foot on the friction-less roofspace.

Isaac pointed his gun and fired as the man fought to stand, sending a bullet into the back of his skull. The man jerked and his head battered against the ground. Isaac reached for his powder horn, then slid back. There was no time to reload, he realized. The last clutch of officers was vaulting towards him. They had been waiting for him to fire.

"Get back, Dee!" he yelled, and moved away from the edge.

Yagharek knocked one man down with a whipstrike at his legs, but he had to withdraw as the officers approached. Derkhan, Yagharek and Isaac moved back from the brink and looked desperately around for weapons.

Isaac stumbled on the segmented limb of a fallen moth. Behind him, the third moth was emitting little cries of greed as it drank. They fused into a single wail, an extended animal sound of delight or misery.

Isaac turned at the sound of the bleating and was caught in a moist detonation of flesh. Shredded innards slopped noisily over the roof, rendering it treacherous.

The third moth had succumbed.

Isaac stared at the dark, lolling shape, hard and variegated, as big as a bear. It was spreadeagled in a radial burst of limbs and bodyparts, dripping from its emptied-out thorax. The Weaver bent forward like a child and prodded the splayed exoskeleton with a tentative finger.

Andrej still moved, though his scissoring kicks were fitful. The moths had not drunk him, but the massive wash of artificial thoughts that bubbled up from the helmet. His mind still worked, bewildered and fearful and locked in the terrible feedback loop of the crisis engine. He was slowing down, his body collapsing under the extraordinary strain. His mouth worked in exaggerated yawns to clear itself of the thick, rotten-smelling saliva.

Directly above him, the final moth had spiralled into the fountain of energy from his helmet. Its wings were still, angled to control its fall, as it dropped like some murderous weapon out of the sky towards the tangled carnage. It bore down on the source of the feast, a clutch of arms and hands and hooks extended in frantic predation.

The militia lieutenant rose a foot or so over the grooved guttering at the edge of the plateau. He faltered and shouted something at his men—". . . ing Weaver!"—then fired wildly at Isaac. Isaac leapt sideways, grunted in quick triumph when he realized that he was uninjured. He grabbed a spanner from the pile of tools by his foot and hurled it at the mirrored helmet.

Something rocked unsteadily in the air around Isaac. His gut tensed and fluttered. He looked around wildly.

Derkhan was moving backwards from the edge of the roof, her face creased with inarticulate horror. She was staring around her in inchoate fear. Yagharek was holding his left hand to his head, the long knife dangling uncertainly from his fingers. His right hand, his whip, was motionless.

The Weaver looked up and muttered.

There was a small round hole in Andrej's chest where the officer's bullet had caught him. Blood was welling out of it in lazy pulses, dribbling across his belly and saturating his filthy clothes. His face was white, his eyes closed.

Isaac shouted and rushed to him, held the old man's hand.

The pattern of Andrej's brainwaves faltered. The engines combining the Weaver's and the Council's exudations skittered uncertainly as their template, their reference, suddenly ebbed.

Andrej was tenacious. He was an old man whose body was collapsing under the oppressive weight of a rotting, wasting disease, whose mind was stiff with coagulated dream-emissions. But even with a bullet lodged under his heart and his lung haemorrhaging, it took him nearly ten seconds to die.

Isaac held Andrej as he breathed bloodily. The bulky helmet lolled absurdly on his head. Isaac clenched his teeth as the old man died. At the very end, in what might have been a twitch of dying nerves, Andrej tensed and clutched Isaac, hugging him back in what Isaac desperately wanted to be forgiveness.

I had to I'm sorry I'm sorry, he thought giddily.

Behind Isaac the Weaver still drew patterns in the spilt juices of the slake-moths. Yagharek and Derkhan were calling to Isaac, screaming at him, as the militia came over the edge of the roof.

One of the dirigibles had lowered itself now until it hung sixty or seventy feet over the flattened roofscape below. It loomed like a bloated shark. A tangle of ropes was spilling untidily through the darkness towards the great expanse of clay.

Andrej's brain went out like a broken lamp.

A confused tangle of information weltered through the analytical engines.

Without Andrej's mind as referent, the combination of the Weaver's and the Construct Council's waves became suddenly random, their proportions skewing and rolling unsteadily. They no longer modelled anything: they were just an untidy slosh of oscillating particles and waves.

The crisis was gone. The thickening mixture of mindwaves was no more than the sum of its parts, and it had stopped trying to be. The paradox, the tension, disappeared. The vast field of crisis energy evaporated.

The burning gears and motors of the crisis engine stuttered to an abrupt stop.

With a crushing implosive collapse, the enormous wash of mental energy was snuffed instantly out.

Isaac, Derkhan, Yagharek and the militia for thirty feet around let out cries of pain. They felt as if they had walked from bright sunlight into a darkness so sudden and total it hurt them. They ached drably behind their eyes.

Isaac let Andrej's body fall slowly to the wet ground.

In the wet heat a little way above the station, the last slake-moth eddied in confusion. It beat its wings in complex four-way patterns, sent coils of air in all directions. It hovered.

The rich trough of food, that unthinkable gush, was gone. The frenzy that had overtaken the moth, the terrible, uncompromising hunger, had gone.

It licked out and its antennae trembled. There were a handful of minds below it, but before it could attack the moth sensed the chaotic bubbling consciousness of the Weaver, and it remembered its agonizing battles and it screeched in fear and rage, stretching its neck back and baring its monstrous teeth.

And then the unmistakable taste of its own kind wafted up to it. It spun in shock as it tasted one, two, three dead siblings, all its siblings, every one of them, insides out, dead and crushed, spent.

The slake-moth was mad with grief. It keened in ultra-high frequencies and spun aerobatically, sending out little calls of sociality, echo-locating for other moths, fumbling through unclear layers of perception with its antennae and clutching empathically for any trace of an answer.

It was quite alone.

It rolled away from the roof of Perdido Street Station, away from that charnel-ground where its brothersisters lay burst, away from the memory of that impossible flavour, veering in terror away from The Crow and the Weaver's claws and the fat dirigibles that stalked it, out of the shadow of the Spike towards the junction of the rivers.

The slake-moth fled in misery, searching for a place to rest.

CHAPTER FIFTY-ONE

As the battered militia gathered themselves and began to peer, once more, over the edge of the roof at Isaac's and Derkhan's and Yagharek's feet. They were wary now.

Three rapid bullets came flying down at them. One sent an officer flying without a word into the dark air beside the roof, to shatter a window four floors below with his weight. The other two buried themselves deep in the fabric of the bricks and stones, sending out wicked sprays of chips.

Isaac looked up. A dim figure was leaning out from a ledge twenty feet above them.

"It's Half-a-Prayer again!" shouted Isaac. "How did he get *there*? What's he *doing*?"

"Come on," said Derkhan brusquely. "We have to go."

The militia were still cowering just below them. Whenever an officer straightened up carefully and looked over the edge, Half-a-Prayer would send another bullet straight at him. He kept them caged in. One or two of them shot at him, but they were desultory, demoralized efforts.

Just beyond the rise of roofs and windows, unclear shapes were descending smoothly from the dirigible, sliding onto the slick surface below. They dangled loosely as they slipped through the air, attached by some hook on their armour. The ropes that held them uncoiled on smooth motors.

"He's buying us some time, gods know why," hissed Derkhan, stumbling over to Isaac and clutching at him. "He's going to run out of bullets soon. These sods—" she waved vaguely at the half-hidden militia below them "—these are just the local flat-foots on roof-duty. *Those* bastards coming from the airships are going to be hardcore troops. We have to *go*."

Isaac looked down and faltered towards the edge, but there were cowering militia visible on all sides. Bullets smacked down around Isaac as he moved. He yelled in fear, then realized that Half-a-Prayer was trying to clear the path before him.

It was no good, though. The militia were hunkering down and waiting.

"Fuck *damn*," spat Isaac. He bent down and pulled a plug from Andrej's helmet, disconnecting the Construct Council, which was still concertedly attempting to bypass the circuit-valve and gain control of the crisis engine. Isaac yanked the wire free, sending a damaging spasm of feedback and rerouted energy bolting down the line into the Council's brain.

"Get this shit!" he hissed at Yagharek, and pointed at the engines that littered the roof, fouled with ichor and acid rain. The garuda dropped to one knee and scooped up the sack. "Weaver!" said Isaac urgently, and stumbled over to the enormous figure.

He kept looking back, over his shoulder, fearful of seeing some gung-ho militiaman reaching up to take a potshot. Over the rain, the sound of metallic crunching steps drew nearer on the roof below them in a pounding jog.

"Weaver!" Isaac clapped his hands in front of the extraordinary spider. The Weaver's multifarious eyes slid up to meet him. The Weaver still wore the helmet that linked it to Andrej's corpse. It was rubbing its hands in slake-moth viscera. Isaac looked down briefly at the pile of huge corpses. Their wings had faded to a pale, drab dun, without pattern or variation.

"Weaver, we need to go," he whispered. The Weaver interrupted him.

. . . I TIRE AND GROW OLD AND COLD GRIMY LITTLING . . . the Weaver said quietly . . . YOU WORK WITH FINESSE I GRANT AND GIVE YOU BUT THIS SIPHONING OF PHANTASMS FROM MY SOLE SOUL LEAVES ME MELANCHOLIC SEE PATTERNS INHERE EVEN IN THESE THE VORACIOUS ONES PERHAPS I JUDGE QUICK AND SLICK TASTES FALTER AND ALTER AND I AM UNSURE . . . It raised a handful of glistening guts to Isaac's eyes and began to pull them gently apart.

"Believe me, Weaver," said Isaac urgently, "this was the *right thing*, we saved the city for you to . . . to judge, to weave . . . now that we've done this. But we need to go *now*, we need you to help us. Please . . . get us away from here . . ."

"Isaac," hissed Derkhan, "I don't know who these swine are that are coming but . . . but they're not militia."

Isaac stole a glance out over the roofs. His eyes widened incredulously.

Stomping purposefully towards them was a battery of extraordinary metal soldiers. The light slid from them, illuminating their edges in cold flashes. They were sculpted in astonishing and frightening detail. Their arms and legs swung with great bursts of hydraulic power, pistons hissing as they stormed closer. Little glimmers of reflected light came from somewhere a little behind their heads.

"Who the *fuck* are those bastards?" said Isaac in a strangled voice.

The Weaver interrupted him. Its voice was suddenly loud again, purposeful.

. . . BY GOODNESS ME YOU CONVINCE . . . it said . . . LOOK AT THE INTRICATE SKEINS AND THREADLINES WE CORRECT WHERE THE DEADLINGS REAVED WE CAN RESHUFFLE AND SPIN AND FIX IT UP NICE . . . The Weaver bobbed excitedly up and down and stared at the dark sky. It plucked the helmet from its head in a smooth motion and threw it casually out into the night. Isaac did not hear it land. . . . IT RUNS AND HIDES ITS HIDE . . . it said . . . IT IS ROOTING FOR A NEST POOR FRIGHTENED MONSTER WE MUST CRUSH IT LIKE ITS BROTHERS BEFORE IT GNAWS HOLES IN THE SKY AND THE CITYWIDE COLOURFLOW COME AND LET US SLIDE DOWN

LONG FISSURES IN THE WORLDWEB WHERE THE RENDER RUNS AND
FIND ITS LAIR . . .

It staggered forward, always seeming to teeter on the edge of
collapse. It opened its arms to Isaac like a loving parent, swept
him quickly and effortlessly up. Isaac grimaced in fear as he was
taken into its weird, cool embrace. *Don't cut me,* he thought fervently, *don't slice me up!*

The militia peered furtive and aghast over the roof at the sight.
The enormous, towering spider stalked edgily this way and that,
Isaac tucked lolling like some absurd, vast baby under its arm.

It moved with sure, fleeting motions across the sodden tar and
clay. It could not be followed. It moved in and out of conventional space with motions too fast to see.

It stood before Yagharek. The garuda swung the sack of mechanical components that he had hastily gathered over onto his
back. Yagharek delivered himself thankfully to the dancing mad
god, throwing up his arms and clutching at the smooth waist between the Weaver's head and abdomen . . . GRAB TIGHT LITTLE
ONE WE MUST FIND A WAY AWAY . . . sang the Weaver.

The weird metallic troops were approaching the little eleva-
tion of flat land, their mechanical anatomy hissing with efficient
energy. They swept past the lower militia, terrified junior officers
who gazed up in astonishment at the human faces peering intently from the back of the iron warriors' heads.

Derkhan looked round at the encroaching figures, then swallowed and walked quickly over to the Weaver, which stood with
humanoid arms wide. Isaac and Yagharek were perched on its
weapon arms, their legs scrabbling for purchase across its broad
back.

"Don't hurt me again," whispered Derkhan, her hand flickering over the scabbed wound on the side of her face. She hol-
stered her guns and raced across into the Weaver's terrifying,
cradling arms.

The second dirigible arrived at the roof of Perdido Street Station
and threw out ropes for its troops to descend. Motley's Remade
squadron had reached the top of the rise of architecture and was
vaulting over without pause. The militia gazed up at them,
cowed. They did not understand what they were seeing.

The Remade breached the low rise of bricks without hesitation, only faltering when they saw the Weaver's huge and skulk-

ing form scampering to and fro across the bricks, three figures jouncing like dolls on its back.

Motley's troops stepped back towards the edge slowly, rain varnishing their impassive steel faces. Their heavy feet crushed the remnants of the engines that still lay split across the roof.

As they watched, the Weaver reached down and grasped hold of a quailing militiaman, who wailed in terror as he was dragged up by his head. The man flailed, but the Weaver pushed his arms away and cuddled him like a baby.

. . . OFF AND ON TO GO HUNTING WE WILL TAKE OUR LEAVE . . . whispered the Weaver to all present. It walked sideways off the edge of the roof, seemingly unencumbered, and disappeared.

For two or three seconds, only the rain sounded fitful and depressing on the roof. Then Half-a-Prayer let off a last volley of shots from above, sending the assembled men and Remade scattering. When they emerged carefully, there were no more attacks. Jack Half-a-Prayer had gone.

The Weaver and its companions had left no trail, and no trace.

The slake-moth tore through currents of air. It was frantic and afraid.

It sounded every so often, letting out a cry in a variety of sonic registers, but it was unanswered. It was miserable and confused.

And yet beneath it all, its infernal hunger was growing again. It was not free of its appetite.

Below it the Canker flowed through the city, its barges and pleasure boats little grubs of dirty light on the blackness. The slake-moth slowed and spiralled.

A line of filthy smoke was drawn slowly across the face of New Crobuzon, marking it like a stub of pencil, as a late train went east on the Dexter Line, through Gidd and Barguest Bridge, on over the water towards Lud Fallow and Sedim Junction.

The moth swept on over Ludmead, ducking low above the roofs of the university faculty, alighting briefly on the roof of the Magpie Cathedral in Saltbur, flitting away in a pang of hunger and lonely fear. It could not rest. It could not channel its rapacity to feed.

As it flew, the slake-moth recognized the configuration of light and darkness below it. It felt a sudden pull.

Behind the railway lines, rising from the shabby and decrepit architecture of Bonetown, the Ribs rose out into the night air in a colossal sweep and curve of ivory. They made memories eddy in the slake-moth's head. It recalled the dubious influence of those old bones that had made Bonetown a fearful place, somewhere to be escaped, where air currents were unpredictable and noxious tides could pollute the æther. Distant images of days clamped still, being milked lasciviously, its glands sucked clean, a hazy sense of a suckling grub at its teat, but nothing being there . . . memories caught it up.

The moth was utterly cowed. It sought relief. It hankered for a nest, somewhere to lie still, recuperate. Somewhere familiar, where it could tend itself and be tended. In its misery, it remembered its captivity in a selective, twisted light. It had been fed and cleaned by careful tenders there in Bonetown. It had been a sanctuary.

Frightened and hungry and eager for relief, it conquered its fear of the Bonetown Ribs.

It set off southwards, licking its way through half-forgotten routes in the air, skirting the blistered bones, seeking out a dark building in a little alley, a bitumened terrace of unclear purpose, from where it had crawled weeks ago.

The slake-moth wheeled nervously over the dangerous city and headed for home.

Isaac felt as if he had been asleep for several days, and he stretched luxuriously, feeling his body slide uncomfortably forward and back.

He heard an appalling scream.

Isaac froze as memories came back to him in torrents, let him know how he had come to be there, held tight in the Weaver's arms (he jerked and spasmed as he recalled it all).

The Weaver was stepping lightly over the worldweb, scuttling across metareal filaments connecting every moment to every other.

Isaac remembered the vertiginous pitch of his soul when he had seen the worldweb. He remembered a nausea that had wracked his existential being at the sight of that impossible vista. He struggled not to open his eyes.

He could hear the jabbering of Yagharek and Derkhan's whispered curses. They came to him not as sounds but as intimations, floating fragments of silk that slipped into his skull and became clear to him. There was another voice, a jagged cacophony of bright fabric shrieking in terror.

He wondered who that might be.

The Weaver moved quickly across pitching threads alongside

the damage and potentiality of damage that the slake-moth had wreaked, and might again. The Weaver disappeared into a hole, a dim funnel of connections that wound through the material of that complex dimension and

emerged again into the city.

Isaac felt air against his cheek, wood below him. He woke and opened his eyes.

His head hurt. He looked up. His neck wobbled as he adjusted to the weight of his helmet, still perched tight on his head, its mirrors miraculously unbroken.

He was lying in a shaft of moonlight in some dusty little attic. Sounds filtered into the space through the wooden floors and walls.

Derkhan and Yagharek were raising themselves slowly and carefully onto their elbows, shaking their heads. As Isaac watched, Derkhan reached up quickly and gently felt the sides of her head. Her remaining ear—and his, he quickly ascertained—was untouched.

The Weaver loomed in the corner of the room. It stepped forward slightly, and behind it, Isaac saw a militiaman. The officer seemed paralysed. He sat with his back against the wall, shaking quietly, his smooth faceplate skewwhiff and falling from his head. His rifle lay across his lap. Isaac's eyes widened when he saw it.

It was glass. A perfect and useless model of a flintlock rifle rendered in glass.

. . . THIS WOULD BE HOMESTEAD FOR THE FLEETING WINGED ONE . . . crooned the Weaver. It sounded subdued again, as if its energy had ebbed from it during the journey through the planes of the web . . . SEE MY LOOKING-GLASS MAN MY PLAYMATE MY FRIENDLING . . . it whispered . . . HE AND ME SHALL WHILE TIME AWAY THIS IS THE RESTING PLACE OF THE VAMPIR MOTH THIS IS WHERE IT FOLDS ITS WINGS AND HIDES TO EAT AGAIN I WILL PLAY TIC-TAC-TOE AND BOXES WITH MY GLASS-GUNNER . . .

It stepped back into the corner of the room and set itself down suddenly with a jerk of its legs. One of its knife-hands flashed like elyctricity, moving with extraordinary speed, scoring a three-by-three grid onto the boards before the comatose officer's lap.

The Weaver etched a cross into a corner square, then sat back and waited, whispering to itself.

Isaac, Derkhan and Yagharek shuffled into the centre of the room.

"I thought it was going to get us away," mumbled Isaac. "It's followed the fucking moth . . . It's here, somewhere . . ."

"We have to take it," whispered Derkhan, her face set. "We've almost got them all. Let's finish it."

"With *what*?" hissed Isaac. "We've got our fucking helmets and that's *it*. We've not got any weapons to face the likes of that thing . . . we don't even know where we damn-well are . . ."

"We have to get the Weaver to help us," said Derkhan.

But their attempts were quite fruitless. The gigantic spider ignored them utterly, wittering quietly to itself and waiting intently, as if waiting for the frozen militia officer to complete his move in tic-tac-toe. Isaac and the others entreated with the Weaver, begged it to help them, but they seemed suddenly invisible to it. They turned away in frustration.

"We have to go out there," said Derkhan suddenly. Isaac met her eyes. Slowly, he nodded. He strode across to the window and peered out.

"I can't tell where we are," he said eventually. "It's just streets." He moved his head exaggeratedly from side to side, seeking some landmark. He re-entered the room eventually, shaking his head. "You're right, Dee," he said. "Maybe we'll . . . find something . . . maybe we can get out of here."

Yagharek moved without sound, stalking from the little room into a dimly lit corridor. He looked up and down its length, carefully.

The wall to his left slanted steeply in with the roof. To his right, the narrow passage was broken with two doors, before it curved away to the right and disappeared in shadows.

Yagharek kept crouched down. He beckoned slowly behind him, without looking, and Derkhan and Isaac emerged slowly. They carried their guns loaded with the last of their powder, damp and unreliable, aiming vaguely into the darkness.

They waited while Yagharek crept slowly on, then followed him in faltering, pugnacious steps.

Yagharek stopped by the first door and flattened his feathered head against it. He waited a moment, then pushed it open slowly, slowly. Derkhan and Isaac crept over, peered into an unlit storeroom.

"Is there anything in there we can use?" hissed Isaac, but the shelves were empty of everything except dry and dusty bottles, ancient decaying brushes.

When Yagharek reached the second door, he repeated the operation, waving at Isaac and Derkhan to be still and listening intently through the thin wood. This time he was still for much longer. The door was bolted several times, and Yagharek fumbled with all the simple slide-locks. There was a fat padlock, but it was resting open across one of the bolts, as if it had been left for a moment. Yagharek pushed slowly at the door. He poked his head through the resulting gap and stood like that, perched half in, half out of the room for a disconcertingly long time.

When he withdrew, he turned.

"Isaac," he said quietly. "You must come."

Isaac frowned and stepped forward, his heart beating hard in his chest.

What is it? he thought. *What's going on? (And even as he thought that a voice in the deepest part of his mind told him what was waiting for him, and he only half heard it, would not listen for fear that it was wrong.)*

He pushed past Yagharek and walked hesitantly into the room.

It was a large, rectangular attic space, lit by three oil-lamps and the thin wisps of gaslight that found their way up from the street and through the grubby, sealed window. The floor was littered with a tangle of metal and discarded rubbish. The room stank.

Isaac was only fleetingly conscious of any of this.

In a dim corner, turned away from the door, kneeling up and chewing dutifully with her back and head and gland attached to an extraordinary twisted sculpture, was Lin.

Isaac cried out.

It was an animal wail, and it grew and grew in strength until Yagharek hissed at him, unheeded.

Lin turned with a start at the sound. She trembled when she saw him.

He stumbled over to her, weeping at the sight of her, at her russet skin and flexing headscarab; and as he approached he cried out again, this time in anguish, as he saw what had been done to her.

Her body was bruised and covered with burns and scratches, welts that hinted at vicious acts and brutalizations. She had been beaten across her back, through her ragged shift. Her breasts were criss-crossed with thin scars. She was bruised heavily around her belly and thighs.

But it was her head, the twitching headbody, that almost made him fall.

Her wings had been taken: he knew that, from the envelope, but to see them, to see the tiny ragged stubs flit in agitation . . . Her carapace had been snapped and bent backwards in places, uncovering the tender flesh beneath, which was scabbed and broken. One of her compound eyes was crumpled and sightless. The middle headleg on her right and the hind one on her left had been torn from their sockets.

Isaac fell forward and held her, closing her into him. She was so thin . . . so tiny and ragged and broken, she was trembling as she touched him, her whole body tense as if she could not believe he were real, as if he might be taken away as some new torture.

Isaac clutched her and cried. He held her carefully, feeling her thin bones beneath her skin.

"I would have *come*," he moaned in abject misery and joy. "I would've *come*, I thought you were *dead* . . ."

She pushed him back just a little, until she had space for her hands to move.

Wanted you, love you, she signed chaotically, *help me save me take me away, couldn't he couldn't let me die till had finished this* . . .

For the first time, Isaac looked up at the extraordinary sculpture that rose above and behind her, onto which she was spreading khepri-spit. It was an incredible multicoloured thing, a horrific kaleidoscopic figure of composite nightmares, limbs and eyes and legs sprouting in weird combinations. It was almost finished, with only a smooth framework where what looked like a head must be, and an empty clutch of air that suggested a shoulder.

Isaac gasped at it, looked back at her.

Lemuel had been right. There was, strategically, no reason at all for Motley to keep Lin alive. He would not have done so for any other captive. But his vanity, his mystical self-aggrandizement and philosophical dreamings were stimulated by Lin's extraordinary work. Lemuel could not have known that.

Motley could not bear for the sculpture to remain unfinished.

*   *   *

Derkhan and Yagharek entered. When she saw Lin, Derkhan cried out as Isaac had done. She ran across the room to where Isaac and Lin embraced and put her own arms around the two of them, crying and smiling.

Yagharek paced uneasily towards them.

Isaac was murmuring to Lin, telling her over and over how sorry he was, that he thought she was dead, that he would have come.

Kept me working, beating and . . . and torturing, taunting me, Lin signed, giddy and exhausted with emotion.

Yagharek was about to speak, but he snapped his head suddenly around.

The tramp of hurried feet was audible in the corridor outside.

Isaac stood, supporting Lin as he came, keeping her enfolded in his embrace. Derkhan moved away from the two of them. She drew her pistols and turned to face the door. Yagharek flattened himself against the wall in the shadow of the sculpture, his whip coiled and ready.

The door burst open and hammered against the wall, sprang back.

Motley stood before them.

He was silhouetted. Isaac saw a twisted outline against the black-painted walls of the corridor. A garden of multifarious limbs, a walking patchwork of organic forms. Isaac's mouth dropped open in amazement. He realized as he watched the shuffling goat- and bird- and dog-footed creature, as he saw the clutching tentacles and knots of tissue, the composite bones and invented skin, that Lin's piece was taken, without fancy, from *life*.

At the sight of him, Lin went limp with fear and the memory of pain. Isaac felt rage begin to engulf him.

Motley stepped back slightly and turned to face the way he had come.

"Security!" shouted Motley from some unclear mouth. *"Get here now!"* He stepped back into the room.

"Grimnebulin," he said. His voice was quick and tense. "You came. Didn't you get my message? Bit *remiss*, aren't you?" Motley stepped into the room and the faint light.

Derkhan fired twice. Her bullets tore through Motley's armoured skin and patches of fur. He staggered back on multiple legs with a bellow of pain. His cry became a vicious laugh.

"Far too many internal organs to hurt me, you useless slut," he shouted. Derkhan spat with fury and edged closer to the wall.

Isaac stared at Motley, saw teeth gnashing in a multitude of mouths. The floor shook as people pounded along the corridor outside, racing towards the room.

Men appeared in the doorway behind Motley, waved weapons, waited uncertainly. For a moment Isaac's stomach pitched: the men had no faces, only smooth skin stretched tight over their skulls. *What kind of fucking Remades are these?* he thought giddily. Then he caught sight of the mirrors extending backwards from the helmets.

His eyes widened as he realized that these were shaven-headed Remade with their heads turned one hundred and eighty degrees, specially and perfectly adapted to dealing with the slake-moths. They waited now for their boss's orders, their muscular bodies facing Isaac, their heads turned permanently away.

One of Motley's limbs—an ugly, segmented and suckered thing—shot out to indicate Lin.

"Finish your godsdamned *job*, you bugger bitch, or you know what you'll get!" he shouted, and hobbled towards Lin and Isaac.

With an utterly bestial roar, Isaac pushed Lin to one side. A spray of chymical anguish burst from her. Her hands twisted as she begged him to stay with her, but he was launching himself at Motley in an agony of guilt and fury.

Motley shouted wordlessly, meeting Isaac's challenge.

There was a sudden loud concussion. An explosion of glass scintillas sprayed across the room, leaving blood and curses.

Isaac froze in the centre of the room. Motley was frozen before him. The ranks of security were fumbling with their weapons, shouting orders at each other. Isaac looked up, into the mirrors before his eyes.

The last slake-moth stood behind him. It was framed in the ragged stubs of the window. Glass still dripped around it like viscous liquid.

Isaac gasped.

It was a huge, a terrifying presence. It stood, half crouched, a little way forward from the wall and the window-hole, various savage limbs clutching the floor. It was massive as a gorilla, a body of terrible solidity and intricate violence.

Its unthinkable wings were wide open. Patterns burst across them like negative fireworks.

Motley had been facing the great beast: his mind was captured. He gazed at the wings with an array of unblinking eyes.

Behind him his troops were shouting in agitation, levelling weapons.

Yagharek and Derkhan had been standing with their backs to the wall. Isaac saw them in his mirrors behind the thing. The patterned sides of its wings were hidden from them: they were still with shock, but not in thrall.

Between the slake-moth and Isaac, sprawled on the boards where she had fallen in the ragged cascade of glass, was Lin.

"Lin!" shouted Isaac desperately. *"Don't turn round! Don't look behind you! Come to me!"*

Lin froze at his panicked tone. She saw him reach backwards in an appallingly clumsy gesture, step hesitatingly towards her without turning round.

She crawled slowly, very slowly, towards him.

Behind her, she heard a low, animal noise.

The slake-moth stood, pugnacious and uneasy. It could taste minds all around, moving on all sides, threatening and fearing it.

It was unsettled and nervous, still traumatized by the slaughter of its siblings. One of its spiny tentacles lashed the ground like a tail.

Before it, one mind was captive. But the moth's wings were spread out wide and yet it had captured only *one* . . . ? It was confused. It faced the main mass of its enemies, it batted its wings at them hypnotically, trying to pull them under and send their dreams bubbling to the surface.

They remained resistant.

The slake-moth grew panicked.

The security behind Motley shifted in frustration. They tried to push past their boss, but he had frozen at the threshold to the room. His enormous body seemed fixed, his various legs planted hard on the ground. He gazed at the slake-moth wings in an intense trance.

There were five Remade behind him. They were poised. They were equipped specifically to defend against slake-moths, in case of escapes. In addition to small arms, three wielded flamethrowers; one a spray of femtocorrosive acid; one an elyctro-thaumaturgic barb-gun. They could see their quarry. But they could not get past their boss.

Motley's men tried to aim their weapons around him, but his towering bulk occluded their line of fire. They shouted to each other and tried to devise strategies, but they could not. They gazed into their mirrors, watched the huge, predatory moth under Motley's arms and limbs, through gaps in his outline. They were cowed by the monstrous sight.

Isaac stretched his arm back, reached for Derkhan.

"Come here, Lin," he hissed, "and *don't look behind you.*"

It was like some terrifying children's game.

Yagharek and Derkhan shifted quietly, moving towards each other behind the moth. It chittered and looked up at their motion, but it remained more wary of the mass of figures before it, and it did not turn round.

Lin slid fitfully along the floor towards Isaac's back, his clutching arms. A little way from him, she hesitated. She saw Motley, transfixed as if amazed, gazing past Isaac and over her, captivated by . . . something.

She did not know what was happening, what was behind her.

She knew nothing about the moths.

Isaac saw her hesitate, and began to howl at her not to stop.

Lin was an artist. She created with her touch and taste, making tactile objects. Visible objects. Sculpture to be fondled and seen.

She was fascinated by colour and light and shadow, by the interplay of shapes and lines, negative and positive spaces.

She had been locked in the attic for a long time.

In her position, some would have sabotaged the vast sculpture of Motley. The commission had become a sentence, after all. But Lin did not destroy it or skimp in her work. She poured everything she could, all her pent-up creative energy into that one monolithic and terrible piece. As Motley had known she would.

It had been her only escape. Her only means of expression. Starved of all the light and colour and shapeliness of the world, she had focused in her fear and pain and become obsessed. Creating a presence herself, the better to beguile her.

And now something extraordinary had entered her attic world.

She knew nothing of the slake-moths. The command *don't look behind you* was familiar from fables, made sense only as a moralistic injunction, some heavy-handed lesson. Isaac must mean *be quick* or *don't doubt me,* something like that. His command made sense only as an emotional exhortation.

Lin was an artist. Savaged and tortured, confused by imprisonment and pain and degradation, Lin grasped only that something extraordinary, some utterly affecting sight had risen up behind her. And hungry for any kind of wonder after the weeks of pain in the shadow of those drab, colourless and shapeless walls, she paused, then quickly glanced behind her.

Isaac and Derkhan screamed in terrible disbelief; Yagharek called out with shock like some livid crow.

With her one good eye, Lin took in the extraordinary sweep of the slake-moth's shape with awe; and then she caught sight of the gusting colours on the wings, and her mandibles clattered briefly and she was silent. Enthralled.

She squatted on the floor, her head twisted over her left shoulder, gazing stupidly at the great beast, at the rush of colours. Motley and she stared at the slake-moth's wings, their minds overflowing.

Isaac howled and stumbled backwards, reaching out desperately.

The slake-moth reached out with a slithering clutch of tentacles and pulled Lin towards it. Its vast and dripping mouth slid open like a doorway into some stygian place. Rank citric spittle drooled across Lin's face.

As Isaac grabbed backwards for her hand, staring intently into his mirrors, the slake-moth's tongue lurched out of its stinking throat and lapped at her headscarab briefly. Isaac shouted again and again, but he could not stop it.

The long tongue, slippery with saliva, inveigled its way past Lin's slack mouthparts and plunged into her head.

At the sound of Isaac's appalled yells, two of the Remade trapped behind Motley's enormous bulk reached over and fired erratically with their flintlocks. One missed completely, the other clipped the slake-moth's thorax, eliciting a brief dollop of liquid and an irritated hiss, but no more. It was not the right weapon.

The two who had fired shouted at their fellows, and the small squadron began to shove at Motley's bulk, in careful, timed thrusts.

Isaac was clutching for Lin's hand.

The slake-moth's throat swelled and shrank, its gristly throat swallowing in great swigs.

Yagharek reached down and grabbed the oil-lamp that stood by the foot of the sculpture. He hefted it briefly in his left hand, raised his whip in his right.

"Grab her, Isaac," he called.

As the slake-moth clutched her thin body to its thorax, Isaac felt his fingers close around Lin's wrist. He clenched hard, tried to pull her free. He wept and swore.

Yagharek hurled the lit oil-lamp against the back of the slake-moth's head. The glass broke open and a little spray of incandescent oil spattered over the smooth skin. A burst of blue flame crawled across the dome of the skull.

The slake-moth squealed. A flurry of limbs whipped up to batter out the little fire as the slake-moth jerked its head back momentarily in pain. Instantly, Yagharek snapped his whip with a savage stroke. It smacked loud and dramatic against the dark skin. Coils of the thick leather wound almost instantly around the slake-moth's neck.

Yagharek pulled hard and fast, with all his wiry strength. He drew the whip absolutely tight and braced himself.

The small fire kept stinging, burning tenaciously. The whip cut off the slake-moth's throat. It could not swallow or breathe.

Its head lurched on its long neck. It emitted strangulated little cries. Its tongue swelled and it lashed it out of Lin's mouth. The spurts of consciousness it had tried to drink clogged up in its throat. The moth clawed at the whip, frantic and terrified. It flailed and shook and spun.

Isaac hung on to Lin's shrunken wrist, tugging at her as the moth twirled in a hideous dance. Its twitching limbs flew away from her, clutching vainly at the thong that choked it. Isaac pulled her clear, dropped to the floor and scrabbled away from the rampaging creature.

As it turned in its panic, its wings folded and it turned away from the door. Instantly, its hold on Motley was broken. Motley's composite body stumbled forward and collapsed on the floor as his mind crawled back together. His men pushed over him, picking their way past a tangle of his legs into the room.

In a hideous drumming of feet the slake-moth spun. The whip was wrenched from Yagharek's hands, tearing his skin. He staggered back, towards Derkhan, out of range of the slake-moth's razored, spinning limbs.

Motley was standing. He stamped quickly away from the beast, passing back into the corridor.

"Kill the damn thing!" he shrieked.

*   *   *

The moth danced in a frenzy into the centre of the room. The five Remade stood in a little clutch around the door. They aimed through their mirrors.

Three jets of burning gas burst from the flamethrowers, scorching the vast creature's skin. It tried to shriek as its wings and chitin roared and split and crisped, but the whip prevented it. A great gob of acid sprayed the twisting moth square in the face. It denatured the proteins and compounds of its hide in seconds, melting the moth's exoskeleton.

The acid and the flame ate swiftly through the whip. Its remnants flew away from the spinning moth, which could finally breathe, and scream.

It shrieked in agony as fresh gouts of fire and acid caught it. It hurled itself blindly in the direction of its attackers.

Bolts of dark energy from the fifth man's gun burst into it, dissipating across its surface area, numbing and scorching it without heat. It screeched again, but hurtled on, a sightless storm of flame, spitting acid and flailing ragged bone.

The five Remade moved back as it stumbled madly for them, following Motley into the corridor. The intense moving pyre slammed into the walls, igniting them, fumbling for the doorway.

From the little hallway, the sounds of fire, spewing acid and quarrels of elyctro-thaumaturgy continued.

For long seconds, Derkhan and Yagharek and Isaac stared up dumbfounded at the doorway. The moth still shrieked just out of sight, the corridor beyond was radiant with flickering light and heat.

Then Isaac blinked and stared down at Lin, who slumped in his embrace.

He hissed at her, shook her.

"Lin," he whispered. "Lin . . . We're leaving."

Yagharek strode quickly over to the window and peered out over the street five floors below. Next to the window, a little jutting column of brick extended out from the wall, becoming a chimney. A drainpipe snaked up beside it. He stood quickly on the windowsill and reached up for the guttering, tugged it quickly. It was solid.

"Isaac, bring her here," said Derkhan urgently. Isaac lifted Lin up, biting his lip at how light she was. He walked quickly with her to the window. As he watched her, his face suddenly broke into an incredulous, an ecstatic smile. He began to weep.

From the passage outside, the slake-moth keened weakly.

"Dee, look!" he hissed. Lin's hands were fluttering erratically in front of her as he cradled her. "She's *signing*! She's going to be all right!"

Derkhan peered over, reading her words. Isaac watched, shook his head.

"She's not conscious, it's just random words, but, Dee, it's *words* . . . We were in *time* . . ."

Derkhan smiled in delight. She kissed Isaac hard on the cheek, stroked Lin's broken headscarb gently.

"Get her out of here," she said quietly. Isaac peered out of the window, where Yagharek had wedged himself into a corner of architecture, on a little extrusion of brick a few feet away.

"Give her to me, and follow," said Yagharek, jerking his head up above him. At the eastern end the long sloped roof of Motley's terrace joined with the next street, which jutted perpendicularly south in a descending row of houses. The roofscape of Bonetown stretched out above and all around them; a raised landscape; linked islands of slate over the dangerous streets, extending for miles in the darkness, sweeping away from the Ribs to Mog Hill and beyond.

Even then, devoured alive by tides of fire and acid, stunned with bolts of obscure energy, the last slake-moth might have survived.

It was a creature of astonishing endurance. It could heal itself at frightening speeds.

If it had been in the open air, it could have leapt up and spread those terribly wounded wings and disappeared from the earth. It might have forced itself up, ignoring the pain, ignoring the scorched flakes of skin and chitin that would flutter around it filthily. It could have rolled into the wet clouds to douse the flames, wash itself free of acid.

If its family had survived, if it had been confident that it could return to its siblings, that they would hunt together again, it might not have panicked. If it had not witnessed a carnage of its kind, an impossible blast of poisonous vapour that enticed its brothersisters in and burst them, the moth would not have been insane with fear and anger, and it might not have become frenzied and lashed out, trapping itself further.

But it was alone. Trapped under brick, in a claustrophobic warren that constricted it, flattened its wings, left it nowhere to go. Assailed on all sides by murderous, endless pain. The fire came and came again too fast for it to heal.

It staggered the length of the corridor in Motley's headquarters, a white-hot ball, reaching out to the last with ragged claws and spines, trying to hunt. It fell just before the top of the stairs.

Motley and the Remade looked on in awe from halfway down, praying that it lay still, that it did not crawl over the lip of the stairway and tumble flaming onto them.

It did not. It was still while it died.

When they were sure the slake-moth was dead, Motley sent men and women up and down the stairs in quick columns, carrying sodden towels and blankets to control the blaze it had left in its wake.

It took twenty minutes before the fire was subdued. The beams and boards of the attic were split and smoke-fouled. Massive footprints of charred wood and blistered paint stretched the length of the passage. The smouldering body of the moth rested on the top of the stairs, an unrecognizable pile of flesh and tissue, twisted by heat into an even more exotic shape than it had had in life.

"Grimnebulin and his bastard friends'll be gone," said Motley. "Find them. Find where they went. Track them down. Trace them. Tonight. Now."

It was easy to see how they had escaped, out of the window and onto the roof. From there, though, they could have gone in almost any direction. Motley's men shifted, looking uneasily at each other.

"Move, you Remade scum," raged Motley. "Find them *now*, track them down and *bring them to me*."

Terrified gangs of Remade, of humans, of cactacae and vodyanoi set out from Motley's terrace-den, off into the city. They made pointless plans, compared notes, frantically raced down to Sunter, to Echomire and Ludmead, to Kelltree and Mog Hill, all the way to Badside, over the river to Brock Marsh, to West Gidd and Griss Fell and Murkside and Saltpetre.

They might have walked past Isaac and his companions a thousand times.

There was an infinity of holes in New Crobuzon. There were far more hiding places than there were people to hide. Motley's troops never had a chance.

On nights like that one, when rain and streetlamp light made all the lines and edges of the city complex—a palimpsest of gusting trees and architecture and sound, ancient ruins, darkness, catacombs, building sites, guesthouses, barren land, lights and pubs and sewers—it was an endless, recursive, secretive place.

Motley's men made their way home empty-handed and afraid.

Motley raged and raged at the unfinished statue that taunted him, perfect and incomplete. His men searched the building, in case some clue had been missed.

In the last room on the attic corridor, they found a militiaman sitting with his back to the wall, comatose and alone. A bizarre, beautiful glass flintlock lay across his lap. A game of tic-tac-toe was scratched into the wood by his feet.

Crosses had won, in three moves.

We run and hide like hunted vermin, but it is with relief and joy.

We know that we have won.

Isaac carries Lin in his arms, sometimes hauling her over his shoulder apologetically when the way is tough. We race away. We run as if we are spirits. Weary and exhilarated. The shabby geography in the east of the city cannot restrain us. We clamber over low fences and into narrow swathes of backyards, rude gardens of mutant apple trees and wretched brambles, dubious compost, mud and broken toys.

Sometimes a shade will pass across Derkhan's face and she will murmur something. She thinks of Andrej; but it is hard that night to retain guilt, even when it is deserved. There is a sombre moment, but under that spew of warm rain, above the city lights that bloom promiscuous as weeds, it is hard not to catch each other's eyes and smile or caw softly in astonishment.

The moths are gone.

There have been terrible, terrible costs. There has been Hell to pay. But tonight as we settle in a rooftop shack in Pincod, beyond the reach of the skyrails, a little way north of the railway and the squalor of Dark Water Station, we are triumphant.

In the morning, the newspapers are full of dire warnings. The Quarrell *and* The Messenger *both hint that severe measures are to come.*

Derkhan sleeps for hours, then sits alone, her sadness and her guilt finally given space to flower. Lin moves fitfully, in and out of consciousness. Isaac dozes and eats the food we have stolen. He cradles Lin constantly. He talks of Jack Half-a-Prayer in wondering tones.

He sifts through the battered and broken components of the crisis engine, tuts and purses his lips. He tells me he can get it working again, no problem.

At that I come alive with longing. A final freedom. I want it badly. Flight.

He reads the pilfered papers over my shoulder.

In the climate of crisis, the militia are to be given extraordinary powers, we read. They may revert to open, uniformed patrols. Civilian rights may be curtailed. Martial law is mooted.

But throughout that blustery day, the shit, the filthy discharge, the dream-poison of the slake-moths is sinking slowly through the æther and on into the earth. I fancy I can feel it as I lie under these dilapidated planks; it subsides gently around me, denatured by the daylight. It drifts like polluted snow through the planes that entangle the city, on through layers of materia, leeching out of our dimension and away.

And when the night comes, the nightmares have gone.

It is as if some gentle sob, some mass exhalation of relief and languor sweeps the city. A wave of calm gusts in from the nightside, from the west, from Gallmarch and Smog Bend to Gross Coil, to Sheck and Brock Marsh, Ludmead and Mog Hill and Abrogate Green.

The city is cleansed in a tide of sleep. On piles of piss-damp straw in Creekside and the slums, on bloated featherbeds in Chnum, huddled together and alone, the citizens of New Crobuzon sleep soundly.

The city moves without pause, of course, and there is no let-up for the nightcrews in the docks, or the battering of metal as late shifts enter mills and foundries. Brazen sounds puncture the night, sounds like war. Watchmen still guard the forecourts of factories. Whores seek business wherever they can find it. There are still crimes. Violence does not dissipate.

But the sleepers and the waking are not taunted by phantoms. Their terrors are their own.

Like some unthinkable torpid giant, New Crobuzon shifts easily in its dreams.

I had forgotten the pleasure of such a night.

When I wake to the sun, my head is clear. I do not ache.

We have been freed.

This time the stories are all of the end of the "Midsummer Nightmare," or the "Sleeping Sickness," or the "Dream Curse," or whatever other name the particular newspaper had coined.

We read them and laugh, Derkhan and Isaac and I. Delight is palpable everywhere. The city is returned. Transformed.

We wait for Lin to wake, to come to her senses.

But she does not.

That first day, she slept. Her body began to reknit itself. She clutched Isaac tight and refused to wake. Free, and free to sleep without fear.

But now she has woken and sat up sluggishly. Her headlegs judder a little. Her mandibles work: she is hungry, and we find fruit in our stolen hoard, give her breakfast.

She looks unsteadily from me to Derkhan to Isaac as she eats. He grips her thighs, whispers to her, too low for me to hear. She jerks her head away like a baby. She moves with a spastic, palsied quivering.

She raises her hands and signs for him.

He watches her eagerly, his face creasing in incredulous despair at her fumbling, ugly manipulations.

Derkhan's eyes widen as she reads the words.

Isaac shakes his head, can hardly speak.

Morning . . . food . . . warming, *he falters,* insect . . . journey . . . happy.

She cannot feed herself. Her outer jaws spasm and split the fruit in two, or relax suddenly and let it fall. She shakes with frustration, rocks her head, releases a cloud of spray that Isaac says are khepri tears.

He comforts her, holds the apple before her, helping her to bite, wiping her when she drips juice and residue across herself. Afraid, she signs, *as Isaac hesitantly translates.* Mind tiring spilling loose, art Motley! *She shakes suddenly, peering around her in terror. Isaac shushes her, comforts her. Derkhan watches in misery. Alone, Lin signs desperately, and spews out a chymical message that is opaque to us all.* Monster warm Remade . . . *She looks around.* Apple, *she signs.* Apple.

Isaac lifts it to her mouth and lets her feed. She jigs like a toddler.

When the evening comes and she falls asleep once more, quickly and deeply, Isaac and Derkhan confer, and Isaac begins to rage and shout, and to cry.

She'll recover, he shouts, as Lin shifts in her sleep, *she's half-dead with fucking tiredness, she's had the shit beaten out of her, it's no wonder, no wonder she's confused . . .*

But she does not recover, as he knows she will not.

*   *   *

We ripped her from the moth half drunk. Half her mind, half her dreams had been sucked into the gullet of the vampir beast. It is gone, burnt up by stomach juices and then by Motley's men.

Lin wakes happy, talks animated gibberish with her hands, flails to stand and cannot, falls and weeps or laughs chymically, chatters with her mandibles, fouls herself like a baby.

Lin toddles across our roof with her half-mind. Helpless. Ruined. A weird patchwork of childish laughter and adult dreams, her speech extraordinary and incomprehensible, complex and violent and infantile.

Isaac is broken.

We move roofs, made uneasy by noises from below. Lin has a tantrum on our journey, made mad by our inability to understand her bizarre stream of words. She drums her heels on the pavement, slaps Isaac with weak strokes. She signs vile insults, tries to kick us away.

We control her, hold her tight, bundle her away.

We move by night. We are fearful of the militia and of Motley's men. We watch out for constructs which might report to the Council. We watch carefully for sudden movements and suspicious glances. We cannot trust our neighbours. We must live in a hinterland of half darkness, isolated and solipsistic. We steal what we need, or buy from tiny late-night grocers miles from where we are settled. Every askance look, every gaze, every shout, sudden flurry of hooves or boots, every bang or hiss of a construct's pistons is a moment of fear.

We are the most wanted in New Crobuzon. An honour, a dubious honour.

Lin wants colourberries.

Isaac interprets her motions thus. The faltering charade of chewing, the pulsing of her gland (an unsettling sexual sight).

Derkhan agrees to go. She loves Lin, too.

They spend hours on Derkhan's disguise, with water and butter and soot, ragged clothes from all over, foodstuffs and the remnants of dyes. She emerges with sleek black hair that shines like coal-crystals and a puckered scar across her forehead. She holds herself hunched and scowls.

When she leaves, Isaac and I spend the hours waiting fearfully. We are almost totally silent.

Lin continues her idiot monologue, and Isaac tries to answer with his own hands, caressing her and signing slowly as if she were a child. But she is not: she is half an adult, and his manner enrages her. She tries to stalk away and falls, her limbs disobedient. She is terrified of her own body. Isaac helps her, sits her up and feeds her, massages her tense, bruised shoulders.

Derkhan returns to our muttered relief with slabs of paste and a large handful of variegated berries. Their tones are lush and vivid.

I thought the damn Council had us, *she says.* I thought some construct was after me. I had to wind through Kinken to get away.

None of us know if she was really being tracked.

Lin is excited. Her antennae and her headlegs quiver. She tries to chew a finger of the white paste, but she trembles and spills it and cannot control herself. Isaac is gentle with her. He pushes the paste slowly into her mouth, unobtrusive, as if she ate for herself.

It takes some minutes for the headscarab to digest the paste and direct it towards the khepri's gland. As we wait, Isaac shakes a few colourberries at Lin, waiting until her twitches decide him that she wants a particular bunch, which he feeds to her gently and carefully.

We are silent. Lin swallows and chews carefully. We watch her.

Minutes pass and then her gland distends. We rock forward, eager to see what she will make.

She opens her gland-lips and pushes out a pellet of moist khepri-spit. She moves her arms in excitement as it oozes shapeless and sopping from her, dropping heavy to the floor like a white turd.

A thin drool of coloured spittle from the berries streams out after it, spattering and staining the mess.

Derkhan looks away. Isaac cries as I have never seen a human do.

Outside our foul shanty the city squats fatly in its freedom, brazen again and fearless. It ignores us. It is an ingrate. The days are cooler this week, a brief ebbing of the relentless summer. Gusts blow in from the coast, from the Gross Tar estuary and Iron Bay. Clutches of ships arrive every day. They queue in the river to the east, waiting to load and unload. Merchant ships from Kohnid and Tesh; explorers from the Firewater Straits; floating factories from Myrshock; privateers from Figh Vadiso, respectable and law-abiding so far from the open sea. Clouds scurry like bees before the sun. The city is raucous. It has forgotten. It has some vague notion that once its sleep was troubled: nothing more.

I can see the sky. There are slats of light between the rough boards that surround us. I would like very much to be away from this now. I can imagine the sensation of wind, the sudden heaviness of air below me. I would like to look down on this building and this street. I wish that there was nothing to hold me here, that gravity was a suggestion I could ignore.

Lin signs. Sticky fearful, *whispers Isaac snottily, watching her hands.* Piss and mother, food wings happy. Afraid. Afraid.

PART EIGHT

Judgement

CHAPTER FIFTY-TWO

"We have to leave."

Derkhan spoke quickly. Isaac looked up at her dully. He was feeding Lin, who squirmed uncomfortably, unsure of what she wanted to do. She signed at him, her hands tracing words and then simply moving, tracing shapes that had no meaning. He flicked fruit detritus from her shirt.

He nodded and looked down. Derkhan continued as if he had disagreed with her, as if she were convincing him.

"Every time we move, we're afraid." She spoke quickly. Her face was hard. Terror, guilt, exhilaration and misery had scoured her. She was exhausted. "Every time any kind of automaton goes past, we think the Construct Council's found us. Every man or woman or xenian makes us freeze up. Is it the militia? Is it one of Motley's thugs?" She kneeled down. "I can't live like this, 'Zaac," she said. She looked down at Lin, smiled very slowly and closed her eyes. "We'll take her away," she whispered. "We can look after her. We're finished here. It can't be long before one of them finds us. I'm not waiting around for that."

Isaac nodded again.

"I . . ." He thought carefully. He tried to organize his mind. "I've got . . . a commitment," he said quietly.

He rubbed the flab below his chin. It itched as his stubble re-grew, pushing through his uneven skin. Wind blew through the windows. The house in Pincod was tall and mouldering and full of junkies. Isaac and Derkhan and Yagharek had claimed the top two floors. There was one window on each side, overlooking the street and the wretched little yard. Weeds had burst out through the stained concrete below like subcutaneous growths.

Isaac and the others barricaded the doors whenever they were in: slipped out carefully, disguised, mostly at night. Sometimes they would venture out in the daylight, as Yagharek had now. There was always some reason given, some urgency that meant the vague trip could not wait. It was just claustrophobia. They had freed the city: it was untenable that they should not walk under the sun.

"I *know* about the commitment," Derkhan said. She looked over at the loosely connected components of the crisis engine. Isaac had cleaned them up the previous night, slotted them into place.

"Yagharek," he said. "I owe him. I promised."

Derkhan looked down and swallowed, then turned her head to him again. She nodded.

"How long?" she said. Isaac glanced up at her, broke her gaze and looked away. He shrugged briefly.

"Some of the wires are burnt out," he said vaguely, and shifted Lin into a more comfortable position on his chest. "There was a shitload of feedback, melted right through some of the circuits. Um . . . I'm going to have to go out tonight and rummage around for a couple of adapters . . . and a dynamo. I can fix the rest of it myself," he said, "but I'll have to get the tools. Trouble is, every time we nick something we put ourselves even more at risk." He shrugged slowly. There was nothing he could do. They had no money. "Then I have to get a cell-battery or something. But the hardest thing is going to be the maths. Fixing all this up is mostly just . . . mechanics. But even if I can get the engines to work, getting the sums right to . . . you know, formulating this in *equations* . . . that's damn hard. That's what I got the Council to do last time." He closed his eyes and rested his head against the wall.

"I have to formulate the commands," he said quietly. "*Fly.* That's what I've got to tell it. Put Yag in the sky and he's in crisis, he's about to fall. Tap that and channel it, keep him in the air, keep him flying, keep him in crisis, so tap the energy and so on. It's a perfect loop," he said. "I think it'll work. It's just the *maths . . .*"

"How long?" Derkhan repeated quietly. Isaac frowned.

"A week . . . or two, maybe," he admitted. "Maybe more."

Derkhan shook her head. She said nothing.

"I *owe* him, Dee!" Isaac said, his voice tense. "I've promised him this for ages, and he . . ."

He got the slake-moth off Lin, he had been about to say, but something in him had preempted him, asked if that was such a good thing after all, and appalled, Isaac faltered into silence.

It's the most powerful science for hundreds of years, he thought in a sudden rage, *and I can't come out of hiding. I have to . . . to spirit it away.*

He stroked Lin's carapace and she began to sign to him, mentioning fish and cold and sugar.

"I know, 'Zaac," said Derkhan without anger. "I know. He's . . . he deserves it. But we can't wait that long. We have to go."

I'll do what I can, promised Isaac, I have to help him, I'll be quick.

Derkhan accepted it. She had no choice. She would not leave him, or Lin. She did not blame him. She wanted him to honour his agreement, to give Yagharek what he wanted.

The stink and sadness of the damp little room overwhelmed her. She muttered something about scouting out the river and she left. Isaac smiled without warmth at her half-hearted excuse.

"Be careful," he said unnecessarily as she left.

He lay cuddling Lin with his back to the foetid wall.

After a while he felt Lin relax into sleep. He slipped out from behind her and walked over to the window, looked out over the bustle below.

Isaac did not know the name of the street. It was wide, lined with young trees all pliant and hopeful. At the far end, a cart had been parked sideways, deliberately creating a cul-de-sac. A man and a vodyanoi were arguing ferociously beside it, while the two cowed donkeys drawing it hung their heads, trying not to be noticed. A group of children materialized in front of the motionless wheels, kicking a ball of tied rags. They scampered, their clothes flapping like flightless wings.

An argument broke out, four little boys prodding one of the two vodyanoi children in the group. The fat little vodyanoi backed away on all fours, crying. One of the boys threw a stone. The argument was forgotten quickly. The vodyanoi sulked a brief moment, then hopped back into the game, stealing the ball.

Further along the road, a few doors down from Isaac's building, a young woman was chalking some symbol onto the wall. It was an unfamiliar, angular device, some witch's talisman. Two old men sat together on a stoop, tossing dice and laughing uproariously at the results. The buildings were bird-limed and grotty, the tarred pavement punctuated with water-filled potholes. Rooks and pigeons threaded through smoke from thousands of chimneys.

Cuttings from conversations reached Isaac's ears.

". . . so he says *a stiver for that*? . . ."

". . . damaged the engine, but then he was always a cunt . . ."

". . . don't say nothing about it . . ."

". . . it's on Dockday next, and she copped a total crystal . . ."

". . . savage, absofuckinglutely savage . . ."

". . . remembrance? For who?"

For Andrej, thought Isaac suddenly, without warning or reason. He listened again.

There was much more. There were languages he did not speak. He recognized Perrickish and Fellid, the intricate cadences of Low Cymek. And others.

He did not want to leave.

Isaac sighed and turned back into the room. Lin squirmed on the floor in sleep.

He looked at her, saw her breasts pushing at her torn shirt. Her skirt rode up her thighs. He looked away.

Since recovering Lin, twice he had woken with the warmth and pressure of her against him, his prick erect and eager. He had rubbed his hand over the swell of her hips and down into her parted legs. Sleep had rolled off him like fog as his arousal grew and he had opened his eyes to see her, moving her beneath him as she woke, forgetting that Derkhan and Yagharek were sleeping nearby. He had breathed at her and spoken lovingly and explicitly of what he wanted to do, and then he had jerked backwards in horror as she began to sign babble at him and he remembered what had happened to her.

She had rubbed against him and stopped, rubbed him again (*like some capricious dog,* he had thought, appalled), her erratic arousal and confusion absolutely clear. Some lustful part of him had wanted to continue, but the weight of sorrow had shrivelled his penis almost instantly.

Lin had seemed disappointed and hurt, then she hugged him, happily and suddenly. Then she curled up in despair. Isaac had tasted her emissions in the air around them. He had known she was crying herself to sleep.

Isaac glanced out at the day again. He thought of Rudgutter and his cronies; of the macabre Mr. Motley; he imagined the cold analysis of the Construct Council, cheated of the engine it coveted. He imagined the rages, the arguments, the orders given and received that week that cursed him.

Isaac walked over to the crisis engine, took brief stock of it.

He sat down, folded paper in his lap, and began to write calculations.

He was not worried that the Construct Council might mimic his engine itself. It could not design one. It could not calculate its parameters. The blueprint had come to him in an intuitive leap so natural that he had not recognized it for hours. The Construct Council could not be inspired. Isaac's fundamental model, the conceptual basis of the engine, he had never even had to write down. His notes would be quite opaque to any reader.

Isaac positioned himself so that he worked in a shaft of sunlight.

The grey dirigibles patrolled the air, as they did every day. They seemed uneasy.

It was a perfect day. The wind from the sea seemed constantly to renew the sky.

Yagharek and Derkhan, in separate quarters of the city, enjoyed their furtive times in the sun, and tried not to court danger. They walked away from arguments and stuck to the crowded streets.

The sky was riotous with birds and wyrmen. They flocked to buttresses and minarets, crowding the gently sloped roofs of militia towers and struts, coating them in white shit. They stormed in shifting spirals around the Ketch Heath towers and the skeletal edifices in Spatters.

They scudded over The Crow, wove intricately through the complex pattern of air that rose above Perdido Street Station. Rowdy jackdaws squabbled over the layers of clay. They flitted over the lower hulks of slate and tar at the station's shabby rear, descending towards a peculiar plateau of concrete above a little brow of windowed roofs. Their droppings fouled its recently scrubbed surface, little pellets of white splattering against the dark stains where some noxious fluid had spilled copiously.

The Spike and the Parliament building swarmed with little avian bodies.

The Ribs bleached and split, their flaws worsening slowly in the sun. Birds alit briefly on the enormous shafts of bone, launching themselves free again quickly, seeking refuge elsewhere in Bonetown, skimming over the roof of a smoke-damaged black terrace, in the heart of which Mr. Motley ranted against the incomplete sculpture which mocked him with unending spite.

Gulls and gannets followed rubbish barges and fishing boats

up along the Gross Tar and the Tar, swooping down to snatch organic morsels from the detritus. They wheeled away to other pickings, to the offal-piles in Badside, the fish market in Pelorus Fields. They landed briefly on the split, algaed cable that crawled out of the river by Spit Hearth. They explored the rubbish heaps in Stoneshell, and picked at half-dead prey crawling through the Griss Twist wasteland. The ground purred beneath them, as hidden cables hummed inches below the ragged topsoil.

A larger body than the birds rose up from the slums of St. Jabber's Mound and soared into the air. It sailed at a massive height over the western city. The streets below became a mottled stain of khaki and grey like some exotic mould. It passed easily above the aerostats in the gusting breeze, warmed by the noon sun. It maintained a steady pace eastwards, crossing the city's nucleus where the five rail lines burst out like petals.

In the air over Sheck, gangs of wyrmen looped the loop in vulgar aerobatics. The drifting figure passed over them serene and unnoticed.

It moved slowly, with langorous strokes that suggested it could increase its speed tenfold suddenly and with ease. It crossed the Canker and began a long descent, passing in and out of the air over the Dexter Line trains, riding their hot exhaust briefly, then gliding earthwards with unseen majesty, descending towards the canopy of roofs, weaving easily through the maze of the thermals gusting up from massive smokestacks and little hovels' flues.

It banked towards the huge gas cylinders in Echomire, spiralled back easily, slipped under a layer of disturbed air and flew steeply down towards Mog Station, passing under the skyrails too fast to be seen, disappearing into the Pincod roofscape.

Isaac was not lost in his numbers.

He looked up every few minutes at Lin, who slept and moved her arms and wriggled like a helpless grub. His eyes looked as if they had never been lit up.

In the early afternoon, when he had worked for an hour, an hour and a half, he heard something clatter in the yard below. Half a minute later there were footsteps on the stairs.

Isaac froze and waited for them to stop, to disappear into one of the junkies' rooms. They did not. They moved with a deliberate tread up the final two flights, making their careful way up the noisome steps and halting outside his door.

Isaac was still. His heart beat quickly in alarm. He looked around wildly for his gun.

There was a knock at the door. Isaac said nothing.

After a moment, whoever was outside knocked again: not hard, but rhythmically and insistently, repeatedly. Isaac stalked closer, trying to be quiet. He saw Lin twisting uncomfortably at the sound.

There was a voice outside the door, a weird, harsh, familiar voice. It was all grating treble, and Isaac could not understand it, but he reached out for the door suddenly, unsettled and aggressive and ready for trouble. *Rudgutter would send a whole damn squadron,* he thought as his hand closed on the handle, *it's bound to be some junkie begging.* And although he did not believe that, he was reassured that it was not the militia, or Motley's men.

He pulled the door open.

Standing before him on the unlit stairs, leaning slightly forward, sleek feathered head mottled like dry leaves, beak curved and glinting like an exotic weapon, was a garuda.

He saw instantly that it was not Yagharek.

Its wings rose up and swelled around it like a corona, vast and magnificent, feathered in ochre and smooth red-stained brown.

Isaac had forgotten what an uncrippled garuda looked like. He had forgotten the extraordinary scale and grandeur of those wings.

He understood what was happening almost immediately, in some inchoate and unstructured way. A wordless intimation hit him.

Following it by a fraction of a second came a massive gust of doubt and alarm and curiosity and a slew of questions.

"Who the fuck are you?" he breathed, and: "What are you fucking doing here? How did you find me . . . What . . ." Half-answers came unbidden to him. He stepped back from the threshold quickly, trying to banish them.

"Grim . . . neb . . . lin . . ." The garuda struggled with his name. It sounded as if he was a dæmon being invoked. Isaac jerked his arm quickly for the garuda to follow him into the little room. He closed the door and pushed the chair back up against it.

The garuda stalked into the centre of the room, into a sunlit patch. Isaac watched it warily. It wore a dusty loincloth and nothing more. Its skin was darker than Yagharek's, its feathered head more mottled. It moved with incredible economy, tiny snapping movements and great stillness, its head cocked to take in the room.

It stared at Lin for a long time, until Isaac sighed and the garuda looked up at him.

"Who are you?" Isaac said. "How did you fucking find me?" *What did he do?* Isaac thought, but did not say. *Tell me.*

They stood, slim, tight-muscled garuda and fat, thickset human, at opposite ends of the room. The garuda's feathers were shiny with sun. Isaac stared at them, suddenly tired. Some sense of inevitability, of finality, had entered with the garuda. Isaac hated it for that.

"I am Kar'uchai," the garuda said. Its voice was harder even than Yagharek's with Cymek intonations. It was difficult to understand. "Kar'uchai Sukhtu-h'k Vaijhin-khi-khi. Concrete Individual Kar'uchai Very Very Respected."

Isaac waited.

"How did you *find me*?" he said eventually, bitterly.

"I have . . . come a long way, Grimneb . . . lin," Kar'uchai said. "I am *yahj'hur* . . . hunter. I have hunted for days. Here I hunt with . . . gold and paper-money . . . My quarry leaves a trail of rumour . . . and memory."

What did he do?

"I come from Cymek. I have hunted . . . since Cymek."

"I can't believe you found us," said Isaac suddenly, nervously. He talked quickly, hating the pervasive sense of ending and ignoring it aggressively, blotting it. "If you did the damn militia can for sure and if *they* can . . ." He strode quickly back and forth. He knelt down by Lin, stroked her gently, drew breath to say more.

"I am come for justice," said Kar'uchai, and Isaac could not speak. He felt suffocated.

"Shankell," said Kar'uchai. "Meagre Sea. Myrshock." *I've heard about the journey,* thought Isaac in anger, *you don't have to tell me.* Kar'uchai continued. "I have . . . hunted across a thousand miles. Seek justice."

Isaac spoke slowly, in rage and sadness.

"Yagharek is my friend," he said.

Kar'uchai continued as if he had said nothing. "When we found that he was gone, after . . . judgement . . . I was chosen to come . . ."

"What do you want?" said Isaac. "What are you going to do to him? You want to take him back with you? You want to . . . what, cut off . . . more of him?"

"I have not come for Yagharek," said Kar'uchai. "I have come for you."

Isaac stared in miserable confusion.

"It is up to you . . . to let justice be . . ."

Kar'uchai was relentless. Isaac could say nothing.

What did he do?

"I heard your name first in Myrshock," said Kar'uchai. "It was on a list. Then here, in this city, it came back again and again until . . . all others melted away. I hunted. Yagharek and you . . . were linked. People whispered . . . of your researches. Flying monsters and thaumaturgic machines. I knew that Yagharek had found what he sought. What he came a thousand miles for. You would deny justice, Grimneb'lin. I am here to ask you . . . not to do that.

"It was finished. He was judged and punished. And it was over. We did not think . . . we did not know that he might . . . find a way . . . that justice could be *retracted*.

"I am here to ask you not to help him fly."

"Yagharek is my friend," said Isaac steadily. "He came to me and employed me. He was generous. When things . . . went wrong . . . got complicated and dangerous . . . well, he was brave and he helped me—us. He's been part of . . . of something extraordinary. And I owe him . . . a life." He glanced at Lin and then away again. "I owe him . . . for the times . . . He was ready to die, you know? He could have died, but he stayed and without him . . . I don't think I could have come through."

Isaac spoke quietly. His words were sincere and affecting.

What did he do?

"What did he do?" said Isaac, defeated.

"He is guilty," said Kar'uchai quietly, "of choice-theft in the second degree, with utter disrespect."

"What does that *mean*?" shouted Isaac. "What did he *do*? What's fucking choice-theft anyway? This means *nothing* to me."

"It is the only crime we *have*, Grimneb'lin," replied Kar'uchai in a harsh monotone. "To take the choice of another . . . to forget their concrete reality, to abstract them, to forget that you are a node in a matrix, that actions have consequences. We must not take the choice of another being. What is community but a means to . . . for all we individuals to have . . . our *choices*."

Kar'uchai shrugged and indicated the world around them vaguely. "Your city institutions . . . Talking and talking of individuals . . . but crushing them in layers and hierarchies . . . until their choices might be between three kinds of squalor.

"We have far less, in the desert. We hunger, sometimes, and thirst. *But we have all the choices that we can.* Except when someone forgets themselves, forgets the reality of their companions, as if they were an individual *alone* . . . And steals food, and takes the choice of others to eat it, or lies about game, and takes the choice of others to hunt it; or grows angry and attacks without reason, and takes the choice of another not to be bruised or live in fear.

"A child who steals the cloak of some beloved other, to smell at night . . . they take away the choice to wear the cloak, but with respect, with a surfeit of respect.

"Other thefts, though, do not have even respect to mitigate them.

"To kill . . . not in war or defence, but to . . . *murder* . . . is to have such disrespect, such utter disrespect, that you take not only the choice of whether to live or die that moment . . . but *every other choice for all of time* that might be made. Choices beget choices . . . if they had been allowed their choice to live, they might have chosen to hunt for fish in a salt-swamp, or to play dice, or to tan hides, to write poesy or cook stew . . . and all those choices are taken from them in that one theft.

"That is choice-theft in the *highest* degree. But all choice-thefts steal from the future as well as the present.

"Yagharek's was a heinous . . . a terrible forgetting. Theft in the second degree."

"What did he *do*?" shouted Isaac, and Lin woke with a flutter of hands and a nervous twitching.

Kar'uchai spoke dispassionately.

"You would call it rape."

Oh, I would call it rape, would I? thought Isaac in a molten, raging sneer; but the torrent of livid contempt was not enough to drown his horror.

I would call it rape.

Isaac could not but imagine. Immediately.

The act itself, of course, though that was a vague and nebulous brutality in his mind *(did he beat her? Hold her down? Where was she? Did she curse and fight back?)*. What he saw most clearly, immediately, were all the vistas, the avenues of choice that Yagharek had stolen. Fleetingly, Isaac glimpsed the denied possibilities.

The choice not to have sex, not to be hurt. The choice not to risk pregnancy. And then . . . what if she had become pregnant? The choice not to abort? The choice not to have a child?

The choice to look at Yagharek with respect?

Isaac's mouth worked and Kar'uchai spoke again.

"It was my choice he stole."

It took a few seconds, a ludicrously long time, for Isaac to understand what Kar'uchai meant. Then he gasped and stared at her, seeing for the first time the slight swell of her ornamental breasts, as useless as bird-of-paradise plumage. He struggled for something to say, but he did not know what he felt: there was nothing solid for words to express.

He murmured some appallingly loose apology, some solicitation.

"I thought you were . . . the garuda magister . . . or the militia, or something," he said.

"We have none," she replied.

"Yag . . . a fucking *rapist*," he hissed, and she clucked.

"He stole choice," she said flatly.

"He *raped* you," he said, and instantly Kar'uchai clucked again.

"He stole my choice," she said. She was not expanding on his words, Isaac realized: she was correcting him. "You cannot translate into your jurisprudence, Grimneb'lin," she said. She seemed annoyed.

Isaac tried to speak, shook his head miserably, stared at her and again saw the crime committed, behind his eyes.

"You cannot *translate*, Grimneb'lin," Kar'uchai repeated. "Stop. I can see . . . all the texts of your city's laws and morals that I have read . . . in you." Her tone sounded monotonous to him. The emotion in the pauses and cadences of her voice was opaque.

"I was not *violated* or *ravaged*, Grimneb'lin. I am not *abused* or *defiled* . . . or *ravished* or *spoiled*. You would call his actions rape, but I do not: that tells me nothing. He *stole my choice*, and that is why he was . . . judged. It was severe . . . the last sanction but one . . . There are many choice-thefts less heinous than his, and only a few more so . . . And there are others that are judged equal . . . many of those are actions utterly unlike Yagharek's. Some, you would not deem crimes at all.

"The actions vary: the *crime* . . . is the theft of *choice*. Your magisters and laws . . . that sexualize and sacralize . . . for whom individuals are defined abstract . . . their matrix-nature ignored . . . where context is a distraction . . . cannot grasp that.

"Do not look at me with eyes reserved for victims . . . And when Yagharek returns . . . I ask you to observe our justice—Yagharek's justice—not to impute your own.

"He stole choice, in the second highest degree. He was judged. The band voted. That is the end."

Is it? thought Isaac. *Is that enough? Is that the end?*

Kar'uchai watched him struggle.

Lin called to Isaac, clapping her hands like a clumsy child. He knelt quickly and spoke to her. She signed anxiously at him and he signed back as if what she said made sense, as if they were conversing.

She was calmed, and she hugged him and looked nervously up at Kar'uchai with her unbroken compound eye.

"Will you observe our judgement?" said Kar'uchai quietly. Isaac looked at her quickly. He busied himself with Lin.

Kar'uchai was silent for a long time. When Isaac did not speak, she repeated her question. Isaac turned to her and shook his head, not in denial but confusion.

"I don't know," he said. "Please . . ."

He turned back to Lin, who slept. He slumped against her and rubbed his head.

After minutes of silence, Kar'uchai stopped her swift pacing and called his name.

He started as if he had forgotten she was there.

"I will leave. I ask you again. Please do not mock our justice. Please let our judgement be." She moved the chair from the door and stalked out. Her taloned feet scratched at the old wood as she descended.

And Isaac sat and stroked Lin's iridescent carapace—marbled now with stress-fractures and lines of cruelty—thinking about Yagharek.

Do not translate, Kar'uchai had said, but how could he not?

He thought of Kar'uchai's wings shuddering with rage as she

was pinioned by Yagharek's arms. Or had he threatened with a knife? A weapon? A fucking *whip*?

Fuck them, he would think suddenly, staring at the crisis engine's parts. *I don't owe their laws respect . . .* Free the prisoners. That was what *Runagate Rampant* always said.

But the Cymek garuda did not live like the citizens of New Crobuzon. There were no magisters, Isaac remembered, no courts or punishment factories, no quarries and dumps to pack with Remade, no militia or politicians. Punishment was not doled out by backhanding bosses.

Or so he had been told. So he remembered. *The band voted,* Kar'uchai had said.

Was that true? Did that change things?

In New Crobuzon punishment was *for* someone. Some interest was served. Was that different in the Cymek? Did that make the crime more heinous?

Was a garuda rapist worse than a human one?

Who am I to judge? Isaac thought in sudden anger, and stormed towards his engine, picked up his calculations, ready to continue, but then, *Who am I to judge?* he thought, in sudden hollow uncertainty, the ground taken from under him, and he put his papers down slowly.

He kept glancing at Lin's thighs. Her bruises had almost gone, but his memory of them was as savage a stain as they had been.

They had mottled her in suggestive patterns around her lower belly and inner thighs.

Lin shifted and woke and held him and shied away in fear and Isaac's teeth set at the thought of what might have been done to her. He thought of Kar'uchai.

This is all wrong, he thought. *That's just exactly what she told you not to do. This isn't about rape, she said . . .*

But it was too hard. Isaac could not do it. If he thought of Yagharek he thought of Kar'uchai, and if he thought of her he thought of Lin.

This is all arse-side up, he thought.

If he took Kar'uchai at her word, he could not judge the punishment. He could not decide whether he respected garuda justice or not: he had no grounds at all, he knew nothing of the circumstances. So it was natural, surely, it was inevitable and healthy, that he should fall back on what he knew: his scepticism; the fact that Yagharek was his friend. Would he leave his friend flightless because he gave alien laws the benefit of the *doubt*?

He remembered Yagharek scaling the Glasshouse, fighting beside him against the militia.

He remembered Yagharek's whip savaging the slake-moth, ensnaring it, freeing Lin.

But when he thought of Kar'uchai, and what had been done to her, he could not but think of that as *rape*. And he thought of Lin, and everything that might have been done to her, until he felt as if he would puke with anger.

He tried to extricate himself.

He tried to think himself away from the whole thing. He told himself desperately that to refuse his services would *not* imply judgement, that it would *not* mean he pretended knowledge of the facts, that it would simply be a way of saying, "This is beyond me, this is not my business." But he could not convince himself.

He slumped and breathed a miserable moan of exhaustion. If he turned from Yagharek, he realized, no matter what he said, Isaac would feel himself to have judged, and to have found Yagharek wanting. And Isaac realized that he could not in conscience imply that, when he did not know the case.

But on the heels of that thought came another; a flipside, a counterpoint.

If withholding help implied negative judgement he could not make, thought Isaac, then helping, bestowing flight, would imply that Yagharek's actions were *acceptable*.

And that, thought Isaac in cold distaste and fury, he *would not do*.

He folded his notes slowly, his half-finished equations, his scribbled formulae, and began to pack them away.

When Derkhan returned, the sun was low and the sky was blemished with blood-coloured clouds. She tapped the door in the quick rhythm they had agreed, bundling past Isaac when he opened it.

"It's an amazing day," she said with sadness. "I've been sniffing quietly all over the place, getting a few leads, a few ideas . . ." She turned to face him and was instantly quiet.

His dark, scarred face bore an extraordinary expression. Some complex composite of hope and excitement and terrible misery. He seemed to brim with energy. He shifted as if he crawled with ants. He wore his long beggar's cloak. A sack sat beside the door, bulging with heavy, bulky contents. The crisis engine was gone, she realized, disassembled and hidden away in the sack.

Without the spread-out mess of metal and wire, the room seemed utterly bare.

With a little gasp, Derkhan saw that Isaac had wrapped up Lin in a foul, tattered blanket. Lin clutched at it fitfully and nervously, signing nonsense up at him. She saw Derkhan and jerked happily.

"Let's go," said Isaac in a hollow voice that strained with tension.

"What are you talking about?" said Derkhan angrily. "What are you *talking* about? Where's Yagharek? What's come over you?"

"Dee, *please* . . ." whispered Isaac. He took her hands. She reeled at his imploring fervour. "Yag's still not come back. I'm leaving this for him," he said, and plucked a letter from his pocket. He tossed it nervously into the centre of the floor. Derkhan began to speak again and Isaac cut her off, shaking his head violently.

"I'm not . . . I can't . . . I don't work for Yag no more, Dee . . . I'm *terminating our contract* . . . I'll explain *everything*, I promise, but let's *go*. You're right, we've stayed much too long." He flicked his hand at the window, where the evening sounded boisterous and easygoing. "The fucking *government* are after us, and the biggest damn gangster on the continent . . . And the . . . the Construct Council . . ." He shook her gently.

"Let's *go*. The . . . the three of us. Let's get out and away."

"What *happened*, Isaac?" she demanded. She shook him back. "Tell me now."

He looked away quickly, and back at her.

"I had a visitor . . ." She gasped and her eyes widened, but he shook his head slowly. "Dee . . . a visitor from the fucking *Cymek*." He held her eyes and swallowed. "I know what Yagharek did, Dee." He was quiet as her face rearranged itself into a cold calm. "I know what he got . . . punished for.

"There's nothing holding us here, Dee. I'll tell you everything— *everything*, I swear—but there's nothing holding us here. I'll tell you while we . . . while we go."

For days he had been in an awful lassitude, distracted by crisis maths and utterly, exhaustingly despondent about Lin. Quite suddenly, the urgency of their situation had come home to him. He realized their danger. He understood how patient Derkhan had been, and he understood that they must leave.

"Godsdamnit," she said quietly. "I know it's only a few months, but he . . . he's your friend. Isn't he? We can't just . . . can we just leave him . . . ?" She looked at him and her face creased. "Is it . . . what is it? Is it so terrible? Is it bad enough that it . . . that it cancels everything else out? Is it so terrible?" Isaac closed his eyes.

"No . . . yes. It's not that simple. I'll explain when we go.

"*I'm not going to help him.* That's the bottom line. I can't, I fucking can't, Dee, I fucking *can't.* And I can't see him, I don't want to see him. So there's *nothing* here, so we can go.

"We really must go."

Derkhan argued, but briefly and without conviction. She was gathering her tiny bag of clothes, her little notebook, even while she said she was not sure. She was caught up in Isaac's wake.

She scrawled a tiny addendum to the back of Isaac's note, without opening it. *Good luck,* she scribbled. *We will meet again. Sorry to disappear so suddenly. You know how to get out of the city. You know what to do.* She paused for quite a long time, unsure of how to say goodbye, and then wrote *Derkhan.* She replaced the letter.

She wrapped her scarf about her, let her new black hair slide like oil over her shoulders. It rubbed against the scab left by her ruined ear. She looked out of the window, to where the sky grew thick with evening, then turned and put her arm gently around Lin, helped her walk in her erratic fashion.

Slowly, the three of them descended.

"There's a bunch of guys over in Smog Bend," Derkhan said. "Bargemen. They can take us south without any questions."

"Fuck, no!" hissed Isaac. He looked up from below his hood with wide eyes.

They stood at the end of the street, where the cart had acted as goal for the children hours before. The warm evening air was full of smells. There were loud disagreements and hysterical laughter from a parallel avenue. Grocers and housewives and steelwrights and minor criminals chatted on corners. The lights were emerging with the sputter of a hundred different fuels and currents. Flames in various colours sprang up behind frosted glass.

"Fuck no," Isaac said again. "Not *inland* . . . Let's go *out* . . . Let's go to Kelltree. Let's go to the docks."

So they walked together slowly south and west. They skirted between Saltbur and Mog Hill, shuffling through the busy streets, an unlikely trio. A tall and bulky beggar with a hidden face, a striking crow-haired woman and a hooded cripple walking in unsteady spasming gait, half-supported and half-pulled by her companions.

Every steaming construct that walked past made them duck their heads uncomfortably away. Isaac and Derkhan kept their eyes down, talking quickly under their breath. They glanced up nervously as they passed below skyrails, as if the militia streaking above them could sniff them out from all that way above. They avoided catching the eyes of the men and women who lounged aggressively on street corners.

They felt as if they held their breath. An agonizing journey. They were tremulous with adrenalin.

They looked around them as they walked, taking in everything they could as if their eyes were cameras. Isaac snatched glimpses of opera posters curling ragged off walls, twists of barbed wire and concrete embedded with broken glass, the arches of the Kelltree rail-link that branched from the Dexter Line, hovering over Sunter and Bonetown.

He looked up at the Ribs that loomed colossal to his right, and he tried to remember their angles, exactly.

With every step they pulled themselves free of the city. They could feel its gravity receding. They felt light-headed. As if they might cry.

Unseen, just below the clouds, a shadow drifted lazily after them. It turned and spiralled as their course became clear. It swept giddily in a moment of lonely aerobatics. As Isaac and Lin and Derkhan continued, the figure broke off its circles and shot away at speed through the sky, heading out of the city.

Stars appeared and Isaac began to whisper goodbye to The Clock and Cockerel, to Aspic Bazaar and Ketch Heath and his friends.

It stayed warm as they made their way south, shadowing the trains, into a wide-open landscape of industrial estates. Weeds escaped from lots and encroached onto the pavement, tripping the pedestrians that still filled the night-city, making them swear. Isaac and Derkhan guided Lin carefully through the outskirts of Echomire and Kelltree, bearing south, the trains beside them, heading for the river.

The Gross Tar, shimmering prettily under the neon and the gaslight, its pollution obscured by reflections: and the docks full of tall ships with heavy furled sails and steamboats leaking iridescently into the water, merchant vessels drawn by bored seawyrms chewing on vast bridles, unsteady factory-freighters that bristled with cranes and steamhammers; ships for whom New Crobuzon was just one stop on a journey.

In the Cymek, we call the moon's little satellites the mosquitoes. Here in New Crobuzon they call them her daughters.

The room is full of light from the moon and her daughters, and empty of all else.

I have stood here for a long time, Isaac's letter in my hand.

In a moment, I will read it again.

I heard the emptiness of the decaying house from the stairs. The echoes receded for too long. I knew before I touched the door that the attic was deserted.

I was away for hours, seeking some spurious, faltering freedom in the city.

I wandered into the pretty gardens of Sobek Croix, through fussing clouds of insects and past the sculpted lakes of overfed fowl. I found the ruins of the monastery, the little shell displayed proudly at the park's heart. Where romantic vandals carve their lovers' names onto the ancient stone. The little keep was deserted a thousand years before New Crobuzon's foundations were laid. The god to which it was consecrated died.

Some people come at night to honour the dead god's ghost. What tenuous, desperate theology.

I visited Howl Barrow today. I saw Lichford. I stood before a grey wall in Barrackham, the crumbling skin of a dead factory, and read all the graffiti.

I was foolish. I took risks. Did not remain carefully hidden.

I felt almost drunk with that little snatch of freedom, eager for more.

So I returned at last through the night, to that hollow and forsaken attic, to Isaac's brutal betrayal.

What breach of faith, what cruelty.

I open it once more (ignoring Derkhan's pathetic little words, like some dusting of sugar on poison). The extraordinary tension in the words seems to make them crawl. I can see Isaac striving for so many things as he writes. Bluff no-nonsense. Anger, stern disapproval. True misery. Objectivism. And some weird comradeship, some shame-faced apology.

... had a visitor today ... I read, and *... under the circumstances ...*

Under the circumstances. Under the circumstances I will flee you. I will turn and judge you. I will leave you with your shame, I will know you from the inside and I will pass on and I will not help you.

... not going to ask you "how could you?" I read and I feel weak suddenly, truly weak, not as if I will faint or vomit but as if I will die.

It makes me cry out.

It makes me scream. I cannot stop this noise, I do not want to, I shriek and shriek and as my voice grows, memories of warcries come to me, memories of my band racing in to hunt or fight, memories of funereal ululation and exorcism wails but this is none of these, this is my pain, unstructured, uncultured, unregulated and illicit and my own, my agony, my loneliness, my misery, my guilt.

She told me no, that Sazhin had asked for her that summer; that as it was his gathering-year she had said yes; that she wanted to pair exclusively as a present to him.

She told me I was unfair, that I should leave her immediately, respect her, show respect and leave her be.

It was an ugly, vicious coupling. I was only a little stronger than her. It took a long time to subdue her. She clawed and bit me every moment, battered me viciously. I was unrelenting.

I grew infuriated. Lustful and jealous. I beat her and entered her when she lay stunned.

Her anger was extraordinary and awesome. It woke me to what I had done.

Shame has draped me since that day. Remorse came only a little later. They gather about me as if to replace my wings.

* * *

The band's vote was unanimous. I did not contest the facts (it entered my mind to do so for the briefest moment and a wave of self-loathing made me retch).

There could be no question about judgement.

I knew it was the correct decision. I could even show a little dignity, a tiny shred, as I walked between the elected finishers of the law. I was slow, shuffling with the enormous weight of ballast attached to me, to stop me fleeing and flying, but I walked on without pause or question.

It was only at the last that I faltered, when I saw the stakes that would tether me to the baked earth.

They had to drag me the last twenty feet, into the dried-up bed of the Ghost River. I twisted and fought at every step. I begged for mercy I did not deserve. We were half a mile from our encampment and I am sure that my band heard every scream.

I was stretched out cruciform, my belly in the dust and the sun driving upon me. I tugged at my bonds until my hands and feet were absolutely numb.

Five on each side, holding my wings. Holding my great wings tight as I thrashed and sought to beat them hard and viciously against my captors' skulls. I looked up and saw the sawman, my cousin, red-feathered San'jhuarr.

Dust and sand and heat and the coursing wind in the channel. I remember them.

I remember the touch of the metal. The extraordinary sense of intrusion, the horrific in-out-in-out motion of the serrated blade. It fouled with my flesh many times, had to be withdrawn and wiped clean. I remember the breathtaking inrush of hot air on tissue laid bare, on nerves torn from their roots. The slow, slow, merciless cracking of bone. I remember the vomit that quenched my screams, briefly, before my mouth cleared and I drew breath and screamed again. Blood in frightening quantities. The sudden, giddying weightlessness as one wing was lifted away and the stubs of bone trembled shatteringly back into my flesh and ragged fringes of meat slithered from my wound and the agonizing pressure of clean cloth and unguents on my lacerations and the slow stalk of San'jhuarr around my head and the knowledge, the unbearable knowledge that it was all about to happen again.

*   *   *

I never questioned that I deserved the judgement. Even when I fled to find flight again. I was doubly ashamed. Crippled and shorn of respect for my choice-theft; I would add to that the shame of overturning a just punishment.

I could not live. I could not be earthbound. I was dead.

I put Isaac's letter in my ragged clothes without reading his merciless, miserable farewell. I cannot say for sure that I despise him. I cannot say for sure I would do other than he has done.

I step out and down.

Some streets away in Saltbur, a fifteen-storey towerblock rises over the eastern city. The front door will not lock. It is easy to clamber over the gate that supposedly blocks access to the flat roof. I have climbed that edifice before.

It is a short walk. I feel as if I am sleeping. The citizens stare at me as I step past them. I am not wearing my hood. I cannot see that it matters.

No one stops me as I climb the huge building. On two levels, doors open very slightly as I walk past on the treacherous stairwell, and I am stared at by eyes too hidden in darkness for me to see. But I am not challenged, and within minutes I am on the roof.

One hundred and fifty feet or more. There are plenty of taller structures in New Crobuzon. But this is high enough that the block rears out of the streets and stone and brick like something enormous emerging from water.

I stalk past the rubble and the signs of bonfires, the detritus of intruders and squatters. I am alone in the skyline tonight.

The brick wall that contains the roofspace is five feet high. I lean on it and look out, to all sides.

I know what it is I see.

I can place myself exactly.

That is a glimpse of the Glasshouse dome, a smudge of dirty light between two gas towers. The clenching Ribs are only a mile away, dwarfing the railways and the stubby houses. Dark clutches of trees pepper the city. The lights, the lights of all the different colours, all around me.

I vault easily onto the wall, and stand.

I am on top of New Crobuzon now.

It is such an enormous thing. Such a great wallow. There is everything within it, spread out under my feet.

I can see the rivers. The Canker is about six minutes' flying time away. I stretch out my arms.

The winds rush up to me and hammer me with joy. The air is boisterous and alive.

I close my eyes.

I can imagine it with absolute exactitude. A flight. To kick out with the legs and feel my wings grab the air and throw it easily earthward, scooping great chunks away from me like paddles. The hard slog into a thermal where the feathers plump and prime, spread out, drifting, easing, gliding up around in a spiral over this enormity below me. It is another city from above. The hidden gardens become spectacles to delight me. The dark bricks are something to shake off like mud. Every building becomes an eyrie. The whole of the city can be treated with disrespect, landing and alighting on a whim, soiling the air in passing.

From the air, in flight, from above, the government and militia are pompous termites, the squalor a dulled patch passing quickly away, the degradations that take place in the shadow of the architecture are none of my concern.

I feel the wind force my fingers apart. I am buffeted invitingly. I feel the twitching as my ragged flanges of wingbone stretch.

I will not do this any more. I will not be this cripple, this earthbound bird, any longer.

This half-life ends now, with my hope.

I can so well picture a last flight, a swift, elegant curving sweep through the air that parts like a lost lover to welcome me.

Let the wind take me.

I lean forward on the wall, out over the tumbling city, into the air.

Time is quite still. I am poised. There is no sound. The city and the air are poised.

And I reach up slowly and run my fingers through my feathers. Pushing them slowly aside as my skin bristles, rubbing them mercilessly the wrong way, against the grain. I open my eyes. My fingers close and clutch at the stiff shafts and oiled fibres on my cheeks and I snap my beak shut so I will not cry out, and I begin to pull.

*   *   *

And a long time later, hours later, in the deepest part of the night, I step back down through that pitch stairwell and emerge.

A single cab clatters quickly through the deserted street and then there is no sound. Across the cobbles, beige light drools down from a guttering gasjet.

A dark figure has been waiting for me. He steps into the little pool of light, and stands, his face shadowed. He waves slowly to me. There is a fractional moment when I think of all my enemies and wonder which this man is. Then I see the huge scissoring mantis limb with which he greets me.

I find that I am not surprised.

Jack Half-a-Prayer extends his Remade arm again and with a slow, portentous movement, he beckons me.

He invites me in. Into his city.

I step forward into what little light there is.

I do not see him start as I pass out of silhouette and he sees me.

I know how I must look.

My face a mass of raw and ragged flesh, bleeding copiously from a hundred little punctures where the feathers left my flesh. Tenacious fluffs of down that I have missed patch me like stubble. My eyes peer out from bald, pink, ruined skin, blistered and sickly. Trickles of blood draw paths along my skull.

My feet are constricted again by filthy strips of rag, their monstrous shape hidden. The fringes of feathers that segued into their scales are ripped clean. I walk gingerly, my groin as raw and newly plucked as my head.

I tried to break my beak, but I could not.

I stand before the building in my new flesh.

Half-a-Prayer pauses, but not for very long. With another languorous stroke, he repeats his invitation.

It is generous, but I must decline.

He offers me the half-world. He offers to share his bastard liminal life, his interstitial city. His obscure crusades and anarchic vengeance. His scorn for doors.

Escaped Remade, fReemade. Nothing. He does not fit in. He has wrested New Crobuzon into a new city, and he strives to save it from itself.

He sees another broken-down half-thing, another exhausted relic that he might convert to fight his unthinkable fight, another for whom existence in any world is impossible, a paradox, a bird

*that cannot fly. And he offers me a way out, into his uncommu-
nity, his margin, his mongrel city. The violent and honourable
place from where he rages.*

He is generous, but I decline. That is not my city. Not my fight.

*I must leave his half-breed world alone, his demimonde of
weird resistance. I live in a simpler place.*

He is mistaken. •

*I am not the earthbound garuda any more. That one is dead.
This is a new life. I am not a half-thing, a failed neither-nor.*

*I have torn the misleading quills from my skin and made it
smooth, and below that avian affectation, I am the same as my
citizen fellows. I can live foresquare in one world.*

*I indicate him thanks and farewell and turn away, stepping off
into the dim lamplight to the east, towards the university campus
and Ludmead Station, through my world of bricks and mortar
and tar, bazaars and markets, sulphur-lit streets. It is night and I
must hurry to my bed, to find my bed, to find a bed in this my city
where I can live my foresquare life.*

*I turn away from him and step into the vastness of New Crobu-
zon, this towering edifice of architecture and history, this com-
plexitude of money and slum, this profane steam-powered god. I
turn and walk into the city my home, not bird or garuda, not miserable crossbreed.*

I turn and walk into my home, the city, a man.

Don't miss this captivating fantasy epic by
China Miéville

THE SCAR

Finalist for the Hugo Award, Philip K. Dick Award,
Arthur C. Clarke Award, and The British Science
Fiction Award

"Miéville's world is a place of sprawling architecture and creatures . . . A world where treachery is expected and mutilation commonplace, where taxes might be collected in blood, and librarians tear pages out of books. It is a fantastic setting for an unforgettable tale."
—*The Cleveland Plain Dealer*

A mythmaker of the highest order, China Miéville has emblazoned the fantasy novel with fresh language, startling images, and stunning originality. Set in the same sprawling world of Miéville's award-winning novel, *Perdido Street Station*, this latest epic introduces a whole new cast of intriguing characters and dazzling creations.

Published by Del Rey
www.delreydigital.com
Available in paperback wherever books are sold